In a Dark Wood Wandering

IN A DARK WOOD WANDERING

WANDERING

A Novel of the Middle Ages

HELLA S. HAASSE

Revised and Edited by Anita Miller
from an English Translation from the Dutch
by Lewis C. Kaplan

ARROW BOOKS

Arrow Books Limited
20 Vauxhall Bridge Road, London SW1V 2SA

An imprint of the Random Century Group

London Melbourne Sydney Auckland Johannesburg
and agencies throughout the world

First published in Great Britain by Hutchinson 1990
Arrow edition 1990

Printed and bound in Great Britain by
The Guernsey Press Co. Ltd
Guernsey, C.I.

ISBN 0 09 974470 8

CONTENTS

INTRODUCTION

This novel, written in Dutch, was first published in the Netherlands in 1949; it has never been out of print. Hella Haasse's interest in the Middle Ages—and especially in the fifteenth century—had begun when she was a child in Batavia in the Dutch East Indies (now Jakarta, Indonesia). Her attention had been captured when, in 1924 at the age of six, she had seen a portrait of Queen Isabeau in her tall, veiled headdress. At once, she says, "I wanted to know all about that person." This interest persisted: "While most boys and girls my age were collecting stamps or pictures of film stars, I collected books, articles and pictures about the Middle Ages." In 1938 or '39, while she was a student at the University of Amsterdam, she came by chance across an edition in the library of a collection of the poems of Charles d'Orléans, and everything she had read and thought about the fifteenth century crystallized around him.

During the German occupation, Hella Haasse chose to leave the University, where she had been studying Scandinavian languages and literature, rather than sign a statement of loyalty to the Reich, as all students there were required to do. She went instead to the Amsterdam Academy of Dramatic Art and, upon graduation in 1943, joined a theatrical company managed by Cees Laseur, one of Holland's foremost actors—but only for a short time: the war was too overwhelming. She turned instead to research into the life and times of Charles d'Orléans and after the war began a play on that theme which grew into this novel.

In the fall of 1945 her first book, a volume of poetry, was published, and in 1947 her first work of fiction appeared: *Oeroeg*, a novella about the relationship between a Dutch and a Javanese youth. The success of this book—about 300,000 copies are now in print—encouraged its Dutch publisher to issue the massive medieval novel entitled *Het woud der verwachting*: literally, the Forest of Long Awaiting, a metaphor popular with medieval poets and one used by Charles d'Orléans himself. The book was hailed immediately by Dutch literary critics as a major work. In 1950, in a review in English in the *Times Literary Supplement*, it was called "monumental", scholarly and admirably lucid, with characters which "take their place as living human beings".

At this point the scene shifts to Chicago, where Lewis C. Kaplan was working as a postal clerk, a job he had held since 1939 when he left the WPA Federal Writers Project. The Chicago post office at that time was a haven for literary refugees from the Depression; Mr. Kaplan worked with Nelson Algren, Jack Conroy, Willard Motley and the future Chicago bookseller Stuart Brent. Mr. Kaplan's first love was translation. His method was to spend many months with dictionaries and grammar books and then to embark on the translation of works which he deemed worthwhile and which otherwise would not be available to the English-speaking world. In this way he had translated three novels from the Portuguese: Enrico Verissimo's *Crossroads* and *The Rest is Silence*, published by Macmillan in 1943 and 1946 respectively, and Graciliano Ramos's *Anguish*, brought out by Knopf in 1946. In the early fifties, Mr. Kaplan had begun to familiarize himself with Dutch. Through his job in the post office, he had access to foreign periodicals and he scanned the Dutch reviews in search of worthwhile material for translation. In 1953 he came across comments on *Het woud der verwachting* and was attracted to it not only because the reviews were universally enthusiastic, but because it appeared to be a work of epic dimensions and he preferred large canvases.

Mr. Kaplan contacted Hella Haasse through Querido, her Dutch publisher, who passed his letter on to her; they added that they knew Mr. Kaplan: he was a German refugee who had worked for a time, after the war, in their offices as an editor and had then moved to England. Accordingly, the author gave Mr. Kaplan her blessing. Mr. Kaplan, who had been born in Chicago in 1911 and had lived there all his life, and had never implied otherwise, set to work immediately upon receipt of the Dutch volume, unaware that the people at Querido had apparently confused him with another Kaplan. He worked steadily every evening and on weekends, although his health was not good; his heart had been affected by a childhood attack of rheumatic fever. Within five years, but with no further contact with Hella Haasse, he had completed his first draft of the book. In 1958, when he had revised the first 150 pages more or less to his satisfaction, he became very ill. The night before he was hospitalized, he stood—too sick to sit or lie down—using the television set as a desk in his small Chicago lake-front apartment, still at work on the manuscript. A few days later, he was dead.

His widow, understandably distraught, disposed of all his effects. His Dutch books she donated to Deering Library at Northwestern University; the manuscript itself, which had no title page or identification of any kind, she put in a black briefcase which she stowed at the back of a closet where it was to remain for twenty years. During that time Hella Haasse thought occasionally of Mr. Kaplan and the English version of *Het woud der verwachting*; it seemed to her that he was taking a considerable time to complete his work, but she knew that he had tackled a formidable task and, with commendable sensitivity, she hesitated to give him the impression that he was being rushed. Her writing career and her role as the mother of two daughters were taking all her attention; in 1959 she received one of two International Atlantic awards for Literature from the Atlantic Cultural Commission of NATO; in that twenty years she produced at least a dozen novels and she had achieved a reputation as one of the Netherlands' foremost authors, and was to go on to win many more prizes and honors.

In the late 1970s a fire broke out in the Kaplan apartment. Mrs. Kaplan enlisted the help of her son Kalman, who at the time was a research assistant and guest lecturer at Harvard University, to clean up the ensuing mess. In the course of clearing out a closet, Kalman Kaplan came across the black briefcase and asked his mother about its sopping contents. Mrs. Kaplan knew only that it was the work her husband had been doing before he died. Dr. Kaplan dried out the sheets with some difficulty, and then attempted to find out what this manuscript was since, as we have said, it was untitled and had no author's name. He sent it off to a publisher in Michigan who responded that it appeared to be some sort of saga, like *The Thorn Birds* or *Gone With the Wind*. But they did not publish fiction.

Fortunately, shortly after this, Mrs. Kaplan came up with a piece of paper with "Hella Haasse" written on it. Dr. Kaplan, now armed with a name, telephoned the Library of Congress, who gave him the Dutch title and the Dutch publisher. This was in 1979. Although he contacted Querido immediately, Dr. Kaplan did not hear from the author until 1982; some confusion had apparently resulted from a change of directors at Querido and because Hella Haasse had been in the process of moving from Holland to France. In the meantime, Dr. Kaplan copyrighted his father's manuscript under the title *The Forest of Expectations*. Finally, in 1982 Hella Haasse gave Dr. Kaplan permission to market the translation, subject to her approval of it.

At this time Dr. Kaplan was teaching in the psychology department of Wayne State University in Detroit. On a visit to his mother in Chicago, he happened to see an article in *The Chicago Tribune* about our publishing house. He phoned me, and I told him to bring the manuscript to us so we could look at it. Dr. Kaplan carried a cardboard carton up to our offices in the old Mandel Building on the Chicago River; it contained an 1100-page manuscript divided into five or six sections, each section held together at the top by two large metal rings. He gave me also a separate manuscript of the first seventy-five pages of the book cleanly typed, because his father's pages were basically worksheets: it had been Lewis Kaplan's practice to look up Dutch words and type their English definitions on each line, often with snatches of Dutch; when he went back for his revision, he crossed out the words he had decided not to use; occasionally he crossed them all out and wrote the chosen word above them, or added a possible alternative in handwriting in the margin. This of course made the translation very difficult to read.

Therefore, I read Dr. Kaplan's seventy-five pages and on the strength of them we signed a contract for the book. With historical fiction, one always hesitates: does the author have a sure hand and a real insight into the period? Although I knew virtually nothing about medieval French history, I recognized immediately the sweep and scope of the drama unfolding here; this was unquestionably a serious and impressive work. It was in essence an uncompleted manuscript, and I was prepared to do a considerable amount of editing. I was sent a copy of the Dutch edition, but I set it aside since I knew no Dutch. I began to write out what I considered a coherent revision of Mr. Kaplan's translation; I had to write it, so to speak, in order to read it. I filled notebook after notebook in the evenings and on weekends, on airplanes and in hotel rooms. Like Mr. Kaplan, I was prevented by the press of business from working on the book on weekdays. When I had completed and typed each hundred pages or so, I sent them to Hella Haasse, along with questions about things that puzzled me, for her comments and corrections. In this way the new manuscript grew and was nearly complete by early 1988. All medieval French and some of the pages dealing with the sojourn in Pontefract castle which had eluded Mr. Kaplan, Hella Haasse herself translated for me. She is fluent in English and has in fact translated Iris Murdoch's *The Bell* as well as some medieval English poetry into Dutch.

I had a manuscript, but I was uncomfortably aware that I had polished and rearranged Mr. Kaplan's sentences and that, since I had not looked at the original text, I might have carried the prose, inadvertently, far from the rhythm of the Dutch prose. I felt I had no choice but to follow in Mr. Kaplan's footsteps by procuring a Dutch dictionary and painfully fighting my way through the Prologue in Dutch. I discovered that I had indeed smoothed away a good deal of the vigor and liveliness of Hella Haasse's style. Accordingly I revised the first fifty pages working against the Dutch text, and the author made further emendations. I called upon a Dutch friend, Nini Blinstrub, who lives in Chicago, and she spent a long afternoon with me, going line by line over some scenes that I had felt to be murky or confusing. I then went carefully over the last hundred pages of the book and over all scenes that seemed ambiguous, to make sure that they corresponded in tone and meaning with the Dutch original. I had learned also that Mr. Kaplan had worked from an edition of the book containing passages which the author had cut from later editions; it was necessary to check constantly against the Dutch text to make sure that these passages were also excluded from the English translation. Finally, Hella Haasse flew to Chicago in March of 1989 to go over the book with me line by line as Nini Blinstrub had done with a limited number of pages. Thus—although I am uneasily aware that nothing is perfect in this world—both Hella Haasse and I are satisfied that the following pages offer a faithful English version of a book which I, like

Lewis Kaplan, am convinced is far too important to be kept from readers of English.

The question of the title was a knotty one: the author was not happy with "The Forest of Expectations"; "verwachting" does not mean "expectations" but "long awaiting". There is no real English equivalent. Since we were fortunate to have a son who specialized in Renaissance literature, we turned to him and he suggested the line from Dante that resulted in the present title. Hella Haasse was delighted with "In a Dark Wood Wandering" and that now seems to us to be the only possible English title for this work, although we spent weeks agonizing over it.

Here then, after forty years of accidents and disasters, and as a direct result of Lewis Kaplan's remarkable choice of avocation, is an unforgettable chronicle, rescued from its wanderings in the wilderness.

—Anita Miller
Chicago, Illinois
May, 1989

CAST OF MAJOR CHARACTERS
NOVEMBER 24, 1394

❧

Valentine Visconti, Duchess of Orléans.
> Wife of the King's brother, Louis d'Orléans, daughter of Gian
> Galeazzo Visconti, Lord of Milan.

Charles VI, King of France.
> The elder son of Charles V, who was also known as Charles the
> Wise.

Isabeau, Queen of France.
> The wife of Charles VI.

Louis, Duke of Orléans.
> The younger son of Charles the Wise; brother to Charles VI,
> husband of Valentine Visconti.

Philippe, Duke of Burgundy.
> Also known as Philippe the Bold (Philippe le Hardi). Brother
> of Charles the Wise and therefore uncle to Charles VI and Louis
> d'Orléans. He is married to Margaretha of Flanders; their son is
> Jean de Nevers.

Jean, Duke of Berry.
> An obsessive aesthete, collector and bibliophile. The patron of
> the famous Book of Hours. Also a brother of Charles the Wise
> and therefore uncle to Charles VI and Louis d'Orléans.

Louis, Duke of Bourbon.
> Brother-in-law of Charles the Wise and therefore uncle to
> Charles VI and Louis d'Orléans on their mother's side (Queen
> Jeanne).

The Royal House of Valois

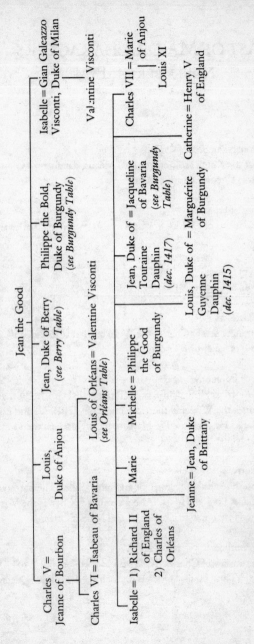

THE HOUSE OF ORLÉANS

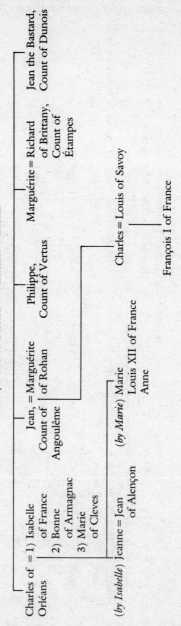

Louis, Duke of Orléans = Valentine Visconti

- Charles of Orléans = 1) Isabelle of France 2) Bonne of Armagnac 3) Marie of Cleves
- Jean, Count of Angoulême = Marguérite of Rohan
- Philippe, Count of Vertus
- Marguérite = Richard of Brittany, Count of Étampes
- Jean the Bastard, Count of Dunois

(by Isabelle) Jeanne = Jean of Alençon

(by Marie) Marie
Louis XII of France
Anne

Charles = Louis of Savoy

François I of France

THE HOUSE OF BURGUNDY

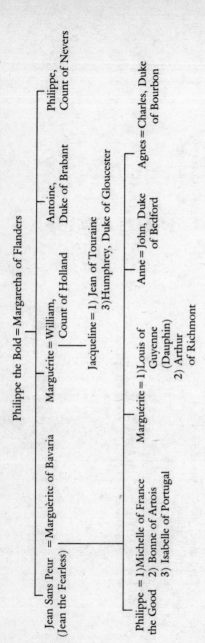

Philippe the Bold = Margaretha of Flanders

Jean Sans Peur (Jean the Fearless) = Marguèrite of Bavaria

Marguérite = William, Count of Holland

Antoine, Duke of Brabant

Philippe, Count of Nevers

Jacqueline = 1) Jean of Touraine 3) Humphrey, Duke of Gloucester

Anne = John, Duke of Bedford

Agnes = Charles, Duke of Bourbon

Philippe the Good = 1) Michelle of France 2) Bonne of Artois 3) Isabelle of Portugal

Marguérite = 1) Louis of Guyenne (Dauphin) 2) Arthur of Richmont

THE HOUSE OF BERRY

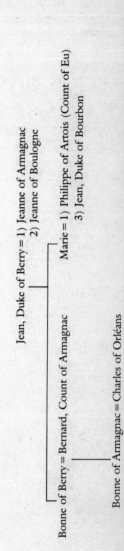

Jean, Duke of Berry = 1) Jeanne of Armagnac 2) Jeanne of Boulogne

Marie = 1) Philippe of Artois (Count of Eu) 3) Jean, Duke of Bourbon

Bonne of Berry = Bernard, Count of Armagnac

Bonne of Armagnac = Charles of Orléans

PROLOGUE

(NOVEMBER 24, 1394)

Nel mezzo del cammin di nostra vita
mi ritrovae per una selva oscura,
che la deritta via era smarrita.

In the middle of the journey of our life,
I found myself in a dark wood,
For the straight way was lost.
— Dante Alighieri

alentine, Duchess of Orléans, lay in her green-curtained bed of state, listening to the bells of Saint-Pol. The church was not far from the royal palace—only a stone's throw away. The pealing of the bells swelled into a heavy sea of cheerless sound; Valentine folded her hands over the green coverlet. The christening procession of her fourth son, Charles, had left the palace.

The people of Paris, crowded behind the wooden barriers set up to protect the procession, strained to see Charles VI, the god-father of the royal child, and the King's brother Louis, the father, preceded by torchbearers, noblemen, high dignitaries of the Church and clergy. Following Charles and Louis were their uncles: Philippe, Duke of Burgundy, and the Dukes of Berry and Bourbon.

The King walked faster than the solemnity of the occasion dictated; the agitated movements of his head and his aimless, wandering stare betrayed his unfortunate mental condition even to the uninitiated. But the spectators' attention was riveted on Louis the Duke of Orléans, because of his smile and splendid clothes, and on Isabeau the Queen, surrounded by princesses and royal kinswomen and followed by many ladies-in-waiting. In the midst of the women's crowns, veils, pointed headdresses and trailing, ermine-trimmed mantles, the infant Charles d'Orléans was carried to church for the first time.

Valentine's weary body lay beneath the coverlet. She stared at the women busying themselves at the hearth, at the open cupboard filled with platters and tankards, the torches set along the walls in their iron brackets, the green wall hangings of the ducal lying-in chamber. Before the hearthfire stood the cradle on small wooden wheels in which Charles had slept from the moment that, washed, rubbed with honey and wrapped in linen cloth, he had been entrusted to the care of his nurse, Jeanne la Brune. Women hurried back and forth from the adjoining room, filling the platters on the sideboard with sweets and fruit, bringing green cushions for the benches along the walls. The torches gave off a stupefying smell of resin; their heat, together with the heat of the hearthfire, was almost unbearable in the tightly-closed room. The Duchess broke into a sweat.

Her body had been worn out by four confinements in four years' time. But more exhausting still, perhaps, was the pace of court life—an uninterrupted series of dances, masquerades and banquets. On Valentine Visconti, exhaustion worked like a poison. At her father's court in Pavia, she had loved the small elegant gatherings frequented by poets and scholars, the debates and word games, the music played in her own chambers. Gian Galeazzo Visconti, although denounced as a tyrant and a sorcerer, had a more acute eye for learning and the fine arts than the pretentious inhabitants of Saint-Pol.

The glitter of the torch flames, reflected in the gold and silver plate on the sideboard, hurt her eyes. She closed them and sank away instantly into a deep pool of exhaustion, a darkness without rest, riddled with the voices and stifled laughter of the women. It seemed to her that the walls of Saint-Pol vibrated with sound like the walls of a gigantic beehive. The entire enormous palace, with its complex structure which linked halls, chambers, towers, bastions, inner courtyards, annexes, stables and gardens, enclosed her like a honeycomb of cells, buzzing with bees. She was aware all at the same time of members of the household running up and down the stairs and through the corridors; of the continuous uproar in and around the kitchens, larders and wine cellars where the christening meal and the banquet were being prepared; of the stamping of hooves and the jingle of weapons and armor in the guardrooms; of the chirping and twittering of birds in the great indoor aviary; of the roaring of lions—the King's menagerie—in their winter quarters. And more disturbing than all this was the ceaseless cacophony of the bells. She murmured prayers and endeavored to lose herself in thoughts of the ceremony nearby in the church of Saint-Pol, where even now her son was receiving baptism over the basin hung with gold brocade. She thought of her brother-in-law the King who, as godfather, had to hold the child in his right arm throughout the christening. She had been told that he was pleased at the birth and the planned festivities.

For the first time in months, he had left the castle of Creil where he was confined, to show himself to the public. His relatives, warned by physicians, watched him anxiously, fearing a sudden renewed outburst of madness. Valentine felt a heartrending pity for the King, of whom she was as fond as he was of her. The news two years earlier of an unexpected eruption of his illness had upset her no less—although she reacted in a different way—than it had upset the Queen. Despite her displays of desperate grief, Isabeau believed— or professed to believe—that recovery was possible; Valentine, on the other hand, perhaps because of her swifter Southern intuition, knew that the germ of madness, always present in the King's child-like, capricious nature, had now put down roots that were inerad-icable. To some degree, Valentine shared the view that a madman was little more than a dangerous animal; but the thought of her brother-in-law imprisoned in the barred balcony high above the walls of Creil, gazing down from his cage at the nobles of his retinue who were playing ball in the dry moat below, filled her with horror and compassion. Although she knew that Isabeau's grief was sincere, she could not remain blind to the avidity with which the Queen had taken over the administration of the court, and the Duke of Bur-gundy the control of affairs of state.

She had little faith in the physician Guillaume de Harselly, how-ever capable he might be. She no longer believed that illness could be banished by confession and exorcism. The previous winter she had found another physician's recommendation for a cure even less beneficial; the King should be kept away from the Council and all state business; he should be diverted with various amusements. As a result, Saint-Pol became a madhouse where the music was never silenced, where the uproar of balls and drinking bouts never stopped; where Isabeau, evening after evening, on the arm of Louis d'Orléans, led the rows of celebrants in their multi-colored finery, and the King, actually somewhat recovered, clapped his hands in time with the music and looked on eagerly at each new entertainment.

The torchlight pricked Valentine's closed eyes; the heat of the lying-in chamber made her think of the endless nights spent under the canopy of tapestries and fading flowers at the side of the King, who enjoyed having her near him and would not allow her to withdraw. As she looked down from the raised platform upon the crowd in the overflowing hall, it often seemed to her that she was in a purgatory more cruel and terrifying than the one the Church had taught her to fear. The statues in the niches of the cathedral, the spewing monsters, the devils and gargoyles which looked down upon Paris, grimacing, from the exterior of Notre Dame, had come to life in the grotesquely-masked dancers illuminated in the torchlight: in the women whose high headdresses were decorated with horns and rolls of stuffed cloth, in the men whose wide pleated sleeves looked like the wings of bats and who wore sharply pointed shoes like the beaks of alien beasts.

Valentine moved her head restlessly on the pillows. The rush of milk made her feverish. The normal cure for this, the feeding of her child, was denied to her: that was taken care of by the wet nurse who sat by the hearthfire, a cloth folded over her breasts. A chamberwoman threw some logs on the fire; the flames leapt high in the recesses of the hearth.

Flames had put a premature end to the wild masquerade which Isabeau had held in January to celebrate the marriage of her friend and confidante, the widow of the Sire de Hainceville. The celebration of a second marriage offered abundant opportunity for unbridled pleasures, jokes full of double entendres, reckless debauchery. An endless train of guests danced hand in hand through the hall. And the King, infected by the general atmosphere of wild elation, allowed himself to be seduced into joining a game of dressing-up invented by some noblemen who wanted to terrorize the women for sport.

In a side room they had their naked bodies sewn into garments of thin leather smeared with pitch and then strewn with feathers; they put on feather headdresses to make themselves look like savages. So attired, they leapt shouting among the dancers who dispersed in panic in every direction, to the onlookers' delight.

The Duchess of Berry, the very young wife of the Duke's uncle, sat beside Valentine under the canopy. She recognized the King by his build and laughed uncontrollably at his antics, which were wilder and more excited than those of the others. Louis d'Orléans entered the hall, drunk, with a lighted torch in his hand, accompanied by some friends; the savages rushed over to him and began, crowded together, to dance around him. The shouts of the bystanders drowned out the music. A scuffle broke out, in the course of which the feathered headdresses caught fire.

In nightmares, Valentine still heard the screams of the living torches, hopelessly doomed in their tight garments; they ran in circles, frantically clawing at themselves, or rolled howling over the floor. Isabeau, who knew that the King was one of thé dancers, collapsed at the sight of the flames. But the young Duchess de Berry, tears of laughter still on her cheeks, wrapped the train of her dress around the King and was able to smother the fire. The others burned half an hour longer, but they did not die for several days.

Valentine moaned aloud and threw her hands over her face. This caused a stir among the women near the door. Someone came quickly to the bed; it was the Dame de Maucouvent, who looked after Valentine's oldest son Louis.

"Madame," she said, curtseying low, "the procession is returning from the church."

The Duchess opened her eyes—she was still overcome by the memory of that hellish night which had caused the King to have another, and prolonged, relapse. She gazed for a time at the trustworthy, somewhat faded face of the Dame de Maucouvent. "Help me," Valentine said at last, holding out her arms.

The woman helped her to sit up, wiped the perspiration from her face and spread the deeply scalloped sleeves of her upper garment over the coverlet. The pealing of the bells began to subside.

The Dame de Maucouvent put a silver dish filled with sweetmeats and spices on Valentine's lap. Custom dictated that the mother of a new-born child quit her bed during the King's visit to offer him refreshment with her own hand. The women took the lids from the jugs on the sideboard; a fragrance of warm hippocras filled the chamber. The voices of arriving guests could be heard in the antechamber; pages opened the door to the lying-in room and the King entered quickly, walking between rows of torchbearers and curtseying women.

Valentine, who had not seen him since the early spring, was so shocked and horrified by his altered appearance that she forgot her manners and remained sitting in bed. She watched him approaching her, slovenly in his rich clothing, his eyes distended with nervous mirth. Behind him, on the threshold of the chamber and in the anteroom, stood the royal kinsmen and the court. The baptized child began to wail.

Hastily the women pulled back the coverlet and Valentine, supported by the Dame de Maucouvent, set her feet on the floor.

"Sire," Valentine whispered, lifting the dish toward him. She was blinded by a sudden dizziness; two ladies of the court held her firmly under the arms while the King, dawdling like a child, poked among the delicacies in the dish.

"Take this, Sire, it is a deer," Valentine said softly, almost in tears to see him staring uncertainly at the sugar beast in his hand. Over his shoulder she caught the Queen's eye, cold and full of suspicion. Louis, Valentine's husband, leaned against the doorpost, toying with his embroidered gloves; he held them before his face to conceal a yawn. The King clutched the piece of candy and raised his eyes for the first time to Valentine's face.

"A deer?" he asked, motioning for the dish to be removed. "A deer? Yes, surely, a deer. You are right, Madame my sister-in-law, Valentine, dear Valentine. A deer. You know of course that a deer brings me luck? You know the story, don't you?"

His eyes strayed about the room. No one said anything.

"I'll tell you what happened to me," the King continued in a confidential tone, walking along with Valentine who was being led back to bed. "I was already crowned, although I was still only a boy. I was hunting in the forest of Senlis . . ."

The Queen, the Dukes of Burgundy, Berry, Bourbon and Orléans, the prince and princesses of the royal House and all the counts and barons and their ladies, as well as the women who carried the infant Charles, followed the King into the lying-in chamber. They accepted some of the hippocras and candied fruit offered by the Duchess's women and exchanged knowing looks. It was not for the first time that the King talked in front of them about this youthful experience, which held great significance for him.

"Know then, Valentine," said the King. He bent over his sister-in-law and took one of her cold hands in his. "At a crossroad I came upon a deer. I did not shoot it. It let itself be taken by hand. It was like the deer of Saint Hubert, but instead of a cross it wore a collar of gilded copper—what do you say to that?—and on it was written in Latin . . ." He placed the spread fingers of his left hand over his mouth and looked with glistening eyes at Valentine, who smiled sadly at him. "On it was . . . well, what *was* written there? . . . In Latin?" he asked suddenly, with an impatient stamp of his foot.

One of the nobles stepped forward and bowed. "*Caesar hoc mihi donavit,* Sire," he murmured, sinking onto one knee beside the bed. His long red sleeves trailed behind him on the carpet.

"That was it! 'Caesar has given me this collar'," continued the King, speaking so quickly that he stammered. "That is to say, the deer was more than a thousand years old. Think of it, Valentine! Was that a good omen or not? Well?" He tugged at the hand which he still clutched tightly.

"It was a good omen, Sire," the Duchess said in a flat voice. She was constantly aware of Isabeau's eyes; the Queen stood near the bed, staring at her husband.

"I thought so too—no, I'm sure of it!" the King said loudly. "I dreamed of a hart on the eve of the battle of Roosebeke. And didn't I win a glorious victory there? Who dares to deny that? I was twelve years old then, no older. But you should have seen that battlefield . . . Ten thousand dead, ten thousand, all because of *me*." He struck his chest, panting with excitement. "*I* won it; it was I who gave the signal for the assault. When I finally had the flag hoisted again, the sun broke through the clouds for the first time in five days . . . Wasn't it so? Wasn't it so? . . . Mountjoye for the King of France!" he cried hoarsely, stepping down from the platform on which the bed stood.

Isabeau made a movement toward him, but he stepped back, looking at her with anger and fear.

"Who is this woman, anyway?" he said to the courtiers standing near him. "What does she want from me? She is always bothering me. She wants to *touch* me. Send her away!"

Valentine's lips parted in terror. What she had heard whispered these past few months was true . . . that the King did not recognize his wife and refused to see her. It was true. Isabeau turned white, but her mouth remained pulled down in an expression of contempt. She stood in the middle of the lying-in chamber, broad and heavy in her ermine-lined mantle, the train held up by two ladies of the court. On her head she wore an extraordinarily tall crowned hat, under which her face looked small and full, with almost lashless eyes, round cheeks and well-shaped lips. On her breast above the square deeply-cut bodice, jeweled stars trembled with her heavy breathing.

Valentine's cheeks burned with shame at the insult inflicted on the Queen; she nodded to her women. The platter with the candied fruit was passed around once more. Although the child was now in its cradle, it did not stop crying. It was carried into an adjoining room.

The King showed no sign of quitting the chamber. He allowed a chair to be brought to him and sat down next to Valentine at whom he stared fixedly without speaking. The court, which could not leave before the King gave the signal for departure, stood in a half-circle around the bed. The Duchess found this wall of bodies, of faces wearing formal smiles, immensely oppressive. She could not sit upright because of the roaring in her ears, which rose and fell at regular intervals. Although no one betrayed impatience by word or look, she knew only too well what thoughts were hidden behind those courteous masks.

The King's affinity for his sister-in-law was no secret; from the moment she had arrived as Louis' bride in Melun to celebrate her marriage—Louis then was still Duke of Touraine—Charles had openly manifested signs of the greatest affection for her. He had paid all the costs of the wedding fêtes, had issued orders that the municipal fountain should gush milk and rosewater as it had at the Queen's formal entry into the country some years earlier, and had heaped gifts upon Valentine. But the affection which, before the King became ill, had been a mark of favor that increased the respect of the court for Monseigneur d'Orléans and his wife, evoked a different response when it was evinced by a madman. The contrast between the King's almost morbid fondness for his sister-in-law and the aversion he showed for Isabeau, was glaring. Indignation, derision, perverse enjoyment of someone else's discomfiture—all these feelings undoubtedly existed behind those polite smiles.

Isabeau had sat down too; she turned to whisper to Louis d'Orléans, who stood behind her. The Duke of Burgundy finally decided to put an end to this painful waiting. He took off his hat and approached the bed. He had been Charles' guardian and the real ruler of France in the first years of the kingship. Now he had completely regained the power which had been threatened when the King, full-grown, had chosen other advisors. He bent down and spoke to Charles as though he were speaking to a child, with his stern impenetrable face close to the King's.

"Sire, my King, it is time."

"So soon?" the King asked impatiently. He had taken off his rings and set them on the edge of Valentine's bed. Now he picked them up one by one and dropped them into the Duchess's lap. "For the child—from his godfather," he said with a smothered laugh as he arose. "Valentine, dear Valentine, don't forget to come and visit me tomorrow, or the day after tomorrow."

He kissed her on both cheeks, stroking the damp braids on either side of her forehead. The Duke of Burgundy drew him away. The King looked back. "Be sure to remember," he muttered. The courtiers stepped aside to make way for him. Isabeau took leave of her sister-in-law, but her kiss was no more than a fleeting touch with pursed lips; her eyes remained cold. The ladies-in-waiting picked up the Queen's train.

The old Duke of Bourbon, Charles' uncle on his mother's side, took Isabeau's hand and led her out of the room; the court followed. Even before the anteroom door had closed, Valentine fell backward upon the pillows. The heat in the lying-in chamber was unbearable, but custom forbade anyone to let in fresh air before the mother had taken her first walk to church. Not the Dame de Maucouvent nor any of the other women could unlace the Duchess's bodice to make her breathing easier because Louis d'Orléans, who had stayed behind in the room, came and sat on the edge of the bed. The women withdrew to the hearthfire.

"Well, my darling," said Louis, smiling. He stooped to pick up his wife's handkerchief from the floor. "Our brother the King has been quite generous today." He took the rings which lay scattered over the bed and looked at them carefully, one by one; finally, he slipped one onto his index finger. "How are you feeling today? You look tired."

"I am tired," answered the Duchess. She did not open her eyes.

There was a brief silence. Louis looked down at his wife's face, which had an ivory tint in the green reflection of the bedcurtains. In a sudden rush of warmth and pity, he reached for her hand which lay weakly, half-open, on the coverlet. She turned her head slightly toward him and her narrow lips curved into a smile—a gentle smile, not without melancholy.

"Maître Darien brought me our new son's horoscope this morning," Louis went on. "He says the child was born under a lucky star."

Valentine's smile deepened. Her husband rose to his feet.

"Adieu, Valentine." He pressed her cold fingers. "You should sleep well now." He stepped easily from the dais, tossed his right sleeve over his shoulder, saluted the women and left the room.

The Duchess beckoned. The Dame de Maucouvent came quickly forward and removed the heavy crown from her head.

Louis d'Orléans went directly to the armory, a room adjacent to the library. That portion of the palace of Saint-Pol which he and his household occupied was no less sumptuous and was, in fact, more elegantly furnished than the apartments of the royal family. The armory reflected, in a small way, the opulence with which the Duke liked to surround himself. A Flemish tapestry depicting the crowning of Our Lady covered two walls with the colors of semi-precious stones: dull green, rust red and the dark yellow of old amber. Facing the arched window hung racks of Louis' weapon collection: daggers with wrought-gold sheaths, swords from Lyon, Saracen blades, the hilts engraved with heraldic devices and set with gems, the scabbards covered with gold and enamel.

Three men stood talking before the fire; they turned when Louis entered. They were Marshal Boucicaut and Messires Mahieu de Moras and Jean de Bueil, noblemen of the Duke's retinue with whom he was on very friendly terms. They bowed and came toward him.

"Well, gentlemen," Louis said; he flung his gloves onto a chest. "You were able to see the King today."

De Bueil strode to a table where there were some tankards and goblets of chased silver—part of Valentine's dowry—and at a nod from the Duke poured out wine.

"The King is undoubtedly mad," said de Moras, fixing his eyes upon Louis with a trace of a smile on his heavily scarred face. "To whom do you want us to drink, Monseigneur?"

"To the King—that goes without saying." Louis sat down and raised the goblet to his lips with both hands. "I don't want you to misinterpret my words—not for anything."

"Monseigneur of Burgundy is not present," said Jean de Bueil with a significant look. Louis frowned.

"I've noticed that seems to make little difference," he remarked, sipping the wine slowly. "My uncle hears everything, even things which I never said and which I never had any intention of saying. Things which I don't even *think*," he added. "For Monseigneur of Burgundy, Satan himself couldn't be any more evil than I." He began to laugh and set the beaker down.

"It's a good thing that he can't hear you speak so lightly of the Enemy," said de Moras. "I doubt that would help your reputation much—in the inns and the marketplace . . ."

"I've heard it said that men suspect you of sorcery, my lord," said Jean de Bueil; at Louis' nod he refilled the goblets. "You have brought astrologers from Lombardy . . ."

Louis interrupted him with a gesture. "I know that. Don't they say too that my father-in-law, the Lord of Milan, has signed a pact with the Devil? The learned gentlemen of the Sorbonne are behind this; they hate me so much that they would even learn sorcery if with that they could cause me to vanish from the earth. My father-in-law is anything but pious, and perhaps he does know more about the Devil than is good for him. But I vastly prefer him to the bellowing clerics who can only expel wind."

Marshal Boucicaut looked up quickly. "Monseigneur," he said earnestly, "talk like that can give rise to misunderstanding. Everyone who knows you knows that you are a devout Christian."

"You are not abreast of the times," Louis said sarcastically. "If you were, you would know that things are not what they appear to be. Do you know what the common people call the chapel of Orléans? 'The Monument to Misrule' . . . *my* misrule, do you understand? Building it was the penalty I paid for my sins. And don't forget above all that this spring I set fire to the King—to say nothing of the six noble gentlemen who did not come off as well as he did."

"You can mock, Monseigneur," said Boucicaut coolly, "because you know that with us your words are in safekeeping. But you must remember as well as I do how the people behaved the day after the unfortunate accident."

"They came by the hundreds to Saint-Pol to see the King himself and to curse us," Louis said, the ironic smile still on his lips. "They would have torn the Duchess and me to pieces if a single hair on his head had been scorched. The people think a great deal of the King."

"They would think as much of you if only they knew you," Jean de Bueil said staunchly. Louis stood up.

"You ought to concern yourself with reaching a good under-standing with the people of Paris, my lord," Boucicaut said in a low voice. "You will become regent if the King dies."

Louis turned quickly and stared at the three men, his hands on his hips. "*If* the King dies, indeed," he said finally. "May God grant the King a long and healthy life."

He walked to a window and stood looking out, his back to the others. Beneath the windows in this part of the palace was an en-closed garden with a marble fountain in the middle, surrounded by galleries. The trees, to which a single half-shrivelled red leaf still clung here and there, loomed mournfully through the autumn mist. The turrets and battlements of the palace walls were barely visible on the other side of the courtyard. The Duke turned. The three young noblemen still stood near the table.

"You're right, Messires. I joke too much," Louis said. "And I must certainly not make jokes about such worthy gentlemen as the doctors of the Sorbonne. And now enough of these things."

He took a lute from one of the tables and handed it to Jean de Bueil. "Play that song of Bernard de Ventadour's," he said, sitting down. In a clear voice de Bueil began to sing:

> Quan la doss aura venta
> Deves vostre pais
> M'es veiare que senta
> Odor de Paradis . . .

Two servants entered the room; the arms of Orléans were em-broidered on the cloth over their breasts. One of them began to light the torches along the wall; the other approached the Duke and stood hesitantly before him because Louis sat listening to the song with closed eyes. Jean de Bueil ended the couplet with a flourish of chords; the Duke of Orléans opened his eyes and asked, "Why have you stopped, de Bueil?" Then he noticed the servant. "Well?" he asked impatiently.

The man slipped onto one knee and whispered something. The peevish expression vanished from Louis' face; he smiled at the servant absently, absorbed in thought. Finally he snapped his fingers as a sign that the man could go and rose, stretching, as though to shake off every trace of lassitude. "Forgive me, gentlemen," he said. "I am needed elsewhere." He saluted them and walked swiftly to disappear behind a tapestry where the servant held a hidden door open for him.

De Bueil took up the lute again and softly played the melody of the song he had just sung. "Things are allotted queerly in this world," he remarked, without looking up from the strings. "The King is a child who plays with sugar candy. And Monseigneur d'Orléans deserves a better plaything than a ducal crown. We are not the only ones who think so."

Boucicaut frowned and rose to leave. "But it's to be hoped that everyone who thinks so is sensible enough to keep quiet about it for the time being," he said curtly. De Moras was about to follow him; he turned toward the young man with the lute.

"Don't worry about it, de Bueil," he said. "No man escapes his destiny."

In one of the towers of the ducal wing was a small room to which few had access. Louis d'Orléans had turned this room over to his astrologers: two of them, Maître Darien and Ettore Salvia, could carry on their experiments here in privacy, working with the powders and liquids which they were attempting to transmute into gold. Other, stranger things undoubtedly took place in this murky chamber into which, on the brightest day, little light seemed to filter through the small greenish windowpanes.

The usual appurtenances of the magic art lay spread upon a table shoved up against the window: parchments, shells, glass vials filled with liquids, rings, balls and mathematical symbols forged from metal. A pungent odor of burnt herbs hung in the air. In this room two men awaited the Duke. One was Ettore Salvia, an astrologer from Padua whom Galeazzo Visconti had sent to his son-in-law with warm recommendations. He sat hunched forward on a bench beside the table. His companion, a filthy fellow clad in rags, stood behind him, staring at the door with the tense look of a trapped animal. When he heard footsteps, Ettore Salvia sprang up. Louis entered the room.

"Have you been successful?" he asked the astrologer who fell to his knees before him. "Stand up, stand up," he added impatiently, "and tell me what you've found."

Ettore Salvia rose to his feet. He was taller than Louis; he stood between the hearthfire and the wall, his shadow extending over the beamed ceiling. He stepped aside and pointed to the other man who too had fallen to his knees at Louis' entrance—his eyes, sunken under a bulging, scarred forehead, glistened with terror.

"Who is he?" Louis asked, seating himself. "Stand up, man, and answer."

"He cannot do that, my lord," Ettore Salvia replied swiftly and softly. "They cut out his tongue a long time ago—for treason."

Louis laughed shortly. "You haven't been squeamish about choosing an accomplice."

Salvia shrugged. "There are not many to be found for the sort of mission you wished carried out," he replied evenly, with downcast eyes.

A flush crept over Louis' face; he was on the point of responding sharply, but he checked himself. "The important thing is that you bring me what I asked for," he said coldly.

Salvia spoke some low words to the ragged man, who groped in the folds of his garment and drew out a small leather sack, wound around with cord. Perspiration stood on his forehead. "He is afraid of the consequences," remarked the astrologer, handing the sack to Louis. "He hid for two days and two nights under the gallows and he thinks he may have been detected."

Without a word Louis took a purse from his sleeve and tossed it onto the table. The mute snatched it up and concealed it among his rags. Salvia smiled contemptuously; he turned and stood watching the Duke of Orléans. Louis had opened the leather sack and removed a smooth iron ring; it lay now in the palm of his hand. He feigned a calm interest, but the astrologer knew better. To him the young man was as transparent as the figures of veined blown glass with which Venetian artisans ornamented their goblets—thus he anticipated the questions on Louis' lips.

"There is no possible doubt," he said mildly, without emphasis, as though he were giving the most trivial information. "This ring lay twice twenty-four hours under the tongue of a hanged man. This fellow here swears to it. He did not take his eyes off the gallows—no one apart from him touched the corpse after the execution."

Louis raised his hand, signalling that enough had been said. Salvia fell silent. A trace of a smile gleamed under his half-closed eyelids. A ring which had undergone that treatment became a powerful amulet: it made its bearer irresistible to women. Apart from preparing a single potion, which had only served to strengthen a dormant inclination, Salvia had never been required to render the Duke this sort of service. Louis' youth and charm had always smoothed his path to each bower in which he wanted to make an offering to Our Lady Venus. But now he desired Mariette d'En-ghien, a demoiselle of Valentine's retinue; she was still very young and had been in the service of the Duchess only a short time. The customs of Saint-Pol seemed strange to her; she came from the provinces. Her reserve excited Louis exceedingly, because he could not fathom whether what lay behind it was genuine modesty or a refinement of the art of seduction.

Her eyes, which she so seldom raised to his, were green: the grass in spring-time could not be greener, thought Louis, consumed by passion. The desire to possess Maret—her pet name—dominated him completely, so overwhelmingly that he had resorted to what was for him so revolting a measure as the ring which he held in the palm of his hand. This amulet, worn on a chain on the naked body, could not help but make the conquest easy for him.

The Duke of Burgundy, about to depart from Saint-Pol with his attendants to return to his own dwelling, was interrupted by some gentlemen from Isabeau's retinue who delivered the request to him that he visit the Queen before he left. Accompanied by some trusted friends, the Duke went with Isabeau's messengers; he found the Queen in one of the vast gloomy halls which had once served as a reception and meeting room, but was now seldom used.

Isabeau preferred the castle of Vincennes; if she had to reside at Saint-Pol she stayed mostly in her own apartments which, al-though not spacious, were comfortably furnished. However, there were too many eyes and ears there—a confidential conversation was impossible; greater security was offered by these deserted salons in the old section of the palace.

The Queen sat near the hearth. The projecting mantelpiece was decorated to the ceiling with immense sculptures in relief: twelve heraldic beasts and the figures of prophets in pleated robes. Along the walls hung somber tapestries depicting hunting scenes. Some wax candles burned on a table before Isabeau. The silk damask of her clothing and her jewels glowed crimson and violet in the can-dleflames and the light of the setting sun which streamed in through the windows behind her. In a dark corner of the room the Duke saw a few court ladies and other members of Isabeau's retinue; he ordered his own followers to remain near the door and approached the Queen. He knelt before her despite the stiffness of his limbs. He attached great importance to the conventions and was particularly punctilious about the expression of all due marks of respect. Not the difference in age between Isabeau and himself, not the fact that they tolerated each other only out of self-interest, nor that he was essentially the more powerful of the two, could prevent him from the performance of these ceremonies. Three times he allowed himself to be encouraged by the Queen to rise, before he stood up.

Isabeau, who usually enjoyed Burgundy's voluntary—although purely formal—self-abasement, was in no mood for compliments. She was frowning and her full lips were pursed; with her that was always a sure sign of annoyance. She sat erect with her hands on the arms of her chair. She had put aside her robes of state and so, despite the fact that her garments had been cleverly altered by her seamstress, it could no longer remain a secret that she was pregnant again as a result of the rapprochement between herself and the King during Charles' short period of relative lucidity in the spring. There was a general sentiment that a second son was needed; the Dauphin was weak and frail. Isabeau had already lost two children who had suffered from the same lack of vitality. That she, with her strong healthy body, apparently was not capable of giving the country a robust heir was a disappointment and a source of amazement to many people. But the sickly blood of the most recent generation of France's royal House seemed to be predominant.

The Duke of Burgundy waited. The candlelight seemed to emphasize the sharpness of his features; the shadows lay deep around his nose and in his eyesockets. He held his mouth rigidly closed; Isabeau knew that only carefully tested and rehearsed words passed those lips. She had become accustomed, during the years when Charles was underage and Burgundy acted as his guardian, and now again during his renewed regency—which actually amounted to single-handed control of the government—to look for double, even triple, meanings behind the Duke's words. Despite the fact that she considered him to be dangerous, she had a great deal of admiration for him. She recognized the similarity between them: like him, she was intent on working to her own advantage, on safeguarding her own position, on amassing gold and property, and on building power for herself. And she knew now that it was he whom she had to thank, in the main, for her marriage. His own children were married to members of the Bavarian royal house, whose possessions in the Netherlands Burgundy craved. Nothing could be more precious to him than a stronger bond between France and Bavaria. Isabeau had found that she could learn a great deal from him. Already she knew how to keep secret any plans of hers which ran counter to his. Now she concealed her growing desire for power behind a show of docility.

"The King is not well," she said abruptly, without preamble. Her manner of speech was unique in that court: she had never completely lost her foreign accent and had the habit of using short sentences, coming right to the point without the fashionable flowery circumlocutions and paraphrases.

"Madame, I regret the incident in the apartments of the Duchess of Orléans," said Burgundy in a low voice, without looking at her. "The King must, indeed, be far from well to demonstrate publicly an inclination which—"

"Be still!" Isabeau cried. A dark flush spread over her face. The Duke of Burgundy fell silent; the released arrow quivered in the target.

"How is he now?" Isabeau asked after a moment. "You brought him back to his chambers? What is he doing?"

"The King is resting for a while. He was extremely excited." Burgundy's tone was, as usual, unruffled. "I believe that the physicians do not find it advisable for him to appear at the christening feast."

"That's absurd!" Isabeau tossed her head; the pear-shaped pearls trembled in her ears. "Why can't he come to the table? A meal is less tiring than going to church. I do not want them to bring food to his chamber," she announced with sudden brusqueness.

The Duke looked at her directly for the first time, and raised his eyebrows. "What objection can you possibly have to that?" he asked. Isabeau glanced toward her courtiers who stood talking in low voices in the farthest corner of the darkening room. She did not answer at once but stared, her face averted, at the fire, while she toyed with an ornament which the King had sent her when they were first married and he was staying in the south of France: a small golden triptych with a tiny mirror in the back.

"The King is bewitched," she said finally, leaning toward him.

Burgundy's eyes did not change expression; only his mouth showed a trace of satisfaction.

"Madame, may I ask on what grounds you base your opinion?"

"Someone came to me—a man from Guyenne—his name is Arnaud Guillaume," replied the Queen without looking at the impassive face opposite her.

"Came to Your Majesty?" The Duke's lips barely moved. Isabeau felt the reproof. She raised her head defiantly. "I had him brought—I had heard about him," she said shortly. "He believes he can protect the King against sinister influences. He knows all about magic . . ."

"Magic?" repeated Philippe. Isabeau shrugged. She let the gold triptych drop into her lap and looked at him almost defiantly. "What else helps against sorcery?" she asked haughtily. "We see all the time how little comes from the measures of the learned physicians. The King no longer recognizes me." She lowered her eyes and fell silent.

The Duke of Burgundy maintained the silence. A new fruit had ripened on the tree which he had so carefully planted.

"Maître Guillaume says," Isabeau continued, "that those who bewitched the King are concentrating all their energies to prevent his recovery."

"Why should anyone—" the Duke stressed the last word. "—cast a spell upon the King? Does the King have enemies then, Madame?"

Isabeau looked into his eyes. "*I* have enemies," she said. "They bewitch the King in order to remove *my* influence on him. There are those who want to use him for their own purposes. You know that, Monseigneur. The Duchess of Orléans . . ."

Burgundy raised his hand.

"Madame, my Queen," he said evenly, "is there any reason to mention names between us? We both know that a highly-placed man at the court dabbles in politics . . ."

"I don't mean that," the Queen replied hastily. She was fond of Louis d'Orléans. She found it in her interest to protect her brother-in-law. On her mother's side Isabeau came from the Visconti family, to which Valentine also belonged. But since Gian Galeazzo had come to power in Milan and damaged the interests of her Bavarian kinsmen, mutual forbearance had chilled to mutual enmity. "Before his marriage there was no talk of political dabbling," she said significantly. The Duke smiled. Isabeau continued more vehemently.

"Surely everyone knows how the tyrant of Milan came to power—the poisoner Gian Galeazzo!"

"Madame." Philippe knelt before her again. "It might be well to allow this Maître Guillaume the opportunity to do what he can. The King is in a really pitiable plight. He has broken his glass goblets because he was displeased by Your Majesty's coat of arms."

"The arms of Wittelsbach?" asked Isabeau fiercely. "But all the tableware bears my coat of arms next to the King's. He himself gave the order to have it engraved."

Burgundy bowed his head. "The King did not recognize the coat of arms. He trampled on the splinters—he defiled them."

Isabeau stood up so suddenly that her long sleeves brushed against his face. She folded her arms over her protruding stomach and choked with rage. Philippe arose also and made a gesture as if to support her. But the Queen quickly composed herself.

"Arnaud Guillaume is in the palace," she said tensely. "I can have him summoned. We should speak to him as soon as possible."

"In the presence of my lords Berry and Bourbon," added Philippe, involving his fellow Regents in the affair with ceremonial modesty. "I shall see that they are told."

"In my apartments, then," said the Queen, who was still trembling. "It's too cold here."

The Duke of Burgundy struck a silver cymbal which stood upon the table next to the candlesticks. The group of ladies moved forward, preceded by the Comtesse d'Eu, Isabeau's mistress of ceremonies, who placed a mantle about the Queen's shoulders.

Isabeau walked slowly from the hall, leaning on Philippe's arm. Torchbearers appeared at the door. The Queen's red train and Burgundy's long violet sleeves seemed to flow into each other, variations of one color. The retinue of courtiers followed them at a leisurely pace.

The room in which the Queen and the Regents met resembled a bower: the tapestries that hung along the walls were so thickly embroidered with flowers and leafy tendrils that their blue background was barely visible. Isabeau sat under a canopy. A greyhound crouched before the old Duke of Bourbon, who urged it to show off its tricks. The Queen looked on with an absent smile. Burgundy and his brother, the Duke of Berry, stood at a table which held some books. They were examining a breviary which had been commissioned not long before by Isabeau. Both men were bibliophiles, especially Berry, who spent vast sums of money on books. His castle of Bicêtre contained countless art treasures; painters, writers and sculptors made pilgrimages to his court where they were hospitably received and where their work was paid for with annual allowances and life-long annuities.

Philippe too had been busy for some years putting together a library of ecclesiastical, didactic and historical documents which he had found in his Burgundian and Flemish residences. His motivation, however, was different. While his late brother Charles V had been interested primarily in acquiring knowledge, and Berry was an aesthete, the Duke of Burgundy believed that a ruler must be a Maecenas if he wanted to see himself and his deeds glorified in the art of his time.

Berry held the Queen's breviary up to the candlelight to get a better look at one of the miniatures. He was sixty-five years old, corpulent, with the somewhat slack features of one who had indulged too abundantly in the good things of the earth; there were bags under his eyes and the drooping flesh of his chin and cheeks was an unhealthy color. He wore his hair cut short like Philippe's, but his was curled. The cloak which enveloped his shapeless body was of green and gold brocade, trimmed with marten fur. The Oriental pomades with which he liked to be regularly massaged surrounded him with a penetrating aroma.

His brother looked with disapproval at the thick, beringed fingers turning the pages. Philippe's austere appearance caused Berry, by contrast, to look almost like a gaudy parrot. The Duke of Burgundy cherished a secret contempt for his brother, who had no aspirations beyond the collecting of books and curiosities and the beautification of Bicêtre where he spent most of his time with his wife, who was almost fifty years younger than he.

"Look, look," said Berry keenly. "These initials have been overlaid with gold leaf. By God, there is no handsomer script anywhere! Oh yes, I concede that its production was demanding—the cost of time and paper. But what nobility of form!" He held the book out at arm's length; the candlelight glinted on the golden ornaments between the blue-and-green-painted vines which framed the text. His small sharp eyes sparkled; he clicked his tongue a few times in admiration and closed the book. Burgundy took it from him and examined the clasps mounted on the leather covers.

"I must say, Madame, the book is magnificent." Berry went up to Isabeau and stood before her. "I congratulate you. I must have the man too—who is it? Hennecart? Beautiful work—superb work! But at the first opportunity I'll let you see a few pages from my new breviary. Maître Paul of Limburg and his brother are illuminating the calendar. I don't exaggerate when I call it a miracle. One would swear that the flowers could actually be plucked from the grass and that in the next moment the crows would come flying up out of the snow. The initials are especially beautiful—like these here—but in vermilion—"

"Actually, where is that man now?" Burgundy broke testily into the flood of his brother's words. He put the book back on the table. The workmanship of the clasps was exceptionally exquisite, and they were mounted with cabochon garnets and pearls. He didn't doubt that it had cost the Queen a considerable amount of money.

Isabeau turned toward him. "He's being fetched," she replied coldly. "I gave instructions that he should not be brought directly here. It was necessary first for Messeigneurs de Berry and Bourbon to become acquainted with our intentions."

The Duke of Bourbon stopped playing with the dog. The animal sprang toward him in invitation, but he paid no more attention to it. Isabeau ordered it to lie down.

"I cannot say that I find this new plan to be entirely as favorable as it looks," Bourbon said slowly. His caution in all matters was well-known. During deliberations he bored Berry and roused the impatience of Isabeau and Burgundy. "Why should we encourage behavior that is known to engender suspicion and discontent everywhere? Isn't it wiser for us to stick to remedies which can bear the light of day? In the long run the wisdom of the physicians and the mercy of the Church will help the King much more."

"In the long run!" Isabeau's eyes became hard as glass. "Hasn't this lasted long enough then? Two years of misery and worry and the King's condition has grown worse, if that's possible. Surely by now everyone knows that all the sacraments of the Church can do nothing against witchcraft . . ."

"Madame, Madame!" Berry raised both hands in warning. "Your Majesty does not realize what she is saying."

Isabeau crossed herself. "That is no blasphemy," she said with hauteur, to hide her confusion. "But I'm at my wits' end! What has happened to the King does not come from natural causes. That's obvious," she continued more heatedly, bending forward to stare at the three Regents.

Berry made a gesture more eloquent than words, that signified his benevolently impartial attitude toward this problem. Burgundy stood silent; he betrayed his irritation only by rubbing the thumb and forefinger of his left hand together. Isabeau saw it. She attempted to control her nervousness, beckoning to the dog, which came to her immediately and laid its head in her lap.

A door, hung like the walls with flowered tapestries, opened suddenly to admit two men: Jean Salaut, the Queen's private secretary, and Arnaud Guillaume. Both knelt before Isabeau and the Regents. Arnaud Guillaume wore a stained, patched garment, something between a tabard and a cassock; with his long, filthy hair, his bony, emaciated face, he looked like one of the half-crazed anchorites who mortified themselves for the salvation of mankind. His fasts and flagellations, however, were undertaken with intentions far less than holy. Although he knelt, his demeanor was not in the least humble.

While the secretary addressed the Queen, Guillaume's cold eyes traveled without a trace of timidity over the people in the room: the waiting Dukes who eyed him with extreme reserve, and Isabeau who, with apparent unconcern, was allowing the dog to play with her golden triptych.

"That is good, Maître Salaut," the Queen said. "You may go now."

The secretary arose and, after the prescribed bows, backed to the door, which he shut noiselessly after him. There was a brief silence. The three Dukes stood motionless; the Queen did not stir. If it had not been for the panting dog which snapped playfully at the shiny toy in Isabeau's lap, the royal group could have been painted against the colorful flowers and vines of the wall hangings. Finally, Bourbon spoke.

"You come from Guyenne?" Guillaume bowed his head in assent. "You call yourself a monk," Bourbon continued. "To which order do you belong?"

The man raised his bright, icy eyes to the Queen.

"I thought I had been called here to cure the King," he said, "not to be held accountable for a past which is of little significance."

"This is an extremely impudent rascal," Berry said half-aloud. He raised his perfumed gloves to his face. Philippe of Burgundy put his arms akimbo and set one leg on the step leading to the Queen's chair.

"Then you believe you can cure the King," he said curtly. "By what means? Think before you answer; there is no pardon here for frauds."

"Your Grace has no need to be afraid of fraud," Guillaume replied in his crude, hoarse voice. "I'm sure of my powers. Here in my breast, under my habit, I carry a book which gives me power over everything living—over the four elements and over all the substance and matter which they contain. Thanks to this book of wonders, I could be ruler of the planets—if I wanted that; I could alter their courses. Aren't the astrologers saying that a comet has appeared which will bring a calamity to France, the death of men and beasts, drought and destruction of all the crops standing in the fields? I could call forth another comet from the heavens, a comet which no one knows about and no astrologer has ever seen—more powerful than the first, so powerful it could thrust the deadly one out of its orbit."

"What sort of book is that?" asked the Duke of Berry inquisitively. The person of this filthy ascetic repelled him, but his curiosity had been aroused by the mention of the wonder book. Guillaume smiled slyly and pressed his crossed arms more tightly against his breast.

"The book is intended for a few eyes only," he said. He made a cringing bow in Berry's direction. "Besides, Your Grace would not be able to read the characters. The writing is older than mankind itself, older than Adam, the father of us all, who left us in original sin."

Berry's nostrils flared in contempt. He took a few steps toward Isabeau and spoke to her in an undertone. "I consider this the most revolting deception. Send this man away, Madame."

"Or force him to show you what he is hiding under his habit," Burgundy said impatiently. "You've used your whip well against less arrogant dogs."

Berry threw him a cold, angry look. Long ago he had given up all hope of emulating his brother's gift for administration. In the period before the King came of age, Berry's all-too-obvious mismanagement of his assigned provinces had provoked Burgundy to criticize him sharply; later, Berry suspected, not without evidence, that his older brother had had a hand in the King's removal of Languedoc from Berry's control. He had never forgiven Philippe for that.

"I'm sure that you can hold your own in matters like that, Monseigneur," Berry said, in his courtly, biting voice. "No one ever did me the impressive honor of calling me 'the Bold' because I managed to get a place at the table for myself with my fists."

Bourbon raised his head quickly and Isabeau turned pale. The sorcerer, momentarily forgotten, suppressed a smile; he grasped Berry's insinuation. The Duke of Burgundy's enemies always claimed that he did not owe his soubriquet of "the Bold" to his valiant conduct on the battlefield of Poitiers, but to the public childish squabble for precedence between him and the late Duke of Anjou at the coronation feast of Charles VI.

The Queen, who had reason to fear a personal quarrel between the Regents, came hastily between the two of them.

"My lords, my uncles," she said, "this is no time for discord. Maître Guillaume has been recommended to me by highly-placed persons in whom I can place my trust. There are many people at the court who have consulted him with good results. What does it matter whether he lets us see his book? The important thing is the advice he can give us. Go on, speak further," she said to Guillaume. "No one will force you to show the book. But bear in mind that you will need more than words to convince us."

The ascetic cast a quick, malicious glance at her.

"Convince?" he muttered. "How can I prove what was disclosed to me in a state of grace? In the land of the blind, it is I alone who can see. Secret signs have revealed to me by God's grace, that our King has been bewitched—within these walls the Devil and all the hellish powers have been conjured up to ruin His Majesty."

"Enough, man, enough," said Bourbon. "What are you saying? Have you any accusations to make against anyone? Can you name names?"

"Monseigneur, there is a man who watched for two days and two nights under the gallows at Montfaucon where a thief had been hanged. Do I need to tell you, my lord, what use the corpses of criminals are put to?"

Hastily Isabeau crossed herself. Parts of the bodies of the hanged were used for conjuration, a dreaded practice. "This man," continued Guillaume, "I saw today in the palace."

"How is that possible?" Burgundy asked smoothly. "The palace is not an open marketplace where anyone can come and go."

"No, Monseigneur." Guillaume bowed again, his arms crossed over his breast. "But he was not alone. He was in the company of the black astrologer, the southerner, about whom there has been much talk."

"Salvia," Burgundy said, raising his brows. "In the service of Orléans," he added, throwing a glance at Isabeau. The Queen caught his look, but her own eyes remained cold and hard. "From Milan," she amended in a flat voice. "Salvia of Milan, a trusted friend of *Gian Galeazzo*." She stressed the last words to make it clear to Burgundy that she rejected any other association. The Duke shrugged and then bowed in agreement. "It is as Your Majesty wishes," he said evenly.

During this exchange Bourbon stood staring at the ascetic with knitted brows; now he took a step toward Isabeau. "Now that we have established that this fellow is telling the truth, what measures must be taken here? The simplest thing would be to subject Salvia as well as the body snatcher to an interrogation."

Guillaume's eyes lit up. Isabeau made a hasty defensive gesture. "That seems unwise to me. We would be exposed. What we do here must not be aired in public."

She gave a sign to Berry, who stood closest to the table. He dropped a silver ball into a dish provided for that purpose; the prolonged jingling sound summoned the secretary Salaut from an adjoining room. While Isabeau instructed the secretary to give Guillaume lodging in the palace and pay him a certain sum in advance, Burgundy continued to stand with his hands on his hips and one foot on the step of the chair, staring at the ascetic. He was not in the least interested in the continually changing series of doctors and their methods of treatment, although he gave the appearance of taking an active part in the discussions. This time, however, it was quite different: he suspected that in Arnaud Guillaume he had found a useful instrument at a bargain price. Guillaume bowed directly to him; he responded with a cold glance from under half closed lids. He was quite sure that Guillaume understood where his profit lay.

"Bah!" Berry said contemptuously when the door had closed

behind the two men. "Do you really believe, Madame, that this lout is capable of doing anything for the King?"

Isabeau had risen and kicked the heavy train of her gown to one side. She felt deadly tired and no longer capable of arguing.

"Why not?" she said irritably. She did not care for the Duke of Berry with his exaggerated interest in art and artists; she found him untrustworthy and, although less dangerous than Burgundy, altogether insufferable. She knew that he had lashed out at Guillaume mainly because he had not been able to acquire the book in question; undoubtedly he had expected her to cooperate with him by ordering the sorcerer to give it up. Isabeau did not believe for an instant in the sincerity of the Dukes' solicitude for the madman's welfare; she knew that the plans of his royal uncles did not depend in any way on the King's recovery. On this point Bourbon was the least calculating of the three; and the only one whose compassion for the King was genuine. Usually Isabeau found it easy to play the diplomat at gatherings like these; an appetite and talent for intrigue were in her blood. Now however she was suddenly overcome by depression bordering on despair; she was painfully aware that she stood completely alone and that today and in the future she must brace herself firmly with her back against the wall, to protect everything that she considered rightfully hers. She was in the heart of the Kingdom, apparently safely hidden like the stone in the core of a fruit; but on all sides greedy worms were eating through the rich pulp. With a wave of her hand, she prevented Berry from elaborating on his opinion.

She walked past the Regents, who bowed to her politely, to a door opposite the one through which Salaut and Guillaume had vanished; she had to bend her head to one side to prevent the top of her crowned headdress from touching the door frame. The white greyhound bounded after her.

"You forgot yourself just now, Monseigneur," said Burgundy to Berry, who was beginning to draw on his gloves.

The Duke of Bourbon made an impatient gesture. "There is no sense in stirring up old ashes," he remarked, approaching Burgundy. "Monseigneur de Berry was somewhat hasty."

"I don't care about haste." Burgundy shoved aside the arm with which Bourbon attempted to restrain him. "My brother of Berry is not hot-blooded enough to blurt out things which he does not customarily think . . . and say. What you think leaves me cold," he added, the bitter lines around his mouth becoming sharper, "but what you say, especially what you say about me publicly, touches me deeply. In your eyes then, I am a braggart, a squabbler? And have you no respect for the name which I bear with honor?"

Berry shrugged. He stood half-turned away from the light, and the shadow which fell over his heavy face made him look a little like a toad, an impression intensified by his ample glossy greenish clothing.

"Have you earned my respect then, brother?" he said affably, but not without malice. "Have you, on your side, furthered *my* interests, or at least not worked against them since you have been occupying a position of power—or say rather, *the* position of power? You have not given me much inducement to honor you or your name."

Burgundy frowned and sat down, stiffly erect as always, on the bench under the canopy.

"I have had no reason to approve of the manner in which you have been able to arrange your affairs," he said coldly. "God knows there is chaos in all the provinces, but the mess in Languedoc and Guyenne surpasses anything we have had to contend with in the dominions. You can't expect anything better, of course, when you refuse to lower taxes. No sensible governor lets himself go so far for the sake of miniature paintings and carved towers."

"No, you manage another way," Berry said; he struck the edge of the table angrily with his right-hand glove which he had not yet put on. "You marry the rich heiress of Flanders and let the roast goose melt in your mouth. You have no trouble being generous and lifting the tax burden. Nevertheless, I have heard it said that you are not averse to extra income, either, if you are able to squeeze it out somewhere without damaging your good name. There are many within these borders who curse your name already, lord brother."

"It is not unpleasant or dangerous to live in Burgundy or Flanders," Philippe replied calmly, "and if anything should occur or be expected to occur there which would stir up discontent, I would be prepared to look into the matter. But it may be as you say—that I am called 'the Bold' because I thrust Anjou away from his place at table—I am, in any case, not so cowardly that I let my tax collector be burned by the populace to make up for my foolish actions."

The Duke of Berry raised his glove and took a step forward. Hastily Bourbon placed himself between him and Burgundy, who remained motionless in his seat.

"My lords!" Bourbon exhorted them. "This is really going too far. All these things lie behind us. Wouldn't it be more sensible to confine our discussion to the present?"

"Agreed, agreed, worthy lord," Burgundy said, without taking his eyes from Berry. "But can he deny that I am right? Six years ago when the King, our pitiable nephew, went to see how the land lay in Languedoc—because the laments of the people were audible even here—he could not quiet them in any other way except to allow them to burn your treasurer, Messire de Betisac. I have a good memory, brother. Does it still surprise you that the King found it prudent to deprive you of authority for a considerable period of time?"

"The King, the King!" Berry threw his glove on the floor. "Slide everything onto the shoulders of that poor soul again. You gave him good counsel, you knew what you were doing."

"Don't make yourself ridiculous, brother." A shadow slid over Burgundy's cold, crafty face. "How much influence did I—or any one of us—have after the King thanked us so politely in the great Council at Reims for our help? Do you think that I would try to press my advice on him when he so clearly preferred those fools, the Marmousets, that haughty set of climbing burghers and priests whom he loved to call his 'Council'?"

"It's not difficult to talk about hating," said Berry. "No, Monseigneur de Bourbon, why do you enjoin me to be silent? I'll say what I think fit to say. My brother is so eager to condemn the way we received our dismissal at Reims. But what have you done about it, Burgundy? Have you presented any resistance or tried to avenge yourself?"

"You did that yourself already, brother, didn't you?" answered Philippe drily. "Cardinal de Laon, who so cleverly and venemously explained to the Council that our nephew Charles was capable of ruling by himself—not long after that, the Cardinal was no more. Wasn't that poison? Surely, *you* know about that," he added ironically.

"Messeigneurs!" The Duke of Bourbon threw a quick glance at the door through which Isabeau had vanished. "In heaven's name, remember where we are. The walls have ears. The room next door . . ."

"A room full of women!" Berry gave an ugly laugh. "They are used to hearing—and seeing—less beautiful things whenever they wish. You are even crazier than our nephew the King," he went on to Burgundy, "if you are attempting to insinuate that I . . ."

"Have I contended such a thing?" Burgundy laughed softly and put his fingertips together. "I only know the facts, brother. I know that you were not especially obliging when the King asked you to march with your vassals to Brittany to seek out the suspects."

"By the body of Christ!" Berry swore with a gesture of impotent rage. "You distort everything. Did you want to cooperate then? Or Bourbon here? No, my lord of Burgundy, you cannot throw dust in my eyes. I know damned well who always has the final say here. Oh, yes, you can insist that you were pushed into the background when our nephew took advice from the Marmousets, but you knew enough to reach your goal by going through back roads. You are slyer than a fox, brother. And I never doubted that I had you to thank for the matter of Languedoc."

"You are so certain of your case." Burgundy rose. "Undoubtedly you will be able to tell me why I played such a nasty trick on you." He looked fixedly at his brother over Bourbon's head. The Duke of Berry, who had become so excited that beads of perspiration glistened on his forehead, cried, almost choking with rage, "Why, why? Do I know why? So much goes on in that cunning heart of yours that I wager only the Devil knows your thoughts—and perhaps not even he, for you are too wily even for him. Are you going to tell me that you did not want Languedoc for yourself? You are forever swallowing up land, brother. Look at the map. You wind yourself around the heart of France like a serpent. *I* don't know where your avarice will end . . ."

Burgundy walked down the steps leading from the bench, shrugged, and took his velvet hat from a chest nearby. The Duke of Bourbon, taking this as a sign that this painful conversation was over, heaved a sigh of relief. He picked up Berry's glove which lay near him and returned it to its owner.

"Look upon all this as belonging to the past, Monseigneur," he said in a low voice. "You—didn't you?—returned Languedoc to the King . . ."

Burgundy laughed; a short, dry laugh filled with derision.

Bourbon, who had maintained the calm demeanor of the mediator long enough, lost his patience.

"I find it deeply mortifying, my lords," he said heatedly, "that we should be busy splitting hairs when it is in our interest to work together harmoniously. There is no authority in France today except our own. We have a heavy responsibility before us, my lords."

Burgundy smiled sarcastically, but Berry burst out, "Words, words! Don't play the hypocrite, Monseigneur de Bourbon! We know each other too well, I'm afraid. It's perhaps better not to describe the interests which we pursue here."

"I see to my delight, brother," said Burgundy, who was already at the door, "that you have found for the nonce a new opponent to argue with. Good-bye, my lords. The baptismal feast of little Orléans will be lively this evening if we come to the table in our present frame of mind."

In the great inner courtyard next to the stables, servants had been holding horses in readiness for some time for the Duke and his retinue. Burgundy's coal-black stallion, Charlemagne, kicked up the earth impatiently with his front hooves. On the harnesses and saddles, the copper and silver ornaments glittered in the steady light of the torches held high by the servants. A glimmer of light streamed out too from the open stable doors, through which could be seen a swarm of grooms and horses. The men were busily cleaning harnesses and tending to the beasts in the stalls. An acrid odor of hay and manure met everyone who came into the vicinity of these buildings. Dampness hung on the horses in the courtyard. The members of the suite who were already mounted and waiting had great difficulty in keeping their stamping, snorting steeds under control. The Duke allowed one of his servants to throw a fur-lined cloak around him; then he set his foot in a stirrup and deftly swung himself into the saddle. The gates of Saint-Pol were flung open; with a loud clatter of hooves and amid the shouting of the servants and torchbearers who ran quickly alongside it, the ducal train moved off under the archway in the direction of Burgundy's residence, the Hôtel d'Artois.

The evening was chilly and misty; drops of water clung to Burgundy's hat and to the fur of his mantle. The torches smoked with a ruddy glow in the fog. They rode at a fairly quick pace through the narrow streets of the Saint-Pol district; mud and stones flew up from under the horses' hooves. Philippe handled the reins mechanically; his thoughts were elsewhere. He stared fixedly, without seeing it, at the glossy reddish copper band between Charlemagne's ears.

He had been unusually patient in allowing Berry to talk so much; he had listened because he had a deep aversion to commonplace wrangling. He found it diverting that his brother was so well aware of the nature of the relationship between the two of them; the fact that Berry lacked the pride and tact to preserve a courtly, arrogant silence about these matters was, to Burgundy, merely further proof that Berry had no talent for the craft of diplomacy. Indeed, Burgundy knew that he himself was not blameless in the matter of Languedoc; a resentment, never openly acknowledged but carefully stored away, was the thing that had motivated Philippe to work against his brother at that time.

In 1385, the Duke of Burgundy had come up with a plan to attack England directly as part of—and perhaps as a way to end—the drawn-out war between France and that island. He knew how to turn the head of the King, then seventeen years old and married for only a short time to Isabeau, with promises of great new military victories. The plan was received enthusiastically by the nobility, all of whom had sufficient motivation to want to plunder and extort tribute from the inhabitants of the English coast.

About 1400 vessels had been assembled, most of them only fit for boating and as senselessly and grotesquely dressed up as the pugnacious young noblemen themselves. Even now Burgundy could not think of that fleet without irritation: silvered masts, gilded prows, multi-colored silk pavilions on the decks, streamers and banners on which all of French heraldry seemed to come to life as the colorful ensigns fluttered in the wind: lions and griffins, dragons and unicorns. And even more ludicrous than this, an entire wooden city, complete with houses and palaces, loaded onto seventy-two cargo ships—a city intended to shelter the whole army after it disembarked on English soil.

An invasion at that moment offered Burgundy an unparalleled opportunity for influence over English-Flemish relations. If everything had gone as he had planned, Burgundy might have become the most powerful man on the continent, but his dream was too daring: too many in his circle hated him and were jealous of the apparent ease with which he moved piece after piece on the political chessboard. His brother Berry had been one of these for a long time, and was well aware that the plan depended mostly on taking advantage of the propitious moment to set out to sea and attack; if that moment were allowed to slip past and the departure of the fleet were delayed, winter storms would make the voyage impossible. While Burgundy waited in Arras with the army of nobles, biting his lips in impatience, Berry lingered in Paris with the King, dawdling and delaying. A marriage was arranged between Berry's son and the King's youngest sister; the festivities held everyone's attention. It was not until the middle of September that the King arrived in Arras.

The crossing was still possible because the weather was holding, but now Berry, and his indispensable army, remained absent. Despite letters and urgent messages, he could not be shifted from his intentionally dilatory course. He finally came in December when the storms were breaking out, the nights were long and dark and the sea growled around England. Burgundy had to give up his plan. He suffered this setback in his own way, without in any respect allowing his resentment and rage to be seen. Instead of literally setting his sails to the wind, he did so figuratively: he altered his course in the inimitably adroit manner of the politician and began seeking rapport with England.

For him this policy might possibly yield much more favorable, if costly, results than the naval expedition would have been able to do. So, after all, he did not regret the failure of his plan, for which France bore the enormous cost. And although Burgundy did not betray by word or deed that he was aware of Berry's role in the failure, he did not forget it.

The horses' hooves clattered on the pavement of the inner courtyard of the Hôtel d'Artois. Philippe dismounted before the main door. He threw his cloak, heavy with dampness, to one of the nobles in his retinue and strode swiftly into the palace. In the rooms where he was accustomed to spend his time when he was at home, he found his son, Jean, Comte de Nevers. The young man was standing near a writing desk, slowly turning over the pages of a manuscript. He closed the book and turned when his father entered.

"You are late, Monseigneur," he said, with a formal bow.

Burgundy greeted his son with a frown. "I missed you at the christening ceremony," he said curtly.

The corners of Jean's mouth turned down in an expression of contempt.

"If I had to attend christenings for all of Orléans' offspring—legitimate as well as illegitimate—" he began, but a glance from his father silenced him. He went to the hearth and spat into the fire.

"You know what I mean," said Burgundy sternly.

"Yes, in that respect I am not so good a diplomat as you, my lord. I cannot dissemble. God knows I would like nothing better than to wring Orléans' neck—I find him too much beneath contempt for me to dirty my sword or my dagger on him."

"You know my position." Burgundy looked at his son, who now stood with his back to the fire. The wax candles on the reading desk illuminated his somewhat sharp, oldish face; he had his father's keen eyes and a sour mouth with a full lower lip. He was rather small and badly built: his upper body was disproportionately heavy, a trait that was exaggerated by the short pleated jacket he was wearing.

Jean de Nevers and Louis d'Orléans held much the same position in the Kingdom; they were about the same age, all but equal in rank and well-matched in acumen. Louis had many enemies at court, but he had no fewer admirers; with unparalleled luck he managed to maintain his position in all circumstances and avoid unfortunate entanglements. Nature had not withheld a single gift from him.

Jean, on the other hand, lacked all the qualities which could have made him shine: his mind, forceful and caustic rather than quick-witted, did not show to advantage in the courtly world of Saint-Pol, where his surly character won him few friends. Ever since his boyhood, the preference shown to Orléans had been a thorn in Jean's flesh. He had his father's uncommunicative disposition. Resentment burned in him, a constantly smouldering fire nourished by countless petty incidents involving his cousin: a precedence at a banquet, a victory in a tournament, the admiring glance of a woman, a word of praise—and more than all this, Louis' own airy amiability, even toward Jean himself—his adaptability and dashing courtliness.

At a fête given by the King a few years before, Jean de Nevers had found his wife Marguérite in Orléans' arms. Earlier in the festivities he had already had reason to complain about her roving glances, her attention to the banter of the King's younger brother. Because no one was sober and the momentum of the celebration could not be interrupted, the affair did not result in an altercation or a physical fight.

The day after this evening of indulgence was more bitter for Jean than any which came from simply drinking too much wine. He was assailed by doubt and rage; he was not sure now what exactly he had seen in his drunken condition; he did not know what to believe or what to do. There were no witnesses; Marguérite remained silent, Orléans behaved with courteous indifference. Spies, servants with sharp eyes, could discover no signs of an illicit love affair. But Jean, wracked by jealousy, saw signs where there were none: a poem filled with allegory, which the Duke of Orléans had written and which he read aloud at a court fête, Jean took to be a hymn of praise to his wife's beauty. His self-possession deserted him completely and he let himself go into frenzies of hatred. Of all those who worked for Burgundy, secretly fueling hostility against Orléans, he was the most industrious; he supervised the men in his father's service who were trying to enflame the people. And it was he who came up with the notion of using Louis' dabbling in the occult as a weapon against him.

Jean was driven to these methods by his father's prudence; he himself would much rather have allowed his bottled-up loathing to explode into violence. But his father firmly and resolutely opposed any form of assassination, including the poisoned cup. So Jean could only wait, brooding in solitude on the rancor which embittered his life. Because he did not have the ability to feign amiability or even indifference, every moment he spent in Orléans' presence was a torment for him. He kept away from the court, but etiquette had assigned his wife a place among the Queen's ladies, so he could not forbid Marguérite to go to Saint-Pol. He bided his time, taking refuge in the library of the Hôtel d'Artois or in various of his many country estates, venting his fury in hunting and sport.

"In truth, I know your position," he said in response to his father's look of cold disapproval. "But I repeat once more: I am incapable of so much diplomacy. Wild horses could not have dragged me to that christening this afternoon."

"You're a fool," Burgundy said, rising from the bench onto which he had sunk. "And the future of your landed inheritance is very dim if you persist in carrying this attitude into other areas of your life. But I know you better than you know yourself. I have confidence in you—you're shrewd and you're capable of looking ahead. Like me, you learn from experience; you're guided by the adage 'what three know, the whole world knows'. But in God's name, control yourself. Don't let yourself be carried away by your emotions. I know what rage means, I know passion, but I'd sooner seal my mouth up with iron locks and my hands with chains than speak or act too quickly."

A semblance of a smile flitted over Jean's clever, pointed face; he shrugged. In many respects he found his father too cautious; he felt more in sympathy with the Italian tyrants who did not hesitate to employ any means to get what they wanted. He hated not being able to express his urge to action; he cursed his indolence. His restlessness drove him to keep abreast of all news of events at home and abroad, all public disturbances, all military operations, preparing himself to choose sides and participate as soon as the opportunity arose. He considered it a serious deficiency that he had never won fame on the battlefield and looked for the chance to come into the flower of his manhood in that respect.

"I waited here because I wanted to speak with you, Monseigneur," he began, coming away from the hearth. Burgundy paused on his way to the door.

"I have very little time," he said crustily. He did not want to reveal how tired he was. His shoes, which had gotten wet during his ride home, were uncomfortable. And he had to change clothes for the christening fête. "I cannot avoid my obligations as easily as you do," he said without turning around. "I must return to the palace."

"Too bad." Jean laughed shortly. He waited a moment, but the Duke did not move. He knew his son; though he rarely allowed himself to be tempted into expressions of feeling, he was worried about Jean de Nevers. Their conversations were always somewhat formal; they never approached friendly intimacy. Nevertheless, he knew that Jean would never have asked for an interview if he did not already have a carefully-weighed plan of action. So Burgundy returned to the bench.

"It's not necessary for you to come to an instant decision." Jean sat down opposite his father. "All I want is your opinion in principle." He stopped a moment, rubbing his long, bony forefinger along his nose—a gesture which was also characteristic of Burgundy.

"You are undoubtedly aware of what has been going on in Hungary. King Sigismund's couriers have been visiting us too often recently, and their stories are too alarming to be ignored. Those messengers aren't coming here for nothing, my lord. Actually, I have the impression that this business is being passed off too lightly at court."

"No wonder Sigismund is uneasy—if it is true that the Turks are massing on the Hungarian border. But what do you mean to imply? Surely this would be an exceptionally ill-chosen moment for France to send an auxiliary army to Hungary."

"I do not agree with you, Monseigneur." Jean de Nevers leaned toward his father, with both hands on his knees. "On the contrary, I am convinced that there is great enthusiasm for a crusade against the Turks now. For the last few years there has been no military undertaking of any importance. And surely there are enough men in France who are eager to demonstrate their dexterity with weapons outside the jousting field. It would be really wicked to encourage our knighthood to believe that they should be contented with dancing, playing the lute and composing love songs." He snorted derisively and laughed. Deep in thought, Burgundy stared at his son.

"If we should be in a position to raise an army," he said slowly, with the traces of a smile at the corners of his mouth, "presumably you do not intend to play a subordinate role."

"Then I will take the leadership upon myself. I consider that I am completely capable of it."

"No one could accuse you of false modesty, my son," said Burgundy ironically. "But as I have already said, I am afraid that the moment is not auspicious. It requires a good deal of trouble and expense to gather the money and materials for that kind of enterprise. I don't believe that I can permit a claim for new taxes now—there's a limit to everything."

"I'm convinced that almost everyone who bears a name of any consequence will respond to the summons. This matter cannot be put off for long, my lord. Sigismund's messengers who are here at the moment will shortly be leaving. I am eager to give them a satisfactory answer to take back with them. We have to anticipate that the Hungarians could be destroyed if the Serbian army perishes at Kossovo."

"Yes, yes." Philippe nodded somewhat impatiently. "We will talk about this later at a more convenient time. Come to me tomorrow after early mass," he said, saluting his son in farewell.

Jean de Nevers bowed, and remained in that position until the Duke had left the room. Then he walked slowly back to the reading desk, his brow wrinkled in thought and his lower lip thrust forward. He trimmed a candle and resumed reading the letters of the Apostles, beautifully written on heavy parchment with the initial letters done in red and gold. The candles and the hearthfire cast a deep glow over the furniture, the dark carpets and the beamed ceiling.

Queen Blanche, the widow of the King's great grandfather, who had been dead for more than forty years, entered the lying-in chamber. She was the last descendant of the generation of the beloved and lamented Philippe the Fair who, as the first prince of the House of Valois, had now almost passed into legend. In a certain sense she was considered to be the head of the entire royal family. Although she lived in retirement in her castle at Néauphle in the province of Seine and Oise, the family listened to her advice, valued her judgment and kept her informed about everything that happened. She always attended the fêtes of the royal family.

Queen Blanche was about sixty-four years old, stately and beautiful in a way different from any other woman at court. The mourning which she had not laid aside in the forty years of her widowhood made her appearance all the more impressive. Past a row of deeply curtseying court ladies and chamberwomen, she walked to Valentine's bed, her long mantle trailing after her.

The Duchess of Orléans, refreshed after a deep sleep, lay on her back against the pillows, her face framed by two brown braids.

"Well, Valentine?" said Queen Blanche cordially; she seated herself on a stool which the chamberwomen had placed hastily beside the bed. The Duchess smiled and attempted to sit up and kiss the older woman's hand. Blanche held her back.

"Lie still, darling. You must be tired enough after the reception here this afternoon. You are as white as a waxen votive image. Was it difficult this time?"

"Ah, no." Valentine shook her head. "Only I am so tired," she added in a whisper. "I feel as though I will never find the strength to get up again. God knows it is a sinful thought . . . but sometimes I wish I had died in the childbed."

"Hush, hush, ma mie." Queen Blanche leaned forward to block, from the ladies of her retinue who stood together at some distance behind her, the sight of tears gliding slowly down Valentine's cheeks. "Don't give in. Be brave. Life is hard for women—no one knows it better than I, ma mie; we must endure much sickness, grief and solitude before God delivers us. We are puppets; another will manipulates the strings, never our own. There is nothing for us except resignation and patience, Valentine, till the end of our days. Pray for strength to the Mother of God who had to bear more than any other woman on earth."

Valentine nodded; she could not restrain her tears.

"And as far as my lord of Orléans is concerned," continued the older woman softly, "there are worse husbands, darling. He is always courteous and obliging, and he does not neglect you—Harken to the testimony," she added, smiling as the infant began to wail in the adjoining room. "All men are like that, ma mie—unruly and violent when they are young and foolish in their old age. A white neck, a pair of pretty eyes—no more is needed to bring their blood to a boil. Look at me, child, I know what I am talking about. When I was eighteen years old I was chosen by the King to be the Dauphin's bride. I was pretty—prettier than these wax dolls here at the court. La Belle Blanche they called me in Navarre. My God, where does the time go?"

Her smile deepened, wise, full of humor, and spread to the laughter lines around her bright, childlike eyes, black and round as Morello cherries.

"The King had never seen me; he allowed me to come to Paris with my father to draw up the marriage agreement. I found my cousin the Dauphin not unpleasant—a little thin, but at least young and lively enough—and he was eager to have me; he made no bones about it. Then the King saw me and I did not become the wife of the crown prince; I became the Queen. My bridegroom was almost sixty years old. Do you think that I did not shed bitter tears, Valentine, when I had to stand beside that old man at the altar and still be silent? It pleased God to summon my husband two years after our marriage—perhaps you are thinking that I had little reason to complain about that. But my blood was young, even though I wore mourning—and I had no children. No, ma mie, you don't know your own wealth."

"Don't think that I am ungrateful, Madame," said Valentine. She was a little livelier; color had come into her cheeks. "When I was a child I had already learned that there is not much sense in dreaming too much. In Pavia too, reality was hard and bitter. But within the last few years it seems as though everything happens at once. I hardly solve one problem before another one appears. It is not so much about the death of my children or about—about Monseigneur d'Orléans . . ." she went on quietly after a slight pause, while her fingers burrowed into the embroidery of the coverlet. "I believe that sorrow is the portion of all women . . . that does not make it easier to bear. But there are things one can learn to accept."

Queen Blanche smiled in compassion. She saw through Valentine's heroic attempt at self-deception.

"What is vexing you then, ma mie? I want nothing better than to help you . . . if that lies in my power. A sympathetic ear can also be a help, if no advice is possible."

"The King," whispered Valentine, with a sidelong glance at the ladies-in-waiting. "I worry about the King." The older woman leaned forward; the lappets of her veil fell over the blanket.

"We do not need to pretend with each other. You know as well as I do that the King's illness is incurable. It still amazes me that it took so long for the seizures to come upon him. I saw it in him when he was only a child—he was restless and filled with strange notions. Indeed, his mother, Queen Jeanne, also suffered from a weakness in her head; there were times when she could not remember anything, not even her own name, nor her rank, or recognize the faces of her children. She suffered terribly when she came to herself again and everyone suffered with her, for she was a sweet lady, Queen Jeanne; after her death her husband said of her that she had been the sun of his kingdom—a somewhat pale sun, perhaps." She smiled, lost in memory. "But it was well put and it expressed what many people felt. She had grace and charm—two important qualities, which Monseigneur d'Orléans inherited from her."

"The King does not want to recognize the Queen," Valentine said, looking up at Blanche's face. "The Queen suffers because of it. This afternoon when they were here—he thrust her away from him. My heart bled for her; she loves the King so much."

"Loves . . . !" said Queen Blanche, not without mockery. "Pure madness. That is the love of the doe for the buck, the ewe for the ram. It is irresistible in the spring and when the leaves fall, it is over."

Valentine shook her head.

"You cannot say that, Madame. I was with the Queen when

they brought her the news of the King's first attack of madness in the forest of Mans; I saw how the blow struck her. It was as though she had lost her senses herself. And doesn't she do what she can for him? Each day while he was there, she sent a message to Creil to ask him if he wanted anything. I have heard it said that she stands weeping outside his door when he does not wish to see her. Oh, but I feel with her too," she continued vehemently. "It is unbearable to know that someone you love is close by and unreachably distant and . . . gone . . ."

"The Queen has a staunch advocate in you, ma mie," the older woman said shrewdly. "And she does not deserve it."

A flush flooded into Valentine's face; she lowered her eyes.

"I know very well that the Queen cannot abide me," she murmured, almost inaudibly. "That is also one of the things that pains me. I understand it—the discord between Bavaria and the Visconti . . ."

"And more yet . . ." Queen Blanche nodded significantly. "Much more yet—and that is worse. You know what I mean."

"Yes, my God!" whispered the Duchess of Orléans; she raised both hands in a gesture of despair. "But I do not *want* that at all— I cannot help it. I love the King very much . . . he has always been kind and gentle to me . . . but surely no one would dare to say . . ."

She pressed the palms of her hands against her cheeks and turned her head slowly from side to side. "The Queen cannot think that, Madame; she knows there is nothing between the King and me but close friendship . . ."

"As far as that is concerned, you have certainly never given her cause for complaint," Blanche agreed. "The King usually sought and found his pleasures far from the palace with wanton women and peasant girls—shabby amusement for a king! But the Queen could not be angry about that—no one is jealous of an hour's nameless love. Oh no, ma mie, envy of you suits her convenience remarkably well; she *wants* to believe that she has a reason to blame you."

Valentine raised herself slightly from the pillows; two bright red marks stained her cheeks.

"So much is being said," she whispered. "I don't know what to think. One of the chamberwomen overheard a story they are telling in the streets . . . They say I let a poisoned apple roll into the nursery while the Dauphin was playing with my little son."

"Hush—that's foolishness." Blanche half-rose from her seat and pushed the young woman back among the pillows. "Lie still now, Valentine. Your face is glowing with fever. Don't you know that kind of talk is meaningless? Why, your little Louis could have eaten the apple himself."

She stroked Valentine's cheek soothingly, but she kept her eyes cast down to conceal her look of alert disquiet. She had heard that strange story. Isabeau did not always do her work with caution. Valentine moved her head back and forth over the pillows as though she were in pain; her lips were dry from thirst. Queen Blanche noticed this and beckoned to one of the young women nearby; she asked her to bring a spiced drink.

"I feel danger everywhere," whispered Valentine. "Perhaps I am imagining it, perhaps it is not true. God grant it is not true. But I don't know . . . my feelings have never deceived me about things like that . . ."

"Yes, yes," the older woman nodded, sighing, while she took the goblet from the waiting-woman and helped Valentine to drink. "Try to go to sleep now, ma mie. It wasn't sensible of me to let you talk so long."

"I can't sleep now," said the Duchess of Orléans. She waved the beaker away after she had taken a few sips. "I should like someone to read to me; that would distract me from my thoughts. I am too tired to read myself; perhaps the Dame de Maucouvent can come sit with me . . . with the Histories of Troy which I was reading before my confinement."

"I shall send her." Blanche rose. The ladies of her suite came up quickly, ready to push away the chair and to pick up the Queen's long train when she descended from the dais. She bent over Valentine again. "Be brave," she whispered within the shelter of the falling veil which hid both their faces. Then she left to enter the adjoining room.

A few of Valentine's ladies stood around the wet nurse who was holding little Charles at her breast. The infant's wrinkled, red head seemed smaller than the rounded breast from which he suckled. He moved his little hands aimlessly back and forth, and made loud smacking sounds, to the delight of the young women. As Queen Blanche entered the room, they moved aside and curtsied. The wet nurse made an effort to stand up.

"Please sit, la Brune," Blanche said, with a wave of her hand. The child, who had lost the nipple, turned his head to left and right.

He was bound to a small oblong cushion, stiffly wound about with bands of cloth.

"A healthy youngster," said the wet nurse proudly. "And he suckles well, much better than Monseigneur Louis did at his age."

Blanche smiled and brushed her forefinger lightly over the baby's little cheek, as cool and soft as fine silk. She let her eyes travel over the room, which, like the lying-in chamber, was hung with green tapestries. Two beds of state stood there, richly made up with pillows, cushions and counterpane.

"Is the Dame de Maucouvent not here?" she asked one of the young women. "The Duchess would like someone to read to her." The girl curtsied, colored with shyness and replied in the negative. The Dame de Maucouvent was in the nursery, putting Monseigneur Louis to bed. Queen Blanche frowned and cast a look of quick concern toward the lying-in chamber. She was about to send for the governess when another young woman stepped forward.

"Let me sit with Madame," she said. "I can read."

Blanche had the impression that this offer did not sit well with the other women: their faces stiffened almost imperceptibly, their eyes were hostile. The young woman who stood before her was hardly more than a child; tall and slender, with white, almost translucent skin. She kept her eyes lowered modestly and her hands folded over her breast in the manner prescribed by etiquette, the upper part of her body bent slightly backwards and her head held a little to one side. The Queen was pleasantly impressed by the voice and appearance of this girl, whom she had not seen before among Valentine's retinue.

"Good. Go then, Mademoiselle," she said, "and take the Histories of Troy with you."

The young woman curtsied; before she arose she looked directly at Blanche, a flashing glance, green as clear deep spring water. Those wonderful eyes struck the Dowager-Queen particularly—they reminded her of an old, half-forgotten love song which described the leaves of an early spring. She felt for a moment as though she stood in the cool spring wind in the meadows near Néauphle-le-Château.

"Who is that?" she asked, staring after the newcomer. The women exchanged significant looks—her own women as well as those of the Duchess of Orléans. But their silence lasted so long that it impinged on the respect due to the Dowager-Queen. A lady of the court hastened to reply in the subdued, expressionless tones of a subordinate.

"Madame, that is the Demoiselle d'Enghien."

Servants in short jackets, with napkins slung over their shoulders, jostled past each other on the spiral staircase leading down from the dining hall to the kitchens. They carried great platters on their heads and some smaller ones at the same time on their widely outstretched arms. A double curtain of worked leather, weighted on the bottom with lead, hung at the entrance to the hall, from which rose the talk and laughter of the guests, the clatter of tableware and the sounds of music. Those servants who carried fowl took them first to the carving tables which stood at the entrance; those who had fruit, pastry and wine brought them directly to the guests.

The feast celebrating the christening of Orléans' youngest son was being held in a long narrow hall made even narrower by the existence of two rows of flecked marble pillars. At the end of the hall opposite the servants' entrance stood a dais where, against a background of tapestries, the royal guests sat at table.

Above the colonnades were galleries where the musicians and a few courtiers were. A great number of torches were burning; pages ran back and forth continually tending to these sources of light. Several of the Duke's house dogs lay on the mosaic floor, gnawing bones and growling whenever the servants came too close to them. The musicians in the gallery played without pause on their wind and brass instruments. A dwarf squatted behind the grating of the balcony, his face pressed against the opening between two bars, gazing down at the company on the dais below him, and especially at Orléans, who was chatting politely with his neighbor, the young wife of the Duke of Berry. Later in the evening, to honor her and Queen Isabeau, the dwarf would be brought to the table in a pastry to recite a couplet composed by Louis.

The Duke wore a crimson garment with voluminous sleeves, so densely stitched with series of his favorite emblem, the crossbow, that from a distance one could not tell whether the background of the cloth was red or gold. The Duke was in an exuberant mood; the Duchess of Berry, who was easily amused, shouted almost unceasingly with laughter.

On Orléans' other side sat the Queen, silent and lost in thought. Dull fatigue weighed more heavily upon her than her crown and necklaces. She smiled mechanically whenever her brother-in-law spoke to her, replying with automatic motions of head and hand. She looked often at the King who sat next to her, but as far away from her as possible, in a corner of the bench under the royal canopy. He was pulling at the threads of the tapestry with his knife and muttering unintelligibly. He had been brought to the table despite the physicians' advice. At the beginning of the meal, diverted by the bustle and stir around him, he had sat motionless and attentive, without a glance or a word for Isabeau.

Because he toyed with his food like a child, his sleeves and tunic were soon spotted with bread crumbs, grease and wine. Finally he became restless. He could not get up from the table and walk around when he wanted to, as he did in his own rooms. The Queen bit her lip. It seemed to her that everyone was staring at the royal seat as if it were a stage framed by tapestries and festive garlands.

Charles overturned his goblet; wine sopped onto the freshly baked white bread which nobles, kneeling respectfully before him, had put upon his plate. He bit his nails, scratched his thinning grey-blond hair. Because of the long confinement in Creil, his face was as pale as wax; his nose was sharp, deep grooves ran from his nostrils to his mouth, which looked sunken and old, because he had recently lost some teeth. He was only a few years older than the Duke of Orléans, but the disparity between them appeared to be one between a very young and a very old man. The softness of Charles' faded, enflamed eyes made his appearance all the sadder; they were the windows through which his spirit looked out, the captive in his cage, forever isolated from the world. From time to time the involuntary contractions of his cheek muscles caused his face to contort into a grimace.

He listened at last to the whispered entreaties of Burgundy, who sat beside him, and leaned back into the shadow of the canopy. He seemed to have lost all interest in food and festivities. He mumbled and poked the point of his knife between the brightly colored threads of the tapestry beside him. Burgundy, soberly dressed in a garment of black Flemish cloth which had cost a fortune, and with his hat glinting red with rubies, sat eating with a cold smile, as though he noticed nothing. Only the censoriously compressed lips of his wife Margaretha betrayed disapproval.

The Duke of Bourbon, however, could not conceal his displeasure; he was still upset by the dispute with Berry. He was deeply offended by the accusation that he would work exclusively for his own interests now that he was once more a regent. Naturally, like Berry, Anjou and Burgundy, he had not hesitated, in the period before Charles came of age, to take advantage of any opportunity for profit that came his way. But he was no longer particularly interested in worldly affairs. He stood, he believed, at the brink of the grave; his health was failing. Moreover, he was extremely fond of the King, in whom he had always seen a resemblance to his sister, the late Queen Jeanne. Was it guilt that made him eager now to set himself up as a protector of the royal family? That was what Berry had the audacity to assume.

Bourbon saw him sitting at the other end of the table, looking all but ridiculous in a garment of flowered brocade trimmed with ornaments, like a heathen Turk. From Berry his glance shifted to Isabeau, whose forced smile he did not see through. He blamed her for the stupid decision to allow the King to come to the table and expose his scandalous behavior to the derision of the court. Bourbon listened without interest to the remarks of his neighbor, the Duchess of Burgundy, whose mind he found as cold and materialistic as her Flemish estates.

Berry followed their conversation from a distance; he knew Bourbon's antipathy to Philippe's wife and secretly rejoiced that protocol had made them neighbors at table. He himself was seated between two comely, flirtatious princesses, his own wife Jeanne and the young wife of Jean de Nevers, Marguérite, of whom it was whispered that she had received Louis d'Orléans in her bower, although there was no proof of that.

The Bishops of Saint-Denis and Saint-Pol and other dignitaries of the Church, as well as the Dukes of Bar and Lorraine, sat at both ends of the horseshoe-shaped royal table. Queen Blanche did not attend the christening feast; the sober life at Néauphle had given her a distaste for prolonged repasts. She had gone with her retinue to one of the palace chapels to offer candles in honor of the newborn baby. At the lower tables sat nobles from Orléans' most trusted entourage: the Sires de Garencières, de Morez, de Béthencourt, Jean de Bueil and Marshal Boucicaut. The servants in their dark green livery constantly carried in new dishes—haunches of venison, pork, capon and other fowl, stuffed with truffles or cooked in sour sauce, all accompanied by compotes, by spiced meat pies and egg dishes. The two tall buffets on either side of the tables were loaded with platters piled high with pyramids of fruits, raisins, dates and nuts. The Duke's precious silver plate, the jugs and goblets which Valentine had brought him as part of her dowry, stood displayed there. The servants filled graceful decanters from almost man-sized narrow tankards with wines from Bordeaux and Burgundy, mead spiced with honey and currants, malmsey and sweet hippocras. The music continued without pause; minstrels appeared on the balcony and started singing the couplets of Bernard de Ventadour, so beloved by Orléans.

"Listen!" The Duke interrupted himself. "Can there possibly be a more perfect way of praising the pleasures of love? 'M'es veiare que senta—odor de paradis . . .' " he sang in a warm but rather unsteady voice. " 'It seemed to me there wafted a scent of paradise . . .' "

"You use music as an easy excuse to back out of the argument," cried the Duchess de Berry with playful indignation. "I call everyone to witness! Monseigneur d'Orléans neglects his duties in the service of Lady Love, he refuses to answer the question which I put to him in the name of all those who profess true courtesy. Can Your Majesty not compel him to answer? A royal command has more weight than one from a woman like me, who am Monseigneur's mistress neither in rank nor in matters of love."

Her loud, clear voice drew everyone's attention to the center of the royal table. She glanced laughing from Isabeau to Marguérite de Nevers, who smiled in cold contempt, but without embarrassment, as though she were only indirectly involved in the conversation. The Queen, startled from her brown study, turned mechanically toward the speaker.

"What questions?" she asked, with a forced smile.

The young Duchess of Berry repeated loudly, "I asked Monseigneur, 'Fair sir, which would you prefer: that one should speak ill of your beloved and you should find her good, or that one should speak well of her and you should find her evil?' "

"By heavens!" exclaimed Berry. He wiped his fingers on a linen cloth which a page held out to him. "That is a real poser for a court of love. Poets will have to be called on to answer it; I fear that even the eloquence of Monseigneur d'Orléans is no match for it. What do you think?" He turned to the Countess de Nevers.

Burgundy frowned; his wife's face became cold and vigilant. They suspected that hidden allusions were being made to the rumored infidelity of their daughter-in-law, under the guise of light-hearted banter, and they felt it as an attack upon the honor of their House.

The Countess de Nevers waved her hand and said modestly, "It would not be proper for me to give my opinion before the Queen has spoken." Thus she diverted attention from herself.

"The question is directed to Monseigneur d'Orléans," Isabeau said. She did not feel capable at the moment of playing clever word games. Louis, tapping his ring against a goblet in time with the music, shrugged his shoulders and smiled. "I can give you the answer that Courtesy prescribes," he said, "which is that I would rather think my lady good and find her evil, than the reverse, if I could preserve her honor in that way, and her reputation. In all likelihood I would also deal justly in accordance with the true state of affairs, for il est vérité sans doubtance: femme n'a point de conscience, vers ce qu'elle hait ou qu'elle ame . . . Woman has no conscience at all about what she hates or what she loves," he concluded, quoting a stanza by Jean de Meun. He bowed in ironic apology to his two dinner partners. The Duchess of Berry turned away, apparently offended, and Isabeau was not amused. Her eyes were cold behind the thin veil of gold gauze which fell from her high, two-horned headdress over the upper part of her face. Berry laughed loudly and raised his goblet.

"Bravo!" he called out. "Now we are back again where we ought to be, debating the value of women's love. Where is Madame Christine de Pisan, who regaled us so recently at my brother of Burgundy's with so passionate a defense of the honor of women? She is an excellent poet, my lord." He leaned across the table to cast a mocking look at Burgundy. "And she knows how to be grateful to her benefactors; I read the eulogies which she dedicated to our brother. 'Benign and gentle' she called him, the eternal crab. They say that she even praised his piety and bravery. In truth, that is a remarkable talent that you have taken under your protection . . . Chastity!" exclaimed Berry in melodious, polished tones which were more biting than playful. "It's no wonder that

Christine sings of chastity, now that she lives so near to Madame de Nevers!"

The Duchess of Burgundy put a soothing hand on her husband's sleeve; the sober gesture did not go unnoticed—surely not by Berry, who derived satisfaction from this small act of vengeance. Nevertheless, Marguérite bent her head as though in gratitude for this supreme praise; it was impossible to guess her thoughts.

Bourbon said quickly, to bridge the painful silence, "Even here in the court I can mention a passionate defender of true courtesy. I think it is not by chance that the excellent Christine has so many words of praise for the Marshal Boucicaut."

Louis burst into laughter and beckoned to one of the cup-bearers who carried a tankard through the hall. The man hastened to him, filled the Duke's cup to the brim and, at his request, took it to the Marshal who sat at one of the two tables beneath the dais. Boucicaut rose and drank to Louis, not without wondering what had caused this signal honor, because he could not hear the conversation at the royal table.

"Fair sir," cried Orléans, "drink to the health of the virtuous women whom you have praised in your ballads. Here we are involved, as usual, in combat over the Book of the Rose. How could it be otherwise? It seems that for lack of bloodier fights we must break our lances now continually in the service of Love. I fight under the banner of the Rose, to the vexation of Monseigneur de Bourbon, who has chosen you as his champion. I defy you, Boucicaut, with this beaker of wine—choose your weapons and come into the arena."

Boucicaut raised his grave young face to the Duke. The rigid carriage of his lean, sinewy body, the hair clipped short around his high forehead and his black garb distinguished him from his gaily dressed, somewhat boisterous table companions. He was barely thirty years old; great personal bravery and thoughtful acts had won him the title of Marshal a few years before, during a crusade in the East. After he had returned the goblet to the waiting servant, he said with his usual calm gravity, "It is true, my lord, that I hold women in high esteem and I have vowed to serve all equally, regardless of rank or age."

"Ho ho, fair sir." Berry interrupted him. His eyes glittered with spite and his face was bloated by wine and heat. He found the young Marshal, notwithstanding his blameless conduct, to be faintly ridiculous. "You say you serve all, regardless of age or rank? But what do you think of ugly women, without charm, and especially of evil, malicious ones, such as there are—alas!—enough among us, to the distress of Dame Venus herself?"

"I serve all," replied Boucicaut with a slight bow.

Isabeau sighed. The conversation held little interest for her. She was warm, the weight of her clothing and jewels was beginning to oppress her sorely. Moreover, the King had become restless again; he had pushed himself forward on his seat so that he was sprawling halfway over the table, muttering incessantly. Burgundy tried in vain to calm him down; when he finally attempted to pull the King back onto the seat by his arm, a small struggle ensued, in which goblets and plates were knocked off the table.

Orléans signalled to his steward. The leather curtains in front of the servants' entrance parted and a procession of servants, dressed as savages, festooned with leaves and fruit, carried in a huge tray holding a mountain landscape made of cake and sugar round a lake on which swans were floating; this was intended as a compliment to Isabeau, who was meant to recognize her native country, Bavaria. Armored knights brought in the gigantic pie from which the dwarf would emerge later on, and there were also silvered birds filled with sweets and pastry, and a fountain which spouted different kinds of wine to the sound of cunningly concealed carillons. Last of the cortege were jongleurs, singers and musicians displaying their skills before the tables. This diversion distracted the guests' attention from the King; he himself showed a childish interest in the great pie which had been set down before the royal seat on a tray standing on wooden trestles. The dwarf, clad as a herald for the occasion, appeared through an opening in the top of the pie and directed a speech in rhyme to Isabeau and the other women. Margaretha of Burgundy, who was wiping the wine from her husband's sleeve, considered the whole spectacle rather shabby, compared to the entremets and richly ornamented dishes which were customarily served at festivities in her native Flemish cities.

"Is that not Madame Valentine's Italian dwarf?" she asked Burgundy in an undertone. The King, hearing that beloved name, became restless once again. "Valentine, Valentine," he repeated, rising from his seat. His dilated eyes strayed from one face to another. "She is not here," he said, in fear and impatience. "Why haven't they invited Madame my sister-in-law? Let her come here at once. Instantly." He pulled nervously at Burgundy's shoulder.

— *51* —

The dwarf fell silent in confusion; even the musicians, who stood playing at the lower tables, put down their instruments. Good manners prevented the guests from staring at the royal table, but an oppressive silence suddenly prevailed. The blood drained from the Queen's face. She bent toward her husband, whispering.

"But Sire, the Duchess of Orléans is lying-in; it is impossible for her to come here. We sit at the feast in honor of her son, whom you yourself held at the font today." She offered him her hand, inviting him to sit down. But the King drew his cloak tightly about his body, and with a cry of aversion withdrew to the farthest corner of the bench.

"There she is again," he said, a catch of agony in his voice. "Go away! Begone—don't look at me like that. What does she want of me? Let her be gone! Valentine, Valentine!" he screamed, pounding his fist against the sidewall of the canopy.

"Sire!" hissed Isabeau sharply, white to the lips. "Don't forget who or where you are. You are the King of France!"

"Who says that?" Shuddering, Charles gripped the sculptured armrest of the bench with both hands and half-turned toward Burgundy. "That is a lie! Why do they insist that I am the King? Begone, leave me in peace! Do not believe this idle chatter, my lords and ladies," he went on loudly to his table companions. "It is a slander, the King will surely punish those who say it when he gets wind of it."

Burgundy stood up resolutely, but Isabeau, driven by now to extremes, thrust him back. She was torn by shame and impotent rage. She gripped Charles' hand so tightly that her nails tore his flesh. "There are the lilies and escutcheons of Valois. You stand before the throne, Sire. Surely you must know you are the King himself."

Charles shrieked in pain and fury and wrenched his hand free. In his anguish he fell against Burgundy, who threw an arm around his shoulders to keep him on his feet. The King's face was white as chalk; foam appeared between his lips. Isabeau, who had never before seen him like that—she had not been present during his attacks of madness at Creil—stepped back and sought support against the edge of the table.

The guests sat motionless; servants and musicians withdrew into the shadows of the colonnades. The dwarf slid from the pie and crept timidly away under the drooping folds of a table cover.

"Hush now, Sire, hush," said Burgundy, attempting to take hold of the King's resistant body. "No one will do you harm; you are among friends. Now sit down calmly; do. We will summon the man who juggles burning torches."

But the mention of fire woke in the King's disordered brain recollections of the fearful night which had brought on his second period of madness. He shrieked and struck out wildly about him. Bourbon moved quickly to pull the dagger from its sheath on Charles' girdle and get the weapon out of the madman's reach, remembering what had happened in the forest of Mans, where the King in his frenzy had stabbed two noblemen of his retinue.

"Your Majesty," the Duke of Burgundy began, but he was not able to finish. The King spat on the lilies on the canopy, tried to tear the tapestry, making derisive, scornful gestures.

"Away, away with that weed!" he screamed. "Take the plants away! Majesty, majesty—it is all blasphemy! My name is George— my escutcheon bears a lion pierced by a sword. I am a valiant knight! To arms! To arms!" His lips turned blue; his eyeballs turned up, showing the whites of his eyes.

"In God's name, call a physician," said Louis d'Orléans with vehemence. "My lords, forgive the disturbance. The King is gravely ill. I regret that I did not cancel this banquet—under these circumstances."

Jean de Bueil left the hall quickly, followed by a few retainers. The Archbishop of Saint-Denis approached in long, trailing purple robes and held a cross before the King, while he moved his lips in prayer. The King, somewhat restored to himself by the wine which someone had sprinkled on his forehead, shook his head fearfully.

"Let him rest awhile—give him a chance to breathe." Orléans had come under the canopy. Now he took one of the King's ice-cold hands in his. "Brother—do you not know me?" he said softly, insistently. "Come sit by me here, and let us talk awhile together. Tell me about the sword and helmet which our father gave you when you were a child."

The sick man shivered; he seemed to shake off his frenzy, like a wet dog shaking off drops of water. He blinked his eyes.

"Come, now." Louis tapped the cushion of the bench. Burgundy looked at the Archbishop with raised eyebrows.

"It seems that Monseigneur d'Orléans really knows a treatment which is mightier than any treatment from the Church," he remarked in an undertone. Isabeau, still breathing heavily, gave him an angry look, but remained silent. The veil was damp on her temples; her legs could no longer hold her. Leaning on the Duchess of Berry, she sank into her seat. The King slumped against his brother's shoulder. Seen together, the likeness as well as the frightful disparity between the two was startling: one face was like a twisted reflection of the other.

"Yes, brother," said the King, who recognized Orléans and at that moment began to speak to his brother as he had done in their childhood. "That was a wondrous story, with the weapons—they hung over my bed. I had to choose . . . how was it again?" He became lost in thought; his head drooped over his breast. Orléans gazed down at him with a smile which was not without bitterness.

There was some disorder at the tables. Food remained untouched on dishes and platters. The chimes of the wine fountain played monotonously without pause. The guests at the lower tables talked softly to one another, following the advice of Boucicaut, who thought as little attention as possible should be paid to the King's condition.

A door opened under the portico and Jean de Bueil re-entered the hall with Maître d'Harselly, a few other of the King's physicians, two valets and an old retainer who enjoyed the King's special confidence, and who was always with him. The doctors' presence was linked in the King's consciousness with unspeakable bodily and spiritual torments; he was beside himself again. Neither persuasion nor gentle compulsion could induce him to accompany the court physicians. Finally, they had to carry him away by force past the tables, guests, musicians, servants and the ever-growing group of spectators in the gallery.

"Valentine, Valentine!" shrieked the sick man desperately before the doors shut tight behind him and the doctors. Immediately Louis d'Orléans signalled to his servants; music sounded again from the balcony, cup-bearers and table servants hastily resumed their work. A few dogs played in the hall with some feathers which had dropped from one of the silvered birds decorating the platters; the dwarf slipped away unnoticed between the pillars of the gallery. Orléans sat down beside the Queen. For the first time he saw a look of cruelty in the set of her mouth. She threw her brother-in-law a glance he had never seen in her eyes before.

"Valentine," she murmured, almost without moving her lips.

"Always Valentine. This situation is becoming unbearable, Monseigneur."

Louis shrugged. "The King is like a child," he responded softly, beckoning to a cup-bearer to fill her goblet. Isabeau, however, laid her white, fleshy hand over the mouth of the goblet. The page bowed and moved on. "Will you not drink with me, Madame?" The Duke of Orléans spoke with an astonished smile that only partly disguised his wounded feelings.

"It is a situation that must be remedied," continued Isabeau, her eyes fixed on his face. Orléans laughed, somewhat irritated. He did not understand. After a pause she said in a cold voice, "You can do much to prevent greater difficulties in the future, my lord." A shadow crossed Louis' face; he bit his lip. Because the mood among his guests was still constrained, he felt obliged to attempt to restore the lighter atmosphere. While he looked about, trying to think of a way to re-open the conversation, his eyes met those of Berry, who sat staring at him, rather shapeless in his colored brocade, slowly turning his beaker in his hand.

"Really, in all the excitement we have forgotten to drink to the health of the baptized child," Berry declared with a malicious smile. "Would *this* not be the time to wish him prosperity and a glorious future?" He raised his goblet. "Charles of Orléans, long may he live!"

It was not long past midnight when Louis set out for the room which the people of Saint-Pol called "the chamber where Monseigneur d'Orléans says his prayers." He went there frequently and stayed long, especially on those days when circumstances prevented him from going to the chapel of the Celestines. An odor of frankincense and a profound silence, all the more soothing after the hubbub in the dining hall, greeted him when he opened the door. After the dessert there was a rowdy atmosphere at the tables because of the wine and the wit of Louis' six jesters who were famous for their insolent subtleties. Orléans retained an unpleasant memory of Berry's flushed face, the empty uncontrollable laughter of his young wife, Isabeau's barely veiled anger. Over the creased damask, strewn with bread crumbs and fruit pits, the enemies had traded gibes and taunts, encouraged by the forced mirth of the other guests who boisterously approved of everything the fools said as they walked past the tables.

After the Queen's abrupt departure, the banquet had ended.

Orléans had already ordered his chamberlain to arrange a tournament in honor of his new son, to make up for the abortive christening feast. Walking through the narrow draughty corridors he had deliberated whether he should still go to the chapel of the Celestines. But after the strains of the evening he longed for the perfect tranquillity of the chapel. Kneeling in the fragrant twilight on the mosaic tiles, under which his two eldest sons lay buried, he sought to recover the shadowless peace, the serene faith untainted by guilt, which he had known as a child. The cold, quiet room which he entered now awoke memories of his childhood; it was here that he and his brother used to kneel together, leaning against the knees of their governess, the Dame de Roussel. Charles, the elder, could recite all the prayers fluently, without mistakes, and he did it willingly, with scarcely concealed pride; Louis, who could not yet speak clearly, had enough difficulty kneeling and concentrating on keeping his small hands together at the same time, could only stammer after the governess: "Ave Maria—full of grace . . ."

He shut the heavy door carefully behind him. A perpetual lamp, hanging from long chains, stirred slightly in the draught. The shadows on the face of the image of the Virgin alternately faded and deepened, so that there seemed to be life in the painted eyes and the artfully carved, smiling lips. The Mother of God wore a gilded crown on her head and the cloak which enveloped her as well as the child was stitched with gold thread and jewels. Something in the pale, narrow wooden face reminded him of his wife, equally delicate and pale, who lay beneath the coverlet of her lying-in bed. Was it the sad, patient smile, or the way she held her head, slightly inclined to one side, under the heavy crown? Shame and remorse welled up in Louis, a bitter, scalding wave; he dropped to his knees before the statue, his fists pressed against his forehead. He did not notice the icy coldness of the stone floor. In the silence he heard the throbbing of his heart and the gentle crackling of the hot wax of the altar candles dripping onto the candleholder. He felt overwhelmed by melancholy, the inevitable reaction to tension and great excitement; by sorrow for vanished innocence and childish happiness.

What had become of the two boys in their matching brocade cloaks; the King's two small sons who had learned their prayers kneeling here? Where had the sounds of their voices gone? And the jingling of the bells on the harness with which, each in turn, they played the part of the horse? Somewhere within these walls their

excited cries must still echo—when they played at battles and tourneys with friends Henri de Bar and Charles d'Albret, each window
niche had become a fortress, each mosaic tile a territory to be conquered. Although Louis was still a young man, it seemed to have
been an infinity since he had come here as a child and as a youth.
He remembered his father clearly, although he had been barely
eleven years old when Charles V had died. The King usually sent
for his sons when he sat in the library, his favorite room, between
stacks of manuscripts, beautifully ornamented pages in vellum. To
collect books, and sit poring over them in a quiet room behind walls
which shut out the outside world, was the only desire he had which
approached passion. His library was housed in one of the towers of
the Louvre, his imposing castle which dominated Paris with its high
battlements and pointed roofs. Bars had been placed before the
windows to prevent birds from flying in and damaging the books.

The King loved to bring his little sons here and show them
about, after what seemed like an endless climb up the circular staircase which wound between the white walls of the tower. Louis still
vividly remembered those hours: first the small procession on the
stairs, his father in front, his thin, slightly misshapen body wrapped
in a fur-lined mantle, black like all his clothes, and with a velvet
hood on his head, intended to protect him against headache and
cold draughts; behind him came Charles and Louis, apparently
climbing the stairs with all the decorum expected of the sons of a
king, but in reality counting the steps under their breaths or trying
to push past each other on the narrow landings; and last came the
librarian, Giles Malet, who, after the King's death, would be librarian
in Louis' ducal household. Later, at the tables piled with manuscripts, the conversation between father and sons took on the character of an examination, a random test. The King, leaning against
a reading desk, quietly and patiently asked questions in Latin, which
he chose to use on these occasions; thoughtful, beautifully constructed, eloquent sentences, strewn with quotations from his favorite writer, Aristotle.

When Louis thought of his father, he remembered him so, teaching, his pale face with strong arched eyebrows in the shadow of his
hood; the long nose had the tint of old ivory. He had a large, sensitive
mouth. It was a face that gave a preponderant impression of sadness
and suffering; it was clear from the lines that ran from his nostrils
to the corners of his mouth that old age had come to him prema-

turely; but his brown eyes were sharp and lively, the eyes of a man of great understanding and clear insight.

Charles V seemed to have been born old. Before he came of age, he had known enough trouble to make him realize the relativity of all things under the sun. In his sickly body lived a spirit which coldly and calmly surveyed a France ravaged by war and pestilence, a welter of famine, chaos and boundless misery, in which he began to create order, following a system that did not meet with a positive reaction from the people around him, the pretentious and haughty nobles who had not only lost battle after battle against the English invaders, but had brought their own country to the point of ruin by squeezing the commoners and peasants dry. He rendered them harmless by surrounding himself with advisors from the bourgeoisie, men who were tirelessly zealous in their newly awakened social consciousness. Gradually, by proper organization of the armies, he freed the country from the pillaging bands of roving mercenaries who came from all over; he let the English exhaust themselves on unimportant skirmishes—now on the coast, now deeper in the land again; buildings rose up—forts, palaces, the towered Louvre, the Bastille and a long series of connecting halls in Saint-Pol.

The King was extremely frugal and sober; he had no desires to be gratified at the cost of the exchequer and the prosperity of the country. Day after day he kept punctually to a regimen of work and relaxation. The pleasures of the table meant nothing to him; he ate little meat and drank diluted wine. He loved his family, his work; above all, however, he loved his books—and the writers, philosophers and astrologers who lived in great numbers at his court. France had raised itself from the morass of misery into which it had fallen; the eyes of all Christendom were fixed again upon the heart of the Western world.

"Le Sage" he was called in his time; the wise, the thoughtful one. So he was seen, with his books and his scriveners, governing from his library; so Louis saw him when he thought of his father: leaning against his reading desk, the fingers of one hand between the pages of a manuscript, and the other hand—permanently paralyzed as a result of the poison given him as a youth by his archenemy Navarre—resting in the folds of his mantle.

As long as the King lived, much care was expended on the education of both boys—a succession of excellent tutors instructed them in all accomplishments essential for princes of the blood and, perhaps because of the direct supervision of the King, this instruction was more thorough than would have been the case in other circumstances. And as was customary with him, the father looked to the future. He was rightly concerned about his health. The inheritance he was leaving—a reviving France, barely-allayed hostilities with England, discontented nobles who waited, hand on sword, in their castles for a chance to rehabilitate their positions, and an awakening populace of commoners and peasants—this inheritance was a dangerous toy for children or reckless youths. In addition, ambitious rivals, the King's brothers, waited near the throne—the avaricious Anjou, the crafty Burgundy, the cold, sensual Berry and his brother-in-law Bourbon, meddlesome and pompous—in truth, a pack of vultures which could never be feared enough.

Therefore, the King set up a guardian trust consisting of various high dignitaries of the Church and some of his advisors—among them Philippe de Maizières and Clisson, later constable of France. These men were part of the group which the King's brothers and knights referred to tauntingly as 'the Marmousets'—the fools. Charles V expected that these tested servants would be a temporizing influence on the far-from-disinterested Regency of the Dukes. At the same time he decreed that his son should be considered to have come of age on his fourteenth birthday.

Even as the King lay dying, the Dukes swooped down upon the Regency. With their armies they came riding from their domains to challenge one another in turn for the greatest power. The King lay in his death agony, surrounded by his court; at his feet knelt his sons, his friends, his devoted servants. While he was receiving the sacraments, a bitter argument raged in the anteroom between his brothers which resulted in Anjou ransacking the deserted rooms of the palace. Furniture, golden tableware, jewels were carried off with no further comment. Anjou withdrew as regent; with the plundered gold he could carry on a war for the possession of Sicily, to which he lay claim. Bourbon, Berry and Burgundy now fastened their claws in earnest into the crown of France, which at Reims had been placed on the head of a twelve-year-old boy.

Louis remembered it as though it were yesterday: the colorful silk banners rippling in the breeze along the stone pillars; the reflection of the flicker of wax candles in the golden censers, in the jeweled ornaments, in the burnished steel of armor.

He knelt behind his brother on the altar steps, holding in both hands the sword Joyeuse which had belonged to Charlemagne and which had been brought from the royal treasury for the occasion. Even more than the sight of the slender figure of his brother in his royal robes of gold and purple, the legendary sword filled Louis with pride and awe. Where his childish fingers grasped the hilt, the hand of the great Emperor had once rested. He thought it a good omen that he had been given the sword to carry, a sign that he was destined to perform valiant deeds.

After their father's death, both boys had drawn even more closely together, perhaps in reaction to the surveillance with which the Dukes had surrounded them behind a mask of courtesy. But the time for childish games was over for good; Charles fell prey to Burgundy's powers of persuasion; seduced by the prospect of heroic deeds on the field of battle, he allowed himself to lead an army into Flanders to subdue the regions which had risen against French rule; thus, without being aware of it, he played into the hands of Burgundy, whose power in Flanders had been firmly established by French victories in Roosebeke and elsewhere. Louis had fervently hoped to go to war, too; he was wisely kept at a safe distance from the battlefield by sensible elements in the Council. They did not entertain the possibility that some accident would befall the young King; they thought only that it was prudent to keep the successor to the throne close at hand. Among the Marmousets, those ministers who had served his father and who had not been banished by the Regents, he found sharp-witted and objective advisors; one of them, Philippe de Maizières, a man advanced in years, was uncommonly fond of Louis and only for his sake remained near the court which had lost the sobriety characterizing it during the reign of Charles V. Louis delighted in this wantonly sensual and luxurious atmosphere. He had too ebullient a personality not to be the first among those dancers, those devotees of Our Lady Love, addicted to gambling and hunting.

Although he was still a boy, barely on the brink of manhood, Louis was quite aware of the impression which he made upon women. They seemed to be wherever he went, all sorts of women, with light and dark eyes, their hair done in a thousand different ways, in long graceful garments, sparkling with costly jewels, infinitely more beautiful than the cold, chaste saints who looked down upon him from altar panel and tapestry. Small wonder, then, that he soon became familiar with the games of the Courts of Love. And he dreamt meanwhile of other conquests as well. He was now four-teen years old and considered to have come of age. The young King gave him the Duchy of Touraine as well as many other estates and castles along with their titles and revenues. At the same time, a bride was found for him in Italy, an heiress to vast land holdings. Val-entine, however, was nothing more than a name to the young man—a name linked to long negotiations about the dowry of 30,000 gold florins, the city of Asti and other citadels with mellifluous names: Montechiaro, Serravalle, Castagnole. Louis took active part in the discussions and helped to choose the officials who would represent him in his new dominions. He and Valentine exchanged gifts; they were now betrothed.

Time did not hang heavily on his hands while he awaited the coming of his bride; in a campaign against the Duke of Gelre, Louis could at long last play a role. The boy had grown into a man; the sprightly, quick-witted child had developed a diplomatic skill to be reckoned with. The eyes of the Duke of Burgundy fixed on his youngest nephew; he did not plan to lose sight of him again. He attempted to gauge the feelings of Louis' friends, trying cautiously to discover causes of enmity toward him; he needed to know where the young man's power and where his vulnerability lay. He consid-ered the King to be a good-natured but rather muddle-headed young fellow, easily influenced and quickly distracted by all sorts of fan-tasies. In addition, Charles' health was already affected by dissipa-tion. Louis seemed to be without hereditary mental or physical taint; this, in addition to his popularity at court, made him a figure of great importance in the political theatre which Burgundy, the pup-pet-master, wished to control. However, it soon became all too apparent that Louis had no intention of dangling helplessly from Burgundy's strings. The young man, courteous and urbane, went his own way. Those districts and provinces which he had over the years received from the King or had been able to acquire himself, seemed to cluster around the heart of France, a well-plotted zone of strategic bases upon which Burgundy looked with suspicion.

In August of the year 1389, Valentine Visconti came to Melun to be joined to Louis in matrimony. It was there, outside the castle, amid the thick deep greenery of the midsummer meadows, that bride and bridegroom met each other for the first time, under the bright August sky filled with white drifting clouds. She had come to meet him, stepping forward from a group of Lombardy noblewomen;

against the background of their flowing garments embroidered with gold and precious stones, she stood out in simple elegance, more sophisticated than any finery: in her deep scarlet bridal dress she appeared to rise up from the ground like a flame; the radiant light of the summer day seemed to burn within her, a bright glory behind her eyes and skin.

Kneeling now on the cold stone floor before the statue of the Mother of God, Louis mourned the loss of that summer bliss, the pull of more gross pleasures which had taken him from Valentine's arms. What did it matter that he respected her for the purity of her character, that he turned to her for her unfailing sympathy, that he considered her his kindred spirit, sharing his interests in the arts and sciences—if all that were not enough to pacify his restless heart? The amber and ivory of her beauty often seemed to pale for him— he looked for more glowing colors and voluptuous curves; he did not disdain the full ripe fruit beckoning in the foliage of the orchard, even though he held a lily in his hand.

Apart from all this, Valentine's dowry required too much of his attention. Galeazzo Visconti released the gold florins with great reluctance; the money reached his son-in-law only in driblets. In addition, matters did not go smoothly in Asti and the cities of Lombardy because the nobles there did not wish to pay Louis the homage of vassals. Thus it was imperative that Louis go to Lombardy. Once he arrived in Italy and came face-to-face with his crafty father-in-law, Louis became painfully aware that the possession of Asti and its surrounding countryside—and, even more, the relationship with the Lord of Milan—would embroil him in endless difficulties. Not only the interests, but also the enemies of the Visconti would be his; on the other hand, as lord of domains in Lombardy he was obliged to maintain good relations with all subjects and neighbors, even though this was not in accord with Galeazzo's politics. Visconti was like a spider in a web of intrigue; left and right he seized what he liked; weaving, meanwhile, cunning new threads. He lay in wait for more important plunder than a handful of Italian cities; he had made a firm decision to utilize his relationship with powerful France.

Louis was offered the prospect of a crown, a kingdom on the Adriatic Sea, artificially created by a group of ambitious men working behind the scenes: the Avignon Pope, Clement VII, who wished to move to Rome; Galeazzo, who wanted to be crowned king of Tuscany and Lombardy; the heirs of Anjou, who still hankered after the throne of Sicily; and, finally, Burgundy, who supported all these ambitions in return for certain compensations, for it would be most convenient for him in the future if Louis were safely tucked away on the Adriatic coast, far from Saint-Pol, far from France.

It was to be expected that the attempted execution of these plans would encounter fierce resistance in Italy. The battle continued to rage in a series of skirmishes and negotiations between the involved parties: Florence, Bologna, Padua, Milan, the mighty city of Genoa as well as Savona—all threatened, directly or indirectly, by the intrigues of Gian Galeazzo, and by rapacity and treason within their own camps. Genoa, the city most torn by civic discord, was the one weak spot in all the turbulence; the conquest of Genoa would be a milestone on the road to the Adriatic kingdom.

At this point the King, and Gian Galeazzo as well, shifted responsibility for the entire undertaking onto Louis' shoulders— Charles because he was tired and sick, already touched by madness; and the Lord of Milan calculatedly. With gold and promises, Louis mustered an army of mercenaries and adventurous nobles with their followers. He sent messengers to everyone to hold themselves in readiness for the campaign; at the head of his troops he placed Enguerrand, Lord of Coucy, who for years had been one of his closest friends and who was one of the most able military commanders in the realm. At the same time, Louis pressed Pope Clement for a bull of authorization which would lend this enterprise the look of legality. The Prince of the Church in Avignon was not ready for this; to be sure, he wished eventually to pluck the fruits of the campaign and tread the path to Rome that Louis had cleared for him. But he did not consider it expedient at that time to announce his interests in the affair. Louis was disappointed but not surprised. He sent Enguerrand de Coucy to Lombardy.

Many of the problems seemed on the point of being solved when suddenly the Western world was violently upset: in September the Avignon Pope, Clement, died unexpectedly. No stone thrown into an ant hill could have caused a greater commotion than this death caused in a shaken and divided Christendom. So many new problems piled up that Louis, dismayed, set politics aside for the moment. Impelled by a longing for inner peace, he went on a pilgrimage to

Asnières where he owned a castle in the neighborhood of a monastery and a church. However, Valentine's approaching confinement brought him back to Paris toward the end of November.

Kneeling in the chapel of his house, he remembered the many hours of meditation he had spent in Asnières, far from war and ambition, far from the court and temptation. With a bitter smile he thought of the priests, urging him at confession to control his desires; it was easy enough to be chaste and disinterested within the white walls of his cell, listening to pealing bells and pious hymns. But who could engage in the life of the world outside without being caught up in passion? Louis had learned from the behavior of dignitaries of the Church in the environs of the court and especially from the conduct of Clement and his cardinals in Avignon that even the purple robes of prelates did not protect them against sin.

Lust and greed, the Devil's companions, often hid behind masks. There were moments when Louis felt almost choked by the wickedness of the world. At those times he lost the light cynicism with which he managed to adjust to every circumstance; he felt like the serpent which the sculptured Mother of God trampled under her small foot. Nor did his uneasiness cease in this hushed room redolent of incense.

He crossed himself and rose to his feet. He knew that he was going to spend another sleepless night when he went to bed. The thought crossed his mind even in this sacred place, of an alternative; there were houses in Paris where, with women and dice, one could temporarily escape from reality. He struck himself scornfully on the mouth with his gloves, which he still held tightly in his hand. Then he quickly left the room.

He walked to the door which led to his own private apartments, but paused with his hand upon the door-ring, staring at the sentry who stood leaning against the wall, asleep. The torches in metal brackets, placed at regular intervals along the walls of the corridor, burned with a soft crackling sound; the man stirred in his sleep.

Orléans turned and moved cautiously to a low door at the other end of the passage, behind which a spiral staircase wound down through one of the many towers to the ground floor. The icy night air and the odor of damp earth rushed to meet him as he opened the door to the inner court. The wind had driven away the fog and the clouds; the moon stood reflected in pools of water left from early evening showers. Between the narrow cobbled footpaths which traversed the court in the shape of a star, small shrubs had been planted. In the center of the star stood a fountain.

Louis stood leaning against a pillar of the gallery which bordered one side of the court and gazed at the blue slate roofs of Saint-Pol and its numerous towers, wings and galleries looking like a mysterious labyrinth in the cold moonlight. Behind a series of narrow windows a weak glow could be seen: these were the apartments of Valentine and the women. Louis sighed and with one hand began to hook closed the cloak which he had thrown over his shoulders after the banquet. He could feel the metal ring which Salvia had brought him that morning pressing against his breast beneath his shirt; he pressed it with his hand.

He had caught only a glimpse of Mariette d'Enghien when he had visited his wife with the King's retinue; when the girl became aware of his glance she had retreated behind a group of ladies of the court, like a deer fleeing into the wood to escape the approaching hunting party. He crossed his arms and hid his hands in the wide folds of his cloak. Startled by the sound of a light step on the stones of the gallery, he turned quickly. The moonlight, shining through the rosettes cut into the stone arches, cast a pattern of silvery patches onto the floor; in the light could be seen the face and figure of his squire, Jacques van Hersen, whom he had dismissed for the night when he left the table. The youth knelt. "My lord," he said.

"What is it?" Louis asked curtly. He was annoyed at the interruption.

"Don't you need me, Monseigneur?"

"Now that you have found me, you can come with me." Louis turned his back to the page and entered the garden.

They passed under the arched gate into the gardens of Saint-Pol, which were surrounded by high walls. The young trees, planted only a few years before, stood in rigid rows along the paths; wrapped in straw against the winter cold they looked like grotesque figures, suppliants, assassins, dancers, stylites. In the summer, lilies grew here, and bright-colored columbines in flower beds; rosebushes and hawthornes divided the garden into small lawns adorned with fountains and bird houses. Now the hazy moonlight hung over branches and twigs, bare hedges and leafless arbors.

The Duke walked rapidly; without slowing his pace he pulled the hood of his cloak over his head. By now it was obvious to the page where they were going; the path Louis was taking led directly to the buildings of the Celestine monastery, a pile of towers and roofs outside the palace walls. Before the Duke opened the door in the garden wall which led to the monastery, the page turned to look back once more; but the spacious gardens lay deserted and almost shadowless in the moonlight. Seen from this spot the steep walls and peaked towers of the palace of Saint-Pol seemed almost unreal: an enchanted castle suspended between heaven and earth, a dream vision woven out of moonlight and clouds.

"Come, young man," said Louis impatiently from the darkness.

Quickly, Jacques followed his master through the low arch and shut the door. They stood in a roofed passage, with small windows on one side, through which the moonlight cast elongated white strips onto the ground. The Duke was at home here. In this place he had his own prayer cell where he spent certain days each year leading the life of a monk, wearing cap and cord and walking barefoot on the stone floors. His old friend and councillor lived here, Philippe de Maizières, who had retired among the Celestines shortly after Louis had been declared of age.

Louis hesitated a moment before the door of the chapel which had been built onto the cloister walls. He did not enter, but walked in the opposite direction until, past stairs and corridors, he entered the nearly dark dormitorium. Abruptly he stopped, with a half-suppressed cry of terror.

The page stepped forward quickly. "What is it, Monseigneur?"

Louis laid a trembling hand on the young man's shoulder, seeking support, but he spoke words of reassurance.

The page let his dagger slide back into its sheath, but stood peering suspiciously into the darkness. There was only one patch of light in the hall, a square of moonlight under the little window cut high into the wall. But this bluish, misty light only intensified the surrounding darkness and silence. A cold shiver climbed between Jacques' shoulderblades; for a moment he felt a blind urge to bolt. The Duke's footsteps sounded quicker than before. They reached the door giving access to de Maizières' rooms. Louis tapped at the wooden door, his usual quick, short signal; he entered without waiting for a reply.

The former councillor to the King occupied two adjoining white-walled cells with vaulted ceilings. A life-sized image of the crucified Christ hung directly opposite the door; in the flickering light of a perpetual lamp the wounds seemed to glitter darkly with coagulated blood. A soft rustling came from the adjoining cell; after a few moments de Maizières appeared, an old man in a cowl.

"Forgive me for arriving at this late hour," Louis said before de Maizières could speak. "If I had not known that you seldom sleep after midnight, I would not have come. I needed to talk to you."

The old man stepped aside and motioned him to enter.

"You don't look well, Monseigneur," he said, pushing the manuscript he had been reading to one side of the table. "I cannot say that the rest in Asnières has done you good. Nor has the celebration of your son's birth. What's the matter? Your hands are shaking," he added, lapsing into that familiar tone with which he had sometimes addressed Louis the child.

"Maizières," said Orléans softly, "if it is true that a man can foresee his end . . ." He paused. "I know well enough that I have been fortunate in my undertakings," he continued, more softly still. "But now it seems I am running out of time. I do not believe I shall live long, Maizières. I have seen Death himself tonight."

The old man raised his head quickly. He shaded his eyes with one hand against the glow of the candle which stood on the table between them and scrutinized Louis sharply.

"In the dormitorium, Death passed before me," Orléans said, while they stared into each other's eyes. "If I had put out my hand, I could have touched him—he was so real. Don't say that I imagined it—I was thinking about other things. Without wishing it, without being prepared for it, I suddenly felt the chill which emanated from him and I saw him too, although it was dark all around me. How else would I know that he can transfix one with a stare from eyeless sockets—that he whispers without tongue or lips?"

"You came from a banquet, my lord. Drinking the wine and listening to the music, you had perhaps given no thought to the fleeting nature of pleasure. Death frequently surprises men at such moments. Perhaps it is as well that you were reminded of more important matters."

Louis stifled the anger which welled up in him at these words; he forced himself to smile courteously as usual. "If I can be charged with no worse debauchery than attending my son's christening feast . . ." he tried to joke, but broke off.

"God knows, Monseigneur, that you waste enough time on

matters which are in essence perhaps as senseless as debaucheries," said de Maizières in a low voice, folding his gaunt hands before him on the table.

"What do you mean by that?" Louis did not look up; his fingers drummed the table top.

"You know very well what I mean, Monseigneur, but it cannot harm either of us if I repeat my meaning within these walls. I have told you often enough that I believe you waste your time on enterprises which fade away like rings on the water. What is the point of looking for conquests in Italy when a hundred paces from your palace gate there is chaos which cries out for quick action?"

Louis bit his lip and frowned; although he paused for a moment to collect himself, his voice held an undertone of impatient annoyance.

"Did *I* ever initiate these enterprises, as you call them? Do you think I would be stupid enough to put my hand all alone into that hornets' nest on the other side of the Alps without support from the King or the Pope? But by the time the King became ill too much had happened—I could not withdraw. I had to carry on even though my father-in-law and Pope Clement had deserted me. You don't need to worry about me any longer, because nothing will come of my kingdom on the Adriatic Sea now that the Pope is dead. If I were to persist in carrying on my purpose in Italy, the brotherhood of former fighters would presumably unite against me."

"I am delighted that you see things this way, my lord. I was afraid you might not abandon the enterprise in spite of recent events. There are more serious problems here now. You have an extremely responsible position, and one which puts the obligation upon you of forgetting your personal interests. Now that the King cannot reign, *you* must act in the name of the Crown."

Louis laughed softly; the bitterness did not escape de Maizières.

"I wish you would deliver this speech sometime to my uncle of Burgundy, who sees—or professes to see—only self-interest in everything I do, and who does not hesitate to tell everyone that I am busy undermining my brother's throne. As though everything I have done had not been worked out with the King when he still had his health—and since he became ill—for the last two years I have acted only in the interests of France. Those provinces which have been allotted to me—along with the whole Italian affair— behind all this is only the necessity to act in French interests. My lord uncles would never act as champions of the Kingdom, if it came to that . . . my brother knows that *I* would never turn against him— on the contrary. It's laughable the dark motives the Duke of Burgundy sees behind every gift of land."

He leaned toward the old man and went on with passion.

"And now, this summer, as you know, the King confided the country of Angoulême to me. When he was lucid, we spoke of it together—he saw himself that it was of the utmost importance that a region so close to the English front should lie in trusted hands. If the war party conquers in London, all treaties are meaningless. Can you see my lord uncles marching to defend Paris? But you can well imagine that any new acquisition on my part gives Burgundy an opportunity to spew new venom. Ah!"

He made a sound of deep aversion and clenched his fist on the table.

"I don't like to speak this way about my kinsmen, and God knows I would make every effort to maintain good relations—but sometimes I feel like someone who must dance in a field of thistles, whirling gracefully in complicated steps, without being scratched or pricked for otherwise . . . it is like a picture from a nightmare."

He bent forward, pressing his fists to his forehead and gave a short, despairing laugh. De Maizières heard him laughing and, more than by bitter words, the old man was alarmed by this laughter, which sounded like sobbing. Never before had Louis lost control so openly. De Maizières sat motionless, too shocked to speak. However, Louis knew how to recover himself quickly. He looked up, smiling in his usual ironic manner, and said, "Fortunately, courtesy does not forbid me to choose my weapons in this secret combat. If my uncle of Burgundy is as cunning as they say, he will understand the significance of my having taken a thistle for my new device, my having conferred the title Comte d'Angoulême on my new-born son . . . and my having instituted an order, the order of the hedgehog, in his honor."

"It seems to me that you ought not to waste your time on childish skirmishes with emblems and titles," said de Maizières acidly. "Now what was it you wished to discuss with me, my lord?"

"The Queen wishes my wife to leave the court. She has wanted that for a long time. But there never was a valid reason and in truth there is none now either, although the Queen is making every effort to find one, with the help of Madame of Burgundy, who begrudges my wife first place at the court. There are strange rumours circulating—I shall not repeat them—you know about them, perhaps?"

De Maizières shook his head and Louis continued quickly.

"I consider it demeaning to pay attention to these kinds of stories, but I am positive this is creating feelings against my wife who deserves such treatment less than anyone. I think she suspects something already, and if she knew the Queen's real purpose, she would go away at once, and she would not come back unbidden even if the stars fell from heaven. The situation has become so tense that I must do something . . . but what? I would like to spare my wife humiliation, but I cannot send her away without a reason. Sometimes I think I should quit Paris for good, with Valentine and the children."

De Maizières stood up so abruptly that his sleeves swept the loose pages of a manuscript from the table to the floor.

"My lord! You cannot possibly mean that. Will you deprive us of the only hope we have left since your father died? Monseigneur, you have never stood on the field in the heat of battle—if you had, you would know the meaning of desertion—"

The blood rushed into Louis' cheeks. He rose also.

"Yes! Desertion!" De Maizières continued in a voice trembling with emotion. "Even high treason, my lord! At this moment France has no other king but you. I know it is a thankless role you must play, concealed behind the throne, threatened on all sides. But you cannot be permitted to abandon the role even for a single instant, my lord; no one realizes better than I how much disappointment you have swallowed, how upsetting your situation is—but you must not give way."

"Quiet! Be still now, Maizières," Louis said roughly, putting his hand on his tutor's shoulder. "You are talking drivel about kingship, secret or otherwise. I sit concealed behind the throne and I am exposed to gossip from all sides, it is true, but I am more like an unwanted house animal, an unwelcome dog, than a secret wearer of the crown."

"Monseigneur, Monseigneur." De Maizières folded his hands. "You have more influence than you seem to realize—infinitely more. The place you occupy cannot be allowed to fall vacant, under any circumstances. You have never needed to tell me that you serve the interests of France. I know it; I know you too well to doubt it. You must go on serving those interests, my lord, you are the only one who can."

"Don't make me out to be better than I am," Louis said shortly. "I might not be France's champion if my interests did not happen to coincide with those of the Kingdom. I am only human."

"The Queen maintains relations with Bavaria, and the interests of Bavaria are not identical with those of France. The Dukes will not interfere with the Queen's plans if they are not interfered with themselves. And so the Kingdom crumbles, my lord, like a dry crust of bread. There will be hunger, rebellion, rapine, boundless misery—and the English will manage adroitly to profit from this chaos."

"And now you want me to struggle like a second David against Goliath—with no weapon except a sling and a handful of pebbles? Do you really take me for a child then, Messire de Maizières?"

"I take you for a man who knows his obligations," said de Maizières, his head bowed. "I am no star gazer nor fawning courtier. I can't make all sorts of encouraging predictions. It's more than possible that you will find only frustration, my lord."

"Or a speedy death," Louis said. He thought he felt again the palpable cold he had encountered in the dormitorium. He pulled his mantle tight and moved toward the arched doorway.

"Are you leaving already, Monseigneur?" De Maizières did not stir.

"I wish to hear early mass in the chapel of Orléans," said Louis. "What else can I do then but submit to the fate which awaits me? God grant me more humility and patience." He stood for a moment staring at the black and white mosaic tile of the floor. "Do you know, Maizières," he went on, in that eager, boyish manner which made him so likeable, "something happened to the King and me when we were still children. Have you forgotten it? I was eleven years old—my father had been dead only a short while. We were hunting in the forest of Bouconne near Toulouse, with my uncle of Burgundy and Henri de Bar—I even believe that Clisson was with us . . ."

"Indeed I have heard of a wall painting in the monastery of Carmes," said de Maizières with a vague smile, "which was brought there about ten years ago in memory of a miracle performed by Our Lady. And I know there is a hunting party in it . . . in a dark wood, surrounded by wolves, deer and other wild animals."

"That is the one I mean." Louis turned and walked back to the table; he stared into the candle flame as he talked, lost in memory. "Night overtook us in the middle of the forest and we could not find our way. The horses were frightened; they did not want to go on, because somewhere near us wolves were howling. Besides, it was pitch dark—a heavy, overcast sky without a single star—and we had wandered off from the servants and torchbearers.

"The King fell from his horse; the animal was skittish because it sensed my brother's panic. I remember how we stood near each other, in despair in the darkness. Then my brother made a vow: that he would offer the value of his horse in gold to Our Lady of Good Hope if we escaped safely from the forest. Not long after that, we saw the torches of the hunting party through the trees. The monks of Carmes near Toulouse had dedicated a shrine to Our Lady of Good Hope. They had our adventure painted on its walls as an example."

"Why do you tell me this story, Monseigneur?" asked de Maizières, raising his tired, slightly enflamed eyes to the young man. "What is the connection between a childhood adventure and the things we were talking about just now?"

"Doesn't it seem to you that we have, all of us—the King and I and our good friends—wandered off into a forest of the night, filled with wolves and sly foxes? The darkness holds endless danger; we are stranded with no torch to protect us. But even if the King were to offer now all the gold of France I am afraid that no Lady would save us from darkness and disaster. There is no Good Hope for us, Maizières. We are lost in the Forest of Long Awaiting, a wilderness without prospect," said Louis, employing an image much in vogue with the poets to express the frustration of hopeless love. "The Forest of Long Awaiting," he repeated, deriving a kind of mournful pleasure from the sound of the words.

De Maizières, who was not susceptible to poetic phrases, sighed and shook his head. He had become tired and chilly during the conversation. Besides, a bell could be heard pealing somewhere in the monastery, a sign that the night had ended.

Isabeau woke startled from a chaotic dream; she lay clammy with sweat under the heavy, fur-trimmed coverlet, her heart beating against her throat. At that moment the bells began to chime for early mass in the chapels of Saint-Pol and in the churches and cloisters of Paris. A wave of relief swept over the Queen, although her body ached with exhaustion. The prospect of having to wait a few more hours for daylight, she found unbearable. She turned her head toward the hearth, where her chambermaid Femmette sat dozing by the fire.

"Femmette," said Isabeau loudly. The woman sprang up with a startled cry, clutching to straighten her wrinkled kerchief. When she saw the Queen's dark eyes fixed upon her, she knelt hastily on the carpet before the bed.

"Forgive me, Your Grace. I was asleep. It was so warm by the fire."

"Good," said Isabeau curtly. "Help me get up now."

She had thrown back the bedcover and shivered in her damp chemise. The chambermaid, who had been accustomed for years to obey Isabeau's wishes blindly, now ventured a timid suggestion: the Queen had gone late to bed, the ladies of her retinue who had to help her dress were not yet in the anteroom; the Queen's condition made a longer rest advisable.

Isabeau sighed, irritated, her lips pressed together. If she was goaded, she could burst into a stream of invective. The control she had to exert toward kinsmen and dignitaries of the court taxed her nerves to the limit. She was used to taking out her frustration on her servingwomen. Now too she had to make an effort to hold back her anger; the chambermaid was already kneeling beside her, putting slippers on her feet. Femmette, who saw that the Queen was in a bad mood, remained silent; usually Isabeau spent the few minutes before she received her ladies listening to the chambermaid recount the gossip going the rounds of the city and the palace—the idle talk, the words caught on the sly—but now she was too distracted and annoyed. She had a cloak put round her shoulders and walked heavily to her prayer stool.

The tolling of the bells and her own disordered thoughts made it impossible to concentrate; she prayed mechanically. While the beads of her rosary slid through her fingers, she thought of her plans for the day—she would go to the Audit Chamber to insist on a speedy settlement of her annuity; she would discuss with Salaut, her secretary, the gifts she must offer to relatives, court and servants on New Year's Day; she had to accept the resignation of the King's physicians—especially Harselly, whom she considered a stubborn, opinionated bungler—who had dared to attribute the King's illness to an excess of wine and love. Then she wanted to dictate some letters to Salaut; she longed for the presence of her brother, Ludwig of Bavaria, who since her marriage had often resided in France. Whenever Isabeau, in the treacherous solitude of court life, felt a need for someone with whom she could be her real self, without reserve, she sent a message to Ludwig, who was usually to be found somewhere nearby, hunting and drinking with French barons.

Isabeau had stopped praying; the rosary hung motionless between the folds of her robe. She was startled when the sound of city bells ceased; the steady chiming had put her into a sort of trance, a borderland between sleeping and waking, in which the events of her life, the countless plans and desires which controlled her, assumed an almost tangible form. She rose with an effort, leaning heavily against the prayer stool.

Femmette, who had not dared to disturb the Queen's devotions in any way, was about to go through to the anteroom to inform the mistress of ceremonies that the Queen was awake. But the Queen called her back and pushed aside the tapestry before another door. The chambermaid, anxious to comply with her mistress's wishes, hurried after Isabeau with a candle to light her passage through the dark, quiet rooms. They came to a low, heavily bolted door, studded with iron lilies, which led to the chambers where the King resided; there had been a time when the door had stood open always so that the couple could reach each other at any hour of the day or night. Against this door, now locked on both sides, Isabeau often leaned, listening, trying to hear what was happening on the other side; sometimes she heard stifled cries, and the monotonous murmur of voices of doctors and servants; but most of the time—as now—a deep, almost ominous silence prevailed. The Queen walked quickly past the door, along the corridor which joined the royal apartments with those of the Dauphin and the three small princesses.

From the fields surrounding the palace, which stood at the extreme edge of Paris, came a cold morning wind, blowing through the shutters and carrying with it a stench of rotting garbage; the great municipal sewer, the Pont-Perrin, emptied into a ditch along the embankment, not far from Saint-Pol. Isabeau averted her head. The stink of spoiled food and other refuse called up her intense dislike of the people who swarmed through the narrow streets, of their constant needs, their incessant complaining and petitioning. Poverty and filth aroused Isabeau's anger, never her compassion.

Because it was her duty to do so, she ordered coins thrown to the rabble of beggars when she rode out in her coach or in a palanquin. But she could not muster the friendly smile and sympathetic words which the King dispersed so readily on these occasions even to the most disfigured and filthy beggars. She looked with friendly condescension upon merchants and tradesmen; the benefits of their labor came eventually, to be sure, into her exchequer; her existence justified theirs. But the jostling mob of paupers inspired her only with a secret terror; their hoarse cheers seemed to be filled with veiled menace.

Carefully, the Queen opened the door which led to the series of apartments occupied by the royal children. She chose to visit them, unannounced, in the early morning when they were still asleep, so she could see them without being bothered by them. Isabeau wanted to be proud of the Dauphin and the three small princesses; she wanted to be proud of their good looks, fine manners, pretty clothes, the power that would be theirs, the important marriages they would make. It was the love of a chess player for the precious pieces on her board; in it there was no trace of tenderness, of concern with the thousand little joys and sorrows of a child's life; the affection with which the Duchess of Orléans held her babies in her arms filled Isabeau with mild derision; a throne was not a nursemaid's stool. She kept strict watch over her children's governesses and tutors; they were fortunate children to have a mother who went to such lengths to see that they were raised as future bearers of crowns should be raised.

The children's nurses were busily raking up the hearthfire; they quit their work when the Queen entered, and paid her proper homage. Apart from that, there was a deep silence in the darkened room. Isabeau walked to the bed in which the Dauphin slept and thrust aside the curtains. The child lay on his back in the center of his bed; damp hair clung to his forehead. His mouth was open; he breathed heavily, wheezing. As usual Isabeau told herself that the child's pallor, the shadows under his eyes, his whistling breath were symptoms of a passing indisposition, not sickness or even weakness. With almost childish obstinacy she dismissed the words of the doctors who compared the child's health to the King's. The child stirred in his sleep, perhaps disturbed by the light which the Queen held aloft. His lids flickered, showing the whites of his eyes. At that moment he bore a remarkable resemblance to the King as she had seen him the previous evening, writhing in Burgundy's arms. Isabeau quickly dropped the curtain.

Passing through the adjoining room where the governess still lay sleeping, Isabeau entered the princesses' room. Isabelle and Jeanne lay together in a large bed like a scarlet tent; the reflection of the freshly raked hearthfire on the red cloth cast a glow on their small faces under their tight muslin nightcaps. Marie, the youngest, about a year old, slept in her cradle; her arm covered her face so that Isabeau could not see it. Marie had been born at a time when the King seemed recovered, and had been dedicated, out of gratitude, to the service of Our Sweet Lady of Poissy; a small pawn placed on Isabeau's chessboard, not for wordly gain this time, but to buy God's favor for the King of France.

The dawn had colored the horizon a bright pink above the hills and fields of Saint-Pol when the Duke of Orléans left the chapel, followed by Jacques. The morning mist drifted low over the lightly frozen ground; the palace rose from the gardens as though from a hazy gray sea. The Bastille, at the extreme edge of the city, stood outlined steep and dark against the lightening sky. The park of Saint-Pol lay exactly in the sharp angle formed by two municipal walls on the right bank of the Seine; behind the Celestine monastery flowed the river, bisected by the island of Louviers. In the west loomed the city, with its dozens of churches, cloisters and castle towers, the irregular roofs of the houses crowded closely together on both sides of the narrow streets. Paris had been silent before the church bells began to ring; now the city was awake.

In the early morning those who were employed in the fields surrounding the ramparts walked out to them through the countless gates; the day's work began in the streets, in the marketplace, on the quays along the Seine, in the offices of the Provost, in the shops, granaries, mills and slaughterhouses, and in all of the 4,000 taverns of Paris.

In the Hôtel d'Artois—the residence of the Duke of Burgundy—it was the custom to arise at dawn. Philippe and Margaretha, out of an unswerving devotion to duty, attended early mass; in addition, the Duke chose to receive the officials of his household and to handle the countless matters connected with the provinces in the early morning hours. Also, on this November morning the room adjoining the reception hall was filled with waiting people: burghers, merchants, farmers, clergy, lawyers, many holding petitions in their hands. Behind a tall wooden partition stood a few peasants from the domains in Burgundy; they had been called to account because they had been negligent in paying the taxes due on the vintage. The grey light filtering through the small, high windows made the room seem bleaker and colder than it was. The more self-assured among those who waited walked back and forth, stamping softly now and then, and rubbing their hands. But those who were here for the first time stood, intimidated, against the walls, shivering in their best clothes.

It took longer than usual for the first visitor to be called in; the Duke's scriveners and secretaries glanced curiously at the door which led to Burgundy's apartments. The Duke did not come; he was talking with his wife. Margaretha sat in a deep window niche, staring through small, slightly cloudy panes at the land behind the adjacent city wall. The autumn morning light lay pale on the hills of Montmartre. Burgundy stood, hands behind his back, one foot on the step leading to the seat in the window niche.

"It was too late to begin yesterday. There are a few things I am eager to learn, Madame."

"Do not forget, my lord, that people are waiting for you," remarked the Duchess, her eyes still on the hills.

Burgundy frowned. "Am I master in my own house or not?" he asked testily.

The corners of Margaretha's mouth moved in an imperceptible smile, more eloquent than any answer. She folded her hands in her lap, a sign that she was ready to listen.

"In the first place," Burgundy began coldly, "I am anxious to hear how it happens that the Queen can speak privately with so loathsome a fellow as the beggar from Guyenne, about whom you have no doubt heard."

The Duchess of Burgundy shrugged placidly, looking at her husband from the corner of her eye.

"I thought we had agreed at the time," Burgundy continued, "that every contact between the Queen and the outside world would take place through you. You have the opportunity to observe everything that happens in Her Majesty's apartments."

"The Queen is not a child," said Margaretha. "I cannot lie down like a watchdog on her threshold. But there is no reason to be dissatisfied with me; I do what I can."

"Yes, I know that." Philippe now stood on the step of the window niche. "And as a matter of fact no harm was done, this time. But that does not mean that similar visits will be harmless in the future. After the Queen, you are the first lady at court, Madame."

"Forgive me, my lord, but I am not," said Margaretha. Her small mouth seemed to become smaller, her glance sharper, a sign that Burgundy's dart had found its mark with malice aforethought. He bowed his head as though suddenly aware that he had made a mistake.

"Good. You are right, Madame, ma mie, you are only the third lady of France—but it lies in your power to be the first, if you wish."

"I do what I can," Margaretha repeated. She turned her head away and stared unseeing at the buildings which lay between the Hôtel d'Artois and the ramparts. She thought of the humiliation she had endured at the court: at each more or less official function where both she and the Duchess of Orléans had been present, Margaretha had duly given precedence to the much younger woman, with deep curtsies. She punctiliously observed protocol, but the deferential words lay like gall and wormwood on her tongue and the faultlessly executed curtsies were torture to her. That Valentine invariably treated her with kind respect only exacerbated her resentment. She could not forgive the Italian woman for her amiable disposition and her honorable character which made every intrigue against her seem tasteless and reprehensible. Margaretha was only too well aware that the task she had taken upon herself—to drive a wedge between the royal family and Orléans—demanded from her words and actions of which she was secretly ashamed. This feeling of guilt lay deep within her. It gnawed at the roots of her self-esteem and created a constant state of discontent which was reflected in the drooping corners of her mouth.

"I know you do everything in your power," Burgundy said, somewhat less coldly. "Yesterday I had an opportunity to observe that the Queen is firmly convinced that Madame d'Orléans is an accomplished practitioner of the black arts. But we must take care that the Queen does not choose Orléans' side now; on the contrary, it is desirable that the same shadow should fall over husband and wife. I would like to know if my meaning is clear to you."

The Duchess of Burgundy gave him a sharp look; two luminous points lay motionless in her black pupils.

"I understand perfectly," she replied at last. "But I fear it will not be easy. Do not forget that the Queen's aversion to Madame d'Orléans is almost innate. Furthermore, it is seldom difficult for one woman to hate another—reasons can always be found. And the role which Monseigneur d'Orléans fills for the Queen cannot be taken by anyone else. She needs him; therefore he will remain in her favor—even if he were the foul fiend himself. The Queen has a real hunger for pleasure and amusements; who would help her prepare all those masquerades and balls if Monseigneur d'Orléans were not there?"

"I am only amazed that he still finds time for another less harmless pastime," said Burgundy drily. He walked across the room where, on the opposite wall, hung a Flemish tapestry, depicting the birth of Mary. He stood motionless before it, filled, as always, with deep pleasure; not so much because he was struck by the splendor of crimson, peacock blue and red gold, but because this precious work of art belonged to him.

"Alas, what a pity," said Margaretha from the window niche, "that our son Jean shows so little interest in affairs at court. The Queen does not like him, although she does her best to hide it. That makes Orléans' position considerably stronger."

Burgundy frowned, nodding; he ran his finger along the letters stitched in gold thread on the lower edge of the tapestry.

"Now is also the time to discuss Jean," he said, without turning. "He has asked me to allow him to lead a crusade against the Turks. Do you know about this?" he broke off to ask, and saw her nod.

"Not directly from him. And not in detail, but enough to know that we must encourage the venture as strongly as possible."

"I think so too." Philippe walked back to her across the tiled floors, with measured steps. "It will mean great expense, but we must raise the money. Naturally, I am not opposed to it; I see the substantial benefits of such an enterprise. Besides, Basaach is a danger to Christendom; he is not a man, but a ravenous beast. And now it seems that Orléans promised help to the Hungarians some time ago—a considerable sum of money, if I am correctly informed, and also various gentlemen of his court with their men."

"Orléans cannot possibly leave now." Margaretha smiled and smoothed her wide sleeves. "Though that might possibly be a solution . . ."

The Duke of Burgundy stood and looked at her.

"That is foolishness," he said sharply. "You know that it is impossible for me to exert any influence here, especially now that the King's condition leaves so much to be desired. I wish Jean to go; I have thought a great deal about it and I believe it would be unwise to neglect this opportunity. He must take the best men who can be found. I am thinking of sending messengers to Enguerrand de Coucy in Italy. He is the only one who knows what a campaign in the East means."

Margaretha looked up quickly, like a greyhound pricking up its ears.

"But the Sire de Coucy leads Orléans' troops in Italy," she said. "His return would cause considerable delay there. I thought the state of affairs in Italy had your full support, my lord."

"Yes, so it did. But Pope Clement is dead and without him this Italian venture has little purpose. In any case, I need the Sire de Coucy now. I can offer him better employment for his abilities— the best is not good enough for me, now that a son of Burgundy marches off to war."

"This will create a great sensation," said Margaretha thoughtfully, "especially in England." She paused to arrange her long, fur-trimmed train carefully about her feet; a cold draught had swept across the floor. Then, casually, she gave him the news which she considered the most important part of the conversation.

"Froissart has returned from England," she said. "He has petitioned the Queen for an interview. Quite by accident I heard something about the intelligence he brings. It should be of interest to you, my friend."

"What are the important tidings which have reached your ears, my dear wife?" Burgundy sat down in the window niche next to her. The Duchess folded her long, rather bony hands over each other; on her forefinger was the ring engraved with the Flemish motto of the Burgundies: "Ic houd". I keep.

"King Richard wishes to remarry," she said slowly. "He asks if an embassy would be well received here. It seems to be his intention to ask the King for the hand of the small Isabelle. My informant was quite certain of his business."

The Duke of Burgundy sat quietly; he gazed at his wife, absorbed in thought.

"If that is really true," he said at last, "then it is the best news I have heard in a long time. A marriage between France and England would make war impossible—or at any rate most undesirable. We cannot underestimate the advantages, ma mie. A war with England would cause the interests of France and of Flanders to be so diametrically opposed to each other that I would have to tear myself in two to satisfy both. I may assume then that you will support Froissart's errands whole-heartedly and that you will point out to the Queen the advantages of the proposal. For my part I shall speak with the King myself—at least so far as that is possible."

"And . . . Orléans?" asked Margaretha, rising. She liked order and punctuality; she was annoyed that her husband had delayed his audiences. The Duke helped her descend the step from the window niche and walked slowly with her to the door.

"Orléans will undoubtedly be against it," he said. "For that reason it is extremely important that decisions be made before he can exert any influence."

The Duchess stopped and drew the long, rustling train of her dress over her arm.

"Such things usually reach his ears more swiftly than I would wish. Orléans is on his guard."

"I know it." Philippe thrust aside a tapestry to let his wife through the door. "And he does not hide his knowledge, as you may have noticed last night. I shall have to put up strong barriers against him."

"God be with you, my lord," said the Duchess of Burgundy ironically.

She was gone, dropping the curtain while Philippe was still making his formal bow. Donning his velvet hat, the Duke strode to the audience chamber.

At dawn Louis d'Orléans sank onto his bed fully clothed, hoping to snatch a few moments of sleep. But because he lay quiet, breathing regularly, his valet Racaille assumed that he was sleeping; he approached cautiously and began to pull off Louis' muddy shoes. The fire roared in the hearth, for the morning wind was blowing into the chimney; early sunlight gleamed through the small round cut glass window panes. While the servant busily loosened the laces of the Duke's clothing, loud insistent voices could be heard in the anteroom; a chair was pushed noisily aside.

Racaille went quickly to the door, fearing that Louis' friends had come to remind him of a pre-arranged morning ride, repast or hunting party. Two gentlemen-in-waiting, along with a page, panting from having raced up many flights of stairs, were standing in the anteroom.

"Where is Monseigneur?" demanded one of the gentlemen. He seemed excited, and attempted to peer past Racaille into the bedroom.

"Monseigneur d'Orléans is asleep," the servant replied curtly. He was angry at this invasion, but angrier still at the carelessness of Monseigneur who seemed to think he could live without sleep, wandering God knew where while sensible people were getting their good night's rest. But the gentlemen insisted on an audience.

Louis heard the voices through a dreamy mist. Although he did not wish to be disturbed, he opened his eyes and called, "What is it, Racaille?" The gentlemen appeared in the doorway.

"My lord," said one, "a courier has just arrived from Lombardy with a message from Messire Enguerrand de Coucy."

"Well?" Louis heaved himself onto his elbow.

"The city of Savona has surrendered, Monseigneur, even before a siege could begin." The courtier spoke in a loud, important voice. "The city fathers wish to conclude an alliance with you regardless of Genoa's position."

Louis sat up and swung his legs onto the step next to his bed. Racaille hurried to bring him clean, dry shoes. The two noblemen, who had expected expressions of pleasure, or at the least, approval from the Duke, stared at him in surprise. Louis sat expressionless while Racaille tightened the buckles on his shoes.

"So," he said finally, "very pretty. A success for Chassenage and Armagnac's mercenaries. Although the Gascons will be sorry they could not use force of arms. If all this had happened in the spring or during the summer," he continued, standing up, "I would have had more reason to rejoice." He walked to the window: the gleam of the morning sun on the blue roofs of the towers was almost blinding. He squinted, but did not turn; he had no wish for further conversation with the two noblemen who stood uncertainly in the doorway.

"Send the courier to me when he is ready," Louis said, with a dismissive gesture.

Later in the day Louis set out for his wife's apartments. As always, he felt the need to share important events and considerations with her. Some time had passed since he had last talked seriously with Valentine; in recent months he had not wanted to tire her with discussions about the Italian campaign or the matter of the papal elections.

The Duchess of Orléans lay propped up on pillows in the large state bed; two damsels stood on steps on either side, plaiting her hair into braids. She had slept better than she had for days and felt refreshed insofar as she could in the stuffy air of the hermetically sealed chamber. A smile glimmered in her eyes as soon as she saw her husband enter; the court ladies withdrew immediately to an adjoining room. Louis greeted her with more warmth than he had shown in a long time. His eagerness for a willing ear and loving attention woke an almost reluctant surge of affection in him. Valentine's bright golden brown eyes were fixed upon her husband as he moved a bench beside her bed and sat down; her cheeks were flushed and a smile quivered at the corners of her mouth. She folded her hands before her on the coverlet. She was filled with deep contentment bordering on bliss because he had come to her; although at the same time she was conscious, to her sorrow, that he had not sought her so much as the comfort of her counsel.

Although Gian Galeazzo's daughter was by no means in full agreement with Milan's policies, she had no choice but to endorse the plans made or inspired by her father—especially those in which Louis was involved. The Tyrant of Milan had tried repeatedly to use Valentine to exercise influence on both his son-in-law and the King, but she refused to allow herself to be used in that way, although she was willing to involve herself in negotiations or make recommendations. She knew that appearances were against her, especially in the eyes of Isabeau and her Bavarian kinsmen—it seemed almost unnatural that the daughter should not blindly serve the father's interests.

"Savona has surrendered," Louis said, after he had asked about the state of her health and the health of their small son. "Enguerrand de Coucy's courier arrived in the palace this morning. I talked briefly with the man—he was dead tired; he seems to have ridden day and night without stopping."

"Is that good news then?" she asked. Louis bent forward, tracing lines with his finger on the velvet edging of the coverlet, and shrugged. After a short silence, he said, "De Coucy has appointed

Jean de Garencières captain of the fortress of Savona, and left a fairly substantial garrison behind. But I have the impression that the people of Savona have a few tricks up their sleeves—they are willing to support us in future action against Genoa, so long as the campaign lasts—provided we pay them a monthly stipend—and not a small one, either."

"The alliance with Savona is not insignificant," said Valentine. "It will make both Genoa and Florence uneasy."

Louis laughed shortly.

"I don't trust any of them," he said. He smoothed the velvet with his hand. "In the course of years I have finally come to see what they understand over there by the word 'negotiation'. While the city fathers come to offer the keys and a long list of conditions, their ambassadors slip out through a back door to reach an agreement with our bitterest enemies. In any case, victories in Italy don't mean much to me, as long as I do not have the support of the Church; this alliance with Gian Galeazzo alone is no recommendation—quite the contrary. I hope you won't mind, ma mie, if I speak frankly. If I were to take up residence in those vanquished lands, I would live as safely as a lost sheep among wolves—although perhaps that image doesn't fit me too well because I am neither guileless nor helpless. And besides . . ." He leaned sideways against the edge of the bed, crossing his arms under the cover of his long green sleeves. ". . . why should I pursue conquests in distant lands when God knows I can well serve my country here even if it is only as a pot watcher? I have repeatedly been able to accomplish things, either directly or through the exercise of influence—which I suppose is the same thing—things that I knew the King would approve of if he were able to understand them. The Dukes will never take my brother's wishes into account, insofar as they do not agree with their own plans. In those moments when the King's head is clearer he often tells me how he approves of the way I have handled this or that matter—you know that yourself, my dear. I hope that my brother's illness is only temporary . . ."

"Yes," said the Duchess of Orléans softly, but without conviction; she turned her head away to conceal the anxiety in her eyes. "God knows that I pray every day for his recovery—whatever else they may say about me . . ." Her voice quivered with suppressed tears. Louis looked up quickly.

"Madame," he said, almost sternly, "you must rise above gossip. I would be very sorry if your self-esteem were to be jolted by the idle chatter which travels round from time to time . . ."

"Alas, it is no idle chatter," said Valentine; her voice still shook. She made an effort to restrain her tears, the treacherous, embarrassing tears which threatened to overwhelm her in times of physical weakness. "It is not gossip, my lord, you know that as well as I. It is a bulwark of hatred and slander, which is being constructed stone by stone. Don't think that I am blind and deaf," she continued, in a vehement whisper, clasping her hands tighter. "In the streets of Paris they are saying I wish to kill the King . . ."

"Hush, hush, Valentine," Louis interrupted, reaching for her hand across the coverlet. The fact that she was aware of all this upset him greatly. He had not expected it.

Valentine continued to speak swiftly and angrily.

"They say that at my departure, before I left for France, my father said to me, 'Farewell, daughter; see to it that when we meet again you have become the Queen.' But, my God, that is . . . Surely everyone knows that I left without saying goodbye to my father, who was then in Padua. It grieved him enough that we could not bid each other farewell."

"Hush, hush," repeated Louis, angry at the suffering she had borne because of the malice of stupid people. But Valentine went on.

"They see sufficient proof in my coat of arms, I'm sure. Yes, it sounds foolish, but it is true . . . You know what people are like, they even create the evidence they wish to believe."

Involuntarily, Louis' eyes glided to the coat of arms stitched in gold on the bed curtain behind his wife's head: a field, divided in two, displaying a lily of Valois on the left, and on the right the adder which symbolized Milan, a viper about to devour a child at play. Who could deny that it was an image which inspired little confidence? Louis felt the throbbing of his wife's pulse under his hand; he was overwhelmed by deep compassion.

"I don't know," he said, withdrawing his hand from hers. "This is becoming a most painful situation. Most likely I shall have to dissuade you from visiting the King more often than is strictly necessary."

"That is impossible," said Valentine in a dead voice. "I do not go to him, he comes here—and against that I am helpless. It does him good. With me he is often more cheerful and placid than anywhere else; it is wonderful to see how at times he is completely his old self again; he talks sensibly about all sorts of things—even though it lasts only a few moments," she concluded, with a sad smile.

The couple gazed at each other in silence, each lost in thought. They were, thought Valentine, like solitary trees which sometimes take root in the stony soil of mountain tops. Exposed to rain and lightning they stand; clouds drift past them, by degrees wind and weather polish them to stumps as barren as the rocks around them. When, as a bride she had crossed the Italian Alps, Valentine had seen such trees on steep crags, hanging over precipices, pressed obliquely by the wind, scorched black by bolts of lightning. Everything which still bore foliage at that altitude seemed fated to come to a frightful end.

A door opened and two women entered the lying-in chamber: the Dame de Maucouvent and the nurse with the baby in her arms. They were followed, as protocol required, by two rows of demoiselles from Valentine's retinue. Mariette d'Enghien was one of the last pair; as soon as she saw Orléans, she pulled back as though she wished to leave, but her companion held her hand. Louis, who rose when the women entered, greeted the Dame de Maucouvent and lifted the veil which partly covered the small Charles; nothing more was visible of the sleeping child than a pink face as large as a fist. Smiling, the Duke walked past the curtseying maidens; the glance which he cast upon the bent head of Mariette d'Enghien did not escape Valentine's notice; stretched out under the coverlet she watched her husband while the pounding of her heart almost suffocated her.

FIRST BOOK:
Youth

Je suis celuy au cueur vestu de noir.
I am he whose heart is dressed in black.

— Charles d'Orléans

I. Louis d'Orléans, The Father

Se j'ay aimé et on m'amé, ce a faict amours; je l'en mercie, je
m'en répute bien heureux.
If I have loved and have been loved, it was Love that made it
so. I am grateful to Love, I am fortunate.
— Louis d'Orléans, in a letter.

n a July day in the year 1395, the King sat in the open veranda which bordered his rooms on the garden side of Saint-Pol. A green canopy had been set up over him to protect him from the blazing sun; on both sides of it tapestries hung down to the floor. Inside this tent, the King had been playing for a considerable time with oversized, gaily colored cards; he arranged them on the table before him, built tottering towers, and now and then swept them all together with trembling fingers. The court physician, Renaud Fréron, personally appointed by Isabeau after de Harselly's dismissal, walked back and forth over the red and white tiles of the gallery, his hands behind his back. A few courtiers stood, bored and weary, in the shade under the archways.

The aviaries had been brought outside to amuse the King; birds of all sizes and colors hopped twittering about the gilded cage. The hot white light quivered above the slate roofs of the palace; for more than a week the sun had shone from a cloudless sky—the heat grew from day to day, scorching grass and shrubs. The streets of Paris lay deserted as though the city had been struck by plague: the stench of garbage hung over the squares and along the banks of the Seine. Under the bridges the river water flowed sluggishly, turbid, full of silt and filthy. Only in the fields outside the walls of Paris work continued without interruption, despite the scorching heat. The farmers wanted to get the grain inside the barns before the storms began. From the windows of Saint-Pol and the outlying castles, the mowers could be seen moving over the fields like tiny specks; the sun flashed on sickles and scythes. Half-naked, dripping with sweat, the men cut row after row of stalks of grain. The women came behind them, with cloths bound around their heads and shoulders, stooping and squatting, binding the sheaves. Blinded by sun and sweat, swarming with flies, they gathered the bread for the city of Paris, fodder for the beasts.

The King, who had stacked the cards neatly, pushed them to one end of the table and sat quiet, with downcast eyes, waiting for his brother Louis d'Orléans and the Provost of Paris, whose presence he had requested. The haze in which his mind had been enveloped continually since the previous year, had lifted. He recognized the people in his suite, was aware of events and joined in the festivities honoring the delegation which had arrived from England to make a formal request for the hand of the child Isabelle.

Although the physician Fréron had, on the Queen's insistence, advised him to rest and avoid state affairs, the King wished to take advantage of the brief respite between periods of insanity. He knew only too well that the calm clarity, the comfortable feeling of being free, would not last long; that he would be overcome again by mortal fear, fierce pain in his head, darkness filled with hellish visions—but when? How? He saw with despair how much time had passed since he had last been sane. He could still remember hazily a few of the things which had happened afterward; a conversation with his sister-in-law, the Duchess of Orléans, who lay in bed—why? When? And the birth in January of his youngest daughter, Michelle. Charles shook his head slowly, and pensively bit his nails. He had a strong desire to see Valentine; he had wanted to send her a message but he gathered from what the courtiers said that she was no longer in Saint-Pol. Shame and pride prevented him from asking questions of the gentlemen of his retinue who sneered at him haughtily, or smiled at him with compassion. Only from his intimates could he learn about those things which interested him deeply. He considered himself fortunate that his brother was nearby and that the Provost was an able, honest and upright man, who knew how to hold his ground in the face of all opposition.

The King was secretly relieved that the pressure of business prevented Isabeau from coming to see him. The full responsibility of receiving the English legation rested upon her shoulders. Above all else, he feared an interview with his wife; although no one alluded in his presence to the affronts which he, blinded by madness, had offered the Queen, he knew enough. He remembered Isabeau's tears and reproaches, her nocturnal revelations; frozen with horror at his own unwitting cruelty, he had lain listening to her whispers.

That had been in the spring of the previous year. What have I said or done since then, he thought uneasily. He looked quickly and diffidently at the courtiers who chatted under the arched entrance. Before him on a table stood a silver tray heaped with fruit; he removed the peaches one by one and raised the tray before his face. He did not yet have the courage to complain about the absence of mirrors from his rooms, because he surmised, with considerable anguish, the reason for this absence.

Now, partially concealed within the tapestries, he looked at himself in the polished bottom of the tray, touching his cheeks and forehead with clammy fingers; his lips parted involuntarily in disbelief and horror. The sound of footsteps and voices reached him from the adjoining corridors; the birds twittered loudly and beat their wings against the bars. Hastily, the King set the tray back on the table. He saw his brother approaching; Louis' lips trembled with emotion.

"Sire, my King," he said, kneeling before the King without taking his eyes from his brother's face. "Are you well again?"

The King patted the cushioned bench. "Come sit beside me," he said in a low voice, "and tell the others to leave us alone."

Gentlemen and pages retired to the end of the gallery; Renaud Fréron, annoyed, continued his pacing back and forth. The King was receiving against his advice; he feared Isabeau's displeasure. The brothers sat side by side under the canopy: Louis, tanned from frequent exercise in the open air, his posture that of a man who knew how to control every muscle of his body; and Charles, pale, drab, huddled together like an old man.

"Tell me, how goes it with you, brother?" said Louis, laying his hand on the King's. "Are you free from pain now? Is your head clearer? Nothing has made me so happy in a long time as this—that we can speak together in good health."

"I am like someone who has temporarily exchanged hell for

purgatory," replied the King with a melancholy smile. "No, I feel no pain, but I suffer even more from uncertainty." He looked at his brother timidly, from the corner of his eye. "I cannot remember anything," he whispered, with a sigh.

Louis was silent. He could find no words to express the pity which consumed his heart. The King sat very still, huddled within the folds of his mantle, blinking his slightly inflamed eyelids.

"You must tell me everything now," he went on, after a pause. "No one knows how long I shall be able to busy myself with affairs of state. Have you kept a watchful eye, brother, in spite of everything, as you promised me?"

"I have been vigilant," said Louis, in an equally soft voice. He picked up the playing cards from the table and fanned them out; there was the smiling Queen, who bore a falcon on her wrist, the armored King, and the Jester with bells on his cap.

"Yesterday I received the English delegation in an audience," the King went on. "It seems I gave them permission to come here just before Christmas."

"Our uncle of Burgundy was strongly in favor of it," said Louis lightly, while he examined the handsome cards one by one. "And so Messeigneurs de Berry and Bourbon gave their consent also—at last. As to the Queen—the Bavarians maintain friendly relations with England. There is no better and easier way to strengthen an alliance than by contracting a marriage, especially when one is so indirectly connected to the bride that no financial obligation is entailed."

"What do you think, then, brother?" asked the King without looking up; he was preoccupied with braiding and unravelling the fringe of the tablecloth. Orléans smiled bitterly.

"I agree with those who say that it's senseless to conclude a treaty between two kingdoms which still have a few more years of armistice between them. And it is meaningless politically, because I don't believe it is possible to end hostilities. And it will be a crime against the child Isabelle who will suffer if the war goes on when she is queen over there."

The King shrugged. "They are here now," he said hesitantly. "They bring gifts and friendly letters from King Richard. This Norwich—he's Earl of Rutland, isn't he?—he seems to be a capable, courteous ambassador. Richard must really crave peace," he added doubtfully, "if he approaches us and leaves us to name the conditions."

"Ah!" Louis made a passionate gesture. "Don't think that England—to say nothing of Burgundy—will fare badly after a treaty has been signed. I'm even willing to assume that Richard does not intend to fight again—why shouldn't I? They say he is a trustworthy man, ready to settle any dispute quickly. But it remains to be seen whether a new armistice will really mean the end of raids and looting. For two years I've been working on the plan you and I discussed before you became ill the first time. Surely after Poitiers and Crécy anyone who knew anything about it could see that our soldiers were no match for the English bowmen. It's incredible that none of our captains thought of teaching our fellows to use English weapons. Now I have that in hand; you can rest easy. Now most towns and cities have bands of archers who can use handbows as well as crossbows. That was really useful last year in Normandy and Brittany when the English kept raiding the coast."

He was silent for a moment, and the bitter lines appeared again at the corners of his mouth. "It's really hard to have to watch the constant efforts of our noble lords to disband well-trained groups of fighting men. They are so frightened of rebellion that they would sooner hand the land over to the English."

The King's sigh was so deep that it was almost a groan. The physician turned on his heel abruptly and came toward him. The King, who, not without reason, hated and feared Fréron, began to ramble, but he managed to pull himself together and call out with a semblance of his former authority that he wished to be left in peace. Fréron backed away, bowing, and joined the group of attendants.

"I do not want that man near me anymore," the King said nervously. He drew the curtain and shifted the bench so that the physician could not see him. "He takes too much blood from me; I am weak and dizzy from it. No, no, brother, let me finish! God knows when I will get the chance again. I commiserate with you," he said vehemently, pushing away the beaker which Louis offered him, "your lot is more difficult than mine. Few will thank you for your efforts, and you will be thwarted at every turn—and I am not able to help you. God, God, why don't they kill me when the madness comes upon me!" Tears trickled from under his enflamed eyelids; he sat motionless, a shattered man.

"Be still now, control yourself." The Duke of Orléans spoke almost roughly. "I do what I can, but I cannot move mountains.

We must help ourselves, brother, the wolves are stealing through the snow; they will not spare us. I shall have to put up with great frustration, but I do not propose to abandon the struggle because of that. I shall be too clever for Burgundy. He thinks he has put me in checkmate by effecting the marriage pact with England; but he is mistaken once again, our lord uncle. I shall seek my strength where he has sought it himself—in friendship with Richard of England. I have already taken steps to that end."

The King wrinkled his brow; he could hardly grasp the state of affairs, so much had happened since he had last been lucid. He strained to understand. A fierce throbbing behind his eyes warned of the onset of a headache. He put a hand to his forehead and sank back in his seat.

"Am I tiring you, brother?" Louis spoke self-reproachfully. But the King quickly shook his head. "Tell me more," he whispered. "Do you advise me to continue negotiations then?"

"You don't have any alternative. The English lords are here and the Queen has let them know they can call upon Madame Isabelle this afternoon. The Dukes are meeting continually to define conditions. Take a piece of advice from me . . ." He leaned toward the King and laid a hand on his knee. "Insist on the insertion of a clause in the treaty which excludes Madame Isabelle from succession to the throne—even from inheriting French territory. Be royal with a dowry, brother, but demand that clause!"

The King bit the knuckles of his left hand. He gazed into his brother's face, so close to his own: he saw the healthy glow under Louis' brown skin, the long, muscular hand raised in warning. The King shuddered with disgust at his own decrepitude.

"You could insist upon it," he said, groping for words. "You are always there, aren't you?"

Louis sighed with impatience.

"This is too important," he said emphatically. "God be praised, you are now able to enforce your views in this matter. They have kept me in the dark about everything, as usual: Burgundy has seen to it that I was kept busy elsewhere. Do you know anything about our difficulties with the Pope?" he asked, after a brief, prudent silence.

The King nervously shook his head. For a few moments Louis stared into space. It was a difficult task to enlighten the King; nonetheless he wanted to tell him as much as he could, for the Regents would no doubt attempt to force their views upon him during his temporary recovery.

"Can you remember," Louis went on slowly, "that you allowed a poll to be taken among the clergy more than a year ago, on the advice of the University? They favored then making concessions on behalf of re-elections."

"Yes. True." Charles still spoke hesitantly. "But—surely—they were correct—these doctors at the Sorbonne, were they not? You have always disagreed with them, brother, haven't you?"

Louis shrugged. "That is beside the point," he said testily. "I admit that I could not—and cannot—tolerate their blatant arrogance. 'Rectify and judge—*et doctrinaliter, et indecialiter.*'" Softly he mimicked Gershon's hoarse voice. "They act as if they know everything. Besides, they supported Rome, which was to be expected—the learned doctors almost always come here from abroad. They cursed Avignon whenever they spoke. But then last fall Pope Clement died . . ."

The King nodded a few times; his eyes began to shine.

"Yes, yes." He talked fast. "I know all about it. I signed letters to the Cardinals at Avignon, asking them not to choose a new pope."

"The Cardinals left the letters unopened and immediately chose Pedro de Luna." Louis' laughter was jeering; he was thinking of his own hopes at the time. "I thought then that this was a positive action, because I knew that Luna supported cession. Well, I soon had reason enough to doubt his good intentions. The University did not leave us in peace; daily it sent doctors and orators to plead the cause of cession. Then this spring Monseigneur de Berry and I went to Avignon with an embassy from the Sorbonne. We talked with de Luna day and night but he is a sly fox who does not let himself be tempted by promises—not even for a moment. And what is the result? A pope sits in Avignon—his name is Benedict—who never for a single moment considers resigning his office in order to have a second ballot. And so farewell to the unity of the Church."

"My God," said Charles softly. "How are we to find solace to ease the pain of existence when our comforter, the Church, is torn by discord and dissension?"

Louis made an irritable gesture. "The Church, the Church . . . Sometimes I think that we ought to seek our solace, as you call it, anywhere where there are no priests and prelates. Who can enlighten us in our dark ignorance? For we are in the darkness, brother, we hardly dare to feel our way . . ."

The King was becoming restless. He felt tired and hot. "What are you babbling about now?" he muttered. "What you have just told me is bad enough, but what can I do about it? What do you expect of me? Where is Madame d'Orléans?" he asked suddenly, sitting up straight. "Why hasn't she come to visit me yet? I would like to see her. It is a long time since she was last here—is she ill? Why don't you answer me?" He looked at Louis with suspicion. Orléans sat with bowed head.

"My wife is no longer in Saint-Pol," he said finally, without looking at the King. "She lives in the Hôtel de Béhaigne—she has been there since January, since she went to church after the birth of our son Charles."

The Hôtel de Béhaigne was one of the many houses which Louis d'Orléans owned in Paris. It was comfortably furnished and set amid beautiful gardens.

Two red spots appeared on the King's cheekbones. He too lowered his eyes. "Why?" he whispered, inexplicably choked by feelings of guilt and shame.

"Your friendship for Madame d'Orléans has aroused suspicion and mistrust," said Louis formally. "I thought it advisable that she should leave Saint-Pol."

"My God," said the King, "this is a gross insult. Is Burgundy behind it?"

Louis shrugged. "It can't be tracked down. You might as well try to surprise a viper in his hole as try to trace the origin of an ugly rumor; you know that as well as I, brother."

The King, already restless and overwrought, could not restrain his emotion. He hung over the arm of the bench, racked by sobs. In vain Louis attempted to quiet him with soothing words, rebukes, promises.

The physician, Fréron, who had not taken his eyes from the royal tent even for an instant, approached in haste, followed by the King's old valet. Despite the physician's mild manner and his courteous, even submissive demeanor toward the Duke of Orléans, he retained an aura of cold determination, verging on brutality. Fréron was considered to be a skillful doctor; only Isabeau knew that he put his own interests before the welfare of his royal patient. It required no effort for him to do what his predecessor, de Harselly, would never have done; at Isabeau's request he administered to the King potions and powders prepared by the exorcist Guillaume; sometimes he brought the ascetic into the King's bedroom at midnight to perform spells in secret.

As Louis d'Orléans emerged from under the canopy, the physician cast a venomous glance at him; he intensely disliked the King's brother, who always argued against him as well as against Arnaud Guillaume. Orléans bit his lip; he blamed himself for his impulsiveness. But he knew from experience that he must take quick advantage of the King's lucid moments before Isabeau or the Regents could stop him from speaking privately to his brother by taking up his time with trifles. Isabeau and the Dukes were preoccupied at the moment with the important visit of the English nobles, but they would notice the King's recovery soon enough.

"Rest now, Sire my King," Louis said gently to the sick man who, supported by his valet, had taken a draught of some medicine; the physician stood nearby, watching coldly. "I shall come back later; there is still a lot to talk about."

The King nodded and waved his hand. He had recovered himself somewhat, but his lips still trembled and his eyes were bloodshot.

A stir ran through the group of nobles standing at the other end of the gallery. The Provost of Paris, de Tignonville, preceded by sentries and pages from the royal retinue, and accompanied by a secretary and a few clerks, appeared at the gate which joined this section of Saint-Pol with the state rooms. Orléans acknowledged the magistrate's grave salutations and took formal leave of his brother. "The birds should be brought inside; it is too hot," he said to one of the pages as he left the gallery. Fréron, who had given the order to bring the birds outside, blinked several times.

The King invited de Tignonville to sit opposite him under the canopy. "Don't talk about my health, Messire. I want to use these few hours which God has granted me to put my affairs in order."

De Tignonville, an older man with a tranquil, sober demeanor, closed his eyes in a gesture of understanding. He nodded to the secretary who stepped forward with some rolls of vellum: accounts, surveys, petitions. While de Tignonville was busy with these papers, the King hurriedly removed the pile of playing cards from the table.

"How goes it in Paris?" he asked, staring uneasily at the many closely written pages which the Provost was carefully smoothing out before offering them to him.

"The city is sorely concerned for Your Majesty," replied de Tignonville slowly, "and also about the schism in the Holy Church. The populace is disquieted and fearful; the winter was severe. There is much suffering in the city and around it and now the land is stricken by drought. I have often noticed," he continued after a pause, "that in times of stress, men behave in different ways: some seek penance and a sober life; others fall into crime and licentiousness. So it is in Paris, Sire: there are processions and gatherings in the churchyard of the Innocents—but the taverns and bordellos are as full as the churches and the Châtelet, the pillory and Gallows Hill are overcrowded. I do not believe that such a rabble has ever roamed through the city streets as in recent years. The houses are falling down, the streets are filthy. I do not bring you good news, Sire, but I bring you the truth."

The King sat huddled together for a few minutes, without touching the papers spread before him. In the green reflection of the tapestries his was the face of a drowned man—flabby and translucent, drained of blood.

"How can the body be healthy when the mind is ravaged by disease?" he murmured, almost inaudibly. "Surely savagery and disorder must prevail in the cities of France, de Tignonville; for when the King was well, he had neither the inclination nor the insight— and now that he wishes to do his duty like a good prince—God knows—he has lost his senses." He turned his head from side to side as though he were in pain.

The Provost sighed and said nothing.

Louis d'Orléans walked slowly through the reception halls in the old part of the palace, followed at a distance by Jacques van Hersen and two gentlemen of his suite. The halls were crowded; the arrival of the English envoys had drawn nobles and dignitaries to Saint-Pol from far beyond the confines of Paris. Orléans acknowledged their formal greetings with brief replies; he had no desire to chat or even to exchange civilities. He knew this behavior was unwise; he was making his displeasure clear to all these people. But at the moment he was not capable of masking his real feelings.

He set out for his own apartments; although his official residence was the Hôtel de Béhaigne, he spent six days a week in Saint-Pol.

He dismissed his followers and withdrew to the dusky coolness of the armory. Here he was seized by the same feelings of despondency which had overwhelmed him during the winter and spring; in his uncertainty and anguish at his own helplessness, he paced back and forth between the wall hangings with their autumnal colors and the racks of swords and knives. He thought bitterly how unrewarding the task was which he had taken upon himself; the only thing he was striving after was to undo Burgundy's work, to weaken the Regent's every move by a counter-move. He could not see yet where his actions were leading; he could not himself take control of the situation by pushing Burgundy off the stage. He thought of himself as one of those water insects called whirlygigs which are in constant motion but never make any headway. He moved incessantly between Isabeau, the Duke, the King, almost always a little behind events. If he should ever move a little ahead, his uncle of Burgundy was hot on his heels. Valentine's removal to the Hôtel de Béhaigne, the abortive negotiations with the Pope at Avignon, the plans for the royal marriage—these were all personal defeats for him.

He knew that he had to act again to thwart Burgundy, that he had to change his plans and do what Burgundy least expected him to do, and he knew that this behavior smacked of desperation; he hated this constant maneuvering, these abrupt changes of direction. His attention had been diverted from the Italian situation: Gian Galeazzo had been made Duke of Milan by the Holy Roman Emperor, Wenceslaus; this expanded the tyrant's power. Louis guessed that in the future his father-in-law would want to settle his own affairs without any outside help. And it was doubtful that Pope Benedict of Avignon would abdicate of his own free will, especially after what had happened in the spring. The advocates of cession found a staunch supporter in the Duke of Burgundy; for that reason Louis considered throwing his own support to the Avignon Pope, however much he distrusted him, but first it was his duty to revise his attitude toward the English question. The only thing he could find no solution for was Valentine's exile; he watched helplessly as the enmity against her grew day by day in the royal circle at court— although they sent her letters and gifts—and among the people of Paris.

Louis d'Orléans stood motionless before one of the arms racks, his hands behind his back. He had once heard a tale of a knight whose evil fate hung around his neck day and night in the shape of a demon. Now he himself felt the constant weight of a leaden, oppressive presence. Even at the hunt, or at games, or during the brief amorous adventures which he pursued from a craving for oblivion, he was never free from the burden of melancholy. He thought of his brother the King, huddled apprehensive and distraught under the green tapestries of his pavilion, afraid of the physician, of new attacks of madness.

Over the course of a few years the good-natured, pleasure-loving young man had become a wreck, a hopeless invalid, who tried vainly in moments of lucidity to make up for what he had frittered away during the ten years of his reign. This man, tormented by feverish bewilderment, wore the Crown of France. His hand, which could not hold a glass of wine without spilling it, all too quickly took up the pen to sign decrees and edicts, the significance of which he could not possibly grasp. He alternated rapidly between suspicion and unquestioning trust: if in the morning he allowed himself to be convinced of something by Louis, at noon he let himself be equally persuaded of an opposing view by Burgundy. Louis knew that this was true, from his own experience; not infrequently after a talk with Burgundy the King had revoked a decision which he had made earlier at Louis' insistence.

He sighed and resumed his walk through the armory. The Holy Virgins who were leading Mary to her Coronation in Paradise smiled down from the walls, the stiff folds of their garments spread around their feet over the celestial fields. Among roses and lilies, Saint Catherine, Saint Barbara, Ursula, Veronica, walked in procession wearing crowns and veils like worldly princesses. Louis gazed at their sweet, mysterious, laughing faces, at their hands, folded demurely on their breasts. Mariette d'Enghien had looked like that as she stood among the women of Valentine's entourage. Neither his considerable powers of persuasion nor the magic ring which the astrologer Salvia had brought him seemed able to shatter her resistance. She spurned gifts, thrusting them shyly but firmly away; whenever, in the seclusion of house or court, he endeavored to approach her, she stood motionless, with lowered eyes, in anguished apprehension. Had it been any other woman, Louis would undoubtedly have abandoned his hopeless courtship earlier; he did not usually go to such pains for the sake of beauty alone. Besides, he never needed to, for women as a rule offered themselves before he was even ready to approach them. He did not know himself why he desired the Demoiselle d'Enghien more desperately from day to day; in the couplets which he sent her he compared her to a meadow buried under snow, to a frozen crystalline mountain brook or an icy spring wind. She seldom answered him when he spoke to her; sometimes she only looked at him and her glance was green and sparkling—something smouldered there, which he did not understand. He tried to forget his chagrin and annoyance in the arms of other women; fleeting adventures with strangers encountered in streets or taverns; a few days' fling with a court lady of the Queen's, the frivolous wife of a nobleman who lived in Saint-Pol. Valentine he treated with the greatest delicacy; since her confinement she had not yet regained her strength, and although she hid it well, she suffered from the calumny which threatened to make her life in Paris impossible.

Louis smiled sardonically, gazing at the placid saints on the wall hanging. "Has she a talisman which protects her from love?" he said in a low voice. "But why is she uncertain then? She flees, but she herself does not know why." An enticing image rose before him: Maret, her auburn hair loose upon her shoulders, her chaste garment about to slip away . . . He covered his eyes with his hand and turned hastily from the tapestry.

Valentine, Duchess of Orléans, sat in a small bower in the ornamental garden of the Hôtel de Béhaigne. Trees shaded the grass; within the border of wallflowers and lilies, a fountain leaped from a marble basin. Surrounding the garden was a hedge of clipped shrubs; it was like a fragrant green chamber. Shadows and droplets from the fountain cooled the air; the dry, stifling heat which burned down on stone and sand outside the garden did not reach the women in the arbor. Valentine was bareheaded and wore a light undergarment; on her lap she held a harp, a beautifully painted instrument which she had brought with her from Lombardy. Around her in the grass lay rolls of music. She played the harp with great dexterity; writers eagerly offered her their compositions.

She did not play now, but brushed her fingertips along the strings of the harp, absorbed in thought. She had sent all the women who had kept her company during the course of the morning back into the house, except for Mariette d'Enghien. The girl had requested an audience with her. Valentine knew very well where it would lead; she dreaded a conversation but at the same time she yearned to hear the truth. Intuition told her that Mariette d'Enghien abhorred lies and secrecy. The girl could not flatter; she lacked the taste for intrigue.

The Duchess of Orléans, who watched her constantly, had had the opportunity to compare Maret with the young ladies of her retinue who were adept at court ceremony. At first she was somewhat surprised at Mademoiselle d'Enghien's modest self-possession, her brusque speech, her look of inward reserve. Her companions made fun of her for what they called her country manners; it was known that she came from an isolated province, having spent her childhood in an uncomfortable, remote castle among kinsmen who did not concern themselves with courtly ceremony. However much Valentine might loathe the fact that Mariette seemed to captivate Louis as no woman before her had ever done, she could not help admitting that the girl's honesty and cool simplicity were artless and disarming. She did not believe that a love affair was going on between her husband and this quiet, shy young woman. On the contrary, she knew instinctively that there could be greater danger in the relationship evolving from Louis' uncontrollable passion and Mariette's cool resistance than from one of mutual ardor. Confused by anguished grief, Valentine surveyed the situation: she had been given no reason to demand an explanation, to utter a reprimand or even a warning.

The Duchess of Orléans thought sadly of the day—four or five years ago—when she heard for the first time that her husband had sought the favors of a pretty bourgeoise. She had summoned the woman and threatened to punish her if she ever yielded to Louis again. Many hours of exasperation and disillusionment had followed that first painful interview, but never again had she called any of Orléans' paramours to account. She could not hold Mariette d'Enghien to account; she had no proof, not even justifiable suspicions. But Maret sought an audience.

The two young women sat facing each other in the shadow of the shrubbery. Spots of sunlight quivered on their clothes, on the scrolls of music, and on the thick short grass. Even the birds were silent in the heat. No single sound rose from the nearby streets.

"Madame," said Mariette d'Enghien quietly, fixing her large bright eyes on Valentine, "I implore you to dismiss me from your service."

The Duchess made an involuntary gesture of surprise; she had not expected this.

"Do you wish to return to your family, Mademoiselle?" she asked gently. "The dismissal of a maid of honor from the royal suite is a serious matter—it could create a mistaken impression; I would like to spare you that. I am not dissatisfied with you," she added quickly; she regretted her familiarity immediately, for Maret turned pale with shame and annoyance.

"I do not have to go home," she replied slowly, with her eyes down.

Unconsciously, Valentine continued to stroke her harpstrings; soft, vague sounds issued from under her fingertips.

"Where can you go then, Mademoiselle?" she asked, not looking at the girl.

Mariette folded her hands stiffly in her lap.

"As it happens, Madame, I have consented to become the wife of Sire Aubert de Cany, who serves in the King's retinue."

Now Valentine raised her head quickly; between the braided tresses her small narrow face seemed paler than usual.

"I had not heard that a promise of marriage existed between you and the Sire de Cany," she said.

"My kinsmen arranged the matter. Messire de Cany will ask for the King's consent. But that is a mere formality, if I understand properly. No one can hinder the marriage."

Valentine's heart throbbed so loudly she felt it must be audible in the deep silence. She attempted to ask in a light, jesting tone the question which tormented her.

"Your heart was not then at the Court of Orléans during the time that you served me, Mademoiselle?"

Mariette stood up; the folds of her dress rustled over the grass.

The Duchess saw that the girl's green eyes were filled with tears; her mouth, however, remained firm and her expression austere.

"My heart was with you, Madame," said Maret, almost roughly. "That is why I am leaving. I beg you to excuse me now."

Valentine released the harp and took Mademoiselle d'Enghien's hand in her own.

"Can we not speak honestly with each other?" she whispered. Mariette stood motionless; the Duchess felt something in the girl tighten with resistance; the hand which she held firmly was cold despite the heat.

"Madame," said Maret d'Enghien with an effort, "it is my wish to become the wife of Messire de Cany. He is a noble man, Madame . . . too good to be deceived. Where I was raised they had little sympathy for adultery, and no pretty words for it. So I was taught; I cannot think otherwise. It is a great honor for me to marry a man like Messire de Cany, whose views are no less strict."

"Maret, Maret." The Duchess of Orléans was moved by an emotion which she could not name. "Is this an escape?"

A spark of impatience flickered in Mariette d'Enghien's eyes.

"You doubt my courage and the firmness of my will, Madame," she said. Valentine sighed and released the girl's cold, damp hand. The damsel stooped to pick up the rolls of music.

"May I go now, Madame?" she asked at last. Valentine nodded.

"I wish to remain out here a little longer," she said, attempting to regain her usual airy, benevolent manner. "Send my women— but not too quickly."

Mariette curtsied and left the enclosed garden. The Duchess of Orléans sat motionless, gazing after her. That this resilient young body, this firm mouth and deep green eyes had aroused Louis' lust disturbed and alarmed her, but she could understand it. Her sorrow deepened as she realized that within Maret lay the power of enchantment—a power which, precisely because it was so deeply concealed, was more irresistible than any beauty and grace of form.

Was it perhaps the strength to resist, once she had made up her mind to it? Valentine stood within the hedges of her garden like a prisoner; the fountain murmured in the silence. Coolness seemed to have vanished from the arbor with Maret's departure; despite the shade, hot air rose from grass and shrub. The water dropped into the brimming basin of the fountain like a rain of tears. The odor of the wallflowers reminded her suddenly of the sweet but poisonous perfume which her father in Milan gave freely to those who had lost his favor. She thought of her youth, spent in the gardens and palaces of Pavia, amid greater opulence and greater cruelty than she had known since then; she thought of her girlhood, her deep sadness over the misery of the world, her yearning for warmth and happiness, all the vague forebodings of future sorrow which had already disturbed her under the radiant skies of her native land. She knew while she sat motionless amid the greenery of the arbor that storm clouds were gathering on the horizon of her life. She was condemned to wait as though she were the victim of some evil spell until the tempest burst loose above her—until wind and hail blighted and tore the delicate blossoms of her ornamental garden.

Queen Isabeau received the English legation in the palace of Saint-Pol. The English lords had insisted on seeing the bride as soon as they reached Paris. Although the eight-year-old Madame Isabelle had not yet reached the marriageable age, it was still possible to conjecture what sort of flower would develop from such a bud. The King's eldest daughter, deeply impressed at being the main object of interest at the ceremony, stood behind Isabeau, hand-in-hand with her brother the Dauphin. The royal delegation stood in the reception hall of the Queen's apartments. Isabeau had ordered the walls hung with new, beautiful tapestries, patterned with crowned doves of peace, golden against a dark red background. Except for the Queen and her two eldest children, only the Duke and Duchess of Burgundy, the mistress of ceremonies, Madame d'Eu, and Marguérite de Nevers were present; in the rear of the hall were a number of members of the King's Council, among them the Chancellor, Arnault de Corbie, who had spoken at the assembly in favor of accepting the marriage proposal. The King was not there; they had decided to present the English lords to him when Isabeau's reception ended. Louis d'Orléans led the envoys to the dais where the Queen stood beside her children. Isabelle freed her hand with some difficulty from the Dauphin who was, as usual, confused by so many strange faces.

"My daughter," the Queen said, smiling; she put her hand on the child's shoulder. But Isabelle needed no encouragement. She knew what was expected of her; maternal counsel had not been wasted on the precocious, haughty little princess. Folding her hands on the front of her stiffly embroidered dress, the child walked to the edge of the dais; she wore a crown and veil like an adult and held her fingers tightly together to avoid losing her rings. The Earls of Rutland and Nottingham knelt in homage.

"My lady," said Rutland in slow, careful French, looking up at the controlled, smooth childish face. "God willing, you shall be our mistress and Queen of England."

A silence ensued. Nervously, Isabeau clenched her fists; she stood too far away from the child to help her. She smiled at the envoys, but her eyes were uneasy. The royal kinsmen, the retinue, the members of the council, looked on; the English lords knelt with bowed heads. Outside the arched windows the sunlight was blinding; flies buzzed in the silence. Isabeau breathed quickly; she wanted to help her daughter. If Isabelle was anxious, she did not show it. She stood impassive in her state dress, which cast a gold reflection on the tiled floor, and kept her fingers pressed carefully together. With the interested respectful smile required by etiquette on her face, she stared straight before her over the heads of the envoys, trying to remember what words she was supposed to say. She was not frightened but annoyed at having stupidly forgotten the phrases she had studied so diligently. Behind her she heard her mother's nervous cough; a feeling of apprehension crept over her. Behind the English lords stood her uncle of Orléans. Playfully he put his hand over his heart. The child realized that he was trying to attract her attention; he closed his eyes in reassurance, and bowed his head. The blood rushed to Isabelle's cheeks—now she remembered what she must say. The high-pitched, childish voice did not quaver; it seemed as though she had deliberately paused for effect, to heighten the impression she made.

"Messires," said Isabelle, "if it shall please God and my father that I become Queen of England, then am I well content, for I have always heard it said that I shall then be a mighty sovereign."

Carefully she put out her five tightly closed fingers and requested the Lord Marshal to rise. The envoy took in his own the childish hand bedecked with heavy rings and allowed himself to be led to Isabeau by his future Queen. Isabeau was deeply moved, but more from relief than from maternal pride. The child had made an excellent impression; the English declared that their fondest expectations had been surpassed. They praised the appearance and behavior of the princess—above all, they admired her self-possession and well-chosen words. Isabeau listened to the envoys in silence, still smiling. Now that the reception, the high point of five months of negotiations and preparation, had been a success, she had achieved her goal—at least in regard to the English marriage. Isabelle seemed in every way a perfect bride for a king. So far as the signing of the marriage contract was concerned, Richard's spokesmen would presumably raise few objections. New labors awaited them.

Isabeau withdrew; she had sent away the children with their nurses. The Englishmen set out together with the Duke and Council members to pay their respects to the King in his apartments.

In the coolness of her bedroom, Isabeau attempted to prepare herself for the meeting with her husband. During the last few days she had seen him only at state dinners. She knew that he was somewhat recovered, but strangely enough, this filled her more with apprehension than with hope. She could not identify the sickly, prematurely aged man who avoided her eyes, with the King her husband. The passion was dead which had driven her into his arms a year and a half ago; instead of pity she felt aversion, as though for a stranger. But she could not shun him, even if she wished to; she needed his co-operation. She had to bend him to her will as long as he was capable of judgment.

Isabeau, who suffered sorely from the heat—after her last confinement she had gained even more weight—allowed them to remove the high headdress and all her jewels. While her chamberwomen busied themselves about her, she stared sullenly, her lips pursed, at the potted shrubs blooming along the wall. Her brother Ludwig had arrived with news that in all its aspects required careful consideration. Isabeau knew from experience that Ludwig had a sharp nose for being on hand when important events took place; she trusted his judgment implicitly. She had heard that the German electors intended to depose the Emperor; Wenceslaus the Drunkard had in the course of years convincingly proven his ineptitude. A new candidate for the throne of the Holy Roman Empire had already appeared in the person of Ruprecht of Bavaria, Duke of Heidelberg, a member of the Wittelsbach family. Isabeau's kinsmen were strong supporters of Ruprecht; they had never forgiven Wenceslaus for conferring the title of Duke of Milan upon their arch-enemy Gian Galeazzo. It was a matter of winning France to Ruprecht's side. Ludwig who, with some justification, saw in his sister the strongest advocate of the Wittelsbach interests, considered that his goal was very nearly accomplished. Isabeau, on the other hand, was not quite as certain of success; many influential members of the court favored Wenceslaus—pre-eminent among them was Louis d'Orléans. Isabeau saw a possibility of influencing the court in Ruprecht's favor only with Burgundy's support. She considered that she might win the Duke and Duchess over to the Electors' plan; in large measure Burgundy and Bavaria shared the same interests.

In her brother's presence, Isabeau had already spoken to the Duchess of Burgundy; but Margaretha, always cautious, said only that she would need time to consider in tranquillity before she could respond. The Queen was positive that Burgundy would be told that same day and that the couple would act appropriately. And indeed Margaretha took advantage of the fact that Isabeau would be alone after the reception, to continue the discussion. The Duchess of Burgundy, alone of the highly-placed women of the court, entered Isabeau's chambers unannounced; she assumed that her role as the Queen's right hand guaranteed her this privilege. Isabeau, who disliked the cold, all-too-shrewd Fleming, would not have allowed this presumption if she were not convinced of Margaretha's value to her. She forced herself, therefore, to smile when the Duchess of Burgundy appeared in the doorway. Philippe's wife considered it unwise to irritate Isabeau by showing too much self-confidence; she could hardly believe that she could enter the Queen's presence again and again without ceremony. She entered in her slow, stately manner and curtsied deeply.

"Does it please Your Majesty to receive me?" she asked, knowing that Isabeau would acquiesce. The chamberwomen withdrew.

Margaretha politely declined the proferred chair. She remained standing at a proper distance from the Queen, her hands folded together on her breast. She spoke first of all of the successful reception; she praised the child Isabelle and wished the Queen joy in the brilliant debut.

"Yes," Isabeau said impatiently. "Have you considered meanwhile what you will say to the Duke of Bavaria?"

Margaretha raised her brows slightly; she could not become accustomed to Isabeau's lack of finesse.

"One cannot form a judgment on a matter of such importance in a few days, Madame," the Duchess of Burgundy parried in respectfully gentle rebuke. "We have never been supporters of the Emperor Wenceslaus, as you know. But Your Majesty knows also that the Emperor has many friends here at court—that the Duke of Orléans your brother-in-law is well disposed toward him." She paused and shot Isabeau an inquiring glance. "I take it that it is worth a lot to Your Majesty to win the King to your point of view."

"I know that in all circumstances the opinion of Monseigneur of Burgundy is extremely important," the Queen said irritably. She picked up a comb from the table and ran it through her thin hair which hung loose to her shoulders. Isabeau had had good reason to introduce the fashion of wearing elaborate headdresses which concealed the hair.

"Well, Madame," said Margaretha softly, "my husband has heard with interest the news from Germany. Your Majesty may rest assured that he will study the matter thoroughly. I think that he may still find an opportunity to speak with the Duke of Bavaria before His Grace leaves the court."

Isabeau nodded; she was not displeased to hear this.

"And now I should like to discuss another matter with your Majesty." The Duchess of Burgundy's voice became rather brusque. "It concerns my granddaughter, my son Jean's oldest child. It is a year now since Monseigneur my husband spoke to the King about the possibility of a marriage between Marguérite and the Dauphin. Such an arrangement would be highly beneficial to our mutual interests, Madame. Moreover, as it happens," she moved a few paces closer to the Queen, "my sons have sons—and Your Majesty a very few young daughters for whom, I believe, plans have not yet been made."

Isabeau dropped the comb into her lap.

"Monseigneur d'Orléans also has two sons," she replied, with some hauteur. "And I seem to recall that the King has already made an agreement with Orléans concerning the Dauphin."

The Duchess of Burgundy gave a short, malicious laugh, while her cheeks flushed with anger.

"There is no assurance that Monseigneur d'Orléans will ever have a daughter. Such an agreement can have little value. I hope with all my heart that Your Majesty can convince the King to make a wiser decision, especially in the light of the news from Bavaria."

"Yes, yes." Isabeau sighed and threw back her head. A familiar feeling of rebellious rage swept over her. How much longer must she allow them to dictate to her? "You say I have so much influence with the King," she burst out hotly. "Has it not been obvious in the last few months that it is not I who have influence with the King?"

"Ah, Madame," said Margaretha, with emphasis, "a clever wife can always influence her husband. We all saw how the King turned to you before the illness overcame him. Your Majesty undoubtedly knows how to charm the King." She paused a moment and then continued. "It seems to me that your Majesty can begin by ordering that the door be unbolted which separates your apartments from the King's."

Isabeau sprang from her chair. The Duchess of Burgundy saw that she had said enough; she backed from the room, curtseying deeply once again.

In the course of the day the weather changed. The sky clouded over; a heavy mist began almost imperceptibly to cover the dazzling blue of the sky. Within a few hours it became dark; the summer lightning darted over the hills. The reapers worked hastily to haul the sheaves inside the barns until they were halted by the rain which tumbled down in torrents; earth and sky became indistinguishable from each other. The crash of thunder echoed incessantly from the walls and high towers of Saint-Pol.

The great reception rooms were crowded. The hundreds of nobles who were sojourning in the palace to honor the English envoys and had been driven from the gardens and fives courts by the storm, were seeking amusement in cards and dice. Louis d'Orléans had managed to shake off his despondency; he was in a boisterous mood and moved from table to table, joking loudly with the players.

The rain squalls whipped through the inner courtyards, a wet mist blew through the windows and corridors as far as the great halls. Torchlight flickered on the walls. Orléans was offered a place at each gaming table as he approached it, but he waved his glove, watched the game for a short while and then moved on, humming to himself.

In a side room Jean de Nevers sat with friends, playing dice at a table strewn with gold pieces. A crowd of spectators—members of de Nevers' suite—stood around the table.

"Ah, cousin," Louis cried loudly, pushing his way through, "I see that you are seriously occupied, raising money for your crusade against the Turks. How many tents and lances have you assembled by gambling today?"

Jean de Nevers looked up. He could not bring himself to smile.

"You need not tell me how good the wine was," he replied sarcastically. "Your breath tells me that already, cousin, and in any case your infantile behavior does not lie. Not that I begrudge you the drink," he continued quickly, when he saw that Louis, still laughing, was about to move away. "You can raise your spirits with food and wine. You do not need to fight."

"Ah la . . ." Orléans said slowly, in the same jocular tone. "It is not my fault, my dear cousin, that we have never measured our strength in a duel . . ."

Jean began to get up, but his friend Philippe de Bar, who sat beside him, put his hand on his arm. Jean curled his lip.

"It may interest you to know," he said, "that everyone who has a name and can hold a weapon has declared himself ready to come with me. But no doubt you knew that already. Your old friend, the Sire de Coucy, who has served you so well in Lombardy, will have brought you the news."

"The Sire de Coucy is too busy organizing your crusade, cousin." Louis tossed his glove in the air and caught it. "It is a wearisome job to recruit soldiers and arm them, even for an experienced general—one who has no time for games or idle chit-chat."

Nevers flushed darkly; he clenched his fist on the table in an effort to control himself.

"Well, that depends," he said in a voice choking with anger. "There are reports that there is much merriment at the court of your father-in-law, Gian Galeazzo, although he sends auxiliary troops to the Turks."

It became suddenly very quiet around the gaming table. The rain clattered against the roofs and the thunder crackled and boomed. The side room was crowded with spectators; it was the first time since the banquet in the abbey of Saint-Denis that my lords of Orléans and Nevers had publicly betrayed their enmity. Louis stood motionless, the glove in his upraised hand. He was no longer smiling.

"If I did not know, cousin, that spreading slander had become second nature to you, I would perhaps in all seriousness take up arms for my father-in-law," he said, forcing himself to speak calmly, despite the wine he had drunk. The dark, piercing eyes of Jean de Nevers were fixed upon him; the others waited for him to lose his self-control. For a moment Orléans was tempted to throw his glove into that face distorted with hatred and contempt. Only in combat between the two of them could they give vent to their mutual feelings. Louis knew that Burgundy's son would like nothing better than to attack him—especially if the challenge for the fight between kinsmen came from Orléans himself—but Louis would not permit this just yet. It would be particularly ill-advised at this moment to engage in a public brawl with the House of Burgundy. He contented himself, therefore, with shoving his glove into his belt and announcing to the bystanders with a smile:

"My lords, things will have come to a sorry pass when we can no longer joke with one another at the court of the King of France. Perhaps you would have taken it better, cousin, if I had begun by asking you whether you had squandered your tents and lances."

He saluted Nevers and left the room with a nod and a cheerful word for everyone who spoke to him. But he was filled with shame and anger; he craved more wine and the boisterous excitement which could be bought in many of the public houses of Paris. He sought out among the players a few intimate friends who usually accompanied him on his nocturnal expeditions through the city, and beckoned to them to follow him.

Isabeau sat beside the King. The burning candles illuminated the parchment covered with close writing, that lay on the table. The King, already exceedingly weary after a day of conversations and receptions, and upset by the storm, squinted nervously at the papers which Isabeau had put before him; here he could see with his own eyes what it cost the Treasury to maintain the Queen's palaces, estates and properties, what money she was forced to pay out for clothing and entertainment, what gifts she had given to kinsmen and household on New Year's Day, on the occasions of fêtes and holy days.

"I do not do this to upset you, Sire," she said. Her tone was soft but business-like. "I do not like troubling you with numbers and lists, but the Audit Office must make a decision about my income. I have been waiting almost two years now for an adjustment. First they assigned me a number of estates which are too remote from one another. To collect taxes I would need an army of officials. Now they tell me again that I shall receive more lands when Queen Blanche dies. But that must be codified somehow. I have no real assurance. I have my household and my children to feed and to clothe. It is an impossible situation that I must beg the Audit Office for every livre."

Isabeau spoke hotly. She had brought up the subject as soon as she was left alone with her husband. The King looked at her strangely; he had a vague recollection of another Isabeau, a fresh, blooming young Isabeau always ready for laughter and kisses, with no interest in anything resembling official documents and numbers. The plump, bejeweled woman who sat facing him bore no resemblance to the Isabeau to whom he had once sent a golden triptych as a token of his love. Her dark brown eyes were hard; they looked at him without tenderness. They were alone together for the first time in a year and a half, and she spoke of revenue, territories— gold, gold, gold!

"I shall instruct the Audit Office to settle the matter at once," the King said wearily, shoving the papers away from him. "And to fix the annuity which you will be paid upon my death, Madame." He turned his head to listen to the crackling of the storm. "How it rains," he continued nervously. "Could the flood have started like this in Noah's day? We don't deserve a better fate."

Isabeau did not answer; she tightened her lips and began to put the papers together. From time to time she glanced at the King. Wine, cake and fruit stood untouched on the table. The wall hangings stirred in the draughts. The roaring of the wind and rain drowned out all other sounds, giving the King and Queen a feeling of utter seclusion in the heart of the palace. They sat for a while, facing each other in silence, Charles with uneasy, wandering eyes, Isabeau staring vacantly at the golden candle holders. But the silence oppressed the Queen. She began to talk quickly, in a forced way, about her children: about the Dauphin, who knew his prayers by heart; about how dignified Isabelle was during the reception. She mentioned her discussion with the convent where Marie would be accepted and she talked about the infant Michelle whom she had named after the King's patron saint. The King listened uneasily, tapping his fingers on the table top; he rocked back and forth in his chair, rubbing his face and his clothes. He sensed his wife's feeling of aversion toward him, and he was frightened by this hard-eyed stranger.

They were both relieved when Colin de Bailly, a nobleman of the King's retinue, entered the room and requested an audience for a messenger from Lombardy who had been waiting for more than half the day in one of the anterooms. The King remembered suddenly that as early as that morning he had given instructions to let the man wait. He declared himself ready to hear the messenger.

The Italian brought a letter from Gian Galeazzo. The Duke of Milan wrote stiffly that he had been shocked and dismayed to hear the news from France, which he hoped would prove to be false.

There were, he wrote, reports concerning the exalted and excellent lady, his daughter, the Duchess of Orléans, of whom it was apparently being said that she attempted to impede the King's recovery by means of sorcery. He expected that the King, may it please God to grant him good health, or the King's closest relatives, would spare no efforts to refute publicly the malevolent rumor—that the slanderers would be tracked down and then suitably punished.

As he read the letter, the King became very excited.

"Who said that? Who dares to say that?" he repeated; trembling with agitation, he crumpled the sleeves of his mantle into a wad. "Is that why she went away?" he asked abruptly. He stared at his wife; she read the letter, smiling oddly. He watched her eyes move to and fro under her eyelids. Isabeau let the letter fall onto the table as though the parchment were tainted. She shrugged.

"Lombardy is the cradle of the black arts," she said loftily. "Everyone knows that."

The King shook his head with impotent violence. "But who dares to accuse our dear sister?" he asked, nearly weeping; his lips trembled.

"Who?" Isabeau's voice shot out, suddenly shrill. "Who, Sire? The people of Paris throw stones at her carriage when she ventures outside the walls of her Hôtel de Béhaigne. The servants here will tell you that the people call her the Witch of Orléans. Her rooms swarm with soothsayers and alchemists . . . her servants disfigure corpses . . ."

"Who says that, who says that?" screamed the King; the blood rushed to his head, sweat stood on his upper lip. The Queen was frightened; was the madness overcoming him again?

"I have someone in my service," she said, calming herself. "A man who possesses remarkable powers of healing. With his own eyes he saw—"

"That living corpse?" The King leaned over the edge of the table and stared at Isabeau with distended eyes. A horrible image came into his memory: a face like a death's head appearing over a candleflame between the bed curtains at midnight. "The man who lays dead frogs on my breast and forces stinking powders down my throat? Is it he, the necromancer, who accuses Valentine? Get away! Get away!" he cried suddenly, stamping his feet with rage and striking the table. "I'll have him hanged, the filthy swine . . . ! De Bailly! The watch!"

Isabeau rose hastily.

"Sire," she said, attempting to quiet the King by a soothing tone, "Arnaud Guillaume tends you with my approval. My lord of Burgundy is aware of it. Be calm, be calm, Sire . . ."

"He slanders our sister-in-law!" The King sank back in his chair, still gasping with excitement. "Our brother of Orléans and his wife are dear to us, Madame, very dear to us. I want Valentine to return to Saint-Pol at once."

"Sire, Sire . . ." Desperately Isabeau moved toward him; she pulled at her train, which was caught on the table. "Rest now. Any excitement is dangerous. It is for your sake that I—that it was suggested that Madame d'Orléans leave the palace."

"But I will not see those frauds again," the King muttered, suppressing his rage in the folds of Isabeau's long sleeves. The Queen had thrown her arms around his neck. "Send them away, the physicians and the . . . the . . . Deliver the liar to Orléans—let my brother punish him, the slanderer!"

"Yes, yes." She began anxiously to whisper the endearments that had been customary between them so long ago. These words so long unspoken seemed strange on her lips. She closed her eyes so that she would not see that distorted, sweating face so close to hers. Filled with bitter aversion, she held the King in her arms; she knew that she could maintain her position only by feigning passion, at least as long as his temporary recovery lasted. He sat quietly relaxed against her, occasionally racked by a small shudder. Isabeau's caressing hands roused half-forgotten sensations within him . . . Did she still exist, the wife whom he had once known, did she forgive his madness? Without looking at each other, they exchanged a kiss.

Tears sprang into the King's eyes; he wanted to heap gifts upon his wife, to reward her for her devotion and patience; he could not thank her, could not admire her enough. Isabeau thought of the many plans she wished to bring to fruition, of the concessions she could wheedle from him on family affairs, on questions of money, on foreign and domestic policy. The Florentine emissaries were waiting for an answer; how could she induce him to send help to Gian Galeazzo's enemies, especially now that it was clear he wished to keep the Duke of Milan as a friend? How could she prevent Valentine from nestling once more within the walls of Saint-Pol?

✣ ✣ ✣

In March of the following year, the Duchess of Orléans quit Paris. From day to day the threats of the incited populace increased in intensity—she was now openly suspected of attempting to poison the King and his children—until it was impossible for her to remain any longer in the Hôtel de Béhaigne. Crowds gathered repeatedly before the gates, screaming for justice: why were witches being condemned every day when the most evil sorceress of all remained at large because of her rank? Louis d'Orléans' armed servants drove away the troublemakers, but they came back often, and each time in such large numbers that the roads leading to the Hôtel de Béhaigne were impassable. When it became known, in late autumn, that the King had gone mad again, suspicion and hatred of Valentine boiled over.

The subject was brought up before the Council; in the presence of the Regents a councillor demanded the speedy removal of the Duchess from Paris. Louis replied with vehemence: although he feared for Valentine's safety if she remained in the Hôtel de Béhaigne, he felt that her departure from the city would be regarded as an open admission of guilt. He knew, moreover, that this would cause a separation between him and his wife. He must, if he did not want to give up his activity in the political sphere, live in Paris, or at any rate in the immediate neighborhood of the King and court. Finally, he was forced to yield; after New Year's Day preparations began for the Duchess's journey.

It was Louis' wish that she should leave the city in a regal manner, with a procession of carriages and armed riders. Her household and a great retinue of servants accompanied her; she conveyed tapestries and furniture, works of art, books; dwarfs, musicians, a physician, a librarian and her court poet, Eustache Deschamps, would share her exile.

On a windy day in early spring, Valentine rode out of the gates of the Hôtel de Béhaigne. The people, packed together in the streets, watched silently as the procession filed past them toward the royal palace. The Duchess remained invisible behind the closed curtains of her coach. At the great inner court of Saint-Pol she alighted; Louis d'Orléans greeted her there and escorted her to the Queen's anterooms. The demoiselle who had carried Valentine's train now adjusted its heavy folds over her mistress's arm. Without attendants, the Duchess of Orléans bade her formal farewell to Isabeau.

The Queen sat on a chair beside a made-up ceremonial bed, surrounded by a large number of high-born women: Margaretha of Burgundy, Marguérite de Nevers and the young Duchess of Berry stood in order of rank beside her. In a deep silence Valentine made the three curtsies prescribed by etiquette. She was dressed in heavy mourning; in September Louis, her oldest son, had died from an intestinal ailment. Isabeau released the Duchess of Orléans from her third curtsey more slowly than was customary; only after some minutes did she reluctantly extend her hand to her sister-in-law as a sign that she could rise. There was a brief pause; then Margaretha of Burgundy stepped toward Valentine to render her, for the last time at the court, the homage due to the second lady of France.

"Well, my fair sister." When the long ceremony had been properly executed, the Queen spoke, with some hauteur. "I hear that you are going to leave us, to visit the lands and territories of Monseigneur d'Orléans." This was the official reason for Valentine's departure.

"Yes, Madame," replied the Duchess of Orléans in a low but steady voice. "I am going to the castle of Asnières in Beaumont. It must be really lovely there in the spring."

Isabeau smiled, not without malice, and ran her thick ringed fingers over the arm of her chair. "When do you plan to return?" she asked sweetly. Margaretha of Burgundy looked up quickly and frowned in disapproval.

"Madame, that rests with God alone," Valentine said calmly.

The Queen looked away; the sentences she had so carefully prepared, the words which, under the cloak of ceremonious friendliness, had been intended to wound, would not leave her lips. She was conscious that she could scarcely hurt that slender woman with the sorrowful eyes who stood before her, and who bore a deeper grief than any insult could inflict. A vague feeling of shame stirred in Isabeau; for one lightning moment, she almost wished she could undo the enmity that she had roused against Valentine, that she could take back the slander.

Curtseying three times once again, Valentine prepared to leave the Queen; the ladies curtsied to her, each in their turn. Among them was the Dame de Cany, Mariette d'Enghien, who had, since her marriage, entered the Queen's service. Valentine smiled at her, but with a heart filled with pain; she knew that Louis desired the chaste, faithful wife even more fiercely than he had the shy maiden of the past.

In the anteroom the damsel again took up Valentine's heavy train; the Duchess of Orléans left the palace of Saint-Pol on her husband's arm. Before she climbed into the coach, she looked up once more at the rows of windows, the galleries and battlements. Somewhere within those grey walls was the King, raving with fever and madness, kept like a ferocious animal behind bolted doors. She had not seen her brother-in-law since the day of the christening, a year and a half ago. She whispered a farewell, her eyes dimmed with tears. Then she seated herself in the carriage; she pushed aside one of the leather curtains so that she could see Louis, who would accompany the procession on horseback part of the way.

Riders and carriages began to move; slowly the heavy vehicles rolled over the inner court; the restless horses strained forward. The people who had gathered outside the palace stared in silence at the handsome painted carriages, the armed horsemen, the standard-bearers and heralds. They caught a glimpse of Valentine's pale profile; they saw Louis who, clad in gold and black, rode on a spirited horse. Finally, in one of the coaches a small child could be seen, who sat prattling on his nurse's lap, unaware of the uproar around him— the sole surviving child of Louis and Valentine, their last born, Charles d'Orléans.

The departure of the Duchess of Orléans created less disturbance than had been initially expected. Before long the minds of the royal court, of the city of Paris, of all France, were engrossed with a more important event: the army which was to fight against the Turks marched out of Paris, commanded nominally by Jean de Nevers but in actuality by Enguerrand de Coucy. The army consisted of groups of knights and barons, accompanied by squires, bowmen and foot soldiers. Nobles without retinues and able-bodied men without leaders could also be found among the troops. The largest contingent of followers belonged to the four Princes of the blood, Comte d'Eu the Constable, and the Sires de Coucy and Boucicaut. Most of the nobles, especially those who had never before been to war, had spared no expense on equipage for themselves and their retinues. The ranks bristled with banners and gleamed with caparisons embroidered with gold; silk tents and silver dinnerware were conveyed in processions of wagons; ships came down the Danube laden with victuals and vats of good wine. A train of camp followers brought up the rear.

In October, the young Queen of England—the child Isabelle, who had been married by proxy to Richard II—departed for Calais, where she would meet her husband and embark with him for England. Never had there been a more splendid exodus. All royal personages and nobles of high rank at the court set out for Calais in the bridal train. Richard, having stayed on in France for a few months to settle the details of the marriage contract, had been, with his retinue, the guest of the Duke and Duchess of Burgundy in Saint-Omer. In addition to the Dukes of Rutland and Nottingham, who had come the previous year as envoys, the English King was attended by the Dukes of Lancaster and Gloucester who fiercely opposed peace with France; they delayed the negotiations at every turn.

Burgundy did not view this without concern; the war party in England was becoming more powerful every day—of what benefit would the royal marriage be, and the peace treaty provisionally set until 1426, if the princes and the people still strongly wanted war?

Accompanied by her father—the King was at this time relatively calm, if he could not be called lucid—and by the Dukes of Orléans, Berry and Bourbon, Isabelle reached the coast. On the beach, a city of tents had been set up, glittering with gold, azure and purple, decorated with banners. Four hundred English, and four hundred French knights in armor, bared swords in hand, formed a double hedge between the two tents of the Kings.

At ten o'clock in the morning the Kings went bareheaded to meet each other, Charles attended by Lancaster and Gloucester, Richard by the Dukes of Berry and Burgundy. The King of France, who looked very ill, kept his eyes fixed on the ground before him; the glint of sunlight on the swords and armor of the guard of honor was making him uneasy. After they had dined, Isabelle was delivered to her husband. Surrounded by duchesses and countesses of the two kingdoms, she appeared in the tent, a small eight-year-old girl, pale with excitement. When she placed her hand in her father's, the King seemed to realize for the first time where he was and why he was there. He cast a timid glance at those present.

"I regret," he mumbled, "I regret that our daughter is still so young. If she were fully grown, she and our son from England could celebrate this day with greater joy."

Isabelle looked up uncertainly. The royal kinsmen and their wives stifled smiles. Richard saw the child's confusion; he found the little girl charming in her state dress covered with golden lilies. He replied quickly, "Father-in-law, we are exceedingly pleased with the age of our new wife. If France and England should ever be united in love as I hope I shall one day be with my wife, no power on earth could ever disturb our peace."

He took Isabelle's hand from her father's; while the court bowed, he whispered to her that a beautiful dog, white as snow and with a golden collar, awaited her in England. The child gazed up silently into his shrewd, friendly eyes. She thought he was a much more impressive king than her father; he was not so young as her uncle of Orléans, but surely he was taller. Her hand warmed in his. After many ceremonial farewells, the King and Queen of England embarked with their retinues. They arrived in Dover the same day.

At first, his wife's departure had left Louis feeling gloomy. His melancholy would not yield to hours of prayer and meditation in the Celestine monastery, nor to continual concentration on affairs of state, nor yet to absorption in games and the hunt. Jealously he had watched the departure of the crusaders; at that moment he could conceive of no more enviable lot than had fallen to these men, who were free to seek valorous adventure. *He* could—and this thought especially tormented him—have been riding at the head of the armies, instead of Jean de Nevers. The state of affairs in Italy had grown increasingly confused; the cities of Florence, Genoa, Savona, Adorna, played a double-dealing game with one another and with France and Milan; negotiations which accomplished nothing, pacts which none of the parties observed, equivocal statements which only clouded the issues further.

It seemed to him often during the course of that year that every enterprise he undertook or had ever undertaken was doomed to failure. The negotiations with the Pope in Avignon had collapsed; the Prince of the Church, entrenched in his city, had solemnly declared that he would never be dislodged. The University incessantly pressed for action, while the princes of Europe, on the other hand, whose opinions and help had been requested, answered generally in an evasive way. No one seemed to want to involve himself with this painful matter of the schism. The King was hardly in a condition to render a judgment. Berry and Bourbon chose to remain aloof. And because Burgundy always worked more and more zealously for cession, Louis felt constrained to support the authority of Avignon. At the moment, however, he could not do much; there was too much discord and dissension, and in any event the public was distracted by the crusade and the marriage of the princess.

In the month of August, Louis visited his wife in the castle of Asnières, on the occasion of the birth of his son Philippe—named not without irony after the Duke of Burgundy. During this visit Louis had an opportunity to devote his full attention for the first time to little Charles. The child was now about two years old, of a rather delicate constitution and, in his father's opinion, a little too quiet and gentle. He would sit for hours in the same spot in the garden or hall playing with a stone, a flower, a piece of colored cloth.

"Doesn't he ever laugh, this son of mine?" Louis asked the Dame de Maucouvent. She replied that the child was grave because Valentine had been depressed during her pregnancy, and because his first year had been spent in the Hôtel de Béhaigne in an atmosphere of tension and uncertainty. Louis picked the child up and let him play with his gold chain and the hilt of his dagger, which was shaped like a rolled-up hedgehog. The child stared at the gleaming ornaments with bright grey-green eyes, but he did not attempt to touch them or crow with joy as his dead older brother would have done.

To Valentine, Louis gave costly gifts and a considerable sum of money to spend on decorations for her apartments. But he did not stay very long with his wife; he had to return to Paris to help with preparations for Isabelle's bridal journey.

The days he spent in Saint-Omer gained significance for Louis chiefly because he met a remarkable and interesting man there: Henry Bolingbroke, the eldest son of the Duke of Lancaster. In this taciturn, somewhat rough and moody young man, Louis saw a companion in distress: here too was a gifted, ambitious prince's son who condemned his government's policies. Orléans and he were about the same age—it was natural that, among the other princes, they should seek each other's company at meals and at the hunt. Their relationship hovered on the brink of friendship; they got on well with each other, but despite jests and courtesies neither of them forgot that they pursued absolutely opposed interests. Secretly each attempted to gauge how useful the other might be to him in the future. Their parting was comradely enough to awaken in Richard of England and the Duke of Burgundy the hope that Lancaster's son could perhaps be won over to the peace.

Toward the end of November, the King of France and the Regents returned to Paris. Orléans took advantage of a temporary improvement in the King's condition to enlarge his landed property considerably and to acquire command of the usufruct. When all the relevant documents had been signed, he saw with satisfaction that his possessions were, in extent and value, hardly second to those of any other princes of the blood. The Dukes, greatly angered by this move, commented on his avarice. So the Christmas season came— but peace was still far off.

Following an ancient tradition, the King of France gave an elaborate banquet on Christmas Eve, at which not only royalty, the court and eminent officials sat at table, but also numerous burghers. In addition, on the ground floor of Saint-Pol an open table was provided for the people of Paris. The Christmas feast of 1396 was not less lavish in any way than its predecessors; as always, vast amounts of game and pastry appeared on the tables, and plenty of good wine was on hand. In the palace banquet hall, high-ceilinged and wide as the nave of a cathedral, the King entertained his guests. It was very crowded and sweltering; so many torches were burning that one could almost believe one was dining in daylight. At the royal table, beside the King and Isabeau, who was pregnant again, sat the Dukes of Burgundy and Berry with their wives; old Bourbon and Louis d'Orléans, surrounded by a number of highly-placed people, including many wives of men who had gone to Turkey with Jean de Nevers. Since early summer, little or nothing had been heard of the crusaders; the messengers repeatedly dispatched by the King to Hungary and Italy had brought back only vague reports.

The mood at the Christmas feast, at least at the royal table, was constrained. The King stared sleepily at the performance in the center of the hall, a battle between armored knights and a dragon; Isabeau, weighed down by her ungainly body, did not feel up even to feigning interest in what was going on around her. Conversation at the table was dull, despite the wine; even Louis d'Orléans, who was usually the center of attention on these occasions, spoke little. His glance wandered again and again to a certain spot at one of the lower tables where, among the lords and ladies of the royal retinue, beside her husband, the Dame de Cany sat, dressed in dark green. Aubert de Cany showed his wife every conceivable attention, but Mariette did not laugh and seldom responded—she was constantly aware of Orléans' eyes upon her. Whenever she raised her head she saw him, sitting next to the royal chair; he rested his chin upon his fist, scarcely touched his food but took some wine. When their eyes met, the young Dame de Cany was overcome once more by the emotion which had tormented her day and night during her service with the Duchess of Orléans. Her heart began to thump, slowly and violently. She forced herself to look only at her husband, or to keep her eyes on her plate. But she heard nothing that was said to her and could scarcely remember where she was.

About nine o'clock in the evening, a commotion started at one of the entrances to the hall; the sound of raised voices was audible above the hubbub at the tables. Out of the throng at the door a man appeared, booted and spurred, in torn clothes, sweating and exhausted. He crossed the hall, heedless of the sham fight that was going on there and threw himself, still breathless and unable to speak, onto his knees before the King. At first no one knew who he was; Louis d'Orléans finally recognized the dirty, deadly tired man as Jacques de Helly, one of the knights of de Nevers' retinue, a vagabond and adventurer who had the reputation of being very familiar with the routes to the East. The King looked at him apathetically, without comprehension; his expression did not change when de Helly cried out hoarsely, "Sire, my King, I come from Basaach's camp—our army was destroyed near the city of Nicopolis on Saint Michael's Day!"

At the royal table there were gasps; many sprang from their seats. The news spread quickly through the hall; there were exclamations of fright, the clatter of chairs; then, under the standards and banners, under the thousand torches, it became quite still. The performers vanished quickly through a side door; only the scaly cover of the dragon lay in the middle of the floor, a painted rag.

"Monseigneur de Nevers, the Lords de Bar, de Coucy and Boucicaut, and twenty-three others are prisoners," murmured de Helly, almost inaudibly. "Their lives are not in danger because Basaach intends to deliver them in exchange for ransom."

"And the others?" Orléans leaned toward him over the table.

Jacques de Helly hid his face in his hands.

"Basaach ordered all those who did not perish in battle to be put to death," he said in a smothered voice. "No one is left alive except those whom I named, and me. I don't think anyone else can have escaped the slaughter."

Louis took firm hold of the King who, thinking that the meal had ended, was about to get up.

"Give the names of the survivors," Orléans said shortly.

The knight obeyed; although his voice was low, everyone heard him in that deathly quiet room. A woman shrieked; it was the signal for a great outbreak of weeping and wailing.

For little Charles d'Orléans, the days passed as peacefully and at the same time as festively as a procession which he had once seen at the church of Asnières. First of all, there were the many journeys, the purpose of which he did not understand; but he went through the colorful landscapes with great delight. Standing at the carriage door, he looked out over the wooded hills, the vineyards and fields, the sloping land softly green and brown, the broad sparkling rivers. Sometimes the fields were filled with flowers. If they rode through a forest the greenery murmured over their heads; sometimes red and gold leaves hung on the trees and rustled and crackled mysteriously under the carriage wheels. The sky was black with swarms of birds. Sometimes he had traveled, wrapped in furs and velvet, with a hot stone under his feet; then the trees were bare, streaks of snow lay on the fields and the wind blowing through the narrow openings of the carriage made the court ladies shiver. The child was later to remember clearly that everything about those journeys fascinated him: the steam that the horses exhaled, the parcels and things that they brought with them, the soldiers and horsemen who rode beside the carriages and the handsome standards flying from their lances.

Charles always lived with his mother, little brother and all the gentlemen, ladies, demoiselles, servants and pages in other castles: from the outside they looked alike, one and all; he could not remember all their names, there were too many of them: Châteauneuf, Blois, Montils, a whole series of them—but if you tried to follow a familiar route along passages and staircases, you could make a bad mistake. Only the little windows, the thick walls and circular staircases were the same everywhere. Charles always slept in his own bed because that was taken along. And in every inner court of every castle he had his own painted wooden horse to play with.

The child did not trouble himself about the how and why of all this moving: he was easily satisfied and happy; the world teemed with things one could amuse oneself with. He did not notice that he always played alone; he could amuse himself with a small stick, a stone, a piece of colored glass. His mother's maidens tried to teach him games—tag, hide and seek, leapfrog—but although Charles played willingly, he was not really interested. He preferred to look out through the narrow peepholes of tower or gallery over the land which, bathed in sunlight or covered with shadowy clouds, alternately glowed and faded. He could see the roofs of the small houses clustered in a hamlet around the citadel, and the tapering steeples of a church or a far castle against the horizon. It was not so much this looking at what could be seen through the windows that he loved; it was rather the standing still, the waiting, which enthralled him—that curious feeling that at any moment a miracle would happen. What—he did not know. He knew about miracles only from stories he had heard and from wall paintings in churches and chapels. An angel with golden wings, holding a lily in his hand, who appeared to the Virgin Mary . . . he had heard it said that that was a great miracle. And the dead man who rose up again, and the pilgrim's staff on which roses began to bloom. No, he did not expect anything so amazing as that.

The Dame de Maucouvent, his governess, usually put an end to his secret pleasures. The tower stairs and galleries were too dangerous for a five-year-old child, he could easily break his neck. So then he had to go to the room where his little brother Philippe pushed himself in his walker, where the women sat the whole day talking to one another or yawning and looking out of the windows as soon as the Dame de Maucouvent showed her heels. Eagerly, Charles went by himself on secret searches through the vast, usually empty halls, where the tapestries stirred mysteriously against the walls. His mother told him about the tapestry pictures: in one castle the tapestry told the story of Charlemagne, in another of Saint-Louis, or Lancelot, or Theseus and the Golden Eagle. The figures of heroes and saints seemed to come alive in the dusky halls; in the evenings, in the light of wax candles and torches, Charles saw their eyes glitter and their lips move; their heads nodded, they raised their hands, the dogs sprang through the brushwood, the horses reared; yes—he could even hear the banners flapping.

He did not tell anyone about these fantasies, not even his mother, whom he loved more than anyone else. He was glad to sit close to her on winter afternoons when the corridors were dark and uneasy feelings lay in wait for him on the silent steps, in the empty doorways. His mother sat by the fire and played the harp or embroidered with golden thread. The light gleamed in the little colored jewels in her necklace and in her eyes; she told long stories which he found splendidly thrilling, although he did not completely understand them. Or she sang songs with her maidens, very sad songs. Often she sat silent. At those times she put her arms around her small son and held him close against her. An odor of honey and roses wafted from the deep folds of her dress. Charles looked close up at her sweet face, her narrow pale lips and her soft tresses. Her sighs made him feel sad. It was always something of a relief when she had the chess set brought to her so that she could play with Marie d'Harcourt, or when she told the librarian, Maître Giles Malet, to fetch a book— one of her breviaries with little paintings in gold and azure, or the great book of King Arthur.

In the spring, Charles' mother became livelier, but at the same time more restless; then she usually wanted to travel to castles as yet unvisited. The prospect of a carriage ride quickly reconciled Charles to the bustle in the inner rooms, the running back and forth of women and servants, the moving of pieces of furniture, carpets and other household goods. Later, when summer came, with sun and flowers and deep greenery, his mother hurried each day to leave the castle and sit outside on the grass, braiding garlands or gathering herbs. Often too she went horseback riding; the harness was studded with gilded knobs and embellished with tiny bells; golden tassels hung from caparison and saddlecloth. So she rode to the hunt with a falcon perched on her glove. Charles' mother never looked so beautiful as when she returned home after such an outing, with flushed cheeks and bright eyes. She talked a lot to Charles about his father, who was the King's brother, a courageous knight and a splendid figure like the heroes of the romances.

That idea was strengthened on the few occasions when he saw his father. Surrounded by horsemen in armor, he came riding over the bridge and courtyard on a magnificent steed; when, with spurs jingling, he entered the great hall, he knelt to salute Charles' mother, who waited for him in the seat of honor. When his father stayed with them, the castle overflowed with people, and each evening there was a feast; long tables were added to accommodate all the guests. After the meal the minstrels Colinet and Herbelin, who were always with his father, sang songs and Gilot the Fool somersaulted along the tables. Later, gifts, brought from Paris on donkeys, were brought in: mantles of silk and gold for Charles' mother, household linen, fur and leather, silver dishes, books; for Charles and Philippe, mantles like the ones grown-ups wear, in green or black, embroidered with emblems: thistles, vines, heraldic wolves. Once Charles was given a leather case which held three combs and a little mirror; he wore it proudly on his girdle.

Then during his father's visits, there was hunting; that was quite a spectacle. Early in the morning, while it was still dark, a sleepy nursemaid held Charles, wrapped in a blanket, up to a window so that he could look down on the inner courtyard where torches burned, servants kept dozens of restless dogs together on long leashes, horses stood stamping and snorting. All day long the child could hear the blaring of the hunting horns in the forest, and the furious baying of the dogs. Later he found the deferred booty less attractive: he was filled with pity and revulsion when he saw the stiffly outstretched legs of the does, their great glazed eyes, the wild boar black with congealed blood, the limp bodies of the hares, and the dead birds, a heap of feathers stuck together.

Charles most admired his father when he blew on his hunting horn—no one made a prettier sound than he did. Sometimes, to please his little son, Louis, outdoors in the gallery or somewhere in the castle gardens, blew for him all the signals he knew, along with little melodies which he made up on the spot. These sounds remained linked in Charles' memory with the image of a castle looming dark against the light of a pink evening sky, the twilight fragrance of herbs, flowers and earth. Always early in the morning his father was suddenly gone; each time these departures took Charles completely by surprise; he was angry then because no one had warned him.

Once—it was the middle of winter, when the trees stood frosty-white in the fields—there was a great feast. They were living then in a castle called Épernay: Charles remembered that because the journey there had required unusually long and full preparations. The castle was filled with so many tapestries and candlesticks, cushions and valuables, that Charles asked himself if it were Christmas, but no one seemed to have time to tell him anything. The Dame de Maucouvent kept her eye on the chamberwomen who folded and spread the linen; Charles' mother supervised the polishing and display of the gold dishes and tankards; servants hammered in the stables; the court ladies embroidered crowned initials on a set of new bedcurtains. At last Charles was fetched to be fitted with a small cloak that glittered with gold and precious stones. Now he heard something about what was going on. The Emperor of the Holy Roman Empire, Wenceslaus, was coming to see Charles' parents; the Dame de Maucouvent told him this while she knelt before Charles to see if his state robes sat upon him properly.

"Emperor Wenceslaus, Wen . . . ces . . . laus," she repeated. "Say that once, Monseigneur."

"Wen . . . ces . . . laus," said Charles hesitantly. The Dame de Maucouvent seemed to be very excited; her headdress was all on one side, which was not her usual custom, and her dress was rumpled. Later that evening his mother came to sit on the side of his bed; she laid her narrow, cool hand against his cheek.

"Tomorrow the Emperor is coming here, child," she said.

"Wen . . . ces . . . laus," whispered Charles quickly, to show that he remembered this remarkable name. His mother smiled. "Your father is bringing the Emperor to Épernay," she went on. "The Emperor is coming to see you. Don't forget that; be brave and carry yourself like a true knight. You are growing so big, my little son. Kneel before the Emperor when you are brought before him and say, 'Welcome, Sire.' "

"Welcome, Sire, welcome, Sire," repeated Charles; he no longer knew whether he was dreaming or awake.

The day dawned with great hubbub and activity; from the kitchens where work had gone on all night, rose the odor of venison and fresh bread; servants in festive livery lit fires in all the halls. When clarion calls and the sound of trampling hooves were heard, Charles was not able to go and look out the window; he stood waiting in a corner of the great hall with the Dame de Maucouvent and his nurse Jeanne la Brune, both of whom wore new, fur-trimmed mantles in honor of this occasion. His father entered, followed by a train of knights and pages; he was leading a fat man with a red, smiling face to the seat of honor. For the first time in his life Charles saw his mother curtsey three times, very deeply; he held his breath. On the lake of the castle of Montils lived a black swan; in her rustling black dress, his mother curtsied the way the swan alighted with outspread wings on the surface of the water. After that he had to come himself. He did his best, kneeling before the fat man who chuckled looking down at him, and saying, "Welcome, Sire." It was over in a moment. The Dame de Maucouvent brought him back to the nursery.

After the meal he was sent for again. The Emperor's face was still redder than it had been in the morning; he hung back in the seat of honor and roared with incessant laughter. Even when Charles' father rose to speak, he went on sniggering and chortling.

"Charles, my son," said the Duke of Orléans, "it has pleased our lord, the Emperor, to promise you as your wife, his niece Elisabeth, the heiress of Bohemia."

"Ja, ja, ja!" cried Wenceslaus in a hoarse voice, throwing himself back and forth in his chair, "Bravo, bravo!"

"Thank the Emperor," Charles' father went on calmly, but the child could see from the fixed look in his eye that he was displeased.

"A fine lad, a beautiful child!" Wenceslaus screamed with laughter. "He must drink; wine, wine!" He flourished his goblet so that wine spattered over the table. Charles took a few hasty swallows from the beaker which his father held before him. He knew now that the Emperor Wenceslaus was dead drunk and he was afraid of drunkards. His mother signalled to him with a reassuring nod of the head that he could leave.

"Come, come, she is getting a handsome dowry!" roared the Emperor, pounding the pommel of his dagger on the edge of the table. "A hundred thousand livres—squeeze that in your fingers!" He spoke French like a street vagrant, with coarse sounds and words, richly interspersed with incomprehensible Polish exclamations and expletives.

"And you," Wenceslaus went on, pointing at the Duke, "as for you, Orléans, I will do what I promised—that is why I came here. I'm really no braggart!" He lunged forward. "I'll call my bishops together—and I'll say to them, by thunder, this is the way it must be! Use your influence in favor of the unity of the Church—the unity of the Church. Keep your eyes on France, I shall say. And I shall not neglect to stress what you have requested of me, Orléans!"

The Duke of Orléans interrupted him quickly with expressions of thanks. Wenceslaus was too drunk to notice the interruption; tears of affection had sprung to his eyes, he hit Louis unceasingly hard on the shoulder. "It's good to talk with you, Orléans," he said, while he tottered up from his chair. "Better than with that brother of yours, the King there in Reims. When he is sensible—I am boozy. When I am sober—he is crazy! But with you I can talk, Orléans, at any time of the day."

Louis bit his lips; the dinner guests were nudging each other and laughing behind their hands. It was common knowledge that anyone who wanted to confer with Wenceslaus had to approach the Emperor before breakfast; that was the only time that he was sober enough to know what he was doing. Valentine, who found her guest's behavior extremely painful, and who, moreover, gathered from Louis' demeanor that the Emperor was busily spreading confidential information abroad, nodded to the musicians and minstrels who were waiting their turn at the back of the hall. Wenceslaus, however, paid no attention to music or poetry.

"Did you see the hateful looks that fat Bavarian was giving me during the conference? Well, did you?" he shouted loudly. "That brother of hers—Ludwig—he was around there too! What are these Wittelsbachers plotting? Do they want to pull tricks on me? What do you think, Orléans?"

Louis sighed impatiently, and shrugged. He knew that Isabeau had gone to Reims filled with suspicion, fearing that an alliance with France would save Wenceslaus from the fate which the Electors planned for him: to depose him in the near future. Although Louis considered the Emperor to be a drunken swine, he wanted to see him retain his throne. If Ruprecht, a Wittelsbacher, were to become Emperor, French interests—or at least French interests as Orléans perceived them—would undoubtedly suffer. A Wittelsbacher would under all circumstances follow Burgundy's advice. In Reims Louis had in passing overheard Ludwig of Bavaria say to Isabeau, "Don't worry, sister. The Drunkard has come here against the Electors' will. He has given himself the death blow."

Louis hoped that the Wittelsbachers were mistaken. In any case he had forged strong ties between Wenceslaus and himself by bringing about Charles' betrothal to the Emperor's little niece. That child could one day inherit the thrones of Bohemia, Poland and Hungary. That which had been denied to Louis might perhaps await his son: a Crown.

Orléans had gone to great trouble to get Wenceslaus to come to France. The Emperor, who was virtually the only foreign prince who had not refused to become involved in Church affairs, was pleasantly impressed by Orléans' continual, overflowing hospitality. He preferred Louis' conversation to the endless dull monologues of Maître Gerson of the University; he certainly preferred Louis' company to that of the mad Charles, the hostile Isabeau, the cold, haughty Burgundy. He said aye and amen to Louis at the meeting in Reims and promised him his support. Although Louis expected few results from Wenceslaus's cooperation, he felt he had, at any rate, accomplished one thing: he had prevented the Emperor from becoming a tool in Burgundy's hands.

The relationship between uncle and nephew had entered a dangerous phase. Until now they had thrashed out their disagreements under the surface; no matter how they despised each other's actions and ideas, they had never become open enemies. At court they behaved toward each other with painful care, giving each other the prescribed marks of honor, and discussing things in a calm, courtly way while their blood boiled. Only occasionally in Council meetings they lost their self-control and attacked each other without mercy. Now, however, the rift between Orléans and Burgundy had deepened—it had become an abyss which no courtesy or appearance of good will could bridge.

In the course of the year France had received a royal guest: Henry Bolingbroke, Lancaster's son, whom Richard II had banished from England. In Paris the fine details of the matter were not known, but the man who had chosen to spend his exile in France was received hospitably and with respect. The King of England reproached his father-in-law for his lack of tact in honoring a rebel who had acted against the execution of the warmonger Gloucester, his kinsman. France was making itself ridiculous by sheltering an enemy. These arguments might have convinced the French court to shun Bolingbroke if reports of the death of the old Duke of Lancaster had not reached Paris at almost the same time, followed nearly immediately by the news that King Richard had seized most of his property to discourage Lancaster's heir from returning to England.

This information roused great indignation in the French court. Richard's conduct was condemned as a breach of chivalry. Influenced by Orléans, who had sworn fellowship with Bolingbroke, many courtiers stood up openly for the exile in one of those bursts of knightly magnanimity which so often militated against their own interests. Saint-Pol donned mourning for the deceased Lancaster and masses were read for him. Then the Duke of Berry entertained the Englishman in his castle in Bicêtre. Louis often spent a few days at Bicêtre while Henry was there in the hope of deciphering his enigmatic character and winning him as a friend and, perhaps, as a future ally. However, during his last visit to Bicêtre, the scales had fallen from Louis' eyes. He was later to think back on those days with bitterness: once, after the hunting parties and banquets, which were exceptionally lavish—Berry inexhaustibly invented new amusements for his guests—Lancaster had unexpectedly betrayed himself over a perfunctory game of chess. He talked about Richard and his government in a way which, to the attentive listener, reflected nothing but hatred and jealousy. Louis kept his eyes fixed on the chess pieces while Lancaster, cold and self-possessed, spoke with apparent casualness—but, with a sensitivity sharpened by experience, Orléans perceived the passion which the other tried so carefully to conceal.

"The King of France is crazy," said Henry of Lancaster harshly, "and that is bad. But there are those in England who consider Richard a more dangerous lunatic. I have never seen anyone risk his crown so recklessly as my worthy cousin. He doesn't seem to understand the simplest elements of reigning—he himself destroys the pillars which support his throne. Only a madman would act like this. Since he became king, he has done nothing but antagonize the people whom he needs the most: the Church, Parliament, the nobility. He puts them off, he kicks them into a corner—he can do that very well. Now he accuses seventeen vassals of high treason, seizes their estates and possessions—and then he sells them back to the former owners because he needs money. Tell me if that makes any sense—apart from the fact that he is conducting a foreign policy which no one can understand."

"I see," said Louis in a courteous tone. But disappointment and distrust crept over him.

Burgundy too came to Bicêtre a few times with a large retinue to visit the English guest. Orléans was sure now that his uncle was following a carefully prepared plan; he was seeking highly-placed allies who had reason, or thought they had reason, to turn against France. Despite all outward appearances, the atmosphere among the royal kinsmen was oppressive; the King, who had been in his right senses only a few weeks before, suffered from violent headaches and renewed fits of melancholy; the Queen was uneasy because there was no news from England—the last report she had was that many of Isabelle's retinue had been dismissed and were on the point of returning home. To her brother-in-law, Isabeau was extremely cool— she knew that he supported Wenceslaus, and in Church matters followed a policy opposed to that of Bavaria and Burgundy. Her brother Ludwig had called her attention to the role played by Orléans; she understood fully for the first time that he was an adversary who should not be underrated. She had considered trying to win him over by pledges and promises, but she rejected the notion. She had—for the moment—strong support in Burgundy. A rapprochement with Orléans could alienate that powerful ally.

In Normandy the summer days went by slowly. The King sat in a cool dark chamber or rode, surrounded by nobles, on a gentle horse, through the vast forests. Louis d'Orléans alternated between his brother's retinue and the Queen's. The members of the House of Burgundy spent the summer in their own domains.

As a gift from the King, Isabeau had received an estate in Saint-Ouen with farmhouses, fields, meadows and livestock; there she spent the beautiful days with her children and her retinue. She wanted to recreate the rustic atmosphere of one of her father's Bavarian mountain retreats, smelling of hay and pigs, where geese fluttered about the courtyard, and where she had run barefoot through the mud with milkmaids and stableboys. She had no desire, of course, to give herself up to these simple pleasures again, although she scattered barley and grain for the fowl with her own hand, and, attended by a procession of court ladies, gathered currants in the kitchen gardens.

It was during one of these visits to the Hôtel de la Bergerie, as Isabeau called her estate, that Louis wandered away from the company and strolled into the forest. From there, among the tall bushes, under the trees, he could see the lords and ladies amusing themselves on the lawn which sparkled in the sunlight. At some distance from the others, one woman stood alone, staring at the edge of the forest. Louis wished that he, like the magician in the old ballad, knew a charm which could bring Mariette de Cany to him to remain always, without a backward glance. Concealed behind the foliage, he watched her. What did she possess that kept his desire for her alive, undiminished, even after long years of fruitless waiting?

Behind the fence which separated the lawn from the field, stood grimy, half-naked children, staring at the glittering spectacle; the children were called again and again by the peasants in the fields, who had been told that the high-born company did not wish to be stared at. Louis laughed softly, glancing at the orchard where Isabeau, dressed in silk and gold, sat eating fruit. The court had come to enjoy country life; they had no interest in country people. He turned away and walked slowly through the long, dark green grass in the shadow of the trees. He could not help but think of two conversations he had had in the past year: one with Boucicaut, newly returned from Turkish captivity; the other with his old friend Philippe de Maizières while he lay on his deathbed. Both had asked him the same questions, reproached him in the same way, asking him whether he sought power to serve his own interests or to look after the welfare of the people.

To Boucicaut Louis had given an evasive answer, but he had been speechless before the old man in his death agony. It was the contest with Burgundy that weighed upon him more than anything else; more than once in the course of the last two years he had even considered seizing the Crown himself so that he could put Burgundy in checkmate. The King's attacks of madness were growing longer and more violent; no one believed now that he could recover.

"Do I really want that?" Louis asked himself aloud. Around him the smooth trunks of the trees rose up from the undergrowth like pillars in the nave of a church; blueberries gleamed darkly amid the low greenery. Both the laughter of the courtiers and the shouts of the peasants sounded far away; he was alone in the deep green silence of the forest. The path before him split into two forks which vanished in the dusk under the trees; he did not know where they led. For a moment it seemed infinitely important to him which path he took. But behind him a cuckoo's call came high and clear in the silence; he turned away without making a decision and went to search for the source of that enticing sweet summer sound.

In the fall the court returned to Paris, to the palace of Saint-Pol. The epidemic had spent itself; it was true that great fires still burned in the public squares and on street corners as precautions, and that near the houses where the sick had lain the pungent odor of vinegar still hovered in the air. But the danger of infection seemed to have passed.

Under a gloomy sky streaked with rain clouds, the royal retinue rode into the city, past the abbey of Saint-Germain de Prés, through the Augustine gate beyond the temple where the royal treasures and the gold of France were stored under guard. The people filled the streets; they were eager to see the King again. The King and Louis rode side by side preceding the carriage where Isabeau sat with the Dauphin. The King sprawled in the saddle, weary after the long ride, his head drooping slightly; he shivered in the chill wind. The crowd on Saint-Michel's bridge shouted, "Noel! Noel!" These cries roused the King from his torpor; he was reminded of the days when he had ridden in triumph under a canopy through streets strewn with lilies. He smiled vaguely at the people along the way. Many of the spectators—especially those who had not seen him for years—burst into tears; they hardly recognized him. Secretly Louis supported his brother; he rode close to the King so that he could hold him by the elbow under cover of his cloak.

In the rue Saint-Antoine, directly in front of the church of Saint-Pol, a commotion broke out among the people. Someone called out, "Down with Orléans, the sorcerer, the traitor!" The armed constables of the Provost, who walked before and on both sides of the procession, pushed their way into the crowd. The horses reared, frightened by the shouting and the people. The Queen's carriage stopped.

During the entry to the city, Isabeau had stared straight before her; the streets, stinking of smoke, the avid faces and the greedy glances of the populace filled her, as always, with a certain secret fear. She preferred to look up at the windows of the castle and the houses of the rich merchants, where well-dressed burghers, nobles and their families looked down on the procession, smiling in greeting. The poverty and hunger of most of the people was apparent in their faces and their clothing; they seemed ravaged by sickness and adversity. Among the artisans, hawkers and little people with their wives and children, among the students and priests, clerks and officials, there appeared everywhere rather terrifying figures who, in the course of the last few years, in ever-growing numbers, from near and far, had invaded Paris. Dressed in rags, dirty and neglected, gaunt, hardened and insolent, they roamed in packs through the city; they made the country roads unsafe, started brawls in taverns, committed murder and manslaughter.

While the constables shoved the uneasy multitude back to a

narrow strip of ground before the houses, Isabeau, with her arm around the Dauphin, looked on with apprehension and anger. She thought she saw two men slink hunched over, to melt among the bystanders. One looked up for a moment, not far from the royal carriage. Isabeau recognized Guillaume the exorcist, whom the King had turned over to Orléans four years earlier. Louis had considered having the man executed, but finally, as a sign of greater contempt, he had released him without questioning him. And not long afterward he had dismissed the astrologer Ettore Salvia, whose glib tongue and inscrutable demeanor had begun to irritate him. Isabeau leaned forward and stared sharply at Guillaume's companion. Both men, however, fought their way to the side street Sainte-Cathérine and vanished into the crowd.

Orléans did not betray in any way that he had noticed the ominous shout or the presence of Guillaume and his comrade; it required all his attention to control the King's horse as well as his own. The Provost's servants cleared a path; the heralds blew the trumpets and the procession began to move again.

Not long afterward the court was upset by the sudden return to Paris of the Dame de Courcy, the mistress of ceremonies, who had been sent to England with Madame Isabelle. The Queen heard the news from a chambermaid in the early morning of December seventh; violently disturbed, she ordered that the King be notified at once. Even before the sun was up, the Sire de Courcy appeared in the palace; he was taken to a small reception hall where the King and Queen, as well as the Dukes of Orléans and Burgundy, awaited him. Isabeau could scarcely control herself during the courteous greetings.

"By God, Messire de Courcy," she cried out at last, half-rising from her chair. "Tell us your news of our daughter, the Queen of England. We hear that Madame de Courcy returned to the city quite unexpectedly last night."

De Courcy did not look up.

"My Lady," he said in a low voice, "the Queen of England has not a single French subject remaining in her service. The entire retinue was summarily dismissed within twenty-four hours by . . . by the King's command."

"I don't believe it!" cried Isabeau; she looked at her husband, but he only twisted his long fingers nervously together until the knuckles cracked. Orléans and Burgundy stood motionless next to each other. "I do not believe it," Isabeau repeated vehemently. "King Richard is well disposed toward us; he would never insult our daughter so grievously."

"Nay, Madame," said de Courcy sadly, "he would not. But Richard is no longer King of England. He has freely delivered the Crown and all to his cousin . . . he who was here last year, the Duke of Lancaster."

Isabeau became deathly pale. She staggered and sat down with an effort.

"Freely? Of his own will?" Louis d'Orléans cried out loudly and derisively. "What does one call 'freely' in England, Messire de Courcy?"

De Courcy mopped his forehead; never before in his life had he been required to perform a more painful task than this.

"The people of London hailed Lancaster as king the moment he arrived in the city," he said. "The Lords of Arundel and Gloucester and many other nobles whose nearest kin King Richard had had killed or banished supported Lancaster. With an armed force they fetched Richard from Conway castle and brought him back to London and locked him up in the fortress they call the Tower of London. My wife tells me that King Richard himself asked for a private audience with . . . with the Duke of Lancaster. They were together for more than two hours and apparently at that time King Richard abdicated his throne. A short time later, in the presence of Parliament, the lords of the Kingdom and the clergy, with his own hands he gave crown and scepter to Lancaster—who has already been crowned in Westminster. He calls himself Henry IV."

"Yes, yes, but my child?" Isabeau clenched her fists. "My daughter, Messire de Courcy, what has happened to my daughter?"

De Courcy shook his head slowly. "All I know, Madame, is that she has been given a new retinue—with only English ladies and lords who have been strictly forbidden to discuss King Richard with her. My wife is completely beside herself because she has been forced to abandon Madame Isabelle," he added softly. The Queen sat unmoving.

The King had listened with his mouth open. When the Sire de Courcy had finished, the King's whole body began to tremble.

"How is it possible?" he asked in that high, whining voice which was typical of him during his attacks of madness. "How is it possible that our son-in-law of England has given away his kingdom as though it were a crust of dry bread? By God and Saint-Michael, how could that happen?"

Now the Duke of Burgundy spoke for the first time.

"Princes often fare badly when they cannot rule. Richard has brought this fate upon himself. He who sows the wind shall reap the whirlwind."

"Precisely, my lord uncle of Burgundy," cried Louis d'Orléans; he had thrown aside restraint now that Burgundy had dared to make such an allusion to the King. "Indeed there are ambitious traitors everywhere who need little encouragement to strike. He who is trusting by nature is easily deceived by such scoundrels."

During these words Burgundy kept his head turned away from Louis, as though he were not being addressed. When Orléans was silent, he sighed calmly, but he did not reply. He walked up to the place where the King sat and said spitefully, "I knew perfectly well this was coming. The marriage between Richard and Madame Isabelle was a senseless undertaking. When the envoys came here four years ago, I warned against the bond . . . "

"That is a lie," said Louis harshly. The Sire de Courcy shivered in dismay; Isabeau raised her head and shot a warning glance at her brother-in-law. Burgundy continued as though he were unaware of any interruption.

"I knew that Richard was unpopular; that almost everyone of any consequence in England had turned against him. And Gloucester, that wily fox, only added kindling to the fire. I explained all that in detail to the Council at the time."

"Again, a damnable lie, lord uncle!" Louis flung himself violently between Burgundy and the King. "You insisted on that marriage; it wouldn't surprise me if you had suggested it in the first place. It was I alone who argued against the marriage before the Council. Your memory can't be that bad!"

Burgundy shrugged. "Worthy nephew, I have no desire to quarrel with you here about this. Surely there are more important matters to discuss right now. The news from England has taken us completely by surprise. But perhaps it is not news to you? At Bicêtre you and Henry of Lancaster were often together . . . "

"My God, my lord of Burgundy!" Louis took a step forward. "What do you mean by that?"

Isabeau gestured; she was white with rage because her brother-in-law and Burgundy had forgotten themselves in front of a courtier. It was universally believed that de Courcy could not be trusted with a secret. Nothing would lend itself more to the spread of gossip than this agitated argument. The King was slumped into the corner of his chair with his head in his hands, too depressed by the news he had just heard to pay attention to the quarrel.

"What should I mean?" asked Burgundy with cold derision. "We know very well that you disliked Richard ever since he said that you were ambitious and dangerous."

"You lie again, Monseigneur!" Louis clenched his fists. "I have never heard that Richard said such things about me! What I do know is that Henry of Lancaster received substantial sums of money from you and that his journey through Brittany was part of a hoax."

Burgundy sniffed scornfully, but his eyes became suddenly hard and watchful. "What I do not underrate is your ability to fabricate. But you are going too far, nephew, if you are trying to convey the impression that Monseigneur of Brittany and I were aware of Lancaster's intentions."

"I will go farther. I say plainly that you wanted this from the very beginning. Madame," Louis turned to Isabeau, "you must suffer my lord of Burgundy and me to carry this conversation to its end. We have gone too far to be silent now."

"You ask my consent to this?" Isabeau retorted furiously. "You forget the King, Monseigneur d'Orléans. Do you give no thought to him, who still commands all of us here?"

The rebuke stung Louis. He thought bitterly how easy it was to forget that the King was not a child. He was about to turn to his brother and beg his forgiveness when Burgundy drawled loudly, "Apparently only you, Madame, are able to remind Monseigneur d'Orléans that he does not wear the crown."

"Damned hypocrite!" Louis struck his upper arm with his fist. "Will you deny, uncle, that you have an interest in the English rebellion? You could not manipulate King Richard: he was too independent. He refused to allow himself to be ordered about by his kinsmen, the clergy, the nobility. Now you have helped Henry of Lancaster and he is obligated to you. Although he will arrive shortly over the sea with an army to fight against France, he will not disturb your lands or your business arrangements. Don't try to make us believe the fairy tale that you serve only the interests of France; I will call you a liar, no matter how often you say it."

For the first time that Louis could remember, the Duke of Burgundy lost his haughty self-control; his face became ashy grey with rage, his voice trembled.

"Tell me, nephew, whether it is for love of France that you maintain relations with an Emperor who is too drunk to sign his own name; that you heap gold and gifts on his relatives from the House of Luxembourg. And tell me whether you accept the cities and provinces so often bestowed upon you simply for the sake of justice, and is it for the sake of justice that you are so well paid from the public treasury for your services?"

The King's lips quivered; he moved his hands quickly and aimlessly over his cloak, over the arms of his chair.

"It is coming again," he said suddenly. He looked helplessly in wild terror at Isabeau. "It is coming over me again. Oh, God, I can feel it approaching; please help me!" He slid from his chair onto his knees, wailing hoarsely. The Queen stood up; her lips were compressed in abhorrence. She knew what would follow; over the last few years she had been present several times when his madness overcame him.

"Take him away," she said in a low, tense voice to the Duke of Burgundy. "Call his people. Send the physicians—quickly."

De Courcy seized this opportunity to slip away unnoticed. The King was crawling across the floor, howling and weeping plaintively; he tried to cling to his wife's skirts, to Burgundy's sleeves. Louis d'Orléans went to the door to call some nobles of the King's retinue who were in the anterooms. After a few minutes the reception hall was filled with people—bringing more lights, a cool drink, some damp towels. This pitiful spectacle had been repeated at regular intervals since 1392; it was always followed by several months at least of complete insanity. Louis helped his brother to stand and held him up; he cursed himself for the altercation with Burgundy which had inadvertently aggravated the King's overwrought condition.

"In Christ's name," the King implored, clutching Louis with mad strength, "help me. It hurts—so much! It is coming upon me again. Oh, God, if anyone here hates me so much that he would torture me like this, let him kill me now, here where I stand, I cannot endure it any longer!"

Louis put his arms around the King and soothed him like a child. He did not see Isabeau and Burgundy exchange glances. While servants and physicians bustled about the King, the Duke of Burgundy and the Queen left the room.

Louis led the King to his apartments. But he could not force himself to watch while the physicians tried crudely to undress the sick man and restore him to his senses. The sound of the King's screams seemed to pursue Orléans into the remote corridors of the palace. In one of the abandoned doorways, he stopped and pressed his face against the icy wall.

"My God, my God," he whispered. "What shall I do? Parry . . . or attack? Frustrate my enemy or fight him to the death? Up to now I have been passive, more or less—but in the name of Jesus Christ, I shall lash out now and woe to him who stands in my way!"

He heard footsteps and turned quickly. A noble from the King's retinue walked past, with a respectful salute. It was the Sire Aubert de Cany.

In his adult years, Charles d'Orléans remembered three incidents which occurred in the year 1400; as a child Charles saw no connection between them. But in retrospect, when he was grown, he saw their underlying relationship. The first was a visit paid to his mother at their castle in Château-Thierry, by the Dame Christine de Pisan. The Duchess of Orléans was in a mournful mood in those days; the old Queen Blanche had died, the only royal woman who continued to behave as she always had, showing kindness to Valentine in her exile and disgrace. She had visited her young friend twice; in her will she bequeathed to her small, cherished gifts: a ring, a precious prayerbook, a breviary with illuminated miniatures. Sorrowfully, Valentine accepted these heirlooms; she felt she was now completely alone. It had been a long time since Louis had paid her a visit. And she was expecting a child in the spring once more. Thus she was doubly glad to see the Dame de Pisan, a noble, generous woman, Italian like the Duchess herself and, moreover, one who knew from her own experience the bitter taste of tears. Valentine found some comfort in the companionship of the poetess; they had much in common. The days passed quickly with pleasant conversation, music and reading.

Charles was often with his mother and her guest; while they talked in the high-ceilinged room hung with bright tapestries, the child sat in his favorite spot in the deep window niche looking out the small, thick, slightly cloudy panes at the winter landscape and the crows' nests in the tall trees around the castle.

Once on an afternoon filled with grey light and squalls of rain, he amused himself by breathing on the curved glass of the panes and then drawing a puppet on the clouded surface with his finger. But when it got dark and he grew tired of that, he caught fragments of the conversation between his mother and the Dame de Pisan; he listened more attentively when he heard mention of his father's name. The lady Christine described a brilliant fête given by the Duke of Orléans on Saint Valentine's Day in the Hôtel de Béhaigne in Paris: she had been there watching the spectacle from a bench set against the wall. She described the elegant repast, enlivened by the music of Orléans' famed minstrels; an allegory was presented with Love and My Lady Fidelity and her retinue. Young maidens wearing wreaths of flowers in their hair, clearly and sweetly sang a new motet, and after the banquet an Order of the Rose had been created in honor of the ladies present. And after that they arranged themselves in long rows to begin the dance. The Dame de Pisan, a widow who would wear mourning as long as she lived, did not join in the dance, but she enjoyed the dancers' pleasure. She watched the ladies and knights move forward slowly and elegantly over the mosaic floor in the great hall of the Hôtel; the dance seemed unending. None of the couples who moved, bowing and turning under the chandeliers, wanted to break the spell.

"With whom did Monseigneur, my husband, dance?" asked Valentine with a sad smile. The glowing splendor of Louis' fêtes in the Hôtel de Béhaigne seemed very remote to her, like images in a dream.

"With the best dancer of all, surely," replied the Dame de Pisan readily. "The wife of Sire Aubert de Cany—I have never seen anyone so graceful."

The Duchess of Orléans bent her head over her embroidery.

"Charles," she said to her son after a prolonged silence, "ask the woman to bring candles. It is getting so dark I cannot see the thread."

The child obeyed, surprised at the change in her voice.

One early spring morning the Demoiselle Marie d'Harcourt came to tell Charles that he had a new brother, Monseigneur Jean d'Orléans. Later they brought Charles to his mother, who lay motionless in bed, white as snow, with closed eyes. The baby was so ugly that Charles turned away in horror; he had expected to see a small child like Philippe, who followed his older brother everywhere on his sturdy little legs. Every day, for a few minutes in the morning and evening, Charles was allowed in the lying-in chamber. His mother sat up now, but she looked strange and thin and she spoke little.

The buds on the trees and shrubbery burst open. A light green haze hung over the tree branches in the forest; the sky was filled with white shining clouds. Charles, less carefully supervised now that his mother and little brother took up all the nurses' time, chose to spend his days watching the falconers exercising the young birds. The hawks were taught to fling themselves upon the prey—which at the moment were heron wings tied to a stick—and then to drop it at a certain spot. Charles was fascinated by this bird training; he watched closely as the falconer bound thin strong cords to the hawks' legs, as they artfully handled stick and hood.

But his mother's first walk to church was also an event; as her nearest male relative, Charles was permitted to lead her by the hand, a task which he discharged with gravity and discretion. The Duchess of Orléans offered the customary taper and gold piece; but her pale lips were pressed tightly together and her eyes were full of tears.

Not long afterward she called her eldest son to her where she stood in the armory, a long, narrow low-ceilinged room where bows, bucklers and other equipment hung, greased and polished, on the walls. The Duchess had ordered her gold and silver plate to be laid out on a table in the middle of the room; it was such a dazzling display of treasure that Charles had to close his eyes when he entered the chamber. Giles Malet, the librarian, and a clerk held writing tools. Valentine explained to the boy that she intended to make her will and therefore she wanted her valuables to be described and counted.

"But I wish to make you a gift today, Charles," she said, leading her son to the table, "because you took your father's place so nobly on my first walk to church since the birth of your brother Jean. I have set two things aside for you, a silver goblet and this . . . "

She took a gold box from the table and raised it for a moment in her narrow pale hand. "Open it, child."

Charles obeyed. In the box were a large golden cross and a bright enameled crucifix with a chain. Somewhat disappointed, the child thanked her. He would have preferred a ring or shiny buckle to wear on his hat, but he understood that this was a more important gift—indeed, a grown-up gift—and that pleased him.

"This is the only comfort the world offers, Charles," his mother said slowly; she closed the box. "Do not forget that when grief overwhelms you, and remember then what I say to you now: life is a long awaiting of God's peace."

"Yes, Madame ma mere," replied Charles, somewhat distracted by the activities of Maître Malet and the clerk. The librarian was dictating while the clerk wrote: "To our dearly beloved son Charles, Count of Angoulême, a silver drinking bowl . . . "

In the afternoon of this memorable day, a messenger arrived from Paris with letters and gifts from Charles' father; the Duke inquired after the health of his wife and children and sent his minstrel, Herbelin, to amuse the Duchess.

Thoughtfully Valentine read the letters; she looked over the bales of velvet and woolens and after the meal received Herbelin. The minstrel, who was a still-young man with black curling hair and an animated expression, was universally loved for his liveliness and his skill at the harp. The Duchess had great respect for him; he had often taught her new songs.

Herbelin played and sang now till late in the evening. Valentine's retinue sat listening as though they were entranced; the Duchess herself sat in quiet enjoyment with her hand shielding her eyes. The dogs were sleeping, stretched out before the fire. Charles, huddled on a small bench beside the hearth, was careful to make no noise for fear he would be sent to bed; he did not want to miss a note, not a sound of the music, clear as raindrops, cool and shimmering like the green river, filled with fragrance and the color of unknown things. He watched Herbelin's long fingers grasp the chords quickly and surely; but more beautiful still was Herbelin's voice, in which could be heard the wind and the peal of church bells, as well as the murmur of water and the clash of weapons.

"One more song, my Herbelin," said the Duchess at last. "It is late and you must surely be tired. Send us to bed with something pretty."

"Madame, if it please Your Grace, I shall play my own composition," said the minstrel, "set to a poem which Monseigneur Orléans wrote a short while ago."

"Monseigneur still writes poetry?" Valentine asked, with an odd smile. But the harp player had already begun. Charles listened breath-lessly; he had never heard that his father could write poetry; he was amazed. The song which Herbelin sang was about a knight who roams through a wood, a forest of long awaiting. Charles did not understand it; he remembered vaguely that his mother had spoken that afternoon about awaiting—but what sort of forest was that? Thorns and thistles and poisonous plants grow there in profusion, sang Herbelin; on all sides danger threatens and there is no escape. But in a still clearing in the forest a tree stands, heavily laden with golden apples. The shining, living fruit tempts the knight, who is weary of his wanderings and suffers from hunger and thirst. He knows that he is forbidden to pluck the apples, for the tree belongs to another. But he snatches an apple and bites into it.

Charles saw his mother's hand close convulsively over the arm of her chair; she sat rigid as though in violent pain. The child moved; he expected her to silence Herbelin. But the Duchess of Orléans said nothing and the minstrel sang further of the knight in the forest of awaiting.

"Who once has tasted of the golden fruit is prepared to risk death and damnation for another morsel. Let no one pity the sinner; he will not give up his place under the magic tree, not even for Heaven itself."

So ended the poem that Monseigneur d'Orléans had written and for which the minstrel Herbelin had composed a melody. Valentine ordered her retinue to bed. As a token of her appreciation, she gave Herbelin a small gold cup which he could wear on a chain around his neck. Absently she kissed Charles good-night; she did not say anything about his staying up so late. She quit the room walking between Marie d'Harcourt and the Dame de Maucouvent, but it was not from fatigue that she stumbled on the threshold.

Charles did not see his father again until the end of the year, when his arrival in no way resembled the stately, festive earlier visits which the child remembered. The Duke did not send couriers abroad as usual; he rode in the evening into Valentine's temporary home, the castle Villers-Cotterets, with only a small following. Servants and court were too stunned to give warning to the Duchess. She sat with Charles and Philippe in her bedchamber; the boys, who were romping on the great bed, noticed that something unusual had happened only when they heard the book which their mother was reading aloud fall to the floor with a thud. They looked up.

Their father stood in the center of the room spurred and booted, with a dark cloak over his leather jacket; his hose and the hem of his cloak were splashed with mud; he looked tired and worried.

The Duchess leaned with one hand on the arm of her chair; she did not rise to greet her husband.

"Children," Valentine said. Her sons had slipped quickly and quietly off the bed. "Greet your father and then go to the Dame de Maucouvent."

That night Charles lay awake for a long time in the darkness, his head throbbing; he asked himself fearfully why his father had looked so strange, why he had arrived unexpectedly, out of breath and exhausted, his clothes splattered and filthy—as though he were in disguise. Charles slept fitfully. Once he was awakened by the sound of voices and footsteps in the adjoining nursery and he saw a light burning under the door.

"Is it day already?" whispered the child. He sat up, but no one came. His little brother Philippe slept soundly and peacefully in the other bed. Presently an infant began to whimper in the nursery. Charles knew instantly that it was not Jean. The child that cries there is a new child that was just born, he thought, amazed. His first feeling was anger and chagrin because his mother had not confided in him this time. Surely his father had come to lead her to church. Charles huddled back into bed and pulled the blankets over his head so that he would hear no more howling.

Because his pride was wounded, he said nothing the following morning. The Dame de Maucouvent, who usually came to wake him and Philippe, behaved as though nothing had happened, but the harsh lines of her mouth showed her displeasure. Jeanne la Brune was busy in the nursery with little Jean, but next to the fire sat an unknown woman with an infant in her arms. Philippe stared at the strange baby with his mouth open. Charles did not betray any surprise because la Brune and the Dame de Maucouvent were watching him.

The two eldest boys were brought to the Duchess. She sat completely alone in the small room which was furnished as a private chapel. Charles had expected to find his mother in bed; he could not remain silent any longer.

"There is a new baby," he said reproachfully. "Why is it not lying with you in the lying-in room?"

Valentine looked calmly at her sons and smiled; the anxiety and bitterness of the past few years seemed to have vanished.

"Come here," she said. "Now listen carefully to what I am going to tell you, and promise me here in this place that as true knights you will repeat it to no one. The infant who came to us last night is not my child. But he is your half-brother; therefore you must love and protect him as you love and protect Jean."

"Half-brother?" asked Charles hesitantly; leaning against his mother's knee he looked close up into her large, shining amber eyes.

"That means," Valentine continued, "that Monseigneur your father is his father also. His mother died in childbirth; and that is why he has come to live with us."

Philippe understood nothing of all this; barely listening, he stared at the reflection of the candle flame in the golden altarpiece. Charles, however, frowned in thought.

"Where is Monseigneur my father then?" he asked at last.

"He is still asleep," answered the Duchess; she gave her oldest son a searching look and then began to stroke his hair gently. He was six years old; did he really understand what she meant?

Charles remained silent as he had sworn he would; he rebuked Philippe when his brother tried to ask him questions about the newest baby. The Dame de Maucouvent gave neither glance nor word to the infant; she walked about with a surly look on her round face, as though she had been personally insulted.

However, the stableboys were less reticent. They spoke once in the courtyard in Charles' presence of the bastard of Orléans who had been taken into the ducal family. Charles knew very well what a bastard was; he had heard a scullery servant's puppy called that. But he did not understand how this word could be applied to his half-brother.

"Why is the little baby a bastard?" he asked his mother later. The Duke his father had been sitting by the fire with his face in his hands; he looked up.

"I want to tell you that it is not always disgraceful to be a bastard," he said before Valentine could reply. "But I forbid you to call your half-brother that, my son, before you are old enough to know what you are saying. His name is Jean and he is Lord of Château-Dun, just as you are Count of Angoulême. Address him as Dunois, that is his rightful name."

"Do not be angry at your half-brother, Charles," said the Duchess gently. "I love him as much as you and Philippe and Jean, child. He really should have been mine . . . " She looked past Charles at her husband, and gave a low, sad laugh. "He was stolen from me, the small Dunois."

The sudden death of Mariette de Cany flung Louis back into the vortex of battle. He had with her—for a few months at any rate—been able to forget the frustrations of the past year: the death of England's former King, Richard; the fall of Wenceslaus, followed by the coronation of Ruprecht of Bavaria. Nor had he enjoyed undiluted happiness at the castle of Épernay, where he had brought the Dame de Cany after they became lovers. She never spoke of love, but her silence was more eloquent than words. Her desperate surrender terrified Louis; it was true that he was profoundly aware of guilt and sin, but he believed his passion could justify the relationship. For Mariette, however, there was no future; it had died, she thought, from the moment that she betrayed Aubert de Cany; she went through a purgatory of humiliation and remorse. Louis blamed her pregnancy for her emotional state; to the end he did not understand her.

"Forgive me that I must flee from you," said Maret before she retired to the lying-in chamber. The pains had already begun, but she held herself erect and refused to allow the women to support her. Louis wanted to cheer her up. He took leave of her lightly, with a joke. "You cannot escape me anymore, ma mie!"

"Alas, it is true," replied Mariette slowly, turning back to face him. "But think of me sometimes, when you cannot find me."

Louis had reason to think of her; when he saw her again, after the confinement, she lay straight and stiff between two rows of burning candles. Without a smile or farewell, she had left him forever.

After the quarrel in the presence of the King, the feud between

Burgundy and Orléans was an accepted fact. Uncle and nephew avoided each other as much as possible, but in the Council passionate reproaches and thrusts burst out at every turn. Their mutual hatred could no longer be hidden; in Paris the rabble taunted Orléans' household with cries of "Burgundy! Burgundy!"

In the beginning of the year 1401, Isabeau's father, Duke Stefan of Bavaria, appeared at the French court to try to conclude a pact between Charles and the Emperor Ruprecht. Isabeau promised to use all her influence. But before she could act, she received a heavy blow: the Dauphin caught a chill and died; he was barely eight years old. Only a few months earlier he had made his solemn entrance into the city of Paris; accompanied by his granduncles and a brilliant procession, he had ridden on horseback through the city to the cheers of the people. Neither the efforts of the physicians nor the masses held in the King's name in all the churches of Paris could save the child. His weak constitution succumbed to an illness which should not have been dangerous. Once more he was brought through the city to Saint-Denis, but now he was borne in a bier intended for dead kings, and weeping had supplanted the cheers. Under the weight of affliction, Isabeau for a time lost all interest in public affairs. She did not trouble Burgundy, who had begun to negotiate a betrothal between the small Marguérite de Nevers and the new Dauphin, whose elder brother lay still unburied.

Mourning for the Dauphin increased Isabeau's worries about her daughter; the eleven-year-old widow of England's King was in Windsor Castle, surrounded by all the ceremony which her station required, but in actual fact Lancaster's prisoner. Delegations from France were allowed to hold brief, formal conversations with her, but all attempts to negotiate her return to Paris and the restoration of her substantial dowry, were frustrated by Henry's cold refusal to respond, which aroused uneasy suspicions. Even Burgundy believed that Lancaster was considering a marriage between his son and the little widow. But Isabeau had other plans, with which the Duke of Burgundy, on second thought, agreed; she wanted to find a husband for her daughter in Germany.

Before summer came, Lancaster decided that keeping the dowry was not worth the loss of popular favor. No king of England had sought a French bride for himself or his kinsmen without penalty. Preparations were made for Madame Isabelle's homeward journey. Meanwhile, Burgundy, with a great entourage, waited in state in Calais.

The prospect of her daughter's homecoming put an end to the depression from which Isabeau had suffered throughout the spring, when she had determined to do penance for the damage she had unwittingly done to French interests and to those who attempted to thwart her over the past years. During a summer storm lightning had struck Isabeau's bedchamber; the violence of the blow, the sight of the bedcurtains in flames, had shocked her into a vow to alter her way of life. But when the storm had passed, and her bedchamber was repaired, the Queen came to see things in another light. She established a church and required weekly masses to be said for the soul of the dead Dauphin. And thus she considered she had done her duty.

Her father, Duke Stefan of Bavaria, had resumed his visits to the French court. He expressed interest in the widow of the Sire de Coucy, who had fallen before Nicopolis. Their daughter was heiress to the barony of Coucy, an extensive and important territory located in Picardy on the borders of Flanders, Hainault and Brabant. It was anticipated that the young damsel would in time cede her proprietary rights in this land to her powerful stepfather of Bavaria. Not only would the domain of Coucy be a brilliant addition to the block of lands belonging to the House of Bavaria, but it was strategically important as a gateway to France. Burgundy, naturally, supported the marriage proposal; as did Isabeau, as did Berry, who occupied himself at Bicêtre collecting exotic beasts. Only Bourbon hesitated; he was not convinced of the wisdom of the marriage. Orléans did not appear at the meetings held to discuss the marriage agreement; he surprised Isabeau and his fellow Regents by buying the barony of Coucy from the heiress. The King ratified by his signature the contract in which the daughter of the Sire de Coucy declared "that in the interest of the Kingdom, she could do no better than to transfer the domain of Coucy to Monseigneur the Duke of Orléans". For the first time Louis tasted triumph; he had overtrumped Burgundy and the Bavarian princes. Their rage and disappointment made it obvious to him at the same time when he must make his next move.

In the midst of Bavarian lands lay the Duchy of Luxembourg; it belonged to the Margrave of Moravia, a kinsman and ally of Wenceslaus. This territory, a wedge between Flanders, Hainault and Brabant, on the one hand, and the states subject to Ruprecht of Bavaria on the other, was strategically crucial. The Margrave of Moravia, who wished at any cost to safeguard his property from the hated Bavarians, suggested that Orléans place Luxembourg under his protection.

The realization that his star was rising stimulated Louis to increase his political activity. While the Queen was absent, he managed to send his friend, Marshal Boucicaut, to Genoa as governor. Boucicaut, who understood and agreed with Louis in everything, performed his duties in an exemplary manner from the first day onward. He managed to maintain order on the other side of the Alps without endangering the peace with neighbor and ally.

Once more Isabeau and Burgundy had bitter reason to bemoan the actions of the King's brother. Each of them attempted, in his own fashion, to outwit him; the Queen, enraged because war against Gian Galeazzo was out of the question while Boucicaut was governor of Genoa, entered heart and soul into the intrigues of Emperor Ruprecht; Burgundy, meanwhile, struck elsewhere. Through artful political maneuvering, he brought the Duchy of Brittany within his sphere of influence.

Louis was in a grim mood, chiefly because of Burgundy's successful countermove. The King, more gravely ill than ever, was unapproachable; he seemed, in fact, scarcely human. Almost every day Isabeau received envoys from Germany; Louis was aware of this, although the Queen attempted to behave as though nothing unusual were happening. The Dukes of Berry and Bourbon remained aloof, wishing to see which way the cat would jump. In the Council all was confusion and discontent; it was impossible to steer a steady course with so many conflicting opinions. Louis d'Orléans craved an outlet for his feelings of hatred for Lancaster and Burgundy; he challenged his former brother-in-arms to a duel. It occurred to him to do this after he had seen his niece, the little Isabelle, move pale and mournful through the halls of Saint-Pol, still accorded the dignity and respect of a queen. She had carried back from England an attitude of injured majesty which seemed almost ludicrous in so young a child, but the grief in her bright round eyes was real. She had loved King Richard deeply; he had always been kind to her.

"And he loved me too," said the child, sobbing. "He lifted me in the air when he took leave of me before he went to Ireland, and he must have kissed me forty times." When Madame Isabelle said this, her tears would not stop flowing.

Louis felt deep compassion for the unthroned Queen, the child who had become a widow before she became a woman. It would be extremely difficult to arrange so brilliant a marriage for her again. Before long she would, perhaps, be forced to set aside the high rank which she now bore so self-consciously. She sat surrounded by princesses and duchesses, arrayed in the state robes of her dowry, in furnished apartments set aside for Her Majesty, the Dowager-Queen of England. But all the ceremony, all the homage and pomp, could bring no color to her small, stiff face. Upset and angry, Louis felt it was his duty to do what the French court apparently considered unnecessary; he flung himself forward as his niece's champion and challenged Lancaster to single combat.

The Englishman replied dryly that he found the proposal ridiculous; he had no inclination to fight with one who was his inferior in rank.

In fact, things were not going smoothly for England's new monarch; he discovered all too quickly that one cannot learn to rule in a few days. With Burgundy's help he managed to achieve an extension of the peace treaty with France. He was so distracted by internal affairs that he had no time even to think about attacking French soil. Louis, believing that France should not be cheated of the chance to strike at England while it was weakened by dissension, played his trump card against Burgundy. In the summer of 1402 he set out with a great entourage for Coucy, which was favorably located near the border, and entered into negotiations with representatives of the Margrave of Moravia for the purchase of Luxembourg. The agreement was reached without difficulty. For the sum of 100,000 ducats Moravia sold the Duchy to Orléans. Louis went almost immediately to his new domain where he approached the lords of the region and bound them to him in the traditional way with gifts and grants. Thus a dangerous rift was opened in the Bavarian sphere of influence by Louis d'Orléans; in case of war he could rely now on an army of vassals and their followers. Both Orléans and Burgundy had adopted highly provocative stances; neither could move now without mortally wounding his adversary or being mortally wounded himself.

One afternoon in May, 1403, Isabeau, on returning from a stroll in the gardens of Saint-Pol, accompanied by her entourage, heard with surprise that the Duke of Orléans had requested an audience with her; he had been waiting for a considerable time in the ante-room. Relations between the Queen and her brother-in-law had grown extremely chilly over the past few years; they spoke to each other only on state occasions and maintained the illusion of mutual courtesy only for the sake of appearances. Isabeau was involved with Burgundy's policies; she was on the side of Burgundy and Bavaria, and she did not trust Orléans. During the past few months she had begun to show her disapproval by openly avoiding him.

Isabeau set out for her favorite room; it was a chamber hung with flowered tapestries next to the reception hall. She knew that the King had held audience that morning with Louis d'Orléans and a great number of clergy. Charles was somewhat better at the mo-ment; for a short time he could once again busy himself with affairs of state.

While Isabeau awaited her brother-in-law's arrival, she fanned herself impatiently with a handkerchief and sniffed repeatedly at a gold-filigree ball filled with sweet-smelling herbs. Presently the doors opened and the Duke of Orléans was announced. Louis entered the Queen's room and bowed; although neither word nor gesture left anything to be desired, Isabeau detected under his courtly demeanor a cold self-assurance which made her very angry; it seemed to her that Louis must already have accomplished his purpose.

"Well, my lord?" The Queen was cold and haughty in her turn. "To what do I owe this honor?"

Louis ran his eyes over the rows of noble women. Margaretha of Burgundy stared past him, her face hard and grey as though it were hewn from stone; the Countess de Nevers smiled politely; her eyes were icy. Louis, who under other circumstances had seen those eyes gleam with a different emotion, raised his brows ironically. The other ladies of Isabeau's suite kept their eyes fixed demurely on the floor.

"Send your women away, Madame," replied Louis. "What I must say to you is intended for your ears only."

The Queen wanted to deny his request curtly; she could see that Margaretha of Burgundy expected her to do so. But in that case she feared that Orléans would not speak, and she felt it was her duty to find out what he was up to. Therefore she commanded her women to withdraw; the Burgundy women, deeply offended, led the others from the chamber.

"I have been with the King," said Orléans, as soon as the door had closed behind the Queen's retinue. "Perhaps Your Majesty does not know that he has once more recovered his health?"

Isabeau looked up in surprise. "Naturally, I know it . . . "

"You have not visited the King for weeks," said Louis, looking at her steadily, "although he sends you messages repeatedly. He has complained of it himself, Madame."

"But that is not true!" The Queen made a vehement gesture; the perfumed ball rolled to the floor. "I have been to see the King twice with the Dauphin. A day does not go by without my inquiry into the state of his health."

"Oh, yes, very good, Madame," said Louis impatiently, "but you choose to misunderstand me. The King is your husband."

Isabeau's face and plump neck turned deep scarlet; she lowered her eyes. It was extremely quiet in the room: birds could be heard in the park, and the shouts of nobles on the fives-courts.

"I do not want to," the Queen burst out harshly. "I cannot. Jesus, Maria. I do not want to any more."

Louis d'Orléans gazed at Isabeau's broad fingers; she was wringing her hands with a strength that seemed to belie their softness.

"What do you mean, Madame?" Louis asked gently; he was moved despite himself by her distress. She sat huddled together.

"I have had ten children, Monseigneur," she replied, struggling to suppress her anger and embarrassment. "Don't you see that it is a miracle that I have been able to go on like that when the King has been almost continuously insane? I have brought seven children into the world since he went mad." She fell silent. Louis picked up the perfumed golden ball and held it out to her.

"I am afraid of the King," Isabeau continued vehemently. "Everyone knows how he threatens me when he has an attack. He can change so that he is hardly recognizable; he has driven me from his rooms with blows and abuse. Must I endure all that forever? Is there no one who will have compassion for *me*—who will try to imagine what I go through?"

In that silent room, that bower of bright embroidery, they sat and stared at each other. Louis d'Orléans had the sudden feeling that he had never met this woman before. She was fat and faded and no longer even resembled the fresh, robust princess whom he had greeted as his brother's bride in Melun. But her desperation moved him more than all the memories of happier days. The thought crossed his mind that perhaps all Isabeau's political maneuvering was simply an attempt to escape from the agonizing nightmare of her married life. He felt ashamed that he had never before considered her behavior in this light. And as an admirer of women, he quickly respected her for the dignity and pride with which she had borne her silent, secret despair. Involuntarily he relaxed his stiff demeanor; his tone became gentle, his eyes lost their coldness.

He smiled at the Queen as he had smiled only at little Isabelle— with understanding and compassion. He so closely resembled the King as he had been fifteen years before that Isabeau's heart began to ache in a queer way; she began to weep for her vanished happiness.

She is only a woman after all, Louis thought, gazing down on her bent head. By God, she is also lonely. Burgundy has taken advantage of her misery. It occurred to him that the cold pride which he had always disliked in Isabeau was only a mask behind which she concealed her feelings. Can she be guided? he asked himself. Could she possibly be amenable to reason? If she is on my side, then I have won the battle. Burgundy uses her, but apart from politicking he gives her nothing in return. Of course she is a woman— how could I have forgotten that? thought Louis, in mounting astonishment. She wants to be understood and not pitied. My lord uncle does not perceive things like that.

"I understand your situation, Madame." He spoke softly and warmly. "Please don't think I am blind to the sacrifices that have been demanded of you. But the King is so fond of you when he is well, and we can only guess at the shame and remorse he must feel for the anguish he causes you. I know how painful it must be for you to speak about these things with me. The King has taken me into his confidence because I am his closest blood relative. And he knows that I put his welfare before anything else." Isabeau looked at him doubtfully. "Perhaps we don't agree about that, Madame," he added quickly, still with a pleasant smile.

The Queen dashed her tears away, upset that she had lost control of herself, although she was well aware that she had aroused Orléans' sympathy.

"The King has now two sons, Madame," Louis went on, somewhat more coolly now that he saw she had regained her composure. "Neither is robust. If something should happen to the Dauphin or his brother—which God forbid—France would have no successor to the throne."

"I am amazed that it is you who lets himself be used as a go-between," Isabeau said with irony. "In that case the throne would pass to your heirs, my lord."

Louis rose and bowed. "I am afraid that we do not understand each other," he replied coldly. But the Queen entreated him to remain.

Isabeau's moods changed quickly. Her tears had left no trace; her grief had given way to the cautious calculation so basic to her nature. She began to weigh the possibility of a return to the friendly relationship of the past. Under the pervasive influence of Burgundy and his wife, court life had been reduced to empty ceremony. Isabeau sorely missed the imaginative exuberance of Louis' fêtes. She missed the careless delight, the surrender to intoxicated pleasure. In her desire for happiness she forgot that youth cannot return, that what is finished cannot be repeated. What weighed most strongly in Louis' favor at the moment was the fact that he was unlikely to curtail in any way what she regarded as her rightful income. Burgundy, who seized every opportunity to push his expenses and debts off onto the public treasury, was always demanding greater frugality of Isabeau. Under the guise of concern for public monies, he dogged her footsteps, spying zealously on all her expenditures, no matter how petty. This niggling surveillance irritated her beyond measure, but she had to put up with it because she needed Burgundy.

She considered, staring thoughtfully at her brother-in-law, how pleasant it would be if the person upon whom she relied for political guidance were also indulgent and forbearing toward her in other respects. She had often toyed with the idea of keeping Orléans close at hand; but she had done nothing about it because he did not seem sufficiently important to her interests. But now he had shown that he was a match for Burgundy; in her eyes there was no greater proof of capability.

"My lord," said Isabeau, fixing her dark brown, somewhat adamant gaze upon Louis, "I shall try in my prayers to reflect upon what you have said to me today. God knows, I am a person of good will. But there is a limit to everything. Sometimes I feel as though the King were dead. I cannot feel love for the creature who has taken his place."

Louis d'Orléans took the hand which she held out to him and helped her to rise.

"I have spoken to you only at the behest of my brother, the King," he said most courteously, as though the subject were closed. "I understand your objections only too well, Madame. And now, if you will allow me, I shall call your women."

Isabeau's smile held a trace of her former coquettishness; she almost forgot that she was no longer beautiful, that she was not really an innocent victim: it was not out of patience and timidity that she had accepted the King's advances over the past ten years. Castles, treasures, great sums of money had been the price of her love.

Orléans had known how to accomplish his ends with the King. The sale of valuables had not been enough to defray the enormous expenses he had incurred for the purchase of Coucy and Luxembourg. Since the possession of these two properties benefited the realm, it was obvious that the realm should help to pay for them. And Louis managed to convince his brother that an eye should be kept on England. Henry of Lancaster would undoubtedly resume the wars as soon as a good opportunity presented itself. Therefore it could only be wise policy to prepare now while circumstances in England guaranteed a postponement of hostilities.

By royal decree all of France was compelled to contribute, for three years, a sum equal to what had been raised for Isabelle's dowry. This time, however, the clergy, who had previously been spared, were not exempted. Their indignation knew no bounds. Burgundy, who was already offended because he had not been consulted in the matter, did not hesitate to support the clergy. In his own domain he did not encourage the populace to raise the tribute— quite the contrary, in fact. He continually encouraged them not to pay it.

The Parisians had become alarmed by the presence in and about the city of bands of soldiers—Picards, Luxembourgers and armed men from Gelre who said they served the Duke of Orléans, and other troops from the Burgundian dominions of Artois and Flanders. The Elector of Liège, Johann of Bavaria, was Burgundy's guest in the Hôtel d'Artois; the army he had brought—chiefly archers and lansquenets—were lodged in the quarters of the city near the palace. Fear of civil war mounted with each passing day.

The city of Paris sent a delegation to the King petitioning him to put an end to this disorder. The population was assured, in the name of the King, that the troops quartered in the city were not dangerous in any way; their support was paid for, and any infraction of discipline would be severely punished. In spite of these assurances, the city lived in constant fear; many departed but most armed themselves and laid in provisions, as though they were preparing for a siege.

And now a new kind of life began for Charles d'Orléans. His time as a small child had ended; playtime, with no obligation except the faultless recitation of morning and evening prayers, was over. The nine-year-old was taken from the care of the Dame de Maucouvent; he was now too old to have a governess.

The Duke of Orléans sent his secretary, Maître Nicolas Garbet, who had studied theology, to the Château-Thierry, where Valentine lived with her children for increasing periods, to tutor Monseigneur Charles, Count of Angoulême. Charles eagerly awaited the arrival of Maître Garbet; for a long time he had been impatiently waiting to learn to read. He thought that there could be no pleasure greater than to be able to decipher the rows of beautiful characters in the books which his mother had had so carefully illuminated and bound—unless it was plying the pen. He drew figures in the sand with a stick, pretending that he was writing a story across the enormous page of the courtyard. For hours he would study the densely written leaves of King Arthur's Histories, of Ovid's Metamorphoses, or the Gospels. He did not know what was written there, but he was filled with deep satisfaction at the sight of the rectangular pages covered with letters surrounded with gaily colored tendrils, the initials against the gilded background. He obeyed with reluctance when his mother urged him to go out and play with his brother.

"You have time for learning, child," Valentine said. "You can find pleasure in books when you have forgotten how to play."

So he rode hobby horse with Philippe in the courtyard or hopped on the pavement of the corridors and halls. Little Jean watched his brothers from the sidelines but Dunois, who was not yet four years old, always wanted to play. He plunged headlong between his older brothers without fear of stumbling or falling, a resolute child with sturdy legs and strong little hands. He spoke little and never cried, but when he wanted to accomplish something, his will was inflexible. Charles and Philippe thought of him as being as old as they; from time to time they remembered with surprise that their indefatigable playmate was younger than Jean, the timid, apprehensive toddler. They did not seem to care that Dunois was only their half-brother and a bastard to boot. He was part of the family, sharing their food and clothing; he slept in bed with Jean and was treated by strangers and inferiors with the same respect accorded the other children of the Duke. Valentine loved him uncommonly well; she was proud of his healthy good looks, his thriving body and spirit.

Her own sons were less robust, paler and more easily tired than he. Charles was short-winded; she found him too quiet, too introspective for a nine-year-old boy. Inclined to day-dream herself, she wanted to spare him the fate that befalls sensitive natures; it was better for him, she thought, to be able-bodied and alert. However, the arrival of Maître Garbet meant that Charles' spirit had to be guided into other channels, at least for a time; in a sense she was forced to abandon him.

With flushed cheeks the child watched while the tutor opened his leather bag of books. They were placed on the table in the study room: the Katholicon, Latin grammars, the works of Cato, Terentius, Sallustius and Cicero, the Doctrine of Alexander de Villedieu. Nicolas Garbet, a thin, vivacious man not much taller than Charles himself, rushed about, chattering incessantly. He directed the servants who carried the books, told Charles what the thick leather covers contained, recalled aloud what Monseigneur d'Orléans had told him to tell the Duchess. His sleeves fluttered as he made short, choppy gestures. Charles noticed that his shoes were worn down—that did not surprise him, for Maître Garbet did not stand still for a moment.

The lessons began the following day. Valentine had insisted that Philippe be there too; she hoped that the presence of the younger child would slow things down somewhat and put a necessary rein on the enthusiasms of Maître de Garbet and the studious Charles. So seated side by side at the long table, the brothers became acquainted with the ABCs; slowly they read psalms from a little book which Hugues Foubert, illuminator of manuscripts, had made for them at Valentine's request. Above their little black cloaks—they wore in mourning for their grandfather Gian Galeazzo, who had died suddenly in Milan—their young faces were taut and grave as they wielded the pen stiffly, the tips of their tongues between their teeth.

Before long they began to learn Latin words, followed by conjugations, declensions and what-not. Then logic, rhetoric and arithmetic. Charles, especially, made rapid progress. Philippe was more playful; he wanted to be done so that he could go out and amuse himself. When lessons were over, Charles usually lingered in the room filled with books and writing implements. Maître Garbet, always busy himself—he was writing a theological treatise in poetic form—encouraged the boy to remain. The shouts and laughter of the younger boys echoed outside; they stormed and defended sand hills, threw stones and shot arrows at wooden targets or leapt breathlessly over barricades of sticks, while Charles sat on in the quiet study, his arms resting on the edge of the table.

He was continually overcome by amazement that a world filled with adventure and beauty could rise from behind the black letters; that within a single page, a life could unfold, that death and heroism could be enclosed in a few strokes on the paper. He read a line aloud as soon as it was taught to him: there rode Perceval through the forest; on the mountaintop could be seen the citadel of Montsalvat. The words "mountain" and "forest" called up a variety of images for the boy: he saw leaves hanging, dark and gleaming, and heard the splashing of a hidden brook; the horses' hooves left deep tracks in the moss. The sunlight glowed red on the mountainside, and glinted on the windows of the castle, an eagle rose screaming from his craggy nest.

Reading in the study, Charles lost all track of time; he was completely immersed. In the summer he did not notice the flies buzzing along the walls or the scratching of Maître Garbet's pen. In the winter he did not hear the wood crackling on the hearth and he never remembered the exact moment when a kindly hand had set a candle down beside him.

The many journeys and processions had ended; they lived now almost the whole year around in Château-Thierry. During this period Charles and his mother became very close. They talked and read together, and enjoyed the minstrel's songs. For the first time the boy realized something of his mother's unhappiness. He knew now that she had been exiled from the court in Paris and why; he knew too that she had fresh reasons to be sad. Although she never complained and talked about herself with reluctance in his presence, Charles sensed with the sharp intuition of a precocious child what oppressed her spirits.

His father came to visit them very often now, always with a large entourage, usually attended by lords from his provinces or from Luxembourg. But Louis paid little attention to his sons when he stayed at Château-Thierry; there was so much to discuss with Valentine and important guests that no time was left for the children. Charles, observing him from a distance, admired him greatly. He had never seen such a handsome and splendidly dressed man as his father—he could not help identifying him with the heroes of the romances, with Perceval, Lancelot, Arthur and Aeneas. He knew his mother felt that way too. Often he saw her looking at her husband—the glow in her eyes was almost frightening.

As a rule the Duchess chose to dress in black; she rarely wore jewels. But when Monseigneur visited Château-Thierry, she appeared dressed like a princess, wearing necklaces of precious stones. The child Charles observed the transformation breathlessly; at these times he became aware that his mother was an uncommonly beautiful woman, tall and slender—her hair was golden brown, like leaves in October. The Duke greeted her with courtly elegance, and behaved toward her throughout his stay with deference and gallantry—but in his eyes the boy never saw the look of burning ardor which he sometimes detected in the eyes of his mother.

In the course of time another child had been born, a girl, baptized Marie d'Orléans. But she did not lie long in the green-curtained cradle; even before their mother had risen from the lying-in bed, Charles and Philippe were called to take leave of their sister, who lay in the folds of her shroud like a pale wax doll.

In the spring of 1404, the Duchess of Orléans received a letter from her husband containing important news, especially for Charles. Louis and the former Emperor Wenceslaus had agreed to nullify the marriage agreement between Charles and the young Elisabeth von Goerlitz. A new bride had been found in the person of Madame Isabelle, the fourteen-year-old widow of King Richard of England. The marriage would, it was true, be put off for several years because of the youth of the groom, but the betrothal would be announced as soon as the formalities had been concluded.

The Pope consented to this marriage between cousins; the King declared that Isabelle's dowry would be 100,000 gold florins, two-thirds of which Orléans would use to buy territory in France.

In the autumn Louis d'Orléans took his oldest son with him to Senlis for the hunt, and to meet the royal personages at the court. Dressed in handsome garments which were—as usual—heavily embroidered with thistles, crossbows and nettles, the boy walked beside his father between rows of high-placed lords. Never had he seen such a magnificent display of horses, carriages, pennants, colorfully-clad servants and pages. The counts and barons and their wives glittered with gold and precious stones; under a red silk tent the King sat, Charles' uncle and godfather.

The boy was disappointed. He knew quite well that the King was sick, but still he had expected a more impressive figure than this thin, shrunken man with waxen face and red-rimmed, restless eyes. However, the King greeted him with great geniality; he called Charles first "worthy nephew" and later "our son"; he gave him beautiful gifts and the promise of an annuity. Charles thanked him with downcast eyes, a little flustered because everyone was looking at him. It was precisely this boyish embarrassment which roused admiration; people found him a well-made, mannerly youth. They said he had his father's nose and mouth, but Valentine's eyes. The Duke of Orléans was pleased with the impression his son had made; he gave the boy a signet ring and a horse as souvenirs of his days at Senlis.

That winter brought much snow and rain; in early spring the swollen rivers overflowed their banks; the wind was raw. During the bad weather a new illness broke out, characterized by violent headaches and loss of appetite. Almost no one escaped this sickness but only a few died of it. Among these few was the Duke of Burgundy.

On an evening in the spring of 1405, a great number of people were gathered in the rooms of The Golden Stag, a tavern in the rue Barre du Bec, not far from the Hôtel d'Artois. The doors were barred so that no one else could enter; inside, only a couple of torches were burning. The innkeeper was called Thibault the Dice-Player because he could always manage to provide a sequestered room where one could drink wine and gamble undisturbed for any conceivable stakes.

If he was paid well and promptly, Thibault asked no questions—his rooms were notorious as a gathering place for those who wished to amuse themselves or transact business without attracting attention. The sheriff's servants were reluctant to enter there; Thibault's tavern was frequented by armed people who, day or night, were all too ready to draw a knife. Scuffles usually became bloodbaths; no one bothered to distinguish between opponents and companions-at-arms, they went at each other for the sheer enjoyment of the fight itself and the chance to cut some purses and steal some valuables. Those who had no business there avoided not only The Golden Stag, but the rue Barre du Bec because of it.

On the evening in question the gathering in Thibault's rooms had a prearranged character: the men sat or stood almost one on top of the other around a table which served as a rostrum, listening to an orator who, despite his off-putting appearance, possessed to a high degree the ability to enthrall his audience. His filthy rags were held together by a rope about his middle; his long hair hung over his shoulders. There in the tavern no one was present who would find it in his interest to inform the officials that Arnaud Guillaume was preaching rebellion against Orléans; he had therefore pulled off his bonnet. However, his two companions who sat at the table did not want to be recognized: their cloaks were pulled up over their chins, they had drawn the lappets of their hats down across their cheeks. Without moving, silent, they sat staring at the men around them. Arnaud Guillaume spoke in the style that had served him so well throughout his earlier career: slowly, in a low voice that appeared to quiver with deep emotion. Thus had he practiced exorcism over the head of the sleeping King.

" . . . And what happened to the gold which you fellows paid at the cost of so much sacrifice, brothers?" asked Guillaume, with upraised hands. This question ended a long speech in which he had once again described the misery caused by taxes imposed the previous year. He waited a moment; an angry murmur rose from among his listeners.

"Was it really spent on those things which the tax collector knew how to list so nicely? Are the forts strengthened, the troops armed, the winter stores laid in? And even if that should have chanced to happen—I doubt it seriously, brothers, but suppose that they are—what then? How will you fellows fare in a new war, with robbery and murder . . . your houses looted, your cattle stolen, your fields laid waste, your wives and daughters dishonored and you yourselves perhaps strung up on the nearest tree? For so it goes always, men, so it goes, where there is war, and the plunderers are mostly the soldiers who are supposed to protect you! It is you people who are the victims, brothers, *you* who will be defeated, not the enemy, for they strike back! Do you want to see your good money used for your own destruction? No, men, no, you don't want that. You don't, but Orléans does—the warmonger who will serve his own interests with your lives!"

"But—" a voice called from the densely packed crowd—"you said that our tax money is not being spent for anything."

"Precisely, friend; well put. Your gold pieces have gone in another direction."

A man raised his hand and cried, "Gone, gone? They lie heaped up in a tower room in the Louvre!"

"They did," continued Guillaume, raising his voice, "but two nights ago a wagon drove up in front, guarded by armed men. They loaded the gold onto the wagon, friends, not a single écu is left lying in the tower of the Louvre. Who did that, brothers? Come, think about it, who can always use money for himself and his royal sweetheart?"

"Come, come," mocked a young man who sat astride a stool directly below Guillaume. "Make us believe that you have looked at the King in bed!"

The adventurer from Guyenne had expected such an objection. Pronouncing an oath loaded with frightful curses—which one dare not misuse—he declared that he had indeed enjoyed that privilege. This raised great interest, and great suspicion. One of Guillame's companions nudged him and in a sharp tone added some words the spectators did not understand. The ascetic began to speak again.

"Who has seriously endangered your salvation, brothers, by forcing you to give obedience to the Anti-Christ at Avignon? Couldn't the wise and pious scholars at the Sorbonne have shown you a better way to true grace? It seems clear now from all the facts that neither Orléans nor Avignon has any intention of complying with the conditions which our clergy at the Sorbonne had put forward. The old order reigns; he who kisses the ground before Avignon's feet is rewarded with high office and decks himself in purple. And the priests and bishops who remain loyal to the True Faith would rather perish from hunger and thirst then deal with you, friends, for you are being driven straight into the Devil's arms. And who is responsible for this?

"It's not necessary—is it?—for me to name the adulterer and sorcerer who wants to involve you in a war with England out of his own self-interest . . . who lines his purse with your hard-earned money . . . who means to destroy the Dauphin and all the King's children so that he can place one of his own brood on the throne . . . who carries on openly with the Bavarian, and helps her to drain the country's treasury to get clothes and valuables!"

He paused to catch his breath and looked about him with glittering eyes. It had become quiet under the smoke-blackened beams of the ceiling; the flickering torchlight played on the faces of his listeners. There were men there from every layer of the population, but whatever their occupation or business, they all had reason to feel dissatisfied or fearful. "Come," Guillaume said, after a brief conversation with his companions. "You yourselves have so rightly complained with bitterness about the way you were forced to pay tribute. The sheriff's men follow the tax collectors, in order to drag anyone who refuses to pay off to prison. On your doors and shutters are painted the arms of Orléans, your lord and master, who, draped with a fortune in gold, hunts or dances, while you sweat. And what can you do about this? May I remind you of Messire Jean Gilbert de Donnery, who last week in the presence of Orléans' officials dared to say that it would be better to hang Monseigneur than to allow him to govern? Now Messire Donnery hangs from the gallows and the Duke of Orléans has gone with the Queen to the castle of Saint-Germain. What is he doing there, brothers?"

A loud, coarse laugh rose from the group of bystanders. Arnaud Guillaume made quick use of their good humor.

"But believe me, friends, there is no reason to despair. The people of Paris—what am I saying?—the people of the entire Kingdom have always a friend and protector in a highly-placed man—do I need to mention his name?—who would like nothing better than to continue the work of his noble father. Ah, brothers, listen to reason before it is too late! Take a stand before you bitterly regret your indecision. The man I refer to—a gallant knight, a mighty prince—is your protector. He is outraged at the excessive taxes which are imposed on you . . . yes, he urges you not to pay the tribute . . . he takes personal responsibility. He is devoted to peace and the preservation of the armistice—help him, give no more money for warmongering. He strives along with the pious clergy of the Sorbonne for cession—support him, refuse to obey Avignon. He champions the cause of our unfortunate King, of our defenseless Dauphin. He has set himself the task of working against Orléans in every way—Orléans, the accomplice of the Evil One, who with his late father-in-law conspired with the Turks to destroy our Christian knights at Nicopolis. Yes, this fearless hero to whom I refer," cried Guillaume, carried away by his own artificially inflated enthusiasm, "this hero, friends, will be on his guard to make sure that the King's innocent young daughters do not marry the son of a poisoner, a witch, whom you yourselves have driven out of the city!"

While the listeners shouted their agreement, one of Guillaume's companions threw an open purse onto the table: gold and silver coins rolled into all the corners. The ascetic from Guyenne raised his voice once more over the ensuing uproar.

"Thibault, Dice-Player! Wine for all my good friends present here! In the name of our benefactor and protector, a drink! He intends the best for you, brothers, he is a brave man, a high-minded man, a man who would rather give away money with both hands than knock a single denier out of your pockets. God and the Virgin for Burgundy!"

The shrieks of response were momentarily overwhelming; the walls resounded with the shouting. The landlord, a man in a leather apron, pushed his way with difficulty to the wine vats which were stacked against the rear wall of the room, and knocked the bung from a cask. Jars and beakers were quickly given out; within a few minutes the tavern had become too small. Doors and windows were thrown open; men streamed from the hot, stuffy tavern into the cool air. Thibault the Dice-Player, busily filling the cups for a second round, saw, not without uneasiness, knives flashing near the place where the purse had fallen.

"Let the fellows quarrel," said a voice near his ear; one of Guillaume's companions stood next to him, and slid a handful of gold pieces into the pocket of Thibault's apron. "Don't forget what was said here tonight and take care that it is spread abroad."

"Certainly, Messire," answered the landlord nervously; it was not the first time that he had played host to this trio. He thought that the speaker and his friends had come from the Hôtel d'Artois. Therefore he added, "But I am running into danger. This is less innocent than gambling or fighting, Messire. Who will protect *me* if Orléans sends his men after me?"

The stranger leaned forward so that the lappets of his black hat fell loose. The light from the candle stuck on top of the wine casks shone on his face: the large, sharp nose, the mouth with its protruding lower lip, the small but fierce eyes. Thibault gasped and stared; then he fell to his knees and let the wine stream out.

"Get up," said Jean of Burgundy harshly. "Control yourself. Do as I order and don't worry about your life. Send your friends through the city—you know the way—and tell them to repeat what Guillaume has said, in the halls, on the bridges, in the market, in the outskirts of the town. Choose some trustworthy men, send them to the Hôtel d'Artois. Watchword: 'the hour is coming—the time approaches—.' Understand?"

The landlord nodded and went back to the wine vats. The three visitors quickly pushed their way out through the knots of drinking, fighting, loudly wrangling men. Soon they were swallowed up in the dark street.

Burgundy's death caused what he had tried so painstakingly to prevent during his lifetime: a rapprochement between the Queen and Orléans. Jean of Burgundy inspired Isabeau with an inexplicable fear and aversion; she found him ugly, clumsy and disagreeable. Not for a moment did she consider making the son heir to the confidence which she had given the father. The Queen had been offended by the manner in which he had come to the court after his father's death and announced himself as the Duke of Burgundy. His arrogance, his rough manners, lost for him whatever good will he might have possessed, especially in Isabeau's eyes. Under these circumstances it was natural that Isabeau should renew her alliance with her brother-in-law. Now that Burgundy was dead, Berry and Bourbon scarcely set foot in Council or court, and Burgundy's son did not appear to be trustworthy, the Queen could seek support only from Louis d'Orléans. Gradually they had dropped the coldness of the past few years; they conferred together, carefully avoiding all points on which their opinions might diverge. Once again Orléans played the role of royal host at Isabeau's side; at those times the Queen noticed how much her brother-in-law had changed over the years. He had lost much of his spontaneity, his natural bouyancy; but in its place were qualities that Isabeau found more attractive: a certain hardness, reticence and the ability to act quickly, at the precise moment. His mind, always simply brilliant, had now become sharp and incisive, flashing with menace, or making a deadly strike, as he chose. In short, he was now a mature man, and an extremely appealing and courteous one to boot.

Isabeau, encountering her brother-in-law face to face almost every day, could not hide from herself, after a relatively short time, the fact that her feelings for him were no longer only friendly. She did not resist this emotion; she did not wish to resist it. She was thirty-five years old; she had sacrificed the best years of her life to a madman who cursed her in his delirium and who terrorized her during his periods of so-called sanity by his strange words and inexplicable behavior. It was true that her sacrifice had some material purpose, but nevertheless she had suffered. At first, after the birth of her last child, she had wanted only to rest and dabble undisturbed in politics. But suddenly she began to crave the joys of love, to feel a longing that was all the more violent now that youth and beauty had gone forever. Her innate pride would not allow her to choose a paramour from among the nobles of her retinue; but toward the King's brother, who was already in many respects her husband's substitute, she did not feel such scruples. In this way could she not wreak on Valentine Visconti the vengeance which Gian Galeazzo had escaped through death? And Louis, bound to her by love, could perhaps serve her interests in other ways. The more she thought about it, the more attractive such a relationship appeared to her to be.

When Isabeau was with Orléans, she allowed herself to be dazzled by his charm; but when she was alone, when she saw her faded face in her mirror, she was seized by anguished uncertainty. If she had not desired Orléans, she would have been less upset, less vulnerable; she might even have responded to his flirtatiousness with cynicism or indifference. Isabeau did not completely lose her head; she was much too cold for that, too self-involved. She was restless, capricious and irritable; now she decided to hold a fête, then a hunting party—or an excursion to the Hôtel de la Bergerie or a picnic in the gardens of Saint-Pol, or perhaps a pilgrimage to cloisters and chapels. She left state affairs alone; even letters and messages from Bavaria went unanswered for the moment. For the first time in her life she scarcely thought about her children—the court noticed this with great astonishment.

The King heard of it when he was feeling slightly better again. He summoned the Dauphin to him and asked the child how long it had been since he had last seen his mother. The boy was frightened by the manner and appearance of the sick man: the King sat filthy and neglected in a darkened room. The Dauphin hesitated, but at last he said haltingly that his mother had not been near him for three months; his nurse took care of him and treated him with affection. When he heard that, the King burst into tears; he thanked the nurse for her devotion and presented her with the only valuable possession he could lay his hands on at that moment—his silver goblet. From that time he was seized by a melancholy apathy; he did not bathe nor change his clothes for months at a time; he slept and ate whenever he felt like it. Covered with sores and vermin, he squatted in a corner of his bedchamber. His physicians and servants, no longer under the Queen's watchful eye, troubled themselves about him as little as possible. They gave him his food and left him alone.

Louis d'Orléans could have put an end to this shocking state of affairs—but now he seldom visited his brother. Since he had allowed himself to be named Lieutenant-Governor of the realm once more, he was completely absorbed in his official duties. He spent months fortifying his castles, providing whatever supplies were needed for fortifications in the environs of Paris and Normandy. With regard to Jean of Burgundy, Louis followed the policy symbolized by his device of the thistle and stinging nettle: to prickle, to sting, to scratch severely the foot which tried to trample upon him. Toward Isabeau he was gallant; he wished in this way to influence her to declare null and void the marriage agreements between her children and Burgundy's children.

As soon as he got wind of this, Jean hurried back from Flanders. The King was not in a condition to receive him; the Queen and the Duke of Orléans had left Paris—they had set off with a great retinue to pay an official visit to the cities of Melun and Chartres. The Dauphin had been instructed to join them; he had ridden out of Paris with his own entourage only a few hours before Burgundy's arrival, accompanied by Ludwig of Bavaria who, alarmed by Isabeau's prolonged silence, had come to see how things stood. This fact settled the matter for Burgundy. With a company of armed horsemen, he rode at full gallop through the city, to the dismay of the people, who could not imagine what was going on.

Jean of Burgundy overtook the royal travelling party near Juvisy; horsemen and carriages came to a standstill and the Dauphin thrust his head out of the window of the palanquin to see what the cause of the delay might be. Burgundy asked the royal child to return with him to Paris, at first on his knees, and in the most respectful language; but before long, when the boy hesitated and appeared reluctant, in a less courteous manner. Finally he gave his followers the command to encircle the palanquin. So Jean of Burgundy conducted the Dauphin as well as the Dauphin's uncle of Bavaria back to the city, with a show of weapons and a flourish of trumpets, as though he had saved the heir to the throne from mortal danger.

The news spread throughout Paris like wild fire: Orléans and the Queen had tried to lead the child into an ambush, but thanks to the speedy appearance of Jean Sans Peur, the good and valiant hero, the Dauphin was now healthy and unscathed in the Louvre. The Rector of the University proceeded there with a company of learned gentlemen to give public thanks to Jean of Burgundy for his loyalty and devotion to the King's welfare.

Under these circumstances, the people, gathered into crowds in the streets, shouting with jubilation and excitement, were only too quickly disposed to lend an ear to those men who, here and there standing on a cask, a stone, the steps of a house, cursed Orléans and praised Burgundy to the skies. A few days later, in the name of the King and Council, orders were given to the city to begin to prepare itself for attack; from the storage rooms of the Châtelet iron chains were brought which could block the streets and wall off the districts. Meanwhile, Burgundy's allies and vassals, the Lords of Liège, Limburg and Cleves and their men, marched in great numbers into the city.

Jean of Burgundy was far from displeased with this state of affairs; but he felt compelled to justify his frenzied behavior, to give the appearance of well-considered action to his fit of rage. He sent to Parlement a declaration of protest, signed by him and his two brothers, expressing their indignation at the King's neglected condition, the irresponsible levying of taxes, the disorderly management of the royal domains and the corruption in the courts of justice. With real, inimitable skill, he knew precisely how to present himself as the accuser, the man who could lay his finger on the sore spot.

Swift as an arrow this perception of him caused him to rise in public favor.

Meanwhile Louis d'Orléans and Isabeau were at Melun. The Queen was assailed by doubt and anxiety: in the long run her publicly flaunted rapprochement with Louis might damage her interests more than it helped them. Burgundy seemed very sure of himself and he had, if the news from Paris were to be believed, public opinion with him. No matter how she wracked her brains, she could think of no way she could return in dignity to the city unless it was under Burgundy's protection or together with Orléans at the head of a triumphant army of troops. While Isabeau brooded in her apartments in the castle of Melun, Louis d'Orléans spent his time as profitably as possible, gathering his strength.

He summoned his vassals from all parts of his domains and sent couriers to his allies at home and abroad. To Melun came the Dukes of Lorraine and Alençon with 1,400 nobles and an army of men. All these soldiers had to find lodgings in the environs of Melun, to the considerable concern of the peasants and burghers. Orléans' messengers hurried to get to the cities throughout the Kingdom before Burgundy's messengers did; letters were delivered and placards posted warning against the scandalous libel which would soon reach from Paris to the farthest corners of France. The Duke of Orléans vowed that he would take suitable action to lay all these rumors to rest; until then he was counting on the loyalty of the people.

While he busied himself with these and similar matters, a delegation from the University was announced. Louis received them in a frame of mind that was anything but humble. The learned doctors, who had expected to find him cast-down and intimidated by Burgundy's actions, quickly realized their mistake. Considerably sobered, they recited their petition, taking care to greatly soften its lofty and peremptory tone.

"The University hopes with all its heart," said the spokesman in a low voice, with downcast eyes, "hopes with all its heart that peace will prevail in the Kingdom. In short, it desires nothing so ardently as a reconciliation between Monseigneur and the Duke of Burgundy."

Louis, who had listened impassively, let them wait before he answered. Finally, looking over their heads, he said coldly, "In my opinion it was not wise of you to express so openly your approval of the conduct of my cousin of Burgundy. You know that he acts against me. I do not need, surely, to remind you that I am the King's brother, and that in view of the state of his health and the Dauphin's extreme youth, it is I whom you must obey. It seems to me that you would do well to restrict yourselves to intellectual and spiritual concerns; you can safely leave the administration of the government to members of the royal House and the Council."

He paused and snapped his fingers impatiently. The learned doctors of the Sorbonne remained motionless, staring at the floor. They felt it expedient to assume a chastened demeanor.

"And as for a reconciliation between my lord of Burgundy and me . . . I was not aware that my cousin and I were at war. Where there is no war, gentlemen, there is nothing to reconcile. You have my permission to withdraw."

He waited, his face averted, until the delegation had left the room. Then he set out for Isabeau's apartments, to tell her his plans. He intended to return with her to Paris the following Saturday, accompanied by his entourage of allies and vassals amounting to more than a thousand men.

Isabeau, who suffered in warm weather from swollen, painful limbs, sat before the open window while her maid Femmette massaged her feet. Louis had become accustomed over the course of the year to being admitted to the Queen's presence without ceremony; he was struck now by Isabeau's obvious embarrassment, by the haste with which the maid straightened her mistress's garments. While he stood on the threshold of the chamber making gallant little jokes to put Isabeau at her ease, a thought struck him, swift and blinding as a flash of lightning.

He had treated the Queen with the familiarity, the camaraderie, of a kinsman; with a gallantry that was perhaps not always brotherly or simply friendly, but quite natural between a man and a woman of their age. Louis had noticed with some satisfaction how the Queen had revived in his company, he rejoiced with her over the return of her enjoyment of life and profited from it himself. He had known in advance that their friendship would be blown out of all proportion; given the facts of court life, a love affair between the Queen and him would seem only too credible. He knew that Isabeau was extremely offended by this slander, but he considered her sensible enough to put up with a little annoyance if her self-interest was involved.

However now, on entering the Queen's chambers in Melun, Louis suddenly realized the real reasons for the Queen's contentment as well as for her rages—her blush, her glance, something indefinable about the way she quickly concealed her large swollen feet under the hem of her dress—these told him, more plainly than words. The discovery filled him with horror; he knew only too well what the consequences would be if he wanted to continue in her good graces. Nothing is more dangerous than the disappointment of a woman who thinks that she is in love, especially when her nature is essentially hard and wilful. Burgundy was waiting with Isabeau's brother in the fortified city of Paris; the Queen's inner uncertainty, moreover, was evident. If Orléans did not manage to bind her to him, he would drive her irrevocably into the camp of the enemy; he knew her too well not to fear the ease with which she could leap from one extreme to the other.

He thought of the King his brother, a defenseless invalid; of Valentine, to whom he had been faithful since the death of Mariette de Cany. While he moved slowly into the room he stared at Isabeau: at her greedy mouth, her soft hands which would release only reluctantly anything that came into their grasp. Stifling the great despondent sigh which welled up in him, he bowed deeply before the Queen, whose smiles could no longer be misconstrued.

The next day he sent couriers to the city of Provins with a hundred golden écus to buy roses for Her Majesty.

When Jean of Burgundy learned that Orléans was approaching the city with an army, he ordered his horse to be saddled, and rode to the palace where the Council was assembled.

"Well, Messeigneurs," he called contemptuously to Berry and Bourbon who sat among the peers of the realm, "what I predicted is happening. Orléans is on his way to Paris with about 2,000 men; Alençon and Lorraine are with him, and the Queen rides in the procession. Don't say now that he comes in friendship, although his reply to the lords of the University might perhaps have led you to believe that."

Bourbon rose, with some difficulty, and held up his hands in a placatory gesture.

"No one can tell our nephew of Orléans not to gather men around him, now that you have armed half the city!"

Jean of Burgundy kicked his long riding cloak to one side.

"It is no accident," he remarked, "that Orléans' banners carry the motto 'I challenge' in defiance of my own device 'I hold'. Well, this time he can count on a warm reception. Most quarters are fortified—the burghers have been given weapons and students who can handle pitch and stones as well as Latin are waiting outside the bridge. Yes, the brave citizens intend to defend themselves and me, my lords. They know where their interests lie!"

Bourbon threw up his hands, looking helplessly about him, but Berry who, like an old bird of prey on a branch, surveyed the hall from his elevated chair, said ironically, "But that means civil war." He declared himself ready to work with both sides to reconcile their differences. This attitude reflected the line he had taken since his illness.

After due deliberations the Provost of Paris, de Tignonville, was sent as the head of a delegation to meet Orléans in the name of the Chancellor and the chairman of Parlement. De Tignonville and Louis had always gotten on well together and Louis, following de Tignonville's advice, sent an announcement to Paris that, for the sake of the populace and in order to preserve peace in the Kingdom, he had voluntarily renounced armed conflict, although he had every right to attack. Jean of Burgundy, not wishing to hurt his reputation as the people's benefactor, had no choice but to lay down his arms.

Most of the troops billeted in and around the city were sent home. Once more Isabeau entered Paris, but this time the festive note was struck only by the gay trappings of her procession. The people stood in silence, darkly watching as the entourage wound through the streets. There were gold-brocaded palanquins, plumed horses, a plethora of banners and canopies, but the escort was armed to the teeth and the smiles of the beautiful ladies were joyless.

On the following day the royal kinsmen proceeded to Notre Dame where, before the Queen, the Dauphin, the Dukes of Berry and Bourbon and a great number of dignitaries, Jean of Burgundy and Louis of Orléans shook hands in a formal show of mutual apology. From a distance it seemed a noble gesture, but those who stood close by were later to recall vividly not the handshake but the look in both men's eyes.

On the twenty-ninth of June, in the year 1406, Charles d'Orléans married his cousin Isabelle, once Queen of England. The wedding was celebrated in Compiègne; on the same day the King's second son took to wife the small daughter of the Countess of Hainault. Charles, carefully coached by his mother about what he must say and do at the altar and at the great receptions, seemed a good deal more at ease than he had been a few years earlier at Senlis. His father's presence gave him self-confidence; he could see now with his own eyes that his father was indeed the most powerful man in the Kingdom. The boy spoke little, but noticed everything; it was not natural for him to push himself forward.

In a hall where, in the torch and candlelight, the pomp and splendor of the chivalric romances seemed to become reality, Charles met his bride for the first time. She stood amid queens and princesses, under a canopy embroidered with lilies; she was clad in gold, azure and purple. Charles, kneeling before her, dared not raise his eyes higher than the gleaming hem of her dress: she was so much older than he, weighed more than he did, and—most important—was already the widow of a king. He felt he could not possibly be worthy of this high and noble lady. He was—and he knew it better than anyone else—still a boy, and not accomplished in chivalry. He knew little of courtly behavior, and even less about dancing and love-making. The only women he knew were his mother and the ladies of her court and the beautiful queens about whom he read in his favorite books. In short, he was not yet thirteen years old, and deeply conscious of his disadvantages as a bridegroom.

Isabelle greeted him courteously, but her voice lacked warmth and she did not smile. She was sixteen years old and almost a head taller than her intended husband. No one would ever know about the tears she had shed over the humiliation of this marriage to a small boy who was, moreover, her inferior in rank. Isabelle had been long accustomed to controlling her emotions in a royal manner; she was determined to conceal her dismay at any price, in order to avoid pity or ridicule. Pale and impassive, she stood once more in bridal finery among her ladies. Charles d'Orléans she ignored; she felt his embarrassed uncertainty, and this added to her irritation. Standing beside Isabelle, Charles did his best to follow his mother's advice and make up in outward dignity for his insecurity.

He was distracted momentarily when the heralds raised their trumpets to announce the approach of the Duchess of Holland and Hainault with her little daughter Jacoba of Bavaria, the bride of the

King's second son. The opulence displayed by the Princess from the Netherlands and her retinue surpassed anything ever seen at Saint-Pol—to the considerable annoyance of Isabeau, who was jealous of her kinsmen's wealth. This rivalry went on during the entire week of festivities: where France was arrayed in silver, Hainault gleamed with gold; ten Flemish knights escorted the bridal procession to five French; and the largesse distributed among the attending populace at the request of the Bavarian bride was more than royal.

For the first few days Charles enjoyed the crowds, the pageants, tournaments and solemn services; banquet followed upon banquet; the music did not seem to stop even for an instant. But finally the festivities tired the boy, who was accustomed to a life of routine, without much excitement or diversion. After the marriage ceremony, he sat, sleepy and silent, at the great banquet given in honor of the two young couples. Isabelle, seated beside him on the garlanded bench, did not speak; on the other side of the table were the prince and his bride, young children who barely understood what was happening. The adults at the royal table, after the obligatory speeches and toasts, wasted little more attention on the bridal couples. They became involved in lively conversations. It was rare for so illustrious a company to come together; there were many questions to be asked, and much to talk about and, after cups of wine, much to joke about and to argue about.

The Countess of Hainault wished to take her small son-in-law to her castle in Quesnoy. Isabeau did not want her child to leave. The advantages and disadvantages of his departure were discussed in detail by the royal kinsmen.

For Charles, who could scarcely keep his eyes open, the impressions flowed together; the red and gold of his father's clothes, the women's sparkling headdresses, the long purple row of clergy; the light of the setting sun glowing in the stained glass windows in the festive hall, the profusion of splendidly served dishes. He was just dozing off when Isabelle pulled roughly at his arm.

"You cannot fall asleep now," she whispered sharply; in her indignation she forgot all ceremony. "You will disgrace me. You must sit up straight and behave properly, even though you don't like it. We cannot run away!"

Her words jolted Charles back to reality; he was wide awake instantly from sheer astonishment that the cold, elegant Isabelle could behave unexpectedly like the ladies of the court in Château-Thierry. Hastily he began to apologize, but stopped in confusion when he noticed that her eyes were filled with tears. She did not wipe them away but sat motionless, her lips compressed; she stared fixedly at the head of the table where Isabeau sat, as hostess, between Orléans and Burgundy.

"I'm dreadfully sorry," said Charles hesitantly. "I did not intend to offend you, Madame."

Isabelle shrugged scornfully; her eyes were still on her mother.

I shall never forgive her for this, thought Isabelle, once Queen of England and now only Countess d'Angoulême. She has mortified me only to win the favor of Monseigneur d'Orléans. She would just as soon I go away—my eyes and ears are too sharp. I hate her—I hate her—and I will never forget it, not if I live to be a hundred.

So thought Charles' young wife in fury and despair. Her rage was not directed so much at her father-in-law as at her mother, although she knew that Orléans had become the Queen's lover the previous autumn. He had always treated Isabelle with obvious affection. Only he had been willing to take arms to avenge her grief. True, Isabelle was bitterly disappointed in her childhood idol; but she blamed her mother, whom she thought hard and grasping, and who, once she had set her mind on something, refused to budge. With deep horror, Isabelle had witnessed the arrival at Saint-Pol of Odette de Champdivers, a young girl of her own age, born of a noble family, brought to share the King's bed now that Isabeau had found love elsewhere.

"Why are you crying?" asked Charles, tormented by guilt. "I promise I will not fall asleep again. I'm not sleepy any more anyway. Shall I tell you about Château-Thierry?"

Isabelle nodded; anything was better than a yawning bridegroom and a weeping bride. There were enough jokes circulating about them already. Charles, delighted that he could evince his good will, spoke quickly.

"I have magnificent books, Madame. Do you know the history of Perceval of Gaul? My tutor, Maître Garbet, says no one in the Kingdom has a finer library than Orléans. Maître Garbet has written a poem in Latin in honor of you and me on the flyleaf of my Sallustius. I can recite it to you, if you like." Charles thought a moment—yes, he still remembered it. Flushed with excitement, he spoke the stately lines:

> *"Anglorum regno pro morte privata mariti*
> *Formoso moribus Ludovici filio ducis*
> *Aurelianensis Karolo Compendii pulchra*
> *Francorum nupsit Isabellis filia regis*
> *Anno millesimo julii sexto*
> *Vicesima nona. Faveant superi precor ipsis . . ."*

He stopped when Isabelle sighed impatiently. Remembering Valentine's wise advice, Charles tried another tack. "My mother has beautifully trained falcons, Madame. Four white ones are named after the four sons of Haimon. Are you fond of hunting? Did you bring your horse with you? In Château-Thierry, we have—"

"I am weeping for the King my father," Isabelle burst out fiercely. "Because he is ill and cannot defend himself. Because of what they do to him. Do you know what happened?"

She wheeled sharply to face Charles and looked him straight in the eye. The youth was taken aback at her vehemence; he glanced quickly around him, but the guests were engrossed in wine and rich food; no one was paying any attention to the children. The Dauphin and little Jacoba of Bavaria were throwing food at each other and squealing with laughter, overjoyed because no one stopped them. Charles and Isabelle sat among their shrieking companions as though they were in an enchanted circle of solitude.

"My father was so filthy, so filthy," continued Isabelle with a shudder. "He got sick from it; he sat covered with boils and sores. If they speak to him kindly he lets them help him, but they treated him with violence. Men with blackened faces forced their way into his room—he thought the Devil had come to fetch him. I heard him scream. Alas, God, my poor father . . ."

"Yes, Madame," Charles said, with downcast eyes. Do all women speak of sorrow then? he thought, astonished. When he had come to Compiègne and seen the streamers fluttering in the wind, he had been inclined to think his mother was wrong; the world was not a vale of tears and grief. Now he was not so sure.

"He cannot defend himself," Isabelle went on in a rapid whisper. "He must look on while they rob and deceive him, my mother and your father."

With some satisfaction she saw the boy's face turn pale with anger and fear. She read his ignorance in his eyes. So Madame Isabelle found suitable employment on her first day of marriage. She bent toward her husband and whispered for a long time into his ear; why should she feel sorry for a stupid boy and spare him suffering? No one had taken pity on her, no one had spared her suffering! Alas, it was a dreary tale she told Charles; he did not understand half of what she whispered to him.

"It is not true," he said at last, close to tears, but he knew it was true. Things his mother had said flashed through his mind; things which had been incomprehensible to him.

"Not true?" Isabelle laughed. "Everyone knows it, everyone talks about how shameful it is. On Ascension Day—I was there myself— a priest from the University preached before the court in Saint-Pol; in front of everyone he rebuked my mother and my lord of Orléans for their adultery. My mother did not dare to punish the man—do you understand what that means? Do you think he would be alive now if he had lied?"

Charles, upset by the picture she called up, pressed his fists to his eyes with a childish awkward gesture. But Madame Isabelle considered that the account was not yet balanced.

"A few weeks ago they were together in the castle of Saint-Germain," she went on, in that sibilant whisper which now filled Charles with dread. "Do you know they nearly died? Surely God wanted to punish them. A storm broke while they were out riding— the horses bolted; if someone had not thrown himself in front of the horses to stop them, they would have run into the Seine, carriage and all. Is that not a sign?"

Charles could stand it no longer; he wanted to leap up and run from the table, escape—he did not know where—but not to Château-Thierry, not to his mother. He did not dare see her again, he thought, overcome by feelings of boundless misery. He wished that all this were not true, that he could wake up instantly as though from a nightmare, in his own bed with the green curtains or over an open book in the quiet reading room. How could he ever return there now that he knew that the tranquillity of his own small world was only illusory? He would never be alone again; everywhere and always Isabelle would be with him, because she was his wife forever. And wherever Isabelle was, there would always be the dreadful thing which she had just told him. He leapt up from the place of honor before Isabelle could stop him and ran from the table without a backward look; while he shoved his way through the crowd of nobles, pages and spectators, he heard behind him the loud, caustic voice of the Duke of Burgundy:

"Look, look, my lord of Angoulême feels somewhat faint! Yes, one celebrates one's nuptials only once . . ." and something else which he did not understand. The walls rang with their laughter.

Charles did not know how long he had stayed hidden in the darkened room when suddenly he heard his father's voice close by. Even in the gloom the boy could see the glimmer of the jewels stitched onto his tunic.

"What is it, my son? Did you drink a little too much?" Louis bent over the boy. "Why have you crept in here? It is not polite to leave your bride. Do you still feel too sick to go back to the table?"

"No, my lord," Charles said in a stifled voice. He could hardly stand the warm touch of his father's hand.

"Have you quarrelled with your wife already?" Orléans laughed softly and pressed the boy's head against his breast. The golden ornaments cut into Charles' forehead; he clenched his teeth and tensed his body. "Come along now," Louis said persuasively, "before people start to talk. The Queen is becoming uneasy. What is the matter with you, lad? Are you bewitched? Come along now and amuse your wife. Does she know what sort of gift you have brought for her?"

Silently, Charles allowed himself to be led back to the festive hall, to his place of honor beside Madame Isabelle, who sat staring at her plate. She wanted to make up for what she had done, but she knew it was too late. She had not anticipated the effect her words would have on her twelve-year-old husband. In a few hours the quiet, childish youth had changed: his head drooped slightly and his eyes seemed suddenly disturbingly wise. But it was impossible for Isabelle to express her contrition or sympathy; she was not capable of such selflessness. She contented herself with behaving in a less unfriendly manner during the remainder of the feast. While dessert was being served, Charles mentioned with hesitation the gift which he had brought her from Château-Thierry: a puppy dog, the pick of a choice litter.

"He knows all sorts of tricks," Charles said, revived somewhat by thinking of the dog. "He is snow white and his name is Doucet."

No one knew—Charles least of all—why Madame Isabelle burst into tears at that precise moment; a storm of violent, unquenchable weeping which cast a pall over the evening's pleasure, and astonished the royal guests. Neither words of comfort nor reprimands, neither music nor fools' play could calm her. Everyone but Isabelle had forgotten that King Richard had given her a white dog as a bridal gift, a white greyhound which once had been a trusted friend, but which had later—Isabelle still cringed at the memory—licked Lancaster's hand.

What was for many the high point of all the ceremonies occurred at the end of a week of celebration: in the presence of the Council, the clergy, nobles and lawyers, Louis of Orléans and Jean of Burgundy swore on the Cross and the Holy Gospels to be friends and brothers-in-arms from that moment on, to protect, assist and defend each other at all times and, so united, to strive against the English who, despite all armistice agreements, had taken possession of Calais, Brest and the other major ports.

Those who knew him well were amazed that Burgundy would enter into such an agreement, but most of the witnesses of the ceremony were delighted that the feud between the two kinsmen seemed to have ended.

After the ceremony, the Queen and Council returned to Paris; Burgundy departed with his entourage for Flanders and Louis d'Orléans brought his son and Isabelle to Château-Thierry where Valentine received her daughter-in-law festively. At first Isabelle had thought that it would be extremely difficult to live in amity with a woman she had been taught from her childhood to despise. But her hatred of her own mother made her feel close to the Duchess of Orléans—were they not both the victims of Isabeau's lust for power?

The girl noticed with admiration Valentine's dignified and forbearing attitude toward her husband; but after Louis departed, Isabelle, purely by accident, saw the collapse of Valentine's defenses against her pent-up misery. For one whole night the two women wept in each other's arms, each for herself and for the other. Both profited from this: Valentine was able to articulate her grief; Isabelle was no longer surly.

While this went on Charles slept unaware in his childhood room; within the green curtains of his familiar bed the fears which he had brought home with him from Compiègne faded into half-forgotten dreams. As he had done before, he listened attentively to the lessons taught by Maître Garbet, and as he had done before, he immersed himself with pleasure in his books while Philippe, Jean and Dunois, strong, agile and cheerful children playing around him, treated their older brother with a mixture of respect and good-natured derision.

"If you had a tonsure now, brother," Philippe called from the door during Charles' lesson, "I could not tell you from a monk. And you are married, too."

Yes, surely he was married. At first he often forgot to show Isabelle the chivalrous deference that was her due at table or when they were entering or leaving church or chapel. But gradually he came to look upon her as a member of the family and to regard her also as his mother's trusted friend and relative. Isabelle lived and slept near Valentine; together they sat embroidering or reading and together they went hunting or tended the flowers in the castle garden.

The Duchess of Orléans thought it was time that her oldest son learned something about his father's affairs. She talked to him about everything that had happened in the past, explained the governance of the varied domains both inside and outside France, and gave him all the news which she received regularly from Paris. Thanks to the discussions in Compiègne, Charles understood something of the political situation; he knew now too that his father with an army of 6,000 men was besieging the city of Bourg, which was occupied by English invaders, and that the Duke of Burgundy was mustering men and weapons at Saint-Omer so that he could advance upon Calais. Although Charles did not share his younger brothers' fierce fascination with military exploits, he followed the development of these events attentively.

He was disappointed to learn that his father had been forced after three months to lift the siege of Bourg; the city seemed impregnable and a plague had broken out among Orléans' men. But he was completely astonished by the news that the King and Council, who from the outset had given Burgundy every conceivable encouragement, had suddenly declared that the preparations at Saint-Omer must cease, and had gone so far as to send threats and warning letters to Burgundy's vassals to stop them from participation. Valentine smiled oddly when she heard these tidings; she and Isabelle exchanged an understanding glance. Charles was indignant; he was certain that Burgundy would be deeply offended by these actions. "Monseigneur of Burgundy sits in Saint-Omer with a whole army," he said. "Much time and money have been spent to gather men and weapons. That order from the King and Council is senseless; what will happen in the city of Calais now?"

"Hush, boy," Valentine replied with unusual tartness. "It is not proper for you to blame the King. I think there is a good reason for these measures; we shall learn soon enough why the Duke of Burgundy was prevented from laying siege to Calais."

The residents of Château-Thierry were to learn these reasons; but not until much later, and in deeply tragic circumstances.

On the twenty-second of November in the year 1407, Louis of Orléans and Jean of Burgundy met once more in the house of the Duke of Berry, the Hôtel de Nesle. This banquet concluded a ceremonial rapprochement between the two cousins. Since the aborted expedition against the English the previous year, they had quarrelled incessantly in private, in the presence of kinsmen, at Council meetings, in writing and through the words of couriers. Burgundy charged Louis with having prompted the King to forbid his laying siege to Calais out of sheer jealousy because his own enterprise had come to nothing. Orléans denied this with the same stubborn conviction. Their behavior caused the kinsmen to fear a fresh outbreak of hostilities.

Berry allowed himself to be persuaded to act as peacemaker; with reluctance he took leave of Bicêtre and his beloved collection for a while and set out for the Hôtel de Nesle, where his young wife usually resided. After long discussions, many admonitions and much advice, Berry finally brought his nephews to the point of declaring themselves ready to conclude a new treaty of peace and friendship, and this time forever. Once more they stood together before the altar, swore an oath and took communion. Berry, not a little relieved to have acquitted himself well of a painful charge, invited Orléans and Burgundy to a banquet; they drank from the same goblet and sat side by side in the seat of honor, Burgundy wearing Orléans' emblems and Orléans in the colors of Burgundy. At the end of the feast Louis invited his cousin to be his guest the following Sunday, and Jean accepted with courtesy.

Orléans saluted his kinsmen now and set out, accompanied by a small retinue, for the Hôtel Barbette, which belonged to Isabeau, and where in recent years she had stayed more and more frequently.

She had ordered it rebuilt and redecorated; new gardens were laid out around the house. It was within easy reach of Saint-Pol. The Queen had lived there uninterruptedly since spring; the court interpreted this as a sign that Isabeau wanted her new pregnancy to be considered her own affair, without concern for state or Crown. Orléans visited her regularly, treating her with a concerned courtesy for which the reason seemed all too apparent.

About the middle of November, Isabeau had given birth to a child who lived only a few days. The Queen lay in her bed, weak and listless; she believed the child's death was a punishment for her adultery. In addition, she was uncertain about her political behavior; now that the first intoxication of her passion for Louis was over, she did not feel inclined to support his plans in every way. When Louis entered her chamber she raised herself slightly and greeted him, but for the first time in a long time there was no trace of softness in her eyes.

"I hear everything has gone extremely well," she remarked, gesturing to a chair that stood beside her bed. Louis sat down. "Will peace remain now between you and Burgundy?" Isabeau continued, somewhat maliciously. "Or do you propose to continue indefinitely this little game of fighting and reconciliation? So much time has been lost. During the Council sessions little is discussed except this quarrel between the two of you."

Orléans shrugged; he looked tired—he had not yet completely recovered from an illness he had suffered at the siege of Bourg.

"If I knew for certain that my cousin was a man of good will," he began hesitantly, but he did not finish the sentence. Isabeau leaned back against the pillows and stretched her fleshy arms in a langorous gesture over the bed cover. "Are you not inclined too quickly to believe the opposite, Monseigneur?" she asked, yawning.

"Burgundy is playing a double game," Louis said wearily, slumping forward with his hand pressed against his eyes. "How could it be otherwise? It's to his advantage. He does what his father did before him—and I don't deny that they both conducted these policies with skill. But that means our downfall." He raised his head and looked at Isabeau who lay eating candied fruit without taking her cold, searching eyes from him. "How can anyone who has witnessed the events of the last few years doubt Burgundy's purpose? Calais lies well-situated near Flanders. He who has Calais and Flanders in his power has little to fear. If Burgundy should wrest Calais from the English—well, I for one refuse to believe that he would ever restore it to the Crown."

Isabeau made a doubting sound; she was in a strangely irritable mood. Although she did not think Orléans was wrong, she wanted to contradict him. Louis looked with pensive resignation at this woman whom, out of calculation and ambition, he had made his own. The relationship had undeniably been advantageous for him; but he despised himself immeasurably for his betrayal of his brother and Valentine—and of Isabeau herself, whose passion, at any rate, had been genuine. Alas, one did not need to have particularly sharp eyes to see that it was all over between the two of them. The death of their child, the fruit of an exceedingly strange relationship, had caused a chill, and disenchantment. Orléans gazed around the small bedchamber in which he had so frequently been a guest; he was filled with bitter melancholy at his own failure. The silk hangings painted with coats of arms stirred gently on the walls; often at night he had lain, restless and discontented, and stared at the lions, falcons and lilies.

He looked at Isabeau, sitting in the large, purple-curtained bed, extremely corpulent in her loose clothing, with a towel wound carelessly around her head. She licked her lower lip as she took the candy from the dish. Orléans lowered his eyes. From the adjoining room came the sound of impatient barking. There, with Femmette and the Queen's ladies, Doucet was waiting, the little white dog which Isabelle had refused to accept. Louis kept the animal near him; it was very attached to him.

"I hope, Madame, that you will speedily recover your health," Louis said, standing up.

From the corner of her eye, Isabeau gave him a long look. "You don't mourn your son, do you?" she asked finally in a muffled voice.

"He needs no mourning," replied Louis calmly, "for he committed no sin and owes God no account of his short life. I consider that he was lucky—what would his place have been among the King's children, Madame?"

Isabeau laughed, a dry, fierce laugh without mirth.

"Why should the King be less generous toward a bastard than your wife has been to the boy—what do you call him? . . . The son of Mariette de Cany?"

Her sharp, malicious words stayed with Louis as he walked through the anterooms, followed by Doucet. He thought for the first time in years of the lovely but austere Maret, who had atoned for her guilt by giving up her most precious possession—her life. He had desired her not only for her youth and beauty, but particularly for that other indescribable quality which lay concealed in her like a precious jewel in a casket. During all the years that he had vainly sought her favor, he had never been able to understand precisely what that captivating and at the same time impalpable element could be. Long after he had conquered her and carried her off, when she lay stretched out, smiling, between candles—only then did he realize what she had represented in his life: a cool purity, chastity, fidelity to an inner law, the power of self-discipline, self-sacrifice and resignation to the inevitable—she embodied all these attributes which he had always aspired to, but had never been able to achieve. Because she could see no possibility of preserving that purity inviolate, she had died.

Not without deep shame could Louis think of Dunois who was stained with his guilt. Isabeau's words called up a number of half-forgotten images and a feeling of strong self-loathing. As so often before, Louis hid this dark mood behind a mask of joviality. No one must see that he walked on knives. He set out for the hall where an evening meal would be served up for him and his entourage, but before he could sit down at the table he was told that a messenger had arrived from Saint-Pol—one of the King's servants wished to speak with him.

The man stood in an antechamber, still out of breath, which surprised Louis slightly; he had been told that the messenger had been waiting for some time.

"My lord," said the man, bowing deeply, "the King entreats you to come to him without delay—he must speak to you at once about a matter which is of deep concern to both you and him."

"I am about to go to table," replied Louis, but the servant continued breathlessly, "You must go immediately, Monseigneur—there is not a moment to lose."

Louis thought that the King had suddenly become seriously ill; he prepared to leave at once, urging the gentlemen of his suite to sit down and eat without him. He left the Hôtel Barbette accompanied by only a few nobles on horseback and Jacques van Hersen, who had once been his squire but who for the last several years had been his personal attendant.

Louis rode a mule, a beautiful beast which he had had sent from

Lombardy. He sat carelessly in the saddle and let the reins hang loose. To conceal his annoyance and anxiety he hummed a tune and toyed with a glove. The dog Doucet leaped forward exuberantly beside the mule; the torchbearers ran ahead. Thus the small procession left Isabeau's residence. Without undue haste the lord and his retinue rode through the Barbette gate and entered the dark alley which led to the rue Vieille du Temple.

It was a mild, humid November evening; it was not raining but a fine vapor hovered in the air. Louis coughed and pulled his cloak closer about him. He saw on his right, by the light of the torches, the building which was called the House of the Effigy of Our Lady, because a statue of the Virgin Mary stood in a niche in its façade. Louis never passed the spot without lifting his eyes to the brightly painted, stiffly smiling image. Now as always he glanced at the old house, which had been empty for years.

At that moment a young woman was standing at the window of her house opposite the House of the Effigy. Her name was Jacquette and she was the wife of a ropemaker, Jean Griffart; she had gone to the window to see if her husband was coming and to take in some washing which she had hung out to dry at noon. The torches in the street belonged to a distinguished company; a gentleman on horseback, attended by a groom and followed at some distance by five or six horsemen, came riding from the direction of the Barbette gate—a small white dog leaped in front of its master. Jacquette Griffart looked down at the procession for a moment— then she turned, intending to put her child to bed. But before she had taken three steps, a loud cry sounded from the alley: "Kill him! Kill him!" With the child in her arms, she hurried back to the window. The nobleman had fallen from his mount—he had slumped to his knees in the middle of the street, bareheaded, the blood streaming from his face.

"Who is that? Who is doing that?" he said weakly, raising his arms as though to ward off a blow. Now armed men swarmed upon him from all sides—they struck home with sticks, knives, axes. The blows echoed in Jacquette's ears; it sounded as though they were beating a mattress, a lifeless thing.

She regained her voice and shrieked, "Murder!", pushing the window open. A stone hissed past her cheek and a man who stood in the shadows under the window shrieked, "Shut up, woman!"

More torchbearers appeared from the House of the Effigy of Our

Lady; by the flickering red glow the woman, softly wailing with terror, saw something formless and unrecognizable lying on the ground. The mule had galloped off in fright; the little dog yelped from a distance away. Jacquette heard the shouts of hurrying men coming from adjacent streets—there was nothing at all to be seen of the riders who had followed many paces behind the distinguished horseman. The squire, however, who had been wounded trying in vain to defend his master during the attack, now began to creep toward him. At the command of a long-haired, emaciated man in a monk's habit, they gave him the death blow; he lay sprawled partially over the body of his lord. Out of the House of the Effigy of Our Lady, followed by a youth leading a horse by the reins, came a tall man, his head covered by a red bonnet. He held a lappet of the bonnet before his nose and mouth, but Jacquette saw the glitter of very dark eyes above the concealing cloth.

"Douse the torches," he said. "Let's get out; he's dead. Come on, don't make any mistakes!"

The man in the red bonnet leaped onto his horse and galloped off down a side street. The armed men followed him as quickly as they could; they hurled their torches away or extinguished them in the mud. Soon the street was plunged into darkness except where a torch still smouldered on the ground beside the dead man.

"Murder, murder!" Jacquette screamed again. She heard her cry taken up in the rue Vieille du Temple and in the rue des Rosiers. From the direction of the Barbette gate, many people came running with torches; before long the street was filled with people. A nobleman in silk clothes flung himself down in the mud beside the two bodies.

"Monseigneur!" he cried desperately. "Monseigneur! Messire van Hersen!"

The squire was still alive; they laid him down on a cloak under the arched doorway of a house. The dying man moaned words unintelligible to the onlookers. "My lord . . . both of us . . . in the Celestine monastery . . . The omen . . . the omen . . ."

The body of the distinguished lord lay in a pool of blood and mud; his skull was cloven in two places so that the brains protruded; someone had lopped off the left arm between elbow and wrist. The hand was found some distance away in a gutter, and placed on a litter with the rest of the corpse. Even before the dead man was borne away, a new calamity struck: flames burst through the ground floor windows of the House of the Effigy of Our Lady. "Fire, fire!" screamed the excited crowd; pails of water were dragged over to quench the blaze.

"In God's name, what was that?" cried Jacquette, who still stood at the open window, trembling with cold and horror; without knowing what she did, she rocked the desperately screaming baby. "Whom have they killed there?"

A man passed by, dragging a bag of sand; he looked up and grinned sardonically, as though he brought good news.

"Orléans!" he replied. "Orléans the blood-sucker, our tormentor! May God rest his soul!"

As soon as the murder was made known at court, a messenger left Paris for Château-Thierry. While the man, bent low in the saddle, urged his horse to greater speed, residents of the castle, still unaware of their affliction, were celebrating the joyful fact that Monseigneur Charles had been born on that day fourteen years before.

II. OF VALENTINE, THE MOTHER

ð

"Rien ne m'est plus, plus ne m'est rien."
"Nothing has meaning any more."
—Motto of Valentine of Milan

n the tenth of December, 1407, the Duchess of Orléans returned to Paris after an absence of eleven years. She arrived in a carriage draped in black, drawn by six black horses; beside her sat her youngest son, Jean, and her daughter-in-law, Madame Isabelle, the King's daughter. Valentine's carriage was followed by an almost endless procession of riders: among them, along with officers of the ducal household, were many of Orléans' vassals with their armed soldiers, friends and intimates.

Valentine was solemnly greeted at the city gate by the most exalted nobility; Berry and Bourbon showed the widow the honor which they had all too prudently withheld from their nephew's wife when she had departed the city years earlier. The Duchess of Orléans sat motionless in the carriage. She was white as snow; her staring eyes were vacant. Isabelle clutched her hand, more terrified by her mother-in-law's icy calm than she had been by the outbursts of despair and savage grief to which Valentine had abandoned herself when she had heard the tragic news. Isabelle had not believed it possible that a noble lady would carry on so, screaming and weeping, lying on the ground in torn clothing. Valentine had been like a madwoman; she had refused food and drink and beat her forehead against the earth, which will never give up its dead.

The small children had been too frightened to come to her; but Isabelle and Charles had kept the Duchess company day and night in the chapel of the castle. Kneeling on either side of the despairing woman, they prayed aloud, not eating, not sleeping, like Valentine herself. Isabelle, who prided herself secretly on having learned to bear suffering while she was still a child, maintained an exemplary attitude like a martyr on a tapestry; even during the long hours of kneeling, she betrayed no sign of weariness. She held the tips of her fingers firmly pressed together, her head erect, her eyes fixed upon the altar.

Charles could not control himself that well; the hoarse sound of his mother's weeping filled him with bottomless horror and compassion. He was tormented also by shame because he could not share her grief—it was true that his father's death had frightened him dreadfully, but he was upset for completely different reasons from his mother. Who had planned this outrageous murder? What was behind all this—was it possible that his father was once more somehow to blame? Charles no longer saw the Duke as a fearless hero without blemish, as he had done in his childhood. No, not since Compiègne. But with the knowledge of his father's faults had come a certain sobriety; he had lost his childish ways forever. He was in a difficult transitional period—he was no longer a boy and not yet a young man. He felt everything passionately, but at the same time he was constricted by the armor of his own clumsiness. He looked with trepidation toward the new, weighty duties which were about to descend upon him.

At the moment when, for the first time, members of his family and servants, bowing deeply, called him Duke of Orléans, a chill seized his heart. He was the head of the family, lord of great and important domains; the dignity of his House rested wholly upon his shoulders.

While his mother, beside herself with misery, lay on the cold flagstones of the chapel, there was chaos and alarm in the castle of Château-Thierry; no one knew what to do, no one issued orders. Charles realized that it was up to him to act—but what did they expect of him? Often during the long, mournful vigil he looked timidly at Isabelle. How could she pray so calmly and with such dignity? This strangely mature maiden was his wife—they shared happiness and sorrow; he wished she could give him some helpful advice. But when he dared to open his mouth, she gave him such a look of warning reproach that he stopped, shamefaced.

After three days Valentine rose from the ground; she sat stony-faced and dressed in black in the great hall and issued commands: messengers were sent to summon Orléans' friends and vassals, while two groups of horsemen and servants were ordered to prepare immediately for a journey—one group to escort the Duchess to Paris, the other to bring Monseigneur Charles and his brothers Philippe and Dunois to the fortified castle of Blois where, during their mother's absence, they would be safe from Orléans' enemies.

Silent, Valentine sat in the carriage during the long journey through the wintry countryside; silent she rode into Paris without a glance at the city which she had left with so much regret eleven years before. Isabelle did look about her: she saw the faces of the people along the way. With curiosity tinged with grim satisfaction, the people of Paris watched Orléans' widow ride slowly through the streets to Saint-Pol.

The Provost de Tignonville and Jean Juvenal des Ursins, the Advocate-Fiscal, waited in the King's anterooms, surrounded by clerks and lawyers; they would tell the Duchess what they had discovered about the murder before she put her affairs in the King's hands. Valentine sat down without a word. Her chancellor and spokesman remained standing behind her. The Dukes of Berry and Bourbon exchanged concerned, even alarmed, glances. At last Berry ended the oppressive silence by asking de Tignonville to speak.

"Madame," began the Provost in a voice that betrayed his emotion, but he swallowed his expressions of sympathy before this woman petrified with grief. He began slowly and precisely to relate the results of the inquiry.

"We have thoroughly interrogated, Madame, the two eye-witnesses: the wife of a ropemaker and a servant from a manor house. Both testified that the assailant seemed to have come from the place called the House of the Effigy of Our Lady—in fact a fire broke out there directly after the crime, but it was quickly extinguished. We know that the premises in question had been unoccupied for many years; a few months ago, however, the owner rented them to a person who said he was a student at the University. He was described as an extremely thin man with long hair, who wore a brown tabard. And the eye-witness, Jacquette Griffart, has told us that the assault was led by a thin, long-haired man in a dark cloak. We have learned that a stranger in a red bonnet gave the command to flee. This same man was subsequently seen in the neighborhood of the Hôtel d'Artois."

At these words Valentine raised her head; the Duke of Berry coughed nervously. The Provost calmly met the Duchess's penetrating gaze, and continued.

"Now it is my opinion, Madame, that we can suspend the investigation in the city itself. It would be better, it seems to me, to question the servants and officials of the royal palaces. The King has already granted me full authorization to enter with my officers wherever I see fit. I have just received similar permission from Messeigneurs Berry and Bourbon."

Valentine nodded; she had not spoken a single word since her departure from Château-Thierry. Escorted by the Dukes and followed by her chancellor and the lords and ladies of her retinue, she walked to the hall where the King would receive her; she held Jean and Isabelle by the hand. At the end of the hall, under a blue and gold canopy, sat a small, wizened man, his nearly toothless mouth half open. His face was covered by a rash, his raised hands trembled, but around his shoulders lay the ermine of royalty. The sight of him affected Valentine as nothing else had—not Isabelle's thoughtfulness, the Dukes' kindly welcome nor the words of de Tignonville. Her lips trembled, her eyes filled with tears. She took a few steps toward him, and sank upon her knees. Jean and Isabelle followed her example.

"Justice, Sire," said Valentine in a choked voice. "In God's name, justice!"

In response to Valentine's return, the Council assembled the following Saturday in the Hôtel de Nesle, the Duke of Berry's house. Most members were already present in the designated hall; the hour of meeting drew near and expired—it could not begin because the Dukes of Berry and Burgundy and young Anjou, who had returned from Italy as King of Sicily, were talking together in a side room.

"Well, nephew, what do you have to tell me that is so important that it cannot possibly be put off?" Berry asked, annoyed at the unexpected delay. "Make haste, the Council sits waiting for you next door."

Jean of Burgundy seemed extremely restless; he could hardly stand still; he struck his thigh repeatedly with one of his gloves. "What does it mean, Monseigneur," he burst out suddenly with passion, "that Messire de Tignonville and his officials request permission to search my home and subject my household to interrogation? How is it possible that you and Monseigneur de Bourbon could have lent your approval to such a senseless and insolent undertaking?"

Young Anjou, who stood at the window, quickly raised his narrow, dark face. "Now that we have given de Tignonville permission to search our residences, you cannot refuse without endangering your good name," he said quietly.

Jean of Burgundy cursed and threw his glove on the floor. He stood motionless for a few seconds, staring straight before him; then he fixed his dark eyes on Berry. "Now then," he said harshly, "why postpone the execution? I did it. You can't have expected anything else; God knows I never tried to hide my hatred of Orléans. I had him killed by a couple of fellows in my service."

"Holy Mother of God!" Berry lifted his hands to his head in horror; he gave a low moan.

"Oh God, Monseigneur, how could you have done that?" Anjou turned hastily from the window. "Not even twenty-four hours after you went together with Orléans to communion and swore on the body of Christ to make peace!"

Jean of Burgundy shrugged.

"The Fiend entered into me," he answered indifferently, with contempt. "A man isn't answerable for his actions when that happens, Monseigneur. You know that."

"Nephew, nephew," said Berry, trembling with emotion. "You have burdened yourself with a dreadful sin—that blood cannot be so quickly wiped away!"

"I haven't filthied my hands with it." Burgundy spoke harshly, holding his hands palm up. "Other enemies of Orléans did that for me. Messire de Courteheuse, the King's valet, lured him into an ambush. The attack was led by Arnaud Guillaume of Guyenne, and the whole plan was devised and worked out by a very clever and useful man whom I can certainly recommend to you for similar things—Messire Ettore Salvia of Milan."

"Orléans' astrologer?" cried Berry, aghast. "I refuse to believe it!"

"Ah come." Jean laughed shortly and bent to pick up his glove. "For money everything and everyone is for sale, Monseigneur de Berry."

"My God," continued Berry, "why didn't Orléans listen to me and have the criminal from Guyenne hanged when he had him in his power? Where are they now, the villains?"

"In safety," replied Jean of Burgundy. "It's no use attempting to find them, my lord. They stand under my protection."

Berry, who had been pacing back and forth, stopped before his nephew again. He looked suddenly very old and tired. "Do you realize what this means?" he asked in a low voice. "You must place yourself at the King's disposal. We must deliberate seriously about this . . ."

Burgundy cut him off rudely. "Monseigneur, you had better stick to your stuffed animals and your collection of holy relics," he said. "Don't meddle in my affairs. I would regret it if you too had to learn to your sorrow that one does not stand in Burgundy's way with impunity."

He spat on the floor before Berry and unceremoniously left the Hôtel de Nesle, stamping and swearing. Inwardly, he was far from confident; he cursed himself for his imprudence. Now that the Duchess of Orléans was in Paris, he considered it not unlikely that the King would order his arrest. After a furious ride through the city, he arrived at the Hôtel d'Artois and went at once to the tower which he had had built in the inner courtyard, a donjon made from massive blocks of stone, where he could entrench himself against impending danger.

In a room on the highest floor he found the men who only a few weeks before had fled in wild haste from the rue Vieille du Temple; Salvia and Arnaud Guillaume were there as well. Most of them lounged on straw mattresses; three or four were playing a listless game of dice. The enforced stay in the donjon had begun, after two weeks, to bore them thoroughly.

"Men," said Jean of Burgundy, "pack up—disguise yourselves and get out of the city. The truth is known; I expect very shortly a visit from the Provost and his bailiffs. Seek shelter in my domains, preferably in Flanders, it won't be difficult for you there. But clear out before it gets dark. Talk to Messire Salvia about the how and when; he knows all about escapes and disguises."

Salvia approached cringing humbly before his new master; the flaps of his red bonnet hung down loosely on either side of his sly, sallow face.

"Where are you sending us, Monseigneur?" he asked tensely.

Burgundy thought for a moment. "Go to the castle of Lens in Artois," he said at last. "Wait there until you hear from me. No, don't bother me with questions," he added irritably as the astrologer bowed again. "Save yourself; conjure up the Devil if you must—it's all the same to me."

Late in the evening a troop of gypsies were seen passing through the outskirts of Paris; they declared that they had leave to spend the night in one of the fields near the ramparts. The following morning no trace of their camp was to be seen anywhere. At midnight the watch at the gate of Saint-Denis was alarmed by loud shouts and the sound of horses' hooves. The Duke of Burgundy, one of the riders said, had to leave the city hastily; Monseigneur did not wish to be interfered with. The watch, who had as yet received no orders to detain Burgundy, opened the gates; the Duke and his followers dashed out at full gallop in the direction of the city of Bapaume on the Flemish border.

While these events were taking place in Paris, Charles d'Orléans and his brother Philippe and half-brother Dunois, were traveling to the castle of Blois. Charles was attended by Maître Nicolas Garbet and Messire Sauvage de Villers, his chamberlain and advisor, along with horsemen, servants and many members of the ducal household. Charles sat on horseback; his brothers, much against their will, had to ride in a carriage. There was so much to see that the boys almost forgot the mournful reason for their journey. The procession had to stop repeatedly in Orléans' domains so that delegations of the populace could greet the young Duke.

They came from everywhere to meet him; in carts along rural roads, by boat and raft over the Loire. Abundant gifts were offered to him: fat capons and beautiful pheasants, loaves of white bread and casks of country wine. Charles accepted the generous gifts and good wishes in as dignified a manner as possible. From his horse he looked down on the weather-beaten faces, the coarse hands, and the bent, warped bodies of the peasants; the dark, anxious looks of the city dwellers. The people, staring at their young Duke, saw against the grey-blue winter sky, the slender figure of a boy in black mourning damask. Most people thought he had friendly eyes.

"Alas, Monseigneur," they dared to say, "be kind to us. Times are hard, and they say it will be a bad winter. We are poor, my lord, we have heavy burdens. Taxes are high, my lord, we beg you to lower them. May God and all the saints bless you, Monseigneur; be generous with us."

Jean of Burgundy's flight had made a deep impression upon the people of Paris who, long biased toward Burgundy, wanted to see in him a benefactor who had delivered them from imminent danger. They thought that the murder could have only good consequences: maintenance of the armistice with England—wasn't it enough that skirmishes took place repeatedly along the coast?—peace in the city; remission of a part of their taxes. There was great need for this, especially in light of the severe winter, which was one of the coldest in memory.

Meanwhile, Valentine, through her chancellor and advocate, demanded punishment of the murderers and especially of the instigator of the deed, a confession of guilt from Burgundy and various forms of compensation for her and her children. But Jean of Burgundy sat safely in Flanders: the snow and cold formed an almost insuperable barrier between him and his kinsmen in Saint-Pol. In addition, the court knew the mood of the people of Paris, who shouted from the rooftops that they eagerly anticipated the return of Burgundy, the defender of their interests, whom they would greet with enthusiasm.

Berry, Bourbon and the young Anjou consulted with Isabeau who, recovered from her illness and fright, participated again in all discussions. To the amazement of the Dukes she seemed to deplore only formally what had happened; she even forgot more than once that an unwritten law forbade one to speak ill of the dead. It was as though her memory of Orléans and her passion for him had died together—or so her behavior would lead one to believe. In reality, she felt secretly relieved; she often thought with remorse and shame that for the sake of a fleeting pleasure she had allowed herself to lose sight of her real interests. Once more messengers went back and forth regularly between her and Ludwig of Bavaria.

"Do not oppose Burgundy too strongly," Isabeau's brother wrote to her. "His situation merits your careful attention. He is Bavaria's ally in the question of Liège. He watches over all our commercial interests with England. Turn toward him, beloved sister, it is to your advantage. Try to hush up this murder business, it won't be much trouble for you because, if I am well informed, Burgundy is the hero of Paris. The opposition is extremely weak; you can handle those old scarecrows, Berry and Bourbon. What constitutes the House of Orléans now? A woman and a few underage, powerless children."

Isabeau took this advice to heart. She could not openly champion Burgundy. Therefore she took the middle way; Berry and Bourbon, who were perplexed by the affair—how could they accuse and punish a kinsman before the whole world?—lent her a willing ear. Bourbon was old and suffered from rheumatism; he wanted nothing so much as to be left in peace. Berry was concerned about his collection; he was heartily tired of all the meetings, discussions and consideration of consequences.

"Speak to Monseigneur of Burgundy," Isabeau said during a serious conversation; she sat, broad and heavy beside the hearth fire, in a dress glittering with gold. "Ask him to surrender the villains. Judge them as they should be judged and after that leave our nephew in peace. The *murderers* will be punished then, isn't that right?"

The Dukes agreed; partly from a desire to be rid of all responsibility and partly too from a secret fear of this woman who fixed her sly, unwavering eyes on them. Berry could not help thinking of a strange, revolting creature which someone had once given him for his collection: it had constantly increased in girth, swelling up to a monstrous thickness; it lay unstirring in its nest, devouring greedily whatever was thrown to it—rats, fish, refuse. It was interested only in food and more food. Bemused by memories of that peculiar beast, Berry offered to open negotiations with Jean of Burgundy.

So it was that Berry, accompanied by young Anjou, left for Amiens in the last days of February. Since the roads were in extremely bad condition, it was a slow and arduous journey, but at last Berry, with a great following, reached Amiens where Burgundy waited with his two brothers. The reception left nothing to be desired.

Burgundy appeared at the meeting as it had been arranged that he would, but he refused to acknowledge his guilt in any respect or to ask forgiveness, or even to surrender his hirelings. He pointed to the emblem that he carried with him: two crossed spears, one dull and the other sharp and pointed.

"It's war or peace as you choose," he said indifferently. "It's all the same to me. I'm ready."

At the last, Berry had to be content with the promise that Burgundy would come to Saint-Pol very soon and plead his case before the King.

The citizens of Paris heard this news with great joy; the court and Council, however, received it with mixed feelings. Many thought that the world seemed turned on its head: was Burgundy coming as the accused or the accuser? Bourbon found it all too much for him; he left Paris. Valentine, deeply offended, made one final effort to approach the King. She received a refusal in Isabeau's name: the King was indisposed.

The Duchess's crepe-hung coaches were once again made ready for a long journey. With her children, friends, vassals and servants, Valentine traveled to the castle of Blois. One carriage contained Orléans' archives; the Duchess intended to seek herself the justice denied her in Paris.

In the first week of March, Jean of Burgundy arrived in the city as he had agreed that he would. He rode at the head of eight hundred horsemen and knights, all armed to the teeth but with uncovered heads as a sign of penance. The streets were crowded with jubilant people; here and there could even be heard shouts of "Noel, noel!" to the great displeasure of members of the King's court and household.

Burgundy took up residence in the donjon of the Hôtel d'Artois; there he consulted with his advisors and advocates about the best way to present his defense. After due deliberation the spokesman was chosen: Maître Jean Petit, professor of theology, member of the University, famous for his fierce eloquence. Day and night, for one whole week, he labored in the Hôtel d'Artois on the text of his speech: a sharply focused indictment of Orléans under the rubric, *"Radix omnium malorum cupiditas*—cupidity is the root of all evil." Placed at the professor's disposal was the person of the astrologer Salvia, the indefatigable collaborator who had, in disguise, accompanied Burgundy to Paris, and who was in a position to add a number of details to the known facts; he was, he asserted, better able than anyone else to furnish evidence for one of the most significant points in Maître Petit's accusation: that Orléans had endeavored, through sorcery, to kill the King and his children so that he himself could ascend the throne.

On the eighth of March, Jean of Burgundy set out for the palace of Saint-Pol. The ceremony would take place in the great hall: two platforms had been set up—one to the right and one to the left of the seats occupied by the royal family. The hall was completely filled with spectators; they stood packed together around the platforms, to the annoyance of the scribes and clerks of the court, who could barely ply their pens in the crush. Jean of Burgundy pushed his way with difficulty to the royal tribunal; the steely glint of armor could be seen under his ample scarlet overgarments. His lower lip protruded; his eyes were hard and scornful; the expression of contempt on his face belied his courtly salutations. The royal personages, dressed in gold and brocade, sat motionless, coldly attentive, under the canopy.

Maître Petit rose, coughed several times and looked reassuringly at Jean of Burgundy who sat on a low chair in front of the royal benches. His scarlet garment had fallen open; the mail at his knees and elbows glittered in the light.

"May I," began Maître Petit in a calm, level tone, "may I, my lords, remind you how in antiquity Judith took vengeance upon Holofernes for the sake of Judea? How the archangel Michael expelled Lucifer from Heaven as we have been taught? Did Judith and Saint-Michael commit any crimes? No! Holofernes was a tyrant; Lucifer a rebel against God. Monseigneur of Burgundy is a loyal servant of the King; the welfare of France lies closer to his heart than to the heart of anyone else.

"You know, my lords, that Orléans was killed on orders from Monseigneur of Burgundy—what conclusions may we draw from that? That Orléans betrayed the King and did harm to France. I shall prove to you over and over that Orléans fully deserved to be labeled a criminal, and criminals deserve to be done away with. I shall now tell you everything the criminal Orléans did to destroy the King's life in so subtle and perverse a manner that no breath of suspicion would ever touch him."

Petit then gave a long summary of the methods used by Louis d'Orléans to achieve his purpose; Salvia had supplied complete descriptions of strange incantations, dreadful magic formulae.

"The criminal Orléans," continued Petit, "wore on his naked body a ring that had lain in the mouth of a hanged man. He did this so that he could impose his will on a woman who refused to let herself be seduced by his promises and sweet words. He wore that charm continuously, even on holy days—during Lent, Easter and Christmas. Ask me not, my lords, how Orléans came to commit these and similar crimes. Remember that he was related by marriage to a nobleman of Lombardy, whom the people there called the foster brother of Satan himself. Do not forget that Orléans' wife was greatly skilled in the black arts."

Petit paused, waiting until the murmur in the room abated somewhat. Then he resumed, raising his voice:

"With the help of the Lord of Milan, Orléans attempted to penetrate the French throne. He had—right here in this court, among you, my lords—an accomplice, a certain Philippe de Maizières, a man of thoughtful demeanor but of evil character. Through the pretense of piety he managed to gain entry to the monastery of the Celestines. Have they tried to fool you about Orléans' piety too? He went to the Celestines at night and at outlandish hours, but it was not to pray or hear mass. Together with de Maizières in a quiet cell, he hatched plots to kill the King and bring France to perdition."

Then the speaker described in great detail how during a palace feast, the King and his friends had been set on fire by Orléans. A murmur of approval went through the hall; the fine points of the affair had, it was true, been forgotten, but everyone remembered that frightful accident.

Maître Jean Petit knew how to weave truth and fiction together artfully into a tale of human greed and wickedness, which his audience received in deep silence. Petit very cleverly left until the very last the argument aimed directly at the emotions of members of the University and the clergy. He outlined at length the miseries of the schism, the significance of the University's desire for cession. He informed his audience also that the only reason Orléans obstructed unification and supported the Pope in Avignon was because the latter had promised him the French throne in the future.

"All in all," concluded Maître Jean Petit, whose voice showed no sign of hoarseness after nearly four hours of talking, "I think that it follows clearly and irrefutably from the preceding that no blame should be attached to Monseigneur of Burgundy because he had had the aforementioned criminal Orléans put out of the way—on the contrary, we are greatly in his debt because he rendered an invaluable service to King, land and people. He deserves to be rewarded with affection and marks of honor. The tidings of his loyalty and devotion should be proclaimed throughout the Kingdom and made known abroad through messengers and letters. So it may be in God's name *qui est benedictus in secula seculorum*—who is blessed forever and ever. Amen! I thank you for your attention. I have finished."

After these words, Petit knelt again before the royal personages, and asked Burgundy if he agreed with this argument. Burgundy uncovered his head and said, slowly and loudly:

"I am in complete agreement with the argument."

Since none among those present seemed inclined to request proof or express doubts, the Duke of Berry declared the session ended, in the King's name.

The following day Burgundy received a document signed by the King which informed him that he was acquitted of all guilt. At the same time he was solemnly invited to resume his seat upon the Council. The King's signature ratified still another document with completely different contents: the children of the Duke of Orléans were deprived of the county of Dreux, the castles and grounds of Château-Thierry, Montargis, Crécy-en-Brie and Châtillon-sur-Marne. That the name Charles VI was written in shaky, blotted, ink-spattered letters by a madman who had no idea of what he was doing, was not thought by anyone to be a point worth consideration.

Isabeau left with her children for the castle of Melun, where she was to meet for prolonged discussions with her brother Ludwig.

Charles d'Orléans stood in one of the deep window recesses of the great hall in Blois and gazed out over the luxuriant landscape of the Loire valley. The broad and glistening river wended its way, bend after bend, between leafy thickets and green hills; the fragrance of flowers and newly-mown grass blew over the field. A triple girdle of ramparts circled the outer wall. Two inner courts separated from each other by moats and fortifications led to the citadel itself, which was flanked by strong towers. In the enormous castle yard were the guardrooms, stables, servants' quarters and dwellings of the officials attached to the ducal household. There also stood the church of Saint-Saveur. The innermost court, situated between the donjon and the chapel, was considerably smaller; it could be reached over a drawbridge. Within these walls Valentine had found a secure refuge for herself and her children.

Charles stood motionless, with his hands behind his back. He was waiting for his mother. The beauty of the summer countryside— the river blinking in the sun, the light clouds—could not dispel the chill from the young man's heart, nor the oppressive presentiments of disaster. After his joyous reception as the Duke of Orléans, he had found his first few weeks at Blois singularly charming; here, for the first time, he was lord and master in his own house. Despite the stifled laughter and amused glances of Philippe and Dunois, he had given orders and instructions; he was consulted on the daily course of affairs in the castle. Assisted by his chamberlain, Messire Sauvage de Villers, Charles had responded to questions, petitions, complaints and reports; he had acquired a taste for independent action. When his mother returned from Paris, he lost this independence. It was true that she kept him punctiliously informed of everything she planned to do, but she seemed to consider it self-evident—to Charles' private annoyance—that her oldest son would agree with her on everything. Little survived of the sweet, gentle Valentine who, with embroidery and harp-playing, had attempted to forget how quickly the sand flowed through the hour-glass.

The woman who now sat from early in the morning until long after darkness fell, at a table strewn with papers, surrounded by clerks and lawyers, garrison commanders and stewards, had no time for hobbies or the pleasure of art. Between the folds of the mourning veil, her sunken cheeks seemed unnaturally pale, her eyes hard and lusterless as stones. When she was silent her mouth was compressed into a narrow line. At her command the castle of Blois and the hamlet of the same name which lay in its shadow, were put into a state of defense; she ordered a store of provisions laid in, the garrisons fortified, and the walls and towers repaired.

Philippe and Dunois enjoyed all this immensely; they could have their fill of armor, catapults, hand- and crossbows. Whenever they had a chance they roamed the great inner court among soldiers and horses, amazed that their mother allowed them to do it. Charles took up his lessons with Maître Garbet once more, although with slightly diminished attention; he was worried about his mother's plans: how did she intend, without allies, to challenge so powerful an enemy as Burgundy? Charles spent considerable time with her each day in the chamber where she conducted her affairs; she showed him the letters and decrees which she signed in his name. The intimate, loving relationship between mother and son seemed to have come to an end.

She displayed a tireless sharpness and objectivity that contrasted strongly with her earlier gentle, tender patience. She caressed only Marguérite, her youngest child, born shortly before Louis' death, and Doucet, the small white dog who had attended its master to the last. Occasionally she smiled with absent sadness at Isabelle.

Charles' wife was eighteen years old; now that Valentine was occupied elsewhere, Isabelle supervised the household and servants, with the same composure and self-possession which she had demonstrated on other occasions. She was very conscientious and seldom overlooked anything. Charles she treated politely, but with a certain irritating impatience. For his part, the young man did not know how to behave toward this tall, pale girl with cold eyes. Sometimes by chance he encountered her tense, penetrating stare; it was as though she looked for something, she expected something from him, but he could not imagine what it could be. He looked away in confusion. Did she perhaps detect the transformation which he was undergoing and which, embarrassed and irritated, he attempted to hide? He was seized alternately by feelings of restlessness and oppression; a sudden, violent urge for action, followed unceremoniously by a longing for quiet and solitude. He did not find peace even in his books any longer; he lay awake at night plagued by restlessness, an inner tension for which no cause seemed to exist. He was confused, queer thoughts came into his head—he did not know where to turn for advice. Once he hesitantly approached Maître Garbet, his tutor whom he admired and trusted, and attempted to confide his troubles, but the old man only looked at him, smiling, over the rim of his spectacles and said, with good-natured mockery:

"Yes, yes, Monseigneur, you are growing up."

This response, and especially the manner in which it was said, Charles found infuriating, but it gave him food for thought. Could that be the solution to the mystery? In the winter he would be fifteen years old, the age at which kings were considered to have attained their majority. The fact that his voice sometimes broke or that his limbs would not always obey him—did all this mean he was becoming an adult? There had been a time when he had wanted more than anything else to be a grown man, so that he could buy books freely, read to his heart's content, journey to distant lands to see with his own eyes the wonders described in the holy stories and the tales of chivalry. Now the future which awaited him as an adult seemed less attractive.

The youth spent his days inside the dark walls of Blois, depressed by these and other thoughts. He loved the castle and principally its setting which unfolded to the horizon in delicate shades of green. In the river he saw reflections of clouds and the light of the sky in summer; it was an infinitely more beautiful picture than those woven into fabrics and tapestries. To his surprise he became aware of a curious desire to put into words what he saw: the sparkle of the sun on the stream, the glow of poppies in the green fields. Secretly he was ashamed of this urge. He had never heard that a man thought about such things.

He heard his mother's train rustling behind him over the leaf-strewn floor. He turned and went to her; silently she allowed herself to be led to the bench under a tapestried canopy. For a few minutes mother and son sat next to each other without speaking; Valentine stared into space. Sunshine lay in broad rectangles on the floor; in its strong light the colors of the fabric hanging along the walls were dimmed by dust and grime. The afternoon was filled with sounds: a cuckoo calling in the thicket by the river, the creak of a water wheel in the village, the stamping of hooves and confused clamor of voices and tools in the inner court . . . Charles glanced sideways at his mother's face; her skin was yellowish, wrinkled around the eyes—he thought she looked suddenly old and tired.

"There are things which I must discuss with you, son," said Valentine. Her soft voice sounded slightly cracked.

"Yes, Madame ma mere," replied Charles; he tried to keep an attitude of courteous attention as he had been taught to do toward grown-ups, but a vague feeling of foreboding was creeping over him.

"You are now almost fifteen. At that age your father and your uncle the King were considered to be mature and responsible. Maître Garbet tells me you have a good sense; he praises the progress you have made. After consulting with him, I have decided to terminate your lessons."

Charles felt a lump in his throat; he made an abrupt gesture of protest.

"Your education has been much too narrow," said Valentine, unmoved. She fixed her dark lusterless eyes upon him. "You are not predestined to be a scholar, son. You are Duke of Orléans, the head of a House, a leader of a party. It is time that we begin to develop those qualities which you must have for a task like that. You are a good horseman, but you have no skill with any weapon."

Charles sighed; his lack of enthusiasm did not escape Valentine's notice.

"You can sit and read later when old age or illness allows you no other diversion." Her tone brooked no contradiction. "I fear, child, that you may already have spoiled your eyes by peering at your letters. Now you must develop your physical strength, exercise your muscles. You will need all that when you ride off to war."

"War?" Charles raised his head; his look was just guileless enough to give his mother pain. But Valentine repressed this sympathetic impulse—she thought she must be pitiless herself if she were to help her son become the man of steel he had to be.

"Why do you think I have called up all these soldiers?" she asked wearily. "It costs a fortune every day to maintain them. If Burgundy will not bend, he must be broken. I shall force him to give me satisfaction, through force of arms if there is no other way. But any army of Orléans' must stand under our personal command—that is to say, under your command, son. You owe that duty to your father, who was so ignominiously murdered. Listen . . ." She turned toward him and took his face almost roughly between her two hands. "Listen, boy. From now on you must be inspired by only one thought, only one desire must impel you—revenge, revenge, nothing but revenge, until the humiliation they visited upon your father and upon us has been expunged in blood. I have never been cruel and vindictive, God knows that. But now I have learnt all too well what fate awaits the meek. Strike before you are struck. That is the only law, son, I can't teach you a wiser maxim. Remember that: revenge, satisfaction. Repeat those words by day and by night. Be aware that you must ignore yourself and everything you love must be set aside until you have achieved your purpose, until your father's death has been avenged, his memory cleansed, your inheritance restored intact to you and your brothers. That work must be pleasing to God, because your father was a noble man who served the interests of the King and the realm."

"Mother," Charles said with sudden vehemence—he slid onto his knees before her. "Mother, they say that my father robbed the King—that he was impious and frivolous."

Valentine raised her hand and struck the young man across the mouth.

"That you should dare to say those words within these walls is worse than treason," she said harshly. "Never speak like that again. Do not question for one moment the truth of what I say to you. I knew your father better than anyone else knew him. He caused me much suffering, many bitter tears, but now it seems to me that the sorrow I had to endure was far less important than the joy he brought to me. Yes, that joy was so deep that now the world has lost its light for me. Nothing has meaning anymore," she concluded, slowly repeating the words which were written in silver against the black walls of her apartments; tears began to fall from her dull eyes—she held a handkerchief before her face.

"I ask your forgiveness, Madame ma mère," said Charles, embarrassed and upset. "But I don't know if I am suited to be the leader of an army. I will learn to fight with weapons if you wish me to. But it is not fitting that I should be in charge of men like Messires de Braquemont and de Villars, who are great warriors."

"You must let me judge what is fitting for a Duke of Orléans." Valentine's face had regained its severity. "You cannot become a leader through talk. You will have the best possible tutors. I don't want any more objections, son. You are still under my guardianship; I am responsible for your education. Sit up straight—throw your shoulders back—you have sat bent over books for too many years. It has not been good for you."

Charles obeyed, but he had to bite his lips to avoid bursting into tears of rage and disappointment. Valentine sighed; she folded her thin hands stiffly in her lap and went on.

"There are still a few important matters I want to discuss with you. Your father contracted huge debts. He had to maintain his court and contribute to the support of his vassals here and abroad. He was forced to borrow a great deal of money at times to pay for his new territories. I want to pay off that debt before we undertake anything else, son, and that cannot be done without sacrifice. We must sell valuables and jewels. I have already made my choices—see if you agree with me, because there are many things among them which belong to you. I believe that if we want to have a large sum of money at our disposal all at once, we shall have to sell a house. I have heard that the Queen wishes to give the Dauphin his own dwelling in Paris. I have recently told her that I am ready to relinquish the Hôtel de Béhaigne to her for ten thousand gold francs. I take it you agree with me?"

The young man nodded; he did not speak. He was overwhelmed by despondency. What could he really say? He did not need to think; everything was being decided for him.

"Furthermore, I have finally received an answer to the letter which I sent to Monseigneur of Brittany in Paris. As you know, I held extensive discussions with him this spring. It is very fortunate for us, son, that he has reason to be dissatisfied with the way Burgundy handled the guardianship and administration of Brittany during Monseigneur's minority. Now that Monseigneur is an adult and his own master, he will no longer allow Burgundy to order him about. In short, he has declared himself ready to enter into an alliance with us even if it means a rupture with his mother the Queen of England. I have had the agreement put into writing; you will be so good as to sign it soon and also those documents which I am sending to the Margrave of Moravia concerning the need to fortify the fortresses in Luxembourg."

"Yes, Madame ma mere," Charles replied in a barely audible voice; he kept his eyes fixed obstinately on the floor. Again they sat side by side in silence, two small black figures against a background embroidered with saints and heroes.

"Charles," Valentine said suddenly, with a trace of the old tenderness in her voice, "you can keep Maître Garbet in your service as secretary, of course. I know that you are greatly attached to him, child. You do not have to lose his friendship."

The young man bowed, but his pale face did not relax. Valentine looked at him, trying to find some resemblance to another, once so loved. She saw in the thin mouth and around the nostrils too, something that reminded her of Louis; but Charles' eyes were different, milder; she missed the flash of irony which had enlivened Louis' glance. The youth's cheeks were beginning to lose their childish roundness. From temple to cheekbone and chin fell the shadow, the outline of maturity, which gives each face its own character. His thick light brown hair, clipped high around the crown, was as curly as it had been in his childhood, but the colorless down on his upper lip and chin was an unmistakable sign of manhood. The Duchess of Orléans almost smiled, but the impulse was too weak to soften the taut mask that was her face. She stood up slowly, leaning on the chair like an old woman; Charles hastened to help her. Together they walked through the long hall; the leaves rustled under Valentine's train and under the soles of Charles' black velvet shoes.

In the last week of August Valentine received a message that she would be received in Paris; she had not been so moved in a long time as when she read the royal letter. With the sealed parchment in her hand, she went to the inner court where, in an area set aside for that purpose, Charles worked with hand- and crossbow under the supervision of the practised archer Archambault de Villars. Valentine, who entered the court accompanied by her daughter-in-law Isabelle, watched her son for a while from the shadow of an arched doorway. The young man stood straight and lean in his leather jacket, at the far end of the shooting range. Slowly he drew back the heavy bow, his eyes squinting. Now the tautly-pulled sinew neared his shoulder; he let go; the arrow whizzed through the air, directly striking the target at the other end of the range. The feathered arrow quivered in the wood. Dunois, who had looked on knowledgeably with tense attention, went up, pulled the arrow from the board and made a chalk mark between the innermost circle and the bull's eye.

"What a beautiful shot," said Isabelle.

The sound of her daughter-in-law's voice struck Valentine; she glanced quickly at her. In the girl's eye she saw something which made her look equally quickly at the spot where Charles stood. After two months of almost uninterrupted physical exertion, he had become more robust. His slenderness had disappeared; he was now lean, but muscular and supple. Horseback riding, swimming, exercises with sword, bow and spear had removed every trace of awkwardness from him; he moved with some of the same ease which had characterized Louis. For the first time Valentine saw that her son was no longer a child but a young man; with amazement she realized that Isabelle already knew this. She drew her own conclusions. The eighteen-year-old Madame d'Orléans went about—it could no longer remain a secret from those around her—bent under her burden of forced virginity. Most women of her age already had one or two children, but although she was married now for the second time she was still a maiden. Her haughty bearing, her cutting coolness concealed her deep sense of shame and inferiority. Valentine had often asked herself, not without concern, what would happen in the future; when must she assign Charles and Isabelle a joint apartment? Isabelle seemed irritated with the quiet, childlike youth. The only feeling Charles evinced toward his wife was a certain embarrassed timidity.

But now Valentine saw in her daughter-in-law's eyes an undisguised interest; more noteworthy still, Isabelle lowered her eyes when Charles, who had seen his mother, handed his bow to de Villars and approached to greet both women. He wiped the sweat from his forehead with the back of his hand; the flush of exertion which had colored his cheeks during the archery had disappeared— exhaustion lurked in the shadows under his eyes. The Duchess of Orléans sighed involuntarily; the young man was not strong; he did his best, but he was hardly equal to the effort which a soldier's education required. Silently she handed him the Queen's letter.

Later—Charles and she had consulted with advisors and lawyers in her apartments—mother and son discussed once again at length the measures to be taken. Valentine believed she must seize the opportunity without delay; she wanted to go to Paris with the evidence she had collected—letters, orders and other documents connected with Louis' affairs—and there choose a qualified spokesman. Her intention was to refute Maître Petit's accusations point by point in the presence of the court, the government and representatives of the Church and the people. She increased her demands. Accompanied by Isabelle, she would go to Paris to gauge the atmosphere in the city and the court. If she found this to be favorable, Charles could follow with a suitable entourage.

The young man agreed to everything; he stood before the table piled high with documents and absently drew diagrams on the wood with his thumbnail. This made Valentine impatient; she was annoyed and disappointed that she saw in him no trace of her own passionate zeal, her vengeful perseverance.

"I trust that you are well aware of your obligations, son," she said at last, standing up to signal that the discussion was over. "What we do now is no whim for me nor child's play for you. We must remain vigilant, even if Burgundy should come on his knees to beg our forgiveness. Do not believe for one moment in the good faith of the hypocrite who had the insolence to hold the edge of the pall covering your father's bier the day after the crime; who went with his victim to communion a few hours before his murder! I want him to be humbled before us, that's obvious—but after that I shall also be prepared for war. There will come a day, Charles, when we will be asked to move swiftly and boldly, you can be sure of that. Take care that you will be ready then in every way; in order to achieve that day you must not relax for a moment, not now, not ever! Is that clear, son? You may go now. I think that your exercise down in the square should be resumed."

Charles shook his head; slowly he unbuckled the straps of the leather bands which he wore on his wrists when he worked with the bow. He gazed past his mother's head at the blue sky outside the arched window; large, gleaming clouds drifted slowly by, a fleet of ships on the way to unknown destinations. He saluted Valentine and left the room.

Where is he going now? thought the mother, overcome by a vague feeling of shame and regret. What is going on in him? What is he thinking?

She walked back and forth in her cheerless room; on the walls hung black fabrics, embroidered with motifs suggesting fountains of tears and with her motto, repeated over and over in pointed silver letters. She passed her days here as though she were in a tomb, surrounded by objects which had belonged to Louis: a missal, a cup, a crucifix, a glove. The dog Doucet, wounded in the attack, lay night and day on a cushion. Valentine now possessed Louis completely; at last he belonged to her alone. He continued to exist for her—nobler, purer, more upright than he had ever been or ever could have been. She was driven only by the need to justify him, to cleanse his memory of every stain—true as well as false. She did not know herself whether her tireless efforts on his behalf made his ideal image clearer every day, or whether her belief in his perfection impelled her to those efforts. The realities of daily existence had been lost for Valentine forever; she did not know whether it was raining or whether the sun was shining; she ate and drank without noticing what was put before her. She concerned herself less and less with her children: the Dame de Maucouvent, grey-haired and rheumatic but more dedicated than ever, cared for Jean and little Marguérite; Philippe and Dunois were looked after by their tutor.

Fervently, Valentine wanted Charles and Isabelle to identify with her struggle. Only similar emotions could constitute any kind of bond; nothing else existed any longer for the Duchess.

For some time she had been hearing a whistling sound in the inner court—the recoil of a bowstring. She looked out the window and saw Dunois in the shooting range. Archambault de Villars was no longer there; a page and a couple of stableboys stood at a distance, watching Dunois as, lips pressed grimly together, he tried to bend the heavy bow, to aim the arrows correctly. Although he was not yet eight years old, he did not seem too young to hit the inside circle of the target if he was not too far from it. The further away he stood the more difficult it was for him, because he did not yet have the strength to draw the bow back far enough. His small, broad face was red with exertion, his short sandy hair tangled and damp with perspiration, but he did not give up. Again and again he picked up the fallen arrows, again and again he marked the holes in the target with chalk. Then he returned to a certain spot and drew the bow once more.

Valentine looked down at him; a strange smile appeared at the corners of her mouth. This boy who was not her son had, since his infancy, shown a strong will, unlike her own children. She saw in him the tenacity of purpose, the blind drive which she now thought indispensable to the present circumstances. Charles did what he was told to do; he performed his exercises for the required time and not a moment longer. Dunois possessed the sacred fire, the inborn passion for weapons and their secrets—and he refused to allow himself to be driven from the field by either fatigue or a feeling of inadequacy.

When, some time later, Valentine looked out the window again, he was still there. Apparently he had hit the target, for he now stood a pace farther away from it. The Duchess of Orléans nodded as though in reply to her own silent question.

Around the vesper hour on the twenty-eighth of August, Valentine rode out of the Hôtel de Béhaigne in Paris; although she had sold the house to the Dauphin, it still remained for a time at her disposal. As before, she had arrived with black carriages, black horses, and a great following clad in mourning; this time too she was attended by Isabelle. As soon as she could, she set out for the royal palace. The King, who had not been in his right mind since the spring, could not receive her; she was admitted into the hall where the Council was gathered, presided over by Isabeau. In the presence of the Queen, the Dauphin, the Dukes of Berry, Bourbon and Brittany, the Chancellor de Corbie, the Constable d'Albret, bishops and archbishops, nobles and prominent citizens, Valentine for the second time presented her petition for justice. With no retinue, accompanied only by her daughter-in-law, she entered the hall; she did not wait for the punctilious ceremonial marks of honor that were her due; like any suppliant she fell immediately upon her knees and from that position delivered her complaint. Isabeau could not understand such indifference to one's rank, such extreme humility; from her raised seat she looked down on her sister-in-law with a disapproving frown.

"Madame," she said, when at last the Duchess of Orléans was silent, "we welcome you to Paris. We assure you that we shall give your petition our most profound consideration and that we will do our utmost to grant it."

Valentine raised her dead eyes to the woman who, all her life long, had been her bitterest enemy. That she herself had once condemned Isabeau for her cruelty, filled her now with a vague feeling of surprise. What did the discord between two women matter in comparison to the catastrophe which had engulfed her since then? She saw on the throne a fat woman dressed in gold brocade, who sat with difficulty on her hard chair. Her obesity aroused aversion and pity rather than hatred; to be sure, Isabeau's eyes were, if possible, brighter and harder than before, but they no longer frightened Valentine.

The Queen, eager to exchange a few words with her daughter, invited both Duchesses of Orléans to accompany her to her apartments at the conclusion of the session. In the room with the golden doves of peace—how well Isabelle remembered greeting the English delegation here—Isabeau received them. She ran her eye swiftly over her daughter's thin figure, her colorless face; she asked a few questions: how was Monseigneur d'Orléans? How old was he now? How did Isabelle like life in Blois—did it suit her? The girl answered politely, but coldly. Isabeau shrugged impatiently. Presently, she turned to her sister-in-law.

"Well, my fair sister," she said, "it's been a long time since we have been together. Much has happened."

"Yes, Madame," replied Valentine without looking up. Isabeau yawned and sat down.

"I ask myself whether you believe you have much to forgive me for," she remarked after a while, glancing aside at Valentine. Isabelle frowned and flushed with annoyance, but the Duchess of Orléans said, in a calm, toneless voice, "Who am I to decide what I must forgive you for, Madame? We are all sinners. In my situation I no longer worry about these things. My father is dead; Monseigneur my husband is dead. There is no need for enmity between you and me, Madame, if my interests are also yours. For the sake of the goal which I have set myself, I am prepared for any humiliation."

Isabeau smiled with narrowed eyes. "What do you mean by that?" she asked, toying with the gilt bells on her sleeve. "Do you mean to say that you consider it humiliating to speak to me?"

The Duchess of Orléans curtsied deeply.

"I mean," she replied softly, "that it is all the same to me, Madame. I am a woman of few words—life might perhaps have been easier for me if I had known how to express myself with facility. It is a great gift to be able to capture in words an image which can move us profoundly. The Dame de Pisan was able to do that when she lost her husband. I have a poor memory for verses, but I remember a song in which she laments: 'I am all alone.' She repeats this refrain incessantly, there is no room in her heart for any other thought. So it is with me, Madame; I am alone, I possess nothing on earth, I seek only justice for my husband—beyond that, I am indifferent to everything."

"Well, well, fair sister." The Queen did not know what to say; she found such mourning, such mortification, completely senseless. Not without secret amusement, she wondered whether Isabelle too joined in this unending funeral procession; she could not help but think that death had often crossed her daughter's path—practically since her ninth year she had worn only black. Tears and reproaches from Valentine—these Isabeau could have understood; her sister-in-law had every justification for them. But this cold grief seemed to Isabeau as strange as Valentine's earlier forbearance. Somewhat curtly, the Queen gave the women of Orléans permission to withdraw.

On the ninth of September, the Duke of Berry rode out the Saint-Antoine gate to greet his grandnephew Charles d'Orléans on a country road. In spite of old age and expanded girth, Berry still sat on horseback; on this day he was uncomfortable because it was exceedingly warm. Besides, the Duke had, as usual, eaten well and drunk copiously. It cost him considerable effort not to fall asleep on his steadily trotting horse; the more so since he was forced to keep his eyes half-closed against the glaring mid-day sun. At the point where the roads to Vincennes and Charenton converged, Berry's escort halted. From the right a procession of several hundred horsemen approached in a cloud of dust.

Berry, now wide awake, perceived that his grandnephew was preparing to salute him; the riders reined in their horses, Charles d'Orléans rode slowly forward. The youth saw an old, fat man whose hat, clothing and gloves were bedecked with uncommonly large gems, slumping sideways in the saddle. His cheeks and chin were flabby pouches; under their heavy lids his small eyes surveyed Charles with sharp curiosity. Berry saw a sad-faced boy soberly clad in black, who sat his horse well and uttered some well-chosen words of greeting. He was not shy. He lacked something—what, Berry could not immediately tell. In the smooth, controlled face opposite him he thought he read listlessness, a lack of resilience, which seemed especially remarkable in one so young. Berry recalled vividly what Louis had been like as an adolescent—passionate in both his enthusiasms and his aversions, but always under every circumstance a plain-spoken, radiant youth.

While they rode to Paris, Berry glanced continually at young Orléans from the corner of his eye; he conversed in his somewhat chilly, easy manner. Charles responded with civility, but as if the conversation did not concern him. However, when the subject turned to books, Charles thawed considerably. Berry was pleasantly surprised; the youth seemed well-read, a presentable Latinist, and he had taste. He has enjoyed a good education, thought the old Duke appreciatively, he is a much more pleasant young man than the Dauphin, that boastful, conceited little know-it-all who can hardly make out his ABCs but who behaves as though he were God Almighty Himself. Orléans acts somewhat elderly, but the lad has seen enough sorrow to make him look somber. He has his mother's eyes. They say that eyes are the windows of the soul; so much the worse for him then, for he will suffer in his life. But be that as it may, he is an acquisition to our royal menagerie!

Berry chuckled softly, but Charles did not notice it; he was busy looking about him. For the first time in his life he rode consciously through the streets of Paris; with his own eyes he now saw the churches and palaces of which Maître Garbet and Marie d'Harcourt and the minstrel Herbelin had told him so often: the squares closely encircled by rows of houses, the busy streets, the thousands of shop signs, the towers with their gilded weathervanes, the handsome gables of the great merchant houses, decorated with wood carvings and statues; he saw the massive towers of the Bastille and—most imposing of all—the shiny blue peaked roofs of the palace of Saint-Pol.

Soon the procession entered under the arched gates; the sentries gave them a respectful greeting; from all sides stableboys and stewards hastened to receive the Dukes and their retinues of nobles. Charles felt as though he was on a plateau set in high mountains. He had never imagined that walls and towers could be so steep, roofs so dizzyingly high. Blois, though powerful and massive, faded into insignificance against these narrow, pointed buildings with their hundreds of corridors and peepholes, pinnacles and battlements. From almost every tower fluttered thin blue pennants embroidered with golden lilies as a sign that the king was in residence within the walls of Saint-Pol.

Charles wished to go at once and pay his respects to his godfather. Berry led him through what seemed to the youth a maze of corridors and galleries to a very quiet wing of the palace. The doors which led to this section were diligently guarded by armed soldiers. Even in the anteroom Charles, who was extremely sensitive to that sort of impression, began to detect a strange, foul odor, such as might emanate from a place where wild beasts were caged. Attempts had been made to dispel the stench by the burning of incense and redolent herbs, but this had succeeded only in making it more noticeable. Old, faded and nearly threadbare fabrics hung on the walls; the windows were small and narrow and further obscured with bars. These dark chambers filled Charles with a feeling of horror and secret anguish. How sick was the King that they could force him to live in a place like this?

Finally they came to a door studded with iron figures; Berry called out that he and Monseigneur d'Orléans wished to see the King—soft footsteps could be heard behind the door; someone pushed a bolt aside. The gentlemen of both Dukes' retinues withdrew to the anterooms as though they wished to avoid an encounter with the woman who appeared now in the doorway.

On the threshold of the King's chamber stood Odette de Champdivers, "the little queen" as she was derisively nicknamed—the paramour whom Isabeau had so opportunely chosen for her husband. Berry greeted her curtly and immediately entered the room; but Charles, who suddenly remembered some court ladies' gossip which he had overheard, stood motionless, uncomfortable and dismayed. He had imagined Odette de Champdivers to be a coarse, bold woman like the trollops with their fierce, shameless eyes and crude gestures who wandered among the troops encamped at Blois. Whenever he heard the word 'sweetheart' he thought of these women, although he knew that this woman was the daughter of a Burgundian nobleman. Odette de Champdivers stood against the open door. She wore a brown dress and hooded cloak like a burgher's wife. Her small, pointed face was also suffused with a brown glow. It was the face of a child, almost an elf, with wise, soft, very dark eyes.

"Come in, my lord," she said amiably, gesturing with her narrow hand. Charles mumbled a hasty greeting and walked past her into the room. The oppressive, acrid air was almost unbearable; he had to make a strong effort to keep from holding his nose. The King sat huddled at the foot of a bed with tied-back curtains; he was biting his nails and looking with hostility at his visitors. The room was barren but neat; flowering plants stood in pots on the window sill.

"Sire," said Berry quickly—in his haste to be on his way he omitted the customary ceremonial formalities. "Sire, your nephew, Monseigneur d'Orléans, requests the honor of greeting you." The King made a few unintelligible sounds and stared about him fearfully. The young woman, who had closed the door softly and carefully, approached and held out her hand to him to help him rise.

"Come." She helped him firmly but lovingly; he allowed himself to be drawn from the bed. "Come, here are Monseigneur de Berry and your nephew. Look at him nicely and greet him—he has come from far away to see you. Come, do not be afraid. I am with you."

"Yes, yes, that's fine." Berry waved his glove impatiently. "Don't force him if he doesn't feel like talking. He doesn't recognize us."

"Oh, yes, I am sure he recognizes you. And he is pleased that you have come to visit him," said Odette de Champdivers, fixing her dark eyes upon Charles. She laughed reassuringly. Never had Charles seen anyone who radiated so much warmth, who inspired such deep confidence. It seemed to him that in spite of her youth she was older and wiser than the oldest and most intelligent people he had ever met; only looking at her gave him a feeling of comfort.

"How is it with the King now?" he asked. Odette de Champdivers shook her head, still smiling.

"He is very ill," she replied, in her tranquil, modest way, "and he suffers a great deal. But he endures his pain with great patience and humility."

Berry snorted with impatience and walked to the door, making it obvious that he wished to leave.

"If sometimes he does *not* do so," continued Odette de Champdivers to Charles, "he cannot help it. He does not always know what he is doing. But he is such a good and friendly man that one must love him."

"Yes," said Charles hesitantly. It was impossible for him to imagine how this young woman could perform her revolting task with so much patience; with so much affection, too. He saw how the King put his hand in hers, for support; how he followed her uneasily with his eyes when she moved away from him. Neither by day nor by night did Odette de Champdivers quit the room where he lived; she was always there to assist him, to comfort him, to clean him when he soiled himself, to admonish him gently when he would not eat or was ill-tempered with visitors. Even in times of deepest mental darkness, the madman had to be assured in one way or another that he was surrounded by a completely unselfish love. Anew each day he got the greatest gift any man could be given: compassion which sees all and forgives all.

"Come along now, nephew," said Berry, who had already opened the door. Charles bowed before the King and, then, no less deeply, before Odette de Champdivers.

"God be with you, Monseigneur." She followed him and showed him out. Standing in the anteroom, Charles and Berry heard the bolt shoved gently back into place on the door.

Not until Charles was outside the gate of Saint-Pol did his depression lift slightly. They rode to the Louvre where Isabeau and the Dauphin had taken up temporary residence; this castle lay at the other end of the city. The procession followed the rue Saint-Antoine, but was soon forced to take the narrower, more tortuous streets striking through the heart of Paris. The populace, long accustomed to the presence in the city of great lords with armed troops from all regions of the realm, paid little attention to the horsemen passing by. Those who recognized the Duke of Berry looked closely at his company, but no one suspected that the young man, stiffly clad in black like a clerk, was the son of Orléans.

So these people are Burgundy's friends, thought Charles, as he rode on, looking down on the turmoil around him; he noticed that a great many of the people carried weapons; that in numerous houses the ground floor windows were nailed up leaving only a small peephole; that an alarming number of soldiers roamed in aimless bands through the streets, throwing a curious eye in passing at the horsemen of Berry and Orléans.

In the Louvre Charles was received by the Queen and the Dauphin. Isabeau looked thoughtfully at her son-in-law; he had grown much taller—who would now say that this youth was still unable to perform his duty as a husband? She did not have much to say to him; she repeated to him only what she had already said to Valentine: she hoped with all her heart that Charles and his mother would be able to refute Maître Petit's argument. Afterward she moved off to a side room with Berry, leaving the two youths alone. The Dauphin, Duke of Aquitaine, was twelve years old, rather thin and pale like all Isabeau's children, but with a large head and protuberant eyes. He wore elegant garments, decorated with golden lacings; he flattered himself that he looked magnificent.

"Fair cousin," said the young Duke of Aquitaine in a sour voice, "they say you have a whole army there in Blois. Is that true?"

"Indeed it is true," replied Charles. He could not bring himself to speak in flowery terms to his perfume-sprinkled royal cousin.

"Then you intend to fight?" asked the Dauphin eagerly. "Because Monseigneur of Burgundy will not yield. I am certain of that."

Charles looked down at the enamelled mosaic of the floor. "That we shall see," he said stiffly.

The Dauphin began to laugh, the forced affected laughter of a badly spoiled child. "Don't think it matters to me one way or the other." He opened a gilded leather pouch which he wore on his girdle, and took out a pair of dice. "Here, throw," he said to Charles, pointing to a table. "The stakes are two golden livres. Do you have any money with you?"

Charles felt little affection for his cousin; when he saw him a few days later in the great hall of the Louvre where Orléans' counterplea was to be read, he found him decidedly ludicrous. The Dauphin was arrayed for the occasion in royal purple, with ermine around his shoulders and a crowned hat on his head; this was to make it plain that he was acting for his father. He sat with Isabeau under the canopy; the places beside them were awarded to the great of the Kingdom and the royal members of the Council. Knights, members of the Council and of Parlement, representatives of the University and many prominent citizens sat as they had sat to hear Maître Petit's speech in Saint-Pol, on platforms erected for that purpose. Great numbers of the populace also had been admitted to the assembly. Only Burgundy was absent; he was laying siege to Liège.

Valentine entered accompanied by Charles, and her Chancellor and by the advocate, Maître Cousinot. The text of the defense, prepared beforehand in Blois and bound as a book, was now solemnly handed over to the Abbé de Sérizy of Saint-Fiacre, whom Valentine had chosen as spokesman. The Abbé proceeded in a clear, calm voice, to read aloud the long speech, which he introduced with the following words: "*Justitia et iudicium praeparatio sedis tuae.*"

Patiently and minutely the Abbé de Sérizy refuted all the charges of attempted poisonings, attempted murder, conjuration. He succeeded in holding the attention of his audience through his choice of words, weaving suitable quotations from Aristotle, Augustine and Cicero into his argument. In contrast to Petit, he did not attempt to make an impression by shouting, using glib phrases, fiercely taking advantage of the reaction of the people in the audience. For this last, he would have had little opportunity anyway because the multitude behind the wooden railings were not at one with him, and attempted again and again to interrupt him through angry muttering and restless shuffling.

"With respect to the King and the royal family, Monseigneur d'Orléans was anything but hostile. Her Majesty the Queen can testify to that if she chooses."

De Sérizy paused and looked toward the royal seats. Displeased. Isabeau raised her brows; coughing and shifting broke out on the platform. Only Madame d'Orléans and her son sat unmoving—she with raised, he with lowered, head.

"Now I come to the final accusation levied by the opposition: that Monseigneur d'Orléans robbed the King and extorted money from the people by the imposition of heavy taxes. My lords, it is truly wonderful that the opposition should reproach Monseigneur d'Orléans in this way. It is a well-known fact that that is a means to which all royal persons have recourse when they need money. May I remind you of the manner in which in the year 1396 the expenses of the expedition against the Turks were defrayed, and how the ransom for Monseigneur of Burgundy was finally collected? Actually, the expedition caused irreparable damage to France.

"Then there is the allegation that Monseigneur d'Orléans attempted by night to steal the gold which is stowed away in a tower of this palace. It is true that he suddenly removed 100,000 gold francs—but he had good reason to do that. Monseigneur d'Orléans had repeatedly sought money to pay the salaries and provide necessities for the troops who must guard our coasts. His opponent, Monseigneur of Burgundy, had refused persistently in the Council to supply the necessary funds. Because the army had a right to prompt payment, Monseigneur d'Orléans was forced, against his will, to take what was not willingly given.

"Members of the opposition," concluded de Sérizy, after a brief pause, turning to the place where Burgundy's lawyers sat, "members of the opposition, take into account the displeasure, even the calamity, which the people of France will have to endure because the soldiers in the service of Burgundy—who pays poorly—roam plundering through the regions between Paris and Flanders.

"Princes, nobles, consider what has happened here. Burgundy has taken a path which can lead only to destruction, a road of treachery and cunning. Men and women of the city, old and young, rich and poor, consider that peace and calm have ended. Between the royal kinsmen glitters the naked sword, and that means war and suffering for you. Prelates, consider that a man has been murdered; that he did his utmost, in spite of everything, to serve the welfare of Church and State. That is why Madame d'Orléans has come here, together with her son, imploring you to give her justice. Remember what Solomon the Wise said in the Book of Proverbs: 'He who deals righteously shall find life and true glory.'"

With these words the Abbé de Sérizy concluded his oration. He had, like Maître Petit, spoken for four hours without interruption. Maître Cousinot, advocate in Parlement, arose now, amid a great tumult from that part of the hall where the people stood packed together; he declared that on the strength of the preceding evidence he had come to believe that the Duke of Burgundy deserved only the most stringent punishment. Bailiffs removed troublemakers from the public area and loudly demanded silence. After that, Cousinot read Valentine's demands.

The Council now withdrew and under the supervision of the Queen, began to deliberate on the reply to be given to Orléans' party. Isabeau, highly displeased by de Sérizy's allusion to her good relations with Orléans and by the way in which the Abbé had depicted Orléans' policies as beneficial—as if to place her own actions in an unfavorable light—declared tartly that she deemed the allegations of Burgundy as well as those of Orléans to be immoderate; she advised the Council to involve itself as little as possible in this dispute between two princely families—in time the hatred on both sides would pass away. Meanwhile, further deliberation could be promised and care taken to see that Paris was fully armed and fortified.

After returning to the hall, the Dauphin in his shrill, childish voice communicated the decision of the Council to the widow of Orléans and her son.

"We are grievously offended by the conduct of Monseigneur of Burgundy," said the heir to the throne in a tone which belied his words. "And we promise you that we shall do whatever is possible to reach the fairest solution."

Valentine and Charles had to remain content with this meaningless response. At first, Charles was inclined to believe that their demands would be granted and that all dispute and discord would come to an end. He said this to his mother, when they sat together that night in the Hôtel de Béhaigne, but Valentine only smiled contemptuously.,

"Put that idea out of your head, son. Our petition is denied. We may find it pretty that the court and the Council exhibit some dissatisfaction with Burgundy. Further than that they will not go. We must help ourselves."

For the first time in his life, Charles dared to speak out openly against his mother.

"What precisely do you want then?" he burst out. He saw Isabelle, in a corner of the room, look up wide-eyed from her embroidery frame. "Can't we rest satisfied with the fact that Burgundy admits committing murder? We hear constantly from everyone that he has no intention of confessing to feelings of guilt or of begging forgiveness. If those in authority do not pursue him, what must we do then? Surely you cannot intend to wage war by yourself? We don't need to interfere with Burgundy; I don't think he intends to get in our way. We have done what we could. If the King doesn't punish Burgundy, it is not our fault. We cannot put France through the agony of a civil war. You yourself heard what the Abbé de Sérizy said."

"Coward." Valentine rose from her seat; she was trembling with rage. "Is your distaste for organization and command so great that you would leave your father's death unavenged? Do you find it so easy to bear your disgrace that you prefer to sit for years beside your father's murderer in the Council and let yourself be bullied by him? Does the honor of your House mean so little to you? Are you too lazy, boy, to take up the sword for the sake of your father's good name?"

"Mother, you distort everything; I haven't said that," muttered the young man. All the color had drained from his face. Tears of rage sprang into his eyes. The Duchess of Orléans made a small, eloquent gesture of contempt. She understood suddenly why the hatred of her father, Gian Galeazzo, had been so dangerous; he too had possessed the ability to gather together all the strength, all the passion that was in him to destroy his enemies. Was this youth, her son, really already tainted by the hereditary character weaknesses of the House of Valois: irresolution, a love of ease? Alas, Louis too had had those weaknesses—she had forgotten it too quickly.

"Do you wish to sacrifice the whole Kingdom?" asked Charles vehemently, trying to detain her as she walked toward the door which led to her bedchamber. "Are you prepared to go that far just to see Burgundy humiliated?"

"Yes, I am ready to go that far," said Valentine proudly, ignoring Charles' outstretched hand. "France will be completely destroyed if Burgundy exercises his power. Do you know the proverb of the gentle surgeon, son? Let us rather cauterize the wound. No, do not contradict me any more. You will admit later that I am right— perhaps when it is too late."

The following morning Valentine ordered everything put in readiness for the journey back to Blois. Without bidding goodbye to the royal family, the Council or those who had assisted her in the matter of the lawsuit, she left Paris with Isabelle and Charles. During the journey she sat huddled in a corner of her carriage, shivering with fever; she had to be carried to bed at once. The physician who was hastily summoned found her condition alarming.

Valentine lay gravely ill at Blois. Considering the nature of her illness, there could be no doubt about the outcome after the first day; the store of will-power from which she had nourished herself since her husband's death was exhausted. For ten long months she had strained her strength to its limits, forcing body and mind to a feverish activity, demanding too much of her constitution. So long as she had hope that her wishes would be fulfilled, so long as she could believe that action would be taken against Burgundy, she had managed to stay on her feet, but she was no match for the bitter disappointment of recent weeks. The blow was the more telling because she had thought her goal was so close. Now each foothold had slipped away from her: the Dukes, the Council faltering from fear, the Queen displeased anew, her own son unwilling to fight for his rights.

Silent, with closed eyes, Valentine lay, day after day, on her bed between the black curtains, the black hangings. She was no longer concerned with those who lived in and near the castle; she hardly heard them speak to her. Charles, on whose shoulders the whole responsibility rested now that his mother no longer concerned herself about anything, had not revoked the orders given by her in the spring; he had in fact toyed repeatedly with the thought of disbanding the troops and sending the vassals home, but he was restrained by the fear of aggravating his mother's condition; and he feared also the opposition and displeasure of the captains and especially of de Mornay, who shared Valentine's views.

Never had Charles felt so uncertain, so melancholy and so burdened with guilt. He knew that his mother's advisors and assistants were privately contemptuous of him for his inclination to remain aloof; they did not show it, but he sensed their criticisms of him: they thought he was a bad son, unworthy to hold the title. Attempting to win their friendship and approval—one can be extremely lonely when one is fourteen years old and without support—he painstakingly performed the tasks in which he had the least interest: he practised with weapons, rode out to inspect the troops, studied the art of war. At night he sought refuge in Maître Garbet's apartment; he tried to find comfort and oblivion in the books which he had loved. But the adventures of Perceval and Arthur now suddenly seemed dull and far-fetched to him; the stately Latin sentences of the classic writers sounded labored in his ears; the holy legends and the stories of miracles were not convincing. How could he immerse himself by candlelight in things which had never happened or had occurred long ago, while his mother pined away from grief, while Burgundy the murderer went his way unpunished, while disaster threatened everywhere and the November wind, like a harbinger of winter's cold, blew its litany along the shutters? For the first time Maître Garbet also seemed like a stranger to him; the little old man, bent day after day over the vellum sheets which he filled with essays on theology and history, seemed very far removed from what disturbed Charles.

Isabelle was confusing too. He did not see her often, because she stayed for the most part in the sickroom, but occasionally she came to him unexpectedly when he sat in the library with maps of roads and rivers and plans of fortresses before him. At first he really believed that she sought him out to bring him special news about his mother; he could not imagine why she tarried, giving him sidelong glances which made him more uneasy than her previous cutting arrogance. She did not say much, nor did she make any effort to draw him into conversation—it was precisely this expectant silence which he found so oppressive. Charles, who could not sit until she requested him to, stood beside her, overcome by shyness and slight irritation. He and she were about the same height; when he glanced at her profile he saw close by the roundness of her pale cheek, her large, grey, slightly protuberant eyes, her slender neck. He was old enough to know that the marriage between them was a marriage in name only; the worldly ladies and gentlemen of Valentine's retinue had not hesitated to tease him continually since the wedding in Compiègne about his neglect of his duties to his wife.

Charles was no longer ignorant, but what seemed perfectly natural and obvious in conversations with pages and grooms in the stables, and in daily business with dogs and house animals, could not somehow be associated with Isabelle and himself. Over the years he had grown accustomed to her constant presence; she belonged in the household and had therefore, despite her sharp tongue and impatient outbursts, the right to respect and affection. The alteration in her manner toward him he found terrifying.

Once when he had offered her his hand to lead her to the door, with a quick gesture she had pressed his fingers against her breast; he felt the restless throbbing of her heart. As a child he had once caught a field mouse. The creature sat in his closed hand, petrified with fear; the tiny body trembled with violent heartbeats. Seized by the same feelings of horror and compassion that he had felt then, he allowed his fingertips to be held against the cloth of Isabelle's bodice; her grip on his wrist did not slacken for an instant. He was forced to remain standing in that position whether he wished to or not. He had retained an unpleasant memory of that incident. Thereafter, he avoided Isabelle.

On the twenty-third of November—the anniversary of the death of Louis d'Orléans—Valentine ordered a mass to be read in her bedroom. Hardly had the odor of incense dispelled, when the Governor de Mornay, who had accompanied the royal procession through the domains of Orléans as far as the city of Tours, urgently requested an audience with the Duchess. He was finally allowed to enter her chamber. The intellligence which he brought confirmed Valentine's worst fears: the Duke of Hainault was in Tours to negotiate with the King in Burgundy's name; both sides seemed equally anxious to re-establish good relations. Isabelle and Charles, who were present at the mass, feared that this news would do great harm to Valentine. However, to their surprise, it seemed to stimulate the Duchess to a final effort.

She was roused from her dull indifference; in spite of pain and fever, weakness and exhaustion, she tried to take measures to protect her children's futures. In the last days of November she gave orders: de Braquemont received instructions to divide the standing army in Blois into special troops and to send these, well supplied with weapons, gunpowder and food, to key positions in Orléans' territory. Once more she wanted it explicitly recorded that Charles would be Duke of Orléans; Philippe, Count de Vertus; Jean, Count of Angoulême and Jean, bastard of Orléans, surnamed Dunois, lord of Château-Dun. At last—December had already made its entrance with storms and bleak rain—she called her children to her.

Philippe, Jean and Dunois, who had not seen her since she left Blois for Paris, did not dare come near the black-hung bed; they could not believe that this emaciated woman was their mother. The skin of her face was tightly drawn over nose and jawbones, her chin protruded sharply—she already looked like a corpse.

"Charles," Valentine said with an effort, while she motioned him with her eyes to come closer. "Charles, kneel down and swear by the Holy Body of Christ, who died for our sins, that you will protect and defend your brothers and your sister, and everything that belongs to them and to you, to the best of your honor, conscience and ability. Swear that you will not rest until you have avenged your father's death, that you will watch and work without ceasing until Burgundy has paid for his crime." She paused, gasping for breath.

"I swear it," said Charles with bowed head.

"Promise me, then," continued Valentine, "that you will keep the memory of your father sacred—you know in what way I mean. Let my body be buried in Blois, but bring my heart to Paris and set it in the tomb near Monseigneur my husband, in the chapel of the Celestines. Promise me," she tried to sit up but could not, "promise me that you will be good . . . to the children here . . . and to Isabelle your wife. And forgive me, you, Charles, and you two children, forgive me for whatever harm I may have done to you. Now come here one by one and say that you forgive me."

They knelt by the bed—Charles, Philippe, Jean and Isabelle; Dunois remained standing a considerable distance away from the others, because the Dame de Maucouvent, who carried little Marguérite in her arms, held him back by the sleeve. But Valentine asked: "Where are you, child?" and stretched her thin hand for him. Dunois knelt close against the edge of the bed and looked at his foster mother with his bright, grey-green eyes; he alone did not weep.

"You will bear the heaviest burden of all, lad," said Valentine; on her lips appeared the old sad, gentle smile. "The inheritance which awaits you is that you will have to fend for yourself. If Monseigneur your father had not been taken from us so suddenly, he would undoubtedly have provided well for your future. I am leaving you some money, child, but it is not much—we of Orléans have become poor. But I am not worried about you—less worried than about my own sons. You are more equal to the task of avenging your father than any of your half-brothers . . . Alas, child, I could not have loved you more if you had been mine. Say that you forgive me, Dunois."

"I shall fight for Orléans and my brothers," said the boy, his forehead pressed against Valentine's hand.

Now the priests, who had been summoned to administer extreme unction, entered from the adjoining room: Valentine's confessor from the house chapel of Orléans and the priests of Saint-Saveur, the church in the forecourt of Blois. Valentine, weeping now, bade her children farewell. Silently she made the sign of the cross over Charles' forehead and grasped the feet of little Marguérite who was not yet a year and a half old, and who understood nothing of what was happening. The child laughed and wriggled in the arms of the Dame de Maucouvent, clutching at the light from the candles reflected in the glittering chalice which the priest held—the governess, blind with tears, stood speechless by the deathbed of the woman whom she had served for twenty long years. They told her she must leave the room; she carried the playful child away.

Charles, praying in a corner of the room, lost all sense of time; he did not know how long he knelt there, murmuring incoherently, until someone shook his arm gently back and forth and said, "Monseigneur, it is over."

The Duchess of Orléans lay with her head thrown back, her mouth open, as though she were about to call out. The sight overcame Charles, shattering his final resistance. He hid his face in his hands and repeated in a whisper the vows he had already sworn to his mother. Women entered the room to lay out the dead Duchess; respectfully they requested that Monseigneur depart.

Charles walked slowly through the empty rooms to his own chamber—through the windows he saw the evening sky, colored yellow above the horizon, steel grey and already filled with stars at the zenith. Crows sat in the leafless trees along the river. In Blois and in the forecourt of the citadel bells began to toll, mourning bells for the Lady Valentine, Duchess of Orléans, who had died at noon on the fourth of December in the year 1408 at the age of thirty-eight, precisely one year and eleven days after her husband was murdered in Paris.

Charles felt his heart lying cold and heavy as a stone in his breast. He sent his valet away; he did not respond to the raps on the door. He flung himself across the bed and thrust his fist into his mouth to smother the sound of his violent convulsive sobs. When he opened his eyes—had he slept?—he saw, vaguely in the darkness, the red glow of fire under the ashes. A small streak of light was visible on the floor by the window; outside, the moon was shining.

Charles raised his head to listen: he thought he heard somewhere in the room a soft rustling, like a woman's dress gliding along the floor. His heart began to thump so violently that he almost choked. He did not dare to look up. He knew that one must call God's name to drive back the dead who can find no rest, but his tongue lay as though it were paralyzed against his palate; he could not speak. Was she trying to urge him once more; did she not understand that he would do what she had asked, did she want to hear him swear an oath again?

In the reflection of the moonlight on the floor he saw a pale white dress; someone stepped up to him and put an arm on his shoulder. It was Isabelle, his wife.

III. BURGUNDIANS AND ARMAGNACS

La guerre est ma patrie,
mon harnois ma maison,
et en toute saison
combattre, c'est ma vie.

War is my fatherland
my armour is my house,
and in every season
combat is my life.
— Folksong

n the first day of March in the year 1409, the populace of the city of Chartres were surprised by the news that royal guests were arriving in great numbers. Workmen in the King's service appeared in the cathedral to construct a dais for the royal chair beside the altar; flags and banners were unfurled as though for a fête. Only when more processions—of nobles, courtiers, horsemen and soldiers—entered Chartres did some information begin to circulate about the purpose of this impressive gathering.

Burgundy and Orléans, it seemed, were ready for a new reconciliation before God and the King; scoffers asked, for the umpteenth time? The people had no opportunity to take part in what promised to be a joyous celebration; it became clear before long that the great lords wished this peace treaty to be a private affair. On the day set aside for the ceremonies a hedge of soldiers stood between the city gate and the cathedral. The square before the church was swept clean, streets blocked off to prevent spectators from flocking in. Thus almost no one witnessed the King's entry; no one saw the sick man, wrapped in a great cloak, helped from his carriage; no one saw the corpulent Queen enter the cathedral wearing a fortune in pearls and rubies, followed by the Dauphin and his young wife;

no one was given the chance to see, close up and with his own eyes, the peers of the Kingdom, the dukes, counts and barons, the cardinals and archbishops, the long procession of figures dressed in purple, gold and black, the indispensable extras in every act of this tragedy of kings.

Unobserved, Charles d'Orléans and his brother Philippe also rode into the city; both wore deep mourning. They were attended by only a small retinue, not more than fifty horsemen; so it was stipulated in the decree which summoned the Duke of Orléans to the meeting in Chartres.

The young man sat straight and silent in the saddle; he dreaded this meeting with Burgundy. He felt guilty because he had yielded to the pressure brought to bear on him by the Council and his own royal kinsmen. Since the death of his mother, they had sent him messengers and mediators without interruption; they knew only too well that it would be easier to make demands upon an inexperienced young man than upon Burgundy. The Duke of Berry had visited his nephew and spoken to him sympathetically, as a man of the world: what was the sense, he asked, in clinging obstinately to desires for vengeance and satisfaction? Why should feelings of enmity exist between the young man and his blood relative? There was certainly no question that reconciliation with Louis had been impossible, that Valentine had been filled with hatred—"but come, Monseigneur; you are too intelligent, too courteous, too pious, when all is said and done, to go on with a feud that can't bring you anything but trouble." With his sharp nose, Berry had sniffed out the arguments which would sway Charles: with broad strokes he painted the suffering and unrest in the country, the terror and aversion people felt for the armies because the soldiers depended upon the farmers and citizens for food and lodging; he did not neglect to point out that the threat of war interfered with the functioning of the government so that important affairs would be neglected or even ignored.

Despite his counsellors' advice that he should not cooperate, Charles did not dare to refuse. He felt swamped by the overwhelming numbers of nearly insoluble problems; he could not choose a position or stand up for a point of view. There were many domains to administer, money matters to arrange, household affairs to manage and guidance to be given to officials—he had to keep an eye on a number of things the existence of which he did not even suspect. He was a husband as well as a brother and guardian, the head of a feudal House of one of France's four most powerful vassal states. He did not know each separate task, but his awareness of the expectations that he would take full control of all these functions together made him extremely receptive to the pressure which was exerted upon him.

Now he had agreed to hear Burgundy's apologies and be satisfied by them. He must play his role, even though he was beginning to question the wisdom of the course; even though he was plagued by feelings of guilt and regret. With thoughts like these he entered the cathedral of Chartres, followed by Philippe.

The light of hundreds of candles could not expel the dusk which hung under the old vaulted roof; the windows glowed dully: smouldering red, autumnal yellow, somber blue. The altar laden with gold, the royal cortege around the throne, the prelates in their ceremonial robes gleamed like treasure which lay sunken at the bottom of a deep shaft. A cold draught swept over the tombstones and made Charles shiver; he felt both insignificant and unimportant in this place. He was ashamed that the House of Orléans was represented so shabbily in the persons of two youths. He sought refuge, as always when he was insecure, in silence and reticence. Precisely because of this, although he was unaware of it, he gave an impression of dignity, of being equal to the situation. In the midst of so much pomp and ceremony, the rather thin figure of the youth, his stiff bearing and quiet face, could not help but arouse sympathy. Thus by his restrained entrance he gained considerably more favor than Burgundy, who came into the cathedral a short time later, attended by twice the number of men which had been stipulated. Jean was accompanied by his advocate, the Sire de Lohaing; they did not waste time upon compliments and ceremonial greetings, but proceeded directly to the purpose for which they had come.

Burgundy, attired in deep blood red, knelt before the King; the advocate followed suit, but remained at some distance behind his lord.

Jean coldly and insolently inspected the royal group and especially the King who looked vacantly before him, and the two sons of Orléans—de Lohaing spoke in a voice which reverberated in the farthest corners of the cathedral.

"Sire, here is Monseigneur, the Duke of Burgundy, your true and humble servant, your nephew of royal blood, who applies to you in connection with the outrage committed by him upon the person of Monseigneur of Orléans, your brother. Monseigneur of Burgundy acknowledges that this outrage was perpetrated with his knowledge and on his authority for your welfare and the welfare of your Kingdom; he stands ready to acknowledge that here again, if Your Majesty wishes. He has heard that his deed has aroused your displeasure, and that causes him great suffering. Therefore, Sire, he beseeches you humbly to receive him once more in your grace and friendship."

De Lohaing stopped, but the rising sound of the last syllables he uttered resounded in the silence; even before the echo died away, Burgundy completed the supplication: "That is my veritable wish, Sire; give ear to it."

The King, who did not understand anything that had been said, remained sitting motionless; his long hair hung over his face, he seemed half asleep. Berry and Bourbon approached and spoke to him in a whisper; the King grumbled a little, but finally cried loudly, "Yes." With this proof of royal favor, Burgundy had to be content. He turned now with a smile to Charles d'Orléans and his brother, Philippe. The advocate inquired, in the same tones he had employed toward the King on Burgundy's behalf, whether the sons of Monseigneur d'Orléans were ready to renounce all thoughts of vengeance. Philippe could not restrain his tears, but Charles listened apparently unmoved; neither by look nor by gesture did he betray what it cost him to hear this purely formal expression of humility; to look into the face of his father's enemy. He felt like shouting loudly that he refused to accept these apologies because he could not believe in their sincerity; that he rejected reconciliation with the murderer, that he would rather choose to continue the feud with fire and sword, even though he himself were to be ruined.

The blood mounted to his head, he took a step forward; but now he saw nearby, on the throne, the sick man's grey face, which looked as though it were covered with cobwebs, and his trembling hands; he was overcome suddenly by a new strong desire: to help this poor madman to wear the crown and carry the sceptre. Was that not also what his father had striven for; could he himself wish for a nobler task? He readied himself to give the cheerful answer which was expected of him; the advocate de Lohaing had just concluded his speech, and Burgundy said, half under his breath, with a look of secret derision, "That I beg of you in sincere friendship, Messeigneurs d'Orléans."

At that moment Charles became acutely aware that the entire reconciliation was essentially a senseless, ridiculous spectacle, undertaken to throw sand in the eyes of the simpletons—among whom, no doubt, they counted him as well. The King knew nothing, the Queen and the Dukes allowed themselves, like weathervanes, to take direction from the strongest wind. Burgundy wanted to be that wind. He expects us to fly away before him like withered leaves, thought Charles, with a new-found grimness. In later years he was to remember this moment in the sparkling twilight of the cathedral as decisive. He understood that in the eyes of many he was the personification of justice which had been trampled underfoot by a merciless ambition. So it went in the world always; the strong prevailed: those who allowed themselves to be oppressed deserved only contempt or pity. Shall it then always be so? thought the youth, embittered and rebellious. Must I bow before Burgundy; my steward before me; one of my farmers before him; a serf before the farmer, and can the serf finally kick his dog if he wants to? Must a man suffer injustice because he is weak—isn't there any defense? I must oppose him, he said to himself, I must move against Burgundy, not from hatred, not from self-interest, but for the sake of a higher justice. How can we live peacefully when the arbitrary acts of a man with a hard fist and an insolent mouth set the law for us? I shall not be weaker than Burgundy—one must assert oneself when injustice seems invincible.

"Yes, Monseigneur," he said aloud, in response to Burgundy's direct question. "I bear no malice against you, and I am ready to make peace with you."

He smiled and looked straight at Jean of Burgundy. It cost him no effort to utter meaningless and nonsensical phrases. Lie for lie, trick for trick, thought Charles, that is the purpose of this whole charade which will be forgotten in a few weeks.

At a nod from the Duke of Berry, he descended from the dais and approached Burgundy to exchange the kiss of peace with him. This symbolic act took place in a deathly silence. Jean of Burgundy watched the young man's tense face draw near; in his eyes he thought he saw something which made him doubt that Charles was indeed so guileless as he had been painted.

At the conclusion of the ceremonies the royal kinsmen and their courtiers assembled in a building opposite the cathedral, where a banquet was to be held. Burgundy and Orléans were to sit on either side of Isabeau. His new insights had brought about a remarkable transformation in Charles: he felt reckless, even elated, able for the first time in his life to exchange jests with his grown-up neighbors at table. Isabeau looked at him, startled and at the same time amused— would her son-in-law now turn out to be a worthy son of his famous, quick-witted father? Burgundy, on the other hand, was not amused by the youth's lively and often trenchant observations. From time to time he thought he saw sitting beside the Queen the cousin whom he had hated more than anything else in the world. The years seemed to slip away; he seemed to find himself again in the festive halls of Saint-Denis, filled with rage and jealousy, watching his wife Marguérite's animated dinner partner.

"Why do you not eat, my lord?" asked Isabeau. "Do you find the wine so bad that you will not touch the goblet?"

Abruptly Burgundy stood up; he could bear it no longer. Assassination, war, intrigue, deception—for these he possessed sufficient patience and self-control; but the gradually dawning realization that he had slain his detested adversary only in appearance—that this man and his power had entered his life afresh in the shape of a youth with the same smile, the same quivering of the nostrils— that realization made him almost choke with rage. He quit the banquet hall as though in flight, under the amazed and displeased eyes of those assembled there. His departure was, understandably, considered to be a bad omen.

Charles felt as though he stood beside a table watching a stranger with an odd resemblance to himself sit eating and drinking; he had never suspected the existence in himself of this outspoken, easy-mannered youth. He heard his own voice raised in jests and laughter, in courteously constructed sentences which held an undertone of ridicule and irony perceptible only to himself. But what were they, those who had gathered here, but a pack of hypocrites? He saw with deep shame Philippe's surprised and indignant glances; it was scarcely three months since they had buried their mother and already Charles behaved as though he had never in his life known a moment of grief.

"I am pleased that my daughter has such a cheerful husband," said Isabeau with a searching sideways glance. "I have often thought that she must surely pine away from boredom there in Blois."

The Queen's remark seemed to drain away Charles' self-assurance as though by magic. He flushed and stared at his plate, crumbling a piece of bread between his fingers.

"We have yet to hear news of our daughter," said the Queen more coldly. "We had expected to see her here today, Monseigneur."

"Madame Isabelle is not feeling well," said Charles, with a quick look at Philippe.

"Is she ill?" asked the Queen sharply and loudly; many of the guests broke off their conversations and turned their heads toward the corner where the royals sat.

"Nay," replied Charles; he felt his ears burning with embarrassment. But he had to speak; the Queen was eyeing him with suspicion. He said as quickly and softly as he could, "She is not ill. That is to say . . . she is . . . she thinks that in September she . . . Her doctor says . . ."

Isabeau threw her head back and burst into loud laughter, which drew more attention than anything which had gone before.

"Surely that is a most unusual way to announce the arrival of an heir, my lord." Isabeau could not restrain herself. Usually prospective fathers were proud at the mere mention of such a thing. Charles gazed straight before him, annoyed and embarrassed. He saw the news traveling from mouth to mouth, beakers being raised toward him, some people laughing secretly—everyone knew that he was not yet fifteen years old.

To Charles' inexpressible relief something happened then which directed attention away from him and his news; the gentlemen of Burgundy's retinue rose in great haste at the lower end of the table. The Duke had sent a messenger to the hall to summon all those in his entourage. The impropriety of this behavior provoked great indignation.

"Does Burgundy forget again that he made peace only an hour ago?" the Chancellor de Corbie asked furiously. "What sort of crazy behavior is this?"

"I shall tell you, Messire!" A small, hunchbacked man in the checkered livery of a jester leapt onto the seat beside the Chancellor; laughing shrilly, he fingered an object which he wore around his neck: a small, flat disc such as priests wore when they received the kiss of peace from the faithful. The object was called a *pax*. "What do you see here on my breast, Messire?" called the fool; he was part of Burgundy's retinue, where his malicious tongue was much admired. "What do you see here? A *pax*. You will say, 'Ah, Messire, do you think I will run to close up shop for a *pax* such as any priest can wear?' But look, look—I turn it round—it is a *lined* peace, as you can see—a so-called peace with a double bottom—do you understand, Messire?" The fool's strident laugh drowned out every other sound; he leaped up from the chair and ran hobbling slightly after the gentlemen of Burgundy's entourage who were moving in groups toward the door. "A lined peace—a peace with a double bottom!" he repeated, jingling his bells.

The guests did not dare to laugh, although the fool had said only what nearly everyone there already thought. None of the secular and spiritual dignitaries who sat at the festive board and drank a toast to the great reconciliation believed in the permanence of the pact. Moreover, the fact that Burgundy had quitted the table without eating or drinking spoke for itself. Curious, sympathetic glances were cast respectfully at young Orléans at the head of the table. It did not augur well for the young man; how could he save himself? Most of them believed that Burgundy would easily make himself master of the barony of Coucy and the duchy of Luxembourg, that he would fleece Orléans when and how he pleased—that would be child's play. Burgundy did not intend to be merciful, nor was there any reason why he should be; the royal kinsmen would let him go his way unquestioned. Why should anyone interfere now that peace between them had been openly announced?

Charles knew this all too well; the assurance with which, in the cathedral, he had resolved to pay Burgundy back in his own coin had vanished. How would he manage? Who would advise or support him? When he finally rose from the table he was tired and filled with somber misgivings. Now in well-chosen words he must take leave of his kinsmen and all the highly-placed, influential persons whom he had met that day. A civil word, a courteous salutation, might win him future friends—he remembered that Valentine had told him that. He rebuked his younger brother who stood yawning, pale with lack of sleep; he would have liked nothing better than to follow Philippe's example: he could scarcely keep his own eyes open.

In the great hall confusion reigned, as it usually did after a feast: spilled food and trampled decorations were strewn over the floor. Pages stood near the partially-cleared tables, waiting to see whether more food or wine would be required. But none of the guests thought of eating any more. Now that the royal family and its entourage had left the hall, no one needed to behave with restraint. Many people strolled about and an equal number had made themselves comfortable and fallen asleep.

At one of the tables a group of older men sat talking. In an undertone they discussed the inauspicious omens and ate nuts which one of them kept cracking almost mechanically. Among this company, which was still reasonably sober, was Nicolas de Baye, clerk of Parlement; he sat listening with his head resting on his left hand. He made a hill of nutshells and then began thoughtfully to draw figures and letters with a sharp piece of shell on the tablecloth. While his friends and colleagues tried to guess at Burgundy's plans and once more reviewed Orléans' poor chances, Nicolas de Baye scratched the outline of a lily into the linen between the wine stains and the crumbs and under it the words, "*Pax, pax inquit propheta, et non est pax*—peace, peace says the prophet and there is no peace." He decided to use this phrase in his account of the ceremonies at Chartres which he would have to prepare in the next few days.

It was April; the skylarks soared once more into the clear sky; the trees wore light-green leaves, daisies were scattered like stars across the grass. The fresh wind, the incandescent clouds, the sparkle of the sun on the stream—who could see all this without feeling a deep desire to melt into the bright beauty of the landscape? Madame Isabelle had become restless within the dense walls of Blois; she wished to escape the castle's chill and shadows. Charles, no less tempted by the hazy golden glow which seemed to hang above the land on the horizon, suggested to his wife that they take a journey; this would be, he thought, a good time to pay a visit to Isabeau and the King who were spending the spring in the castle of Melun.

The young Duchess of Orléans looked forward to the visit with secret trepidation: she feared her mother's hard, probing stare and inevitable questions. But anything seemed preferable to staying in Blois. Now that most of the troops had left, life in the castle was monotonous and quiet. After the unrest and mourning of recent years, both young people longed for the carefree happiness which nature seemed to promise anew each spring. As they rode forth amid a great entourage, surrounded by the green hills, forests and vineyards of the domain of Orléans, they felt in their blood for the first time something of the joy of life which belongs to youth itself.

With flushed cheeks, Isabelle looked over the fields from the window of her palanquin, enjoying the clatter of horses' hooves, the gleaming armor of the riders and the bright colors of the banners. She saw the flocks of birds wheeling in the bright sky, the shrubs along the road sparkling golden-green in the sunshine; on the wind the odor came to her of newly-ploughed earth, of heavy damp soil.

Charles rode at the head of a small group of noble friends. At the village of Olivet they were greeted by the people and offered, following the custom of the country, flat baskets filled with silvery glistening fish, and vats of wine. Charles, increasingly intoxicated by the spring air, not only accepted the gifts but decided to partake of them there as a token of his appreciation. Everyone dismounted outside Olivet in a meadow strewn with flowers; while the fish sizzled in hot oil over hastily-built fires, Isabelle's maidens danced in a circle, the gentlemen galloped their horses across the field and held a tourney, tilting at the ring. Charles flew about at mad speed, pursued in jest by his equally elated companions. He stood in the stirrups, his black cloak streaming behind him like a flag in the wind. Never before had he amused himself that much. Suddenly life seemed a great adventure, crammed with unsuspected possibilities. Had he spent his life dozing over books? Had he passed his days in a grave, melancholy dream-world? Mourning and struggle—yes, that would go on, but wasn't a man free to choose his own company? Nothing could be better than a life so sunny and carefree as this mealtime under a spring sky filled with blue and golden light; as he gave his horse full rein and dashed over the meadow, he vowed to effect friendships and keep peace with those he knew and those he was yet to know, to the end of his days. Why not also with Burgundy? Who would benefit from a quarrel between the two of them? True, the obligation to avenge his father's death weighed heavily upon him, but he could not take that obligation seriously here amidst the flower-strewn fields outside Olivet.

It seemed to him that until this moment he had lived under the influence of other peoples' lives. He had learned to see the world through the eyes of his mother: a menacing, dangerous place where slander and cunning reigned, where enemies crouched to spring on the innocent. Grief and mourning were every man's inheritance— Valentine had often said—happiness could not endure, it was as fine as a mist, as intangible as a shadow. As a child, as a young boy, he had accepted these pronouncements, but now his heart rebelled against this gloomy view of life. Standing in the stirrups, he looked out over the undulating fields, tinted bright green and brown in the spring light; he saw the women dancing in the meadow with wreaths in their hair. Isabelle sat on the grass and sang the refrain of the dance-song. The horses stood farther off, guarded by riders and grooms; the men had thrust lances into the ground adorned with bright banners—a veritable thicket of pennants. The shouts of the tilting and riding nobles filled the air; in the background among the waiting carriages, fires shimmered rosily. Against the hills lay the houses of Olivet arranged about a grey church tower; the Loire gleamed through the leafy boughs. Over all arched the blue-white sky tinted with light like a transparent dome strewn with golden dust. Charles inhaled deeply—this was bliss, he wanted to live like this. When he saw the long rows of servants and pages approaching laden with platters of baked fish and flagons of wine, he rode back to the company laughing and waving his glove.

Later, he lay in the grass beside Isabelle: he watched his wife wind wild flowers into a wreath. The sun stood high now in the heavens; it had grown warmer in the meadow. The courtiers were still occupied with their games and races; the sounds of lute and harp and singing rang in the quiet noon. The horses grazed, the tiny bells on their reins and saddles tinkled softly, the gaily colored saddlecloths of the ambling steeds flapped in the wind. The young ducal couple sat a short distance from their retinue, their faces turned toward the hills; they could almost believe themselves alone. Isabelle still hummed the melody of the dance; Charles, glancing at her from time to time, thought that she had never looked so healthy and contented. Her cheeks were pink, and she had gained some weight, which suited her.

Charles had mixed emotions about the coming of the child; he was more embarrassed and confounded than happy and proud—primarily because he still could not think of the new relationship between Isabelle and himself without constraint. So many things remained unexplained in his own behavior and the way in which Isabelle behaved whenever they came together. To be sure, the aversion he had felt for his older, haughty bride had gone, but a certain element of uneasiness remained. Charles was continually aware that he fell short of the mark, but he did not know how. He understood that love was a more complicated matter than he had once supposed, relying as he had on the words of others. He did not dare to speak with Isabelle about the things which bothered him; she was the last one he would turn to. He had never guessed that it would be so difficult to approach someone; under all circumstances—whether he encountered her now in the great hall amid retinue and guests or found her waiting in the green-curtained bed—she remained equally strange: shy, quickly offended, taciturn and surly. Only once had she shown spontaneous tenderness—on the night of his mother's death. But since then she had seemed to be waiting for something. What did she really want from him? He did his best to treat her with patience and affection; he wished honestly to be a good husband, a devoted friend. He believed staunchly that he loved his wife; it never entered his head that he could do anything else—they had been given to each other, now they must cherish and respect each other. To Charles this was a given. If Isabelle turned away, sighing, began to weep in the darkness or walked past him by day with a smile full of sad resignation, he felt obscurely guilty and depressed. In Blois a really close understanding had never existed between them.

Now in the fragrant grass near Olivet, they experienced something new: the ability to speak with each other comfortably, with gentle joking, in contented pleasure. Charles chewed thoughtfully on a blade of grass: he sampled the tart, fresh taste of the plant sap. He saw a small transparent green insect climbing the deep folds of Isabelle's dress. He caught it and blew it away. Isabelle set her wreath on his head, and laughed. Leaning toward each other, they chatted about things which up to now they had scrupulously avoided—they deliberated about what names they would give their child if it was a son and what names if it should be a daughter; they discussed the invitations to the christening feast and the baptismal service, the appropriate festivities and gifts. Isabelle wanted to order a state bed from Paris; she knew in exact detail how it must look—the figures of the apostles in gold thread on a green background for the canopy, and green velvet for the curtains. While she spoke, Charles gazed at her right hand with which she gestured to describe the bed. He saw the blue veins in her thin wrists; he had often thought that her hands were delicate and weak like an invalid's. With amazement, he listened to her stream of words; he did not know that for years fantasies over this and similar subjects had been Isabelle's only comfort.

"I will also have new mantles," said the young Duchess firmly. "After the christening, shall we get out of mourning? You must order gloves, Charles, and capes. You have had nothing new for more than a year; you are growing out of your clothes."

"Certainly." Charles laughed at her authoritative tone; the Dame de Maucouvent had spoken to him like that when he was a child. "You must take care of these things for me. I intend to buy new horses and falcons; next spring we shall go hunting at Montils, Isabelle."

She looked at him quickly with sparkling eyes.

"Do you mean that?" she asked softly. "Can we leave Blois? I dislike Blois, Charles. It is so gloomy and cold and we have known only suffering there. We have lived all these years as though there were a war, as though we were besieged or pursued. I won't wear black any more, I am tired of mourning."

"Yes, we haven't had much opportunity for celebration," remarked Charles; he ran his finger over the golden embroidery on Isabelle's sleeve. "But it will be different now, I think. I have no desire to let myself be thrust into a war with Monseigneur of Burgundy—or that which he calls peace. At first I thought—trick for trick and lie for lie, but what does a man gain by that? Burgundy still does as he pleases and it makes very little difference to me—I don't care a whit about having power abroad or about winding the government in Paris around my finger."

"You promised your mother . . ." began Isabelle hesitantly. Charles sighed and rested his face in the wide pleats of her dress.

"In the end I will surely get the King to grant my demands," he said. "It seems to me more fitting that Burgundy should be punished by the King than by me."

"You spoke differently when you returned from Chartres." Isabelle touched his head for a moment with her fingertips. "You change your mind quickly, I think."

Charles laughed, embarrassed. "Are you beginning to lecture me too?" he asked, in a low voice. "Don't think that I am too cowardly to fight. I have no desire to exercise an authority which does not belong to me. Burgundy's punishment is a matter for the government. He wants nothing more—does Burgundy—than to get my brothers and me into trouble. You understand, I'm sure, that the easiest thing would be to give him what he wants. But I will not let him have that satisfaction. If he wants to fight me, he will have to violate the agreement which we made at Chartres. Then he will be the disturber of the peace, the spoiler, and that will cost him the King's favor."

"Charles," said Isbelle suddenly, "try to maintain good relations with my mother the Queen. You will have gained much once she is on your side. And listen to me. Be wise and try to get back the land they confiscated from you—or demand compensation. That is your right."

"True." Charles sighed deeply and sat up. "I don't know why," he said, "but I have no desire to talk about these things now. It's such beautiful weather. Look, even the season has taken off its winter cloak and decked itself in green and gold and blue."

He paused, for Isabelle had turned her head toward him in surprise.

"That was prettily put," she said. "Let us also take off our mourning dress—like the season—and go clad in gold and green and blue as though we were to attend a festive ball." She began to hum again, but Charles saw that her eyes were filled with tears. He took her hand in his and looked up. The swallows skimmed through the bright sky, the sun sparkled on the wavelets of the river; moment by moment the world adorned itself with new leaves, new flowers.

Charles and Isabelle did not stay long in Melun. The King was in no condition to see them; he spent his days in a specially guarded tower of the castle, cared for by Odette de Champdivers. Isabeau was distracted; the news from Paris did not please her. Burgundy, apparently convinced that he needed again to present himself to the Parisians as their champion, had ordered an inquiry into the expenditures of money by the officers of the Crown. Isabeau knew only too well what that inquiry would bring to light. The officers of the court administration and the Audit Room were often forced to juggle figures because the Queen neglected to state accurately what she spent, or because she demanded more money than her expenses justified. In the last few years Isabeau had been on a mad spending spree: she had bought land, jewels, furniture, ornaments. The government had been distracted by other matters; nothing more was demanded of the officials concerned than an apparently balanced budget. The Queen was afraid that through Burgundy's probing, most of these transgressions would be unearthed and be traced back to her.

She was too annoyed and uneasy to pay much attention to the visit of her daughter and son-in-law. The young couple did not mind; after a few weeks they went on to Montereau, a castle near Melun that belonged to Charles. They wanted to spend the summer there, but de Braquemont warned that the armed escort was too small to defend that castle if the necessity arose. With some reluctance, Charles and Isabelle returned to Blois in July. After the carefree happiness of the early summer, life within the walls of Blois felt doubly oppressive; although the sun burned on the roofs of the houses and on the fields around the town, Isabelle shivered in her apartments—it was always chilly inside the thick walls. Even the arrival from Paris of the state bed could not put the young Duchess in a more cheerful mood.

At noon on the tenth of September, two women from Isabelle's retinue brought Charles the news that Madame d'Orléans felt suddenly unwell; she had been taken to the lying-in chamber. Charles waited with Philippe. Dusk fell and then night; they passed the time playing chess until midnight, after which Charles sent a page to his wife's apartments. The young man returned quickly to say that according to the physicians the birth of the child would be delayed a few more hours. But he did not mention what he had heard the court maidens whispering—that it was not going well with the young Duchess, that she would have to fight hard for her own life and the life of her child. Unaware of this, Charles spent a sleepless night; he had sent Philippe off to bed and sat alone now, reading by candlelight. The hours crept by slowly; he heard the page speaking in an undertone with a soldier of the guard in an adjoining room—the silence of Blois was broken from time to time by the sound of a dog howling at the moon.

Toward dawn Charles could not bear it; it was impossible for him to distract himself any longer with the tales on the parchment. He took up the candlestick and tiptoed from the room through a side door. Etiquette prevented a husband from coming near the lying-in chamber during his wife's labor; if he wanted to inquire he sent a messenger. Charles had never doubted the wisdom of this custom—now all this secrecy seemed irksome and stupid to him. The first apartment was empty. In the second, Isabelle's court maidens and servant girls knelt, praying aloud for aid and succour for their mistress. The Dame de Travercin, Isabelle's companion, frightened, came swiftly to Charles; her eyes were red from weeping.

"In God's name, Monseigneur," she whispered, "you cannot come here."

"I want to know how it goes with my wife," replied Charles; he had no intention of being sent away without information. It was not necessary for the lady to tell Charles anything now: suddenly, from behind the closed doors of the lying-in chamber came a hoarse shrieking which filled Charles with deep horror. Even in that awful sound he recognized Isabelle's voice.

"Monseigneur, Monseigneur, will you be good enough to go away?" The Dame de Travercin was at her wits' end. "The master of the council and the physicians are with the Duchess. They are doing what they can, Monseigneur, but Madame d'Orléans is having a most difficult time. We do not know how it will end."

Her words echoed in Charles' ears long after he had returned to his own room. He could not sit still; he paced back and forth, pushed open a window shutter, looked outside: a grey line was visible on the horizon, a harbinger of dawn; cocks crowed around Blois and farther away on the farms. A bell began to peal somewhere; the sound brought the young man to awareness of the reality of what was happening behind the closed door. He fled to the chapel in the inner court of the castle.

In the gilded candlesticks on the altar tapers were burning. The lighted altar seemed an island of peace and safety in the gloom of the early morning. He remained kneeling even after the sun had long risen. Philippe joined him.

"What news is there?" Charles whispered; but his brother shook his head without replying. Why must she suffer so? thought Charles, while he murmured mechanically all the prayers he thought appropriate. As the day went on he felt more and more beset by doubt: was this a punishment because he had not kept the promise that he had made to his mother? Must Isabelle do penance for his irresolution, his reluctance to attack his hereditary enemy with fire and sword? Was God's finger pointing at him: could he perhaps free Isabelle from her suffering by swearing anew, this time by all that was holy, that he would not shrink from the destiny that had been laid out for him?

"*Vota mea Domine reddam,*" prayed Charles more loudly. "I shall fulfill my vows unto the Lord." Philippe looked up in fright and astonishment and tapped him on the arm, but Charles wiped the sweat from his face and walked quickly from the chapel. In the courtyard he found one of the doctors, who told him that the progress of the labor showed little change. However Monseigneur must not despair; it might take a few more hours.

It lasted another twenty-four hours; on the afternoon of September twelfth 1409, Madame Isabelle at long last brought a child into the world, a daughter. The baby was healthy and well-formed, but the birth cost the young mother her life. Physicians and nursing women had to stand helplessly by while the Duchess of Orléans bled to death under their hands.

By candlelight and amid the tolling of church bells Isabelle was laid to rest in the church of Saint-Sauveur, beside the spot where Valentine had been buried not quite a year earlier. Tearless, silent and motionless, Charles attended all ceremonies. Then he returned to the castle; in the great hall he accepted condolences, and gave necessary orders: he requested de Braquemont to dispatch couriers to Saint-Pol and to his royal kinsmen in all parts of France. Later he went into the lying-in chamber for a moment; the beautiful state bed stood made up, unused, in the middle of the apartment. The women showed him his little daughter, Jeanne, the name Charles and Isabelle had chosen in the sunny meadow near Olivet: it was in memory of their mutual grandmother, the wife of Charles the Wise.

Silent and surprised, Charles looked at the infant; he felt nothing at all for this little creature, red, naked and helpless as the young earthworms which appear when spring rains disturb the earth. The Dame de Travercin led Charles to a corner of the chamber where some garments were spread out on a chest: the beautifully embroidered mantles which Isabelle had planned to wear after her confinement.

"What do you wish me to do with these, Monseigneur?" whispered the lady. Charles looked at the finery, now so meaningless: gold on green, silver on violet.

"Give them as gifts in my name to the priests of Saint-Saveur," he said after a pause, turning away. "Let them make chausables and dalmatics from them. Perhaps you will be so good as to give me in the near future the names of all the women and maidens who have served Madame d'Orléans. I shall have pensions and annuities paid to them."

The Dame de Travercin curtsied; she would have liked to utter objections, suggest alternatives, but the tone of Monseigneur's voice, the look on his face, imposed silence upon her. Charles left the lying-in chamber. His little daughter began to wail in a thin but penetrating voice; he quickened his step, his head drooping in deadly exhaustion.

In the month of February of the year 1410, Charles set out with a great entourage of armed soldiers for the castle of Gien-sur-Loire; he had chosen the place for a rendezvous with all the great lords and their vassals who had pledged to serve the cause of Orléans. The environs of the castle looked like an army camp; countless tents stood in the fields. Farmsteads and houses were cleared out to serve as lodging for the warriors and stalls for their horses. The peasants who lived there had fled or been driven away from garden and farmyard; the cattle and stores of wine and grain which they had left behind served the always-hungry soldiers as food and drink. The tents and camps swarmed with Gascons, Bretons and Provençals—for the most part rough, brutal men, difficult to control, unreliable, fond of looting and arson and, in battle, truly ferocious cruelty.

When on the bitter cold, misty morning of the twenty-fourth of February, Charles rode through the fields to Gien, he had ample time to review these troops; he knew that the majority of men assembled here were in the service of his new ally, the Count d'Armagnac, with whom he had negotiated since October of the previous year by means of letters and couriers. De Braquemont and de Villars were wont to say that one could know a general by the appearance and conduct of his soldiers; if this were true, thought Charles, he could hope for little good to come from this meeting with Bernard d'Armagnac.

The soldiers who lined the way to watch Orléans' men enter Gien were filthy and unkempt. They were singularly arrayed in parts of old armor, worn-out leather, mantles and coats of mail raggedly pulled together. As they lounged before the houses they had taken over, their demeanor was insolent or indifferent; some wandered in groups over the fields, trying to see what poultry they could catch; others squatted around the great fires which burned here and there among the tents and huts.

The road to Gien was nearly impassable; the horses hurt their legs on sharp crusts of frozen mud, or slipped on ice-covered pools. A stinging cold mist hovered over the land, making it difficult to see. Charles, at the head of his slowly riding, silent escort, saw himself as a traveler in Virgil's underworld—the dark, misty borderland of Hell, filled with faint spectres whom it was wise to leave undisturbed. Charles closed his eyes and hunched his shoulders; the edge of his mantle touched the bottom of his bonnet, giving him the illusion, at least, of shelter against the penetrating damp cold.

Since Isabelle's death he had made no more effort to evade the fate which had apparently been reserved for him. He had resumed operations. His captains de Braquemont and de Villars had at first been suspicious of his air of grim resignation, but later they observed his resumption of operations with growing satisfaction: the garrisons were strengthened, the vassals and their men who had started for home had been recalled, messages had been sent to the allies, the Dukes of Brittany and Alençon. Now that Isabelle's retinue, her maidens and servants, had left the castle, now that her clothes had been given as gifts, her jewels and trinkets put away, and the morning slippers which still stood under the marriage bed had been quickly removed, so that the sight of the small red shoes would not cause Monseigneur sorrow—now that all reminders of the short existence of the young Duchess had vanished, Blois looked more than ever like a fortress, a barracks, with the inner courts and outbuildings filled with archers and foot soldiers. A few women still occupied the series of apartments on the south side of the castle: the old Dame de Maucouvent and some maidservants who looked after the two little girls, Mademoiselle Marguérite, Charles' three-year-old sister, and his daughter Mademoiselle Jeanne. They lived there in a world of their own with scarcely any attention paid to them: two little maidens who could not play a role of any significance in this drama of hatred and revenge.

Charles had reacted to Isabelle's death more with bitter amazement than with grief. Gloomily he asked himself if this were to be his life then: a long journey with no resting places except those of mourning and catastrophe. He had found some verses among the papers which had belonged to his father; he remembered when Herbelin the minstrel had set these words to music: "En la forest de Longue Attente, Chevauchant par divers sentiers. . . In the forest of Long Awaiting, Riding along its many paths. . ." When he was a child, Charles had not understood the imagery; now he was struck by the metaphor and he found the verses harmonious; they awoke a feeling in him which he could not name: they gave him comfort but also profound pain and uneasiness. He often repeated the beginning of the song in his thoughts, or in an undertone. He did not know why he did this; it gave him a feeling of peculiar gratification.

However, he had little time to indulge himself in these kinds of thoughts. He worked together with his captains to raise the army which had been called together after his father's death. And he had many letters to write to the Lords of Coucy and Luxembourg to remind them of their vows of fealty and immediate support in case of need. In January he received assistance from an unexpected source: the Dukes of Berry and Bourbon wrote to him in detail, informing him that they had severed all ties with Burgundy and were disposed to help Orléans' cause. Now that they had publicly proclaimed their withdrawal from the Council and affairs of state, they felt they could justifiably offer Charles their counsel. Burgundy's indifference and insults had driven both old Dukes to frenzy; however, they had had to give way to him. Berry especially was stimulated to renewed activity by the jeers leveled at him. He had initiated the idea of approaching young Charles, who could not oppose Burgundy without experienced assistance.

"He is too young and we are too old to raise and lead armies," said Berry to Bourbon during one of the numerous discussions they held after their resignation. Wrapped in furs and velvet, they sat, two gouty, corpulent old men, facing each other by the hearthfire in one of the halls of the Hôtel de Nesle. Bourbon, who was a trifle dazed and lax, said little; Berry talked a great deal. His small, piercing eyes sparkled; his hands, loaded with jewels, did not rest for a second.

"We have the experience and the ability to open negotiations with the people whom we will need most. He has the name of Orléans and full reason to go to war. What we need now are a few fellows who can fight and a list of ringing names to give substance to the whole undertaking."

Berry was not satisfied with words alone; thanks to his efforts, Bourbon's son, the Count de Clermont, and the Constable d'Albret declared themselves ready to support Orléans in the struggle against Burgundy. Berry's son-in-law, Bernard d'Armagnac, seemed an even more valuable acquisition. Berry congratulated himself on his cleverness in winning over the Gascon to his nephew's side. The counts of Armagnac and their troops were known, and for good reason, far and wide: for more than half a century they had served as mercenaries, both at home and abroad, to anyone who paid them well and did not look too closely at their methods. The Gascons had fought for Florence twenty years before; without scruple they had afterward deserted to the troops of Gian Galeazzo and Louis d'Orléans. Under the leadership of their captain, de Chassenage, they had finally forced Savona and a number of other cities to surrender to France.

Bernard d'Armagnac lent a willing ear to Berry's summons; he was attracted for a number of reasons by the offer to become a pivotal force in Orléans' army. Although he belonged to the oldest and once most powerful family in the Kingdom, the Count d'Armagnac enjoyed little respect; the princes and members of the royal family looked upon him as a brigand, an adventurer, the leader of a pack of plundering brutes. He had never appeared at court; his peers avoided him. When he was not fighting abroad, he was to be found in one of his fortresses in Armagnac, everywhere and always surrounded by troops of soldiers. Although he frequently and loudly proclaimed that a good understanding with his peers did not interest him, Armagnac secretly felt himself to be an outcast. Berry's proposal gave him the chance to get his foot firmly into circles which until that moment had been closed to him. He wanted to nestle permanently into the world of powerful men.

When, therefore, young Orléans, in a personal letter, requested that he come to Gien-sur-Loire, he did not hesitate for a moment. At the head of a constantly expanding army, he rode to the meeting place. In the ranks which followed him there were well-equipped horsemen, many heavily armed, pugnacious battlers who for the most part had been in the service of Armagnac for twenty years or more—but there were also bands of adventurers eager for plunder and murder; vagrants, escaped criminals and half-grown young fellows who would do anything rather than run behind a plow. Like one of the plagues of Egypt they moved through the land, leaving a trail behind them of demolished farms, barns stripped bare and carcasses of slaughtered cattle. So Bernard d'Armagnac came to Gien, where he found the Dukes of Berry, Bourbon, Brittany and Alençon and the Count of Clermont. They awaited only Charles d'Orléans. On the morning of the twenty-seventh of February, a messenger rode into Gien with the news that Monseigneur was approaching; he would reach the castle before the midday meal.

❦ ❦ ❦

"I say, fight!" Bernard d'Armagnac placed both palms flat on the table and looked at his confederates. His yellow-brown eyes glinted in his weather-beaten face, which was full of lines and scars, a face that looked as though it were carved from wood, with high cheekbones and a heavy lower jaw. Among his companions he looked like a giant, taller than they, with a broader, coarser frame. He did not care about his appearance or his behavior: his thick grey hair hung to his shoulders; he wore a stained leather jacket, worn-out boots, a coat of mail on which the lions rampant of Armagnac were already faded. Around him hovered an acrid odor of hay, dogs and horses, of smoke and sweat. He reminded Berry of a beast of prey: the blazing yellow eyes, the hairy wrists and sharp eyeteeth could scarcely be termed human.

The lords sat in one of the empty chambers of the castle of Gien. The castle was seldom occupied and was neglected: the furniture and tapestries which Charles had sent from Blois could not make the cheerless shabby rooms more comfortable—moreover, it was very cold and draughty. The allies had been meeting together since the midday meal. The misty day had passed unperceived into night; for a long time candles had been burning on the table. Leaning forward, Bernard d'Armagnac inspected the other members of the company, one by one: the almost toothless, white-haired Berry, despite his old age keen and ready for fierce repartee, dressed up like a strutting peacock; the young Orléans who spoke little but listened all the more attentively; the Constable d'Albret; Bourbon's son Clermont; the Dukes of Alençon and Brittany. Methods of bringing about Burgundy's downfall had been discussed in great detail; Bourbon, his son and Brittany advocated indirect action: a letter signed by all of them and directed to the King demanding compensation and rehabilitation of Orléans' honor as well as Burgundy's punishment and exile. Berry and the Constable d'Albret held that dispatching such a petition was a waste of time; it would never reach the King's eyes. The Queen and her Council would dismiss it or, in the most favorable circumstances, table the matter indefinitely with vague promises and evasive answers. Bernard d'Armagnac loudly supported Berry.

"I say, fight!" he repeated. "That is our only chance. We must batter Burgundy to a pulp. I am not afraid to risk a fight, my lords. I have stood with my Gascons before hotter fires. Besides, we are in good shape; for more than three years we've been fighting against the English in Bordeaux, and the English-loving Bretons in our midst. Give my men the chance to march against the Flemish peasants—they want nothing better, Messeigneurs. And as for me . . ."

He raised his hands and then dropped them back on the table with a thud. "I have offered my services here; I do nothing halfway." He looked at Charles d'Orléans; his brown chapped lips split into a crooked smile. "I have an interest in the matter too. Burgundy's ally, Navarre, is my hereditary enemy as well as yours, my lord."

"Yes, yes, I know it." The old Duke of Bourbon sighed impatiently. "Fight—that is easily said—but Burgundy's strong; he has powerful allies. He has bought our cousin of Anjou. Ludwig of Bavaria supports him and the Queen protects him."

Berry burst into laughter, the malicious chuckle he often emitted when Isabeau's name was mentioned. "Ah, the Queen," he said with apparent casualness, "she will find that she has been deceived. She imagines she has done something clever by entrusting the Dauphin to Burgundy's care. Like all mothers, she is vain and she is blinded by that vanity; she thinks she controls the Dauphin and through him, Burgundy. Sooner or later she will regret this stupidity. I am completely in accord with my worthy son-in-law Armagnac. We must attack Burgundy, Messeigneurs."

"Orléans hasn't spoken yet," remarked the young Duke of Brittany; he shot a glance from under his heavy black eyebrows at Charles, who sat at the head of the table. "His vote must turn the scale—we are now three against three . . ."

Berry, who had been keeping a sharp eye on his grandnephew—why didn't the boy speak, what did he have in mind?—began to talk quickly, cutting Brittany off.

"The miserable state of the Kingdom, Messeigneurs, calls for acts, not intermediate negotiations. We are all bound to the King by ties of blood; we all owe him fealty and respect. Therefore we are chosen first for the great work I propose to you: we must fight to defeat the King's enemies—fight for the welfare of the Kingdom—that is the task set out for us, my lords! That is why it is our duty, our obligation as honorable men to defend the good name of our late nephew and kinsman, Monseigneur d'Orléans . . ."

"In my opinion that is the principal purpose of this enterprise," said Armagnac, interrupting Berry's flow of words. "So far as I am concerned, Orléans, I will readily admit that I would rather fight for the restoration of the honor of Monseigneur your father than for the King or the people of Paris. I knew your father well. At first I thought of him as only a courtier, an elegant lord without much backbone—but I finally had to admit that he knew what he was doing—he could ply a sword with the best of us, if it came to that, and he had a clever tongue. I never had to wait for pay and compensation for expenses when I fought for Orléans in Italy!"

He flung his whip on the table and moved closer to Charles. "We often agreed about a lot of things," he went on, staring at the young man from the corner of his eye, "Together with your father, I also turned against the English and with good results, believe me. I drove them out of more than sixty villages and they never returned. You buy no pig in a poke when you buy my services, worthy friend; let me manage this business of Burgundy for you. Fight, young man, fight! I don't see any other way for you to achieve your purpose."

He slapped Charles on the shoulder. Then he folded his arms and looked with glinting eyes at the row of faces before him. He prided himself secretly that he was the only real man in this elevated company. Berry and Bourbon were old; Alençon and Clermont both insignificant; d'Albret and Brittany two hotheads, and finally young Orléans—a quiet youth, still almost a child. It seemed a foregone conclusion to Armagnac that he himself would be the leader here—followed and obeyed by men who bore the most impressive names in France, he could ascend a steeper path than ever he would have dared to choose.

All eyes were now fixed upon Charles d'Orléans; he sat erect, in the seat of honor, thinking about all this. He had heard and seen enough by now to know that none of his allies was motivated by overwhelming neighborly love; he had had to buy the support of the Constable d'Albret, just as his father had once had to buy the support of Alençon. Brittany wanted to spite Navarre and Burgundy. Bourbon and Clermont who, under the rule of Burgundy, had had little opportunity to play an important role, hoped that after a victory of Orléans' party they could move again to the forefront. Finally Berry, furious because he had been driven from office, nursed even more rancor against the hated House of Burgundy; the old Duke wanted to settle accounts once and for all with the son for the abuse he had taken for so many years from the father. And as for Armagnac, Charles had watched him during the discussions; he considered him a crafty, callous man, one who would not hesitate to take advantage of the circumstances if there should be war between Orléans and Burgundy.

Charles was afraid that he would lose the friendship of many of his supporters if he chose the troops of savage Gascons to defend his cause. De Braquemont and de Villars had already warned him against it, and what he had seen with his own eyes on the way to Gien did not make him any the less uneasy. However, he knew that it was impossible to get rid of Armagnac now that they had accepted him as an ally and informed him of their plans. It was a matter of controlling him; it had not escaped Charles that Bernard d'Armagnac wished to be lord and master here. The young man realized that he must be very clever if he were not to be deprived of power. He was not yet entirely certain of what to do, but he knew he must speak. He stood up, with his hands resting on the edge of the table before him. In order not to let his attention be diverted, he did not look at the row of faces illuminated by candlelight. He fixed his eyes instead on the escutcheons hanging on the opposite wall.

"I believe," he said, slowly and softly—Bourbon leaned forward with one hand cupped to his ear—"I believe that we must do neither one nor the other; I agree with Monseigneur de Berry that a petition will not help us. I have already had the opportunity of seeing how that works. On the other hand, I do not yet believe that this is the right moment to take up arms; I will not fight before I have made a final effort to persuade the King to administer justice. I propose that we advance upon Paris with our men, that we dispatch a manifesto to the government there, demanding that Burgundy be punished and exiled and offering the King our services, wherever and whenever he desires, to fight against Burgundy, if he should resist the King's measures. We should come with our troops to show that we are able-bodied and prepared for anything. I am ready to hear what you think of this, my lords."

A short silence followed these words. Armagnac screwed up his eyes and thoughtfully gnawed the handle of his whip. He tried to calculate what opportunities Charles' suggestions offered to him. Finally he snorted, made an assenting gesture and threw his whip upon the table. Berry, who had been watching him closely, could not restrain a smile of satisfaction; he nodded slowly and approvingly. Bourbon whispered to his son—both of them, inclined as always to take the middle road, deemed it a most excellent proposal.

Alençon was secretly relieved; like Charles, he felt that the Gascon's behavior would make an unfavorable impression. The Constable d'Albret, who saw his hope of reaping military fame going up in smoke, was vexed, but he did not dare offer any objections now that he saw the attitude of the others. Brittany, with downcast eyes, toyed with the hilt of his dagger.

Charles was slightly stunned at the readiness of his allies to accept his proposal; he had not expected it. He tried to ascertain what motives were playing a role here; during the last months he had become mistrustful enough to attempt to find out what lay behind an all-too-willing agreement. However, he had no time for reflection. Berry had already risen from his seat and said that he and all the others were completely in accord with the solution which Monseigneur d'Orléans, like a second Solomon, had put forward. Armagnac laughed loudly and shouted Berry down.

"Worthy father-in-law, let me get a word in now. I am your man, Orléans, even though I venture to predict to you that it will turn into war sooner or later. Get to work on that manifesto—that is a task for the two bishops which Monseigneur de Berry has brought with him. And tell them at the same time to keep their pens and ink ready to draw up still another document. Look here, why don't I speak frankly, we are all together now."

Shifting his chair so that he faced Charles, he leaned his elbows on his spread knees and tapped the arm of Charles' seat softly with the butt of his whip. "We have a saying in Armagnac: a really true agreement should be sealed with a wedding. Now I am one of those who hold that a bride or a bridegroom form a stronger link between two parties than a couple of signatures or a seal. You are a widower, Orléans, but surely it cannot be your intention to remain one permanently."

Annoyed, Berry gave a warning cough. But the Gascon refused to be driven from the field.

"We can still talk in a business-like way about these things," he continued. "We are among men. Look, Orléans, I have a daughter. I will give her to you with a handsome dowry besides. Monseigneur de Berry, her grandfather, will see to the dispensation. He has already promised me that. I don't doubt that everything will turn out all right."

Berry nearly choked from coughing; he held his sleeve before his mouth. He was crimson with rage and shame. Never had he

seen so tactless a braggart as his son-in-law. No one would doubt
that he had suggested the marriage proposal to Armagnac. Charles
looked up; his eyes betrayed astonishment and antipathy. He was
at the point of retorting that he had no intention of contracting a
new marriage at this time, but Armagnac, who sensed young Orléans' reaction, resumed hastily and still more loudly.

"My daughter Bonne is only eleven years old. You do not need
to see her for the time being if you don't wish it. They tell me that
she's a comely lass, healthy and cheerful. What more do you want?
And I repeat: the dowry is royal with favorable terms—only a few
instalments and a great sum all at once!"

"Forgive me, Monseigneur," said Charles, arising. "I cannot go
into your proposal now. I should like to adjourn the session for
today, at any rate. With my chancellor and the bishops of Bourges
and Nantes I shall draw up the text of the statement tomorrow and
send it to the King with all our signatures."

He bowed and left the chamber.

"You are an idiot," said Berry in an undertone to Bernard d'Armagnac.

The Gascon grinned and stretched himself.

"I have caught him all right," he remarked. "I won't let go of
him. Come, where is the dining hall now? Let's go there, my lords."

"I still do not see how you will set this matter right," Berry
muttered to his son-in-law. While he passed through the door he
slipped his fur-lined hood over his head. The shutters behind the
airholes were for the most part rotten and full of cracks; cold draughts
of wind blew down the corridor. Armagnac, who walked ahead with
great strides, looked over his shoulder at his father-in-law. In the
light of the torches held by servants who had come running to light
the gentlemen on their way to the dining hall, Berry looked like a
malignant gnome; with his crooked fingers, sparkling with gems,
he wrapped his mantle more closely about him; his eyes gleamed in
the shadow of his hood.

"Orléans is as poor as a church mouse," said Armagnac with an
eloquent gesture. "That boy is so hard up for money that he cannot
refuse my offer. Let him think about it for a moment: he will have
to see that he can only gain by this. You said yourself that Orléans
is as pliable as wax—if that's so, we shall have no trouble shaping
him as we wish, father-in-law."

⚜ ⚜ ⚜

The meal was boisterous; since no women were present no one had to watch his words. Although tables had been pushed together, Charles' stewards still found there was not enough room for all the members of the lords' retinues. Men sat, or even stood, eating in the adjoining chambers and in the corridors. After the wine had been passed around a few times, no one bothered with table manners; Bernard d'Armagnac sat with one leg thrown over the arm of the bench and tossed bones to six or seven mastiffs who roamed through the hall. The Gascons and the Provençals set the tone: there was shouting and loud singing and knives were slammed against the table. Armagnac's followers were accustomed to scantier fare in their poor fatherland than they were offered here. They did not let the opportunity escape to enjoy the good things of the earth.

Charles, who had never seen anything like it, made an effort to show no surprise or displeasure; he remembered how the soldiers in Blois, ruled by the captains with an iron hand under his mother's watchful eye, had always conducted themselves in an orderly way, like monks. But this was what happened under the leadership of men who knew no life outside war and adventure, who greedily seized what the day brought, who were free of bonds and obligations. Their eyes and teeth shone; they dominated the tables, drowning out the men who had come with Bourbon, Berry, Alençon and Charles and who attempted to rise to the occasion.

For an instant, Charles felt an impulse to abandon all self-control; he wished he could for once be drunk, shout hoarsely, rest his leg on the table, forget that his name was Orléans, that he wore mourning and had to carry a heavy responsibility. He wanted to be exuberant and unabashed, to curse and mock in a drunken fit, to express his long pent-up bitterness, to give himself up to the wildest, most reckless diversions. The blood mounted to his head; he looked at the goblet which stood on the table before him.

But it flashed suddenly through his mind that he wanted to speak with his Chancellor, with both bishops and with the Sire de Mornay, the governor of Orléans, in his own apartments after the meal. He had already summoned them; it would surely be undignified to discuss, in a drunken condition, so important a subject as the manifesto to the King. He tried therefore to keep his distance from what he saw happening around him. He leaned toward his great-uncle of Bourbon who sat, drowsy and sullen, munching a piece of pastry, and began a conversation with him. Bernard d'Armagnac still had a surprise up his sleeve. When at the conclusion of the meal, the customary dessert—spiced wine— was brought in, the Gascon bawled an order to the men standing by the door. Amid applause, two stableboys led a coal-black stallion into the hall, a vigorous, handsome beast.

"Orléans," said Armagnac, rising, "will you be so good as to accept this horse from me—a warhorse, foaled in my own stables? Perhaps you will find it a more suitable gift to seal our alliance."

Charles went up to the stallion and looked at him; he had not seen such a beautiful animal in a long time. The horse's skin shone like silk, he stood free and erect on powerful muscular legs. The grooms had difficulty restraining him; he reared back wildly and kicked; the straw covering the floor of the hall flew in all directions. He shook his head, snorting, and clouds of vapor streamed from his nostrils. He opened his mouth wide, showing his sound teeth. Charles patted the stallion's flanks and fed him sugar from his hand. He really wanted to own this horse, but he could not dismiss the thought that Armagnac was trying somehow to trick him.

He wished that he knew what lay concealed behind the fierce yellow-brown eyes, behind that boisterous façade, what thoughts were in that head. He thanked Armagnac for the gift; while the horse was being led away, the Gascon proposed a toast to Orléans' health. In accordance with an old custom he flung the beaker over his shoulder against the wall and then strode to embrace Charles. The grooms had delivered the horse to the stableboys outside the door to the hall and now stood expectantly, staring at the royal table. Charles knew what they were waiting for; he had to reward them. It became quiet in the hall; everyone was looking at him. At his own table he saw expressions of indifference, amusement, impatience. A prince did not forget things like that; he had to know how to dispense money smoothly, but not too openhandedly or carelessly—if the knowledge was not innate, it had to be taught by careful education. One could tell a great deal about the character and savoir-faire of a man by the way in which he discharged this honorable duty.

Charles fumbled for the purse which hung from his belt, annoyed at his own negligence. As he loosened the cord, he calculated rapidly to himself. He knew that only some loose silver and a few valuable gold pieces remained in the purse. That was virtually all he possessed; he had been forced to sell books and tableware in order to pay the travel and entertainment expenses of his allies. He could not give the boys the silver coins—that was too little. And he could not give them one gold coin; custom demanded a gift for each of them. He had no choice. He took the two heavy gold coins from his purse and tossed them into the caps which the grooms hurriedly held out to him. This act was received with murmurs and shouts of approval. Armagnac's followers were especially pleased; they saw in the royal gesture a conscious mark of homage to their master. The latter, however, laughed to himself; he suspected that the young Duke of Orléans had nearly ruined himself by his generosity to the grooms.

Charles sat alone in the tower chamber of Gien where he and his advisors had met almost daily for a week. Before him on the table lay the unrolled parchment of the manifesto addressed to the King, written in large, beautiful, even letters. Maître Garbet had labored over it for two days; he was a skilled calligrapher. Charles nodded approvingly and bit his thumb while he pored over the lines. He read the end of the statement softly aloud: "And so we humbly beseech you, most powerful and sovereign Lord, to consider our petitions and take account of the goals for which we strive, to wit: the rightful restoration of Your Sovereign Majesty to the state of honor which is your due. And we beg you further to give us leave to fight in your name for the preservation of liberty and justice in your Kingdom, first for the greater glory of God, secondly for your honor and lastly for the well-being and welfare of your subjects. That this struggle may unite all your truly loyal and devoted subjects, all those genuinely friendly toward you, is the sincere wish of . . ." And here would be appended the signatures of Orléans, Berry, Bourbon, Clermont, Alençon and Brittany.

While Charles stood bending over the document, the leather curtain before the door parted behind him. Even without turning the young man knew who had entered: a musky smell met his nostrils; he heard the clank of mail and the tap of a riding whip against boots.

"Will you not sit down, Messeigneurs?" Charles shoved the parchment to one side. Berry and Armagnac greeted him and seated themselves on a bench under a green canopy. Armagnac had just come from the hunt; he had spent the day in the fields with a number of nobles, killing ducks and rabbits to chase away boredom.

"The document is ready, my lords," said Charles with satisfaction; he found the manifesto nicely worded and beautifully executed. He was content with his work; not for nothing had he lain awake nights reflecting on the precise meaning of a word, choosing a specific turn of phrase. "I trust we can sign it tonight."

"Nephew," said Berry abruptly, "my son-in-law Armagnac and I consider it our duty to warn you. We have learned from a very reliable source that Monseigneur of Brittany will probably refuse to sign the manifesto."

Charles had been walking to his chair; he stopped and stood near the window.

"Why not?" he asked, with quick suspicion. He looked at both faces in the shadow of the canopy. "What do you mean?"

Armagnac began to speak, but Berry swiftly cut him off.

"Burgundy has reportedly offered Monseigneur of Brittany 20,000 gold écus, supposedly at the King's request, if he declared himself ready to go over with all his men to the enemy."

Charles began to object passionately, but Berry raised both hands in a soothing gesture, and went on. "Listen to me—of course it's always possible that he won't sell himself for that amount. But Brittany has huge debts and his quarrel with his mother has not helped him any; he'll get nothing from that quarter. He can't pay his men their wages."

"In short," said Armagnac, "whoever can pay his debts and his soldiers will possess him."

Berry gestured at him vehemently and turned back to Charles. "For two days Brittany has been negotiating with Burgundy's messengers a few miles from Gien. I tell you this to help you: a similar offer in time on your part could prevent you from losing an important ally."

Charles turned and gazed out the grey-green convex window panes. Through the turbid glass he saw vague spots like shapes seen under water. Now he knew the meaning of Brittany's silences and evasive glances.

"I can offer him nothing," he replied. "For I have nothing myself. I am probably poorer than Brittany."

Bernard d'Armagnac rose and approached him slowly with bent head, but his gaze was searching and he smiled with satisfaction, like a patient angler who has finally hooked a fish. He came close to Charles. The warm vapor, d'Armagnac's constant odor of stables, wine and sweat, Charles found suddenly revolting. He found Armagnac's habit of intruding himself intolerable.

"Look here, Orléans," said the Gascon; he attempted for the moment to subdue his raucous voice. "My offer comes to you just in time. If you take my daughter Bonne to wife, you will receive 100,000 gold francs from me—30,000 on the marriage day and the rest in annual payments of 10,000 francs. I shall feed her and clothe her until she is old enough to live with you. Come now, you can't call that a bad offer. Believe me, you can't do anything without money. Your pockets are empty, Orléans—how can you accomplish what you set out to do?"

"We respect your grief, nephew," whispered Berry, who stood now on the other side of Charles, "but think, we princes seldom enjoy the privilege of long mourning. We have other obligations. It seems to me that you ought to accept Armagnac's proposal. The bride is still only a child. And you are over the worst of your sorrow, nephew."

With a heavy heart Charles thought of his empty purse, of the far from encouraging conversation which he had had a few days earlier with his treasurer and the captains of his troops. A feeling of disgust and boundless weariness crept over him. Must he then always allow himself to be ruled by others, was it his fate to be goaded along just those paths which he did not want to take? They were right—without money there were no allies; without allies, no power; without power, no justice; without justice—for him at any rate—no honor, and what man can live without honor? With downcast eyes he pressed the hand which Armagnac held out to him.

All summer long Charles continued to recruit and arm the soldiers; he ordered his castles and the city of Orléans to be fortified. A proclamation was issued in the King's name, banning the taking of service under the Duke of Orléans or his allies; despite this, at least 11,000 men were encamped around Chartres in the autumn. It seemed obvious that Burgundy had suggested this proclamation to the Council since he had raised a large army himself; these Brabanters, Flemings, Bavarians and Burgundians were thrown, for food and shelter, upon the populations of the Ile de France and the countryside north of Paris. Burgundy saw the moment approaching for which he had waited so long: to be in a position to chop up his enemies to his heart's content. He hoped and believed that it would be a massacre without equal, although there were moments when he had doubts: Orléans' inexperienced milksops had sought advice and assistance at the right time. Brittany had not accepted the bribe, which seemed to be proof that Orléans' party—despite all appearances to the contrary—could still come up with funds. All the more reason, thought Burgundy, to nip the growing danger in the bud quickly and for good.

In Paris he carried on a campaign with good results. He succeeded in filling the people with terror over the approach of Orléans' troops; tales were told of the horrible cruelty of the Gascons and Bretons, street orators and agents reminded everyone once again of the sins of the late Orléans. The Provost des Essars, one of Burgundy's most passionate partisans, rode by day and by night through the city, armed and with a great following of horsemen and soldiers—thus the atmosphere of disquiet was heightened. The burghers addressed a humble petition to des Essars: they knew of course that the Provost and Monseigneur of Burgundy would leave no stone unturned to protect Paris, but could the populace not set watches and patrols in each district for greater security? This was precisely what des Essars had wanted—and so it came to pass.

In September when Charles d'Orléans and his allies appeared before Paris—they had arrived with all their troops to hand the manifesto personally to the King—they found the gates closed, the city fortified. In the villages and the outskirts lay the armies of Burgundy.

"Now surely everything has been said and done!" said Bernard d'Armagnac impatiently; he strode up and down, stamping on the plank floors so hard that the dust rose up in clouds. The allies, their commanders, advisors, clerks and chancellors, were in a house at Montlhéry, about seven miles from Paris. The troops had pitched their tents in the fields outside the village where they awaited the decisions of the great lords. In the meantime the troops were not impatient: in the vineyards and orchards ripe fruit hung for the taking; the country people, having learned prudence through bitter experience, seldom ventured into the fields.

"The King has sent letters, the University has sent a delegation, and Her Majesty the Queen was so kind as to come to meet us at

Marcoussis," Armagnac went on. "They beseech us tearfully to send our troops home before we visit the King. We have said no three times. *Now* what do we do, my lords?"

"We have made demands too," remarked Charles; he straddled a bench. Since he had begun to wear leather and mail, his movements had lost that deliberate formality which had always been characteristic of him. He walked and sat like a soldier; not bothering to be courtly in speech and demeanor. These changes were observed with approval by Charles' entourage—finally Monseigneur d'Orléans was becoming a warrior.

"You might as well ask for the moon, son-in-law," said Armagnac contemptuously, "as ask that Burgundy be gone from Paris and the Provost des Essars be dismissed from his post! I do not see your demands being granted, although a hundred times those fellows from the University have declared themselves ready to mediate. In the first place Burgundy pays no attention to the University, when it comes to that, and in the second place those in purple cassocks have their heads set on other things. Believe me, son-in-law, the Council of Pisa is more important to them than a row between you and Burgundy. They take the new Pope more to heart than the King. Don't count on *their* intercession! But seriously now: what do you intend to do? Paris sits sealed shut—a company of my men rode by the ramparts this morning hoping to break a lance, but no one ventured outside. Not even when my fellows fired a dozen arrows!"

"That was surprisingly stupid and reckless," Charles said coldly; he tapped angrily on the edge of the table. He had noticed repeatedly that Armagnac, in spite of decisions made in joint council, gave arbitrary orders, allowed his troops to behave defiantly and tolerated licentious and coarse behavior.

The journey from Chartres to Paris had not passed off without trouble: the closer they came to the city, the more hostile were the people. The fear which the populace exhibited toward Armagnac's men set Charles to thinking. In addition, he could see, every day, how the Gascons and Provençals accepted discipline. Ignoring the express command to preserve order and refrain from acts of violence when they passed through towns and villages, Armagnac's men had plundered right and left as they chose; they flogged those who resisted them and violated the maidens and women who fell into their hands. Sometimes stones and abuse rained down when the soldiers passed through; usually the townspeople hid behind bolted shutters and doors. Charles had been sorely provoked by the brutal, obstinate behavior of his new father-in-law; how could he strive honorably for what he considered his just due when his men behaved like a pack of devils? Neither pleas nor rebukes had any effect upon Armagnac; he listened to everything, but he refused to change his ways. What Charles, his captains and the Dukes of Bourbon and Alençon feared, came to pass: the Gascons' actions stigmatized the entire enterprise. Henceforth the Orléans party, both inside and outside France, were called nothing but Armagnacs. "Armagnac" was the worst term of abuse one could find for an enemy; the accusation "He is an Armagnac" was like a sentence of death.

"I do not understand, father-in-law, why you do not hold your men in check," continued Charles evenly, doing his best to control himself. But passion drove the blood to his head. "Do you want them to call us bad-tempered disturbers of the peace because of our violence? Do you want them to think that we are trying to force war upon the King and Burgundy? We are here to demand justice; we can take up arms only if they refuse us that justice."

Armagnac laughed loudly and spread his arms in an eloquent gesture of scorn and impatience. "By Christ's wounds!" he swore. "Do you seriously believe that there is something behind all those words and formalities? Frankly, I call that blather on both sides. Burgundy is trying to gain time, he hopes to make us uncertain by delay. He thinks our vigilance will slacken after weeks and months of waiting. I am eager to know now, Orléans, what you intend to achieve by dawdling and diplomatic talk. I take it you are pursuing a definite course of action. Don't tell me you are in earnest about your requests for justice and your demands for satisfaction? That would be the greatest farce I ever. . ."

He tossed his ever-present riding whip on the table and approached Charles.

"Even senile old Bourbon still had ambitions," he said in an undertone. "Are you still wet behind the ears then, son-in-law?"

"Will you be quiet now?" cried Charles passionately, glancing at the gentlemen seated at the foot of the table: Alençon and d'Albret with their army captains, officials and priests who belonged to the council of the Orléans party—Brittany had had business to settle elsewhere, and Berry, who did not feel well, lay in bed. "Do not forget that we all wear mourning for Monseigneur de Bourbon."

"Naturally. May God rest his soul." With a mocking grimace Armagnac tugged at the crepe which he, like his confederates, wore bound about his right arm. "Now to business. What do you plan to do?"

Charles rose, "Messire Davy," he said loudly to his Chancellor, "be so good as to read Monseigneur d'Armagnac the letter we received this morning from the King in Paris."

"From Burgundy," said Armagnac, also loudly.

"The messenger says the King is somewhat recovered," remarked the Chancellor. He unrolled the letter and began to read from it slowly and carefully about distress in the city; now that the armies of Orléans and Burgundy occupied the countryside around Paris, the flow of victuals was greatly impeded, yes, made impossible. Food supplies were depleted. Fear of the soldiers prevented the populace from bringing in the harvest—whatever harvest could still be reaped. The King was extremely displeased with the attitudes of both parties. Did the treaty of Chartres mean so little to them? It was the King's wish that Orléans as well as Burgundy and all their vassals and allies should return to their own domains. A board of impartial councillors would henceforth assist the King. The Provost des Essars was relieved of his office.

"That means our first demand is granted," said Charles, motioning to Messire Davy to withdraw. "In the manifesto we declared that we wished to free the King from Burgundy. The King has now taken this measure himself. I am positive he will hear with favor my petition for justice."

"Do you mean to say that I must send my men home without anything to show for their efforts?" Armagnac put his hands on his hips and set one foot on the bench. "They have smelled the odor of roasting meat, and now must they leave the fat drumsticks lying there? What do you think we are, Orléans?"

In November a new treaty was signed in the castle of Bicêtre—a treaty as troublesome and tricky as the preceding one. Berry, invited by the King to resume his seat in the Council, appeared this time also as a peacemaker and chairman of the discussion, much to the indignation of Charles, who could not understand how his great uncle could change his opinion with such rapidity. The Duke of Berry was able to adapt himself to every circumstance with bewildering ease. He pleaded the durability of an armistice and reconciliation between both parties with the same eloquence with which he had advocated war a good half year before. Burgundy himself did not appear; he had sent a number of well-armed envoys with a numerous following. Armagnac had also declined to engage in the discussions. He declared bluntly that the matter was no concern of his. In Bicêtre it was finally decided that the armistice would last until Easter; after that, they would negotiate anew.

In the southerly tower of Blois, Charles wrote a long letter to the King. Respectfully, patiently, driven by the sacred intention to put an end to a situation which one could call neither peace nor war, he set down once more his grievances against Burgundy. He sat in his own room, sober and quiet as a monk's cell. The bed with the green curtains in which he had slept as a child filled the small room almost completely; between both narrow windows stood a cupboard with shelves where he kept his books, and an iron chest containing a few personal belongings: the golden goblet and the crucifix which his mother had given him, a handsome triptych, buckles and rings, his collar of the Order of the Hedgehog. There was no chimney in the room; Charles had to content himself with the heat from the glowing charcoal brazier at his feet. He sat in a chair at a reading desk such as monks used, and wrote page after page in his own hand; he found great satisfaction in this occupation as well as in the careful composition of the letter.

It was snowing outside: the fields around Blois were white, the roofs of houses and barns and the boughs of the trees heavy laden with frost. For days, thick swarms of flakes had fallen from heaven; all sounds were muffled as though they came from far away. All activity had stopped. In the castle and the city the inhabitants lived on stores of provisions piled up over the years. By now Blois contained almost three times as many soldiers, horses and beasts of burden as before; only scanty portions could be doled out if there was to be any hope of survival through the winter without famine. Maintenance of the troops cost Charles handfuls of money; the previous autumn he had had to order his treasures sold in Paris: crowns, chains of honor, a golden ship which had been used as a table ornament, images of saints, candlesticks and jewels. Now the soldiers of the household had been paid to the last denier; whatever remained of the money had to be used for the customary New Year's gifts to members of his household. In order to meet his necessary expenses Charles was forced to borrow small sums from his physician, his Chancellor and substantial citizens of Blois. He himself lived with extreme frugality; in the book in which he listed his personal expenses only three items appeared that winter: a hood, a box of writing materials and a pair of mittens.

Bonne d'Armagnac's dowry seemed finally to amount to nothing more than a drop on a scalding platter. Moreover, there was no guarantee that his father-in-law would keep his word about the payment terms. Charles had seen his new bride only once, during the wedding ceremonies at Riom, one of Berry's castles; of the child Bonne he remembered nothing except that she had black braids and round red cheeks. After the church service she had been taken back to her mother. No one had had the time or the desire to organize a fête.

Charles was pleased that he was not required to keep the girl with him. In Blois there was hardly room for women's quarters, and besides, he could not afford a retinue for the new Duchess. Surely Bonne would not have liked to live in the nursery. Charles seldom visited the apartment where Marguérite played with her wooden dolls and his little daughter crawled on a mat. When he stepped inside and saw the clothes hanging by the fire to dry, or heard the Dame de Maucouvent singing nursery songs in her shrill voice, he fancied himself a child again. It seemed to him at those times only a short while since he himself had lived safely hidden inside the four walls of the nursery, surrounded by toys, protected from worry and pain. He lifted his daughter in his arms. Day by day she was becoming more human, he discovered, easier to understand, a creature of flesh and blood like himself; the frail little doll in the cradle had inspired only wonder and deep pity in him.

Although Blois was blanketed in a winter silence, Charles could not recapture the calm life of the past. The forced inactivity weighed heavily upon him. Writing the letter to the King gave him an illusion, at least, of accomplishment. He poured into the words all his bottled-up energy, all his anxiety to be finished with the task which was his inheritance.

Once again, aided by his secretary Garbet, Charles went over the documents concerning the murder and everything that had happened after it. Once more he had to relive those dreadful, tragic days. Only now did he seem to feel the violence of the blow which had struck him; he had not been able at the time to grasp the full significance of his father's death. A feeling of bewilderment and painful impotence had overwhelmed him when, with Isabelle, he had watched beside his mother who was half mad with grief; now on reading the account of the murder and burial, on reviewing Petit's accusations, going over once more the royal letters informing him of the confiscation of manors and castles, he understood for the first time his mother's courage. Indignation and sorrow made him express himself in a way which perhaps did not belong in so solemn a document as his letter to the King; if he had asked his advisors' opinion they would have told him to mitigate the emotional tone of the letter, and the way in which he had underscored each point in its long list of events.

He forgot that he sat in his quiet room between his bed and his bookcase, that the snow fell silently and unceasingly behind the small window panes, that his feet, near the charcoal grate, were warm, but his fingers stiff from cold. He saw himself in the dark alley where his father's bloody body lay in the mud; later at the funeral mass he saw Burgundy, dressed in mourning, holding the edge of the pall; he saw his mother kneeling in humble entreaty for justice; he relived the empty ceremony in the cathedral of Chartres.

". . . And therefore, my Prince and Sovereign, we implore you— nay, we insist that you give us leave to obtain satisfaction ourselves in every possible way for the murder of our dearly beloved father and lord, may God forgive his sins. We are obliged to do so, we cannot leave it undone with impunity. There is not a man alive, no matter how humble he may be, who will not pursue the murderers of his father to the death. We therefore beseech you to stand by us and help us, as much as it lies in your power, to punish the murderer, liar and traitor. All this I have truly written, so help me God. . ."

The snow had melted and the tepid spring rain was falling when Charles had carefully signed his name to this long and detailed letter. He told his brothers the contents and asked them if they wished to sign their names beside his. This they did, gathered on a spring afternoon in the chamber they habitually used; the silver letters gleamed dully against the black background on the walls: 'Rien ne m'est plus, plus ne m'est rien." Philippe, Count de Vertus, was fourteen years old now, a sprightly youth with charming manners. During Charles' absence Philippe had acted ably as lieutenant-general of Orléans' estates. He patterned himself wholly after his elder brother whose commissions he punctiliously fulfilled. He accepted Charles' decisions without questions; all his life he had heard that Charles was the more thoughtful and sharp-witted of the two. Charles, on his side, found support in Philippe; his brother's carefree disposition, his continually stimulating humor, formed a desirable counterweight to his own retiring, somewhat melancholy nature. But it was his youngest brother, Jean, whom he loved best; Jean, who reminded him strongly of his mother. The nine-year-old was rather small for his age and not particularly robust. He stood somewhat apart from the others—too old for the nursery, too young to take part in business affairs like Philippe, and at the same time not vigorous enough to do as Dunois did and exercise daily in the courtyard of Blois with the soldiers. Louis' bastard son differed from his half-brothers in every respect; he was broad and strongly built, with sandy hair and light eyes. He lacked to a degree the courtliness, the innate dignity which Charles and Philippe possessed. But he lacked also Charles' inclination to melancholy and vacillation and Philippe's easy carelessness.

Dunois consciously followed a well-chosen path: he intended to become a skilled warrior, to lead men in battle, to lay siege to fortresses. He intended when he was older to serve the House of Orléans in this way, so that his half-brothers could devote themselves to matters of state. Already he saw his tenacity rewarded: men praised him for his facility with sword and bow and his proficient horsemanship. Toward Charles and Philippe, Dunois behaved with respect and with a certain reserve: he was only too aware of the difference between his position and theirs. Nevertheless, he showed no trace of humility or envy. Nor was he at all ashamed of his illegitimacy: he was proud to be a son of Orléans; he asked no greater favor of fate than some day to be able to avenge his father's death. Although he did not add his name to the letter, he was present. The others—and he himself too—considered it quite natural that he should enter in all discussions and give his opinions on everything.

"Do you think the King will read your letter now?" Philippe asked after he had carefully written his name, adorning the P with intricate, interwoven lines.

Dunois looked up and asked quietly, "Is Monseigneur de Berry for us or against us this time?"

"I don't know." Charles sighed and shrugged. "He always defends his viewpoints so well that I am inclined afterwards to agree with him. He writes me that he considers himself an outpost in the enemy camp. He believes he can do more for us by exercising influence in the Council and with the Dauphin than by siding with us openly if it comes to hostilities again. I cannot deny that there is truth in what he says. The citizens of Paris have always had high regard for Monseigneur de Berry."

"Is it true that Brittany has deserted us?" Dunois looked worried; he had heard the news from de Braquemont.

"Yes, he wants to remain aloof." Charles sighed again. "But meanwhile I have paid all his men."

"If only he does not go over to Burgundy now, the coward!" Dunois banged his clenched fist on the table. But Charles shook his head and said:

"I believe he has enough reason *not* to do that."

Dunois, who had immediately fallen silent out of courtesy when Charles began to speak, had more to say. He did not want to seem disrespectful, but he could not be quiet.

"Why don't you follow the advice of Messires de Villars and de Braquemont?" he asked. "Why don't you let men come from Lombardy and Lorraine? You can get as many as you want."

"Listen, Dunois, you must leave that to me." Calmly, Charles began to roll up his parchment. "Don't forget that I gave my word of honor at Bicêtre that I would not begin anything until Easter. I—at any rate—intend to keep my word. How can I justifiably complain to the King if I do not obey his wishes? It was to be expected that Burgundy would violate the provisions; thus my case is strengthened."

Philippe and Dunois stared down at the table in some embarrassment. They were surprised at Charles' tart tone. It was unlike him. Their silence was more eloquent than any objections they could raise. For his part Charles already knew their arguments by heart.

"I do not feel responsible for the actions of Monseigneur d'Armagnac," he said curtly. It troubled him deeply that he could not sever his ties with his father-in-law. "He refused to take part in the discussions at Bicêtre; he insists that the treaty has nothing to do with him. It is bad enough that he drags the name of our party in the gutter—I do not see why I should be held accountable for his behavior. Damn it! I have warned him enough—not a day passes that I do not beg him to curb his troops. I believe he is afraid that they will desert if he forbids them to loot and rape. And indeed, alas, words of honor, promises, vows . . . these make little difference to Armagnac—to him they are just meaningless words. By Christ's wounds! What a pity that I fare so ill with the man whom I need most."

He saw his brothers' bowed heads. They sat silently together, three youths dressed in mourning. This is now my family council, Charles thought despondently. He rose with a sigh. These are the only people I can really trust. And for their sakes I must persevere; they are still minors, they have no protector except me. No one but I will fight for their inheritance—no one will put out a hand to restore to them what has been taken from them.

"Forgive me, Dunois, if I spoke harshly to you. I did not mean to do it, brother. I know very well that nothing lies closer to your heart than the honor of Orléans."

Charles walked around the table and patted his half-brother's shoulder. "The world is divided unfairly, Dunois. Our cause would have fared far better if you had stood in my shoes and I in yours."

On the twenty-fifth of July, 1411, the Herald of Orléans appeared before the gate of the Hôtel d'Artois; when he was admitted to Burgundy's presence he read the following challenge in a loud voice:

" 'We, Charles, Duke of Orléans and Valois, Count of Blois and Beaumont, Lord of Coucy; Philippe, Count of Vertus and Jean, Count of Angoulême, to you, Jean, who call yourself Duke of Burgundy. Because of the treacherous and premeditated murder committed by hired assassins upon the person of our greatly revered and beloved lord and father, Monseigneur Louis, Duke of Orléans, despite your vows and expressions of friendship, and because of the further betrayal and crimes committed by you against the respect and honor of our sovereign Prince and King, and against us, we do advise you that henceforward from this hour we shall strive against you with all our power in every possible way. May God be our witness.' "

"You see, Saint-Pol, they put the noose around their necks themselves," said Burgundy. He sat in the room where he received his friends and intimates. Depicted on the heavy Flemish tapestries covering the walls were the birth of Mary, the Annunciation, the sorrowing mother under the cross. Burgundy stood straddle-legged, staring at the splendor of line and color; his hands were clasped behind his back and his underlip, as usual, protruded pensively. He was speaking to the man whom he considered his most valuable collaborator: Waleran, Count of Saint-Pol, descended from the royal family of Luxembourg, Burgundy's right arm, commander of armies and, recently, a captain of the garrison of the city of Paris. The Count of Saint-Pol was a stocky man with a broad, florid face; despite his weight, he moved with the buoyant elasticity of a man who exercises regularly. Stories circulated about the remarkable strength of his hands. He stood with his hands at his sides, listening to Burgundy, his face impassive.

"You accepted the challenge immediately, Monseigneur?" he asked.

Jean de Burgundy laughed curtly and drew a rolled sheet from his sleeve; silently he offered it to Saint-Pol.

" 'We, Jean, Duke of Burgundy, Count of Artois, etc., etc.,' " the Luxembourger read half-aloud; he held the parchment at arm's length and squinted slightly—he was myopic—" 'to you, Charles, who call yourself Duke of Orléans; to Philippe, etc, etc, who have sent us your challenge, etc., etc., know then that in order to put an end to the crimes, conspiracies, sorcery, etc., of the late Louis, your father, and thereby to protect our Sovereign Lord the King, we caused the said Louis to be killed, etc. Since you and your brothers intend manifestly to tread the same pernicious and ruinous path as your late father, we take upon ourselves the task, pleasing to God, of bringing you to your senses and chastising you duly as the liars, rebels and braggarts which you are. In witness thereof we sign these papers with our own seal, and so forth.' Precisely." Saint-Pol rolled up the parchment and returned it to Burgundy. "Precisely. This time you are really in earnest, my lord?"

"This time I am really serious, so help me God," replied Burgundy.

It was clear to Saint-Pol that the Duke was delighted with the situation; it was to his advantage that Orléans had begun by sending him a challenge.

"I am ready," Burgundy continued, always with that secret laughter in his voice and that air of enjoying someone else's discom-

fiture. "So far as I am concerned, Orléans could not have chosen a
better moment. Our troops stand ready. Paris is prepared for a siege.
Let them come—I shall receive them warmly."

"Hm." Saint-Pol ran his palm over his lips and chin. Burgundy
looked at him with a frown. "Don't you agree with me, Saint-Pol?
Out with your objections if you have any."

"Hm," repeated the Luxembourger; he sniffed a few times and
gazed pensively at the scenes on the tapestries before him. "Are we
really so sure of Paris, Monseigneur? Believe me, this matter has
been carefully planned. Orléans' challenge indicates that he feels
pretty confident."

"Do you doubt my influence over the Parisians?" Burgundy
demanded irritably. "Wait and see whom they will choose if it comes
to that."

Saint-Pol thrust his hands under his broad girdle and put his
head back as though he saw something fascinating on the sculptured
beams of the ceiling.

"Things are no longer as they were. In fact I would almost say
that you have squandered the most auspicious moment when you
could have sent Orléans packing. In the course of the last two years
you have made too many enemies. The University too is no longer
well disposed toward you. You have become too powerful, and—
with that power—a little too careless. It is no use to strike me," he
continued impassively, as Burgundy whirled quickly toward him
with upraised hand. "What I say is the truth. You would do better
to acknowledge it."

Burgundy lowered his fist, strode to the other end of the room
and sat down. Saint-Pol did not move. He seemed to be studying
the tapestries with close attention.

"What are you driving at, Saint-Pol?" Jean spoke brusquely; he
tapped the table top angrily with his fingers. "What are you trying
to say? Must I bring more troops into Paris, must I imprison or
exile Orléans' people, must I buy the support of certain men—and
if I must—who are they? Do not come to me now with vague hints.
Facts, Saint-Pol, facts, if you please. But tell me only what I do not
know myself."

"Monseigneur." Saint-Pol leaned toward Burgundy with both
hands on the table. "So far as I can tell, two hostile groups are facing
each other in the city: on the one hand the officers, magistrates and
merchants—in short, everyone who used to enjoy power and a cer-

tain respect; on the other, the people from Saint-Jacques' quarter—the butchers, flayers and tanners with their partisans and all the adventurers and vagrants on the other bank of the Seine. Now my advice to you is this: you must take advantage of this mutual hostility. If you support the Saint-Jacquards, you don't have to fear that the officers and merchants will bring the Armagnacs inside. The butchers and tanners and all the idle rabble will preserve you from any possible traitors in their own camp. Enlist the butchers' guild on your side, my lord, and you have a vigilant army always at your command."

Burgundy frowned, and thrust forward his lower lip in thought. His father's words kept darting through his mind: keep the people as your friend, the people can make and break rulers; never underrate the power of the mob; seek your strength in public favor, my son.

"Arm those fellows of Saint-Jacques then, but do it quickly," he said to Saint-Pol. "Organize the guilds into troops, give them money, ask them their grievances, and make them promises; I don't doubt that you will be able to find your way through those districts. Give them gifts, greet them with courtesy. Evidently you know what pleases those people most. But see to it that they receive weapons and instructions before Saint-Lawrence's day."

"Monseigneur, I think it advisable that you make this request for cooperation yourself," said Saint-Pol mildly, but with determination. "You can accomplish more by personal sympathy than I can accomplish by promises or gifts. There are people, Monseigneur, who will go through fire and flame for a leader. They need to follow, to cling to something. You can be their leader if you approach them in the right way."

Burgundy sniffed contemptuously.

"I have never heard that a member of a royal House had to beg for an alliance with butchers," he cried, leaping to his feet. "A Duke of Burgundy does not beg for a treaty with butchers."

Saint-Pol shrugged and bowed.

"It shall be as Your Grace desires," he said formally. "I thought only that a personal appearance would fully restore the confidence in you which had been somewhat dispelled in the course of the year. The people are still well-disposed toward you, Monseigneur, but already there are many who ask themselves why you have not gone forward with the reforms in the Audit Chamber, why you have not revised the taxes, why you have not restored order in municipal affairs during your administration. You know how difficult it is to keep the people as a friend. But perhaps I do not see these things in their proper light, my lord. In that case I beg you to forgive me. A few days ago I heard a couple of small children singing in the street— 'The Duke of Burgundy! May God keep him happy!' I hope that will always be the wish of Paris, Monseigneur."

He bowed once more and walked backward to the door; as he passed he took his riding gloves from a chest. Burgundy watched him, overcome by an uncomfortable feeling of having made a mistake—worse still, of having made himself ridiculous. He knew that in matters like these, Saint-Pol was seldom wrong; the Luxembourger was a shrewd judge of people, a disinterested and devoted counselor.

"Stay, Saint-Pol," he said curtly even before the other had reached the door. "Sit down here and let us discuss this matter thoroughly."

Saint-Pol put his gloves down again and briskly approached the table. Burgundy told him that he intended to communicate personally with the Legoix brothers. No twitch in his face, no flicker of his eyes, no irony in his voice betrayed his satisfaction as Saint-Pol replied, "Of course. I endorse your plans heartily. I shall execute your instructions at once."

Charles d'Orléans awoke from a deep slumber; it had been a long time since he had enjoyed such a sound, dreamless, undisturbed sleep. He turned onto his back and stretched. What he saw around him in the dusk brought him quickly back to a realization of time and place. He raised himself at once on his elbows and peered through the dawn, listening intently. He lay on the camp bed in his tent. He could hear his pennant fluttering overhead in the wind, horses neighed nearby; further away someone blew a horn. Charles' squire lay curled up on a heap of straw before the curtain which covered the entrance to the tent. Charles leaped from the bed and nudged the sleeping youth.

As the squire sat up, Charles pulled the curtain ropes; a cold morning wind blew in his face. Grey light filtered into the tent.

"Dry weather, clear sky," he muttered. "God be praised. We can finally begin to do something. We have had two days now without rain. I hope the terrain has become a little less swampy. Over here!" he called out to the youth who, still half-blind from sleep, came carrying the leather doublet which was worn under the armor. While his arm and leg pieces were being buckled on, Charles looked outside.

The morning star sparkled over the horizon; the tents of his allies and vassals stood to the left and right of Charles' pavilion, outlined against the clear sky. Banners and ensigns floated from their tops; shields with escutcheons hung over each entrance. As it grew lighter, the colors and armorial bearings painted or enamelled on the flags and shields could be distinguished: the lions, falcons, lilies, crosses and stars in saffron, sable, argent and lapis lazuli. Behind the city of tents lay the army camp. The men had spent the night in the open air, in deserted barns on the field, or under hastily constructed shelters made of twigs, straw and hides. The great fires, which the soldiers had kindled after sunset to protect them at least partially from the night cold, were still burning. An odor of roast meat drifted over the camp. Directly opposite Charles' tent on the other side of the field, rose the roofs of Saint-Denis, a suburb of Paris; above the houses stood the heavy walls and towers of the abbey.

For a week Orléans' troops had besieged Saint-Denis—or rather they had camped around the town, for storm and rain had prevented them from launching an assault. Paris had denied them an entry; the gates were closed, soldiers stood on the ramparts. Armagnac, who had been thoroughly informed of the conditions around Paris, led the army to Saint-Denis; if the village fell, they would have an advantageous base for operations. The people of Saint-Denis had not been fully prepared for the arrival of Orléans' troops. They had not expected that anyone would desecrate by siege so holy a place which held both an abbey and a cathedral. They acted in great haste, pulling down the market stalls to use the wood for shooting weapons and slings. Heavy rainfall brought a welcome postponement of hostilities.

While Orléans' people waited for the sky to clear, the burghers consulted with the Abbot of Saint-Denis. They felt obliged to defend their village for the sake of the people of Paris: bread, firewood and seafish could reach Paris only through Saint-Denis. On the other hand, the Abbot feared that the church and monastery buildings would suffer irreparable damage if there were a siege. He felt responsible for the treasures and objects of art which were stored in the abbey. For that reason the Abbot counseled voluntary surrender. Inside Saint-Denis, opinions on this matter varied widely: the people's terror mounted when somebody on the ramparts reported that

Orléans' army was preparing for an attack. It was rumored in the village that the assault would be led by the Armagnacs, who were feared and detested everywhere.

Orléans now donned his armor. Taking his helmet under his left arm, his sword in his right hand, and followed by his squire, he walked past the tents to the great pavilion where he and his allies met early to eat and talk. Here he found his brother Philippe and Messeigneurs de Bourbon and Alençon, surrounded by nobles of their retinues, already assembled. The Constable d'Albret and Armagnac were not yet present; since dawn they had been busy calling up and instructing the men.

"The weather holds well, my lord," remarked Bourbon after greeting Charles. He was a tall, plump man of middle age, with an affable, but rather weak, face. He had narrow shoulders, bad posture, and looked somewhat ineffectual in a hauberk and coat of mail. His allies considered him something of a dead weight on them; he was excessively cautious, worried constantly, seeing danger or bad luck everywhere; moved slowly and was distinguished by a striking sluggishness in thought and action. In the most favorable circumstances he showed himself to be calm and reliable, just as his old father had been before him; it was perhaps also because of this quality that he had not allowed himself to be swayed by the recent effort of the opposition party to win him over, with his troops and resources, to Burgundy's cause.

"I have just left Monseigneur d'Alençon," continued Bourbon hesitantly, in a low voice, while he bowed to Charles. "We ask ourselves continually whether it is really wise of you to let Armagnac's men lead the attack on Saint-Denis. It is true that they know the neighborhood much better than we do, but after the failure at Ham and the events last year . . ."

Followed by Bourbon, Charles walked to the table which stood in the middle of the tent and let himself be served with bread and meat. Bourbon's words troubled him because they expressed a doubt which he himself shared almost constantly. It had indeed been Charles' intention to let Saint-Denis be taken under the command of de Braquemont and de Villars. He now had a strong, well-equipped army, substantially larger than the previous year, for it had been reinforced by companies from Lombardy and Lorraine. When he had met his father-in-law again in Beauvais a few weeks before, he had believed at first that he was finished with the latter's reck-lessness for the present. Armagnac's soldiers were more squalid and gaunt than ever, their ranks notably diminished, their knapsacks and carts empty, because they had been forced to leave their booty behind at Ham and had had little time for plunder during the flight.

Next to the seemly, well-disciplined troops of Orléans, Alençon and Bourbon, who had recently left fortresses and quarters supplied with weapons and fresh provisions, the men of the Midi looked like a pack of beggars. In addition, it was difficult to handle them; they brought fellow soldiers from other districts into great disrepute, stole clothing and food, horses and weapons, and caused unrest in the army by their raucous, lawless behavior.

"You know nothing can be changed now, Bourbon," said Charles. "Everything has been arranged. All we can to is try to prevent Armagnac's men from looting the city once it falls into our hands. I intend to place the abbey and marketplace under guard. I am counting on you and Alençon to cooperate."

Bourbon made a wry face, but before he could voice his objec-tions, Armagnac and d'Albret entered the tent with their following of armed nobles. Armagnac was in rare good humor. He had already drunk copiously before daybreak; the prospect of combat which would unquestionably result in victory made him jovial and bois-terous.

"Well, son-in-law, what do you have to say about the beautiful weather?" he asked, throwing his armored arm over Charles' shoul-ders. "We could not have hit it better. By starting in early we will have the sun at our back as long as possible. In fact, I venture to predict that you will eat your mid-day meal in Saint-Denis. The village will fall apart like a house of cards, mark my words. They can't do much with the weapons they've put on the ramparts. My men are fresh and pugnacious—they have had an eye on the abbey for a long time now. Well, what is it?" He turned impatiently to one of the knights of his retinue. Near the entrance stood a few armed men belonging to a watch patrol; they requested admittance.

Charles stepped forward and told the men to enter. They re-ported that a number of citizens carrying white flags had just left the Saint-Denis gate. Armagnac snorted contemptuously and hur-ried out. Standing with his hands on his hips, his legs spread, he watched the delegation approach the camp of tents through the dank grass; there were magistrates in dark tabards and surely a half dozen clergy—all older men who held up their mantles while they warily sought a path around pits and pools.

"Well, well," remarked Armagnac. "White flags. They come to request an armistice, Orléans, while they go to fetch Burgundy. Don't let them pull the wool over your eyes!"

Charles' lips were tightly compressed, his eyes dark with anger. He ordered the guards to bring the delegates from Saint-Denis into his tent. Soon the men entered; they knelt and delivered their message.

"Monseigneur, in order to avoid senseless bloodshed, the city of Saint-Denis surrenders to you. Monseigneur, we place ourselves under your protection. We entreat you to spare us the indignity of robbery and mistreatment."

Armagnac moved quickly forward, to stand between Charles and the delegation.

"Son-in-law, they have no right to ask that of us! For a whole week they kept their gates closed and threw stones at our reconnaissance posts. They tried to offer resistance. Surrender cannot mean the same thing for them as for those who open their gates at once. I repeat—they have no right to protection."

The men who knelt before Charles looked up. The Gascon stood in front of them; he blocked their view of Charles. They were afraid that Armagnac would convince his son-in-law. The princely allies and their nobles, however, ranged in a close circle about the group, saw what was hidden from the suppliants: Charles' eyes flashed with fury.

"Be quiet, Armagnac," he said, calmly and coldly. Those who had known his father listened expectantly. "And please be good enough to stand either beside me or behind me, so that I can at least look at these gentlemen while I speak with them. The petition is addressed to me personally—and I grant it. No son of France will plunder Saint-Denis. Even if we had taken the city by storm, I would have forbidden pillage and robbery. It is my express will that there should be no disorder."

He looked searchingly past the row of horsemen; his eyes became fixed upon a robust, erect man in black armor who stood watching the scene. He carried a helmet and battle-axe under his arm.

"Monseigneur." Charles bowed slightly; the warrior stepped toward him and doffed his leather cap, revealing his tonsure.

"My lords, this is the Archbishop of Sens," Charles said, turning back to the envoys. "I confide the custody of the church and abbey of Saint-Denis to him and his troops. I will visit the Abbot myself today with my kinsmen and allies to inform him of my intentions."

"The devil take it, son-in-law, have you lost your mind?" screamed Armagnac, his face purple with rage. "I have promised my men this day's spoils. They have not been paid for a long time, Orléans. I have been so generous with you that I cannot fulfil my obligations to my soldiers. After the reverses of the past few months, my men have a right to compensation. Saint-Denis is rich; the storehouses in the great marketplace are crammed with grain and the merchants' money chests are overflowing. Those people will start earning money again when the war is over; let them help us now, freely or otherwise—what difference does it make to you, son-in-law? The cathedral holds enough gold to keep all the armies of Christendom under arms for as long as they live."

"I repeat," Charles said slowly, "I repeat that I will not tolerate pillage in Saint-Denis. I give you my word of honor, Messires. My troops will occupy the city, but we shall buy our provisions from you."

Armagnac burst into loud, malicious laughter, shoved the listening nobles to one side and hurried to the entrance of the tent, his spurs jingling and his sword striking against his thigh.

"With your leave, son-in-law," he remarked, "you will not go far as a captain if you wage war continually in this way. Buy! Pay! Come, d'Albret. Don't they say that insanity is hereditary in the House of Valois?"

Armagnac and his companions went off through the tents to the soldiers' camp. Charles remained standing silently until the sound of heavy footsteps had died away. He waited until he had completely regained his self-control. The citizens of Saint-Denis still knelt before him. They did not feel as certain as they would have liked. They believed that young Orléans had acted in good faith, but they were not pleased by the Gascon's attitude: he who behaved so brashly toward his superiors in rank would probably pay little attention to a direct command.

"Return to the city and tell them that during the course of the day I shall enter the gates with an army of occupation," said Charles in a more severe tone. "Prepare the Abbot of Saint-Denis for my arrival. You may go now."

The leader of the delegation humbly thanked the Duke of Orléans for his kindness; however, the men left the camp with heavy hearts.

After their departure there was a momentary silence in the tent; Charles stood motionless, staring with knit brows at the ground. Alençon approached him.

"For a moment I thought I heard your father speak, Monseigneur," he said. "He would not have spoken differently to Monseigneur d'Armagnac."

Charles looked up. "Please leave now, my lords. I request all those who belong to my troops to call their men together. Keep yourselves ready. We are going to enter Saint-Denis within the hour."

"We grant your demands, Monseigneur," said the Abbot of Saint-Denis. He stood with bowed head before the table in the abbey refectory, surrounded by a group of clergy. The Duke of Orléans and his brother, their counselors and captains and the Archbishop of Sens occupied the high benches along the wall. "We shall provide shelter for Monseigneur de Sens and his followers in the abbey," the Abbot went on. "Have I understood you correctly that you, Monseigneur, and the princes who have arrived here with you, will not take residence in Saint-Denis?"

"We shall spend the night in our tents," replied Charles, "and station our troops in the local villages and hamlets. Only the army of occupation will remain outside your gates. Now send me some men so that I can arrange to buy provisions."

The Abbot bowed again. He moved his hands uneasily inside the wide sleeves of his cassock and glanced at his priests as though seeking support. "Monseigneur," he began hesitantly, "may we then rely completely on your promise, your assurance, that the valuables in the abbey and in our treasury will be safe?"

"Of course you may." Charles frowned, displeased. The Abbot had already broached this subject several times during the discussion. "It is my intention to hear mass with my allies on the eighth day of the feast of Saint-Denis," he concluded, rising. His colleagues followed his example. "At that time I will be glad to view the holy relics and the tombs of the kings."

"Yes, Monseigneur." The Abbot approached, sighing, to lead

the young man out. At that moment there came from the inner court the loud, confused hubbub of galloping horses, shouts, the clash of arms and the creaking of doors being thrown violently open. Charles and his knights stood stunned; a few fumbled for their swords.

"To the doors!" shouted Archambault de Villars. "Guard the entrances! This may be a trap, my lord. The people of Saint-Denis have admitted Burgundy."

The Abbot attempted to refute these accusations, but there was no need for explanations. At the end of the long passageway which led from the refectory to the first buildings, Armagnac appeared, closely followed by a thick crowd of men from his retinue. With jingling spurs they invaded the refectory. Armagnac was holding his whip; he slammed it against the corridor walls so that the statues trembled in their niches. The Abbot and the brothers retreated to the table. Charles put up his sword and waited until his father-in-law had entered the refectory.

"I came to lend you a hand, Orléans," Armagnac called. He was laughing boisterously, but his eyes were keenly fixed upon Charles. His followers had entered the room behind him; they stood ranged around their commander in a half-circle and smirked at Orléans' men.

"I thought it was clearly understood that I was to come here alone today." Charles made an effort to speak calmly, although the pounding of his heart almost took his breath away. "Messeigneurs de Bourbon and Alençon both understood that."

"Certainly." Armagnac's bright eyes strayed over those present; he stood before his son-in-law, his legs apart, striking the palm of his hand repeatedly with the blade of his sword. "Yes, certainly, Orléans, but don't you really think it an outrage to treat your companions like this? I would not want you to lose the support of my men for anything in the world. I know them, believe me, I know how to deal with these rascals, I know how to make them fierce fighters and keep them pugnacious. Let them fill their bellies and their packs—then you will have the best soldiers, son-in-law."

"What are you trying to tell me by this?" asked Charles. Armagnac and he faced each other, standing on the tiles which shaped a cross in the middle of the refectory, as though they were in an arena.

"Well," Armagnac raised his voice, "I have just given my men permission to take whatever they need from the public granaries. They did not have to be told twice. How those rascals can run!"

It was as though something exploded suddenly in Charles' brain; he did not know what he was doing. He raised his sword in both hands and sprang forward. Steel slid against steel; Armagnac's sword parried Charles'. They stood motionless for a moment, square against each other, their weapons crossed. De Braquemont and the Archbishop of Sens came between them before Charles could strike again.

"Monseigneur," said the prelate in a stifled voice, "this is senseless."

Charles dropped his sword and took a step backward. He shrugged; it was not clear whether he sighed or shivered.

Armagnac snorted a few times to demonstrate his indifference; he was secretly delighted at the looks of dismay on the faces of Orléans' men.

"Come, come, I was only jesting," he said loudly. "Monseigneur d'Orléans does not take this seriously, surely. He will see that I mean well by him, when he hears the news which my scouts have just brought from Paris." He paused for a moment, smacking his lips. Charles stood without moving, his eyes fixed on the floor.

"My lords," continued Armagnac; with pleasure he heard his voice reverberate against the beams of the ceiling. "Know then, my lords, that four days ago an English army landed in Calais. It can reach Paris in a quick day's march. Nay, gentlemen, this time it is not a matter of fighting against the Kingdom; these are auxilliary troops which Burgundy, it seems, requested urgently as soon as he saw that the Flemings had deserted him."

"Monseigneur de Berry has been promised impartiality by England," said Charles dully. Nothing could amaze him now. Armagnac shrugged.

"Come, son-in-law, promises . . . ! However that may be, it is a strong, well-armed troop. We shall thus have something to do speedily, I think. Under these circumstances you will agree with me that we must leave no stone unturned to provide ourselves with money, food and equipment. No one knows how long we shall remain in the field. Look here . . ." He walked past Charles to the Abbot of Saint-Denis, who stood leaning against the table. "We strive for a good purpose: justice and the restitution of honor. That must ring gloriously in your ears, doesn't it? These are still Christian concepts, whatever you may say. They have cost us—me and all our confederates here—handfuls of money, Monseigneur. A greater and better army than ours does not exist anywhere. We will surely gain the victory. But now we are hard up, and we need a trifle to pay our men."

The Abbot made an involuntary gesture.

Armagnac tossed his head back and burst into a roar of laughter. "You have a sharp nose. You smell what I want already." He laid his large, iron-gloved hand on the Abbot's shoulder. "I am well informed; don't attempt to deny it: you are guarding the Queen's treasure in your cellar vaults. Better give me the keys of your own volition—believe me, my methods of persuasion are far from pleasant."

"I forbid it, Armagnac!" Charles cried vehemently, pulling his father-in-law by his riding coat. "This is contrary to all rules. The Queen's treasures are inviolate. Moreover, I have sworn that we would not touch the valuables or the abbey."

"Come, and how shall we conduct war then?" Armagnac asked over his shoulder, without releasing the Abbot. "How will you defeat Burgundy, son-in-law, how do you propose to keep your soldiers friendly? We have sustained enough losses: the English always shoot home like Death itself. You are still inexperienced, Orléans; for once trust the judgment of a man who knows what's necessary. Let me negotiate quietly with these brave gentlemen here. Monseigneur d'Orléans will give you a receipt, naturally," he said to the Abbot of Saint-Denis. "But I wager that Her Majesty will raise no objections when she hears how well her money has been spent. Come forward then: where are the keys?"

In the vaults of the abbey, on the steps which led down there, and even in the inner courtyard, a bitter struggle was already raging among the plunderers; Charles, looking at the colors of the tunics amid the screaming, fighting, half-crazed horde, saw many of his own men—chiefly Lombards from Asti, German soldiers from Wenceslaus' armies, and mercenaries of divers nationalities, who had offered him their services at the last moment. Brutally, the knights had cleared a path to the lowest, most carefully concealed cellars, for themselves and their lord. In the light of the torches the glitter of gold and precious stones could be glimpsed between the shifting bodies of the fighting men: a chest fell open; flashing coins streamed forth. A Gascon who tried to escape unseen, his arms filled with golden candelabra and chalices for the mass, was compelled at knife point to relinquish the booty. The men fell over each other in their haste to snatch the treasure from one another.

In the vault where Isabeau's treasure lay concealed, Armagnac was busily giving directions. The men could not come in here: it was Armagnac's intention to see personally to the chests and their contents. He stood with his arms akimbo before a pile of gold dishes. It was a king's dinner service which Isabeau had earlier stolen from Saint-Pol. The luster of jewels hovered like a brilliant mist over the open chests of treasure. The discovery surpassed even Armagnac's expectations. That his son-in-law stood there watching him did not please him at all. He raised his brows and squinted sideways at the young man who, pale and unmoving, supported himself on his sword as though he were dazed. Suddenly Armagnac grinned; he stooped and snatched from one of the chests a crown adorned with golden lilies, a king's crown worn by the Valois in an earlier time.

"Here, Orléans," said Armagnac. "Here, boy, do not say now that your welfare and prosperity do not lie close to my heart."

He moved quickly toward his son-in-law and pressed the crown upon his head. "If it depended upon me, I would soon call you 'Sire, my Sovereign', and have the king of France as my son-in-law."

Charles snatched off the crown and flung it among the gold dishes and goblets. Armagnac, who had bent his knee before him, made a gesture of mock surprise.

"He throws away the Crown of France as though it were a wilted garland," he said. "I see that Monseigneur still has much to learn."

In the first week of November, a meeting took place in the slaughterhouse of Sainte-Géneviève under the chairmanship of the owners, the three brothers Legoix. In honor of the event the flag-stones of the great room had been purged of blood and filth, the slaughtering blocks and tubs scoured clean. Pickaxes hung in the background. But the stench could not be driven away—the brackish smell, the sharp odor of thousands of pigs and cattle which had been driven in here over the course of time.

The long, narrow slaughterhouse was crowded: by the bleak light of the November day which filtered through the windows mounted high in the wall, the participants in the gathering greeted one another: butchers and skinners, sausage fillers, pastry makers and peddlers, fell-mongers, cobblers and leather-workers; not only the bosses and masters, but also journeymen, servants and apprentices, bare-armed in grimy aprons.

A plank had been laid over a few slaughtering blocks; on it stood those in charge here: Thomas Legoix and both his brothers and the butcher bosses, Saint-Yon and Thibert of the great slaughtering houses.

The oldest Legoix, a giant of a man with a full florid face, kept his eyes fixed intently on the door. From time to time he saluted those who entered with a distracted gesture and shook his head impatiently when his neighbor Thibert nudged him; it was obvious that he expected someone who had not yet arrived.

"Begin now, Legoix, before it gets too dark," said Thibert. "Surely you can still open your mouth. God knows the surgeon must be drawing blood somewhere. An hour from now we won't be able to see each other's noses here."

Legoix continued to shake his head.

"What do I have torches for?" he asked sourly. The answer awoke interest; one of the men who stood around the plank—a peddler—shouted loudly, "Where do you get your torches from, Legoix? There isn't a chip of wood anywhere in Paris. The people in my neighborhood are burning doors and window sills. Do you wander off to Saint-Denis to get kindling wood?"

There was laughter, but without real humor; the effects of the long siege were beginning to be felt. Provisions in the city had run out quickly and the food supply had virtually ceased. As usual in bad times the herds of cattle were the first to go; they were driven to safer quarters by the fleeing peasants to protect them from the besiegers and the roving packs of vandals. The cattle, pigs and sheep which had been wont to feed on the city ramparts had been slaughtered a year earlier to prevent them from falling into the hands of the Armagnacs. For the butchers and related guilds there was therefore precious little work; from time to time they saw an opportunity to bring, with a well-armed escort, a few hundred head of cattle into Paris from outlying districts. Legoix had made use of the encounter of both enemy armies at Montdidier to make hasty conveyance of another herd of cattle. But what did that signify in a city which yearly required 30,000 cattle and 20,000 sheep for subsistence? Prices had shot up fantastically; bread was nearly unobtainable at any price, and as for fruit and green vegetables—they simply did not exist. Those citizens who had gardens, plots of ground at their disposal, could save themselves; they had roots, potatoes, carrots, parsnips and herbs. A man of the people, however, had to do with less; he had to be content with the common people's food in wartime: stinging nettles boiled in salt water.

Thomas Legoix leaped from the platform, shoving aside the bystanders in his haste to reach a man who had just entered: the surgeon, Maître Jean de Troyes. A murmur of satisfaction arose; the surgeon, a lean, dour middle-aged man with extremely penetrating dark eyes, was greatly respected in the butchers' guild; he had connections in the University, was eloquent and was considered both clever and learned.

He waved both his arms in greeting to this assembly and called out joyously, "God be with you, colleagues—for we are colleagues, aren't we? In fact, we exercise the same calling."

He gave Legoix, who led him to the platform, a sidelong glance, and grinned derisively.

"I belong to your guild, Legoix, because I can assert without hesitation that I bleed chiefly swine, cattle and sheep. Greetings, Thibert; greetings, Saint-Yon; greetings, Legoix. Legoix," he continued, waving his hand rapidly at the four men who already stood on the planks, "hoist me up, I am not as nimble as I was a year or so ago."

Thomas Legoix lifted the surgeon as though he were a child and then leaped onto the board himself. The uproar in the butchers' hall had subsided somewhat; the men pressed closer around the slaughtering block, their faces raised. In the front rows stood the guildmasters, the owners of the workshops and factories, the heads of the various branches of the meat and hide industries; men of various ages: some arrayed in furs and rich cloth, others in work clothes. Behind the masters pressed the apprentices, for the most part youths and men from the lowest classes, big-boned, with coarse features, whose doublets and aprons seemed to be permeated with the fetid stench of the work rooms.

The slaughterhouse was completely full; nevertheless still more spectators managed to squeeze inside: ragged students from the colleges of the University quarter, beggars and street loafers who had increased in number since the outbreak of war—they had apparently sensed that something was afoot. Even before Legoix's servants could shut the doors of the slaughterhouse, a troop of vagrants, wrapped in rags, kicked and fought their way inside in frantic haste.

"Men!" roared Thomas Legoix, crossing his sinewy arms, "men, I have something to tell you. The day after tomorrow we leave the city with Burgundy's troops to attack the Armagnacs in Saint-Cloud."

A loud shout of approval greeted this announcement to which the butchers and their partisans had looked forward eagerly ever since the time, late in the summer, when they had accepted arms from Burgundy. Almost daily they patrolled Paris in groups, led by knights and horsemen from the retinue of Count de Saint-Pol, under the colors and emblems of Burgundy—a lily in the heart of a Saint Andrew's cross against an azure field. They called themselves the army of Paris and marched with resounding steps through the streets.

"More than 2,000 of us are expected at Saint-Jacques' gate at midnight," Legoix went on. "Captain Saint-Pol says there are not more than 1,500 Armagnacs lying in Saint-Cloud. Together with Burgundy's men we are surely three or five times as strong."

"Give them hell!" shouted the students, who had climbed onto the cross beams under the roof; they sat there like a flock of famished crows.

"The Armagnacs slander God and offend our beloved King Charles," said Saint-Yon in his gruff, slightly cracked voice. "They cut off their prisoners' noses and ears and say, 'Go back to Paris and show yourself to your crazy king!' "

"Long live the King!" The shouts reverberated under the arched roof. The butchers and journeymen and all the men who stood around the slaughter blocks took up the cry. They stamped on the floor and banged on the walls until the meat hooks jingled.

"Yes, come on, long live the King!" A voice roared above the din. "Away with the Armagnac-loving officials and courtiers who give him bad counsel and stick his money in their purses. Away with Berry, the filthy traitor!"

The man who shouted this was hoisted instantly onto the shoulders of the spectators. He was short and thick-set with a broad face disfigured by strawberry marks. He might have been considered deformed if the bundles of muscles on his neck and arms and his thick, somewhat bent fingers, had not betrayed a strength which dwarves and hunchbacks seldom possess. He had a short, flat nose with wide nostrils; his front teeth protruded so far forward that he could not close his lips. Despite his terrifying appearance, he was highly respected and to a certain extent feared by his comrades and the inhabitants of the Saint-Jacques quarter. When anything happened which frightened and upset people, he did not just grumble and complain like the others; he was always ready to resist with words and blows, to stand up for himself as well as for his friends and acquaintances. His name was Simon le Coutelier. He was nicknamed Caboche and was a skinner by trade.

"By Christ's blood, no more babble!" he roared, emphasizing his words with his raised fist. "We can curse and complain until we turn blue, brothers, but the court wolves and vultures don't give a damn whether we are friendly to Armagnac or Burgundy now. Who is still so foolish as to believe that he will better himself by running after the Burgundians? Get to work, do your own job, lads! Kill those you hate and take what you can't get any other way! What have the politics of the great lords to do with us? We must have grub, a fire on our hearth and money in our pockets, no matter what!"

The servants and youths, the students on the crossbeams and the beggars and vagrants, thieves and pickpockets who stood in the back of the slaughter hall, struck up a deafening roar; knives flew from their sheaths and those who had staffs and cudgels flourished them wildly.

"Simon, Simonnet!" boomed the students in chorus.

"Caboche, you speak like a fool!" cried the surgeon in his high, shrill voice. "You would not go far in the world, man, if you insisted on having your own way every time. There is still room for more thieves and murderers in Montfaucon, even if plenty hang there already, God knows, in bundles like smoked fish, next to each other and above each other and below each other! If we seriously wanted to put an end to the sorry state of affairs, which I don't need to describe, because we get up with anxiety and go to bed with misery— we would have to proceed some other way. All around us disorder and lawlessness are the order of the day; let us at least go to work deliberately and sensibly to create law and order. But first we must drive the Armagnacs from our gates with the help of Monseigneur of Burgundy's troops. We can't do anything while Paris is in danger."

"Do you think I have a mind to fight next to the English dogs?"

screamed Caboche. "Once they have beaten off the Armagnacs they will try to make us a head shorter. Let us lie low, lads, and go our own way, that's the safest course."

"Silence!" Thibert banged the platform angrily with his staff. "In God's name how can we make up our minds if those fellows keep on screeching like that?" He turned to Legoix. "Tell them to hold their tongues. Let's listen now without interruption to Maître de Troyes who speaks here in our name. Quiet!"

Legoix had stood motionless, his arms crossed, after pushing the surgeon forward; he frowned, to be sure, when Caboche took the floor unbidden, but he said nothing. During the uproar which followed the skinner's brief speech, he remained thoughtful, with an expression of uncertainty on his broad, florid face.

"Aye, I don't like it either," he said abruptly to his friends on the platform. "It was an ugly thing for Monseigneur of Burgundy to have brought the English here. How will it end now? They know very well that we don't like them; they couldn't find quarters anywhere in the city. They won't soon forget that either. I don't trust them, these hard-headed sons of whores."

"Use your head, Legoix!" Maître de Troyes wheeled violently toward the owner of the Sainte-Géneviève slaughterhouse. "The English remain here as long as we need them to defeat the Armagnacs and not a day longer. If Monseigneur of Burgundy raises any objections to their departure, we are still here to remind him that we don't want those bastards within our borders. Friends of England have never gotten far here; believe me, Legoix, the Duke knows that as well as we do. Listen, men!" de Troyes continued more loudly, "How often must I tell you: first we get rid of the Armagnac's army and then we can insist that the Council and municipality be purged. We can go far with prudence and patience. Monseigneur of Burgundy needs us badly—don't forget it! Our time will come; we will see to it that peace and prosperity return to every inhabitant of city and farm in France. If the King can't listen or help us, what is to prevent us then from demanding another king for the sake of the people? Yes, it sounds like heresy. . ." He glanced quickly right and left at the astonished, angry faces of the heads of the guilds. "But I only repeat what such learned and devout doctors of the University as Maître Gerson and Maître d'Ailly have asserted all along, that a king who is incapable or evil can and should be dethroned!"

Simon Caboche raised both his hands.

"Then what are we waiting for, friends?" he yelled at the surgeon. "If it is as you say there, we don't need to be ashamed. We are in good company. The big shots of the University you've just named will be sure to give us absolution if we accidentally cut a few more throats than are strictly necessary!"

Thibert banged his truncheon again; Legoix, now really enraged, stepped to the edge of the platform and ordered the skinner to be silent and to put his feet on solid ground—Caboche still sat enthroned on the shoulders of his followers.

"By the Devil, Legoix, do you support these tonsured fools?" Caboche half-closed his small, bloodshot eyes and opened his large mouth in a grimace. "What little dickey bird has chirped in my ear that you curse and damn the friars of Sainte-Géneviève day in and day out—didn't they keep rapping your knuckles for selling meat during Lent?" He grimaced again at his audience. "And it's obvious that you've gobbled up everything you've slaughtered in the past year, friend. You're as fat as a pig before Christmas."

The beggars in the rear of the hall and the students on the beams burst into uncontrollable laughter.

"To the meat hook with Legoix!" someone yelled.

The butcher boss's face turned red; he was at the point of leaping from the platform to attack Caboche, but he was held back by de Troyes and Thibert. With great effort he swallowed his anger and chose the wisest course, which was to join in the boisterous laughter.

"I can see that you don't understand politics, Simon Caboche," the surgeon said acidly. He thought the skinner was a dangerous man; he did not like the way he sat grinning over the heads of his supporters in the calm awareness of his power. The surgeon decided to try intimidation through subtle eloquence. "Violence breeds violence—haven't you seen enough to know that yet? We shall restore order—but like thoughtful men, not like wild beasts. We don't want a repetition of what happened here sixty years ago when the Provost Marcel stood up for the people's rights. He was in too much of a hurry, he acted harshly and violently—and what were the results? Paris lost its privileges; the citizens were plundered more viciously than before. Let's demonstrate that we've learned our lesson from the past. No brute force, no robbery and murder, Caboche. We'll punish whoever needs punishing, but only after careful deliberation, and after trial."

Now that the uproar around them had diminished somewhat, the men became aware of sounds outside the butcher hall. The bells of Notre Dame were pealing; now the bells of Sainte-Géneviève church picked up the message; then Saint-Jacques, Saint-Pol, Saint-Germain l'Auxerrois, Saint-Jean. One by one the churches, the cloisters and chapels joined in; the air was filled with the sounds of all the bells of Paris, large and small.

"What can be going on there?" Thibert asked. "It's still too early for vespers."

Not even Legoix's servants, who entered the murky slaughterhouse with burning torches, could explain these solemn sounds; many of the men hurried outside to join the curious crowds filling the streets in the hope that Paris was suddenly about to be delivered from its besiegers. The peals lessened and died away; shortly after that, word began to circulate from the direction of the Grand Pont that Orléans and Armagnac had been excommunicated and declared outlaw in the church of Notre Dame because they had committed rebellion, robbery and sacrilege. The solemn ceremony had been performed, amidst the ringing of bells and with smothered candles, in the name of Urban, the new pope in Rome. The Duke of Burgundy had been present, along with several high dignitaries of the Church.

"Did you know that, lads?" Caboche asked the men in the hall. He stood in the doorway, his hands under his apron. The students had lowered themselves from the crossbeams, ready at the first sign of trouble to dash away through streets and alleys to their own quarters. The tramps and beggars, who had been the first to vanish when the bells began to chime, had now unobtrusively turned up again. They liked to be near Caboche, whose bold comments gave them the opportunity to revile the authorities in public at the tops of their lungs, to shout complaints, curses and ridicule, to air emotions which must otherwise be prudently repressed.

"Berry—the old swine—has also been declared outlaw," the skinner said. "Was I right when I said the old greasebag was busy selling us hide and hair to the Armagnacs? Come with me to the Hôtel de Nesle, comrades, and let's give him a professional skinning in his own courtyard!"

The noisy crowd pressed around Caboche; a few students had already snatched torches from the rings on the wall. But Thomas

Legoix, followed by his younger brothers, leapt forward from the group of guildmasters who stood in conference near the slaughter blocks.

"Have you gone crazy, Simon Caboche?"

Roughly, Legoix thrust aside the men who had already drawn their knives, bent upon blood and booty—it was said that the vaulted cellars of the Hôtel de Nesle were full of wine and salted meat.

"Are you all stark mad? You couldn't do anything more stupid! If you don't know how to keep your hands to yourself and can't obey our decisions, get out! Blockheads and rioters do our cause more harm than good!"

"I don't give a damn about your blather." Caboche cursed and put his hands on his hips. "Where's the grub? That castle is full of it from top to bottom! Believe me, that pig Berry knows how to live; he takes good care of himself and his pages."

For further news, Maître de Troyes had gone with a few butchers to the great island in the Seine; now he pushed his way back inside past the men who blocked the entrance. He knew from those who shouted and stamped impatiently outside the door, what was going on in the slaughterhouse.

"Listen!" he shouted, hoarse from the effort of trying to make himself heard. "Legoix, Caboche, listen! Berry fled from Paris to-night and the Hôtel de Nesle has been assigned to the Earl of Arundel and his English!"

The angry shouts of the comrades grew louder. They were too hungry and too poor to listen to the voice of reason.

"So the foreigners will fill their bellies with good French food bought and paid for with our centimes!" Caboche leered at the anxious face of Thomas Legoix, who exerted great self-control to keep from assaulting the skinner with his fists. Legoix himself had no love for the English bowmen, but neither had he any stomach for a fight inside the walls of Paris on the eve of a joint action against the Armagnacs.

"Send Caboche and all these fellows away," Maître de Troyes whispered sharply into Legoix's ear. "It's impossible to hold a meeting with the skinner here. He keeps interrupting and confusing the whole issue with his insolent mouth. Tell the men now that they must be at Saint-Jacques gate at midnight tomorrow and then let us go to your house to talk this over with the guildmasters. We don't need all these people here. We have to get away from Caboche's people, those loud mouths and the scarecrows too . . ."

Legoix objected; he was afraid that the skinner and his friends would not leave willingly. However, after a brief consultation with Thibert and Saint-Yon, he ordered Caboche out of the butcher hall. Strangely enough, no one protested. Caboche left at once, followed by nearly all the workers and servants, the students and vagrants. Legoix led those who remained—no more than thirty or forty men—through a hidden passage to his own house which lay beyond the slaughterhouse and its adjoining stables and barns. He was not happy with the silent withdrawal of Caboche and his men. He kept asking himself what the skinner was up to: it seemed obvious that he was up to something—Simon Caboche had never yet shown a willingness to obey a command or fulfil a request without an argument or a show of reluctance. Legoix decided that something must be done about Caboche, even if it meant strangling him with his bare hands, if the skinner persisted by his bestial behavior in endangering the business of the burghers. Legoix had no intention of letting himself or his colleagues lose their authority to a brute who was interested only in his own profit.

The common people, who until recently had looked up to the slaughterhouse owners as powerful protectors and trusted them as leaders, were tending more and more to support Caboche, because he appealed to their basest instincts. The dream of recovering prosperity, public order and moderate taxes under a fair administration would undoubtedly go up in smoke if Simon Caboche were allowed free rein to stir up the hungry mob.

Legoix was forced, more quickly than he had expected, to make a decision about the fate of the skinner. Just before daybreak Maître de Troyes came pounding on his door. The surgeon pointed to the glowing eastern sky.

"That's outside the city," Legoix said. He threw a cloak over his shirt and went up the street with de Troyes. "The Armagnacs have set fire to another town."

"No no, Legoix," the surgeon said despondently. He sighed. "That's the work of our friend Caboche. He convinced five or six hundred men with his wild talk. My apprentice told me that after dusk armed men were seen on their way to an unguarded spot in the city walls. Now they've come back—the ignorant idiots—and they're bragging about their bravery. Instead of the Hôtel de Nesle, they have sacked Bicêtre castle—and set it on fire."

At dawn the streets of Saint-Jacques streamed with people who had taken part in the nocturnal expedition. Those who were not too drunk to talk—they had loaded vats of wine from Berry's cellar onto carts and taken them along—were able to tell marvelous tales about the splendor of the ducal palace. They showed splinters of gold leaf which they had wrenched from the walls, and fragments of Berry's precious stained glass windows. Gold and silver, however, were nowhere to be found—could it really be true that the Duke had stripped himself to the bone to aid Orléans in his struggle? The plunderers had found only the collections famed far and wide: books, stuffed animals, relics of saints in golden shrines. They had thrown the books and beasts into the fire, but they fell eagerly upon the relics. All day, laden with booty, singing and shouting, the butcher apprentices and their hangers-on marched through the streets of Paris, led by Simon Caboche, who had dressed himself in one of Berry's scarlet ceremonial robes, heavy with golden ornaments.

Repeatedly Legoix summoned the skinner to a meeting. At last, with his brothers and associates, he set off for the quarter where Caboche lived, but the skinner appeared only when he was surrounded by followers armed with knives and cudgels.

After midnight more than 6,000 soldiers left Paris under the command of the Duke of Burgundy. While they advanced overland to Saint-Cloud, ships loaded with burning pitch floated down the Seine. So at daybreak the Armagnacs, within their hastily fortified village, found themselves threatened on two sides. The bridges over the Seine and the neighboring wooden barricades went up in smoke, creating a diversion which facilitated the invasion of the village by Burgundy's troops. For hours there was bitter fighting in the village and in the neighboring fields. The garrison of Saint-Cloud—Bretons and Gascons from Armagnac's army—was vastly outnumbered and unprepared for the attack from the city. Burgundy's troops left the dead and wounded on the battlefield to the wolves and ravens and chased the fleeing Armagnacs toward Saint-Denis.

Charles d'Orléans spent the winter at Blois, depressed and embittered. He knew that he owed the failure of his campaign to Armagnac's crude indifference, and to the irresolution and delay of his other allies. And once more Charles had borne the brunt of the defeat. Armagnac had made off with the gold of Saint-Denis. Once more Charles was compelled to raise wages for his soldiers and ransom for the prisoners in Saint-Cloud. The treasury of Orléans was empty: bankers and money-lenders came to Blois to view and appraise the valuables on display, which for the most part were trifles: crucifixes, mirrors, bound books, relic caskets, two gilded birdcages—all of which had belonged to the Duchess Valentine. The proceeds were not nearly enough. Charles had no alternative but to levy a huge tax on the wine and grain in the territory of Orléans so that he could have a substantial sum of money at his disposal.

Now everything seemed to conspire against him. It was true that Burgundy, thinking of ice and snow, had voluntarily refrained from pursuing Orléans' retreating troops, but the winter cold did not prevent the Count of Saint-Pol from occupying the territories of Valois, Beaumont and Coucy. It was impossible for Charles to mount a counter-attack: Bourbon and Alençon, equally threatened by Burgundy's troops on the borders of their own domains, had their hands full. Armagnac wandered with his men as usual from district to district, plundering and destroying at will. Berry had retreated within the strong walls of Bourges, the capital of his feudal state. His couriers traveled weekly to Blois with news and letters; now that he had fallen again into disfavor at court, the old Duke appeared disposed to donate whatever energy and insight he possessed to his nephew's cause.

This time Berry was profoundly grief-stricken and angry: the loss of his power and influence in Paris was nothing to him beside the wanton destruction of his collections. The knowledge that nothing remained of Bicêtre except charred heaps of rubble, that precious manuscripts had been burned to a crisp, stained glass windows smashed, the relics stolen by vandals who could hardly comprehend the value of their booty—the thought of this tormented Berry night and day. In the course of his long life he had never been particularly truthful, upright or merciful; he had lied and deceived, betrayed and blasphemed without scruple whenever it suited his convenience. Now he wept like a child in impotent rage and bitterness over the loss of Bicêtre.

"Worthy Nephew," he wrote to Charles in a private letter, "we cannot go on in this way. You don't have a sou left, and I am ruined.

In order to fortify Bourges I have sold whatever valuables I owned here; my properties in Paris have been confiscated. My beautiful Bicêtre was, as you know, razed to the ground by the rabble which still continue to rob and murder respectable citizens every day. Nephew, I have learned from a good source that they are preparing a new campaign against us: it is said that Burgundy will march upon Bourges after Easter. The Dauphin has been dubbed a knight in Paris; he will lead the army with Burgundy. We are enemies of the state, Nephew, our cause looks bad. That is why I wish to suggest something to you. I have been in touch with the King of England. He has reason to complain because of the manner in which Burgundy treated the auxiliary troops which were despatched to him a year ago from over the sea. Through the mediation of Armagnac and Brittany I have been able to learn the attitude of the King and Queen of England toward the situation in our kingdom. They are willing to send us some reinforcements under certain conditions. I enclose a draft of the treaty in which they list their demands. Think now, Nephew; we have no choice. Decide as quickly as possible; send couriers to Bourbon and Alençon and request them emphatically to do what I advise you to do. This will make probable a quick settlement of the matter. My clerks can fill in the text of the treaty later.

"There is no time to lose, Nephew. Burgundy's army stands at Melun. They have stopped there because the King is unwell, but it cannot be long before they reach Bourges. I expect a siege about Saint-Boniface's day; I can offer resistance for—say—roughly two months, but no longer. Before that time has elapsed, I must have help. Do not delay, Nephew; remember, our cause stands or falls with Bourges. If I am defeated, it will be your turn next at Blois. Your allies cannot help you. Consider all this carefully, sign the blank document and forward it at once. Hurry."

Charles convened his council immediately: his brother Philippe, the Chancellor Davy, the Captains de Braquemont and de Villars, the Governor of Orléans, de Mornay. Hesitantly, with marked reluctance, he told them what the Duke of Berry had written. Amid a silence which held a sharper protest than any spoken argument, he read the points of the treaty: the King of England declared himself ready to despatch at once 8,000 foot soldiers and archers, provided that Orléans and his allies pledged themselves to help him regain Guyenne and Aquitaine to which the English Crown laid claim of old.

The others remained silent even after Charles had finished the letter. They sat motionless around the table, without looking up.

"I am waiting, my lords," Charles said at last, attempting to cover his uneasiness with formality. "I am eager to hear your views on this proposal."

Philippe moved as though he were going to leap from his seat, but he controlled himself and remained sitting with his face averted. The others exchanged glances. Finally de Mornay rose to his feet with a sigh.

"Monseigneur." He paused and stared distractedly out the window at the blue-white, bright vernal sky. "Monseigneur, we have come to a sorry pass when a man must choose between hanging and drowning. I do not know what to advise you. I agree with the Duke of Berry that without swift, vigorous aid from abroad, your armies and your allies' armies will be crushed before the year is out, because they are scattered and weakened and we know now that unity in action and obedience to a central authority are impossible. With the help of the English the party of Orléans would certainly win—for the present, at any rate. The English fight better in France than we do. You would be able to defend your rights yourself, Monseigneur, but at what cost? As for myself, I would sooner lose my life and all that I own than enter into a pact with the enemies of France."

De Braquemont rose too.

"In any case," he said, "what reason do these bastards have to meddle in our domestic disturbances? If they see that we are divided among ourselves, they will be all the more eager to wage war against all of us together. I advise you to let things take their course, my lord. How can you be sure that Burgundy will besiege Blois after Bourges falls? It seems more likely to me that he will turn back, especially now that he has the sick King with him. We will have time to plan then."

"And suppose that Burgundy seeks a reconciliation with England again?" De Villars remarked sharply. "He has already done that once before; is his daughter not half promised to an English prince? If the English come against us even *once*, we are truly lost—because a thousand of these bowmen fight better than the whole of Burgundy's army."

The Chancellor Davy, however, shook his head.

"It is those damnable conditions which make it impossible for us to sign the treaty. England wants our promises now, in black and white. They have learned from Burgundy what happens when one has no written agreement."

"But if we help the English conquer Guyenne—it is high treason!" Philippe exclaimed. He looked imploringly at his brother. "You cannot, we may not do that, Charles."

"Nay," Charles said calmly. "I shall write my uncle of Berry that we cannot accept this proposal. Then we can only march to Bourges with all the men we have here."

That night Charles could not sleep at all: he let the candle burn on the table in his room, and when the tiny crackling flame finally threatened to go out at the bottom of the candlestick, he kindled a new one. He had not taken off his clothes and he could not sit still; with his hands clasped behind his back he paced back and forth from wall to wall, from bed to chest, from table to window. Around midnight there was a soft rap on his door; Charles pushed the bolt aside. From the darkness of the vaulted stairhead Dunois appeared, clad like his brother in doublet and hose.

"What is it?" asked Charles, surprised and slightly annoyed; he did not want to be disturbed now.

"I could not sleep, brother." Dunois sat down on Charles' clothes chest and pressed his hands together between his knees. "I could not help thinking about what you told us today. Is it really so bad with us? Will we lose our war against Burgundy?"

"We will certainly lose," Charles said, shrugging, "unless we get money soon and are able to persuade the soldiers in our service to obey our exact orders. It is our misfortune that our army has a half-dozen commanders who are constantly at loggerheads. If we had discipline and order among us we would not have been defeated so decisively at Saint-Cloud, brother. I don't know where to hide from shame when I remember that day. No wonder our enemies call us empty braggarts."

In silence Dunois looked at his half-brother. Charles had grown thinner, his face had a yellow tint: his outdoor life had made his skin tawny so that he could not be called pale even now, when all the color had vanished from his face. Although he shaved closely, the blue shadow of his beard was always visible on his cheeks and chin. He was so accustomed to wrinkle his forehead in thought that even when he relaxed a crease remained between his eyebrows. He looked much older than his seventeen years: this was noticeable especially in his eyes. He had the weary, mournful, somewhat suspicious look of a man who has been frequently injured and disappointed. He had a habit of looking downward when he wanted to hide his uncertainty—he did this often.

"What happens if we lose?" asked Dunois matter-of-factly.

Charles glanced at him askance.

"That depends. We are outlaws. They could kill us or send us into exile and claim all our possessions for the Crown again. I really don't know, brother. But it does not look very promising."

"What would Monseigneur our father have done?" asked Dunois brusquely. Charles said nothing. He knew only too well that his father would never have allowed himself to become embroiled in such a hopeless and dismal situation; *he* would not have let Armagnac bully him; the Lords of Luxembourg and Picardy would never have deserted *him*. The thought of his father filled him with bitter shame; here he sat, the heir to a great name and to power and vast estates. How had he discharged his task? He had lost half of his lands and all his money and valuables; the blows he had received in his struggle against Burgundy had thoroughly dissipated the glory of the name of Orléans. He had not avenged his father's death nor redeemed the vow he had made to his mother; there was no future for himself, his brothers, his small sister and his child; at best they would be poor exiles.

"What is better now, brother?" asked Dunois in a clear voice. "To defeat Burgundy with the help of the English or to allow ourselves out of loyalty to the realm to be hacked to pieces by Burgundy? I know very well that the English are our hereditary enemies, but you have heard yourself how Burgundy let the butchers take over Paris, how they set fire to the churches and then drove women and children into the flames, how they plunder and murder to their hearts' content. Wouldn't the King prefer to lose Guyenne to the English rather than all France to fellows like the butchers and Armagnac's men? If you win the struggle, brother, and are restored to honor, you will be powerful. If you were the King's right hand you could issue laws to protect the people against rovers and free looters. Perhaps it would be easier then to maintain a vast, well-trained, orderly army to defend the land against foreign invasion, which is something Burgundy will never do."

Charles, who stood by the table, raised his head, startled, and looked attentively at Dunois. He had never heard the youth give so long a speech. Dunois was reticent by nature; he was also unaccustomed to express his opinion unasked. He was about twelve years old, but strong and sinewy as an adult; in his wide fair face his grey-green eyes gleamed, remarkably clear, like the waters of the brooks which flowed through the city of Blois. His thick, sandy hair was clipped so short that he seemed almost bald. He sat in the same position on the chest, hands between his knees, his eyes fixed quietly on Charles.

"So you think I would be no traitor if I did what Berry proposes?" Charles asked gravely, sitting down on the edge of the bed opposite Dunois. "It's merely a question of whether the King will ever think as you do, brother!"

Dunois laughed easily.

"The King himself has eaten and drunk with the Earl of Arundel when he was in Paris," he said. "I know that from La Marche, the Burgundian whom you took prisoner."

Charles sighed and nodded thoughtfully.

"We shall still have to fight the English again for all that," he said finally. "Everyone sees clearly that it must end sooner or later in war. That is why I find this alliance so dishonorable."

"Oh, but the English are perfectly aware of that too." Dunois frowned slightly as though he were surprised that Charles could doubt him on that point. "It is certainly awkward that we need their help now. They will undoubtedly laugh at us because we cannot keep peace in our own lands. But don't you think, brother, that Burgundy is more dangerous than the English?"

Charles sent his half-brother to bed; but he himself remained awake until early morning. Doubt kept him company. He was secretly ashamed of the desires which sometimes crept over him; he felt an urge to relieve himself as quickly as possible of the worries and burdens, the responsibility and unrest, which had fallen to his lot after his father's death. What difference did it make whether he was defeated and exiled? He had demonstrated his good will; the circumstances were stronger than he was. He was always painfully aware of these and similar thoughts. He reproached himself for being cowardly, weak, ungrateful, unworthy. What sort of man was he that he seemed sometimes to lack utterly the will to persevere, the power to act, any impulse to heroism? Dunois' words spurred him to persist anew. What the devil, this was politics; now he must demonstrate his ability as a diplomat. Burgundy had managed to use the English and skilfully move them aside when they had fulfilled their purpose. Must *he* fail where his enemy had succeeded?

Standing before the window, Charles watched the stars fading in the morning sky. He had made up his mind to sign the English treaty.

On a certain day in the middle of June, the army which had arrived in Bourges under the command of the King and Burgundy, prepared for a ceremonial meeting of both parties. A wooden structure, a platform divided in two by a railing, had been erected on the marshy field outside the ramparts of Bourges. Towards noon the Duke of Burgundy and the Dauphin left the royal tents attended by armed nobles, priests and advocates in official robes. Since the mounted heralds, stationed in the field to announce the approach from the city of Berry and his retinue, made no attempt to blow their trumpets, Burgundy and his royal son-in-law continued to pace up and down over the swampy grassland, watched from a respectful distance by their gentlemen-in-waiting. The sun stood high in the sky; it was unusually warm. The Dauphin sighed incessantly; he would gladly have exchanged his heavy gilded cuirass for the silk clothes which had cost him so much money in Paris, but since he had to appear here as a surrogate for his father—they had, after second thoughts, sent the King home—he had to continue playing the soldier. Under the large blue and white plumes which adorned his helmet, in the opening of his visor, the Dauphin's face looked childishly small and peaked. He walked ahead of his father-in-law with a peculiar, exaggerated gait like a strutting young cock with stiff tail feathers.

Burgundy, arrayed as usual in his scarlet mantle, followed, looking surly. For the past few days he had been sorely irritated by the Dauphin's behavior—the fact that this sixteen-year-old brat held an official post did not give him the right to interfere high-handedly in Burgundy's plans and affairs. Burgundy wanted to raze Bourges to the ground, batter it to rubble, force Berry to submit to the paying of tribute, and then march directly on Blois. He had no intention of returning to Paris until he had squared accounts with his enemies thoroughly and for good.

The march to Bourges had not been easy. The army had had to stop repeatedly because of the King's health. Then there were problems with feeding the troops and providing them with war materiel. When he finally reached the walls of Bourges, Burgundy had sent Berry a formal challenge. The old Duke had replied curtly that he was always willing to open the gates to the King and the Dauphin, but not to certain malevolent persons into whose power the King and the Dauphin had unfortunately fallen. The soldiers and burghers crowding onto the ramparts of the city expressed agreement with this in no uncertain terms. They shouted curses at the Burgundians, accused them of holding the King captive, and called them filthy traitors.

Burgundy felt he had good reason to use drastic measures: he ordered battering rams and catapults made ready for an attack; the tall buildings and towers directly behind the ramparts made an excellent target. But opposition to this came from an unexpected source: his son-in-law the Dauphin, who until now had always supported Burgundy's decisions, had resolutely opposed the use of heavy artillery.

Burgundy swore under his breath; the sun burned on the steel of his armor, on the mail covering his neck and arms. With a jerky movement he flung back his heavy red cloak and walked quickly up to his son-in-law.

"Monseigneur," Burgundy said, making an effort to be courteous, "I wish to draw your attention once more to the fact that your method of procedure is dramatically opposite to the resolution which the Council adopted before our departure. As you will undoubtedly recall, we agreed then that we would make every effort to carry this action to a successful conclusion."

"Yes," said the Dauphin impatiently. "That's quite true. But now I wish to put an end to the struggle between you and Messeigneurs, our kinsmen. I find it extremely tedious. It costs an appalling amount of time and money. What kind of life do we actually lead? I have no desire to sit in tents and armed camps for the rest of my life. If my father should suddenly die, I should be saddled with nothing but burdens."

"Are you opposed to purging the Kingdom of rebels and traitors?" Burgundy asked, sneering. "What we do here is in your interest too."

The Dauphin laughed, the shrill, affected titter so characteristic of him.

"Ah, come," he remarked, glancing sideways at his father-in-law under raised brows. It was, thought Burgundy, the selfsame glance which he had always found unbearable in Queen Isabeau. "Ah, come. I fight against kinsmen because they demand satisfaction for the murder of my father's only brother. That is really rather strange, don't you agree?"

Burgundy stood motionless for a moment and then took his son-in-law roughly by the arm.

"Are you with Orléans now?" he asked, with a quick suspicious glance at the group of dignitaries and nobles who stood waiting around the wooden platforms, chatting among themselves. Their armor flashed; their purple and violet state robes and mantles reflected the sunlight. Burgundy reviewed the ranks: he felt suddenly uncertain. The Dauphin had loyal friends and followers. Who of the prelates and knights were traitors, serving Orléans' cause? The thought had already flashed through his mind that the meeting between the Dauphin and Berry might be a trap. He had to be ready for anything and take measures accordingly. A group of trustworthy councillors and proven knights from his own suite would be with him at all times during the discussions; moreover, horsemen and soldiers whose loyalty he could equally trust, stood stationed a short distance from the rendezvous.

"Father-in-law, you search for too many meanings behind my actions," said the Dauphin, annoyed. "How often have I told you that I do not wish to see Bourges destroyed!" He made a long face to let Burgundy see that his patience was at an end, and rattled off his reasons once more in a bored monotone. "Berry has no son; after his death his estates revert to the Crown and I shall get them— that is already decided, as you know. Bourges is a beautiful city; the churches and towers are valuable—it cost a lot of money to build them. I'm not interested in receiving a gift of heaps of rubble, which I should have to clear away and rebuild at my own expense. I have nothing now but barren fields and blighted vineyards. So how can I raise taxes? No thanks; I have no desire for poverty. I see daily from your example how important it is to own thriving estates."

Burgundy thrust out his lower lip. He had deliberately encouraged the young man's taste for luxury by helping him to live extravagantly in order to control him; now it looked as though the youth's demands were getting out of hand. They had reached the end of the small strip of passable ground bordering the swamp; they retraced their steps. Two hundred paces away stood the platform adorned with flags and banners and divided in half by a wooden railing.

"That is all well and good," said Burgundy roughly, "but you cannot disregard the decisions of the Council and negotiate by yourself. Don't forget that the opposition party has been declared outlaw. And don't forget, too, Monseigneur, how much has happened over the past year. By God, you cannot ignore me and my grievances any longer!" he exclaimed abruptly, stopping before the Dauphin. "This whole plan for negotiation is ridiculous, son-in-law. What is there to discuss? De Bar is behind this, I'm sure of it! He is the traitor, he has a brother in Berry's retinue. I've always thought that that alone laid him open to suspicion!"

The Dauphin flushed angrily.

"De Bar stands under my protection," he said excitedly, with a catch in his voice. "I forbid you to attempt to act against him in any way. He is no traitor. No one is going to hurt you, you don't need to disgrace yourself. Now I want to conclude a peaceful treaty with Monseigneur de Berry and my cousins. I have no inclination to carry on your wars. Go and fight to your heart's content without me. The people of Orléans are my kinsmen; they belong to my retinue and should be in my court. Why should I behave in a less honorable way than princes and monarchs in other countries simply because you have a mind to quarrel? I don't have to live like a country bumpkin just because my father is crazy and sick!"

The Dauphin gave an angry shrug and walked more quickly to escape his father-in-law. At that moment the gates of Bourges opened, the drawbridge dropped over the moat and a long procession of horsemen rode out. Burgundy made no effort to overtake the Dauphin; he chewed his lower lip thoughtfully while he watched his son-in-law: the silk tunic, gold breastplate and plume made the heir to the throne appear more helpless and clumsy than he actually was. The armor hindered him; he waddled when he walked. The armor plate on his legs forced him to keep his knees stiff. Burgundy grinned. He always felt angrily ashamed of his own physical shortcomings; it pleased him to notice the imperfections of other men. He ascended the platform behind the Dauphin. Advisors and armed soldiers closed in around both princes. There, protected by a double railing, they awaited the arrival of Berry.

The old Duke approached, with scorn and resentment written

clearly on his features. His opponents had protected themselves from him as though he were a ferocious beast. When he learned what precautions were being taken against him by Burgundy, he had decided to behave in a similar way. He brought only his own advisors to the platform; the horsemen and soldiers who had accompanied him from Bourges remained standing at the same distance in the field as Burgundy's men. For the occasion Berry was clad in armor from head to toe; he refused to give Burgundy the satisfaction of sneering that his uncle was too old and too fat to wear armor. He wore a crowned casque and held axe and sword in his hands. A broad, heavy cloak studded with silver daisies dragged over the ground behind him. Although he could scarcely breathe under the burden of steel and leather, he managed, through great effort, to maintain a stiff, dignified bearing. It was certainly promising that he had been invited to this discussion before a single arrow had been shot or a single stone hurled. The English auxiliary troops had not yet arrived; a postponement of hostilities was certainly welcome. He had no idea what Burgundy and the Dauphin had in mind, but he knew, alas, they had little reason to fear him.

Berry was seventy-four years old. He could not help but notice that his strength was no longer equal to the task which, in rage and bitterness, he had taken upon himself. He was no longer capable of waging war. In God's name, they must cease hostilities at once and if any reasons cropped up for future action, he would not be one of the parties. He had had his fill; he wanted to spend the rest of his life peacefully in a comfortable castle somewhere far from politics and court intrigues. The more he thought about it, the more desirable it seemed to him to settle this matter swiftly. He had doubts—it was not in fact so simple as it seemed and the peace was built on quicksand. But what happened later would not concern *him* anymore, thank God. Orléans could do as he chose; if he received the same conditions that Berry had, he could stop fighting. What the devil, that feud could well be forgotten!

Berry swore solemnly that he would persuade Charles d'Orléans and his brothers to accept the truce; he then handed the keys of the city of Bourges to the Dauphin through two bars in the railing. This action made him heartsick; he could not restrain his tears.

"My uncle is in his second childhood." Burgundy shrugged, looking after Berry—the old man walked somewhat unsteadily back to his escort. "You've had your own way, Monseigneur," he continued loudly to the Dauphin, who was as captivated with the keys of Bourges as a child with a new toy.

In the city of Blois consternation prevailed; two reports had arrived simultaneously: that peace negotiations were being conducted in Bourges, and that the English reinforcements under the leadership of the Dukes of Clarence and Cornwall had landed on the coast. Charles sent desperate letters and envoys to his great-uncle in Bourges who was preparing to leave for Paris. The reply which he received was brief: Berry washed his hands of the whole affair; he had done his best to aid his nephew. If complications had arisen now, it was not his fault. He advised Charles to reach an accord with Clarence and Cornwall as quickly as possible: they would probably be willing to cancel the treaty in return for certain financial considerations. "And come to Auxerre as quickly as possible, Nephew, in order to negotiate the peace personally: if you word it wisely you need not singe your wings at all," Berry concluded.

After he had read the letter Charles sat motionless for a long time with his hands pressed against his eyes. He fancied he saw small, multicolored shapes revolving against a dark background: stars, rings, spheres. They whirled off and on, burst asunder into sparks or shrivelled into dots. Inside his heart it was utterly empty and cold; faith and hope, never completely dispelled despite reverses, had gone now for good, along with his youthful dreams.

Toward his councillors he used a tone which they had never heard from him before: harsh and indifferent; the tone of a gambler who rashly stakes everything he owns on a weak hand. Through the mouths of Mornay and Davy he began negotiations with the English, who from day to day advanced more deeply into the country, roaming aimlessly, plundering with impunity now that they could no longer be sure of war and its booty. Clarence replied that he had never seen so disorderly and riotous a situation as in the Kingdom of France; never had he dealt with such irresolute allies. He would regard this affront to him as healed if he and his men were paid 150,000 écus. The amount made Charles dizzy. Although he did not know yet whether he would be able to raise that sum, he quickly replied that he agreed to the terms, provided the English put to sea before New Year's Day, 1413.

"Agreed. Before January first," replied Clarence, smelling the possibility of a greater profit, "but in that case I must request 60,000 écus more from Your Grace."

Charles wrote bluntly that he saw no chance of collecting such a vast sum; but the cold, matter-of-fact Englishman managed to find a solution, thanks to his advisors. He demanded important hostages who would be freed when the money had been paid. Charles agreed to send hostages at once, on the condition that Clarence's troops would cease their looting during their retreat to the coast. But agreement to this stipulation carried a further price: the English demanded a final hostage, a brother of the Duke of Orléans, of his own choice.

In the presence of loyal friends and members of his household, Charles read aloud Clarence's most recent letter. He hardly dared raise his eyes from the parchment; he could not endure the embarrassed, solicitous, disheartened expressions on the faces of his friends and aides.

'I must send seven hostages," he said at last, returning Clarence's letter to his secretary, Garbet. "Six men from my immediate entourage and one of my brothers."

"Yes, Monseigneur." De Mornay stepped forward. "I know that I speak in the name of all of us when I request that you make a choice *now*."

Charles looked, almost in supplication, at the row of faces. He saw that they still stood motionless, waiting: the captains, the Chancellor, the Governor, his chamberlains, the nobles of his retinue, old Garbet, beside whom sat Philippe and Jean. Philippe tugged at the lacings on his sleeve in ill-controlled excitement. He didn't want exile—he didn't want to go! But he was afraid that he *had* to go and he could not oppose Charles.

"Is there anyone among you who wishes to be excluded, who has urgent reasons?" Charles asked slowly in a low voice, as though each word cost him great effort. The men remained silent.

"Yes, forgive me, but I cannot do it," Charles said suddenly. He made a short, violent gesture of desperation. "I cannot choose."

Archambault de Villars stepped out from the group; he bowed stiffly to Charles and stood at the foot of the table.

"I place myself at your disposal," he said shortly. "I request five others to follow my example. Each knows best for himself what he must do."

Almost immediately Chancellor Davy stood beside him; the Chamberlain des Saveuses and three knights joined Davy. Others who had stepped forward moved back when they saw that the required number had been reached. Charles thanked the volunteers. He knew there was little he could say to them; he was only too well aware of the hopelessness of their position. He might never be able to pay the ransom money: under even the most favorable circumstances, many years of exile awaited them. The silent group at the foot of the table had made a great sacrifice for his sake. He could offer them nothing in return—not even a promise or a word of hope.

He turned to his brothers: he saw Philippe's deep flush and compressed lips; the pale, suddenly adult face of Dunois, who felt himself to be an accessory in the matter and suffered because he knew he could not atone here. The Bastard of Orléans was not highly regarded enough to be a hostage. But now Charles met the dark, tranquil gaze of his youngest brother, Jean.

"Let me go, Charles," said the youth. His voice was still childish. "You can't spare Philippe. You don't need me here. At least this way I can serve you and our House. Let me go, brother, I won't give you any reason to complain about me."

Philippe quickly raised his head and looked at his brother with tense expectation. He saw in Charles' eyes that his elder brother agreed that he could not be spared. Philippe knew he was not going into exile; he thanked all the saints for his deliverance.

Charles went up to Jean and embraced him, pressing the youth's head against his shoulder.

On the day of the Assumption of the Virgin Mary, in a monastery outside the city of Auxerre, peace was restored once more between the parties of Orléans and Burgundy. In the presence of princes, nobles, citizens and prelates, representatives of the Council, Parlement and Audit Chamber, and deputies from all the great cities in the land, Charles dissolved his allegiance with Berry, Bourbon, Alençon and Armagnac, and cancelled the treaty with England, which had just come to light. In his turn Burgundy swore that he would negotiate no more with the enemies of the Kingdom.

On the fields and highways near the monastery of Auxerre, the inhabitants of nearby towns and villages stood in groups, looking at the noble travelers, the horses and wagons, the flags and equipment, at the banquets in the open air, at the sham fights held by the high lords inside an arena cordoned off with gaily colored ribbons. The spectators were gloomy; they could not believe that their anguish and distress had ended. And now the region was afflicted by a pestilence; people said it came from the armed camp before Bourges. All that babble of eternal peace could not dispel the knowledge that every hour men and beasts were dying in the farms and houses in the countryside. For over a century the fear of disease, hunger and war had sunk deep into the hearts of the people. Better times are promised in Heaven, said most men, but Paradise lies far away—we sinners know not where.

To reassure and pacify the crowds huddled in the fields of the monastery, Burgundy and Charles went outside together; they passed back and forth between the decorated tables, sat together on the same horse at the Dauphin's request—Burgundy in front, Charles in back—and rode, amidst the acclaim of the spectators, around the arena. From the monastery chapel, choirboys emerged holding burning candles in their hands. They sang "Glory to God in the Highest" and now the bystanders and participants finally joined this strange game of princes with the most beautiful of songs: "Peace on earth to men of good will, hallelujah, hallelujah!" at first hesitantly, but growing gradually louder, stirred by the pealing bells, the burning tapers, the voices of the choir and the magnificent banners.

Meanwhile the plague raged, the mercenaries of Burgundy and Orléans and all their allies, dismissed from their bond of service, plundered everywhere; Armagnac with his Gascons proceeded to harass the regions between the sea and the Loire, and the English, already in possession of the hostages they had demanded, withdrew to their ships, robbing and burning despite the agreements and promises. "Peace on earth," sang the people, not knowing what the morrow would bring; "Men of good will," hummed the powerful with uneasy and distrustful hearts. "Hallelujah, hallelujah," they shouted all together; bonnets and hats flew off, banners fluttered in the wind. The horse which bore Burgundy and Charles began to rear, frightened by the noise; he had to be held fast so that both riders could dismount without mishap.

Now it so happened that a peasant, Jacques d'Arc by name, lived in Domrémy in Lorraine in those days, and at just about this time his wife gave birth to a child. It was the fifth child and a girl, and she was christened Jeanne.

Charles d'Orléans and his brother Philippe accepted the Dauphin's invitation to accompany him to Vincennes castle. The King's son wished to become better acquainted with his cousins now. Monseigneur d'Aquitaine of Guyenne, as the crown prince was called, had become gradually disenchanted with the manner in which Burgundy still attempted to exercise guardianship over him. The young man had tried a few times to assert his independence, and there were enough men in his suite who encouraged him to rid himself of his father-in-law at any cost. Isabeau, apparently completely on Burgundy's side, tried to influence her son by indulging him immeasurably. She gave him houses, money and valuables, and did not attempt to oppose the frankly licentious life he led.

She thought with regret of the good times of the past; when the Dukes had ruled she had been powerful—now no one listened to her. Her brother, Ludwig of Bavaria, who was continually at her elbow, showed her the way to new influence. The Dauphin was fully grown. He was a shallow, erratic young man who in reality had neither the desire nor the disposition to rule. He was interested in dancing, feasts and carousing, in silk clothes and beautiful jewels. He who succeeded in gratifying his cravings for these things won his confidence completely and could mold him as he wished. Burgundy, once so indulgent toward his son-in-law, began to display more and more irritation when he learned about the amounts of money demanded and squandered by the Dauphin.

Isabeau had to take advantage of this friction if she wanted to rule again through the youth. Accordingly she closed her eyes to her son's excesses; she listened impassively to the hints of the clergy and the complaints of subordinates. What business was it of hers if the Dauphin and his friends drank and danced each night with harlots in the Hôtel de Béhaigne, if they annoyed inoffensive citizens with their wild and not always harmless pranks? She flattered his vanity, loaded him with gifts, whispered new notions into his ear— Isabeau had her fantasies too—and at the same time advised him to seek a fresh rapprochement with the party of Orléans—weren't all the princes of the blood on that path already? The Dauphin considered his mother to be an ugly, self-seeking, disagreeable woman, but he had a still greater aversion to Burgundy who, despite the fact that his son-in-law was the heir to the throne, scolded and nagged him incessantly. Monseigneur de Guyenne felt himself old enough to fill the elevated position to which he was to be called, but he wanted to do it in a suitable manner: in order to be able to give himself up undisturbed to luxurious pleasures, he wished to distribute responsible positions in the government among friends and relatives who were clever enough to prevent disorder and to understand that the wearer of the crown was not to be bothered needlessly.

In Vincennes, the Dauphin overloaded his cousins of Orléans with marks of favor and gave fêtes and hunting parties in their honor. In Philippe, who was completely dazzled by the splendor of court life, and who spent his days intoxicated by joy and hitherto unknown delights, the Dauphin instantly found an enthusiastic, indefatigable boon companion. Charles, however, did not unbend; he could not quickly forget what he had left outside those festive walls decorated with wreaths and garlands. He was filled with bitterness and regret by the thought that he had sacrificed his brother for no purpose, since the English had broken their promises. For the first time in years, Philippe went about dressed in gold and bright colors, but Charles refused to lay aside his mourning. Like a stranger who cannot understand the language of his hosts, he lived among his royal kinsmen and their household. He saw his brother, flushed with excitement and exertion, trying to follow the Dauphin's example in the row of dancing courtiers; beautiful women laughed at the youth and held out their hands to him invitingly.

But Charles sat under the canopy beside the Queen, who found him dull; once, in Chartres, she had thought she had discerned the promise of wit and rare courtliness in young Orléans; now there seemed nothing more to say about him than that he was agreeable and well-mannered. Charles was only too well aware of his inability to join in the exuberance and loose jests of the others; this realization made him all the more silent and monosyllabic, especially since he detected in himself a desire to be as carefree and happy as the elegantly dressed young men he saw around him, leading the women to the dance with light, courtly phrases.

The beauty of the women both confused and enraptured him.

He thought he had never realized that such lustrous warmth and grace existed; in the curve of an arm, the drop of a veil, the lines of neck and shoulders, a timeless enchantment lay concealed, a temptation which Charles felt all the more strongly because timidity and lack of experience made him defenseless. But he did not reveal his emotions; he sat with the older men and talked politics. He considered it his duty to learn the opinions of this group with whom, until now, he had had so little contact. Besides, he felt uncertain: what he had been promised in Auxerre, restoration of honor and property, remained still only words on paper. The Council had not yet convened, Burgundy had gone to Flanders; the restoration of honor existed only in the courteous and sympathetic reception afforded him by the Dauphin.

Charles spoke candidly with only one person while he was in Vincennes. One evening he noticed among the spectators in the banquet hall a thin, middle-aged woman in a dark red gown, with sharply chiselled features and intelligent eyes. He remembered her at once and went up to her, although he knew that etiquette demanded that she, as a subordinate, must salute him first. But he remembered how he, as a small boy, had sat at her feet, between the deep folds of her dress, while she, in a low gentle voice, recited verses to his mother. He found that Christine de Pisan, widow of the Sire de Castel, had changed very little.

He spoke with her at length and often; he found it easy to confide in her. She had known his grandfather, admired his father and had been a friend and compatriot of his mother. He greeted her almost like a kinswoman.

In the twelve years which had passed since Charles had seen her last, the Dame de Pisan had gained renown and esteem; her talents were no longer doubted by anyone; she was the guest and close friend of monarchs and, not the least, among great scholars in wisdom and knowledge. Although Burgundy was her protector, she remained impartial. Charles felt that she could be trusted with his confidences.

When they talked together during fêtes or meals or in the Queen's reception halls, Charles and the poet observed etiquette: she stood or knelt in his presence; he touched on general subjects only, requesting her to instruct him about literature and philosophy. It was soon not unusual for members of the royal household to see

Monseigneur d'Orléans and the Dame de Pisan immersed for hours in conversation. But sometimes Charles invited her to visit his private rooms with no other listener than Maître Garbet. There he told her frankly what he thought and felt, what distressed him, insofar as he could give a clear account of all this himself.

Christine understood him; she knew what it meant to live bitter and aggrieved among carefree people.

"When my husband died, I stood alone in the world, Monseigneur," she said, fixing her calm, intelligent eyes upon him. "From the beginning I had to take care of my children and worry about my closest blood kin. I too had to wage a long and bitter struggle to try to save my inheritance. I did not succeed, my lord. But God has given me the ability to say many things in rhyme. Thanks to that ability I could earn my livelihood and was able to raise my children. Believe me, I know what afflicts you so deeply: to feel isolated, alone in a room full of merry-makers. I could, when I had just lost my husband, sing only of grief and love and you know, Monseigneur, that such songs are fashionable for dancing. I sold my heartache for a handful of gold pieces."

She paused and raised her long narrow hands in a gesture of resignation. "I often thought that no worse fate existed on earth than my own. But, alas, my lord, one becomes older and wiser and one learns from day to day. Now it often seems to me that I wept too quickly over my own grief. I look about me and I cannot understand how I can bear with dry eyes the suffering of France. My lord, my lord, how is it possible that kings and princes can still sleep peacefully at night?"

The Dame de Pisan was able to tell him a good deal about the calamities which ravaged the people: she was no stranger to poverty; often enough she had been close to hunger, cold, pestilence, cruelty and injustice. Her words brought Charles back again to a sense of what he must do.

He took leave of the court and marched south to his castle in Beaumont, which had suffered exceedingly under the occupation of Waleran de Saint-Pol. Philippe he left behind in the Dauphin's retinue; the young man wanted nothing more than that. Before Charles left, Christine de Pisan presented him with a book of her poems, Epistles of Othea to Hector. In exchange, Charles gave her his gold cross; he was not rich enough to reward her with a princely gift of money. His friendship with the poet had warmed his heart. He left Vincennes considerably less embittered and depressed than when he had arrived.

On a rainy, chilly spring day in the year 1413, Philippe, Count de Vertus, rode into the city of Blois; he came from Paris, not with a well-armed escort as befitted one of his rank, but in great haste on a horse chosen at random, attended only by two grooms. Without stopping to change his clothes, Philippe went straight to his brother. He found Charles in his old study, busy checking accounts and receipts with the aid of Maître Garbet and a few clerks. Charles leaped up with a cry of surprise. Philippe was still breathless from his fast ride and hard walk. And he wore a disguise—cloak, bonnet and hose like a traveling merchant, and he was covered with mud and dirt. Philippe did not let his brother get in a word.

"I fled from Paris," he said, while he tugged at the lace of his cloak. "I have ridden for two days and nights without pause, brother. They were close at my heels."

Charles motioned the clerks to withdraw. The faithful Garbet, concerned, remained standing behind the table.

"Come sit down, Philippe," said Charles, "and tell me what happened there." He kicked aside the damp, grimy cloak which Philippe had dropped on the floor, and thrust his brother down on the chair. "A few days ago another refugee arrived here, your physician-in-ordinary, Messire Pion."

"Thank God he is alive. I thought they had killed him," cried Philippe. Charles drew a footstool toward him with his foot and continued.

"Nay, but he was a great deal worse off than you, brother. He came on foot, half-naked and famished. He lies in bed still, too ill to talk much. I know that a rebellion broke out in Paris, that the people are laying siege to the Bastille."

"Alas!" Philippe gestured with impatient excitement. "That was weeks ago—so much has happened since then. The butcher rabble rules Paris; they walk about with large knives and axes. They have fortified their districts as though they were castles. None of those fellows works any longer, they do nothing but patrol the streets and plunder, killing anyone who is not especially dirty and does not shout as loud as they do."

"Yes, yes, I know all that already." With a gesture Charles checked his brother's flow of words. "Are you able to tell me quietly what you know or do you want to eat and sleep first?"

"Are you mad? I'm not tired, brother." Never before had he been in such great danger or been involved in such exciting events. He found that he was extremely well-informed; he could enlighten his brother as well if not better than couriers or letters from the court. "I shall tell you everything in detail. It had already begun when I arrived in Paris with the Queen and Monseigneur de Guyenne. Every day there were riots in front of the palace and fighting in the streets because the King had made peace with us. Of course Burgundy stood behind all this. Each day the butcher folk stood before Saint-Pol screaming for Monseigneur de Guyenne. At last he was forced to appear in a window, whether he wanted to or not. Those people have an orator—a surgeon or some such thing, and he addressed Monseigneur, telling him that he was their only hope, but that he had evil companions and advisors, that he behaved like a profligate and wastrel. Aye, the surgeon said that, brother, and all the time the butcher bosses stood there in their Sunday finery, nodding agreement, but the rabble who are always near them brandished knives and sticks. They wore white bonnets—the bastards, that is their symbol; all Paris walks about wearing them and those who do not wear them are killed. Then Monseigneur de Guyenne— in order to provoke the butchers—donned a cap with long flaps which hung over his shoulders. He looked as though he wore the ribbons of our party!"

With animated gestures he described how the rabble stormed up the stairs of Saint-Pol and forced their way into the halls; how many eminent courtiers had been dragged away, among them Ludwig of Bavaria, the Queen's brother, and a number of ladies of the court who had attended the Dauphin's banquet. The prisoners were locked up in the Louvre and guarded by a growing mob. Burgundy, who had rushed out of the Hôtel d'Artois, had tried to appease the men by facing them and appealing to them himself, but it was useless. Yes, it seemed that even the butcher bosses could no longer control their apprentices and mates. A delegation—Philippe remembered the names Saint-Yon and Thibert—had arrived, imploring Monseigneur's forgiveness for the behavior of the citizen army, but immediately afterward the same troops appeared, led by the former city executive Capeluche, and Caboche, the most notorious rebel of all, and made a new expedition inside the palace walls, this time with the express purpose of seizing and murdering anyone who had ever had anything to do with the party of Orléans.

"I still don't know how I managed to escape," Philippe said, raising his goblet courteously toward his brother before drinking. "I climbed over a wall. A peasant brought me over the Seine in a rowboat. One of Monseigneur de Berry's retainers hid me for a few days in a hovel in the fields outside the Hôtel de Nesle. Then I heard further news: the butchers guard the Dauphin and allow no one near him. Nevertheless he managed to send me a message. Here . . ."

From his sleeve Philippe drew a dirty, crumpled piece of paper on which the Dauphin had written in large sloping letters: "Help me. Recruit troops and allies. They threaten me, they wish to force me to sign over my rights to my brother of Touraine. They demand that I use force against Orléans. Be on your guard. Help me!"

Once more Charles d'Orléans entered into negotiations with his erstwhile allies, Alençon, Bourbon and Armagnac. Incessantly the Dauphin despatched messengers and letters with requests for speedy help. In Paris all was confusion and alarm. The butchers, who wanted to fight the Armagnacs and the English together, were now busy collecting the money required for a campaign. Nobles and wealthy burghers were murdered or driven away and their houses looted.

This time Charles saw himself cast in a new role: now he marched upon Paris not as an opponent of his arch-enemy Burgundy, but as a defender of King and Kingdom, a protector of the reign. Circumstances had undoubtedly never been more favorable for him and his cause. He realized that he had not created these circumstances; he had the rabble to thank, and their rage; he could never have accomplished this by himself. Armagnac appeared with a considerably larger force than before; the Gascon's behavior was as crude and coarsely grasping as ever. Although Charles always treated him with noticeable reserve, Armagnac acted as though there had never been any friction between his son-in-law and himself. He constantly sought Charles' company, sat beside him at council meetings and meals, rode with him, and behaved in general as though he were the confidant and right hand of Orléans. In response Charles could use no weapons except coldness and silence, but he understood very well that Armagnac fervently craved the end which he now regarded as almost within his grasp. He smelled success and wanted to be the first to be considered for favors and gifts when Orléans marched into Paris. Although Charles might thus control his father-in-law's behavior by encouraging his belief that ultimate victory was at hand, he himself looked to the future with fear and misgivings.

On the first of August, Charles appeared before Paris with his armies: he offered the King his help in exchange for the properties which had been taken from him, full restoration of his father's honor and good name. When the people's militia saw the cordon of armed men encircling the city, trouble broke out in their ranks. The men flocked to the marketplace to hear Caboche's response, but before the skinner could open his mouth, here and there among the restless, uneasy mob arose cries for peace. Those who were not part of Caboche's immediate circle were more than sated with murder and pillage, with this harsh and uncertain life. The workshops remained closed, business was at a standstill, the purveyors of food seemed in a constant muddle. The privilege of roaming the city armed to the teeth and letting blood flow with impunity did not outweigh all these inconveniences.

"Peace! Peace! Those who want war step to the left; those who want peace to the right!" cried a voice from the mob. This proposal was immediately echoed and chorused; before long the square re-sounded with shouts from a thousand throats. Caboche's voice was drowned in the sea of sound; he had to look on helplessly while the men, whom until then he had held in the palm of his hand, crowded to the right side of the marketplace. No one dared to remain standing on the left side. This incident had notable consequences: within twenty-four hours the city had completely changed.

The gates were flung open and Charles d'Orléans and his princely allies marched into Paris. The inhabitants of the city, wild with joy, did not bother with half-measures: huge bonfires flamed in the marketplaces and on street corners; here was a chance to dance and drink in the open air until long past midnight. Wine and excitement drove the people to another extreme. Even before dawn broke, Caboche, Saint-Yon, Thibert, de Troyes and a number of butchers and butcher's companions were driven away and their houses looted and put to the torch. In Caboche's lodgings they found a document signed by Burgundy, which contained a long list of names of citizens of Paris; each name was preceded by a sign: D, P or R. Everyone knew what that meant: death, prison or ransom. Many of the names thus marked belonged to people who had always been confirmed supporters of Burgundy. The discovery of this document spelled the end of Burgundy's power. All those who had once been willing to follow him blindly now turned against him. When Burgundy heard that the people in the streets were vying with the Armagnacs to shout, "Burgundian dogs, we will cut your throats!"; that they were beginning to arrest the officials appointed by him and to kill his servants, he considered that he was no longer safe, not even in the donjon of the Hôtel d'Artois. He fled unceremoniously from Paris, leaving his followers behind in peril of their lives.

Burgundy had scarcely reached Arras when he learned that his enemies were advancing under the King's banner to compel him by force of arms to beg forgiveness, and to make amends. So Charles d'Orléans rode into battle beside the Dauphin; before him he saw the silken pavilion covering the carriage where the King sat; over his head fluttered the blue and gold banners of France and the ensigns with the inscriptions "Justice" and "The Right Way". Nevertheless, there were still moments when he thought that he dreamt; sometimes he closed his eyes expecting, when he opened them again, to see the walls of Blois around him, to encounter the desolate landscape at Gien. But this was reality, he was the confidant and favorite of the royal family; they were concerned about him, they defended his cause. Here he was marching to punish Burgundy, supported by the highest authority; he had almost achieved his purpose.

But for all that, he knew no peace of mind. He had only to turn his head to see Armagnac riding behind him, a crafty smile forever on his cracked lips.

The stubborn presence of the Gascon distressed Charles sorely; he could not help thinking of the vultures who often in time of war arch over the advancing armies, knowing instinctively that they need not wait long for the carrion. During the brief time he had spent at the court, Armagnac had already made a number of enemies by his crude and repulsive behavior and unabashed greed. Many saw with trepidation and displeasure that three-fourths of the army with which the King went forth to battle for justice was composed of savage, untrustworthy mercenaries; the memory of their outrages in the outskirts of Paris was still fresh in people's minds.

That the King and the Dauphin had allowed themselves to be persuaded to wear the white band of the Armagnacs on their right arms, thoughtful people considered to be an insurmountable scandal—worse still, a great imprudence: the King had to stand above all parties, and should not identify himself with so disreputable a horde of soldiers. Charles was afraid that those who spoke that way would all too quickly be proven right. Indeed, time had taught him that his fears were only too well-founded: the towns which the army had captured on the way to Arras were, in spite of the King's orders, pillaged and reduced to ashes. Charles saw the city of Soissons after the Gascons and Bretons had rampaged there; as long as he lived the image of the horrors would remain with him: the charred beams and black scorched walls, the mutilated corpses of women and children, the rows of dead hanging on trees and palisades. Over the years he had, indeed, learned to control himself well, but on seeing this senseless destruction, this bestial ferocity, he could contain himself no longer. How could a venture be blessed which owed its success to such behavior?

Charles was not surprised to see that the King's army was stranded before Arras; the city seemed impregnable. Moreover, the camp was ravaged by heavy rains; fever broke out among the troops. The end of the campaign was ignominious: peace negotiations were re-opened once more at the request of the Dauphin, who suffered from the damp climate and was becoming weary. For the fifth time in seven years they entreated Charles to reach out his hand to his adversary. Three times Charles refused. He obeyed only when the Dauphin, enraged by his cousin's persistent refusals, had stalked out of his tent, stamping his foot angrily. But Charles did not look at Burgundy, nor did he speak to him. The King, who had just enough sense to realize that young Orléans was deeply offended, thought that Charles had to be kept satisfied one way or another.

"Let us, for the sake of my brother whose soul is now in Paradise, hold a service in Notre Dame for the dead, when we return to Paris," whispered the sick man, gesticulating quickly to the Archbishop of Reims. "With a thousand candles and torches and black curtains, knights and priests and singing boys, as if it were the funeral of a king. I shall be there too in my prayer chair," he concluded in a mysterious tone, nodding his head like a satisfied child.

So it happened. Before the high altar, heaped with gold candlesticks and flickering lights, Charles heard his father's memory praised by no less a personage than the very learned and eloquent Maître Gerson, who twenty years before, in an equally passionate flow of words, had called Louis d'Orléans a wastrel, a woman chaser and a heretic.

Toward the end of October Charles set out for the castle of Riom, to meet there with his wife Bonne d'Armagnac for the first time in four years.

"I ordered my daughter to come to Riom," Armagnac told him shortly after they had returned from Arras. "She is now fifteen years old, old enough to bear children. You can take her along now, son-in-law, it is growing too expensive for me to keep on supporting her."

Charles realized on this occasion that he had never given thought or word to his young wife. A few years earlier he had dutifully sent her some gifts for the New Year, in honor of her name day—rings, pins, a golden triptych with angels playing the harp. The bride's mother, Berry's daughter, had sent him a letter of thanks in the girl's name; from this he learned that Bonne was well, and thought of him with respect and affection. Charles knew that this was nothing more than a courtly phrase; he had never attached any importance to it. When he had lost contact with Armagnac after the failure at Saint-Cloud, he had also stopped sending Bonne letters and gifts, not so much intentionally as from forgetfulness. Bonne was for him hardly more than a name, he did not think of her, or if he ever did, it was with a certain antipathy because she was the daughter of a man whom he found frustrating and contemptible. Armagnac's words reminded him of Bonne's existence; he realized that she had grown up now and was entitled to the respect due to a Duchess of Orléans, and to husbandly affection and devotion. He could no longer shirk these obligations.

While he rode over the roads to Riom, accompanied by a large retinue of horsemen and servants, he reflected, with the resignation which had become characteristic of him over the last few years, that he ought to be happy to a certain degree with this solution; he was now at an age when a man ought to be married. Although up to now he had had little time or inclination to involve himself with women, passion and desire were not alien to him; he could easily imagine what he had never experienced. He understood now what it was that Isabelle had found lacking in him. Now that he himself knew the torment of sexual deprivation, he thought of his dead wife with compassion. Restrained by inner scruples Charles had not sought the short-lived pleasure which is easily accessible or can be bought with money. In the army camps around Blois, in the camp before Saint-Denis, in the cities through which he had ridden at the head of his troops, there had been enough women ready to oblige him at the slightest sign. Although no one would have blamed him in the least if he had let himself go—on the contrary, his abstinence provoked ridicule and a certain disdain—he suppressed his mounting desires. He longed for something which he himself could not yet clearly visualize; he knew only that gross sensuality, blind passion without anything else, did not attract him. In his solitude and voluntary chastity, he experienced at least the curious sweet feeling of anticipation which had charmed him so when he was a child. He did not discuss these and similar matters; he realized, to be sure, that men found him odd—even his own brothers found him so. Philippe was proud of the casual adventures he had had during these campaigns; Dunois, young as he was, could romp and banter with his half-brother's maid-servants.

At the court of Saint-Pol in Paris, a new world had opened for Charles: a class of women he had never met before lived there. At first he had been deeply impressed with their beauty, the splendor of their finery, their courtly manners and clever conversation, but soon he could not help noticing that in many cases smiling lips and lustrous eyes concealed an inner darkness that he had never imagined. Monseigneur de Guyenne, the Dauphin, already well-schooled in the arts of Our Lady of Love, invited his cousin to attend certain fêtes in a private circle. Charles drank and danced like the others—little by little he had come to understand that it is frequently unwise to behave differently from your fellows—but his heart was bleak with bitterness and aversion. At the Dauphin's request he laid aside his mourning—for the first time since his father's death he wore colored garments: violet and gold brocade, crimson and silver like his royal cousin.

He did not feel at home in this unwonted splendor; he thought he looked like a gilded weathervane, a motley popinjay. The coquettish ladies of the court and the frivolous demoiselles who kept the Dauphin company at his fêtes did Charles no service by demonstrating their interest in him. He despised the crown prince who did not seem to be able to get enough of this kind of life, who spent the nights carousing, the days in gambling halls and bathhouses.

Frequently on these occasions Charles attended the Dauphin's retinue. He knew that it was considered to be a great honor to sit with
the successor to the throne of France in a tub full of steaming hot
water while half-naked bathhouse girls offered them wine and sweetmeats.

When Armagnac told him that Bonne was at Riom, Charles did
not hesitate for a moment; on the contrary, he was delighted to
have a reason to leave the court. The atmosphere at Saint-Pol was
beginning to stifle him; he was amazed that Philippe had no sense
of the chill, corrupt air in that hotbed of intrigue, where the Queen,
immobile in her corpulence, sat watching play and dance with gleaming shrewd eyes while the mad King wandered mumbling through
the halls, followed by insolent, indifferent courtiers—at least when
he did not stand knocking on the bolted door of his chamber,
screaming hoarsely.

Now that at last there was peace, the King could turn to his
favorite diversion: processions and passion plays. To please their
beloved monarch, the people of Paris marched barefoot through the
streets with burning candles in their hands. Little children carried
small flags and pasteboard lilies; they sang hymns of praise and
litanies. The plays were performed in the great marketplace: the Fall
of Man and the Expulsion from Paradise, the story of Cain and Abel,
the Passion of Our Lord and the Crucifixion. Surrounded by retinue
and kinsmen, the King sat on a decorated platform; leaning his head
on his hands, weeping, laughing, shouting, he watched the performance. After it was over he spoke to the players, to the indignation of the Queen and her son.

"I am like you, brothers," he said in a whining voice, while he
shook a handful of gold pieces from his sleeve and distributed them
to the players. "Neither more nor less—a poor comedian. Pray for
me, brothers, pray for me!" He remained standing, babbling and
waving his hands until they dragged him away to his carriage. Since
they had taken Odette de Champdivers from him, he had never
again been completely lucid. The Queen had sent her home when
it appeared she was going to give the King a child; no dangerous
bastards were wanted at the court.

No, Charles was not sorry to see Paris vanish behind the horizon:
he did not know what awaited him, but after what he had endured
he could adjust to anything. So he approached Riom: in the vast
woods that surrounded the castle the leaves glinted russet and amber

in the October sunlight. The undergrowth had already lost its leaves, and a brown glow lay over the fields. Autumn appealed to Charles as no other season did; he felt a certain affinity with the world on the verge of winter, when the land seems strewn with red and yellow gold like a page in an illuminated breviary; when the cry of the birds flying south is both sad and ominous.

The castle of Riom loomed amidst the flame-colored forest; from its peaked roofs and towers fluttered the banners of Orléans, Armagnac and Berry. Charles saluted the people who came running from the small homesteads along the road. A drift of smoke hung over the trees; he saw the glimmer of fires. A group of children ran along with the procession part of the way, but when the ramparts of Riom came into view, they vanished, laughing and shouting, into the forest. The ladies of the house were not yet ready to welcome Monseigneur d'Orléans; Charles deduced this from the confused rushing about of stewards and servants. He had arrived earlier than expected. Because the weather promised to be so beautiful he had left his lodgings at dawn.

Charles was secretly amused; he looked up at the windows facing the courtyard. Behind the thick walls, he thought, they were astir, hurriedly adorning the bride. For the first time a feeling of curiosity crept over him, and even a certain uneasiness. He had no desire to enter the castle. He nodded to a page and rode out the gate. He preferred to spend some time in the forest beyond the ramparts, where the beech trees, with their trunks layered with gray-green moss, rose tall and straight. He let his horse move at a snail's pace; the dry leaves crackled under the hooves. The sound of laughter and singing led him to the spot where the children were playing. He watched them, unperceived, from the depths of the forest. The children danced in a circle; they were filthy and dressed in rags, but their eyes shone and their laughter was carefree. They moved hand in hand. In the center of the circle a girl, her head covered with a blue cloth, stood singing. The tune and the words seemed familiar to Charles: in his childhood he had played a similar game—at a certain moment one had to run hard to try to reach a particular spot before being tagged by the child in the center of the circle. The children flew away in all directions; the girl in the blue kerchief kicked off her wooden shoes and began the pursuit. It was a merry and cheerful sight. Charles was so amused that he decided to give something to the children. Undoubtedly they belonged to the houses and farms of Riom's peasants and servants. The children tumbled over one another, romping and squealing with laughter. The girl had caught someone now; they were beside themselves with delight. They were so absorbed in their game that they noticed the stranger only when he was directly upon them. They stared at him, their mouths open, frightened and confused; the smallest crept behind the girl's skirts.

Charles took a silver écu from his girdle and gave it to the girl with a few friendly words. She did not thank him but stood gazing at him with eyes as amber as the leaves overhead. This gaze astonished Charles; he was not accustomed to be stared at attentively by peasant girls; this gaze was not without a trace of secret mockery, despite a certain diffidence which was far from meek. They stood together under the October leaves, a hushed group: the shy children, the barefoot maid, and Charles, richly clad in gold and brown, on his horse Perceval. The forest was still as death: only the page who stood at some distance behind the trees coughed slightly. He could not understand what his lord was doing there. The spell seemed suddenly shattered; the maid tucked up her skirt and darted away over the leaves, followed by the frightened, screaming children. In a few moments they had all vanished from sight as swiftly as hares and squirrels. Startled, Charles laughed; he wheeled his horse around and rode slowly back to Riom.

The Countess d'Armagnac and her women received him in a lofty hall with white-plastered walls. Charles spoke briefly to his mother-in-law about events at court, his own plans, the arrangements for Bonne's retinue and future position. Charles was at the point of asking where his wife was, when he heard a soft rustle behind him.

"This is my daughter, Monseigneur," said the Countess with visible relief. Charles turned toward his bride; he had to bow deeply to raise her from her curtsey.

"Welcome, Monseigneur," said Madame d'Orléans, offering her cheek to her husband for a greeting kiss. Only when she secretly pressed a silver écu into his hand did Charles recognize her.

For Charles, Bonne was a source of infinite, unprecedented rapture and surprise. No matter what she did, the young man found her continually fresh and captivating; he who had known only sorrow and worry, of whom until now life had demanded only self-mastery and responsible acts, could now bask for the first time in a bliss which was as radiant as it was unexpected. Charles behaved as reticent and solitary natures usually behave under these circumstances: he gave himself wholly, without reservation. His heart was so full of love for Bonne that he knew he could never express his feelings. What he could not put into words or translate into action oppressed him like a pain that nevertheless did not make him unhappy.

The days came and went, but Charles lost all sense of time. The sand in the hourglass, the shadowy streak on the sundial, showed him only that he had spent time with Bonne; they were together everywhere and always—first at Riom, later at Montargis, one of Charles' castles. The young Duchess of Orléans had a sunny, playful disposition; she was slight, swift and happy as a bird; as light as the leaves in the wind, carefree without being frivolous and changeable without inconstancy. She possessed all the qualities which Charles lacked and which he desired: the ability to live easily, without worry, to act boldly on a whim, to laugh heartily, to enjoy the good things in full measure, to be warm and loving without constraint. Everyone—young and old, adults and children, courtiers and servants—loved her. As for Charles, he had the feeling that he could not do without her for a single moment; when she was not there, he longed so much for her that he knew no rest; when he saw her he could think of nothing else. He perceived, in truth, that in Bonne he had found a good woman, despite her youth; she had been wisely brought up by her mother.

The Countess d'Armagnac, whom a hard life had made into a prudent woman without illusions, had not neglected to take into account the possibility that Orléans might one day be an impoverished exile. Bonne could read, embroider and play the lute as befitted a noblewoman, but she also knew how to bake bread, make soap and wash linens. In Armagnac's ramshackle castle, she had learned how to mend clothing again and again; she knew how to be thrifty and keep a sharp eye on servants. Moreover, she had a strong belief that highly placed persons were responsible for the welfare of their subjects. Armagnac's wife, who had made it her task to try incessantly to alleviate the distress caused in and around the castle by her husband's cruelty, had been unable or had not wished to spare her child the spectacle of sickness and misery. Bonne visited the poor, tended the sick, played with the children. She continued this custom even in the castles where she stayed with Charles for only a short time. They traveled together from region to region, surveying the damage to the country estates ravaged by war, reviewing the harvest and the produce from the fields. Bonne had good sense; she was a great comfort to Charles.

Every day he felt greater amazement that she could be a daughter of the loathsome Gascon; nothing about her reminded him of his father-in-law, except possibly the color of her eyes. She resembled her mother; she had in fact seldom seen her father; she feared him and was ashamed of his reputation. Eagerly, Charles heaped gifts upon his young wife; for the first time he regretted having sold all his jewels and ornaments. But Bonne, laughing, disputed his rueful ruminations. She threw her arms about his neck and said that she did not need jewels and rich clothing. "Good health and a happy heart—and of course Monseigneur's love—for me these are the most valuable ornaments."

"You will never lack that last, Bonne," Charles said. "My own fear is that one day you might get tired of it."

Bonne looked at him with shining eyes and shook her head. They were in the bedchamber at Montargis. The fire flared up the chimney, the February wind roared behind the shutters. Charles unbuckled his girdle and put his clothes, one by one, on the chest at the foot of the bed, purposely loitering so that he could watch Bonne, who knelt before the fire in an ample white night shirt, holding a kitten which she had found somewhere. Her long, coal-black curly hair hung down to the floor. She disliked wearing night-caps.

"Bonne," Charles said abruptly, "I am eager to take you back with me to Blois. I feel most at home there. I think you will like it too."

"Yes, of course." Bonne smiled at him over her shoulder. "And there are the two little girls there too. It's time that you looked in on the poor wretches again. But we have to stay here for now, don't we?"

Charles was awaiting a delegation from Asti; in addition the Duchess of Brittany, the wife of his former ally, had announced her intention to pay a visit. The messengers had arrived from Lombardy to pay homage to the young Duke in the name of the people of his domain; but Madame of Brittany's visit was inspired—Charles knew this from the letters—by less agreeable motives. In the past few months Charles had been only remotely conscious of politics; he did not ask for news. But he could not hide from reality behind the fragile walls of his dream castle. He was forced against his will to hear an account of recent events.

The King of England was dead: the son who succeeded him under the name of Henry V had shown himself, after a rather wild, pleasure-seeking youth, to be a disciplined, faithful, austere and ambitious ruler, firmly resolved to complete the conquest which his father, always thwarted by domestic strife, had been unable to finish. With growing self-confidence, the young King had watched the turbulence in France; he believed that God had singled him out to punish the dissolute crowd; England, he thought, had an ancient right to Guyenne, Poitou, Angiers and Périgord, but he believed it would be better and simpler if England and France could be united under one Crown. The time was ripe for swift, vigorous action.

Henry surveyed the game and marshalled his troops. Jean of Burgundy, after his defeat before Paris, had resumed negotiations with England; it was not very difficult for Henry to persuade him to sign a declaration that he would not intervene in the approaching conflict. This done, Henry sent an emissary to France with unheard-of demands: the hand of the young princess Catherine, a dowry of two million gold francs, a series of important territories. It could not be supposed that he expected these demands to be granted; therefore it was quite clear where the matter would lead. Berry and Armagnac, who ruled the Council at the time, kept negotiations going for as long as possible, while they sent couriers to the princes of the realm requesting that they send more men. Charles had received a similar summons. More and more lately he had been receiving news about the state of military operations; Bourbon, Alençon and Brittany were already busy raising troops.

Charles knew that it would be impossible to come to an accord with England in the present circumstances; he too expected war. For Bonne's sake he decided to live, during the visit of the Duchess of Brittany, in a style befitting the name and rank of the House of Orléans. To this end he borrowed money, mortgaging his property. He relished the sight of Bonne, beautifully dressed, moving through festively decorated halls, and presiding at a well-stocked table. The guests were entertained royally with hunts, balls and tournaments. While the Duchess of Brittany and her advisors spoke to him about the need to prepare for war at once—they had heard that King Henry was on the point of taking ship with a large army—Charles, with a smile, toasted his young wife's health. In her honor he had ordered the sleeve of his tunic embroidered with the opening words of a love song which the minstrels sang in parts: Madame, je suys plus joyeulx. . . , Madame, I am overjoyed. My wife, never have I been as happy as I am now.

The moon hid behind clouds; a fine, even, cold rain fell. There was no wind, but the raw damp of the long night seemed far less bearable than a dry cold. On the muddy plain the French army stood with its vast camp of tents: hundreds of bonfires smouldered in the dank mist. Torches flashed like comets through the darkness. Flags and banners hung limply; from the pointed tops of the tents water trickled down the gold and silver escutcheons.

Inside the tents the noble lords sat over their wine, cards and conversation; the men in the open fields tried to keep warm by stamping their feet, running hard or shoving, with curses, for a place near one of the fires. The Gascons and Bretons who, as usual, made up the majority of the foot soldiers, were especially exasperated. They hated campaigns in the northern part of the Kingdom like the plague. At Arras they had had their fill of rain, fog and mud. What possessed the captains to keep waging war in the fall? This was already the night of the twenty-fourth or twenty-fifth of October; winter was at hand. What the devil! The English should have been attacked long before this—as soon as they landed; when they besieged Harfleur; when, enfeebled by sickness and losses, they began their rash, presumptuous march north to Calais across enemy terrain. This view was shared by most soldiers, horsemen and knights. Those who had some knowledge of strategy believed that the Constable and other royal commanders were wrong to cling to the old rules of knightly combat with a formal challenge and a traditional order of battle.

This desire to exact a proper vengeance for the defeats suffered by the French half a century before at Crécy and Poitiers had caused the supreme command to delay endlessly, much to the annoyance of the more experienced soldiers. No one doubted the imminence of victory: that a handful of exhausted Englishmen could be routed without much trouble. It was a matter of fifty thousand against eleven or twelve thousand at the most. The counts and barons would not allow themselves to be deprived of such a wonderful opportunity for military renown. From their treasuries and arsenals they brought forth their splendid armor, ancestral broadswords, crowned and plumed helmets, unrolled their stitched and painted banners, re-gilded their coats of arms. The honor of France was about to be defended against the arch-enemy; the long-awaited moment had arrived. Everyone in the Kingdom who bore a famous name had a grandfather, father or kinsman to avenge. The lions ascendant, the hawks and eagles, the griffins and panthers were ready with pointed claw and cleft tongue—they did not fear the British unicorn.

In an open patch of ground between the tents, heavily armored horses covered with hanging scalloped cloths stood together mo-tionless in the rain; only their eyes gleamed moistly behind the large openings in their almost ridiculous iron masks. Those who were to ride these monsters were already being thrust into their armor. Strad-dle-legged, with extended arms, the knights stood in their tents. Through the drawn-up flaps of the tent-openings, they exchanged words with their friends and kin who were all similarly occupied. Meanwhile, beakers and bowls made the rounds; it was senseless to fast on the eve of such an easy conquest.

The men of lesser rank, camped under tents of hide, wood and straw, showed no more inclination to abstain from the pleasures to which they were accustomed than their lords; they had fetched sup-ply wagons inside the camp, shared food and drink and rolled in the mud with the whores who were part of the army's equipment. The horses, driven together into a gigantic herd between the pali-sades, neighed incessantly, upset by the fires and the rain. Dark shapes loomed outside the reddish fog which hovered over the camp: thickets, a row of trees, an abandoned hut. When the moon became faintly visible through the clouds and the fog, there could be dis-cerned against the night sky the massive towers and ramparts of Agincourt, after which the field was named.

Toward midnight Charles d'Orléans left the Constable's tent where the commanders were gathered—the Dukes of Bourbon, Bar and Alençon, the Counts d'Eu, Vendôme, Marle, Salm, Roussy and Dammartin, the Marshal de Longny, Admirals de Brabant and Dam-pierre and a great number of captains. After long arguments they had decided who would stand at the head of vanguard, center, rearguard and flanks; because each of the great lords coveted a place in the front lines, these ranks would be formed almost exclusively of princes and nobles with their heralds, pages, squires and armed following. Knights of lower rank, horsemen, bowmen and foot soldiers had been relegated to the rear guard.

Charles, who had listened quietly all evening to the battle of words, got up to leave as soon as he heard that he would be one of the leaders of the vanguard; he had confidently sought the post, his rank entitled him to it. He felt little inclination to remain in that company until daybreak. He had agreed to risk a reconnaissance of the English camp, which lay a few miles away against the hill of Maisoncelles. The separate parts of his armor lay displayed in his tent: mechanically he examined the arm and leg pieces, tested the mobility of the scales at the neck and gauntlets. He had a new breastplate of burnished black iron decorated with golden lilies. By the light of the torch overhead, he saw his face reflected vaguely in the glittering surface. He looked away; a shudder of cold apprehension passed through this body. For five long years he had done almost nothing except wander about at the head of an army, but he had never yet engaged in combat—never released an arrow, never used a sword or lifted his shield in self-defense, except for exercise. Charles knew himself well enough to recognize that he had little talent for military heroism, but after all he was a man and naturally he wanted to prove himself. He had not yet killed a knight because he had never enjoyed man-to-man combat. He had planned the reconnaissance so that he could march into battle as a fully worthy knight; he thought perhaps blows would fall on this eve of battle.

Before he left Blois he had exercised vigorously for a few weeks with lance and sword; he had exerted himself to the utmost, especially because Bonne was watching him from the window of her chamber. It was for her sake in the first place that he craved military fame; in addition he hoped to have an opportunity, if the English army should be defeated, to liberate his brother Jean. In any exchange of prisoners Charles' brother would undoubtedly be returned to France. But along with these thoughts a slight fear mounted to his heart, a fear of unknown dangers, of the arrow destined perhaps to strike him, of the enemy who could defeat him in a hand-to-hand mêlée, of the death which he dreaded especially just now. He picked up his sword, a beautiful narrow weapon with a cruciform hilt which his mother had brought from Italy as part of her dowry; for a moment he held it high between the palms of his hands. The blade, catching the glow of the flame, seemed a long line of light. Charles had ordered the weapon consecrated before the altar of Saint-Sauveur in Blois; now at midnight in his tent at Agincourt he entreated once more in a whisper the blessing of God and Saint-Denis on the sword with which he must avenge the dishonor of France and win back his brother.

He heard voices and footsteps outside his tent; the curtain before the entrance was pushed aside and two men in coats of mail and tunics entered: Arthur, Count de Richmont, Brittany's younger brother, and Marshal Boucicaut. Charles had met Boucicaut, his father's great friend and confidant, for the first time only a comparatively short time ago; the Marshal had returned a few years earlier from Italy, ousted by the rebellious inhabitants of Genoa and its environs, who had risen up against domination by the French. Boucicaut had aged greatly: his hair was grey, his figure less upright, but his solemn frank eyes and his self-assurance still inspired confidence. Richmont was a young man of Charles' age, lively, loquacious and restless. He would represent Brittany in the coming conflict.

"Orléans," said Richmont, "we are ready. I see that you too have been wise enough not to wear armor; one can't possibly walk with all that steel on one's back. We just want to see how the land lies with the English. It's so quiet over there; they seem to have put out all their fires. I wonder what they're doing."

Boucicaut shook his head, looked at Charles, and remarked calmly, "They're probably sleeping. They've had an arduous journey—twenty days' march through hostile territory without enough food and supplies. Tomorrow they face a serious challenge—they know that too."

Richmont snorted incredulously and began to pull the hood of his hauberk over his head. "Last week during the battle on the Somme my troops captured a couple of Englishmen. It seems that when they talk among themselves about the size of our army, they say, 'Enough to put to flight, enough to take prisoner, more than enough to kill.' And Henry insists that he is entirely satisfied with the number of his men. He says that God will help him, because the French are a race of sinners."

Charles laughed, but Boucicaut interposed hastily, "Nonetheless it does not behoove us to laugh at King Henry. No one can deny that he is a pious and honorable man who lives soberly and sets his soldiers a good example. It must be said to the credit of the English that they have no wine or women with them, and do not waste precious time with curses and dice. Our army is notorious for licentiousness and crime . . . and rightly. The common soldiers' behavior is an abomination."

Richmont, who was helping Charles put on his coat of mail—Charles had silently begun to make himself ready for the nocturnal expedition—shrugged and said impatiently: "Ah, come, Messire Boucicaut. I know Henry. Don't forget that I lived in England for four years. I have watched the fellow from close by. He can swig liquor with the best of them, and as far as women and dice are concerned, believe me, he needs no instruction there either. Oh yes, he's now God's own right hand or at least he acts as if he were—but I myself think he is nothing but a hypocrite."

"You are probably exaggerating, Richmont," Charles said, carefully buckling on his shoulder belt. "Alas, I cannot say that King Henry is wrong when he calls us a quarrelsome, disorderly mob. God knows we do not seem able to govern the Kingdom as we should."

Young Richmont was not listening. He walked back and forth in the tent, examining Charles' armor spread on the camp bed, testing the point of a dagger on his finger.

"Whatever else King Henry may be," Charles went on, "a coward he is not. He could have entrenched himself within a city when he received our challenge two weeks ago. But no—he came forward and said to us quietly, in a wholly dignified manner, that it did not behoove him to appoint a day or place but that he would meet us in the open at any time. . ."

"Yes, yes, I know all that." Richmont turned with a nervous, jerky movement. "Are you ready now, Orléans?"

"We are taking two hundred men with us, my lord," said Boucicaut. During this conversation he had stood silently at the entrance to the tent. He disapproved of Richmont's familiarity with the King's nephew; when he was young, vassals of the French crown had had better manners. He watched Charles with some concern. He thought that the young man bore himself with dignity and spoke sensibly, but it seemed to him that Charles d'Orléans was a little too mild, that he lacked the fire to assert authority, to be a leader of men.

Louis d'Orléans, when he was twenty years old could, if it came to a crunch, show swift, sharp insight and unflagging persistence. Now it *had* come to a crunch. Boucicaut was astute enough to know that the size of the French army by no means guaranteed invincibility. The supreme command was shared by too many leaders, the diverse troops were thrown together hastily for the most part and were not dependent upon one another for discipline and order; thus morale was affected by mutual jealousy. In addition, Boucicaut disagreed with the proposed plan of organized attack: horsemen would make up both flanks—that would look pretty, but the terrain was unsuitable for it. They had chosen the valley between Agincourt and the adjacent town of Tramecourt as the battlefield. A brook ran the length of the narrow valley; since it was impossible to deploy the cavalry freely there, the Constable had decided that the battle order would be thirty-two rows deep. Boucicaut could see no advantages in this plan either: it would have to lead immediately to a confused hand-to-hand mêlée. He had made his objections clear, but he had not been able to convince d'Albret to change his mind. The Constable's plan had been accepted by a majority.

Charles, Richmont and the Marshal set out to join the men who were to accompany them on the expedition and who were waiting for them behind the farthest row of tents. When the moon, which had been visible through an opening in the clouds, disappeared as gusts of rain began to blow over them, the men hurried into the darkness.

"My God, what mud!" Richmont murmured irritably to Charles, who was behind him. "That promises something for tomorrow. Up to the ankles . . ."

They moved forward through the soft mass of mud. After a while they noticed that the marsh was becoming more solid; presently they began to ascend and found themselves on the sloping terrain before Maisoncelles, the hamlet where the English army was spending the night. Hedges and a series of thickets separated the expedition from the enemy camp. In the air was the unmistakable smell of horses and damp, smouldering wood. The dull glow of an almost extinguished fire was visible here and there through the branches. Richmont remained at the edge of the trees with most of the men while Boucicaut and Charles set out on their scouting expedition accompanied by half a dozen men; they intended to see as much of the enemy camp as they could without being discovered.

Charles was much taken with the idea of being the unseen close watcher of the English; he was more interested in doing that than in coming to blows with them.

The rain abated; the moon broke once more through the clouds. The men ducked hastily into the shadows between the trees. Now the group split up. Charles saw the Marshal move off with a few followers; in a little while he himself chose the road that led straight to the English camp. Two paces from his men, he tripped over a small shrub; he tore his tunic on a branch and banged his foot against a tree trunk. Both times the sound seemed to carry a long way in the silence. But nothing stirred among the sheds and cottages of Maisoncelles; the hamlet seemed completely deserted.

Charles and his men came within about one hundred meters of the camp; they were close enough to see the English sentries in the darkness. A shadow was visible against the vague glow further away between the houses; something jingled there, straw rustled under moving feet.

Charles had undertaken the reconnaissance impelled by the desire for adventure which is innate in every man; but he also wanted to perform bravely so that Bonne would hear of his exploits. While he stood in the misty night before Maisoncelles, the image of Bonne flitted through his head: she must be sleeping now inside the green curtains of her bed, with one hand under her cheek and her black hair spread out like a fan over the pillows. He had often seen her like that by the glimmer of the night light. What did she dream of? The old feeling of loneliness had crept over him at those times; there she was, breathing beside him and yet she was not there at all. He could not bear her to turn away from him, not even in her sleep.

The rain rustled again on the dry leaves under the bushes. Charles heard the English sentry cough. Presently he heard another sound, a muffled chant, a monotonous murmur. He recognized it: thus the murmured prayers of the multitude fill the air in the churches. Charles chose one man from his company, one of his own grooms. Together they crawled through the wet matted grass toward one of the barns. The rain helped them: it poured down heavily and masked the sound of their movements. In the darkness they crept, step by step, past the dank, squalid walls of the hovels of Maisoncelles; abruptly they found themselves in the midst of the enemy camp. A row of sheds and haystacks hid the English, but he who penetrated these barricades could overlook the whole camp.

Most of the soldiers had found shelter in the cottages and barns the owners of which had fled the day before; thanks to some torch-light Charles was able to see about him. It looked as though no one was sleeping, but everyone was silent. Fires burned in the cottages: the men who were huddled together under the shelter of the roofs were busy with their weapons. They sharpened their swords and axes, cut wooden spears and mended leather clothing. Charles and his companion dropped down and burrowed into a pile of straw. Not far from them in a dilapidated stable, archers sat stretching new strings to their bows: crossbows and footbows, man-sized bows which were far from new and which were braced with ends of rope and straps at damaged places. But their owners handled them care-fully as though they were trusted companions. Charles had never seen archers like these before: they were larger and more muscular even than the Picards and Flemings and their sandy hair was worn at an odd length. They worked in intense silence. The same deliberate concentration prevailed everywhere in and around the hovels of Maisoncelles.

Further off stood many dark canvas tents; there Charles saw the faint gleam of helmets and armor. The murmur seemed to come from somewhere close by; between the dark mass of trees and barns behind the tents, lights were visible, torches and small lamps smoked and flickered in the rain. Now men came running on all sides from stables, sheds and haystacks. They knelt in the mire with uncovered heads and murmured the words entreating forgiveness for sin: *"Mis-erere mei, Domine, miserere mei, quoniam in te confidet anima mea."*

Lanterns and more torches were brought. Amid the kneeling men, Charles saw priests standing; one was an old man in a soggy bishop's mantle who turned continually from left to right, his hand raised in blessing. The soldiers were ragged and dirty, in old leather jerkins and dented helmets; knives and axes dangled from their gir-dles, as was usual with peasants. The archers' arms were bare: they wore leather bonnets buckled under their chins. Charles looked in vain for knights: shields, banners or coats of mail were nowhere to be seen. The horses, captured by the English at Harfleur, stood together in rows under hastily improvised shelters. They were prac-tically all beasts of burden, but the soldiers had covered them care-fully with straw and blankets as though they were thoroughbreds.

The soldiers clustered around the huts moved slightly aside; a rider approached on a small grey horse. He was young and bareheaded; a dark mantle was thrown around his shoulders. He gave a few commands in a cold clear voice and disappeared as quickly as he had come. The priests walked on, accompanied by torchbearers; they intoned the litany afresh as a bell sounded. The soldiers returned to their work and silence reigned as before.

Charles was greatly impressed by the behavior of the soldiers in the English camp; the men here prepared for combat in a much more dignified way than the soldiers in the French camp at Agincourt. But although these men had spent the night working and praying, he could not believe that they had much chance of success. On the contrary, now that he had seen their crude equipment, their extremely one-sided army, composed mostly of lightly-armed foot soldiers and bowmen, a French victory seemed to him to be a certainty. He and his men waited for Boucicaut behind the clump of elms below Maisoncelles. The Marshal returned soon enough; he had crept up on the camp from the east and had come to the same conclusion as Charles. Unlike the young man, however, he believed that present weather conditions favored the English: lightly armed troops had more mobility than armed horsemen and spearmen. Boucicaut regretted deeply the decision of the French commanders to refuse, time and time again, the offers of Paris and other cities to send foot soldiers.

They hurried back through the trees to Richmont and his troop: together they walked back again in the direction of Maisoncelles, this time quite openly. And this time their approach was noticed immediately. The watch blew the alarm and the English rushed forward from all sides, thinking that the camp was being attacked by the enemy. When they realized that it was only a challenge to a skirmish, they wisely chose to save their strength. A few hundred men rode out for a brief and rather aimless scuffle. After a few on each side had fallen, the French, as well as the English, withdrew.

Charles' neck was scratched; the warm and sticky feeling of blood under his mail gave him no little satisfaction. Now, he thought, he could take part honorably and justly in the battle; now he was no longer a callow youth. At Maisoncelles he had just killed a man in hand-to-hand combat for the first time. It had all happened so quickly that he scarcely realized it himself, but now that it was over he remembered with a shudder of peculiar excitement the soldier's short scream, and then his fall. Back in his tent he looked at his sword; it bore the traces of his deed. Charles' squire came up immediately to clean the weapon. When he saw the blood-stained cloth, Charles' pride and satisfaction vanished, to his surprise, as though by magic. He was ashamed of this reaction and knew he must not mention it to anyone. He thought bitterly that this demonstrated once more that he was not meant to be a soldier. Nay, he did not have the makings of a hero.

The dawn broke: St Crispin's day, October twenty-fifth, 1415. The first faint glimmer of light appeared hesitantly on the horizon, but the sky remained darkly clouded. True, the rain had stopped, but a heavy fog drifted low over the land. In the French camp the confusion prevailed which is usually the result of divided commands and too little discipline. Forty thousand men were arming themselves; heralds rode about shouting in the midst of the turmoil and blowing with all their might on clarions and trumpets. The heavily armed knights who hours before had had themselves hoisted into their saddles, rode slowly out of the camp, an almost endless procession of grotesque iron dolls adorned with sodden colored plumes and drenched cloaks. They had closed the visors of their helmets and held their lances menacingly before them. In the field the legs of the heavily burdened battlehorses sank into the yellow-brown mud; the riders dug in their spurs and a rain of mud spurted up from under the hooves of the desperately struggling horses; it sucked and bubbled in the soft earth. The drooping saddlecloths and handsome armorplate were soon soiled beyond recognition. Organizing the troops became an unexpectedly difficult task: the Constable d'Albret had competent commanders, but they could not create order in that mass of swarming, entangled horsemen.

Charles, who felt extremely uncomfortable in his heavy armor—inside the stifling helmet he felt shut off forever from light and air—had, with the greatest effort, assembled his own men. He rode through the dense crowd followed by his heralds and Captain de Braquemont, seeking his vassals and instructing them to go to a chosen place on the field where he had ordered his standard fixed; other captains soon followed his example.

The knights and their picked men grouped themselves around the standards; an outline of battle order began at long last to emerge. It looked now as though the valley was indeed too narrow; the warriors stood packed together so closely that they could scarcely move. If a horse took a step forward or backward, a whole row was forced to go along with it. When he saw the ridiculously deep vanguard, Boucicaut lost his self-control. Dukes, counts and barons were crowded together there; their only followers were squires, standard-bearers and trumpeters. It looked impressive, but had the fools learned nothing from what had happened at Nicopolis?

"That was twenty years ago," said d'Albret angrily. "Leave me in peace, Boucicaut, take your place; we have no time to listen to your stories."

"In God's name, make the front wider instead of deeper," the Marshal roared above the noise of the sentries. But d'Albret rode away with a curse, to oversee the progress of the center and rear guard.

Boucicaut pushed his way in beside Charles in the first row. The young man had closed his visor; he was choking from lack of air; his heart throbbed as though it would burst; sweat broke out under the weight of metal.

"God be with us, I can't get my horse out of the mire," said Boucicaut, extremely irritated. "We cannot conduct a charge like this. Why doesn't d'Albret listen? This is sheer folly. Look how those horsemen stand on top of each other! I knew perfectly well there would be no room here for the flanks. Spread out, that is the only way, move the battle to a higher terrain and put only foot soldiers to work here. Is it right that a man who has had thirty years of experience fighting at home and abroad should be shoved aside like a peasant when he comes here with advice?"

Charles moved uneasily. He saw that his horse was sinking ever deeper into the mud; the beast could raise each leg only with great effort. It was light enough now so that the hills could be discerned; among the hedges and groves of Maisoncelles the enemy was visible. Many of them were descending the slopes together in great groups: archers with archers, spearmen with spearmen.

"There is the man," Charles said suddenly, "whom I saw giving orders last night. He there—on that small grey horse, not much larger than a colt."

Boucicaut shaded his eyes with his hand.

"That's the King himself," he replied. "Didn't you know, Monseigneur? I've heard that the English are exceedingly fond of such small horses. They're strong and swift."

Charles leaned forward in the saddle with a cry of amazement. King Henry wore a bright cuirass and was accompanied by a standard-bearer, but nothing else distinguished him from the horsemen around him. The English took their positions with surprising speed; the mud did not seem to incommode them much. But they had chosen high ground for their last stand, less swampy than the rest of the valley. The archers made up the larger part of the army ranks, which now stood lined up in a very broad front four rows deep. The bowmen in the first row thrust sharply pointed wooden lances into the ground, to give themselves the slight protection of a sort of palisade.

The armies faced each other in order of battle. On the one side a forest of banners and pennants, plumes and lances, a packed multitude of knights arrayed in jingling gold and silver metal like participants in a tourney. On the other side of the field a dark row without pomp or splendor: men in leather and coarse wool with flat storm caps on their heads, many barefoot, the majority armed with bows, axes, spears and cudgels.

"By God, they're nothing but common people and workers," cried d'Albret, standing up in his stirrups. "We fight against common villagers today, my lords. Does King Henry think his knights are too noble to be led against us in battle?"

King Henry readied himself for the battle. Someone placed a crowned helmet upon his head; even at a great distance the jewels gleamed on the crown. Alençon swore loudly that he would not rest until he had plucked the gold flowers one by one. Now King Henry rode swiftly along the front of his army; here and there he stopped a moment to speak to the men. Then he dismounted and joined the captains who stood waiting a few paces from the first row of bowmen.

"It is going to begin, Monseigneur," said Boucicaut. He turned to Charles and uttered a request for forgiveness, according to the old rules of chivalry. "Before we march into battle, Monseigneur, I beg you to forgive me for whatever crimes I may have committed against you, even as I forgive you." Charles remembered that this had once been the custom. He bowed to Boucicaut, and in his turn made the same request of the knight on his other side. Everywhere in the vanguard the lords were granting forgiveness to one another. Some even went so far as to embrace each other, insofar as that was possible with mail-covered arms. The English stood astounded by the spectacle.

It was now about ten o'clock in the morning. The rain had stopped, but the sky was overcast with thick grey clouds. A penetrating chill rose from the marshy ground. King Henry stood for a while staring at the French lines, his hands on his hips. Then he spoke briefly to the knight beside him, who ran down the line, whirled around and threw a staff high in the air, shouting, "Now strike!" The men obeyed the command with a chorus of shouts. To the ears of the French chivalry these sounded barbarous and frightening, as though they issued from the throats of beasts of prey. D'Albret signalled for the charge. Charles closed his visor quickly, gripped his lance more firmly in his fist and prepared to do what the men to the right and left of him were doing: rush down at full gallop upon the enemy. He pressed the spurs into his horse's flanks, but it could not move forward. It struggled in vain to free itself from the thick mud.

"Attack! Attack! Saint-Denis for France!" bawled the Constable, hoarse with exertion and excitement. Cursing, the knights tortured their steeds, but it was no use. Even those who had been able to move a few meters sank irrevocably back into the mud which had been churned since early morning by horses' hooves.

While he tugged at the reins, mumbling desperate sounds of encouragement to the horse, a morbid fear crept over Charles for the first time in his life. Through the small eye slits in his visor he saw the English approaching, deliberately, without haste. The archers were feeling for their full quivers. Charles sat on his horse in his black armor covered with scaly ironplate, as though immured in a wall of black-armored bodies; he could neither go forward to fight nor retreat backward. For him and his companions there was nothing to do but wait.

The English stood and drew their bows; ten thousand arrows rained down, almost all at once, on the French vanguard. The Constable dashed away at full speed, hoping to bring the flanks of the army together at once; both squadrons began, with great effort, to move. The horses stumbled and trampled their way through the deep mud in the lowest part of the valley, tightly pressed against each other. But now more bowmen, who had lain in ambush for that purpose, rushed out of the woods in the slopes before Maisoncelles. The cavalry, struck on the flank by a storm of arrows, suffered heavy casualties: of the more than a thousand horsemen, only a few hundred had reached the small stretch of ground between both armies. The wounded, terrified horses no longer obeyed their riders. They reared sideways, snorting, onto the lines of armed knights and did more damage there than the English had done. Men and beasts tumbled over one another; bodies were smashed between steel and steel. Confusion spread through the packed lines; lances were shattered from the violent impact of the first row pressing backward.

The English took quick advantage of the turmoil in the French vanguard; flinging their bows away and arming themselves with pikes and clubs, they fell upon and grappled with the knights who were half-sunk in the mud. Charles, in the heart of the French front lines, saw a chance to remain in the saddle. He had dropped his lance; now he wrenched his sword from its sheath. Boucicaut had leaped from his horse. Charles wanted to follow his example; he knew he should, but he could not draw his feet in their pointed iron shoes out of the stirrups; he saw it was too late. The English were approaching in a virtual mud-storm, shouting at the tops of their lungs. Javelins flew before them.

The horse of the knight next to Charles was stricken mortally; it sagged sideways. The rider fell against Charles and almost knocked him out of the saddle. Charles' warhorse sprang forward, wild with fright; the young man had only enough time to raise his shield, which he had taken from his page when the signal for attack was given. Blows and slashing strikes were already raining from all sides. "Bonne!" said Charles aloud. The blood buzzed in his head, he felt his steed stagger. Around him raged the tumult of battle: the shouts of fighters, the death shrieks of men and horses, the clatter of weapons against armor, and the dull thud of thousands of trampling feet. The English foot soldiers moved through the ranks like reapers through a field of grain; with both hands they swung their spiked clubs and their short axes. The knights and their followers, driven together into groups, defended themselves as well as they could, but they could hardly move. The fallen lay in heaps; they formed barricades, hills of corpses of men and horses, shields and weapons.

Charles fought like one possessed. There was room in his brain for only one thought: he did not want to die, he wanted to live, live and return to Bonne, to Bonne, to Bonne. Without knowing what he did, he muttered the name incessantly. To the rhythm of that beloved name, he hacked at the men who pressed him from all sides like a swarm of hornets. Mortal terror lent him a strength which he had never realized that he possessed. He beat off the attack until his horse sank under him, struck by a javelin. Nevertheless

Charles managed to stay on his feet, up to his ankles in a mash of mud and blood. He continued to fight with undiminished energy; he killed three or four Englishmen, but he began to lose ground against his attackers. While he tried to parry the blows, he glanced about for help. But everywhere around him he saw the same thing: desperate defense ending in defeat. He fancied he saw Alençon still on horseback, with his banner in rags around his neck; he bent forward, his axe struck home, the dead piled up all around him; his horse's saddle-cloth was soaked with blood. Charles saw more. He saw a corpse lying in front of him; he recognized it by its armor. It was Philippe de Nevers, Burgundy's youngest brother, who, despite the Duke of Burgundy's injunctions and threats, had joined the French because he thought it was shameful to stand aside. He lay on his back with his arms spread wide, on top of his squire and a number of knights of his retinue; his visor was open. Charles turned icy cold with fear and horror. He redoubled his efforts to free himself from his attackers. He wanted to escape to the center or the rear, where there was as yet no fighting. I want to throw off my armor, he thought, dizzy and confused. At that instant he received a heavy blow to the head. A burning pain shot through his neck and back. He thought only that this was the end. Then he fell in the mud beside his dead horse.

At first he did not know where he was. Something very heavy lay over his legs; something lighter, soft and limp, over his shoulder and breast. He tried to move but his body felt stiff and painful; a hard band squeezed his loins, arms and wrists. It seemed as though he were floating in a tepid, viscous liquid. Suddenly the truth shot through him: I am alive, he wanted to say, but his tongue would not obey him. He opened his eyes with an effort; his eyelids seemed glued together with the same lukewarm liquid. He knew now that it was blood. He still wore his visor; and since he could not move his arms, he saw no chance of opening it. I must fight on, he thought, more sharply conscious now. At the same moment he realized that he heard no sounds. There were of course the usual noises, but not the cries, the roar of the battlefield. Strangely enough, he heard the wind, and men's voices at some distance from him. Something which jingled and rattled was being dragged across the ground. He thought he heard the same sound further away now—not in one place but everywhere. However, despite the voices and the dragging and clanking, a silence prevailed, which could only mean one thing: the battle was over, the contest decided.

What day was it? How long had he lain here? He moved, but a fierce pain forced him back to immobility. Before the eye slits of his visor there was only a grey luster. Something opaque was covering his head—a cloth, a flag or a tunic. That weight on his legs—he shuddered. He lay among the dead; he must wait until someone came to look for him. Bonne, he thought, and was filled with anxiety. What if they did not find him, what if they let him die here under a heap of corpses? He opened his mouth again, but no sound came from his lips. He exerted his strength to the utmost. Something seemed to tear inside his breast; excruciating pain like a knife thrust lanced between his ribs. But he managed to roll over halfway. He could not move his legs. It seemed an endless time before he was able to draw his right arm toward him; he had to incline his head toward his arm to open his visor. It was jammed, but he managed to twist it open. He lay in the midst of a jumbled mass of corpses, twisted metal, splintered lances. A horse had fallen across his legs; he was sure it could not be his horse. He did not see his horse; it probably lay somewhere under the corpses behind him. A man lay against his shoulder. He wore a starred tunic. Charles could not identify the other dead; they wore closed helmets or were so maimed or covered with congealed blood that their faces were no longer recognizable.

Slowly Charles raised himself until he could look out over the rampart of corpses. He was still so stunned from his fall, so dazed from pain and loss of blood, that the sight of the field of Agincourt could not fill him with terror or amazement. He saw the dead lying as far as the eye could see, heaps of dead—dead men in armor, dead men in gaily colored tunics. Where the French army had stood on the slope between Agincourt and Tramecourt, there were now only trampled fragments of tents, broken carts, great heaps of war materiel.

Evening was drawing in, rain clouds scudded low over the landscape, for the wind had picked up. It was not yet dark. In this hour between light and darkness, men moved in countless groups over the field. Charles recognized them immediately: they were the English bowmen. Such fellows as these had struck him down. What they were doing now was clear enough. They pulled swords, daggers and shields from the piles of corpses, tore off banners and mantles, and stooped searching for valuables—rings, buckles and shoulder-belts. Swiftly and deftly they stripped the dead of helmets and armor; slowly and thoroughly they searched through the heaps of cadavers on the field. Weapons they flung into high piles; valuables were secreted in the pouches which each man carried with him. The looters had not yet reached the place where Charles lay, but he feared they would reach him before midnight. He had only one chance: if the darkness prevented them from discovering him, perhaps he could try to reach the castle of Agincourt by creeping by night through the forest. The Lord of Agincourt was a vassal of Burgundy, but anything was better than being taken prisoner by the English.

He slid cautiously back in the mud and crept as close as possible to the dead. Perhaps the marauders would not reach him. His head throbbed with unbearable pain, and he was thirsty. He sank fever-ishly into a state of semi-consciousness. He thought that he lay in bed in Blois between cool sheets; Bonne approached him with a cup in her hand, holding wine or water, he did not know which. "Let me drink," he whispered and now he really felt moisture be-tween his lips.

It was no dream. Two men supported him under the arms, while a third gave him drink. They had removed his helmet, his head felt wet and cold from blood and perspiration. He was alternately dragged and carried over what seemed to him an endless distance through muddy hollows, up a slope, over rough roots and uneven forest ground. He could not keep his head erect; he lost conscious-ness again and again. Finally he felt himself set down on the ground near a fire, where men spoke to one another in low voices. The sounds of their strange language melted together in one murmur. He was only vaguely aware that his armor had been removed; after that he knew nothing more for a long time.

When he opened his eyes again, he was lying on a straw litter in a tent. The curtain before the opening had been pushed aside; he could look out over a row of barns and hovels; unmistakably those of Maisoncelles. A sentry stood before the tent. It was bright daylight. There was great activity; the English were getting ready to break camp. Pack animals, heavily laden with war booty, passed slowly by. With a shudder, Charles saw the blue and gold banner of France, defaced, torn, stained with blood and mud, laying amid the arms and shields piled high on top of the wagons. He saw a cuirass on top of a cart; it gleamed white with a gold sun on the breast.

"That is Alençon's armor," Charles said aloud.

A man who sat huddled on a heap of straw in the rear of the tent—Charles had not noticed him before—replied.

"Aye, my lord, there go the beautiful toys of France. Gaudy armor and silk flags. Isn't it finally plain now that a war cannot be won this way?"

Charles turned with an effort. "Boucicaut!" he cried. The Marshal raised his thin face and nodded slowly. He wore only a grimy, torn leather underjacket and a pair of shoes. He was not wounded. Charles noticed that he himself was naked under his hide covering; they had bandaged his legs.

"You are not seriously wounded, thank God," Boucicaut whispered hoarsely. "You will be able to sit on a horse today."

"Where are we going?"

Boucicaut sighed. After a moment he answered.

"Wherever it pleases King Henry, Monseigneur. I've heard that we will take ship for England at Calais."

"Exile?" Charles sat straight up, despite the pain in his limbs. "No, no, I don't want that. It is impossible," he cried vehemently. "The Dauphin will surely offer ransom for me."

"Don't count on that, Monseigneur." Boucicaut shrugged in dejection. "That will not happen soon. We are a large company; we represent a vast amount of money: you, Messeigneurs de Bourbon and Richmont, the Counts d'Eu and Vendôme and about 1,500 nobles. I have seen the Sires de Harcourt and Craon and numerous other people I know. Great names all, for whom King Henry can demand a high price. A good deal of water will flow to the sea before an agreement is reached about us. But we can't complain: we have our own pride and ignorance to thank for this catastrophe."

The possibility of death disturbed Charles less than this new prospect of exile in a foreign country. He sat staring straight before him, shivering with cold and weakness, his brow knitted in tense reflection.

"I must send a messenger at once to my wife and brother," he said uneasily. "We can sell our castles and territories. My father-in-law is in Paris: surely he will be able to exert some influence."

"You can try, Monseigneur." Boucicaut shook his head dubiously. "But I fear that you would be the last person King Henry would release. You are the most important of the prisoners; you are being most specially treated. King Henry's personal physician has attended you and bandaged you himself. It is to the advantage of the English to keep you healthy."

The guard who stood before the tent stirred. Charles and the Marshal looked toward the entrance and saw three men approaching: an old knight with a stern, pale face, a soldier carrying clothing over his arm, and a servant with a tray holding white bread and wine.

The knight bowed stiffly in Charles' direction and spoke slowly in French. "My name is Thomas Herpingham, counsellor to King Henry. I understand and speak your language. The King requests that you put on these clothes and eat. Tomorrow at sunrise we leave for Calais. There will be horses for you and the Marshal."

He paused, but Charles did not reply. Herpingham coughed and continued carefully.

"Among the prisoners is a certain de Néry, who says he is your squire. If you set much store by it, we will send him to you."

Charles nodded. He was no longer listening to the Englishman; he was devising a plan. Jean de Néry must escape and carry the news to Bonne. The thought of his wife filled Charles with helpless rage. There she sat now in Blois, still ignorant of what had happened to him. When would he see her again? Reckless plots crossed his mind: he would slip out of the tent that night, seize a weapon and a horse, break out of the camp and ride at full gallop across Picardy to Paris . . .

Herpingham took his leave; now the two men brought forward the food and clothing. With indifference Charles allowed himself to be helped into jacket and overgarment; bread and wine, however, he refused. Later they came to fetch Boucicaut away and Jean de Néry took his place. From his squire Charles learned how the battle had gone. In a relatively short time the English had hacked the vanguard of the French army to pieces; those whom they did not kill were carried off in captivity behind the lines. Afterward, under the personal command of King Henry, the English fell upon the French center which had continued to make a stand. When the troops in the rear guard became aware of the slaughter, they fled to the hills. The center did not hold for long: Alençon, who had boasted that he would pluck the crown from

King Henry's head, was killed almost at once, and this drained the knights of the remnant of their courage. With their surrender the battle was over.

Then while the English were sorting out their prisoners, an alarm sounded from Maisoncelles. A horseman rode at full gallop bringing the message that the Gascons and Bretons from the French rear guard were approaching the field again by a roundabout route, and groups of them seemed intent on pillaging the camp at Maisoncelles. King Henry commanded his men to take battle positions once more; and so that the soldiers could be free to protect themselves from attack from the rear, the prisoners had to be killed on the spot. Two hundred soldiers were assigned to perform the executions. But while the English were preparing to repel the approaching troops, the latter appeared to have abandoned—if they had ever had them— all intentions of mounting an attack. They were seen fleeing over the hills, without so much as a backward glance. The prisoners from the vanguard, held together under guard in another part of the battlefield, were spared.

"Who was killed?" asked Charles, when the squire had finished his report. The youth whispered a long list of names: d'Albret, the Dukes of Alençon and Bar, the Sires de Dampierre, Dammarten, Salm, Roussy and Vaudemont—all those who only two days before had sat together in the Constable's tent so confident of victory. In addition, the governors of Mâcon, Caen and Maux had fallen, along with the martial Archbishop of Sens and innumerable princes and nobles, with their squires, heralds, horsemen and grooms.

"They say we lost more than 10,000 men, my lord," Jean de Néry said, with downcast eyes. "Ten thousand! And the English 1,500, at the most."

Toward evening King Henry himself entered the tent, attended by Thomas Herpingham, who held a torch in his hand. The King drew the leather curtain behind him and stood beside the prisoner's straw cot. Henry had steely blue eyes and a narrow oval face with a high forehead and rather full lips. His hair was cropped short on his round head. He was shorter than Charles but his shoulders were broad and his arms and legs strong and sturdy. Over his hauberk he wore a tunic with the red lions of England rampant.

Charles tried to rise from the straw to greet his visitor. King Henry watched his efforts in silence for a few moments before he said curtly, "Remain lying down, fair cousin; you cannot stand."

His French was almost flawless, but his strong accent made his words sound rough. Charles bent his head and thanked him for the courtesy; he remained lying at Henry's feet, supported by his elbows.

"How goes it, fair cousin?" asked the King, but there was no trace of friendliness in his eyes.

Charles replied dully, "Well, my lord."

"They tell me you do not wish to eat or drink," pursued the King. "Is it true?"

"It is true that I am fasting," said Charles. "It can hardly surprise you that I have no desire for food."

"Hm." Henry raised his thin, sandy eyebrows. "I will give you good advice, fair cousin. Eat what is set before you. It is stupid to go hungry because of regret or shame. I believe that God has given me the victory, not because I am so deserving, but because he wanted to chastise the French. For now it is generally known that this kingdom is a true witches' cauldron of sin and immorality. You probably know better than I what a pack of ruffians the French government is. No one can really be surprised that this situation has aroused God's wrath. In this case I have been only God's instrument, fair cousin."

Henry said all this matter-of-factly, although he raised his voice slightly. He kept his cold bright eyes fixed steadily upon Charles, who at first looked straight before him. But when the King fell silent, Charles gave him a quick, curious glance. He asked himself if Henry really believed what he had just said: the King spoke so dispassionately. There was no emotion in his words, only a chilly pedantry.

"There is nothing more to be said," the King added, thinking that Charles wished to raise some objection. "So it must be from now on, fair cousin. Therefore, lie down."

"Are you taking me back to England with you, Monseigneur?" asked Charles. He could think of nothing else to say. The King's gaze became brighter and more penetrating.

"It is so," he said. "But we will not speak of it now," he continued, when he saw that Charles was about to ask more questions. "We shall give our personal attention to the question of your captivity in due time, in London. I intend to have a serious discussion with you, fair cousin. Perhaps we can reach an understanding."

"Monseigneur," Charles began. He wanted, while preserving the respectful attitude which was Henry's due, to make him understand something of his own anxiety and desires. The King *must* listen to him. But deep in his heart he knew very well that all attempts to win the Englishman over would be futile. So finally he said only, "Will you release my squire, Monseigneur? Add his ransom to mine, I pray you; it can hardly make a difference to so large an amount. I am eager to send a message to Madame d'Orléans before I take ship for England."

"That is true, you are married." Henry raised his eyebrows slightly and looked at Jean de Néry, who stood at respectful attention behind his lord. "Is this your squire? You can let him go as far as I am concerned."

The young man could not suppress a start of surprise. King Henry frowned and turned away with a half nod from which Charles inferred that the interview was over.

Charles was awake all night. He ordered de Néry to repeat over and over all the messages meant for Bonne. On reflection, however, he asked his shieldbearer to accompany him to Calais, where it would be easier for him to find a horse, and where Charles could get pen and paper; he wanted to write a letter himself.

Along with his companions in distress—a dreary group— Charles made the long journey to Calais on horseback. From the hills above Maisoncelles, they surveyed the battlefield once more: the peasants of the district had flocked to Agincourt in great numbers to search for serviceable pieces of clothing and weapons among the half-naked corpses.

In front marched the archers, the red cross of England upon their breasts; they went bowed under the weight of their booty. Henry led the procession, surrounded by flagbearers and heralds. In the rear at the very last the rows of prisoners walked with dragging footsteps and bowed heads, guarded by horsemen. Calais, long in the hands of the English, waited, arrayed in festive finery.

On All Saints Day King Henry entered the city. The noble captives were lodged in a castle close to the harbor. From the narrow grated window of his room, Charles saw, for the first time in his life, the sea, a turbulent grey-green and white stretch of water, a marbled wasteland. A fierce wind was blowing, foggy clouds floated swiftly through the colorless sky. In the harbor Henry's ships lay at anchor, a forest of masts.

Now Jean de Néry prepared for his journey. At Charles' request he was given some money and a horse by King Henry. Charles gave the young man a letter for Bonne and letters for his brother Philippe, for de Mornay, the Dauphin and Bernard d'Armagnac. When de Néry was on the point of departure, Charles took from his own finger a ring intended for his wife: a ring of gold and blue enamel, on which was engraved the words, Dieu le scet—God knows. His father and mother had both worn the ring; day and night it had reminded them of their grievances against Burgundy. Now for the first time the motto acquired another meaning for Charles. He no longer thought about Burgundy; he thought only of Bonne with all the desperate yearning of his twenty-odd years. Dieu le scet. God knows. God knows how much I love her. God knows what I suffer. Only God knows what will happen to me.

On the fifteenth of November, King Henry's sailors hoisted the sails of the ships, which were heavily laden with soldiers, prisoners and booty. Even before they had left the harbor of Calais, an uncommonly strong wind sprang up. Suddenly storm clouds appeared in the northeast; the waves, crowned with foam, rose high. Despite the sailors' warnings, Charles remained on deck. He saw the black-green water swell and fall, he heard the hissing of the spray as it swept past him, the wind whistling through the ropes. The coast of France sank away behind the horizon and with it, forever, Bonne and his youth.

Second Book:
The Road to
Nonchaloir

I. EXILE

Paix est un trésor qu'on ne peut trop louer.
Peace is a treasure which can not be praised too highly.
— Charles d'Orléans

estminster, Windsor, the Tower of London—other names, but everywhere and always the same walls, the same narrow windows. Wall hangings, warm blankets and silver dining utensils were not lacking, but armed men stood before the door and silently accompanied one when one left the comfortable rooms for brief walks. In Westminster and Windsor, one could still fancy oneself a guest in a princely palace, but the sojourn in the Tower carried, despite tapestries and cushions, the unmistakable stamp of imprisonment. Those of royal blood—namely the Dukes of Orléans and Bourbon and the Count de Richmont—had been quickly separated from their less notable comrades in distress. This was hard on Charles, who missed Boucicaut: during the first week of exile a warm friendship had blossomed between the Marshal and himself. Boucicaut's tranquil dignity set a standard for Charles; in Basaach's Turkish dungeons the older man had learned how to endure suffering.

In fact, the Marshal had had an uncommonly interesting life: he could boast of having known the most important men of his time: Charles the Wise, du Guesclin the great Constable, Philippe of Burgundy, Louis d'Orléans, Gian Galeazzo of Milan and so many others—popes and princes, captains and statesmen from all parts of the world. He had seen the East, the remote territories beyond the Danube, Constantinople, Acre, the holy city of Jerusalem; he could give spellbinding descriptions of everything for he was a courtier and a man of letters as well as a soldier. Writing verse was his favorite avocation.

"I always have time for it in prison or during the long day's march in a campaign." He had said this with his calm, kindly smile when Charles had surprised him at that pastime in Windsor Castle. Charles, who lapsed into melancholy when he had nothing to distract his thoughts, began to compose commendably intricate couplets; before long he had reached the point where he and Boucicaut, when they were not playing chess, frequently held pleasant conversations in ingenious verse forms. The proficiency in rhyme which Charles had demonstrated as a child came to his aid now—often in Blois in the last few years he had composed couplets in Bonne's honor for his minstrels to set to music. The lines flowed so swiftly from his pen that Boucicaut, a painstaking versifier, remarked in amazement, "You have undoubtedly inherited the gift from your father, Monseigneur. I remember very well that he could write a really melodious verse when the mood was on him."

Charles thought of the song about the Forest of Long Awaiting and was silent; he could never hear mention of his father's poetry without remembering how Herbelin had sung, how his mother had left the room with unsteady steps, how Dunois had come to them. It was not long before Boucicaut realized that Charles was secretly ashamed of his father, that he listened to praise of the dead man with lowered eyes. Deep in his heart Charles doubted the innocence and good faith of the father for whose vindication he had struggled incessantly for eight long years. From Marshal Boucicaut he heard for the first time an objective portrayal of his father: the Marshal, who had been with Louis d'Orléans almost daily, succeeded in calling up the father for the son, evoking an image infinitely sharper and more convincing to Charles than the one created by Valentine's passionate words or the whispers of courtiers. And for the first time Charles heard an objective evaluation of Jean of Burgundy. Boucicaut had had ample opportunity to become familiar with Orléans' enemy during their long confinement in Turkish dungeons.

Because of these conversations with Boucicaut, Charles began to view the events of the last ten years in a different light. Sometimes it seemed to him that France hung before him like a brightly embroidered tapestry. He looked at the figures from a distance. He saw the men and women of France moving against a background of cities, forests and rivers, vineyards, meadows and fields. He saw that those who wore the crown and mitres, who held a sharp sword or a full moneybag, who were lords over the life and death of the people, paid scant attention to the endless multitudes who stood with hands lifted in entreaty in the shadow of the castles and cathedrals. Those in authority contested each other's crown and scepter; they were motivated only by greed. That wolves devoured the flock, that brigands plundered the pilgrims, that thieves and murderers did their work, that famine and pestilence destroyed the people with sharp scythes—these were no concern of princes and prelates. The more Boucicaut talked to him about the obligation of monarchs and nobles to protect the defenseless people, the more Charles thought he saw the reality depicted in glaring colors; an intense fear for the future of his country crept over him. He had found King Henry's words of condemnation painful, but he knew that Boucicaut spoke from intimate knowledge. His talks with the Marshal gave Charles ample food for thought—this helped him during the first weeks of his captivity to combat the doubt and despair which tortured him as soon as he was left to himself.

Boucicaut forced him by his conversation to think of other things besides his longing for Bonne. The Marshal knew from his own experience the suffering which Charles was enduring, but he knew also that intellectual exercise produces a temporary relief. He feared that the young man had to prepare himself for a prolonged exile; it would do no harm to show him how one hardens oneself for such an ordeal. However, Charles was soon deprived of Boucicaut's company. King Henry assigned most of the prisoners to nobles of his personal entourage; for the present he kept Charles, Bourbon and Richmont for himself. Holding prominent foreign noblemen provided an additional and by no means despicable source of revenue for the great English peers; along with the ransom money, the prisoners were required to pay substantial sums for food and lodging. They could also, if they wished, take a follower into service or have clothing or other useful items brought in from their native country—for an extra consideration. Charles knew that his brother Jean was still a guest of the Duke of Clarence. Despite Charles' efforts they had not yet met, although Jean had sent letters and messages. Clarence, who was out to get whatever he could, demanded an exceptionally high price for his hospitality.

Charles had received permission to transact business through Giovanni Vittori, the Florentine banker who lived in London. Vittori seemed willing to advance Charles large sums of money. But what did four or even six thousand gold écus matter, compared to the fortune, greater than the richest royal dowries, which they would undoubtedly demand as ransom for his brother and himself? Vittori had begun negotiations with Charles' treasurer and solicitors in Paris and Orléans; he had received assurances that everything possible would be done to collect the money for the Duke. Charles was convinced of the good faith of his councillors and officials, but he knew better than anyone else how difficult it would be to raise the money. He tried to think of ways to get it. He made a list from memory of the valuables, tapestries and furniture in his various castles; he even considered selling his properties in Asti. But how were all these things to be arranged?

Vittori was a great businessman with a sharp mind, but he was not the most suitable representative for matters linked to politics. Urgently Charles sought permission to negotiate and to make contact with his Chancellor, secretaries, advocates and advisors. He received no consent to his written applications, but he did receive a promise that some of his officers would be called to a meeting so that he could arrange his affairs—under surveillance, of course.

Now that he had had to give up Boucicaut's company, Charles found it extremely difficult to get through the long days without fits of melancholy and despair. In Westminster and Windsor they had allowed him some distraction—a falcon hunt, strolls in the misty parks, horseback rides. But the Tower was a maze of massive stone walls; a little grass and a solitary tree grew in the courtyard. He had heard that executions had taken place here. "That is why the grass is short and brownish," said Richmont. "The ground is saturated with blood." Charles did not often go to the inner courtyard. Walking in the chill, damp air made him feel even more gloomy, if possible, than staying in his chamber.

A room had been prepared in which Bourbon, Richmont and he could come together to talk or play chess. The narrow chamber had no windows but, high in the walls, some holes had been cut and fitted with shutters. Under the wide chimney burned a good fire, barely dispelling the cold which swept over the flagstones. The only furniture was a table, a bench and a sideboard on which candles burned at high noon. A dozen armed soldiers were always present, under the command of the captain of the watch; a clerk in monk's garb who understood French sat, during the meeting of the princes, on a small bench against the wall, his eyes cast down, his hands concealed within his sleeves. The presence of this silent but immovable auditor irritated the captives more than the clatter of weapons or the stamping, coughing and subdued conversations of the guards who stood in the farthest corner of the room.

Charles found the meetings with Bourbon and Richmont neither diverting nor comforting. It seemed to him that he had never known these men with whom he had associated for so many years. One's true character becomes apparent under adversity—that old saying acquired meaning for Charles for the first time. Bourbon, always cautious and somewhat timid by nature, spent the greater part of the day staring vacantly before him; he was polite and affable to the guards but stingy with tips, evasive when the talk turned to money matters. Although, like Charles and Richmont, he had been given a banker as his solicitor and could have gotten money, his two companions frequently had to pay for his food and lodging. Bourbon seldom carried more than a couple of silver pieces in his purse. He declined to play for money, but looked on eagerly when Charles and Richmont played cards; he calculated the winnings and losses to a fraction of a sou.

At that time Richmont displayed a boisterous recklessness, an insensitive callousness which Charles suspected was a mask for despair rather than actual bravado. Richmont assumed a defiant attitude; he walked humming past the watch, spoke contemptuously of King Henry at the top of his voice and derided and criticized everyone. He was equally hostile to his companions in misery; there were incessant disputes and misunderstandings. Charles, easily irritated himself, began to avoid the company of Bourbon and Richmont. He stayed more and more often in his chamber: a square, spacious, quite comfortably furnished room, with a window overlooking the Thames. He was soon spending the greater part of the day before the small window panes, at least when the fog did not obstruct his view—which was, alas, too often the case. But in clear weather there was a good deal to be seen on the part of the river which was bounded by the two great bridges.

Directly under his window was a triple embankment with a small quay where barges lay moored. Charles knew that in the rampart below there was a low arched waterway; when they had led him into the Tower he had cast a cursory glance at that massive iron gate which hung before the ominous sloshing black water. Ships both large and small moved back and forth continually over the Thames; long narrow freight boats, with twelve oarsmen on each side, flashed quickly by; compared to them the ferries and two-oared rowboats seemed to creep at a snail's pace over the small waves of the river. Along the wharf on the other shore where a number of sea-going ships lay at anchor, there were warehouses and offices. Just as on the Seine, Charles thought; his heart ached. There too were crowds of vessels, there too were houses built on bridges, there too were the moving waters, green and black, flashing with silver reflections.

But for all that, the icy-cold impenetrable fog which drifted in from the sea seemed to Charles an alien and hostile element; it even crept, through cracks in the doors and windows, into his room. He hated nothing so much as the hours spent in the ruddy haze created by candle glow and hearthfire, which caused a prickling in his throat and in his chest when he breathed. When he could not look outside, he sat at the table before the fire. He had a missal and a hymnbook; other books he did not yet own. He could not concentrate on the familiar words; he sat staring at nothing over the open book.

He was with Bonne at Blois; he tried constantly to imagine what she was doing, what she was saying, and to whom. How did she endure their separation? Did she weep, did she think of him? He saw her pale face before him, framed in her black hair; he saw tears gleaming in her large eyes, which he had compared to topazes. He lost himself in her daily routine: now she went to early mass to pray for his safe return; now she was in the women's room giving instructions to the serving maids; now she spoke with de Mornay and with the advocate Maître Cousinot, his Chancellor, about ways to effect his release; now she sat eating at the head of the table in the dining hall; now she lay down to rest in the bed with the green curtains. When Charles imagined this, he put his head in his hands with a muffled sob. He would willingly have given up everything he owned to see Bonne, to speak with her and touch her once more. Sometimes his longing became so intense that he could not remain still. He walked from one end of the room to the other, sometimes cursing softly, sometimes praying. But this gave him no relief. He flung himself on the bed and struck the pillow with his fists, or smashed against the wall behind the tapestry until, exhausted, he realized the senselessness of his behavior. He managed for the most part to control himself if only to hide his emotions from his keepers, who rapped at his door from time to time to see what he was doing.

The wounds on his legs had healed, but he was left with a painful muscle cramp which sometimes bothered him considerably. He slept badly, lying awake on his back for most of the night, listening to the sounds of the fire on the hearth, of the watch coming and going outside his door, of the wind shaking the shutters. All of his past experiences flashed through his mind. He suddenly remembered long-forgotten events, minor incidents from his childhood, faces and voices of people long since dead. He thought of his father and mother, of their lives which had once seemed so remote and alien, but which now seemed familiar, thanks to the illuminating talks with Boucicaut. He thought of the King, so pitiful despite his crown and purple robes; of the Queen with her sly laugh; of the Dauphin who was rumored to be ill—that did not surprise Charles, who had often wondered how the heir to the throne could possibly indulge in so much wine and so much pleasure without damaging himself phys- ically. He remembered now the violent spasms of coughing which suddenly attacked the Dauphin sometimes. And Charles thought of Armagnac, who so far had cleverly managed to keep himself away from the battlefield. He thought of Burgundy, his archenemy, who, strangely enough, now seemed to be a man like other men. Charles did not loathe and disdain him any the less for that, but he saw him in another light—no longer as the embodiment of evil, but rather as one misled by his own passions.

Charles thought of France, of that neglected, impoverished land, threatened on all sides. In the Tower of London he realized what deep misery had befallen his country. What he had not seen when he was there, absorbed as he had been in family feuds and party quarrels, now became clear to him: he had fought only for the interests of Orléans—without understanding that he and his allies were France's only protectors. And very poorly indeed had they acquitted themselves. As his father Philippe had done before him, Jean of Burgundy strove to unite his territories into a kingdom with interests opposed to those of France. England seemed more than ever intent on sinking its claws into the coastal areas and the southern provinces. Although these powers distrusted each other, they would always pull together when it was a question of the subjection of France.

When he reflected upon these things, Charles felt hot with deep shame, fear and despair. His party should have been the party of France, with a duty to protect the King and maintain his authority. Whom had he once heard say these things? Was it Dunois, his half-brother? Yes, he remembered that Dunois had said that, or something like it. "I must communicate with Philippe, with my people," murmured Charles in the darkness of the bedcurtains. "I must know what is happening, what they propose to do, what Armagnac is doing. If Armagnac rules the roost, the end is near. I must warn the Dauphin and the Queen against Armagnac."

Each day he looked forward impatiently to the audience which King Henry had promised him, but the King seemed to have forgotten his promise. He had visited his noble prisoners repeatedly during the first week of their stay in England, and had treated them with the utmost courtesy. But after a while they saw him no more, and heard nothing from him. Not without reason, Charles realized, had he and his two princely compatriots been transferred to the Tower.

The days crept slowly by, varied only by changes in the weather. Charles looked out the window at the ships and the seagulls which circled shrieking over the water; he counted those towers which were clearly visible in bright weather. He now recognized the sounds of London's bells; nothing made him yearn so desperately for home as those recurrent, deep, resounding peals.

Except for his chamberlain, the officers of the guard, the priest who came to hear his confession, and, from time to time, Bourbon and Richmont, he spoke to no one. The world seemed suddenly to contain only a handful of people.

Giovanni Vittori came to see him toward the end of January. The Florentine had lived in northern countries for almost twenty years; first in Bruges, later in London. He spoke Flemish, French and English as fluently as his native tongue. He was a stout but agile man with a small, sharply curved nose and very black, vigilant eyes. He was dressed in furs and velvet like a king, with jeweled stars in his hat. He entered Charles' room as respectfully and courteously as though the Duke still lived in freedom in his own domain, surrounded by pomp and splendor. He observed the required etiquette, inquired after Monseigneur's health and welfare, exhausted himself in countless civilities, and refused three times the seat which Charles offered him. Finally, with an apologetic gesture, he seated himself on the extreme edge of the chair. Charles was silent; he knew Vittori's style—a down-to-earth conversation would undoubtedly follow this display of courtesy. At Charles' nod the valet brought some cake and wine.

"Monseigneur," Vittori began, "I have news from Orléans. I have had a visit from one of your secretaries, Maître de Tuillères. He awaits the King's consent to inform you personally about the state of affairs in your domains, and to receive your instructions."

"Is there any news from Madame d'Orléans, my wife?" asked Charles, without looking at the banker.

The Florentine raised both hands in another gesture of apology.

"Alas, Monseigneur, Maître de Tuillères has said nothing to me about that. But nothing has permitted me to conclude that all does not go well with Madame the Duchess."

"I see," Charles responded curtly. He sighed. He wanted to dash past Vittori, past the rows of guards, out through the inner courts and yards of the Tower, through the gates and over the bridges to the spot where de Tuillères stood, this man who had seen Bonne only a few weeks earlier. But the banker continued.

"We have made an inventory of everything that can be sold, Monseigneur. You have no more liquid assets at the moment. You will have to take radical measures in order to have money at your disposal."

"That's all right," Charles said. "Sell whatever you think best. I agree to everything. Only I do not wish you to make any economies in the households of my wife, my sister and my baby daughter. God knows they live frugally enough already. Of course I still do not know what price they will ask for me . . ."

The Florentine nodded in agreement.

"Naturally, Monseigneur, we can only hazard a guess about that. But you owe 133,000 golden écus to my lord Clarence for Monseigneur your brother. You have obligated yourself to pay the money before the first of July, 1417."

"Then we must attend to that before anything else."

"Tuillères has brought 6,500 écus," the banker went on. "Your subjects' tax money, apparently. Since you arrived here I have advanced you 12,000 écus, my lord. Of these 1,100 were paid out to Clarence's treasurer. I have the receipts."

"In that case of course keep the money from de Tuillères yourself." Charles put his hands over his eyes for a moment. "I hope you will not cheat yourself."

"No, Monseigneur, I am your servant!" Vittori laughed. "I do what I can for you. Look, my lord, the lists . . ." He groped in his sleeve with heavily ringed fingers and produced some scrolls which he smoothed out on the table before Charles. "Furniture, tapestries, an altar piece of massive gold, books . . . these are the most valuable. In exchange for these I can probably get 10,000 écus from colleagues and from my own funds. Worth more? Possibly, Monseigneur, but I dare not guarantee more than 10,000. The rest are trifles—they must be appraised piece by piece. I shall send people to Orléans."

"Vittori," Charles said abruptly, "the King of France once signed an agreement with my late father in which the King made himself responsible for ransom money if my father's sons were to be imprisoned. I heard this from Marshal Boucicaut himself. That document must be found. The Dauphin will—"

"Monseigneur, Monseigneur!" The Florentine sprang from his seat and struck his head with his fists. "Speaking of the King . . . ! The Dauphin of France is dead, Monseigneur! . . . You did not know that? . . . The news has been known in England for some time. Maître de Tuillères mentioned it also. The Dauphin died just before Christmas."

"Dead?" Charles looked away; he did not want to reveal his bewilderment. "I have heard that Monseigneur de Guyenne was sick."

"Aha! Sick, sick," said the banker, shrugging. "Of course they will say that. But the Dauphin was poisoned."

"Are you sure of that?" Charles asked sharply.

Vittori shrugged again; the gesture said more plainly than words that no one doubted that the successor to the French throne had met a violent end. But Charles refused to believe it. He knew how quickly physicians would speak of poisoning when they could effect no cure. He remembered the Dauphin's coughing fits, his feverish flush. He shook his head. But Vittori had more to say. He glanced quickly at the half-open door outside which the watch stood, and resumed, dropping his voice.

"My lord, I know little about your country's politics. I am only repeating what I have heard from acquaintances, reliable men, who I can assure you travel regularly to the Flemish ports on business and have important connections there. It appears that the late Dauphin—may God rest his soul—named your father-in-law, the Sire d'Armagnac, Constable of France, and forbade the Duke of Burgundy to set foot in Paris."

Charles was about to reply with passion, but Vittori shook his head and put his finger to his lips. "My lord, it is probably not the intention of the lords who guard you here that this news should reach your ears. Undoubtedly I am laying myself open to punishment. They believe that I discuss only money matters with you."

"So my cousin of Touraine is Dauphin then," said Charles in an undertone; he was no longer listening to the Florentine. "My cousin of Touraine, who is married to Burgundy's niece, the heiress of Holland, Zeeland and Hainault. That means that if the King should die . . . What is Monseigneur of Burgundy doing?" he asked suddenly; he caught Vittori's arm. "Is there any news of Burgundy?"

"In God's name, Monseigneur!" The banker was becoming seriously alarmed. He tried to wrench his sleeve from Charles' grasp. "In God's name do not forget where we are! My lord, I have taken a vow not to discuss politics . . . I am putting my life in the balance . . ."

"Then you should not have spoken," Charles said roughly. He released the man and turned toward the fire. The news had filled him with fear. Armagnac, Constable! That meant that Armagnac was at the head of the government, the master of Paris! But on the other hand, Burgundy was linked by blood to the new Dauphin—and the Dauphin was in all probability still on Flemish soil—undoubtedly in Burgundy's immediate circle, subject to Burgundy's influence. It was perfectly clear that this state of affairs could lead only to a more violent struggle than ever—if that were possible—and that a victory by either Burgundy or Armagnac could result only in the ultimate ruin of France; in the one case, the Kingdom would be incorporated irrevocably with the Burgundian Bavarian lands; in the other, after being squeezed dry and plundered by Armagnac, it would be left prey to whomever wished to make a bid for power. Now Charles understood why Armagnac had not personally taken part in the battle of Agincourt: the English had rendered him an invaluable service by killing or taking prisoner most of his rivals for power in the Kingdom.

Giovanni Vittori remained standing motionless near the table. He had mixed feelings toward Charles. He felt compassion for the young Duke, who would probably languish in captivity for the rest of his life. Vittori had few illusions about English clemency; as a man of the world, he found it deplorable. On the other hand, as a banker he understood perfectly the attitude of Charles' captors; as long as they had Orléans under lock and key, they had a virtually inexhaustible source of income. And, yes, looking after Monseigneur's financial concerns would also be profitable for him, Vittori; he too found a long captivity to be in his interest. But why allow the young man to pine away without news from home? Vittori wanted to be everyone's friend insofar as he could; the right hand did not always have to know what the left hand was doing.

He glanced over his shoulder at the door; to be safe he occupied himself with rolling up the documents which he had brought with him, while he went on speaking in a low voice.

"Monseigneur, they say that the Duke of Burgundy wishes to lay siege to Paris, but whether this is true I do not know. However there is something else which I can tell you with absolute certainty: the Emperor Sigismund is on his way to Paris to visit the court. There are rumors that he is coming to mediate between your king and King Henry. He is expected here after Easter."

Charles turned around quickly.

"If that is true, Vittori, it is good news," he said with a look of tense excitement. "But how do you know that?"

The banker smiled, pleased; the moment of anger was over.

"Messire de Tuillères tells me that Paris is preparing. King Sigismund seems determined to celebrate carnival there. Some friends of mine at the court in Westminster belong to the company which will welcome the King at Dover."

There was a knock on the door; the nobleman who commanded the guard looked in and signalled to Vittori that the time allotted for the interview had expired. The banker began, with bows and compliments, to take his leave of Charles.

"Vittori, you have rendered me a great service," Charles said quickly and softly. "I shall not forget it. I trust that you will be as diligent for me in the future—there are greater interests at stake than mine alone. Try to use all your influence to see that I speak with de Tuillères. And if you really want to help me, send news of me to the Duchess of Orléans at Blois."

Now that he could hope for freedom, the days seemed longer to Charles. His father had always maintained friendly relations with Sigismund when the latter was King of Hungary. Now that Sigismund had succeeded Ruprecht of Bavaria as Emperor of the Holy Roman Empire, that friendship could yield a rich harvest for Charles. He did not doubt that Sigismund could see to it that he was sent home to France; perhaps the Emperor would even lend him the ransom money—or part of it—himself. Charles awaited the arrival of the monarch with ever-growing impatience; meanwhile he sought in every possible way to get news of events in France.

King Henry suddenly allowed de Tuillères and Maître Cousinot, Charles' Chancellor who had come to England shortly after the Duke's arrival there, to see Charles. Maître Cousinot brought him a letter from Bonne, written by Garbet but signed by Bonne herself. She had remained in Blois, she informed him, with Jeanne and Marguérite. In order to save money in the ducal household, she had dismissed many personal servants. Furniture, silver and censers from the chapel of Orléans had been sold. She had given the proceeds— 500 gold écus—to Maître Cousinot to take to England. She received much comfort and attention from Dunois, who sent Monseigneur his brother respectful greetings and fervent hope for a speedy return.

"Have your wounds healed?" Bonne asked. "Are you well cared for in the Tower? Maître Cousinot is bringing along some bed linens for you, a case with combs, your own razors, six pair of shoes, a half dozen napkins and three large slices of nougat which I have made especially for you. There are almonds in it. I pray for you and I remain until your homecoming and forever after that, your loyal and devoted wife, Bonne d'Orléans."

With great emotion, Charles studied the tapering letters of her signature. They stood on the yellow page beneath the text of the letter, as straight, slender and blithe as Bonne herself. She had embellished the signature by drawing a curling line around it, filled with flourishes. Undoubtedly Garbet had urged her to do that, but it was obvious that she had no talent for calligraphy. However, although the embellishment was a failure, the tiny awkward lines, circling to left and right like festive groups at a procession, inspired him with warmth and hope.

Cousinot's clerk unpacked the shipment; Charles recognized with delight his own worn cases with their shaving blades, combs, scissors, nail files and knives for bleeding. Bonne's nougat, prepared according to a southern recipe, had suffered somewhat in the passage, but never in his life had Charles received a gift with as much joy as he received the sweet white delicacy. Apart from the shipment, Cousinot confirmed what Charles had already learned from Vittori and de Tuillères: that it would be possible to put together a ransom only if lands and castles were sold.

Cousinot advised Charles to mortgage that part of his possessions which were under consideration, and at the same time to hold back for one year the wages and subsidies of his officials and courtiers; to reduce drastically the salaries of the commanders of the garrisons at the castles of Orléans. These suggestions Charles found shocking; he would have thought such actions would be considered only as a last resort.

"Pardon, Monseigneur, do not take it amiss, but you have already reached your last resort," Cousinot responded gravely to Charles' objections. "It is difficult, I know. I myself have always been part of your household. But everyone who is devoted to you and who sincerely wishes your release will accept these actions. We can only hope that you will be able to compensate us in the future. Without these measures you will not be able to accomplish anything, Monseigneur. And certainly your burdens are heavy enough. Everyone in your service is fed and clothed at your expense—you give them shelter and care for them; you have throughout the country a personal retinue of almost one thousand men, my lord. To be sure, that is substantially less than in the time of Monseigneur your late father, but for your purse it is still too large an amount. I am afraid that you *must* sign these documents; it is in your own interest."

While the advocate watched him with friendly concern, Charles, heavy-hearted, signed them. Cousinot saw that the young man was pale; there were dark shadows under his eyes. Cousinot glanced about the chamber. The lodging was decent: tapestries, curtains, silver on the table, enough candles and a good fire in the hearth. He shook his head, sighing and swept his palm over his face. If he found the place depressing during one short visit, how then could Monseigneur keep his spirits up, accustomed as he was to go horseback-riding, to make journeys and stroll through the series of halls of Blois and Saint-Pol? Through the small windowpanes he saw a narrow strip of light, the grey lusterless February sky which presaged rain, rain, always more rain. The small waves of the Thames beat on the embankment with a hissing sound; the cries of boatmen and seamen sounded over the river along with the incessant shrieks of the seagulls skimming across the water in search of food. Cousinot was much impressed with the impregnability of the Tower; a prisoner here was more removed from the world than an exile in Ultima Thule. A real labyrinth of gates and corridors closed off by double doors led eventually to the inner court encircled by the main buildings. Everywhere one could see only high walls, battlements, towers, pinnacles. The citadel was full of guards armed with lances and pikes and wherever one looked one saw heavy bars and doors studded with iron.

"How goes it in Paris, Cousinot?" Charles asked abruptly, shoving the documents aside. "You can speak freely. They brought me news several times last week. I infer from that that King Henry isn't going to keep me ignorant any longer of events in France."

Cousinot folded his narrow, bony hands and nodded agreement.

"How much do you know, my lord?"

"I know that Burgundy lies in wait with an army before Paris, near the village of Lagny," Charles answered slowly, "but that he cannot lay siege to Paris because my father-in-law has fortified the city with his troops from Gascony. I know that Burgundy's men have been beaten time and again in scuffles and skirmishes."

He paused, and looked sharply at the Chancellor.

"I wonder how my father-in-law controls the city of Paris, how he runs things now that he has become Constable."

Cousinot did not look up.

"Monseigneur d'Armagnac rules as tyrants rule in Milan and Venice," he said calmly. "That is to say, the hangman is his right hand and his Gascon hirelings make up his official corps. There are daily executions; when he doubts anyone's reliability, he makes short work of him. The new laws have been abolished. His provost, Messire Tanneguy du Châtel, is a puppet who blindly obeys Armagnac's commands. The citizens have had to give up their weapons—anyone seen with a knife is hanged. Don't misunderstand me, Monseigneur, I don't deny that these kind of actions are the only ones that are respected by certain elements among the people of Paris. We have seen for ourselves what happens when the mob has its way: Armagnac has dissolved the great butchers' guilds—the guildmasters have lost their power. He imprisons, drives out, murders those in Parlement, the Audit Chamber and the University whom he dislikes. Monseigneur d'Armagnac is a savage, but he is intelligent and he is a man of action."

Charles looked skeptical. "Really, you do not have to praise Armagnac because he is my kinsman," he remarked dryly. "I ask myself what possible consequences these vigorous actions can have."

"There have been consequences already, my lord. A pro-Burgundy party has been formed again in Paris—probably larger and more powerful than before, because the new Dauphin belongs to it. For that matter, the Duke of Burgundy is seeking supporters everywhere in the Kingdom; I have heard it said that he goes even to cities which were recently in *our* hands."

"Yes, I have heard that too." Charles sighed and, lost in thought, absently pushed one of the rolls of parchment back and forth over the table top.

"Monseigneur," said Cousinot softly, "have you any idea about what King Henry of England intends to do? I mean, do you think it possible that he will cross the Straits of Calais again soon—or do you think that he will try to reach an agreement either with our King or with Burgundy?"

Charles replied that he had rarely been able to see the King; although he and Richmont and Bourbon had endlessly discussed Henry's possible plans, anything he could say would rest solely on conjecture.

"The King is a riddle to me," he said with a shrug. "At first he treated us like guests. But later we were confined here and forbidden to write or talk to advisors. Now suddenly these privileges have been restored to us. This *must* be connected in some way with the Emperor Sigismund's visit. Do you know anything about that, Cousinot?"

The Chancellor frowned heavily. "The Emperor arrived in Paris the day before I left," he replied. "I saw him for a moment."

"What sort of man is he? He was my father's friend and ally."

Cousinot sniffed. "I can scarcely believe it, Monseigneur. The Emperor Sigismund is cut from the same cloth as his kinsman, Wenceslaus of Bohemia: always drunk, always surrounded by women. When I took ship at Calais I heard it said that he would rather sit in the Parisian bathhouses than with our King in the council hall. I do not expect much from his mediation: he has neither dignity nor influence. Moreover, Monseigneur," Cousinot fixed his piercing dark eyes on Charles and gestured tensely, "moreover I suspect and I fear that King Henry sees you not only as a source of income, but also as a stepping stone in his efforts to gain the Crown of France."

"Me?" asked Charles, fiercely.

"Yes, Monseigneur, you. You and your brother and Messeigneurs de Bourbon and Richmont. I think that King Henry is a bit displeased that the new Dauphin has absorbed Burgundian attitudes along with his mother's milk. Does it seem likely to you that Burgundy will support Henry's claims to the French throne when he can sit on the throne himself through his puppet the Dauphin? No, my lord, I cannot believe it. So thinking of all this, I wonder—what is King Henry going to do?"

Charles had asked himself that question repeatedly since his arrival in England. However, the King remained as enigmatic a personality to the young man as he had been in the tent at Maisoncelles—obliging and gracious, but at the same time coldly disapproving; averse to pomp and splendor but, on his return to London, jealously observing ritual and ceremony; according to his own words determined to make peace with France, determined on a high-minded resolution of all differences, but in reality—this could not be hidden—filled with extreme hostility and some pride. From the day after Agincourt he had steadily maintained that he was nothing more than an instrument of God, but nevertheless he willingly accepted the adulation of his people, and the praises of his entourage.

Charles remembered moment by moment the triumphant procession through the streets of London, so ignominious for him and for his companions in distress; in his mind's eye he saw Henry still, with a large glittering crown on his head, riding slowly along under a red and gold canopy. Exultant crowds blocked his way at every turn; at each street corner, each square, they welcomed him with song, presented allegorical tableaux in his honor, offered him gifts. At long last the procession reached St Paul's cathedral; kneeling amongst armed soldiers, Charles and the French nobles had to watch their conqueror perform his devotions for hours in the glow of candles and against a background of the singing of hymns; a gilded angel dropped from the arched roof to hover in the air above his head swinging a censer. In Westminster Charles had attempted respectfully to engage the King in conversation, but Henry had only bowed courteously and inquired about the progress of a falcon hunt or the response to a stroll in the castle park.

Cousinot's words led Charles anew to deep reflection, the more so since the Chancellor was not content with vague intimations during his next visit to his lord.

"I take it that freedom is worth a great deal to you, Monseigneur," he said, looking attentively at Charles. "Perhaps liberty lies within your grasp if King Henry, like his father before him, should seek a reconciliation with our party because he hopes in that way to achieve his purpose sooner than he could dealing with Burgundy. If that is the case—and I myself am convinced that it is—you have the game in your hand."

Charles did not speak for a while; he went to the window and stood staring out. Rain hovered over the river like a mist.

"I know very well what you mean, Cousinot," he said at last, without turning round. "A few months ago I would probably have welcomed the opportunity to deal my cards so profitably. I long for France, Cousinot, for Blois, for my wife. But since I have been here I have thought a good deal and I see now that Orléans and Burgundy and all their supporters and partisans have together robbed and betrayed France—that we have brought the Kingdom to ruin either wittingly or through ignorance. France is dying, Cousinot. Yes, perhaps I could purchase my freedom by giving that sick country a death-blow; I never thought about such things before. God knows I have used my time badly. But now I am not sure that freedom is worth that much to me."

"Let it be so, Monseigneur," Cousinot replied, after a pause. "Whatever you decide to do, you can count on me. Do you wish me to stay a while longer in London so that I can help you with advice if you need it—in case new information should come up about the Emperor's visit?"

Charles was finally summoned to Westminster where King Henry's own state rooms were being readied for the royal visitor. Surrounded by armed men—as though it were a festive escort, he thought bitterly—he rode to the King's palace. The people in the streets stared at him with curiosity: wasn't that one of the French lords who had mocked King Henry on the night before Agincourt? Why hadn't the foreigner been beheaded?

Charles stared straight before him. It had been weeks since he had been outside in the country air: the fresh wind, the pale March sunshine did him good. The districts along the Thames smelt of fish and damp rope, of river water and silt. Many people were abroad: hawkers and boatmen, warehouse workers and market-goers. Charles, who no longer found the English tongue so strange, heard a few familiar words—the same enticing cries and shouts of peddlers which had reached him in his prison chamber.

King Henry received him in one of the council halls at Westminster. The King sat in a chair under a canopy of carved wood; counsellors and courtiers drew away as the King greeted the Duke of Orléans. There remained nearby only Henry's Chancellor, the Archbishop of Durham, the Dukes of Northumberland and Westmoreland and the Marquis of Kent, all kinsmen and trusted friends of the King. Henry saluted Charles in the usual manner, with a kiss on the cheek; then he gestured him to a seat beside the throne. The high lords stood quietly to one side. Their demeanor, as well as King Henry's, made it obvious that this courtesy was only a prelude to a serious business discussion. Although Henry was plainly dressed, he wore the narrow royal diadem, presumably so that there would be no doubt about the nature of this audience. His light eyes seemed harder and brighter than the stones in the gold band.

"Fair cousin," said Henry in his careful French, "we shall not squander our time in formalities. There is no need for me to inquire after your welfare. I am well informed about your life in the Tower. I know that you eat little, seldom go out, rarely seek the company of your noble companions in distress. May I deduce from this that you find your stay there unpleasant and that a change of surroundings would not be unwelcome to you?"

Charles, who sat up straight with his hands on the arms of his chair, did not move or alter his expression. He watched the King impassively, trying to fathom his intentions.

"You know, of course, fair cousin, that the Holy Roman Emperor is at present in Paris and that he is preparing to honor us with a visit for the sake of peace between this Kingdom and France."

Charles nodded. "I am aware of that, my lord," he said dryly.

"Good." Henry's eyes filled with that sudden light which made his gaze look fierce. "I have great respect for the Emperor Sigismund's desire for peace. I want nothing more myself than to see the differences resolved without bloodshed. I would gladly spare you a second Agincourt." He looked with raised eyebrows at his prisoner. But he saw no change of expression in Charles' dark weary eyes.

"Fair cousin," the King continued after a short pause, "as you know, your fate is dependent in large measure on the progress of negotiations between Emperor Sigismund and me. No doubt he will have something to propose about your release. It would be extremely gratifying to me personally if I could allow you to return to your homeland. So far as peace negotiations are concerned, considering the outcome of the battle at Agincourt and the present conditions in France, it is for *me* to propose terms. You know my claims, fair cousin, don't you? Perhaps it would be helpful now to call them to your attention once again. I hold fast to the treaty of Brétigny: Calais, Montreuil, Boulogne, Aquitaine, Touraine, Angoulême, Anjou and Normandy belong by right to England."

"I do not understand, Monseigneur, why you speak to me of this," said Charles coldly; he glanced at the King's advisors who stood with inscrutable faces in respectful attention beside the throne. "I am Lord of Angoulême, but my House has received the territory as a fief from the Crown. Of the other provinces and regions which you mention, I can tell you even less."

Henry raised his hand and spoke quickly. "I mention this to you, fair cousin, because I believe—and not incorrectly, for that matter—that to some extent you represent France's government here today. You are a nephew of the King, as well as a close kinsman of the Lords of Armagnac and Berry, who—as everyone knows—are now the most powerful men in the Council. No doubt you maintain relations with them."

"Forgive me, Monseigneur, you are mistaken—I can claim neither will nor influence in this matter. True, I have, since contact was granted to me, exchanged a few letters with my kinsmen in France. But I have only concerned myself with the problem of collecting ransoms for me and my brother of Angoulême. With regard to the terms of a peace treaty, I am undoubtedly a most unsuitable person to represent Your Grace to the government of France."

"No, you are exactly the man for that, fair cousin." Henry tapped the arm of his chair impatiently with the great signet ring on the forefinger of his right hand. "I am fully aware of what you have been doing in the past few years; I know what role you play in Armagnac's party. You have brought it a long way; you and your supporters have finally managed to gather the reins in your hands, despite opposition and great obstacles. It is all the more regrettable that the restoration of order in your country should now appear to be an impossibility. He alone can rule who knows how to gain the help and approval of God. But now to business, fair cousin. You know that I have legitimate claims to the French throne."

During this speech Charles sat looking at the rose windows, composed of small azure and blood-red panes which glowed in the sunlight like rosettes of sapphires and rubies. Now he turned his gaze back to the King.

"I know that only the late King Richard could make such claims with some justice," he said slowly. "He was descended from King Edward the Third, who was a kinsman of our royal House. But"— for the first time a trace of irony could be detected in Charles' eyes and voice—"but surely you do not belong to that family, my lord? At least, if I have been correctly informed, your father—may God rest his soul—did not come to the throne by succession."

Henry turned pale with anger. The freckles on his nose and cheeks became plainly visible; they could not normally be seen because the King's face was somewhat tanned by the sun.

"England lays claim to the property of France," he said in a calm, cold voice, after a brief silence. "And I am England, fair cousin. For me that is a fact beyond dispute. You can win freedom only if you acknowledge me as your lawful sovereign: freedom, a considerable reduction in your ransom, retention of your feudal fiefs and the immediate return of all the lands which the Duke of Burgundy has confiscated from you. In addition, an important voice in the capitol at all times. I tell you this straight out, as is my custom; I don't see any reason to beat about the bush with you, fair cousin. In return for my favors I expect support and loyalty from you in word as well as in deed. You and your kinsmen must assure me that you will do your utmost to obtain a written confirmation of my rights, signed by the King. When Charles VI dies, the Crown of France falls to me. I shall take the Princess Catherine to wife; in that way the blood of Valois will retain the throne. I do not think that this can be considered by any means an unreasonable proposal. Thus you have nothing to lose and a great deal to gain. Messeigneurs your fellow prisoners will presumably follow your example when they learn that you recognize my claim."

"I would not recognize the claim even of a direct descendant of Edward the third," Charles responded pensively, continuing to stare at the glowing window. "It is my belief that only my sovereign lord King Charles or one of his legitimate sons can sit upon the throne of France."

"The King is mad and the Dauphin is unquestionably your enemy," remarked Henry. "Loyalty in this case can lead only to your own downfall. Or do you perhaps cherish less noble ambitions with the support of the Lord of Armagnac, fair cousin? You are after all a kinsman of the royal House and death is a striking visitor to the King's sons . . ."

Charles' dark brown eyes—the eyes of his mother, Valentine—began to smoulder. Henry noticed this and said quickly, although not without secret satisfaction, "So far as the death of the late Dauphin is concerned—if it's true that he was poisoned—I am ready to believe that this time the guilt must be placed at the door of the Duke of Burgundy."

"I know little about it," Charles parried politely. "But this has nothing to do with the matter at hand, my lord. I must reject your offer without hesitation. I find it too high a price to pay for my liberty. But I would gladly learn either now or later what sum you demand for my ransom."

Henry's advisors did not conceal their displeasure; the Archbishop of Durham approached the King and whispered to him quickly. Henry shrugged.

"I do not doubt, fair cousin, that you will think differently about these matters after you have spoken with my lords of Bourbon and Richmont. I think it would be wise to postpone your decision for a few days. But not for too long, mind you—for you can understand that it would be exceedingly desirable and might hasten matters considerably if I could give the Emperor Sigismund certain facts directly upon his arrival."

Charles rose and bowed. "I have given you my answer, Monseigneur," he said. "And I can tell you now that my opinion will be shared completely by my lords of Bourbon and Richmont, who are loyal vassals of our King. And now I pray you, give me leave to return to the Tower."

Henry had a few moments' muted conversation with Durham and Northumberland. Then he dismissed Charles with a wave of his hand and a brief nod. Charles' attendants stepped inside to fetch him; the armed escort waited outside the door. Thoughtfully, Henry looked after his ducal captive, his head resting on his hand. Charles d'Orléans was not particularly tall. In his black damask suit—a gift from the English king—he looked somewhat slim and boyish. But he moved with innate dignity; without haste, erect, bowing courteously, he left the room.

The Emperor Sigismund was received in London during the month of April with great pomp and splendor. He expressed his satisfaction with the lavish entertainments. Loudly, in unpolished Latin, he told anyone who cared to listen that, by God, people knew how to live here in England—with plentiful food, pageants, hunting parties—that was men's work. He had been able to detect nothing of the vaunted luxury at the French court. It was a beggarly mess there, bad food and little entertainment worthy of a prince. He had not been able to see the King; he was sick again, but the Queen, at any rate, had done her best to give her guest real pleasure. Now there was a woman who really knew—let it be said and remain between us, my lords—what a man really wants, ha ha, and Sigismund, bowing to the haughty but inquisitive English courtiers, described the delights of Isabeau's nightly balls where all the women were corrupt and all the men played with false dice.

In his youth, twenty years before, at the time of his great campaign against the Turks, Sigismund may have been to a certain extent crude and frivolous, but he was also a brave and well-intentioned man. With the passage of time the coarse lines in his face became more noticeable; a life of war, intrigue, uncurbed licentiousness and callous rule had transformed Sigismund into an unpredictable, brutal, greedy man. He had travelled to France and England chiefly out of vanity. Never before had he had any influence on these once-so-powerful kingdoms. And he was curious to meet Henry, the son of the late usurper Lancaster. Sigismund's desire to help the French King rested mainly on his ancient but still fierce hatred of Burgundy.

The former King of Hungary had never forgotten that he owed his defeat by the Turks to the knights whom Burgundy had brought upon the field.

Strangely, the French said nothing about this old grievance. In fact, Paris was indifferent—no, even downright impudent to him, thought Sigismund; therefore no one should be surprised if his good nature had suffered somewhat under such treatment. Wherever he went, he felt himself mocked and criticized for his behavior, his speech, his predilection for revelry and for the frequenting of houses of prostitution.

In an extremely irritable mood, Sigismund had arrived in London attended by the Archbishop of Reims who would serve as his counselor. But behold! Here were triumphal arches awaiting him, and welcoming committees. Here he was offered lodging in King Henry's state rooms and shown every conceivable evidence of thoughtful hospitality. Sigismund, very much touched by such courtesy—they were careful in Westminster not to remind him of his Slavic origin, his lack of dignity and self-control—was only too happy to lend a willing ear to Henry. Before long he declared that in the event of a peace treaty with France, the advantage must be with Henry; that was only fair under the circumstances.

Over the course of the summer Charles d'Orléans was moved to another chamber in one of the small inner courts of the Tower; one with no view of the Thames. This room was even more luxurious than the other; the floor was covered with hides, the walls hung with beautiful woven tapestries, and there was a comfortable bed and a chair with cushions. But Charles sorely missed the view of the river which had provided so welcome a distraction for him, especially in the spring months when the days were longer and lighter and the bustle on the water seemed to increase constantly. Gazing at the ships, at the people on the other bank, at the traffic on the bridges, Charles had been able to forget, for a while at least, some of the worries which poisoned his life. He received almost no news from France; crossing the Straits was no longer safe and couriers could not obtain permission to come over. Charles was told, of course, that Henry had succeeded in retaining Harfleur after a sea battle near the estuary of the Seine, and that Armagnac had retreated like a beaten dog. And Charles was told again and again that the armies of the Duke of Burgundy, who had signed a peace treaty with England, were rampaging across northern France.

The young man had heard this and similar news, but the news he desired with all his heart—news of Bonne, of Blois, of Paris—was not forthcoming. Since he had been moved to the new chamber, he had often sought the company of Bourbon and Richmont. He and they shared a common fate, and they represented his only remaining link with France. But before long he could not help noticing that a coolness seemed to exist between his former allies and himself. They spoke to him, played cards and chess with him—but apart from that they remained aloof. Sometimes Charles thought that they were afraid of him. They avoided talk about politics, and if they responded to his comments or questions, they did it in a way that made him suspect that they resented him because he had prevented them from accepting King Henry's offer.

Charles' room looked out on a small square in which a few blades of grass pushed up between the paving stones; there was no other greenery. Force of habit brought Charles continually to the window to discover again and again with a slight shock that there was nothing to be seen but stone walls. Once when he stood staring out, with his hands behind his back, his attention was caught by something stirring behind a window opposite his across the courtyard. Charles looked closely and saw, standing in the shadow of the deep window, a man who clutched the window bars in both hands. There could be no doubt that the prisoner across the way had seen him too: he waved to Charles and then stepped back. During the next few days the game was repeated many times. Charles began in his turn to salute his neighbor, who pressed his face against the bars; he was a young man with black hair and the striking waxen complexion of one who had lived indoors for a long time. So far as Charles could see, he wore rich clothing; his demeanor, too, betrayed the nobleman.

Caution at first kept Charles from making inquiries; he hesitated to get the stranger into further trouble. But he learned finally in a circuitous way that the stranger was no other than James Stuart, the Pretender to the Scottish throne, who had been in the Tower since he was a child. When his valet saw that Charles was greatly interested, he brought his master fresh information every day about the other captive.

The King of Scotland—as they called him—was a scholarly man who spent his days writing and studying. He used more candles than any other prisoner because he sometimes lay in bed reading all night long. He wrote poetry too; his wardens could overhear him rhyming aloud when they put their ears to the door. A singular silent friendship arose between Charles and the unfortunate monarch in those autumnal days. They greeted each other in the morning, at noon and in the evening, mimed a conversation on the weather, their respective states of health and other matters which could be communicated in that way. Charles held up one of his few books and indicated that he wanted more to read. A few days later his valet brought him, with a great show of secrecy, a well-thumbed leatherbound copy of Boethius' Consolation of Philosophy. A verse had been written on one of the flyleaves in a language which Charles guessed to be Scottish, since he did not recognize any of the words as English. He was sorry that he could not read the lines; he would have liked to know what thoughts the imprisoned King expressed when his spirit took flight inside those four walls of his chamber. Boethius' book was the first and last token of friendship Charles received from James Stuart. Around All Souls Day his neighbor was missing from the window; when day after day passed without anyone stirring behind the bars, Charles cautiously inquired of his servant whether the King of Scotland was perhaps ill. The man replied that that was not the case; at King Henry's command the prisoner had been sent to Windsor Castle.

Once, Charles received permission to visit his brother Jean. They had not seen each other for four years—years which seemed as long as a man's life. During that time Jean d'Angoulême had grown to manhood; the frail child had developed into a taciturn youth with a troubled look. The brothers sat together for a few hours, talking about the affairs which absorbed them: their hopes and their prospects as well as their past—Blois, their parents and the struggle which had cast so long a shadow over their youth. To Jean, Charles could talk uninterruptedly of Bonne; here was someone who did not know her, but who listened with sympathy. She seemed to Charles nearer, more real, now that he could speak of her and describe her. In the solitude of his room it often seemed to him that she had slipped away from him; desperately he strove to hold her image in his mind's eye to remember the sound of her voice, her laughter. Sometimes he woke at night blithe and light-hearted from a dream which he tried later to evoke once more, but without success.

He felt then that Bonne had been close to him while he was sleeping; he thought he could feel in the darkness the warmth of the place where she had lain, smell the fragrance of her hair upon the pillows. Fruitless were his efforts to call her back, futile his prayers, his agitated thoughts, his seeking for forgetfulness; nothing remained with him except the bitter taste of loneliness. Desperately he buried his head in the pillows.

He could tell these things to his brother Jean—that brought him a measure of relief. However they had no time to indulge themselves for long in such personal conversations; they were not sure they would meet again soon. They had to take advantage of each precious moment.

From a letter from King Henry V of England to His Most Christian Majesty, Sigismund, Emperor of the Holy Roman Empire. January, 1417:

"And so it is a great satisfaction to Us to inform you that Our unquestionable right to the Crown of France has been acknowledged by Jean, Duke of Bourbon, presently a captive living in Our Kingdom and Arthur, Count de Richmont; that the aforementioned Jean, Duke of Bourbon, has declared in Our presence during his stay in Our domain—that We, Henry, have valid claims to the throne of France; that he has bound himself under oath to stake his entire person to realize the terms set forth in the Treaty of Brétigny in the year of Our Lord 1360; that finally he, the aforenamed Jean, Duke of Bourbon, will give vassal service to Us, Henry, as his only lawful and sovereign Lord and Prince and that he will deliver his lands and domains into Our hands if Our demands are not granted by the government of France."

Charles sat writing at the table; without turning his head he asked, "What is it, Chomery?" He had heard the door open and close again. He assumed it was Jean Chomery, his French valet, who often came in and out of the room in this way.

"God be with you, Monseigneur," said a voice behind him.

"Cousinot!" Charles leaped up from his chair, pleased and surprised. "Cousinot, why didn't anyone announce your arrival? Not long ago I received a letter from my brother—he wrote that someone was bringing me money, but not that you were coming. This is a great joy for me!"

"I must speak with you quickly, Monseigneur," the advocate said, in a low agitated voice. "I have been able to get to you by showing the safe-conduct pass they gave me last year when I was in London, but the knight who supervises your wardens was hesitant about it. This time I did not ask for permission to visit you, because I was certain that King Henry would not allow it."

Charles led the Chancellor to the chair under the window, the only spot in the room which—in the summer at any rate and then only around noon—received any sunlight.

"I know that King Henry has not been favorably disposed toward me since I refused to acknowledge him as my sovereign," he said slowly. "He removed me to this room which is definitely darker and gloomier than the one I had, but apart from that I haven't noticed any sign of the King's displeasure. I realize that I may expect few visitors or letters because of the war."

"You know nothing then; I did not think that you could possibly know anything." Cousinot glanced at the door. Outside there was as usual the sound of footsteps and soft jingling; a couple of soldiers passed back and forth before Charles' door. Charles looked attentively at his Chancellor: he had rarely seen such excitement in that habitually controlled face.

"Monseigneur," said Cousinot softly and urgently, "I shall try to tell you everything as briefly as I can. I fear they will come to fetch me away at any moment. The Dauphin died a week ago in Compiègne; your father-in-law the Sire d'Armagnac requested me particularly to inform you that the Dauphin had a fistula in his left ear; he would not want you to believe the rumors which are going round the English and Burgundian camps. Our new Dauphin, Monseigneur de Viennois, is in Paris under the personal protection of the Sire d'Armagnac whom he considers his advisor and confidant in every respect."

Charles took his Chancellor firmly by the elbow.

"Cousinot," he said, "do not tell me what Armagnac has instructed you to say. Tell me what you think of all this yourself. In God's name speak plainly."

Cousinot kept his searching eyes fixed on Charles; the corners of his narrow pale lips twitched almost imperceptibly.

"I do not believe in the fistula, Monseigneur," he said. "I believe that the Sire d'Armagnac felt the reins of power slipping from his grasp and that he resorted to a damnable, unworthy means of re-assuring himself of that power. Burgundy held all the cards, because the Dauphin was completely under his influence—it was precisely then that Armagnac remembered that he too had one of the King's sons near him—Monseigneur Charles, the youngest. The new Dauphin is still only twelve or thirteen years old, I believe, and his wife's kinsmen, the princes of Anjou, have become, as you know, increasingly disposed toward Armagnac in recent years. Now Armagnac holds the Dauphin before him like a banner."

"The King has no more sons," Charles said, in soft surprised dismay. "No other successor to the throne except this . . ." He remembered the new Dauphin well; he had met him in Paris after the siege of Arras: an uncommonly ugly child, with a large head and the same rickety legs as his brothers. In the features of Messeigneurs de Guyenne and de Touraine could be seen at least something of the charm which Charles VI had had as a boy, but the youngest son was, bluntly, ugly. He had a high globular forehead, prominent ears and bulbous despondent blue eyes. That the fate of France should rest in the hands of this timid, uncertain youth seemed to Charles little less than a catastrophe; he had heard years ago that the King's youngest son had inherited his father's feeble nervous constitution. Those who said this then were able to supply many occurrences which bore out their point. Charles remembered their words with fear and horror.

"I realize fully what this means, Cousinot," he said slowly at last to the advocate who sat looking at him with attentive concern. "The shift of power will bring with it such great, far-reaching consequences that I hardly dare to think about it. So my father-in-law of Armagnac is expecting that those who support the Dauphin will join the Armagnac party. If he succeeds he will be a singularly powerful man."

"Monseigneur, do you realize what this means for you? Armagnac's party is yours. You can be carried on this stream to the throne of France. You must not forget that the Dauphin is weak in body and very probably also weak in mind. King Henry has undoubtedly also drawn this conclusion. Every day you become a more dangerous opponent for him, and by the same token a more valuable prize. Believe me, Monseigneur, we must bend all our efforts to effect your release. We must not reject a single effort, no matter how trifling it may seem. But you must understand that Burgundy will do anything to stop you from returning. Listen!"

Quick booming footsteps could be heard in the corridor outside Charles' room, along with jingling spurs and the harsh voice of Sir Robert Waterton, the nobleman who commanded the guard. Cousinot rose from the bench.

"Give me the order, my lord, to communicate some important information in your name to the King of England. Trust me now, I am your devoted servant; I know very well what I am doing. Monseigneur, if you love liberty, give me the order, for as surely as Christ died for us, they will not release you under any other terms."

For a moment the images flashed past Charles which had floated temptingly before his eyes night and day since Agincourt: the ship cutting quickly through the waves on the voyage home to France, the yellow coastline of Calais, the welcome on native soil, the cities and fields of the Ile de France, Paris, the hills along the Loire, the shape of Blois against the sky, the pointed towers of Saint-Sauveur, the battlements of the donjon, his entry over the drawbridge, over castle yard and inner court to the gate where Bonne was standing, weeping and laughing and beaming . . .

Now he saw Robert Waterton enter the room, followed by the officers of the guard; he saw Cousinot's tense, almost supplicating look. The word "yes" was on his lips, but still he hesitated. Swear fealty to King Henry for reasons of diplomacy? But this is high treason, he thought, confused, and remained silent. With an eloquent gesture of despair, Cousinot left the room at Waterton's command.

From a written command from King Henry V of England to the knight Sir Robert Waterton, June, 1417:
". . .we charge you to convey immediately, under heavy guard, Charles, Duke of Orléans, at present a prisoner of war confined in the Tower of London, to Pontefract castle in York, where he will remain for an indefinite period . . ."

The sand flows through the hourglass, a ruddy mist, forming at first a barely visible layer and then gradually a growing hill. Before one fully realizes it, the lower globe is completely filled; an hour has gone by, a long precious hour of a life which seems suddenly to consist of a terrifying number of such hours. He whose life it is sees the sand slipping away with comingled feelings of fear, regret, impatience and despair; he sees that the passage of time is at once pitilessly slow and unmercifully fast. In those glass spheres his hours are counted out, the precious wasted hours. The lost hours become days, the days flow into weeks, the weeks create months and before long the months have turned into a year.

To one who thinks in that way the winds, clouds, rain, sunshine and moonlight can be only dismal portents. The gleam of stars comes and goes behind the window, a ray of the sun, a streak of moonlight creeps over the walls. The seasons change; he sees the leaves of the great trees wither and fall in the field outside the castle; he sees the trees standing for four long months like branched candelabra under the wintry sky; on a certain day in spring he sees a light green cloud hovering between the grey branches, and finally he sees, in the midst of summer, the heated air quivering about the full-crowned trees.

All this the prisoner of Pontefract sees when he stands before his window. He can see over the outermost wall of the castle. Between the double row of battlements there is a passage where a sentry, wearing a storm hat and with the red cross of England on his breast, paces continually back and forth, back and forth.

Many different men take their turn at guard duty there; the garrison at Pontefract is a large one. When the prisoner at his window begins to recognize the faces of individual sentries he realizes with bitterness that he has come full circle once more, that time has once more stolen a piece of his life away. Every six hours another watch . . . He has seen the same men repeatedly; he thinks, There goes the Redhead, there's Black Beard—there's Scarcheek, there's More-Than-Six-Feet-Tall . . . How many hours, how many hours, in God's name, how many hours must have passed before he could learn to recognize these people?

He searches, as he looks out the window, for something that will not change, something that cannot measure time. No, the sky will not do: clouds float by, gleaming white, radiant in the summer— perhaps they are the same clouds which will sail later over Blois, perhaps throwing a swift shadow over Bonne's upturned face. In the autumn the clouds are more shapeless: torn, scudding low over the land; occasionally they are too heavy with rain to reach the horizon; they break over Pontefract and cause the recluse in his tower chamber the further torment of listening for hours or days to the murmur of falling water, a sound which brings only a deceptive oblivion. He dreams with open eyes and thinks he is elsewhere—he hears someone laughing and someone sobbing; the sobs form a melody that he sang long ago—Madame, je suys plus joyeulx, Madame, I am overjoyed. He puts his hands over his ears so that he can no longer hear the sound of the rain, but he cannot banish that gentle, incessant tapping which becomes Bonne's voice, bewitching him by night even more distinctly than by day.

He would rather listen to the wails and ravings of the winter wind which seems never to leave Pontefract in peace, but which howls and bellows round the towers, by turns fierce and melancholy, always a fearful visitor. The prisoner lying sleepless under a fur coverlet feels a cold draught brush along his cheeks and forehead, despite the fire and the shelter of the bedcurtains; the candle flame flickers, the thin tapestries billow in and out, in and out. The mice rustle behind the walls, gnawing and nibbling on the wood, trying to reach the crumbs under the table. The man in the bed—a good warm bed—waits for day. He awaits the first shrill cockcrow, the slight drop in the wind, the odd droning sound which fills the darkness just before the break of dawn; he listens for the sounds in and out of Pontefract—the changing of the guard, the summons to work—a trumpet call, the rumble of footsteps on stair and gallery, the neighing of horses, the clatter of armor and weapons. He awaits the pealing of the church bells; the church spire is visible by day over the tops of the trees in the fields. When at last his servant enters with the morning drink and washing gear, opens the shutters before the windows and rakes up the fire, the prisoner sits up in bed with a sigh; the daily struggle begins anew.

Summer and winter he gazes at the horizon, the faint, undulating line between the clump of trees behind the ramparts of Pontefract; and the line, ascending here, descending there, remains the same despite the seasons; the profile of York is always the same to the man who stands alone by the window and finds a certain comfort in the sight of this dependable horizon. He comes to know the hazy northern sunlight, the piercing biting cold of winter whenever he sees the clods of dark earth lying in the fields; he discovers the secret of the summer dew which rises in the early morning and after sunset and hovers in long streaks low over the earth. He knows all the birds and their calls; from the way in which they wheel, climb and skim, he can tell whether a storm or gale is approaching, whether the day will bring rain, whether it will be an early winter, whether spring is approaching.

He can see how, over the course of many weeks, the planets and the stars change their positions in the nocturnal sky; in September sparks rain across the blue-black abyss; in the winter the stars sparkle coldly as the icicles which festoon the outsides of his window. With autumn the winds bring him familiar smells: of rotting leaves and mushrooms, of morning mist, of leather trappings. Far away in the forest he hears the horns blowing, the excited barking of hounds and the pounding of hooves on the ground. The birch trees stand in the meadow bedecked in red and gold and drop leaf after leaf—the largesse of nature. The beauty of these trees torments the prisoner like no other image. He remembers a certain autumn-red forest outside the ramparts of Riom, a splendid spring in another kingdom—how long ago was it now, four, five years?—he remembers riding on horseback through rustling leaves in the still November sunlight; he remembers Bonne laughing, mounted on her horse Mirabel.

On such days the young man, watching in the tower room of Pontefract, cannot remain standing by the window; he steps into the shadows and paces with his hands behind his back, as he is wont to do. Sometimes he sits motionless by the hearth, reading. The books are arranged carefully on a table beside him: Aristotle's Politics, a Chronicle of Jerusalem Reconquered, a book on medicine, an edition of Boccaccio—these are the works which Maître Cousinot had brought along for the prisoner during his last visit. Most of the time the young man can completely forget himself and his surroundings by losing himself in a book; his spirit skims lightly and easily through a world of wisdom and colorful fantasy. But this flight is not always an unmitigated release for him—a word, a wish, a thought can pull him back to the present—and that return is worse than no escape at all.

He sets to work diligently, mindful of the advice given him by his friend Marshal Boucicaut; he is allowed once more to possess paper and writing materials and day in and day out he does the work of monks and clerks: he copies books, collects maxims, writes in his beautiful uniform script a small commentary on Cato's Disticha. His chamber servant Chomery, Sir Robert Waterton and those among the guard who are nobly born and who are admitted to the presence of the prisoner, see him invariably occupied in this way through the long winter: a figure dressed in black, on his head a velvet cap with flaps, sitting erect at his table; the parchment sheet hangs over a sloping reading desk, Monseigneur's right hand moves slowly, purposefully, forward over the lines marked in red. His eyes are fixed on his work and he is apparently absorbed in it; his pale lips are pressed firmly together; every now and then he knits his brows for a moment—the fixed staring wearies him. When he is spoken to, he puts his pen carefully down and gives a courteous reply, but he never smiles. Robert Waterton himself, a man hardened by constant exposure to the open air, to hunting and war, assumes, not incorrectly, that the prisoner suffers from the lack of physical exercise. He permits him to take walks in the inner court, although there is no mention of this in King Henry's warrant.

But after a few days the captive declines the pleasure: he chooses to stand by his open window, rather than to proceed through a little section reserved for that purpose, enclosed on all sides by high walls, where he walks around like a horse on a treadmill, watched by a half-dozen armed soldiers.

When a swift foaming stream flows into a stagnant pool, at first the water rushes forward; small waves fan out from the main-stream—but slowly the last ripples subside and the surface of the pool becomes a dark mirror. Thus the soul of the prisoner in Pon-tefract castle becomes immobile, like the stagnant pool. The current is stilled; whatever falls onto the surface floats for an instant and then sinks into darkness. There are only reflections there, fleeting images: clouds, treetops, a bird in flight, long grass stirred by a breeze.

The prisoner on occasion vividly relives moments of his child-hood: he closes his eyes and suddenly the years slip away. He finds himself once again in the stately castles of Valois with their melodious names: Montargis, Montils, Asnières, Beaumont, Crécy-en-Brie. He is a child, tip-toeing through the high-ceilinged rooms; the noon sun streams, filled with dancing particles of dust, through half-opened shutters. By this golden light he sees kings and heroes strid-ing across the walls. Saints pray, fair women smile, playing the lute or releasing a falcon into the air. As the white unicorn moves through the forest, he looks askance at the child with a large lustrous eye.

Beyond, in the flower-strewn meadow, are prancing beasts; deer, hounds, hare and, in the background, peacocks with wide-spread tails.

Like one enchanted, the child steals through the silent rooms, inhaling the odors of old woodwork and dusty hangings. He comes to a chamber hung with green tapestries; embroidered on the heavy fabric are small angels in stiffly pleated golden garments, blowing on clarions and trumpets. He goes through a low door and stands staring in amazement: he is in a room where, on hangings of colored silk interwoven with gold thread, children bathe in the small trans-lucent waves of a river.

Finally, he stands for a long time before a tapestry depicting a lord and his lady seated at a chess board set with red and gold pieces. This picture always fascinates him, because the knight looks like his father: a narrow face, a courteous smile, and, in the eyes, the enig-matic expression, at once restless, mocking and appealing, which surprises the child anew each time he sees his father. For years, day after day, the small boy plays in these rooms amid the red and gold and green splendor of the tapestries; the walls of the chambers in his father's castles are like so many pages of a gigantic storybook. Here the heroes of Antiquity, his own ancestral kings, the holy men and women of the legends, come to meet him. Large as life, they beckon to him to join them in their jewel-toned world, among flowers and leafy vines, or in the shadows of enchanted forests; they show him the vistas of their horizons, or the views from the windows of their palaces: a field of golden-yellow corn, a spring garden, hills blue against a dark sky. Between blooming hedgerows, Lady Venus holds court; she sits there on her throne, surrounded by her chan-cellors and chamberlains, the members of her council and her retinue; and all who wish to be her subjects are led to her by her son, the God of Love. The child has been told that this is an allegory; his tutor Maître Garbet has quoted those lines from the Roman de la Rose which he considers suitable for childish ears.

But soon the boy no longer needs explanations. The mysterious glowing colors of the tapestries, their harmony of line and form, awaken a response in his heart. The figures in the tapestries are his secret companions: the concepts of courtliness in his schoolbooks take on for him the physical appearance of these fair, slender, beau-tifully dressed ladies, these proud knights, these militant saints and humble martyrs.

Long years of worry and warfare have not left time for thoughts like these; harsh reality has driven away the creatures of the imagination, whose essence is symbolic. But now they come to share the prisoner's solitude; they glide into the silence of his aimless fleeting hours, carrying oblivion in the folds of their garments. They knock at the door of the prisoner, who dreams the day away over his books, absorbed in thought, who remains awake throughout the night— a colorful procession of allegorical figures: Grief, Affliction and Hope, Sorrow, Faith, Desire, Solace, Fortune, Memory and Melancholy, Love and—lastly—Death. The stages of his life appear before him: Childhood and Youth arrayed in the rich trappings of images from a turbulent past.

One day, to amuse himself, the prisoner begins to write in the light, flowing style characteristic of him, a story in rhyme about his life. Words and images glide effortlessly from his pen; he does not need to exert himself; he needs only to describe what is being enacted in his imagination, an allegory in which he himself plays a role among symbols come alive. Love and Youth, ideal in feature and form, stride through his dream like royal figures embroidered in red, gold and green with tapering fingers and sweet mysterious smiles. He himself, the mere mortal, moves among Love's subjects as he once walked among the courtiers in Saint-Pol, uncertain and shy, awkwardly polite, unable to express the admiration and longing which he feels—a stranger in the Court of Love.

This new pastime has a strange effect on the prisoner. He has begun it out of boredom and a vague, melancholy nostalgia for the carefree childhood that vanished all too quickly. As he writes, the young man regrets the past and thinks bitterly of the reality of his youth; he knows the pleasures of courtly love only from hearsay; he was never allowed the time and freedom to mature gradually, in the green-gold April of life, into a man. He reads over his poem; it seems to him to be dull and artificial; the meaning behind the allegory is obscure. During the long hours of his sleepless nights he calls up, word for word, line for line, the ballads which he once composed for Bonne and which he intended his minstrels to sing at supper. He improves the rhyme and metaphor of these stanzas, once written all too hastily.

When he grows tired of reading Aristotle, or when he is not in the mood to annotate Cato's Disticha, he jots down these reconstructions. He cuts a large sheet of vellum into eight parts, creating a booklet in which he can write his ballads. Carefully, in red ink, he decorates the initial letter of each poem with vines and flowers; he has plenty of time for this monkish work.

"Radiant and fresh, rich in Youth's treasures, laughing eyes, red lips and sweet soft voice . . . These are the virtues which adorn my Lady . . ."

But the words which he sets down so carefully on the page before him become his implacable enemies; they do not distract him, but force him to relive the feelings which inspired him the first time he wrote them. The desperate burning desire which tortured him in the first years of his solitude, and which he thought he had overcome, assails him again. Behind the lines Bonne's intangible image lurks enticingly. The time which has passed since their last meeting, the distance and the silence between them, have transformed her. She is no longer the sweet friend, the young wife; she is now the beauty, the seductress incarnate. She has become beauty, love, youth itself, an infinitely distant star.

The prisoner of Pontefract falls victim to the divinity which he himself has inadvertently evoked in light graceful words. Poetry is his only means of relief; there is no other. Song follows song, and all speak of his sense of loss, his yearning, his unquenchable grief and the hope of freedom which lives in him still. These ballads are substitutes for the letters which he is not allowed to write; he manages, within the limitations of poetic form, to express what he could not put into words even if he were permitted to write letters. What began as a diversion has become a need for him, a necessity. Just as wine never quenches thirst but continues to reawaken it, so each verse embodies in itself the germ of the next verse. When he has completed the envoi, the first words of a new poem well up in him— a complaint, a hymn of praise, an expression of desire . . .

He knows all too well that in the world outside Pontefract, waves are tossing in the wind while he himself sinks into stagnant waters. From time to time his servant picks up gossip which is circulating among Waterton's men. So over the years the lonely young man in the tower chamber hears disquieting news, vague rumors which seem to echo frightful events taking place far away in France. The prisoner thinks these rumors seem very credible in every way: he knows the players and the stage; he does not go so far as to doubt even the strangest and wildest tales.

Burgundy, who wishes at any cost to get control of the new

Dauphin, has gone into the field with large armies, while the King of England conquers town after town in Normandy without opposition; secret negotiations are being carried on between Burgundy and the exiled Queen; she seems suddenly to have been taken off to the city of Troyes, which belongs to Burgundy. Proclamations are delivered: "Armagnac's authority in Paris is unlawful; the true government is in Troyes. Queen Isabeau will rule France along with Burgundy in the name of the King who is too ill to hold the reins of government. All those who follow Armagnac are committing high treason."

So the Kingdom then has two governments.

The prisoner of Pontefract hears with mounting concern how his father-in-law Armagnac struggles vainly against the rising tide of public hatred. A rebellion breaks out in Paris and the burghers themselves bring Burgundy's troops inside the city. The first to attack Armagnac's supporters are the butchers and their apprentices who had once been banished from the city and who are blinded by the lust for blood and vengeance.

Is there any truth to the dreadful stories which the valet Chomery whispers in his master's ear? The names of Simon Caboche and of Capeluche the executioner are heard once more; there is talk of a savage, starved mob ready to seek revenge for years of enforced wanderings. In the streets, in the houses, in the churches, there are piles of corpses; in the midsummer heat, burial pits could not be dug fast enough. The prisoner believes unreservedly that murder is being committed for the sake of murder. He does not doubt for an instant that the great lords and nobles of Burgundy's army are the equal of the plundering rabble in cruelty and greed. In addition, he thinks it is more than likely that disease will break out from the rotten stench which must fill the city.

When Waterton comes at last to tell him that the Constable d'Armagnac had been seized and killed, and that his naked corpse had been exposed for three whole days (in order to ensure that he would be recognized, he had been adorned with the insignia of his own party: white bands, which in this case had been sliced from his own skin), when Waterton tells him this, the prisoner betrays neither amazement nor horror. He can believe it.

Now that his father-in-law is dead and the power of the Armagnacs appears to be on the wane, the prisoner has only his followers and kinsmen to turn to. He writes urgently, in detail, to

Bonne, to Philippe, to Cousinot, to his brother of Angoulême, whose ransom still does not seem to have been collected. It is not long before he receives an answer. It comes in the person of the devoted Chancellor who must once more undertake the journey by sea and land to bring his master news and a bag of gold. A small amount of gold—the collections have been scant, there is nothing left to be sold; it has cost a great deal of money to fortify the castles of Orléans!—has already been delivered to Giovanni Vittori in London.

Cousinot sits facing the prisoner at the table; Waterton, who insists on being present at the meeting, stands at the window; he listens attentively to every word of the conversation. Before being admitted to his master's presence, Cousinot has been searched for weapons and secret documents, but nothing incriminating has been found. The Chancellor is noticeably more subdued and somber than in the past. The thin hair at his temples is now completely grey; his cheeks are hollow. He slumps wearily in his chair.

The journey to Pontefract has been long and tiring and since his last meeting with his lord, Cousinot has led a life of privation in the impoverished cities of Orléans, in the barren castle of Blois. He finds the prisoner greatly altered—not so much outwardly as in his bearing and attitude. The young man appears to be indifferent, distracted; he seems to be only partially present, although he asks and answers questions in his usual courteous, tranquil manner. He listens impassively to the news: the partisans of Orléans and Armagnac have now entrenched themselves in the provinces and in the hastily fortified castles in the heart of the Kingdom.

Messeigneurs de Vertus and Dunois are incessantly recruiting troops again, preparing fortresses for attack. Cousinot gives a long list of those who have been appointed captains and heads of garrisons. Waterton coughs and comes to the table; he does not consider this information essential.

"Any news of my wife?" asks the prisoner; for the first time Cousinot sees a gleam in the rather dull, dark brown eyes. The advocate has consciously avoided this subject until now. He fears that Monseigneur will not find the news to his liking.

"Madame d'Orléans no longer lives in Blois," he responds quickly, without looking at the young man. "It was considered advisable for many reasons that she should return to her mother. There are a number of former allies who are willing to come back to our party now that Monseigneur d'Armagnac is dead . . . but they wish to be certain that we do not fall under the influence of Armagnac's nearest kinsmen."

A blow on the table by a clenched fist silences him. Waterton, back at the window again, turns hastily around, but the prisoner has already regained his composure. He swallows the words which rise to his lips.

He asks only, "Where is my wife now?"

"Madame d'Orléans is with her mother in the Cordelier convent in Rodez," says Cousinot, with bowed head. "Monseigneur Jean d'Armagnac, her brother, has declared himself ready to pay her a yearly stipend so that she can at least provide for her own needs in a suitable manner. Your daughter and your sister, my lord, remain at Blois. We could defray the costs for only two servant girls for Mesdemoiselles."

"That's all right, Cousinot." The prisoner waves his hand. There is silence for an instant in the gloomy tower chamber. Sir Robert Waterton grows impatient.

"May I implore Your Grace to proceed with the interview? The King has permitted you this visitor so that you can arrange your affairs."

Again sums are discussed. Cousinot takes out sheets of accounts, statements of receipts and expenditures. The young man reads in silence; finally he signs the necessary papers.

"I see that we still owe my lord of Clarence 75,000 écus," he remarks with a sad, somewhat mocking smile, as he returns the documents one by one to Cousinot. "I fear my brother of Angoulême and I will have to find the Philosophers' Stone, if we do not wish to remain under lock and key for the rest of our lives. In God's name, Cousinot, see first to my brother's ransom. I have promised him that."

Sir Robert Waterton interrupts the conversation once more.

"Perhaps Messire Cousinot would do better to inform you, my lord, that your party's position is almost hopeless. Now that the Queen of France and the Duke of Burgundy occupy Paris once more, and have taken the King under their protection, it does not look as though your allies can go on resisting—despite the fact that the Dauphin might be on their side—which I, for that matter, strongly doubt. I believe rather that your Armagnacs *force* the prince to choose their side. Messire Cousinot should make the state of affairs emphatically clear to you: the government of France is inclined to accept King Henry's proposals; the Dukes of Bourbon and Brittany too, have, as you know, come to their senses. It seems to me, Monseigneur, that it is high time that you also should be convinced that your resistance is foolish. Perhaps you will give your Chancellor letters to take with him, in which you instruct your kinsmen and partisans to join with the government in granting King Henry's rightful demands. I want once more, my lord, to call to your attention the fact that any other course can have only catastrophic consequences. Your party and the Dauphin's have supporters only in the central provinces and in the far south. The rest of France is in the hands of the Duke of Burgundy and our own troops. It will undoubtedly interest you to know that King Henry's forces have by now taken the city of Rouen."

The young man, who has sat listening with averted face, leans suddenly toward his Chancellor and asks incredulously, "Can you really say without stretching the truth, Cousinot, that Monseigneur of Burgundy and the Queen view these English conquests with equanimity—that they are doing nothing at all to protect the country and the throne?"

The Chancellor looks at Robert Waterton for a moment.

"Yes," he replies, "God knows I can, Monseigneur. I am deeply grieved that I must answer thus. But as matters stand in the Kingdom now, she who wears the crown and her mightiest vassal find it more advantageous to surrender the land to the enemy than to defend it. In the Council they are preparing to negotiate with King Henry. Forgive me, Monseigneur, but that is the truth."

"You hear that?" Robert Waterton has been charged by a high authority to exert pressure on the Duke of Orléans—not physical pressure, of course, that is unnecessary; there are many methods available to the man who is practiced in such matters. Solitary confinement creates an uncertain state of mind; and in addition it rouses an almost desperate craving for freedom at any price. A piece of discouraging news, the vacillation of his advisors—these can be the decisive thrust. Waterton thinks that the prisoner is ripe for persuasion; he is already trying to decide how he will presently inform King Henry that Orléans has acknowledged England's sovereignty, that the King for his part need no longer be concerned about any organized resistance in France. The knight looks expectantly at the young man, who continues to sit motionless. Cousinot is torn by an inward conflict: although he hopes his lord will soon be free, he cannot refrain from making a comment, perhaps out of pride.

"Monseigneur," he says, clearly and calmly, "there is some comfort in all this misery. I know—I receive proof of it every day—I know that the people of France and the greater number of our knights will not suffer themselves to be tempted to betray King and Kingdom as quickly and easily as Burgundy has done. God knows there has been enough wrangling and discord among our people, but with my own eyes I have seen bitter enemies unite in anger over what is now happening in France. The government abandoned the besieged city of Rouen to its fate; I cannot tell you what the populace must have gone through before they surrendered. Even many Burgundian sympathizers are coming to their senses; they are learning from experience that their leader is not acting in the interests of the French people. Believe me, Monseigneur, the Duke of Burgundy has at the moment only the appearance of power. The people are clamoring for action against the English invaders; they demand that the Kingdom be defended. They already distrust Burgundy more than you can imagine. If I wanted to give you a truthful answer, I will have to say this—the situation over there is miserable. King Henry is gaining ground daily and it looks as though his demands will shortly be flatly accepted by Burgundy and the Queen—God only knows on what terms. But all France will know, Monseigneur, that those who want to fight to keep the lawful government can find a place under the banner of Orléans. And apropos of this, I find it most auspicious that Monseigneur the Dauphin is in our ranks—"

"That is enough. Messire!" Waterton cries angrily. He walks over and opens the door. "The interview is over. I doubt greatly that you will have the opportunity to speak with Monseigneur again. You do him more harm than good by behaving in this way. It's not my fault if you did not come prepared to settle your business affairs."

The prisoner has risen too. He holds his hand out for the Chancellor's farewell.

"Cousinot," he says, looking his visitor calmly in the eye, "here are my orders for my brothers of Vertus and Dunois, for my captains and officers and all my allies, vassals and partisans: I wish them to place themselves completely under the authority of Monseigneur the Dauphin and his council. If I understand you correctly, Cousinot, our party has become the party of the Dauphin and of France. I can do little but pray God to help Monseigneur de Viennois and ourselves to uphold the honor of the Kingdom and to show them the road which leads out of the wilderness. Urge my brothers to place the interests of the Dauphin above all else. If this should mean a delay in my deliverance, so be it, in God's name. Send this to my wife, if the occasion arises."

Waterton takes the stiff rolled parchment from the prisoner and unrolls it. When he sees it is only verses, he rolls it up again and hands it to Cousinot with a shrug.

"Tell her that I am well," the young man goes on. "Other than that, I have nothing more to say. God be with you, Cousinot. I am exceedingly grateful to you for your loyalty and your service. Perhaps we shall meet again—perhaps not."

The Chancellor kneels before his lord and salutes him with great courtly deference. Suddenly he knows with certainty that he will never see the Duke again. He would like to say something, to express somehow the affection for the young man which he has felt from the days when he served the Lady of Orléans and her son for the first time. At this moment he recalls vividly the assembly in Paris at which the Abbé de Sérizy had delivered his impassioned defense of the Duke of Orléans; it is as though he sees Valentine sitting once more among the hostile courtiers with her son at her right hand. Again through Cousinot's head flash the words he murmured when he first saw the somber lad in mourning: "These are exceptionally young shoulders to bear the weight of such an inheritance; I fear that Monseigneur will sink beneath it." He cannot hide from himself the fact that his lord has staggered under the burden; he searches for words to express his devotion in spite of everything to the young man who has demonstrated at the least a great dignity, uncommon in one of his age.

"Monseigneur, forgive me if I have ever doubted the wisdom of your views, of your actions. I have often argued against your proposals."

Waterton, who is standing by the door, snaps his fingers. The prisoner helps his visitor rise and leads him himself a few steps to the entrance.

"I am well aware of what you want to say, Cousinot," he says; his nostrils quiver in his light, somewhat bitter, laughter. "You need not apologize. We live in stormy times which demand great men, capable leaders. It is my misfortune that I am neither a great man nor an able leader, Cousinot: I am only a man of good will, but the political game is beyond my comprehension. I don't have the ability to turn cards to my advantage. Go now, my dearest friend, God be with you and with France . . . Remember my brother of Angoulême," he calls out before the heavy door slams shut behind Waterton and Cousinot. In the gloom of the hallway he sees the face of the departing Chancellor for the last time. He raises his hand in salute. Then he is alone again.

Je fu en fleur ou temps passé d'enfance,	I was in blossom in my childhood,
Et puis aprés devins fruit en jeunesse;	But before I could come to fruition I was knocked, green and unripe from the tree
Lors m'abaty de l'arbre de Plaisance,	Of Plaisance by my mistress Folly;
Vert et non meur, Folie, mà maistresse.	Therefore Reason who redresses everything
Et pour cela, Raison qui tout redresse	At her pleasure, without wrong or misprision,
A son plasir, sans tort ou mesprison,	Rightly in her very great wisdom
M'a a bon droit, par sa tresgrant sagesse,	Set me to ripen in the straw of prison.
Mis pour meurir ou feurre de prison.	
En ce j'ay fait longue continuance,	Here I have stayed since that time,
Sans estre mis a l'essor de Largesse;	Not allowed to soar into Freedom;
J'en suy contant et tiens que, sans doubtance,	I am content and think without doubt
C'est pour le mieulx, combien que par peresse	That it is for the best, although disuse
Deviens fletry et tire vers vieillesse.	Has caused me to become wrinkled with age.
Assez estaint est en moy le tison	The torch of foolish desire has almost
De sot desir, puis qu'ay esté en presse	Burned out in me since I have been stored away,
Mis pour meurir ou feurre de prison.	Set to ripen in the straw of prison.
Dieu nous doint paix, car c'est ma desirance!	God give us peace, for that is my desire!
Adonc seray en l'eaue de Liesse	Then the waters of Delight will soon
Tost refreschi, et au souleil de France	Refresh me and the sunlight of France
Bien nettié du moisy de Tristesse;	Clean the mould of Sadness from me;

J'attens Bon Temps, endurant en
    humblesse.
Car j'ay espoir que Dieu ma
    guerison
Ordonnera; pour ce, m'a sa haultesse
Mis pour meurir ou feurre de
    prison.

Fruit suis d'yver qui a meins de
    tendresse
Que fruit d'esté; si suis en garnison,
Pour amolir ma trop verde duresse,
Mis pour meurir ou feurre de
    prison.

Humbly, I endure to await the
    Good Days,
For I hope that God will cure me;
He must have intended this when
    He
Set me to ripen in the straw of
    prison.

I am a winter fruit, less tender
Than summer fruit, so I am kept in
    store
To soften, to become less green and
    hard,
Set to ripen in the straw of prison.

Silence reigns in the tower chamber of Pontefract. Never has it been so difficult to endure as in the days following Cousinot's visit. Once again the lonely tenant is restless: books cannot distract him, he cannot forget himself in the polishing of verses, he tries without success, by thinking and writing about Bonne, to regain the near contentment he felt before the Chancellor's arrival. His desires were the desires of love; his sorrow mostly regret for the happiness which had so quickly fled, and dread that he would experience this happiness no more. But despite the bittersweet memories, despite melancholy and fits of violent despair, life had never seemed to him to be intolerable. He had spent his days in stagnation; only effortless song moved him—and yet in spite of all this he had had a vague feeling of satisfaction. But now he cannot recover that blessed calm, that indifference to the world and its turbulence. He is forced to think constantly of what Cousinot had said. He is tormented by concern: anxiety for Bonne and the fate which has befallen her—the fate of an impoverished woman who must seek shelter in a convent; anxiety for Philippe and Dunois who have inherited the heavy threefold task of guarding the dukedom, collecting ransom, fulfilling feudal obligations; anxiety for the defenceless little girls in Blois, anxiety for the outraged and violated Kingdom of France. Since his earliest childhood, he had always punctiliously performed his religious devotions without, however, becoming emotionally involved in the significance of prayer and ritual. Year in, year out, filled with reverence, he had attended the ceremonies, public and private, which play so great a part in the life of a Duke of Orléans: the flicker of candles, the smell of incense, the singing of the mass and the glow of gold and rich colors were somewhat intoxicating to a mind so amenable to beauty as his. He knows well the concentration of prayer, the emotion caused by the words of Our Lord—but it is only now in this period of his imprisonment that he becomes fully conscious of the suffering of Christ—he can experience now what was formerly only a vague notion.

Here in this chamber of Pontefract he offers prayers, morning, noon and evening, to the image of the crucified Christ which stands on a table before an open triptych of painted wood. For the first time he understands, in the deepest recesses of his heart, the meaning of the figure nailed to the Cross—the wounded, emaciated limbs, carved faithfully from ivory, contorted on the Cross in more than physical pain. The prisoner raises his eyes to the image and sees on the crucifix the dead of the battlefields, the tortured inhabitants of Soissons, Saint-Denis and all the other cities occupied and ravaged by soldiers; he sees the stiffening corpses of victims of cruel warfare—the dead children, the ravished women; he sees finally the image of the horrors he knows only from hearsay: the dry moats outside besieged Rouen where women, children and old people huddled together for days, half-naked under the open sky, driven out of the city gates by the starving garrison, hurled back by the besiegers, condemned to rot like garbage.

The courtly emblems recede for an instant; he cannot express in the elegant and melancholy language of the love couplets dedicated to Bonne, the sensations which now overcome him. The self-possession so carefully cultivated and assiduously maintained forsakes him as it did at the time of his mother's death, the rapine of Saint-Denis, the murders at Soissons, the desperate combat in the field of Agincourt. He paces restlessly back and forth; a thousand plans, a thousand thoughts, flash furiously through his brain. He wants to break out of this prison, to be free of the oppressive stone walls around him, at whatever cost. He wants to escape and, with his newly won insight and sense of responsibility, put himself in the service of his country, its defenceless King and ignorant Dauphin.

But the door, banded with iron hoops, remains firmly closed; the grating before the window does not budge, well-armed guards who understand no French replace each other on the small landing before his door. From time to time the valet enters, or Waterton, or an officer of the watch; always the wind, the mice behind the wainscoting, the rain, the indeterminate sounds which are often heard in old walls. He knows that in this castle of Pontefract, King Richard died suddenly twenty years before, under mysterious circumstances—how? Why? He has heard the rumors; now that Henry reigns, the son of the usurper, no one dares to rake up these tales, but the memory hovers over Pontefract.

Suddenly he must recall the words which he overheard when he was a child; he hears his father's voice murmur about solitary confinement in darkness, of hunger, of massive brutal chains. Pontefract—Pontefract ... the word once echoed over the ducal tables at Asnières and Beaumont, in the quiet of Lady Valentine's bedchamber. A word like any other word to the child who listens casually; nothing more than a sound conveying a vague sense of menace. Now the prisoner thinks of his royal predecessor; was it perhaps here, on this spot, that Richard, weighed down with jangling chains, waited for the end? The Richard of whom he has heard from his first wife Isabelle ... a man who, without pity, orders the peers of his kingdom to be summarily executed, but who, when he goes off to war, takes his leave with kisses and tears ...

He tosses uneasily from one side to the other of his bed. Will it go with him as it once went with Richard? Do darkness, hunger and thirst await him too? Or perhaps an assassin's dagger—poisoned food? Doesn't King Henry know as well as he himself that it can take a very long time for the ransom to be collected—and would the Englishman release his captive even if he were offered the whole amount at once?

The weeks glide by, shrouded in gloom and uncertainty. Suddenly there is a perceptible change: Sir Robert Waterton, who until now has visited the prisoner daily for the sole purpose of inquiring dutifully after the latter's health, finding out if he has any feasible requests, and checking on the situation in general—Sir Robert Waterton one afternoon—and soon by chance every afternoon—pays a fairly prolonged visit. At first he makes a visible effort to throw off the cold, official demeanor of the warden, to become suddenly courteous and chatty. On these occasions he does not come in cuirass and coat of mail, but dresses as a courtier. The multi-colored garments make him look heavier and broader; it is obvious that he is uncomfortable in his long overgarment and velvet hat with scalloped lappets, all brand-new and cut according to the latest French fashion. He still wears his red-brown hair long. He walks toward the prisoner, frowning, but with a forced smile. Two servants from Waterton's household carry wooden trays heaped with fruit, wine, and cake, and place these upon the table.

The young man who stands reading at his desk looks up with raised brows. Finally he accepts Waterton's invitation to take a seat; oddly, the knight has dropped his reserve. He no longer behaves toward his noble guest like a prison keeper, but like a host. The two discuss the weather, the hunt, horses and dogs, weapons—even, casually, books. Waterton does not like to read. They drink together and after a while a chessboard is fetched. The knight's game reflects his character: he is crude, without guile and purposefully deliberate. The prisoner, a skilled chess player since childhood, wins effortlessly again and again. In this way a considerable amount of time passes. Again Waterton visits the young man. They chat, drink and play chess, the knight behaving with forced joviality, the Duke with obvious mistrust beneath his cautious manner. Politics is not mentioned, although more than once the conversation seems to be tending in that direction. Waterton's clear anxiety to avoid that precise subject increases the prisoner's suspicion.

When for several weeks the knight has spent the late afternoon hours with him in this way, the prisoner knows with certainty that these visits have a definite purpose, that wine and friendly conversation are intended to pave the way . . . to what? Charles waits; from time to time he watches his warden attentively, trying to read something in the small greenish eyes which are sometimes fixed upon the chess pieces in almost childish desperation. At long last one day, Waterton begins to talk about the military situation in France in a tone which is too emphatically indifferent to be genuine. He gives an imposingly long list of names: the cities in Normandy and Picardy which are occupied by the English—some after siege, the most, however, after a pragmatic surrender by the citizens.

"The populace knows that King Henry permits no plunder, his soldiers are well-disciplined," says Waterton. "The people can continue to cultivate their fields and carry on trade. They will quickly see that King Henry's government provides them with security and prosperity."

Charles does not reply; he sits staring at his silver goblet, which he turns slowly between his thumb and forefinger. Waterton continues.

"In any case it's senseless for the cities to offer resistance. Sooner or later they must lay down their arms; no one will be able to help them—not the government, not anyone acting in the name of the Dauphin and your—forgive me—*his* party. I doubt, for that matter, I doubt whether any auxiliary armies could check King Henry's advance. Our troops are exceptionally well-trained, and our methods of combat are different, better than those which are clung to on the continent.

"Indeed, it has become very clear in the course of the last hundred years that methods of waging war have changed, my lord. It is generally held here that war is not a tourney; the time is over when battles are fought at prearranged places according to prescribed rules. Speed and efficiency and equipment mean more than a pretty show of arms. I continue to be surprised that in France they refuse to see this. Take the siege of Rouen—there stood the lads again upon the ramparts with catapults and barrels of pitch—mere expedients that could cover only very short distances and only against attacks on solid ground. But King Henry has ended this obsolete custom of literally storming a fortress. Have you heard anything yet about this new method? He makes use of what we call trenches, in which the men are protected from projectiles. Behind the trenches we mount heavy weapons—great machines that fling stones over a distance. It's remarkable that you have not thought of this yourselves."

"Probably we will learn from King Henry's victories," Charles replies with a slight ironic smile. "One could hardly remain blind to the advantages of your methods of warfare. Harsh tutors produce the most diligent pupils, as you know."

"Hm." Waterton casts a quick glance at his companion. "Do you believe then, my lord, that before long France will offer an organized resistance? Perhaps you are better informed about the situation there than I?"

Something in the knight's tone makes the prisoner look up.

"I thought that King Henry was at the point of concluding certain agreements with those who—according to him—represent the French Crown," he says smoothly, but his dark brown eyes suddenly become extremely sharp and vigilant. He sees suspicion, curiosity and some suspense in the Englishman's gaze. The conversation, stumbling until now, takes a decisive turn. Although Waterton does not admit it in so many words and lets no information drop, Charles senses what is happening in France. The talks between King Henry and the French government have broken down—a hitch has occurred somewhere—but where? Waterton does not seem unwilling to give him a hint about where the cause of the difficulty lies, and soon the young man knows how he must interpret his warden's remarks: Burgundy, in exchange for complying with King Henry's wishes, has made certain demands, and the King finds these demands excessive and, moreover, dangerous. If France will not give herself willingly, she must be taken by force. But that is possible only if Burgundy remains neutral. If Burgundy exchanges his neutrality for hostility to the English, King Henry will need the help of another French party in order to hold his ground.

Slowly but surely the prisoner manages to learn the truth behind Waterton's words: Burgundy seeks an approach to the Dauphin for greater security. He can do this now, because the Dauphin's party no longer carries the stamp of Orléans or Armagnac. It is also clear what King Henry is aiming at—since he is uncertain about Burgundy's intentions, he turns anew to the only one who could cooperate with him to influence the Dauphin: Orléans.

The prisoner manages during the course of this conversation to learn still more. Waterton repeatedly shows an unusual interest in Monseigneur's short-lived contact with the man who calls himself the King of Scotland.

"It was no secret to us that—by means of gestures—Your Grace was able to hold conversations with James during the last months of his residence in the Tower," he says.

"Yes, I guessed as much when the King of Scotland was transferred to Windsor," the prisoner answers, with a smile. "I'm very sorry. Now I shall never have the opportunity to return the book which he so kindly lent me."

Waterton's eyes rest on the table where the manuscripts are piled. The young man beckons to his servant who stands near the door with both of Waterton's retainers, ready to serve their masters if they want anything.

"Give me the King of Scotland's book."

Waterton frowns suspiciously when Boethius' Consolation of Philosophy is placed before him. The prisoner turns to the fly-leaf and points out five or six lines written in the King's own hand.

"Will you do me the favor, Sir Robert, of telling me what is written there?"

The knight bends quickly over the book; his eagerness convinces the prisoner that suspicions have been entertained about the extremely brief friendship between the two princely exiles. After a few moments Waterton looks up.

"It is a poem," he says curtly, but not without a spark of amusement in his small green eyes.

"I thought so too. Please be good enough to translate it for me, Messire. You know that I also divert myself with rhymes. I am naturally interested in the work of a colleague."

Waterton strokes his beard; finally he shrugs and complies with the request. He reads aloud in his somewhat hesitant, stiff French.

" 'Come, all who wish to greet these May mornings . . . The hour of good fortune has struck for you . . . Sing with me: go hence, winter, be off. Come, summer, time of sweet sunny days.' "

"Well, well." The prisoner smiles. "That is prettily put. It has been worth waiting two long years for such a message."

"What do you mean by that?" Waterton asks sharply, slamming the book shut. "Do these words perhaps have a meaning known only to you and James of Scotland?"

The young man raises his brows and his smile vanishes.

"Now it is clear to me what you are aiming at, Sir Robert, but I'm afraid that this time you're on the wrong track. I have had no opportunity to correspond with King James and one cannot discuss politics in sign language."

"*King* James?" says Waterton, looking at him askance. He sighs; the task which King Henry has entrusted to him is far from easy. To fight, organize, protect fortresses, exercise surveillance—these are things Waterton can do competently. But this wary fumbling behind the mask of polite conversation, these diplomatic skirmishes, go against his grain. The other will not commit himself. Waterton has known that from the beginning. In his reports he customarily characterizes the prisoner as courteous, self-controlled, mild-mannered and apparently co-operative—in short, a completely inscrutable character; he concludes from this that there is something hidden here.

He tells the King the results of the conversation—an extremely meager report. "Monseigneur does not mention it, but one should not conclude from this that in spite of all precautions he is not or has not been in touch with the Dauphin of France or the Pretender to the Scottish throne. He appears to know nothing about the national disturbances in Scotland. He seems to be tranquil as usual, reads, writes, stands and stares for long hours out the window. During interviews he behaves as though he does not understand Your Majesty's purpose."

King Henry's reply suggests a new task for Waterton.

"Win his confidence. Give him more freedom. Invite him to your house. Make him realize that it is of the greatest importance to him to conclude a treaty with Us."

Charles d'Orléans walked slowly back and forth in the orchard of Pontefract; although he had been permitted these strolls for some time now, he was surprised each time anew by the freshness and fragrance of the air. He could hardly believe that he could at one time have experienced this pleasure without restraint. He had gone through the seasons burdened always with cares and worries; he had noticed only incidentally the beauty of leaf and flower, the happiness that came from feeling the sun on one's face, of inhaling deeply the odors of earth and green grass.

He was not alone; Sir Robert Waterton's wife walked beside him, carefully holding her dress away from the dewy grass so that the hem would not get wet. Waterton's children, two boys and a small girl, ran in front of the grown-ups, romping and shrieking as healthy children do. An abundance of still-green apples and pears hung from the trees; the air was filled with the tart scent of unripe fruit. Although the orchard was large and well-tended, the soil was obviously poor: the grass was scanty, the apple trees were stunted.

The garden lay in the lea of Pontefract against the ramparts but inside the castle moat; the high walls of the castle were overgrown here with ivy. Close to the water's edge was Lady Waterton's flower garden, where wild roses and foxglove tried to blossom. Charles remembered the magnificent gardens of Saint-Pol and Vincennes, but he praised the flower beds of Pontefract's Lady; it was apparent that they were the result of the expenditure of a great deal of loving care and that she was proud of them. She was still a young woman, not much older than Charles himself. She had bright blue eyes and fresh cheeks and the hair which peeked from under her headdress was jet black. That hair, that quick trusting smile, and something about the way she walked, reminded him constantly of Bonne.

The first time he saw Lady Waterton he had been struck with pained surprise at the resemblance; for a moment he could not take his eyes from her. Sometimes when she walked beside him without turning her head toward him, it seemed to him that he was walking beside Bonne herself. He was conscious of her graceful movements, of the luster of her black hair—burning desire consumed him then. He had to exert the utmost self-control to restrain himself from seizing her in his arms to test the illusion by touch or embrace. But when she spoke in her laborious, somewhat twisted French, in her high, timid voice, he returned to reality. She was a stranger; her eyes were bright but rather shallow and her mouth was thin-lipped. Waterton, who was usually busy in the mornings, had undoubtedly instructed his wife to accompany the noble prisoner on his walks; her presence and the children's were probably intended to help the young man to forget that, outside the low wall of the orchard and kitchen garden, an armed guard was standing.

Lady Waterton, who had never participated in court life and who had a diffident nature, performed her task with reluctance at first, but she soon decided that it was not so difficult as she had feared it would be to keep Monseigneur amused. He was young, courteous and unassuming, and he hit it off very well with the children. At first his foreign gallantry embarrassed her; she was not accustomed to receiving so many compliments. But the Duke's friendliness won the day; gradually she lost her shyness and chattered with him as eagerly as she did with her children and her chambermaid. Charles found her stories delightful. Her restricted view, the relative insignificance of her experience, provided exactly the diversion which he needed. She told him things her children had said and done, she described dramatically how a cat had attempted to pounce on her pet bird, how the fabric on her loom was progressing. She asked him a number of questions too: was it true that the women at the French court wore trains six feet long and hats two ells high? Was Queen Isabeau really so fat that she had to be pushed around in a wheelchair? Had she heard correctly that there was a market in France where servants and servantmaids were put up for auction?

Smiling, Charles answered all these questions in the affirmative; how far away, how ludicrous, court life and street brawls over there seemed to him as he walked under these fresh fragrant trees. Thus he passed nearly every beautiful day in the orchard of Pontefract in the company of Waterton's family. The children were greatly attached to Charles, although they could not talk with him. They knew no French and invariably burst out laughing when Charles tried to speak to them in English.

Once when the children were not present, the time spent with Waterton's wife took on a different character: despite the mutual efforts to carry on a light and unconstrained conversation, an awkward silence fell between them from time to time. Under the low, leafy roof of the orchard, or on the stone benches in the flower garden, Charles became conscious of something which he had almost forgotten in the solitude of his tower chamber: he was a healthy young man. His blood could find resignation less quickly than his heart, and his heart, God knew, was still filled with as much pain and disquietude as on the first day after Agincourt. The emblematic figures which had peopled his dream world were less seductive than the fresh young woman beside him, who looked so much like Bonne. To a certain extent it was his longing for Bonne which attracted him to Lady Waterton. He was quite aware that he could not call this feeling love. The fear of disillusionment which irrevocably follows upon sated desire kept him from paying court to her in earnest. Further, he had no desire to offend Waterton. But he was well aware of the pitfalls hidden in these encounters. It did not escape him that Waterton's wife took pains to please him, that she secretly watched him from the corner of her eye when they walked together. He often dined now with the knight and his lady; after dinner they played chess. On rare occasions they spoke more frankly now about politics.

Waterton liked his prisoner very well, although he did not want to admit it. He thought that once one became accustomed to Monseigneur's French manners and his great formality, one discovered behind the rigmarole a cordial and straightforward personality. A boy the Duke was not; he had apparently acquitted himself valiantly at Agincourt; further, it was undoubtedly true that he used his intelligence and managed to conduct himself in adversity like a man. Waterton punctiliously discharged the task which had been imposed upon him: to endeavor to win young Orléans for England's King. That he failed in this did not, to his surprise, either sadden or annoy him. Secretly he respected the prisoner's tenacity; courage and control were necessary for the maintenance of firm opposition during long years of solitary confinement without any practical hope of liberation. Waterton found this resistance to be senseless in itself—who could seriously stand up against the tide of King Henry's power?—but he had to admit that Orléans' conduct was chivalrous, if also useless. He noticed the change in his wife since she had been accompanying the prisoner on his walks; he saw that she sat dreaming over her needlework or prayer book, that her thoughts caused her to blush. He watched the Duke attentively, but found no reason to put an end to the friendly association. Waterton was not jealous by nature; he assumed, moreover, that his wife knew her duty and that Orléans was wise enough not to bring down a hornet's nest about his ears. However, he remained on his guard and treated his prisoner with cool restraint.

"It is a good year," said Lady Waterton, smiling, as she stood on tiptoe and bent the branches of a ripe pear tree sideways. "We're not always certain for long about the harvest here. This is a barren country, Monseigneur. Our summers are rarely warm and dry enough and there is a cold wind in every season."

"I have noticed that, Lady," Charles replied. She looked at him over her shoulder.

"But you haven't been behind those hills there. It is swamp and moor, a sheer morass, inhospitable and bleak, even in midsummer. There are no areas like that in France, are there? You have plenty of vineyards and green fields, huge forests. This is a lonely, cheerless land. Those of us who live here are missing a great deal."

"Pontefract is one of the King's fortresses. Thus you are forced to remain here for my sake, isn't that right? I can only hope that King Henry will transfer me quickly to more southerly parts, Lady. Then I would not feel so guilty about your situation."

"Do you believe what people say, that we here in England have more sluggish blood and less grace and merriment than people in other lands?"

Charles took the hand which she extended to him and led her under the arch of fruit trees to the flower garden; behind the green currant bushes the roses glowed. The children were kneeling in the grass at the water's edge and throwing stones and twigs into the moat.

"I can hardly judge that, Lady, for I myself have had little opportunity to learn what you call grace and merriment. I believe, though, that our blood is not governed by wind and cold or loneliness but rather by the strength of our emotions."

Lady Waterton sighed; her fingers moved involuntarily over Charles' palm. As soon as she became aware of this, she blushed and glanced in quick confusion at her children. She and Charles sat down in silence on the bench. The young man gazed at the distant hills, tinted lavender in the morning light. Inhospitable swampy moor country, he thought, they have packed me well away in Ultima Thule. I could not escape even if they let me.

He felt the warmth of Lady Waterton's arm against his side. The bench was small and narrow; they were forced to sit more closely together than good manners allowed. She remained motionless, her eyes cast demurely down at the flowers in her hand, but Charles knew that she wanted him, with all her heart, to be aware of her proximity. He turned toward her, he saw the black glossy bound tresses resting against her fresh cheek. He saw too how under her innocent lowered eyelids and quivering lashes, her glance was filled with tense expectation. Charles, who was a witness, practically daily, of Waterton's somewhat rough, kindly indifference toward his wife, felt some compassion for her. Pity and lust are handy bedfellows, he thought with irony. He rose so abruptly, despite his politely apologetic gesture, that the young woman, startled, dropped her flowers. The children came running in the hope that he would lift them in his arms and swing them around, as he so often did. But Monseigneur did not seem to be in the mood for roughhousing; he stood in silence near the rosebushes.

At mealtime Waterton arrived with important news: he could say with certainty this time that discussions between Burgundy and the Dauphin had taken place in earnest. A meeting had been convened at Montereau on the Yonne, where the Dauphin was staying temporarily.

"According to what they say, the Dauphin of France is an extremely timorous and very young man and, as you know, his Council consists almost exclusively of Armagnac sympathizers. The old Provost of Paris, Messire Tanneguy du Châtel, is his Chancellor. If these people are willing to lend their cooperation to arrange the meeting, then it is almost a foregone conclusion that the parties in this case will unite against King Henry."

Waterton paused and stared searchingly at the prisoner, his eyes narrowed between his reddish lashes.

"That is important news," Charles said.

"Hm! However much you rejoice to hear that France is apparently preparing to oppose us, do you realize the results such an alliance will have for you? Do you consider it likely that Burgundy will work for your release, or that the Dauphin will do anything for you so long as he works together with Burgundy?"

"I am convinced that I shall be forgotten." Charles smiled ironically and drank from his beaker. "So long as Monseigneur the Dauphin and the Duke of Burgundy serve the same interests, they will do well to forget that I too belong to their party."

"You understand this then?" Waterton went to sit down; he was becoming tense. "Don't you realize that you can no longer count on support from France and that for your own self-preservation you must take the hand which King Henry holds out to you? Don't you see that you can win only if you recognize the English claims?"

"Don't misunderstand me; I consider the news from France to be exceptionally favorable," said Charles, bowing slightly to Waterton. "I shall thank God on my knees if it is true that an end has come to the civil war and the hostilities between the King's vassals. I would consider myself blessed if my freedom was the price for the unity of the Kingdom."

"Won't you think it over thoroughly once more, my lord?" Waterton asked, after a brief pause. "You understand, surely, that they are going to ask me very soon for your reply. Wouldn't it be a good idea if before you decide, you exchange some thoughts with your brother Monseigneur d'Angoulême about this matter? Perhaps his opinion differs from yours."

"My brother thinks as I do."

The knight began to reply, but Charles shook his head. "Sir Robert, it is futile to speak any further about this."

"But—by Saint George and Our Lady, do you find it so pleasant to sit in confinement year in and year out?" Waterton struck the table with both fists; the beakers shivered. "Have you had enough of life, do you wish then to attempt nothing new?"

"Ah . . ." Charles' pale lips twitched in a fleeting smile. "It is my misfortune to be of royal blood, Messire. I must certainly uphold my position whether I want to or not. No one has ever asked me what I personally would enjoy doing. Since I was never truly able to render my country a service in the days when I was still in touch with things, I must do what I can now that I am condemned to patient long suffering. The least anyone can ask of me is that I be loyal to those parties in my country which support the royal House."

"Even if those parties do not lift a finger to bring about your release?" Waterton snorted in scornful anger and emptied his beaker at one draught.

"Messire, to change the subject—I would consider it a great honor if you would permit me to offer a few gifts to Madame your wife and your children."

Charles signalled to Chomery, who stood behind him. The servant immediately removed a box from his girdle and put it on the table before the young man.

"While I was still in London I was sent a few trifles from Blois," Charles explained. He brought forth a gold drinking cup and three belts of worked silver. "Lady, you would do me a great favor if you would accept these things from me for yourself and your children."

The young woman flushed violently. She moved to put out her hand but when she saw Waterton watching her sharply, she stopped and lowered her eyes. The knight snapped his fingers; the servants who had been waiting at the table retreated to the door.

"Forgive me, Monseigneur," Waterton said curtly. "But these are rather costly gifts which you offer my wife. Perhaps this is the custom in France, but here we are not so open-handed without sufficient reason."

"But there is a reason." The young man looked calmly at Waterton. "These are farewell gifts."

"So far as I know, there has been no talk of your leaving us."

"No." Charles looked into his eyes. "But I greatly fear that I have trespassed far too frequently and too long on Madame your wife's time, Sir Robert. In the pleasure I derived from her delightful company, I have perhaps forgotten that she has things to do apart from strolling in the orchard with an idle lord, which I have now become. Perhaps, too, I have caused your young sons to neglect their morning lessons. You have done me a kindness for which I shall remain fervently thankful to you always. I entreat you as a personal favor, Messire, to let me give these gifts—a token of thanks for some sunny, carefree hours."

Waterton cleared his throat. He accepted the drinking cup and the silver belts from Charles, looked appreciatively at them, and then pushed them across the table to his wife, who sat still unmoving and with downcast eyes beside him. "Thank Monseigneur, my love."

Lady Waterton whispered a few words; her small mouth quivered; she had great difficulty repressing tears of shame and frustration. Charles, who wished to spare her further vexation, asked Waterton to excuse him from the game of chess.

"I shall take you to your room," said Waterton, rising. Both men, followed by the armed guards who were never far away, went through the corridors and series of chambers of Pontefract, hollow empty stone chambers for the most part, unheated and unfurnished. Charles cast a sidelong glance at his warden; he did not yet know how Waterton was reacting to his behavior. The knight remained silent, but when he stood in the tower chamber, at the point of taking his farewell, he said curtly, "You cannot go on without exercise. I can imagine that you have no appetite to walk up and down between the currant bushes below. I have a good horse for you. Do me the honor of going riding with me every day, my lord. In the autumn we can also go hunting—there are fowl in the swamps. It does not matter what the King's orders are," he added with deliberate roughness, when Charles made a movement of surprise. "I take this upon my own responsibility. Good night, my lord."

From a decree of the Council, December, 1419:
". . . that Robert Waterton, knight, is to be relieved of his office; that the keeping of Charles, Duke of Orléans, is henceforth entrusted to Sir Thomas Burton."

En la forest de Longue Actente,
Chevauchant par divers sentiers
M'en voys, ceste année presente,
Ou voyage de Desiriers.
Devant sont allez mes fourriers
Pour appareiller mon logis
En la cité de Destinee;
Et pour mon cueur et moy ont pris
L'ostellerie de Pensee.

. . .

In the forest of Long Awaiting,
Riding by varying pathways
I set out in this present year
On the journey of Desire.
My stewards have gone on ahead
To prepare my lodging
In the city of Destiny,
And they have taken for me and my heart,
The hostelry of Thought.

. . .

Je mayne des chevaulx quarente
Et autant pour mes officiers,
Voire, par Dieu, plus de soixante,
Sans les bagaiges et sommiers.
Loger nous fauldra par quartiers,
Se les hostelz sont trop petis;
Toutesfoiz, pour une vespree,
En gré prendray, soit mieulx ou pis,
L'ostellerie de Pensee.

I bring with me forty horses
And enough for my officials,
In fact, by God, more than sixty,
Without the pack animals and
  mules.
We shall need quarters about the
  town
If the inns are too small;
However for one evening,
For better or for worse, I shall
  gladly accept
The hostelry of Thought.

Prince, vray Dieu de paradis,
Vostre grace me soit donnee,
Telle que treuve, a mon devis,
L'ostellerie de Pensee.

Prince, true God of Paradise,
Bestow Your grace upon me,
That I may find, as I desire,
The hostelry of Thought.

The bolts were pushed aside, the key rasped in the great lock. Charles d'Orléans, who stood before his reading desk with his back to the door, closed his book; he knew who had entered there. Thomas Burton brought with him, as always, a smell of horses and the outdoors; he always wore leather and mail as a sign of his military office. After a brief greeting, he unrolled a large sheet of parchment and said, "Be so kind, my lord, as to listen to this news which I have received from London. The King has instructed me to inform you about the treaty which the King of France has made with him at Troyes on the twenty-first of May of this year."

"Pray continue, Messire." Charles seated himself on the bench beside the table and fixed his eye on the light rectangle of the window. Thomas Burton cleared his throat, put his gloves under his arm so that he could wield the parchment unhindered and began to read in a dry, cold voice:

"We, Charles, by the grace of God King of France, have found it fit and hereby approve and resolve:

"That with an eye upon the forthcoming marriage between Our beloved son, Henry, King of England, heir and regent of France, and Our dearly beloved Daughter Catherine, our subjects and those of Our aforesaid Son can traffic with one another both on this and on the other side of the sea.

"That directly after Our death the Crown and mastery of France with all the rights and privileges therein shall pass over for good to Our Son, the aforesaid Henry and his heirs.

"That since We are hindered from holding sway by the state of Our health, the royal authority shall, during Our lifetime, be exercised by Our Son, the aforesaid Henry.

"That our aforementioned Son shall labor with all his strength to bring again to Our obedience all cities, towns, fortresses, regions and subjects in Our realm which now show themselves to be rebellious and willing to choose the side of that party which is customarily called the party of the Dauphin and Armagnac.

"That considering the crimes and transgressions committed in Our realm by him who calls himself Charles the Dauphin, We declare that We and Our above-mentioned Son and likewise Our beloved Cousin, Philippe, Duke of Burgundy, shall in no manner negotiate with the aforesaid Charles."

"One moment, Messire," said Charles, raising his hands. "Perhaps you can give me some information here. How is it possible that those who have drawn up this pact have overlooked the rights and lawful claims of Monseigneur the Dauphin?"

"Lawful?" Burton let the parchment drop and eyed the prisoner coldly. "He who at present calls himself Dauphin has no lawful claim to the throne of France, my lord."

"Explain that to me, if you please." Charles felt his self-possession beginning to desert him. "Monseigneur the Dauphin is still the King's only living son?"

Burton shrugged.

"Some doubt has arisen on that precise point," he said casually, while he rolled up the parchment again. "There is evidence that the young man is not the King's son."

Charles stood up. "And who dares to say that?"

"Queen Isabeau herself," replied the knight, with raised brows, as though he found the subject extremely painful. "No one can know better than she."

It was silent in the room for a considerable time. The prisoner walked to the window and looked out; Burton stood on the same spot and impatiently tapped the roll of parchment against the palm of his hand.

"I thought that I had experienced many repulsive things in my life," Charles said at last, without turning round. "'But this really is the worst of all. That a mother could betray her son in such a manner, that a wife could wound her husband so deeply—that is something I would never have thought possible. Has the Queen been so obliging as to reveal the name of the man who enjoys the honor of being the father of France's bastard?"

"There was no need for Her Majesty to do so," replied Burton, apparently indifferent, in the cold, matter-of-fact tone which he invariably employed in conversation with the prisoner. "It is a well-known fact that in the year of the so-called Dauphin's birth, the notorious friendship began between the Queen of France and your late father."

A shudder went through Charles; he clenched his fists on the window sill. Burton had expected an outburst of fear or rage; he knew quite well that he could not have hurt his prisoner more deeply than by uttering these words. The Englishman hesitated. It was almost unthinkable that a man of honor should submit to such an affront. But the man who stood before the window did not move and did not speak.

Burton drew himself up stiffly and said, "I have a further duty to inform you that the Duke of Burgundy was murdered at Montereau on the twentieth of August."

France, jadis on te souloit nommer,
En tous pays, le tresor de noblesse,
Car un chascun povoit en toy
   trouver
Bonté, honneur, loyauté, gentillesse,
Clergie, sens, courtoisie, processe.
Tous estrangiers amoient te suir;
Et maintenant voy, dont j'ay
   desplaisance,
Qu'il te couvient maint grief mal
   soustenir,
Trescrestien, franc royaume de
   France!

Scez tu dont vient ton mal, a vray
   parler?
Congnois tu point pourquoy es en
   tristesse?
Conter le vueil, pour vers toy
   m'acquiter,

France, in times gone by men
   everywhere
Called you the treasure of nobility,
Perceived in you goodness, honor,
Loyalty, learning, wit and prowess;
They burned to follow you.
And now it saddens me to see
The painful hurt that you must
   suffer,
Most Christian, freeborn realm of
   France!

Do you know in truth whence
   comes your ill?
Don't you know why you are
   suffering?
It is my duty to tell you;
You will be wise to listen to me.

Escoutes moy et tu feras sagesse.
Ton grant ourgueil, glotonnie, peresse,
Couvoitise, sans justice tenir,
Et luxure, dont as eu abondance,
Ont pourchacié vers Dieu de te punir,
Trescretien, franc royaume de France!

. . .

You are proud, gluttonous, slothful
And covetous without regard for justice;
You luxuriate in lechery.
Thus God has moved to punish you,
Most Christian, freeborn realm of France!

. . .

Dieu a les bras ouvers pour t'acoler,
Prest d'oublier ta vie pecheresse;
Requier pardon, bien te vendra aidier
Nostre Dame, la trespuissant princesse,
Qui est ton cry et que tiens pour maistresse.
Les sains aussi te vendront secourir,
Desquelz les corps font en toy demourance.

Ne vueilles plus en ton pechié dormir,
Trescrestien, franc royaume de France!

The arms of God are open to embrace you,
He will forget your sinfulness;
Ask pardon, ask for the help of
Our Lady, that most powerful Princess,
Who is your battle cry and honored Mistress.
The saints too will come to aid you,
Whose bodies rest in your domain.
Don't remain asleep, sunken in sin,
Most Christian, freeborn realm of France!

Et je, Charles, duc d'Orleans, rimer
Voulu ces vers ou temps de ma jeunesse,
Devant chascun les vueil bien advouer,
Car prisonnier les fis, je le confesse;
Priant a Dieu, qu'avant qu'aye vieillesee,
Le temps de paix partout puist avenir,
Comme de cueur j'en ay la desirance,
Et que voye tous tes maulx brief finir,
Trescrestien, franc royaume de France!

And I, Charles, Duke of Orléans, poet,
Have written these verses when I am young,
I will avow to the whole world
And confess that I have written them in prison,
Praying to God that before I am old
Peace may have come everywhere,
As I deeply desire from my heart,
And that I may see your sufferings ended,
Most Christian, freeborn realm of France!

In the spring of 1421, Charles received a visit from one of his clerks at Blois. He scarcely knew the man; he was surprised that they had not sent him his secretary de Tuillères or Denisot, the first clerk of his chancellery. The new courier was an insignificant old monk who stared about him helplessly while he was searched by the guards. To Charles' astonishment he had brought along a small, longhaired dog which ran sniffing in through the open door of the chamber even before the watch had finished with the clerk. When Charles bent to stroke the animal, it sprang away from him.

"He allows no one to touch him without my consent, Monseigneur," said the scribe as he entered, bowing deeply. "You know me—I am Jean le Brasseur, once employed in your house chapel at Blois. Monseigneur Dunois sends me to you with money and news about the administration of your estates."

Meanwhile, Burton too had entered the chamber, along with a clerk and an interpreter. The knight observed punctiliously all instructions from London. Every word spoken by the prisoner and by his visitor must be taken down, and if the slightest effort was made to exchange information about the political or military actions of the so-called Dauphin, Burton was to interrupt the interview instantly. Only business affairs, administration of property and news of the family could be discussed. Burton looked with disdain at the messenger from Blois; he thought it amazing that this timorous dullard should have succeeded in traveling all that distance and arriving at Pontefract in one piece.

Charles sat down; the clerk stood humbly before him with the dog in his arms.

"Monseigneur," he said softly—he lisped somewhat, "I come also as the bearer of sad tidings. I have been shocked and deeply sorrowed to learn that you still know nothing about it. Monseigneur, it has pleased God to call to himself your brother, Monseigneur Philippe de Vertus."

Charles rose. The clerk went on with bowed head. "At about the time of the birth of Our Lord, we buried him in the church of Saint-Sauveur. May God give you strength to bear this affliction, my lord."

Charles made the sign of the cross, and put his hand over his eyes. He remained standing that way for a while. Death chooses his victims well—he thought—a young man in the prime of his life; Philippe, my carefree, cheerful brother, my confidant and deputy, the commander of my armies, my friend and childhood playmate.

Now the House of Orléans is represented in France by my father's bastard and two little girls. What have my brother of Angoulême and I to hope for?

"Monseigneur de Dunois has arranged everything," the clerk continued in his high-pitched voice. "In Blois and in all your remaining possessions, everything will go on as usual. Monseigneur de Vertus left a great void, but his death has caused no change in the administration of the dominions or the organization of household affairs."

For the first time Charles looked with attention at the messenger; the man kept his bulging, somewhat melancholy eyes fixed modestly on a point at the height of Charles' girdle, and he spoke in a monotonous drone, as though he were reciting a lesson he had learned by rote. Meanwhile he stroked the puppy, which was almost completely hidden in the folds of his gown. Burton was yawning openly, and the other two men made no bones about their contempt and boredom. But it seemed to Charles that the messenger from Blois was considerably less innocuous and insignificant than he wanted to appear. His whining voice was a little too exaggerated to be genuine, and in his curious bulging eye Charles could detect a vigilant glimmer.

While the clerk gave a dull, true account of the grain and wine harvest, the proceeds of tributes and taxes, expenses in connection with the restoration and maintainance of the castles and annexes, etc., Charles sat tensely watching him. From time to time the man stressed a word in a way that would be noticeable only to a native speaker of French. So under Burton's attentive eye, Charles learned many things worth knowing: out of information apparently limited to administrative matters, he managed to deduce from the messenger's intonation and the way in which he presented the news, that all the citadels of Orléans were strongly manned and fully stocked with great provisions of weapons and food, that hostile troops had invaded the northwestern border areas, that many of the Dauphin's captains and advisors were in hiding in the important cities of Charles' domains, that everywhere military preparations were being made in feverish haste, that all the money that could be squeezed from that neglected and impoverished land was being spent on arms and supplies.

"Alas, Monseigneur," the clerk concluded, while he took some grey linen bags from his girdle and offered them with a bow to

Charles, "this is all we can deliver to you at present—one hundred and eighty-four écus—perhaps it will help somewhat to ease your life here for a few months. Monseigneur de Dunois hopes with all his heart that he will be able to send you more over the course of the summer. Will you be so kind, Monseigneur, as to sign the documents which I had to hand over to Messire Burton on my arrival here? They are authorizations for Monseigneur de Dunois and two deeds for sales of lands."

"Certainly," Charles said thoughtfully. The clerk approached with humility, still holding the puppy.

"Perhaps you would like to hold the creature for a moment, Monseigneur?" asked the monk, gazing at Charles with a rather fatuous smile. He put his head on one side and held the dog out to his master. "I shall then fetch the documents from the lord clerks there, if it pleases you."

It seemed to Charles that the messenger gave a barely perceptible nod of the head. The young man took the dog and set it down beside him on the bench. It was one of those so-called decoy dogs, thin and swift, with bright eyes and a beautiful bushy tail. Charles scratched the animal behind the ears and ran his hand absently over the glossy tail. He left his hand there; a thin, hard roll was tied under the long hair. Charles looked at the monk, who bowed before him.

"A pretty puppy," he said calmly. "Is it yours?"

The clerk opened his mouth in a broad laugh.

"It goes with me everywhere, Monseigneur. If they tell me to make another journey to Pontefract, the dog will come to visit you again."

While Jean le Brasseur was getting the documents from Burton and his clerks, and occupying their attention because of his clumsiness—he dropped the pages, upset an inkwell—Charles busied himself with the dog, which remained docile while Charles, with his nails, tore the threads tying the roll of paper to the tail. When the clerk approached him again, mumbling apologies, the letter was in Charles' sleeve.

Letter from Dunois, Bastard of Orléans, to Charles, Duke of Orléans, Spring, 1421.

"Monseigneur my brother, you will of course have heard what

disasters have afflicted the Kingdom since the treaty of Troyes. King Henry fancies himself lord and master; in the Council, in the University, and in the field, his word is law. He is harsh, austere and proud—so say all who have had any personal dealings with him. Madame Catherine has given birth to a son, another reason for King Henry to think that he has checkmated Monseigneur the Dauphin for good. Monseigneur's name has been removed from the list of the King's sons inscribed on the marble tablet at Saint-Pol. Here and in the Midi we remain loyal to the lawful successor to the throne, and evil rumors are not believed. I assume you know what I am talking about. Monseigneur the Dauphin calls himself, justifiably, the Regent of France. He is eighteen years old and, it seems to me, somewhat shy and with little disposition to independent action. He lets himself be discouraged too quickly. It is our task, Monseigneur, to give him a feeling of certainty, to show him that we have his interest truly at heart. We must support him with our faith and loyalty, and our belief in his legitimate birth.

"Monseigneur, my dearest brother, it does not appear that King Henry's alliance with the new Duke of Burgundy will last long. Philippe of Burgundy does not love the English; it seems that he was treated rather rudely by Henry's envoys in Calais. From what I hear, Monseigneur always finds some excuse when Henry calls upon him to send troops—the English fight practically alone now; a Burgundian is scarcely ever seen in their ranks.

"It is our business to unite all domestic forces under one banner; now that the Kingdom is threatened with complete destruction, it is our sacred duty to maintain unity. I have heard rumors that Arthur, Count of Richmont, intends to offer his services to the Dauphin. I believe we should encourage this strongly. Before anything else I should like to see an agreement reached with Burgundy. The party of Orléans is a thing of the past, lord brother, we must recognize this. There is really no longer a reason for blood feuds since our father's murderer received his just punishment at Montereau. We must be unified if we wish to save France.

"I shall send you the messenger again soon. Have an answer ready if you possibly can and put it in his hands. He will find a way to hide your letter. God be with you, Monseigneur my brother. May He give you strength to bear your bitter lot. The war preparations go on here—you yourself would not wish anything else. But as soon as possible we shall gather the money necessary to ransom you and Monseigneur d'Angoulême. I entreat God's blessing on you. Your servant, Dunois, Bastard of Orléans."

From an official message from London to Sir Thomas Burton: September, 1422.

". . . that on this last day of August of this year of our Lord 1422, our dearly beloved most revered Sovereign and Prince, Henry V, King of England, Regent and Heir of France, departed this life in the castle of Vincennes in France, as a consequence of an intestinal disorder which he contracted during the siege of the city of Cône. The King departed this life reconciled with his Creator. On his deathbed he named as Regents over his son, from today our dearly beloved and highly honored Henry VI, the Dukes of Bedford and Gloucester, from whom you may expect instructions. In connection with the custody of the Duke of Orléans, the following: it was the late King Henry's explicit desire that the aforesaid Orléans should not be freed before the present King shall have attained his majority. If a strict stand is not taken here it is truly to be feared that the said Orléans would abuse the temporary lack of royal authority in order to join forces with those in France who do not acknowledge England's lawful demands. The Duke of Gloucester commands you accordingly to transfer the above-mentioned Orléans to the fortress of Fotherinhay in Northampton."

From the diary of a citizen of Paris, 1422:

". . . so was separated from the world the good King Charles on the 21st day of the month of October, the day of Saint Ursula and the eleven thousand Virgins, who had reigned longer than any Christian monarch in human memory, for he has been King of France for forty-three years.

"Only his chancellors, his first chamberlain, his father confessor and a few servants stood at his deathbed. He lay in state in the palace of Saint-Pol on his own bed, for he had died there; for three days he lay there with his face uncovered, with burning candles around him and a crucifix at his feet and anyone who wished could enter to see him and pray for him.

"Afterward he was laid in a leaden coffin and carried to the chapel of Saint-Pol, where he remained above the earth for twenty days until the Duke of Bedford, Regent of France, had returned from England.

"On the tenth day of November, the body of our late King was brought from his palace of Saint-Pol to the Cathedral of Notre Dame of Paris, accompanied by priests and prelates and the rector and doctors of the University. He was borne as the body of Our Lord is borne on the occasion of the feast of the Redeemer, covered with a heavy cloth of gold brocade, with a crown on his head, a scepter in his right hand, and in his left a gold and silver écu. And above him knights held a vermilion and azure canopy embroidered with golden lilies. And he wore white gloves richly encrusted with precious stones, and the body was enveloped in a mantle of royal purple trimmed with ermine. Behind the bier walked the pages and shield-bearers of the late King, followed by the Duke of Bedford, Regent of France. But there was no prince of the blood in the funeral procession, no blood relative, and that was pitiful to see. And the people of Paris, who had crowded together in great numbers when the body was carried through the streets, burst into sobs and wept and wailed as the procession passed by: 'You go in peace, but we remain behind here in misery and anguish.'

"In the church of Notre Dame two hundred torches burned; wakes were held there, masses read for the dead, and after the Mass they carried the King to the abbey of Saint-Denis to lay him in the earth. And when the King was laid in the grave, the Archbishop of Saint-Denis spoke his blessing, as is customary. And afterward the King's officers and mace-bearers broke their swords and tokens of office in two and threw them in the grave as a sign that their office had ended at the same time as the life of the King. And then the standard-bearers let their flags and banners droop. The sergeant-at-arms stepped forward, accompanied by many heralds and followers, and cried over the grave, 'May God have mercy on the soul of Charles, King of France, sixth of that name, our lawful Sovereign and Lord!' And then, 'God grant life to Henry, by the grace of God King of France and England, our Lord and Sovereign!'

"And then the banners were raised again, and those who stood around the grave called out, 'Long live the King!'

"During the bitter journey to Paris, the Regent, the Duke of Bedford, suffered the sword of the late King to be borne before him as a sign of his own dignity. The people were most angry about this, and murmured. But truly nothing can be done about it. And so ended the life of our very noble King, Charles, in the forty-third year of his reign; during the greater part of that time he had known only calamity and affliction because of the discord between his closest kinsmen. May God in his great love and compassion be merciful to his soul."

A February haze hangs over the streets of Paris and the brownish waters of the Seine. The sun struggles to break through and is visible for a moment before it is lost again in mist and clouds. Despite the damp chill, the streets on the left bank of the Seine are as filled with people as though there were to be a fête or procession. But all similarity ends with the numbers: the silent crowd which flows swiftly past the rows of houses toward the great market-halls is in neither a festive nor a pious mood. A depression hangs over the city of Paris, bleaker and more frigid than the winter mist; it is the realization of complete bankruptcy, of misery without hope. Never within memory has the city been in such dire need of spirtual and physical comfort.

The Four Horsemen of the Apocalypse, Pestilence, Famine, Death and Destruction, have ridden into the city, and will not be moved. The years are notable more for their catastrophes than for their seasons: in the winters, more severe than ever before, thousands die of the cold every day; in the summer thousands more are destroyed by plagues and diseases and—continually—by starvation. When snow comes to the surrounding fields, and the ground is frozen hard, packs of wolves descend on the suburbs, looking for food; children and all solitary homeless wanderers fall prey to these famished beasts. Food, extremely scarce, is almost priceless when it can be procured. As a consequence of war there is little money for wages, and everywhere work is undone: the fields are smothered in weeds, scythes and ploughshares rust, draughthorses and beasts of burden are butchered, barns and stables torn down to be used as kindling. Taxes become higher from day to day: Bedford needs money urgently to carry on the war—his officers and constables show no mercy. The sheriff is a pitiless man who metes out heavy physical punishment for even the slightest infraction of the laws. But the value of money has dropped; a sixteen denier coin is worth no more than two deniers, a beggar's alms.

In the summer of 1424, a swarm of locusts sweeps over the land

and blights the crops in the fields. In dull resignation the people of Paris await the winter, a long harsh winter without food, without firewood; a winter of pestilence and privation. Not a week passes without Bedford's heralds proclaiming fresh English victories to empty streets and deserted squares. And this is even more difficult to bear than cold and hunger. The knowledge that they are being overwhelmed by a foreign power, that they have been abandoned to alien rulers, the awareness of their own impotence and their defeat, deprives the people of their final hope. They have been betrayed. The rebellions and civil wars, the hardships which the country has suffered over the last hundred years seem trifling in comparison to this great infamy. France is lost, it exists no longer as an independent kingdom. There is no reason to believe that the territories occupied by England can be redeemed. Hardly anyone dares even to think of the young man in Bourges in the Midi who calls himself king and attempts to resist Bedford's troops pouring in from all sides. Has he the right to the royal title, the royal power? No one knows. The only person who can know, the Dowager-Queen Isabeau, is tucked away for good, and silent, in the heart of Saint-Pol. Her chambers can be reached only through a maze of deserted, neglected gardens and corridors. The brightly colored tapestries on the walls recall the luxurious, carefree days of the past, but the fountains are stilled, the park is a wilderness, and the windows which once glowed with festive candlelight are dark and empty.

The Queen no longer quits her apartments. Year in, year out, she sees only the walls adorned with embroidered flowers and golden doves; year in, year out, she sits motionless in her wheelchair, she who had loved to travel from Saint-Pol to Vincennes, from Vincennes to Melun, from Melun to Creil and Saint-Ouen, to Chartres and Compiègne, to castles, cloisters, cathedrals. She sits with her back to the window, staring vacantly during the long daylight hours, or she asks for food or her jewel boxes. She eats greedily and carelessly, greasy sauce trickles from her lips over her chin and her mourning dress; she gnaws the small bones of fowl and sucks out the marrow, she spits fruit stones around her. She concentrates fiercely on her jewels. Bent forward, she rummages with gouty fingers among the gold chains and the large gleaming stones; she pulls strings of pearls from the bottom of the pile; she lets fall again and again from the palm of her hand a sparkling rain of rubies and sapphires, gold coins, rings and buckles. If at these moments anyone approaches her, she dismisses him, irritably. Outside her chamber doors her servants stand listening to the jingle of gold, the rustle of ropes of pearls and necklaces. The Queen lives entirely in seclusion; she wishes to hear no news, receive no visitors. She wants to know nothing: her gold is enough for her, and her roast capons—for which, alas, she must pay more each day—and her memories.

The chamber with the flowered tapestry is peopled with silent figures: they glide without sound, almost without motion, past the woman who is sunken, heavily and clumsily, into her wheelchair: Valentine with her sad smile, the young pale Isabelle, Louis toying with his gloves, Burgundy and Margaretha, cold and judging, Bourbon and Berry, two very old men, mistrustful beneath their displays of courtliness, Jean of Burgundy with his cold eyes, the dead crown princes, thin, pale youths bowed under their heavy purple, and last of all Charles, her husband, his eyes distended in madness. It is a procession which comes and goes incessantly, a procession of mists. They do not speak to her, these quiet passersby, they do not greet her, they do not look at her. Without touching the ground they fly past her, by day, by night. They carry a faint odor of dust and decay, of the far distant past. But the Queen does not talk about this, not even to her confessor, who visits her weekly.

From letters sent secretly by Dunois, Bastard of Orléans, to Charles, Duke of Orléans in the years 1428, 1429 and 1430.

". . . we are now virtually bankrupt, Monseigneur my brother; I have little hope that fortune will smile on us in the near future. In more than fifteen years, we have not been in so bad a situation as this, and you know very well what that means. God grant that the King—for here we consider him our lawful king although he has not been crowned at Reims—will realize this and throw off his cursed irresolution. We have suffered many misfortunes because of his inability to act. It is his curse that he allows himself to be led blindly by his favorites; as long as these lords are loyal, everything goes reasonably well; but God help us when traitors predominate, and there are many of them, Monseigneur—that is why the military operations creep along; we mount no organized opposition. A skirmish here or there, nothing more; and whatever the valiant lads—especially our Scottish troops—manage to win, is immediately lost by us again because our cause has no leader. Bedford has at most

20,000 men at arms and these are spread out here and there over the occupied territories. In '24 he defeated our troops at Verneuil with an army of 5,000 men at most; it was a second Agincourt, thanks to the stupidity of the King's favorites. This is Bedford's greatest strength—that he has sharp insight, that he holds the reins firmly in his hands and through his air of self-assurance convinces friend and foe alike of England's superiority. But anyone who uses his intelligence must have seen long ago that all this is bluff, even though it is a massive bluff. We know that in England itself everything is going wrong. If I may believe the rumors, something is brewing in the government; the danger of civil war grows every day. Furthermore, no one can pretend that Burgundy has fraternal feelings toward England—on the contrary, the bonds between the two parties are so fragile that they threaten to snap at any moment.

". . . What I have long expected has happened: the English lie before Orléans under the command of William de la Pole, Earl of Suffolk. They have occupied the Tourelles fort near the bridge over the Loire and have built a great number of fortifications and ditches to the south, west and northwest of the city. If they should succeed in taking Orléans, we are lost; the English will then rule the whole region of the Loire—Touraine, Berry and the Midi.

"Although we can at the moment supply men and provisions without too much difficulty, it does not appear that the city will be able to hold out. I have been captain of the garrison here for a few months now; there are surely as many defenders as there are attackers, but the fellows inside Orléans are listless and discouraged. They have no hope for a better future, they do not believe in an ultimate victory. The populace is desperate and fearful, exhausted by long years of war. This public temper, my lord brother, will destroy us all—unless there is a miracle."

Dunois, Bastard of Orléans, did not believe in miracles; at any rate he did not believe that irresolution, timidity and stupidity could be miraculously transformed into courage, strength of mind and insight. He had, since he had served as captain of the army of the "King of Bourges", learned how to give directions in the face of the King's almost morbid impotence. He knew that this man, with his badly tainted heredity, would never put forth the vigorous effort to make himself worthy of the Crown of France. Authority was in fact divided between the King's mother-in-law, the energetic, ambitious Duchess d'Anjou, and the King's favorites, who were for the most part impoverished knights from the southern provinces, eager for their own profit. These parties did not share mutual interests; they were divided, perpetually involved in disputes and intrigues. While the English—without undue strain on their resources—drew an ever-tightening noose around the heart of France, while roaming bands of every description tormented and harassed the people, the bankrupt court at Bourges concerned itself only with petty scuffles for precedence and favors.

Dunois deliberately kept aloof from the poisonous atmosphere; when, however, his duty called him to Bourges, he armed himself with a stiff silence. He chose the company of captains like la Hire and de Broussart, men calloused and coarsened by continuous battle, unlettered and crude, but trustworthy and as hard upon themselves as upon their men. Dunois had fought side by side with these seasoned warriors against the English; at the defeats of Cravant, Ivry, Verneuil and at Montargis, the single victory, achieved with great effort. The years had passed for Dunois in a long series of sieges and battles, here and there bypassing all towns and castles near the front line, skirmishing, retreating, raiding. But what was the result of all this effort? It seemed to him that he and his comrades were like the men in the legend who attempted to build a dam of sand against the oncoming flood; his work was never completed. As soon as he turned his back the sea ate its way through his defenses again. On the ramparts of Orléans Dunois was overcome with despair. He knew that not more than 5,000 English were camped below the city, that their ranks were constantly being eroded by sickness and desertion. But still he could not persuade the people of Orléans to make any belligerent sallies against the enemy. In essence they were indifferent; they did not care whether the English took the city or not. Indeed, many believed that it would be better for them to surrender as soon as possible.

In February, 1429, Dunois learned that an English convoy was approaching the besieged city from Paris with wagons filled with salted fish for fast days. He decided to risk an attack on the convoy on its route. Messengers rode at full speed to Blois to instruct the Count de Clermont, who was stationed there with his men, to fall upon the English as they approached the city. As a result of Clermont's dawdling—he seemed to suffer from the same unfortunate Bourbon family traits as his father and grandfather before him— the enterprise justifiably failed: the French were decisively defeated, although they far outnumbered the enemy. This defeat, known as the Battle of the Herrings, had a most deleterious effect upon the morale of the troops holding Orléans.

In a final attempt to shake the King from his lethargy, Dunois sent the young captain la Hire to the castle of Chinon. La Hire found the King, timid and distracted as usual, hidden in one of the small rooms reached only through secret doors. He was distressed to hear about the debacle, but he did not know what to say, and still less what to do.

La Hire returned to Orléans bitter and angry; with a string of violent curses—no one knew them better than he—he gave an account of his visit.

"We have to allow ourselves to be butchered here, Bastard," he growled at last. "In the future the King and the fools and villains who cluster around him like lice on a sore head can do the dirty work themselves . . . unless he wants to try the peasant maid from Lorraine first—in Chinon that's all they talk about now. A courier came from Captain de Baudricourt in Vaucouleurs . . . It seems a young girl goes about there with a plan to drive the English out of France and to bring the King to Reims and the King, God keep him well, had nothing better to do than to listen to that sort of drivel. There you have all my news, Bastard."

Dunois, who sat at the table signing vouchers for the payment of wages—a final measure to keep the men satisfied—did not reply at once. He answered, without raising his eyes from the paper, only when la Hire, still cursing under his breath, was preparing to leave the room.

"Let the King divert himself in his own way, la Hire. A child who is occupied in play is no trouble. We shall do our duty, and that is enough."

Dunois spent the following days inquiring in his own way about the girl from Lorraine. He found to his amazement that the people of the city and the countryside knew already in detail about everything she had done. Stories had spread across the Loire, from Domrémy and Vaucouleurs, the district where Jeanne—for that was her name—lived. She was the daughter of a peasant, people said, a sturdy well-behaved maid who tended her father's sheep. But now she had heard voices, from God's Holy Self, or so she thought, which commanded her to free France and crown the King. Despite the protests of her parents and kinfolk, she had gone to Vaucouleurs to Captain de Baudricourt, the King's representative, to ask for safe conduct. Strange stories stubbornly circulated in hamlet and city. An old prophecy, once popular in the Lorraine borderland and now half-forgotten, was revived: a young virgin would one day appear from an oak forest to save the Kingdom. Wasn't there a grove of oaks behind Jeanne's father's property, the remnant of a vast prehistoric forest?

Dunois listened without comment to these tales; he was amused by the gullibility of the people who were ready, on the strength of an old prophecy, to see in this girl from Domrémy the long-awaited Maid who would bring salvation. What did interest and surprise him was Jeanne's courage in holding fast to her convictions in the presence of the captain at Vaucouleurs, and even face to face with the Duke of Lorraine himself. What induced these men to listen to her, to support her proposals? He perceived that, without apparently being aware of it, she had a strange power which revived hope and the expectation of great events. And upon what was this enthusiasm based? On vague rumors, a simple tale which traveled from city to city—that a peasant maid was convinced that she had been sent by God to save the Kingdom. Dunois could not deny that the deep desire in the country for peace and freedom played a considerable part in the affair; nevertheless, day by day it became clearer to him that Jeanne the Maid, as she was now called everywhere, must possess to a considerable degree what he had for years wanted for the King, the commanders of the army and even, secretly, for himself: the ability to re-animate the masses who had lapsed into despair and deep apathy.

From Orléans, he followed events attentively: he heard how Jeanne, dressed like a man and accompanied by a few horsemen, had traveled to Chinon in a long day's journey across the ravaged, impoverished land through partially hostile territory; how she had remained serene and cheerful while her companions wavered, how she had shown herself sure of her mission at all times. This was impressive enough; Dunois was even more impressed to learn that she had not been taken in by an unchivalrous joke that the King had tried to play on her: she had barely glanced at the disguised courtier who sat on the throne, but had pointed out immediately the man whom she persisted in calling the "Dauphin," because he had not yet been crowned at Reims. Her dignified, unassuming behavior had made an impression on the King, but he was even more fascinated by the private conversation he had with her. Neither he nor she told anyone what was said there, but from that time on no one dared openly doubt her words in the King's presence. The favorites wisely kept their suspicions to themselves; it was impossible to resist the growing excitement.

When finally a college of clergymen had, at the King's request, carefully questioned Jeanne about matters of belief and given an unqualified judgment in her favor, Dunois considered this an answer and, in a letter to the King, urged that the Maid be sent to Orléans at the head of a contingent of auxiliary troops and a convoy of provisions. At the beginning of April, he received the news from Chinon: the King had entrusted Jeanne with the command, as he was requested to do.

Around noon of the twenty-ninth of April, 1429, Dunois, together with la Hire and a number of horsemen, crossed the Loire to the village of Chécy to greet the Maid who was advancing from Blois to Orléans along the left bank of the river. It was a clear, warm day; the broad river sparkled in the sunlight. Dunois rode bareheaded. As usual he said little; la Hire, who rode beside him, was more talkative. The captain could not accept the idea that a woman could be expected to perform feats which even experienced soldiers had been unable to accomplish. He was ready to assume that the girl was more brave and devout than most people; otherwise he found the whole affair to be little more than a farce. Dunois listened, now and then turning his head to watch the flat-bottomed barges advance over the river; later in the day they would reach Orléans with the provisions which were their cargo. Once he stood up in his stirrups and shaded his eyes with his hand. The English reinforcements could clearly be seen, encamped on the other side of the river beyond Jargeau opposite Orléans.

In Chécy it appeared that the entire population had left the city to greet Jeanne the Maid, who was coming from the north. When

Dunois and his men rode out of the gates, they found the full force of auxiliary and commissariat troops standing and waiting for them in the fields.

"By my faith, a vanguard of priests!" La Hire roared with laughter.

Indeed, the front lines of Jeanne's army seemed to consist of nothing but friars, led by an Augustine monk who carried a banner depicting the crucified Christ. Dunois paid no attention to la Hire's curses and jeers; he ran his eyes swiftly over the ranks. A white banner was moving toward him, painted with gold lilies and brightly-colored figures. The troops parted to make way for a small procession: a horseman in a white breastplate on a black horse, followed by two shieldbearers and a few armored knights with their grooms and pages. Dunois dismounted and walked to meet them. He saw that the rider in the white cuirass holding the banner was Jeanne. She reined in her horse and looked down upon him with grave bright eyes.

"Are you the Bastard of Orléans?"

"Yes, I am he." Dunois returned her searching look. "Your arrival pleases me more than I can say."

Jeanne frowned; a shadow passed over her open, strong young face.

"Is it true that you gave orders to the captains who came with me from Blois to lead me along the river bank and make sure that I did not do what *I* wanted—that is to go directly to the place where Talbot and Suffolk and their English are camping?"

"Certainly, I did that." Dunois nodded. "It seemed to me and to men who are much more experienced in these matters than I, that it would be wise to avoid a confrontation with the English now."

"In God's name!" cried Jeanne heatedly and so loud that everyone near them hushed to listen. "Do you claim to know more than God, our supreme Lord and Sovereign? I bring you the help and support of God, a greater help does not exist. And God does not do it because of me, but because of the intercession of Saint Louis and Charlemagne. He will not let the English conquer Orléans. He will restore our Duke, Monseigneur d'Orléans to freedom."

"That would be a great blessing—for me and for France," Dunois said earnestly. He was careful not to smile at these childish words, spoken with such fervent conviction. "I have no more heart-

felt wish than this, that God should allow my unfortunate brother
to return to us."

Jeanne stared at him fixedly with her large, very bright hazel
eyes. "That He will surely do, Bastard, for after Monseigneur the
Dauphin, He loves the Duke of Orléans best. And I tell you that
in coming battles, I shall capture many important Englishmen, prisoners of war, whom we can offer in exchange for Monseigneur. It
is a great outrage that the English should attack Monseigneur's cities
and dominions now that he cannot defend them. They do not understand the meaning of chivalry."

Dunois turned his head away. He was both amused and touched.
The word "chivalry" sounded odd enough in the mouth of a peasant
girl who had once spent her time tending sheep. It was obvious that
she did not have the slightest understanding of military operations,
of politics and strategy, of the art of war. That did not surprise
him—how could she know anything about it? What she surely possessed in large measure was that indescribable, inexplicable quality
which a leader has: the air of quiet authority, the ability to overcome
opposition, the steadfast self-assurance, all the more remarkable in
a girl whose grandparents had been serfs. She looked the way an
archangel might be thought to look: radiant and militant. Above
the white breastplate, her fresh broad face with its strong features
shone with the same inner light that must have illumined the faces
of Saint Michael and Saint George when they slew the dragon. Over
her head with its thick short brown hair fluttered the snow-white
banner, painted on one side with the image of God the Father sitting
on a rainbow, and on the other with the golden lilies of France. She
sat her horse well, erect, her long legs stretched to the stirrups.
Behind her, her shieldbearer carried her weapons and a second ensign
depicting Our Lady. A number of prominent captains in the King's
army had come with her from Blois.

Dunois could not hide his pleasure and satisfaction; if anyone
could breathe new life into the enterprise, even if it were only by
her presence, it would be the Maid. He could not and he did not
wish to lose himself in the question of whether she had really been
sent by God or even whether she had the gift of prophecy. He knew
only that she had arrived at a crucial moment. At this time of deep
distress the words of kings, the commands of generals, the inspiration and blessing of the church were no longer important. This,
he thought, was Jeanne's greatest strength, that her arrival, her bear-

ing and her appearance were unlike anything that had ever been seen before. She was completely new, utterly original and as unexpected as miracles always are.

There are able and brave men enough in the army, thought Dunois, staring at Jeanne, but let her come with us. She will give us the unity, the driving force, the enthusiasm which we lost a hundred years ago. She will be for us what the holy banner of the oriflamme was, a mark of God's favor; at least our men must feel that way. And I don't doubt that they will.

"Come, ride beside me, Bastard," said Jeanne suddenly, with a gesture that would have become a king. "And now and later be my right hand when we must fight. You are my friend and brother-at-arms."

While they rode over the road from Chécy to the ferry dock opposite Orléans, Jeanne pursued the conversation.

"Where do the English lie now?" she asked, looking across the Loire.

"Wait till we reach the bend in the river," Dunois replied. "Then we can make out their flags on the fortress of Tourelles."

"They will not wave there much longer," Jeanne smiled, staring before her with wide eyes. Dunois, wanting to discover the secret source of her confidence, said softly, "I ask myself this question: if God wanted to help us, why didn't He drive out the English before this?"

La Hire, riding directly behind Dunois, overheard this and began to laugh, although less boisterously than usual; he could not help being somewhat impressed by Jeanne's imposing demeanor. She won't be able to answer that question so easily, he thought, leaning forward in the saddle to listen intently.

Jeanne became annoyed.

"It is as plain and clear as the day," she said. For the first time her Lorraine accent was noticeable. "If we fight gallantly, God will surely give us the victory. If we remain united and sin neither by word nor by deed against God's commandments, He will help us. We shall not receive the victory as a gift; we shall have to sacrifice blood and sweat for it, Bastard."

"Mort de ma foi, she can talk," said the Breton captain, shoving back his leather casque to scratch his head. Jeanne looked back at him.

"La Hire can swear," she remarked calmly.

"By the eternal pain of Hell! How did you know my name is la Hire?"

"In my troop no one swears any more," she said, still looking back at la Hire. "I have forbidden it. And the very first day I drove away the whores and kept women who bring disgrace upon the army. I tolerate no lewdness and no dirty talk among my men. If you wish to serve in my troop, la Hire, you must leave off cursing. This is a holy struggle."

"Thunder and the Devil! Then I won't be able to open my mouth any more!" La Hire was too taken aback to be offended.

"Say rather, 'by my staff!' " Jeanne advised him good-naturedly, pointing to the captain's truncheon which la Hire, like Dunois and the other commanders, wore on his belt. "Then we will both have our way and God will not be offended."

"By my. . .staff!" mumbled la Hire, dumbfounded at his own docility.

"You manage soldiers well, Jeanne," said Dunois. "That is important. And yet you have always lived far away from war and fighting men, there in Domrémy."

"That's not true, Bastard." Jeanne turned back to look gravely at him. "Year in, year out, our place swarmed with fugitives who had been driven out of their villages and farms by the English and the Burgundians. Many is the time we have given shelter to starving, exhausted people. And we ourselves were once driven into the forests. When we came back, they had set our church on fire and plundered our houses. No, I know very well what war is. I would sit and weep for France if I did not know that my task is to fight for my country instead of spending my time wailing. That is why I was born, you see. I must free France and fetch the Dauphin to Reims—and that I will do. But quick, Bastard, quick, for my time is short."

"Why, Jeanne?" Dunois asked, amazed. But she shook her head and closed her eyes as though in sudden pain. It was clear that she did not want to talk further about it.

Dunois continued, "I wish that you could transfer some of your courage to our King. He has bitter need of it."

Jeanne's eyes lit up again with joy.

"Oh, he feels certain now, Bastard, believe me. He is our sovereign, the lawful heir of France."

"Did you tell him that when you spoke with him at Chinon?"

Jeanne did not answer, although she continued to smile. At a bend in the river Dunois extended his arm. "There lies Orléans."

She stood in the stirrups and looked in the direction he pointed.

"Why don't the English attack us?" she asked, after a few moments. "I thought they would stop us from entering the city."

"The English have suffered many reverses lately. Then too, we now outnumber them. We have to thank our own spineless attitude since the Battle of the Herrings for the fact that they can maintain their fortifications before Orléans. They have calmly spent the winter directly under the walls and we have done nothing to them worth mentioning. They are so certain of the victory that they do not even trouble to fight for it."

"Oh, they are mistaken." Jeanne rode ahead more rapidly, her eyes fixed on the city on the other side of the water. The roofs and towers were outlined darkly against the translucent evening sky, streaked with red and yellow. The river was filled with ships crowded with soldiers and ordinary people who carried flags, banners, torches and garlands of light green leaves. In the evening glow, the auxiliary troops approached Orléans; the men moved in well-ordered ranks along the road, the ships of the convoy glided slowly over the river. What Dunois had hardly dared to hope for, he now saw with his own eyes: the people of Orléans were beside themselves with enthusiasm and joy.

They stared at Jeanne as though she were God Himself; when she rode into the city after crossing the river with Dunois, the army captains and her retinue, the people awaited her in the streets in such vast numbers that the procession could advance only a step at a time. Everyone wanted to see Jeanne up close, to touch her horse or the skirt of her tunic. Many women and children fell to their knees, as was the custom when a religious procession was passing. Jeanne greeted everyone with a smile and spoke to those who crowded nearest to her.

"We shall save Orléans! Be easy, God will drive the English from the land, but we must be brave and strive with all our might, people," she said again and again as she lifted her banner high so that everyone could see the image of God the Father with a globe in His hand.

As they rode through one of the squares, a priest emerged from a church porch holding a crucifix straight before him.

"Stop!" Jeanne said to Dunois. "He thinks I am bewitched. Come here, brother," she called in her clear, penetrating voice, as she stood in the stirrups. "I shall not fly away or vanish in a cloud of smoke!"

To a group of women who offered her their rosaries to touch so that she could consecrate them, she said in good-natured mockery, "Do it yourselves, the rosaries will be just as good."

Dunois felt so happy that he had an urge to laugh aloud. It was almost too good to be true: Jeanne had courage and convictions and healthy good sense besides. During this ride through streets filled with elated, grateful people, a deep affection for Jeanne was born in Dunois' heart. It was a wonderful feeling that in no way resembled the comradeship which Dunois had felt for some men or the passion aroused in him by women. In his eyes Jeanne was neither man nor woman; she seemed a creature of that order to which children and angels belong, serene and simple, without any real understanding of sin and darkness and, out of pure kindness, moved as quickly to pity as to joy.

When he knelt beside her in the cathedral of Orléans, where a welcoming service was held in her honor, an inexplicable wave of fear and grief washed over him for an instant; through a haze of incense he saw the glow of the candle flames on the altar, many pointed fiery tongues quivering white and gold before the dull polished triptych; the voices of the choirboys rose ringing to the vaulted ceiling. Jeanne prayed aloud with open eyes. Glancing at her profile, Dunois suddenly realized that there was good reason for his fear. Those who differ so much from their fellowmen have a hard time in the world. Dunois, who intended to stand beside her and protect her as much as possible by sharing the exceptionally heavy task which she had taken upon herself, understood that there was great danger in success as well as in failure; he knew all too well the atmosphere at the court of Bourges, the King's uncertainty and the inclination of the people in general to shout "Hosanna!" today and "Crucify him!" tomorrow. He put his hands together more firmly on the hilt of his sword and bowed his head in prayer.

On the way to the dwelling of Jean Boucher, treasurer of the Duke of Orléans—Jeanne would spend the night there—she was at her most cheerful.

"Tomorrow the rest of the convoy is arriving," she said to Dunois as they rode through the dark streets accompanied by torchbearers. "I go to meet the men as soon as it gets light. But this time I will do it my own way, Bastard. We enter Orléans along the left bank of the Loire, past the Beauce side between the English fortifications. Believe me now and wait, the English will not even shoot at us from their fortresses. They will not dare to harm us when my vanguard of priests sings "Veni Creator". And when all the provisions are inside the city, we can make a sortie and conquer one of the strongholds. Don't argue with me, Bastard, it will happen as I say. Courage and faith in the power of God—we don't need anything more!"

"Hm," said Dunois, tongue in cheek. "It's possible you're right, Jeanne. You're in command here. I won't oppose you."

"Not I, but this banner leads the armies, Bastard!" Carefully, with her left hand, Jeanne touched the gilded fringe of the great flag. "It will lead us to victory. And then when the enemy is beaten and Monseigneur the Dauphin is crowned in Reims as is proper, we will go and free the Duke of Orléans. If I must, I will cross over to England to fetch him. I have told this to the Duke's daughter and son-in-law too, Madame and Monseigneur d'Alençon whom I visited in Saumur. How long has the Duke been a prisoner in England, Bastard?"

Dunois, his eyes fixed on the torch flames dancing before the procession, answered, "Fourteen years."

Nouvelles ont couru en France	News has traveled in France
Par mains lieux que j'estoye mort;	In various places that I am dead;
Dont avoient peu desplaisance	Some were hardly displeased by this,
Aucuns qui me hayent a tort;	Those who hate me unfairly;
Autres en ont eu desconfort,	Others have been discomforted
Qui m'ayment de loyal vouloir,	Who are loyal and love me
Comme mes bons et vrais amis.	As good and true friends.
Si fais a toutes gens savoir	So I am letting everyone know.
Qu'encore est vive la souris!	The mouse is still alive!
Je n'ay eu ne mal ne grevance,	I have been neither ill nor in pain,
Dieu mercy, mais suis sain et fort,	Thank God, but hale and strong,
Et passe temps en esperance	And pass the time hoping
Que paix, qui trop longuement dort,	That peace, too long asleep,
S'esveillera, et par accort	Will wake and by accord
A tous fera liesse avoir.	Give everyone cause to rejoice.
Pour ce, de Dieu soient maudis	So may God curse those
Ceulx qui sont dolens de veoir	Who are saddened to see
Qu'encore est vive la souris!	That the mouse is still alive!

Jeunesse sur moy a puissance,	Youth still holds me,
Mais Vieillesse fait son effort	But age is making the effort
De m'avoir en sa gouvernance;	To take me in charge.
A present faillira son sort.	Her attempt will fail now.
Je suis assez loing de son port,	I am far away from her port
De pleurer vueil garder mon hoir;	And wish to save my heir from
Loué soit Dieu de Paradis,	tears;
Qui m'a donné force et povoir	Praised be God in Paradise
Qu'encore est vive la souris!	Who has given me strength and
	power
	That the mouse is still alive!

Nul ne porte pour moy le noir,	No one should wear black for me,
On vent meillieur marchié drap gris;	Grey can be bought more cheaply;
Or tiengne chascun, pour tout voir,	Everyone must know it is true
Qu'encore est vive la souris!	That the mouse is still alive!

For Charles d'Orléans in Ampthill castle in the duchy of Bedford, the few letters from Dunois which reach him through Jean le Brasseur and his little dog during the years 1430, 1431 and 1432, are landmarks in a wasteland of aimless time. It is true that his host and warden, the knight John Cornwall, Lord of Fanhope, allows him some freedom; he can walk, ride and hunt in the neighborhood under armed escort. In the castle a series of well-furnished chambers are at his disposal; he has French-speaking servants. Books he possesses in abundance, and if he wishes, he can socialize with nobles from Cornwall's circle of friends. But there are no political discussions; news about the war, about affairs in France, is carefully kept from him. When le Brasseur visits him to submit accounts and documents for his signature, there are always a half dozen men in the room to cut off immediately any but a purely business discussion. Charles does not always succeed in appropriating the letters so artfully concealed under the dog's long hair. More than once he is obliged to return the animal without success because he has not found the opportunity to redeem the message. Under no circumstances does he want his guards to discover this means of securing information; if le Brasseur can no longer visit him, all links between his half-brother and himself are broken forever.

In a flat wooden box which he carries with him always, he keeps the letters: small thin narrow rolls of paper covered closely with writing. At night, by the light of a single candle, carefully screened within the bedcurtains, he reads and rereads countless times the small pages which are all he has of France. Although he learns a good deal and guesses even more, he still cannot form a clear picture of the real state of affairs. Like a blind man who feels unknown areas with his fingertips, he knows the contours of everything which comes within his reach, but he cannot imagine the whole.

So he reads in a letter which he has received early in 1430 that in the previous May the city of Orléans was relieved in four days; the garrison fought heroically under the command of a girl, Jeanne, who is called everywhere the Maid of Orléans. Dunois has not enough space to explain this remarkable leader, but respectful mention of her recurs constantly in his letters. Despite the opposition of the favorite La Trémoille, Jeanne has led the King across enemy territory into Reims and there had him anointed and crowned. Jeanne at the head of 8,000 men purges the area along the Loire of English troops. Jeanne's fame causes the people of Normandy, Picardy and the Isle of France to declare themselves ready to acknowledge the King. Jeanne wishes to free him, Orléans. At Jargeau, Jeanne takes the Earl of Suffolk prisoner and, after consultation with Dunois, releases him for a ransom of 20,000 gold écus and the promise that in England he will make every effort to bring about the release of Charles d'Orléans and Jean d'Angoulême.

"Jeanne, Jeanne," murmurs Charles dubiously; he does not understand how a woman can exercise authority over men like Dunois, Gaucourt, Richmont, Alençon. Do they really believe then that the Maid of Orléans will do what the most experienced commanders have not been able to do? Even the calm, level-headed Dunois now writes with such elation that Charles assumes that everyone in France is intoxicated by hope and new courage. And he cannot deny that according to the information he receives, the King's armies are making good progress.

"The end is in sight," Dunois writes at the end of his letter. "Within a short time we will advance with Jeanne to Paris. I have high expectations that people in the city who are well-disposed toward us will open the gates to us. Perhaps, dear brother, it will not be long before we see each other again."

Considerably less sanguine is the intelligence that reaches Charles three months later. The attack on Paris has been beaten off by the English—the King's troops have had to withdraw over the Loire and the army has even been partially disbanded for lack of money.

And Jeanne? For the first time Charles senses uneasiness and doubt behind Dunois' words.

"It would be better if she were to return to Lorraine," writes the Bastard, "before she is led by her ignorance and presumption to commit grave errors."

After that, almost a year passes before Charles receives another visit from le Brasseur. He is somewhat prepared for bad news; he has heard from the knight Cornwall that ten-year-old King Henry VI was brought to Paris and ceremonially crowned King of both France and England. Charles thinks it is unlikely that this could have happened if the partisans were still active on the other side of the Loire. He has been informed with great pomposity that a certain Jeanne, nicknamed the Maid of Orléans, an inciter of insurrection, a witch, a rebel against English authority and an apostate from the True Faith, was captured at a battle near Compiègne. The brief letter which Charles finally receives from Dunois in July, 1431, confirms this.

"They have betrayed and sold her. She stayed with us too long. Because the King does not need her any more, he has not lifted a finger to save her. At the court of Bourges, they swear by a new prophet, a shepherd from Géveau who for the present finds it safer to flatter and delude the King than to march into battle for him as Jeanne did. The English handed her over to the University and especially to their friend and protégé Pierre Cauchon, the new Archbishop of Beauvais. And, as was to be expected, Jeanne was accused of sorcery. They forced her to confess—I do not know what that means—that she served the Devil. But although she knew perfectly well what was in store for her, she recanted the confession. On the thirtieth day of May, she was burned to death.

"I do not know if she was sent by God. She was brave and devout and she gave us the strength we needed at the critical moment. But she should have seen that her work was finished when she led the King to Reims. She did not want to leave her post, not even when she no longer heard her voices which, she said, told her what to do. She liked to exercise command and to ride at the head of the troops. She liked nothing better than to urge the men on in battle. She didn't want to give up that pleasure. Since the defeat before Paris, I have often called her undertaking foolish and blamed her for her stupidity. But now that I know how she died, I find her no less holy and heroic than the martyrs we read about when we were children. Because of her death many have regained the faith lost when fortune turned against us. Surely the people of France will remember her steadfastness with loving reverence and persevere in the struggle against England. And surely the King will bitterly regret having abandoned her to her fate. For my part, I know I can never again be completely happy now that I can never again meet Jeanne on her black charger with her gleaming banner raised before her, calling, 'Come, Bastard, the dawn is breaking—on to battle, to the attack!' "

Another year crawls slowly by. Some information reaches him in the course of the year, not only through the letters from France; he can infer one thing and another from words dropped by his servants and his English visitors; now and then he overhears a rumor, an echo of events in London and overseas in France and Flanders. Things are not going well for England in those territories which she still holds; riots and uprisings are the order of the day among the population; step by step they are forced from the cities and villages where they had been entrenched. In the government of London the parties of Gloucester and Winchester are quarreling; the evil which King Henry believed he had destroyed has spread over England like a pestilence: feuds between the great lords, dissension at home.

There is little money with which to fight the war, and as a consequence there are not more than four or five thousand English troops under arms in France. Burgundy, officially still England's ally, gives them no support. In England voices are raised, demanding peace. When he hears this, Charles looks forward with almost feverish impatience to news from Dunois. Peace . . . the word which he has not even dared think for many long years—now the thought of it propels him into a state of constant restlessness. Peace is his only hope for freedom; after seventeen years of imprisonment, he knows this only too well. For him and for his brother of Angoulême everything hinges on peace, and now that peace is a possibility and freedom seems within his grasp, he can barely hold out any longer.

In God's name let the King seize this chance, he thinks. Let them see over there that they have never had a more favorable opportunity; things are going so badly for the English that they are willing to withdraw in exchange for land and money. God grant that negotiations begin soon.

En regardant vers le païs de France,	As I was looking toward the land of France
Un jour m'avint, a Dovre sur la mer,	One day at Dover on the sea,
Qu'il me souvint de la doulce plaisance	I remembered the sweet plaisance
Que souloye oudit pays trouver;	Which in the past I found in that country;
Si commençay de cueur a souspirer,	So I could not help but sigh from my heart
Combien certes que grant bien me faisoit	Despite the great good it did me
De voir France que mon cueur amer doit.	To see France, my heart's great love.
Je m'avisay que e'estoit non savance	I thought that it was a foolish thing
De telz souspirs dedens mon cueur garder,	To sit and sigh within my heart
Veu que je voy que la voye commence	When I could see the way begin to open
De bonne paix, qui tous biens peut donner;	To the good peace, which can help us all.
Pour ce, tournay en confort mon penser.	So I began to think comforting thoughts,
Mais non pourtant mon cueur ne se lassoit	But despite this my heart never wearied
De voir France que mon cueur amer doït.	Of seeing France, my heart's great love.
Alors chargay en la nef d'Esperance	Then onto the ship of Hope
Tous mes souhaitz, en leur priant d'aler	I put all my wishes, bidding them to go
Oultre la mer, sans faire demourance,	Beyond the sea, without delay
Et a France de me recommander.	And to remember me to France.
Or nous doint Dieu bonne paix sans tarder!	Now may God give us good peace soon!
Adonce auray loisir, mais qu'ainsi soit,	Then I shall be able, may it only happen,
De voir France que mon cueur amer doit.	To see France, my heart's great love.
Paix est tresor qu'on ne peut trop loer;	Peace is a treasure above all acclaim,
Je hé guerre, point ne la doy prisier;	I hate war; there is nothing in it to respect;

Destourbé m'a long temps, soit tort on droit,	Rightly or wrongly, it has kept me a long time
De voir France que mon cueur amer doit.	From seeing France, my heart's great love.

In the course of the year 1434, the English Council consigned the guardianship of Charles to William de la Pole, Earl of Suffolk—the same Suffolk who, five years before, had conducted the siege of the city of Orléans; the same Suffolk too who, after being captured by Jeanne at Jargeau, had been set free in return for a ransom of 20,000 gold écus. As a man of honor, Suffolk had kept the promise he had made to Dunois: the improvement in Charles' circumstances was due in no small degree to Suffolk's intercession. Since his return to England, Suffolk had pressed the Council repeatedly to entrust the Duke of Orléans to his care.

So at last Charles left the rich wooded hills and valleys around Ampthill with a great escort of horses and armed soldiers, for his new home: the castle of Wingfield, ancestral home of the de la Pole family. Wingfield lay not far from the sea in flat land, some of it grassy, some cultivated, divided by hedges and orchards; small windmills were driven by salty breezes. The smell of seaweed and foam floated over the empty land. The clouds seemed thinner and swifter-moving than in other places. The barren hills outside Pontefract, the forest near Bolingbroke, the stately gloomy parks of Ampthill, had never oppressed Charles' spirits as did this wind-swept, chill, monotonous landscape under a colorless sky. This land was the absolute antithesis of the lush Loire valley, the lost homeland for which, in deep pain, his heart incessantly yearned.

Wingfield Castle dominated the hamlet of Wingfield, a group of cottages and small thatch-roofed farms set in the midst of orchards and kitchen gardens. At the end of the village, directly opposite the castle, was the church; its blunt, stunted towers rose toward the sky. The Earl's castle itself looked extremely forbidding with its ramparts and moats, its corner towers and battlements. Weary and depressed, Charles passed into Wingfield through the heavy arched gate and over the drawbridge. But his reception exceeded all expectations. Suffolk proved to be an amiable and courteous host and his young wife, a granddaughter of the poet Chaucer whose work Charles knew, seemed educated and exceptionally well-read. Both spoke good French, as did the members of all noble families which had come from Normandy. Although Charles had learned over the years to express himself quite well in English, the Earl of Suffolk and his lady, out of a desire to oblige him, spoke only French in his presence. They treated him completely like a guest; he could move freely both inside and outside Wingfield Castle, without the hindrance of an armed escort.

Suffolk was two years younger than Charles, a man in the prime of life. He had been under arms almost uninterruptedly since Agincourt; he had fought in all important battles and sieges and, after Salisbury's death, had assumed supreme command over the English armies in France. But now, as he repeatedly remarked, he was weary of life in the field; after twenty years of fighting, of combat, even the highest military office could not tempt him to remain in France.

"I have my hands full already, managing my estates and settling my personal affairs," he said to Charles one day after mass, as they walked slowly through the nave of Wingfield church.

The pillars in the nave rose up like white tree-trunks which branched high overhead into little fan-shaped arches like leaves in a forest of stone. Before the altar were the tombs of Suffolk's ancestors; on raised slabs slept armored knights sculptured from stone, their hands folded in prayer on the hilts of their broadswords. As usual, Charles spelled out the Latin phrases engraved on the sides of these memorials: "Here rests in God Michael de la Pole, Earl of Suffolk . . . Here the mortal remains of John de la Pole await the Day of Judgment".

"Believe me, my lord," Suffolk went on, "one must have seen as much of war as I to realize that peace is the highest good."

Charles stood still.

"One realizes that even more acutely when one is a caged bird like me," he said, glancing at his host with an ironic smile. "And I am quite certain that you have chosen wisely, Messire. A tranquil life on your own land, surrounded by friends and kinsmen, what more can a man desire? Ambition and the urge for adventure are evil companions. I can't imagine a better life than the one you are leading now. I only wish that I may do the same in France. It is precisely because I long for such a life with all my heart and because I believe that everyone has the right to enjoy the quiet possession of house and hearth—it is precisely because of this, Messire, that I am perhaps the most dedicated champion of peace that you could find anywhere."

Suffolk turned slightly and looked at his guest. He was taller and more robust than Charles and he looked considerably younger. During the long years of forced inactivity indoors, Charles had lost the suppleness and muscular slimness which had characterized him as a young man. His body had become corpulent and soft, his face prematurely faded. Furrows, the signs of bitterness and silent grief, were visible from his nostrils to the corners of his mouth. Although he was not yet forty years old, he walked like a much older man, cautiously, his shoulders slightly bent, slowly, almost unwillingly. Invariably he wore black, without ornaments, in a sober cut; winter and summer he wrapped himself in a fur-lined cloak; inside the castle it was damp and chilly, and he was easily susceptible to gout.

It was difficult for Suffolk, who had not met him before, to believe that Orléans had ever been young; no trace of youth appeared in this quiet, somewhat heavy man. Occasionally, during a discussion of subjects in which the Duke was interested, he seemed to forget his situation sufficiently to cast off his depression and inertia, if only for a brief time. Then a brighter note could be detected in his always pleasant voice, a rare smile sparkled in his eyes, he gestured vivaciously with his exceptionally graceful hands. Melancholy and ennui seemed to leave him in those moments; as if by magic he displayed a spirit and dash which struck a special chord in Suffolk and in his wife, since the nobility were by education and way of life very familiar with French courtliness. Moreover, they respected the prisoner as an individual; it is rare to meet a man who does not under any circumstances lose his self-control or abandon his good breeding. There was no question that his attitude did not result from shallowness or indifference. No one who came into daily contact with the Duke of Orléans could help noticing that he responded deeply to events.

Suffolk became extremely fond of him; true, he sometimes felt that the Duke was too acquiescent, listless, but God in heaven, the man had sat in prison for twenty long years, it was no wonder that his resiliency had broken under it. Suffolk thought it unlikely that this prematurely aged man with his striking interest in intellectual matters, should still desire to play a role in politics. There was no point in holding Orléans in England any longer; anyone who knew anything about what was happening on the other side of the Straits must see that Orléans could do little, either for or against England. Since Henry V's time, the relationship between the two countries had undergone so profound a transformation, domestic affairs had changed so much, that it would be extremely difficult for the Duke, whose focus and concepts were twenty years out of date, to get a true picture of the present situation, let alone involve himself in diplomacy. Suffolk found the government's hesitation to release Charles d'Orléans to be unreasonable. Time and again over the years he had pointed out that it was senseless to prolong this exile. Why not at long last fix the amount of the ransom and set a term for payment? On second thought, why not return Orléans to France on his word of honor and with certain guarantees?

The young Henry VI had bent a willing ear to this proposal, but the Regents and most of the King's advisors were inclined against it. They felt that in Charles d'Orléans and his brother, England held two valuable pawns which they must continue to grasp; perhaps the moment would come soon when they could play these pieces to great advantage. Orléans remained—even if he should be considerably more broken by his captivity than was actually the case—the head of one of the foremost Houses in France; it was a foregone conclusion that he would once more exercise influence, once more make his mark.

Suffolk was privately annoyed about these ridiculous objections raised by the Council. He who had fought in France for more than twenty years knew the situation over there. He knew from his own observations that Dunois the Bastard was the man who really represented the House of Orléans, probably a good deal more ably and energetically than the Duke ever could.

Sometimes when they were together in the great hall, Suffolk quietly watched his guest. He saw Orléans sitting comfortably between the green curtains which he always had hung, according to French custom, on both sides of his chair or bench, bent over the book on the adjustable reading desk, his head propped on his hand. Even indoors he preferred to wear his velvet cap; he had been wearing reading glasses for some years. That finely chiselled, pale, melancholy face with its narrow lips and delicately curved nose was in no way the face of an ambitious, wordly man, a sharp, quick-witted diplomat, a power-obsessed party leader. The books which lay on the reading desk before Monseigneur must surely lead him far from such concerns: The Imitation of Christ, Consolation of Philosophy...

The man who read his own rondelets and ballads to Lady Suffolk from a pile of somewhat yellowed sheets of paper would never want to devote time or effort to political intrigue. At any rate, so it appeared to Suffolk. The two men stood motionless in the nave of Wingfield church, brightly illuminated by the reflection of sunshine on the white walls.

"There could have been peace between France and England long ago," Suffolk said in a low voice. "In '28, even before we lifted the siege of Orléans, there was talk of negotiations. He who calls himself your king did not seem willing then to reach a settlement with us. Fighting went on in your country, partly because of the peasant girl who was later burned in Rouen—a fanatical creature, stupid and headstrong, ignorant of the art of war and incredibly reckless in battle. What is the sense of whipping up the soldiers and the populace when there is no united effort behind these temporary outbursts of enthusiasm? That woman has hurt your country badly with her madness; the people have become rebellious, but they don't have the energy to act."

Charles nodded, his face turned away. Suffolk coughed for a moment and then went on quickly, "In any case negotiations are now going on in earnest between your ... uh ... king and the Duke of Burgundy. Conferences will be held in Arras. This does not interest you, my lord?"

"I ask myself if this will mean peace," Charles said. "I am not at all certain of that."

"Perhaps I can set your mind at rest. Deputies of our government are already on the road to Arras. We shall work with dedication to reach an accord with France. Luckily, capable mediators were found before the discussions began—the papal nuncio Albergati and the Cardinal of Cyprus. Moreover," Suffolk paused and noted with satisfaction that Orléans' dull dark glance was suddenly enlivened by a spark of interest—"moreover, I had news from London today that in a little while representatives of our King will meet to discuss the possibility of a universal peace treaty. I have been summoned to Westminster palace for this meeting."

The spark went out; Charles walked slowly across the stone slabbed floor toward the church door. "Forgive me, Messire, I am not in a position to suggest any action; I do not know the expectations of the parties, but I fear they are so dramatically opposed to each other that no agreement is likely."

"My lord," Suffolk followed swiftly after him and caught him firmly by a fold of his sleeve. He coughed again when Charles looked sharply at him. "My lord, the consensus in London is that the presence of a clever and influential, highly-placed Frenchman would help considerably to advance the discussions in a favorable direction. In short, they would be pleased if you would accompany me to London."

"To act as an advocate of your government's proposals?" Charles responded with an odd smile. "Seventeen years ago they wanted something similar from me." He did not take his eyes from Suffolk's face. "I thought then of honor, and conscience forced me to reject that suggestion without further discussion. Looking back, I am inclined to think that I paid altogether too high a price for that brief moment of satisfaction."

"Are you trying to tell me that you have changed your mind about it now?" Suffolk asked tensely. Still smiling faintly, Charles continued to keep his eyes on Suffolk's face. A number of scars like streaks of light stood out against the Englishman's bronzed skin.

"Do you believe I still have an influence on my countrymen, Messire?"

Suffolk's glance wavered involuntarily. He shrugged slightly.

"Who can tell? You are the Duke of Orléans. They have found you important and dangerous enough to keep you under lock and key."

Charles took his gloves from his belt and slowly and deliberately drew them on, keeping his eyes on the open door through which sunlight streamed into the church.

"Yes, you must understand that I cannot give you an answer now," he said, after a few moments. "Let me have time to think it over, Messire."

The night passed. Charles, leaning back against the cushions piled high on his bed, had blown out the candle which stood beside him; he lay unmoving, his hands folded on his breast, and watched the stars in that part of the sky which he could see from his window. A cool wind brought him the familiar smell of the sea. For the first time—in how many years was it?—he thought of the ship which would one day carry him back to France. France—a long strip of grey sand before Calais. He sighed, but did not move. This time he had only to help himself, said the voice within him with which he was wont to hold conversations: this time freedom was brushing so close against him that he would have only himself to blame if he did not seize it. Charles' heart, heavy as lead from ennui and bitterness, could offer no argument, although he knew quite well that freedom carried a price, and not only in golden écus.

"I am forty years old now," thought Charles, staring at the twinkling night sky. "Whatever still remains of my life I wish to spend in my own house, on my own land, in my own way. God knows that this is not asking too much."

"Bonne," said the voice within him. It rang like an echo, a shadow of sound. Charles had to smile, in deep, bitter surprise. Bonne? He no longer remembered what Bonne had looked like. He could no longer conjure her up before his mind's eye; she was nothing more to him than a name which called up only gratitude for long-past happiness, happiness so radiant that its afterglow had stayed with him throughout the years of grim solitude.

He knew that Bonne still lived in Rodez, secluded in the Cordeliers convent, as any decent woman would be whose husband is in exile. He knew from Vittori's accounting that she was sent money, a certain amount of money regularly. Two or three times in the course of many years news of her had reached him directly: short letters written by a clerk. It cost him a great effort to summon up behind the stiff words the warmth which Bonne surely wanted to express. He did not doubt her loyalty; he understood that she had chosen seclusion inside the walls of the convent in order to feel closer to him, or at any rate to experience loneliness as he did, and that she found comfort in this attempt. Her image eluded him— how could it be otherwise?—but she was present in him even when he did not consciously think of her. Her life was bound to his; neither time nor distance could separate them here on earth.

She seemed most real to him when he turned the pages of what, in melancholy jest, he called his "Thought Book": in songs, rondelets and ballads on the much-thumbed vellum, Bonne lived. Love, desire and the glow of memory had once provided him with the words to recreate her. He could still call up the impotent bitterness with which he had perceived—was it ten, twelve years ago?—that even the rereading of the songs, even his absorption in memories which had once aroused fierce emotions, could no longer stir his heart. He continued as usual to dedicate loving verses to Bonne, but what in the beginning had been a response to bitter need had gradually become an occupation which he cultivated chiefly to dispel deadly tedium; carefully he polished verse after verse, with a cool head and cool senses, seeking to overcome the difficulties of expression within the rigid limitations of artistic form. But as this work went on, Bonne's image became fainter and fainter. Now when he turned the pages of his Thought Book he felt only a facile melancholy for the loss of his beloved, mixed with a mocking recognition of his own self-indulgence.

Since he had come to live in Wingfield Castle, he had thought more often of Bonne than in the past—not so much of Bonne herself as of what she represented: domesticity, a woman's soothing hand, the restfulness, the ultimate peace in which all tensions were soothed away. Secretly he watched Alice, Lady Suffolk, when she was near him. The calm assurance with which she saw to his comfort roused a new yearning in him for the wife who was waiting in Rodez for his return—undoubtedly a strange, mature woman marked by years of solitude—but perhaps precisely for that reason the companion that he needed. He wanted sons and daughters, successors, heirs. He had never before had this feeling, this deep desire to see his children around him, to touch their heads, to name them, to see how one by one they took up their places in life.

His daughter Jeanne was a fully-grown woman, the wife of the Duke of Alençon, probably already a mother, but he knew almost nothing about her childhood. He had no particularly pleasant memories of the few hasty awkward meetings he had had with her. He had become a father at an age when he still needed a father himself. Now he wanted to perpetuate his family.

Return home . . . the feeling which he had learned over the years to repress at the cost of so much anguish, gradually began to stir in his heart more passionately than ever. The night wind seemed to carry, along with the sea air and the scent of the grasslands, the very odor of liberty. While he lay motionless, gazing at the fading stars, waves of excitement and impatience suddenly washed over him; his heart pounded, his mouth went dry.

I know myself a little, he thought ironically, I thought I had learned to reconcile myself to my fate. I thought that nothing could touch me any more. But after twenty years of captivity, my heart throbs more passionately at the mere thought of being able to return home than it did on the eve of Agincourt . . .

The prudent, critical inner voice offered objections: what role must he play in these conferences? What demands would they make of him? Charles did not listen.

"France," he said aloud. "France."

Memories, images, came rushing in upon him from all sides and reason drowned in the flood. He let himself go completely—a rare pleasure. He was there on the country road along the Loire which leads to Blois. The undulant fertile land, gold and green with spring foliage, spread out before him. He saw the flowers sprinkled across the grass, the vines on the hillsides, the sparkle of the water and the great sails of the ships on their way to Orléans. He saw the towers of Blois against the sky. Skylarks soared upward, flashing in the sunshine, swift as an arrow. He was home.

Charles came to himself, realizing that his face was wet with tears.

Most of the envoys who came from across the sea were representatives of the Duke of Burgundy. Charles, who had expected to be put in touch at the outset with deputations from Bourges and envoys from the heads of the feudal Houses, was surprised and disappointed. The thing that he had most dreaded—a connection with the English government in which the intention was that he should be used for their purposes—had happened. On the surface, the authorities appeared to be making no attempts at all to influence him. Charles was present with Suffolk at all discussions; he was treated with great respect by the English and the Burgundians and given all the deference due to his rank. But he was not reassured by this: he realized now, with a feeling of helpless anger at his own credulity, that he was simply a spectator. The meetings, the disputes, the swift, keen resolutions, were performed for his benefit. He did not even know all the facts and those facts which he did know were not put in their proper perspective for him. Consequently, since he wanted to avoid making errors at any cost, he was perhaps more quiet than he should have been if he wished to show them that he was going to stand up for his rights. With incredulous irritation, he watched the arrogant, overbearing behavior of Burgundy's envoys: a crowd of nobles of low rank and rich Flemish merchants decked out like kings, all as self-satisfied and aloof as people can be only when they are sure of their power.

Once he commented on this to Suffolk; his host gave him a searching glance and, after some thought, said, "You should not be shocked at this, my lord. The Duke of Burgundy is the greatest sovereign on the continent."

Charles raised his brows. "Sovereign?"

"Certainly, my lord. Burgundy can scarcely be considered a vassal of the French Crown. It's obvious that he doesn't consider himself a vassal and, indeed, he has no need to do that. His influence is so great and he's so rich that the infidel Turks call him the Grand Duc d'Occidente." Suffolk smiled slightly, looking at Charles. "If a treaty is really effected between your . . . king and Burgundy, it will unquestionably be Burgundy who dictates the terms. And that England is negotiating with France actually means this: England and Burgundy are deciding France's fate together. In fact my lord, if I am to be completely honest, I have to admit that it looks at present as though Burgundy is deciding the fate not only of France, but of England as well. No matter how you look at it, Burgundy holds the cards. No, no, my lord, this is serious; a complete transformation has taken place over the last ten years, and you have to take it into account. You must look upon Burgundy as an independent monarch."

Charles shook his head. "Am I to assume that my cousin of Burgundy has achieved what his father and grandfather struggled for incessantly? Freedom from France for Burgundy?"

"That is exactly the case, my lord. Think about it for a moment. It will make it easier for you to decide what your attitude should be at future discussions. You don't sit opposite representatives of one who calls himself the king of France,"—as a good Englishman Suffolk refused to give Charles VII the title which he believed belonged to Henry VI—"you sit opposite spokesmen for the head of a powerful neighboring state who has enough influence to make his voice heard in French affairs . . ."

"What exactly do they expect of me now?" Charles asked abruptly.

Suffolk saw that he was extremely nervous.

"Yes, this is not simple for you, my lord. You will have to find your way between the various parties. It's your task to make Burgundy amenable to proposals from our side and at the same time to deter the Bourges party—if I may call them that—from introducing proposals which conflict with Burgundy's wishes. It seems to me that you should start by informing yourself thoroughly about the various currents of thought—especially those inside the Bourges party. If what I hear is correct, the Houses are more apt to make concessions to Burgundy than to your . . . king. We would like to reach an agreement with Burgundy and the French Houses together. We regard this as the most favorable solution by far."

"Does that mean you wish to exclude the King of France? In other words, you want me to prepare an ambush for him?"

Suffolk shrugged. "It's difficult to find a name for such political chess moves, my lord."

Charles turned slowly away. They were in an apartment in Suffolk's fortified house in London: a large, handsome dwelling near the royal palace at Westminster. Charles was confused and upset; he had begun only now to realize that it was necessary to combat more than one peril, to overcome more than one obstacle on the road to freedom. He felt as though he were in a maze; his knowledge of place and direction was completely inadequate.

"My God, but shouldn't I have permission to speak with people from my House and envoys from Brittany, Alençon, Bourbon?" he asked at last. "Isn't it possible for me to meet envoys from these domains in Dover or somewhere else along the coast? And I wish to speak to my half-brother, the Sire de Dunois."

"Well, my lord, I personally find this request far from unreasonable." Suffolk shrugged again. "And I shall do what I can to win the Council over to the idea. But I must tell you beforehand that there is very little chance of success. It is believed in the government that you can follow this course of action without any further discussion and that these ambassadors from Bourges and the feudal territories who are already here are completely qualified to make your recommendations known in Arras."

Ah, thought Charles, now they let me feel the whip. A trace of his former watchfulness awoke in him. He thought of himself as an old, lame, half-blind hunting dog still being driven into the open field; the beast is almost useless, but instinctively it goes through the familiar motions: pricks up its ears, sniffs along the ground, pokes into the underbrush. He noticed that Suffolk was looking at him with sober attention, but also with friendly solicitude: clearly his plight touched the Englishman's heart.

He pities me, thought Charles, he thinks I can do nothing more, that I shall fail. Rage flashed through him like a prickling torrent. Something awoke in him which he had never known was there: desperate ambition, the urge for vindication, for self-assertion, the desire to checkmate his adversaries by wily, cunning, knife-sharp maneuvers.

"My lord," said Suffolk suddenly, "permit me to give you some good advice: if you wish to regain your freedom in the near future, seek the friendship and support of the Duke of Burgundy. Show yourself to be amiable toward him—meet his wishes. He is the only man who can help you, Monseigneur; it's your task to see to it that he *does* help you."

From a letter written by the Abbé of the Cordeliers cloister in Rodez to Charles, Duke of Orléans, at Suffolk House, London, 1434:

". . .and it is with deep sorrow, Monseigneur, that we must inform you of the death of Madame Bonne d'Armagnac, Duchess of Orléans, who led so devout and charitable a life within our walls that she stood everywhere in the odor of sanctity."

J'ay fait l'obseque de ma Dame	I have held the funeral of my Lady
Dedens le moustier amoureaux,	In the gleaming chapel of love;
Et le service pour son ame	The requiem for her soul
A chanté Penser Doloreux;	Was sung by Sorrow;
Mains sierges de Soupirs Piteux	The candles at her head, still and bright
Ont esté en son luminaire;	
Aussi j'ay fait la tombe faire	Are sighs of pity;
De Regrez, tous de lermes pains;	She sleeps in a tomb of Regret,
Et tout entour, moult richement,	Painted all round with tears,
Est escript, Cy gist vrayement	And inscribed in golden letters,
Le tresor de tous biens mondains.	Here lies the whole treasure of all wordly bliss.
Dessus elle gist une lame	Above her is a tablet of sapphires and gold;
Faicte d'or et de saffirs bleux,	
Car saffir est nommé la jame	Sapphires for loyalty, gold for good fortune.
De Loyauté, et l'or eureux.	
Bien lui appartiennent ces deux,	Both of these belong to her,
Car Eur et Loyauté pourtraire	For with His two hands
Voulu, en la tresdebonnaire,	God has cunningly fashioned her

Dieu qui la fist de ses deux mains,
Et fourma merveilleusement;
C'estoit, a parler plainnement,
Le tresor de tous biens mondains.

As a portrait of Good Fortune and
   Loyalty;
She was, to put it simply,
The whole treasure of all wordly
   bliss.

N'en parlons plus; mon cueur se
   pasme
Quant il oyt les fais vertueux
D'elle, qui estoit sans nul blasme,
Comme jurent celles et ceulx
Qui congnoissoyent ses conseulx;
Si croy que Dieu la voulu traire
Vers lui, pour parer son repaire
De Paradis ou sont les saints;
Car c'est d'elle bel parement,
Que l'en nommoit communement
Le tresor de tous biens mondains.

Speak of her no more; my heart
   swoons
Over her selfless kindness,
She who was without blame
As men and women attest
Who knew her well;
So I think that God drew her to
   Himself
To ornament Paradise, where the
   saints dwell
For she would be an ornament
   indeed
Whom everyone called
The whole treasure of all wordly
   bliss.

De riens ne servent pleurs ne plains;
Tous mourrons, ou tart ou
   briefment;
Nul ne peut garder longuement
Le tresor de tous biens mondains.

Tears and mourning are useless;
We shall all die, late or soon;
No man can keep forever
The whole treasure of worldly bliss.

One of the conditions in the treaty concluded in Arras in 1435:

I. The King of France, Charles, the seventh of that name, shall in person or through his deputies ask forgiveness of the Duke of Burgundy and express regret for the murder, committed in former times in Montereau, of the late Duke Jean of Burgundy. He shall punish the criminals and/or their descendants and banish them from the Kingdom. He shall pay a compensation to the Duke of Burgundy of 50,000 gold écus.

II. The King gives to the Duke of Burgundy and his heirs in both the male and female lines, all cities in the territory of the Somme, to wit, Mâcon, Châlons, Auxerre, Péronne, Mont-Didier, Saint-Quentin, Amiens, Abbeville, Ponthieu, with accessory landed estates and fortresses as well as the use of the fruits thereof and the right to levy taxes.

III. The Duke of Burgundy is hereby released from the necessity to render feudal service or marks of homage to the King of France.

Priés pour paix, doulce Vierge
  Marie,
Royne des cieulx, et du monde
  maistresse,
Faictes prier, par vostre courtoisie,
Saints et saintes, et prenés vostre
  adresse
Vers vostre filz, requerant sa
  haultesse
Qu'il lui plaise son peuple regarder,
Que de son sang a voulu racheter,
En deboutant guerre qui tout
  desvoye;
De prieres ne vous vueilliez lasser;
Priez pour paix, le vray tresor de
  joye!

Pray for peace, sweet Virgin Mary,
Queen of Heaven and Mistress of
  the world,
Ask the saints to pray and ask your
  Son
To look with favor upon His people
Whom He redeemed with His blood
And put an end to war which
  creates chaos.
Do not grow weary,
Pray for peace, the true treasure of
  joy!

Priez, prelas et gens de sainte vie,
Religieux ne dormez en peresse,
Priez, maistres et tous suivans
  clergie,
Car par guerre fault que l'estude
  cesse;
Moustiers destruis sont sans qu'on
  les redresse,
Le service de Dieu vous fault laissier.
Quant ne povez en repos demourer,
Priez si fort que briefment Dieu
  vous oye;
L'Eglise voult a ce vous ordonner.
Priez pour paix, le vray tresor de
  joye!

Pray, prelates and holy people,
Monks, rouse yourselves from sloth,
Pray, masters and studious clerks,
For war is the death of learning;
Chapels lie in tumbled ruins,
The service of God is deserted.
Pray hard so God hears you
For the sake of the Church.
Pray for peace, the true treasure of
  joy!

Priez, princes qui avez seigneurie,
Roys, ducs, contes, barons plains de
  noblesse,
Gentilz hommes avec chevalerie,
Car meschans gens surmontent
  gentillesse;
En leurs mains ont toute vostre
  richesse,

Pray, ruling princes,
Noble kings, dukes, earls,
High-born lords of chivalry,
For you are overcome by evil men
Who hold your riches in their
  hands;
Lawsuits raise them high in rank,
You see this clearly every day.

Debatz les font en hault estat
  monter,
Vous le povez chascun jour veoir au
  cler,
Et sont riches de voz biens et
  monnoye
Dont vous deussiez le peuple
  suporter.
Priez pour paix, le vray tresor de
  joye!

Priez, peuple qui souffrez tirannie,
Car voz seigneurs sont en telle
  foiblesse
Qu'ilz ne peuent vous garder, par
  maistrie,
Ne vous aidier en vostre grant
  destresse;
Loyaulx marchans, la selle si vous
  blesse
Fort sur le dox; chascun vous vient
  presser
Et ne povez marchandise mener,
Car vous n'avez seur passage ne
  voye,
Et maint peril vous couvient il
  passer.
Priez pour paix, le vray tresor de
  joye!

Priez, galans joyeux en compaignie,
Qui despendre desirez a largesse;
Guerre vous tient la bourse
  desgarnie.
Priez, amans, qui voulez en liesse
Servir amours, car guerre, par
  rudesse,
Vous destourbe de voz dames
  hanter,
Qui maintesfoiz fait leurs vouloirs
  tourner;
Et quant tenez le bout de la
  couroye,
Un estrangier si le vous vient oster;
Priez pour paix, le vray tresor de
  joye!

They have taken the wealth, the
  treasure
Which you need for the people's
  support.
Pray for peace, the true treasure of
  joy!

Pray, victims of oppression,
For your lords are become
  enfeebled;
They cannot protect you
Nor alleviate your suffering.
Honest merchants, your backs are
  sore
From the painful saddle; everyone
  afflicts you,
You have no safe road to travel,
You are in peril wherever you go.
Pray for peace, the true treasure of
  joy!

Pray, gallants who enjoy the festive
  life
And the outpouring of largesse;
War keeps your purses lean.
Pray, lovers who want only to serve
  Love;
The rigors of war keep you from
  your ladies
Who thus often turn their favors
  from you;
And when you hold the end of the
  rope
A stranger comes to take it from
  your hand.
Pray for peace, the true treasure of
  joy!

Dieu tout puissant nous vueille
conforter
Toutes choses en terre, ciel et mer;
Priez vers lui que brief en tout
pourvoye,
En lui seul est de tous maulx
amender;
Priez pour paix, le vray tresor de
joye!

May Almighty God comfort us
And all things on earth, in the sky
and sea,
Pray to him to provide soon for us
all;
He alone has the power to cure all
ills.
Pray for peace, the true treasure of
joy!

II. THE THOUGHT BOOK

Il n'est nul si beau passe temps
que de jouer a la Pensée.

There is no more pleasant way
to pass time than to play
the game of thought.
— Charles d'Orléans

On the eleventh of November, 1440, a glittering procession set out from Saint-Omer to the garden city of Gravelines. Isabelle, Duchess of Burgundy, was riding out to greet a noble guest who was coming that morning from England to Calais. The weather was windy but bright; the banners, scarlet, gold and green, flapped smartly in the breeze; the women's veils floated like wisps of mist.

Everyone in Flanders and Burgundy who bore a noble name had joined the Duchess's retinue, partly to honor the sovereign lady, but mainly out of curiosity to see the man who had lived in captivity far from France for twenty-five years. Isabelle of Burgundy rode under a canopy embroidered with lions and lilies; its long gilt fringe fluttered in the wind. She beamed with happiness and satisfaction; this day was a witness to her triumph, to the success of a diplomatic maneuver which she had initiated and guided.

Isabelle, Burgundy's still-young third wife, was a daughter of the King of Portugal and a princess of the House of Lancaster; she had an uncommonly strong interest in politics and had, since her arrival in Burgundian lands, paid a good deal of attention to the development of government relations, both foreign and domestic. Her husband, who trusted her judgment, often charged her with the direction of conferences and, in general, with all matters that required acumen, patience and tact. He called her his most capable ambassador. Because she was calmer, more thoughtful and gentler than he, and, moreover, understood better than he the art of waiting and, if necessary, temporarily retreating, she was able to render him invaluable service. She had negotiated with representatives of the clergy and of the burghers, received deputations and resolved a number of domestic problems in a most satisfactory manner.

When therefore, in the year 1438, she requested permission to direct the conferences in Saint-Omer concerning the restoration of Flemish-English relations—the hostilities with England had caused great discontent among the merchants, artisans and shipbuilders everywhere in the low countries—Burgundy had consented at once. He wanted to be relieved both of the work and of the unpleasant task of personally seeking rapport with the English, a duty that could not be postponed because of its effect on the prosperity of Flanders. He had heard that across the Straits they had begun to weave cloth and linen with success; at all costs England must be retained as a market for Flemish cloth. The alliance with Charles VII of France had proved on sober reflection to be less advantageous than it had promised to be at the outset; the sickly, timid, irresolute King had shown himself over the years, despite his caution and hesitation, to be a ruler who at least followed a steady course. He had enough insight to surround himself with able advisors and skillful army men. When Richmont, who had been named Constable, retook Paris from the English, the King's authority was recognized once again everywhere in the country, even in those territories still occupied by the enemy.

But then came the nobles and the heads of the feudal Houses who had supported Charles VII after the treaty of Arras, to demand their rewards: Brittany, Bourbon, Alençon, Armagnac, Foix, Lorraine, Anjou and a whole series of counts and barons—all wanted land, money, privileges, high posts in government. The King distrusted them and ignored their demands; he did what his father and grandfather had done in the distant past: he surrounded himself with advisors, both nobles and citizens, who began to review the country's finances and the administration of justice. Since it was too expensive to continue the war with England with troops consisting for the most part of noblemen, their retinues, and mercenaries, he wanted to create a standing army of soldiers who would commit themselves to serve for a fixed period of time.

However, because of this the nobles and independent captains of the army turned against him. The lords openly joined together, feeling all the more justified because the Dauphin Louis had entered their ranks. The Dauphin, a discontented, somewhat sour, but extremely sharp-witted young man, did not attempt to hide his feelings of contemptuous hatred for his father; he entered heart and soul into the conspiracy. Charles VII was aware of this plot to wrest power from him when it began, and made every attempt to frustrate it, but the lords continued to hold secret meetings.

From a distance, Burgundy watched all this attentively. Alençon and Brittany had tried to bring him into the scheme, but he wisely kept aloof, planning to pluck the fruit when it was ripe.

This rebellion of the nobility roused great interest in England, along with the hope that with the help of these malcontents, Henry VI might still be placed on the French throne. Suddenly the Council at Westminster remembered that Charles, Duke of Orléans, who had been in the Tower in the custody of Lord Cobham since 1436, was also a French feudal prince. It could certainly do no harm, in this delicate situation, to allow him to communicate with his peers overseas. The Council referred to the vow which Charles had made three years ago with his hand upon the Gospels to work for peace and support the claims of Henry VI in France.

Thus, when the name of Orléans came up during a conversation at Saint-Omer between the English spokesmen and Isabelle of Burgundy, it was evident that Henry's envoys did not object, under the present circumstances, to allowing the Duke a role in negotiations for a general peace treaty. Isabelle believed that Orléans could function as a sort of link between Burgundy and the French feudal Houses. It was a foregone conclusion that he would be eager to serve Burgundy in return for his freedom. Isabelle, who was not averse to playing a double diplomatic role, adopted Charles' cause as her own. The negotiations were considerably delayed because two parties in England were engaged in a power struggle—one favorably inclined toward the Burgundians and the other against them. But at long last Orléans' ransom was set at 100,000 English marks, a high figure. However, the Duchess of Burgundy managed to raise that sum within the required time of one year.

So she accomplished two feats at once: the restoration of commerce between England and Flanders, and the release of Charles of Orléans. She gathered from her correspondence with the prisoner that his gratitude knew no bounds; he stood ready to render any service in return. While preparations were in progress for the reception of Orléans in the grand manner at the court of Burgundy—the first impression was important—the indefatigable Isabelle was occupied in other ways planning the future of her noble protégé.

In Isabelle's retinue was a young maid of honor, a niece of the Duke of Burgundy who had grown up at her uncle's court. Her name was Marie of Cleves. She came from a family rich in children and because the Cleves, despite their ancient illustrious name, were not amply blessed with wordly goods, the Duchess of Burgundy had taken upon herself the task of marrying off her sister-in-law's daughters and paying their dowries. Aware of the conventional wisdom that a pact was really secure only when it was sealed by a marriage agreement between members of both parties, Isabelle had determined that the Duke of Orléans should take Marie of Cleves to wife. The wedding would bind him to Burgundy. Since in his letters Charles had shown himself willing to accept this proposal, the contracts had already been drawn up, the marriage arranged. Now it was necessary only to await the bridegroom's arrival.

Marie of Cleves was fourteen years old, slender and blonde, with cheerful eyes, but her features were rather coarse; her nose was too large and her teeth were not pretty. Her manners were courtly; she loved to hunt and dance and she played cards well. Duchess Isabelle thought that her foster child would make a most suitable wife for a man who had lived for years in bleak seclusion. The feelings of the bride were not considered; everyone agreed that she could not do better.

Isabelle put a clause in the marriage contract which stipulated that three-quarters of the dowry must be spent on the purchase of castles and estates for the bride and her future progeny.

"If Orléans should go bankrupt because of his ransom, then you will at least still possess your own properties, my dear," the Duchess of Burgundy had explained, with a wordly-wise smile. However, these and similar considerations meant little to Marie. Her thoughts were elsewhere. She knew that her bridegroom was forty-five years old, the age of her uncle of Burgundy, whom she greatly admired. The Duke, with his large supple body and vivacious face, was an extremely handsome man and was also cheerful, generous and courtly—richer and more powerful than any king or emperor of whom she had ever heard. She could not deny that this glittering image had its dark side. It was no secret to Marie, who had grown up too quickly in the anterooms of Madame of Burgundy, that the Duke did not observe the motto which he had adopted upon his third marriage: "Autre n'aray. . . I shall never have another love." Nevertheless, Marie of Cleves hoped with all her heart that her bridegroom would be like Monseigneur of Burgundy; his arrival would crown her fairy tale girlhood which had begun so suddenly when Burgundian envoys had come to fetch her from Cleves. She had left her native land for good—that richly forested marshy country which lay between the Meuse and the Rhine. She had been a child in her father's castle in Cleves, a steep greystone citadel built high on the slope of a wooded hill.

Day in and day out, little Marie had sat at the window. She knew every valley, every thicket, every green hilltop, and every bend of the broad gleaming white Rhine. She followed the river with her eyes until it vanished among the hazy blue hills in the distance. The mysterious Swan Knight who had sought out Elsa of Brabant became a reality for the child; she hoped and believed that if she persisted long enough in her silent vigil he would come to her, too. It was not the ship drawn by swans that she saw approaching, but a glittering golden coach surrounded by armored riders carrying the banners of Burgundy. Her father had raised objections; he was not eager to see his children depart for palaces in Brussels and Ghent from which they would return to him with dainty, fastidious manners. But Marie was his sixth daughter—he could not give her a large dowry. Like a queen, the child rode out of Cleves to take up the unknown life.

Through the small windows of the carriage, she had watched the gradual alteration of the landscape; the wood merged into meadows and orchards expanded into fields of grain and flax. She rode through bustling valleys; the streets teemed with well-dressed, industrious people. In Flanders it always seemed to be market day. The magnificence of the great cities overwhelmed the child, but she became really speechless when she was led into the castle where her Aunt Isabelle lived. She walked across gleaming mosaic tile floors, past walls hung with tapestries; brightly-colored birds sang in gilded cages; in rooms and corridors she met beings who seemed to her to be princes and princesses, but who bowed to her in salutation.

Quickly Marie forgot the castle in Cleves and her frugal childhood there. The glory of Burgundy reflected even on her; she seemed to have become a princess of the blood, exalted, unassailable. She was not troubled by—she scarcely realized—the fact that she was only a pawn on the chessboard of her mightly kinsmen, an instrument with which to confirm treaties and alliances, to draw money, land and possessions into the Burgundian sphere of influence.

Now she was going to be Duchess of Orléans; her bridegroom, they said, had been a powerful man in France, and would surely be so again once he was restored to his own dominions. They showed her the verses which Monseigneur had sent the Duke and Duchess of Burgundy from England in recognition of their efforts on his behalf. Marie imagined her future husband to be a courtly man, dignified, noble, perhaps somewhat melancholy in appearance, made all the more interesting by prolonged exile. Without question he would love and honor her, and dedicate many beautiful verses to her.

Full of expectation, Marie rode between the ladies who followed the Duchess of Burgundy to Gravelines. The damp grey sand spurted up in small clots under the hooves of the brightly bedecked trotting horses; the strong incessant wind blew mantles and veils about; the women in their green and violet dresses looked like so many banners themselves. In the shelter of two sand dunes tents were pitched, adorned with flags and ensigns; a meeting would take place here. Waiting grooms came forward to take the horses; with her retinue of nobles and women the Duchess sought the shelter of the pavilions.

Marie of Cleves stood behind her noble protector, but made sure that she could command a clear view of the sloping dune overgrown with wild grass ... After a short time the blue and gold standards of Orléans became visible on top of the dune; a group of horsemen in fluttering mantles slowly descended, riding toward the ducal tents. Marie watched with pounding heart. The riders dismounted, three of them moved off together to the pavilion, where Isabelle was already coming toward them with both hands outstretched in greeting.

A herald ceased blowing his trumpet and cried out in a loud voice, "The Duke of Orléans, the Earl of Fanhope, Sir Robert Roos."

Two of the lords, a tall, slim, richly dressed knight and a still youthful man in armor, knelt in the sand at some distance from the tent. He who now approached alone was a fairly stout older man, his shoulders bent as though in great weariness. Between the notched flaps of his hat his face looked very pale; deep furrows ran from his nostrils to the corners of his mouth. When he stopped before the Duchess a smile lit his sad, faded face. He knelt and doffed his hat. Marie of Cleves saw that his hair was grey as ashes.

"But he is a very old man," whispered one of her companions, casting a compassionate glance at the bride. Marie flushed with shame and distress and lowered her eyes.

"Welcome, welcome to the soil of Burgundy, Monseigneur," said Isabelle of Burgundy, smiling. "Will you be so good as to rise?"

Charles d'Orléans took the hand which she extended to him and replied lightly, but in a voice quivering with emotion.

"Madame, when I consider all that you have done to effect my release, I can only give myself over wholly to you. I am your prisoner."

At midday the Duke of Burgundy, too, arrived in Gravelines. Both processions—that of Isabelle and her guest, and that of the sovereign lord—met before the main portal of the parish church of the Holy Willibrord. The people—who had hurried from far and wide to see the meeting between Orléans and Burgundy, the protagonists of a now-legendary family feud—pushed forward against hastily-constructed barricades, intent on missing nothing that happened. Heralds had carried communication between the two royal processions and had made sure that both arrived at the same time in the square before the cathedral. Now from both sides the standard-bearers and trumpeters approached, who preceded the royal personages. On the church steps, surrounded by priests and choirboys, stood two bishops who would lead the solemn service: an Englishman and a Burgundian. The crowd shouted loudly, threw their caps in the air, waved pieces of cloth, applauded. "The Good! The Good!" called the people along the road. "Burgundy holds, holds Burgundy!"

Burgundy rode slowly past without acknowledging the cheers, but with a faint smile on his lips. He stared straight before him at the multi-colored flapping streamers and banners behind the barriers at the opposite side of the square. Above his dull black garments (he had not put off mourning since his father's death), his face was stiff and pale with tension. He knew quite well that he had to overcome his aversion to this meeting. Isabelle had smoothed the way for it and the task of making Charles welcome devolved upon Philippe himself. There was no need for him to say much. He saw that under the present circumstances it was senseless to let the feud with Orléans go on; besides, he scarcely knew his second cousin, and he had no reason to fear him. Political interests demanded this reconciliation; there was no other conceivable solution. Nevertheless, he felt guilty; his father and his grandfather would undoubtedly have rejected any agreement with Orléans. But I am not cooperating with him, I am using him, thought Burgundy while he nodded mechanically to his master of ceremonies. The cry of "Largesse!" which rose from the spectators could not be ignored. A storm of small silver coins rained upon the cobblestones, but Burgundy did not react when the elated crowd broke screaming and shoving through the barricades.

The procession had now reached the open square before the cathedral; both sides alighted. Isabelle took her guest by the hand and led him forward; Burgundy was approaching them with slow, controlled steps, his right hand holding the emblem of the Golden Fleece which he wore on a broad chain around his neck. Courtiers and dignitaries remained at a proper distance behind the royal personages. Heralds pulled out their trumpets, the people shouted hurrah, and the solemn voices of the choir streamed out through the open doors of the church.

Charles d'Orléans—who during the ride to Gravelines had attempted to chat courteously with his noble hostess, distracted as he was by the unnerving prospect of the coming meeting—saw that Burgundy was deathly pale; he was no longer smiling. The two men stood facing each other motionless in a strained silence. Both realized that this was the moment when the gap between them should be bridged. Each read in the other's eyes the memories which made friendship between them impossible; between them flashed, as quick as lightning, a human lifetime of combat, deceit, quarrels and mutual hatred, a long series of battles and sieges, of false peace treaties, of intrigues and cunning. The bridge at Montereau, the dark street corner near the Barbette palace, stood between them; the dead mutilated bodies of their fathers, for whose murders neither side had achieved complete satisfaction. So strong was the force of this inherited hatred that both Orléans and Burgundy involuntarily stepped back. Whatever might have appeared on paper or in their minds during the negotiations carried on by couriers or deputies became meaningless now that they stood face to face. Everyone around them waited breathlessly. The sound of the trumpets had died away, the singing in the church had ended. The courtiers waited, the horsemen and armed soldiers of the escort waited, the priests on the steps before the main portal of the church waited, the crowds, suddenly silent, waited behind the barricades. All the flags and banners fluttered in the wind, the horses stamped on the cobblestones, and behind the sand hills the sea glided murmuring over the shore.

Charles saw Burgundy's wide, tight-lipped mouth begin to tremble with uncontrollable emotion at the same moment that his own eyes filled with tears. They stepped forward at the same time and embraced. So they stood for a time, unable to speak. Each felt the body of the other shake with partially suppressed sobs.

Standing before the altar, with the Archbishop of Rochester, the Lords of Fanhope and Roos and a few English lawyers, Charles read in a loud voice declarations which he had made in Westminster Cathedral before his departure from London.

"I, Charles, Duke of Orléans, swear by God's Holy Gospel, which I hold here, that I shall faithfully keep everything contained in the agreements and treaties concluded between the Exalted Sovereign Henry, by the Grace of God King of England, and me, Charles d'Orléans, to wit: that within half a year I shall pay the remaining amount of my ransom, 160,000 gold écus; that I shall bring about a peace with England and France within a year; that if it should prove impossible for me to keep these vows after a year has passed, I shall return of my own free will to captivity. This I swear and affirm. *Sic me Deus adjuvet et haec sancta!*"

From Gravelines the ducal procession traveled inland to Saint-Omer. The procession was disposed to celebration; musicians seated on a painted carriage struck up song after song under the autumn sky; Isabelle's maids of honor laughed loud and clear, the courtiers joked and chatted with one another to the monotonous jangle of the tiny bells on saddles and reins.

Only Charles, who rode between Burgundy and his lady, could not find the proper tone. True, on this first day of freedom he felt slightly drunk, but the English lords still rode behind him with their retinues, and when he glanced over the landscape on either side of the road, he saw, with a feeling of uneasiness, flat marshy meadows, tiny windmills and blunted church towers; he could fancy himself again near Wingfield Castle. The twilight fell swiftly, mist rose from the sluggish rivulets crossing the land; in long rows along the water's edge willow trees, under the constant pressure of the slanting wind, stood gnarled and bare like monsters in almost human form. Here it smelt of mud and dank grass, of fog and salt marshes.

Charles shivered, the chill penetrating his very marrow. In the summer this was rich meadowland, but how gloomy and forsaken, how deadly monotonous it became in cold weather. He felt odd; after the nearly complete isolation of these past years in the Tower, he found it difficult to adjust once more to court life with its intricate ceremonies, its carefully determined social gradations. During his imprisonment he had lost the habit of making a sharp distinction between high and low degree, between lords and servants; he had become inclined to regard each man whom he met as a friend. After the solemn church service in Gravelines he had greeted gentlemen of the Duke's retinue whose names or faces seemed familiar to him— he had repeatedly encountered Burgundy's envoys—but when the Duchess Isabelle raised her brows in surprise and his cousin the Duke turned away with a look of slight displeasure, Charles understood that he was in a court society infinitely more rigid and formal, subject to many stricter distinctions, than even the royal household of France.

The Duke and Duchess of Burgundy seemed as exalted as gods; each act, each word, was accompanied by ceremony; they were addressed only with bent knee and downcast eyes; at every step they were regaled with marks of homage which Charles had seen given only to the King of France and then only on exceptionally solemn occasions. Burgundy does not really have to convince me of his power and wealth, thought Charles, a little annoyed at so much pomp. I would believe in it without all this showing-off. The fact that I am here, that I accept his terms, that I have him to thank for the advance payment on my ransom—all this shows that he has the means to assert his authority. To Charles, the courtiers around the ducal couple were only puppets in an elaborate marionette show. In captivity he had lost the taste for this sort of thing. He made up his mind that in the future, at Blois, he would not put up with such senseless, artificial activity.

But he would not be able to enjoy his return to Blois undisturbed; his thoughts remained shrouded in uneasiness. He would not be alone after his return. The Duchess of Burgundy had presented his bride to him in the pavilion among the dunes outside Gravelines. A child in robes of state who sulks because she finds me too old, he thought when he greeted her with a bow and with courteous words that were perhaps not flowery enough for Marie's taste. After that first meeting she had taken her place again among the Duchess's ladies-in-waiting. Since then Charles had had no further occasion to speak to her. The prospect of the marriage depressed him deeply, although he saw the advantages of such an alliance in the present circumstances.

He did not feel capable of pleasing so young a woman; what did they have in common, what could they talk about together? He felt ridiculous; he was surely not the man to attempt to win the favor of a fourteen-year-old girl. He had forgotten how to practice the art of love; he had spent his life without women except for a few fleeting adventures, brief encounters with ladies and maidens whose names he had forgotten long ago. One of Lady Fanhope's chambermaids, the wife of a knight with whom he used to hunt in Ampthill, a young noblewoman for whom he had composed some verses in English. His memories had faded quickly. Alice, Lady Suffolk . . . thoughts of her he could not shrug away. He was still amazed at the surprise she had in store for him; she appeared to be as cold and chaste as the effigies in Wingfield church, a dignified, grave, thoughtful hostess. But in London, during Suffolk's temporary absence, she had suddenly shown another side of herself and Charles had succumbed in spite of himself. He had plunged into the adventure as a starving man grabs a crust of bread. Afterward he would not remain under Suffolk's roof at any cost, especially not when he saw that his host responded indifferently to any mention of the incident and waved explanations and apologies away with a good-natured, dismissive gesture. It was only later that Charles learned that Suffolk himself had fathered many bastards in England as well as in France.

Later, in the Tower, the prisoner's yearning for female company had vanished. The feeling of guilt which had never wholly left him and the awareness of his own inability to go a-courting after all these years of forced solitude, continued to torment him now that he stood on the threshold of a new era as the bridegroom of an inexperienced child.

Before complete darkness fell, the ducal procession reached Saint-Omer. In the dusk Charles could just make out the high ramparts and towers of the city rising like mountains from the flat land. Outside the gates, awaiting the noble company, stood the notables: the clergy of the abbey of Saint-Bertin and many deputations from the guilds; torchbearers came running and through the arched gate one could see the torchlit square where bailiff's men were having great difficulty in keeping the crowds back so that the procession would have room to pass.

The magistrate of Saint-Omer gave a welcoming speech, addressed mainly to Charles.

"Monseigneur," said the magistrate at the end; bowing deeply he offered Charles the parchment containing the beautifully lettered text. "The population of our good city has grown considerably over the last few days; the people have come here from far and wide to witness your entry and the festivities to be held in honor of your return. They have travelled even from Picardy and the Ile de France to Saint-Omer to welcome you. It is a great privilege for our region to be the first to offer hospitality to Your Grace. Tomorrow, if it pleases you, a delegation will come from the city to bring you welcoming gifts; we hope you will permit us to offer a contribution toward your ransom, Monseigneur."

The bystanders and members of Burgundy's retinue broke into loud cheers in response to these words. Burgundy smiled in approval. When Charles noticed the expression on Burgundy's face, he tensed somewhat; he realized that the friendliness and hospitality of Saint-Omer were part of a carefully worked-out plan.

Amid the blaring of trumpets and in the light of hundreds of torches, they rode through the gate and entered the city. The crowds lining the roads seemed especially eager to shout with joy. Calls of "Long live Burgundy! Long live Orléans! God bless Orléans! Welcome, Orléans!" resounded from street to street, from square to square. Despite his depression, Charles was carried away by the tribute; never before in his life had he been hailed in this personal way. The glow of the torches, the shouts and the applause of the surging crowd mounted to his head; he saluted right and left without troubling himself about the distinguished tranquillity of the Duke of Burgundy and his wife, who sat silent and motionless in their saddles, letting the flood of appreciation wash over them.

Pleasantly tired from all the excitement, Charles at last reached the abbey of Saint-Bertin where a new welcoming committee of high clergy awaited. The travelers dismounted and, preceded by chanting youths and torchbearers, set out for the refectory where the evening meal was to be served.

"There are a number of people gathered there who are eager to salute you, fair cousin," Burgundy said to his guest as they walked. "Surely you must have noticed that your arrival is considered a most important event in my own domains as well as in France. It seems the French cities are awaiting the moment when you will visit them on your way to Blois. Your return home will be nothing less than a triumphal procession."

"It is hard for me to believe that all this homage is for me," Charles remarked smiling; he wiped his hot face with a cloth. "This reception surprises me somewhat. I had resigned myself to the belief that I had been forgotten on this side of the Straits of Calais."

Burgundy raised his brows in ironic amazement.

"Come, come, worthy cousin, you are too modest. How could you be forgotten? The name of Orléans is not one which can be quickly forgotten. From what I hear, your interests have been well looked after during your absence. All you need to do is take up the reins once more. Whether you will have influence and power in the future is entirely up to you." Charles looked in disbelief at his cousin who walked with great composure at his side.

"Too much is expected of me. Don't forget that all these years I have been completely isolated from ongoing events. Of course it is true that some news reached my ears now and then. But I still cannot form a clear opinion about current affairs. The King of England has charged me now with an extremely heavy responsibility."

Burgundy thrust his lower lip forward and smiled; for an instant he looked remarkably like his father.

"When you see where your interest lies, you will have no reason to complain about a lack of cooperation in these dominions and in France, fair cousin."

"My interest?" Charles smiled, somewhat bitterly. "I have only one interest, that of my unfortunate brother of Angoulême, who is still held in England."

Burgundy frowned.

"Nevertheless, you should have been fully informed before you left England," he said, shrugging. "You know that the princes of France see themselves shoved aside more and more often, that they are threatened with the loss of their influence in Council and government, that their ancient privileges are being violated. As the head of a feudal House, you have undoubtedly already chosen sides, fair cousin. You are in good company. Moreover, henceforth you can count on my support—the more so now that I know you will cooperate to further my interests too. But we are approaching the refectory, worthy cousin, and this is neither the time nor the place for a serious conversation, is it? Later, we shall have an opportunity to consult with each other in greater detail.

"And now self-confidence, a lust for life, a good hope for the future, Monseigneur—hold your head high, keep your heart cheerful. Everything here is being done in your honor. We are well-disposed toward you. We rejoice over your safe return, we wish to help you put together the full amount of your ransom, as much as it lies in our power to do it. Come, you are a man of consequence. There's no reason for doubt or despondency."

The light of many torches and candles streamed toward them through the widely opened doors; Burgundy's pages and stewards stood respectfully in rows at the entrance to the hall. Charles could see festively bedecked tables, colorfully dressed guests milling about; in the midst of the brightness and glitter the starched headdresses of the women stirred like sails on the sea. The noble company, led by the abbé of Saint-Bertin and some clerics in ornate vestments, and followed closely by a long procession of courtiers, stepped into the refectory which had been transformed into a banquet hall.

"Welcome once more, Monseigneur," said Isabelle of Burgundy, even before she had taken her place under the enormous canopy. "Here comes someone who wants to be the first to pay his respects to you. I hope our surprise will please you."

From the group of spectators two men stepped foward; one of

them Charles recognized at once as the old Archbishop of Reims whom he had met five years earlier during the conferences in London. The prince of the Church approached him slowly, nodding and smiling, his right hand, on which his large ring sparkled, raised in greeting. The other man remained a few paces behind him. Charles saw a man of medium height, broad-shouldered, with a weather-beaten face and very bright grey-green eyes which looked straight at him attentively; on his chest shone the Order of the Eagle on a wide chain.

"God bless you, Monseigneur," he said, standing before Charles. "I see that you do not recognize me. I am your half-brother, Dunois."

There seemed to be no end to the celebrations and ceremonies in Saint-Omer. Time and again when Charles, exhausted and dazed by so much diversion, so much pomp and festive joy, thought that it must surely end now, Burgundy's heralds and stewards announced new amusements. Tournaments, banquets, processions and contests were the background for the two most important events of those weeks: Charles' appointment as Knight of the Golden Fleece and his marriage to Marie of Cleves. His head was beginning to swim. Since all this commotion was in his honor, he could not shirk his duty. He sat in silence, making an effort to smile politely while he watched the endless tourneys which did not particularly interest him. He could not understand how full-grown men could watch, with enthusiasm and excitement, a spectacle which consisted of gaily attired horsemen hacking away at each other. Since he was the guest of honor, the task of awarding the prizes and addressing the victors fell to him. He did this calmly and pleasantly, using, not without irony, antiquated forms of speech and outdated expressions and often, at the request of the ladies present, adding extemporaneous lines of verse. They applauded him heartily; on every side he heard praise of his mildness, his wit, his patience in adversity. "The good Duke of Orléans," he was called in nearly all the speeches and proclamations. Charles was secretly amused.

So this is the impression I make upon my fellow men, he thought, smiling to himself. Fat and old before my time, tamed forever by adversity, a good-natured lord who can write verses tolerably well. The inner voice which had become so familiar to him during the years of imprisonment seemed to urge him repeatedly to adopt this view of himself. "There it is, accept it, resign yourself to reality, remember how the thrush in the fable perished because it tried obstinately to race the falcons and sparrow-hawks . . ." When he thought like this, the image of Blois rose temptingly before him once more: a safe haven, the last place of refuge, far from politics and intrigue, far from court life, from social obligations, foolish pomp and ceremony. The life of which he had dreamt in England rose before him: a serene existence among trusted friends, books and manuscripts in a world populated with the creatures of his dreams and thoughts. These dreams of the future had faded since he had come ashore at Calais. What he had considered at first to be only a task that had to be performed before he could enjoy his retirement, appeared in another light now that he was surrounded by the ambitious men and women of Burgundy.

In the quiet, secluded chambers of Pontefract, Ampthill, Fotherinhay and Bolingbroke, he had forgotten reality. He had considered the temptations and pleasures of the world to be unimportant because they had vanished from his horizon. In Saint-Omer Charles had walked with open eyes into the net which Burgundy had spread to catch him: the celebrations, meetings, ceremonies and applause, the courtesies and honors had been carefully calculated to make the former prisoner forget his past filled with ennui, resignation and enforced abstinence. They had not missed their mark. In spite of his private annoyance at so much childish idle activity, despite his fatigue and his impatient eagerness to fulfil his obligations as rapidly as possible, Charles felt himself, from day to day, becoming more absorbed in the effervescent life of the court. When, in the midst of fabulous splendor and ostentation, Burgundy hung the emblem of the Golden Fleece around his neck—a distinction coveted by kings and emperors—Charles felt a desire to try to fly once more with the falcons and sparrow-hawks. He did not believe his wings were crippled—not yet. He could still play an important role and render service to his country and its people. If it were true, as Burgundy and his confidants had told him in various discussions, that the King of France wanted to continue the war against England, that he violated agreements, did not keep his promises, allowed himself to be ruled openly by his favorites from the third estate who were bent on smashing the power of the feudal princes for good—if all this were true, it would seem that some intervention was necessary.

He could take it as a sign of appreciation of his abilities that he was wanted as a mediator in this affair, that he was regarded as the man who could, on the one hand, bring about an agreement between Burgundy and the French vassals and, on the other, keep the King informed of the desires and grievances of this powerful group. Wasn't it senseless of him to doubt his own capability when every effort was being made to convince him that he was capable? His growing belief in his own worth was strengthened in no small measure when a legation from Bruges came to petition him humbly to intercede with the Duke of Burgundy for the sake of the city. Some time earlier a disagreement had arisen between Burgundy and the people of Bruges; now they begged Charles, who enjoyed a reputation as a peacemaker, to restore the good relationship between the Duke and the citizens. Burgundy allowed himself to be won over after having given Charles the opportunity to plead Bruges' case in full. When the dispute was eventually settled, Charles could only believe that the favorable resolution was a consequence of his actions.

In this atmosphere of positive self-evaluation, he took Marie of Cleves to wife before the altar in the cathedral of Saint-Omer. He felt he could now allow himself to be led to the bridal chamber by a glittering procession of nobles without any feelings of shame or vexation; he no longer feared being looked upon with contempt or pity. Marie's royal education had not been wasted on her; she did not betray her disappointment by tears or sighs. She bore herself in company with controlled dignity and was amenable and obliging when they were alone together—in itself a rare occurence.

Charles found himself invited more and more often to discussions not only by Burgundy and his council but by other highly placed persons as well. He saw clearly now what Burgundy wanted from him: he must point out to the King of France his dereliction in fulfilling the terms stipulated in the treaty of Arras, and he must prepare a meeting of the feudal princes. Burgundy also wanted Charles to swear loyalty to the treaty of Arras and approve all the points covered in the treaty. On this occasion some differences arose for the first time between guest and host. An adder lay concealed in the grass; undoubtedly Burgundy also wanted to hear declarations of guilt and remorse over the murder which had been committed at Montereau. Charles, however, declined to express these sentiments; he had had nothing to do with that business. Dunois, summoned to swear an oath of allegiance, had no intention of recognizing the treaty of Arras. His refusal finally led to a heated exchange of words on the subject between Charles and Dunois.

"I have sworn fealty to the King," said Dunois. "Besides, I can have no peace as long as Burgundy has disassociated himself from the Crown. Apparently the King has no intention of putting up with this in the long run."

"But the King has not rejected the treaty!"

"The King is not so simple-minded as people here seem to think," Dunois said slowly. "He has more brains than we thought. Just because he does things that many people don't see eye to eye with, doesn't mean that he lacks insight. For me, he remains the man who is first in the Kingdom; I consider it my duty to serve him."

"My God, in your letters you haven't always sounded like such a willing subject, brother!" Charles, who was sitting at a table before a spread of documents, took off his spectacles and tapped them angrily on the back of his hand. "I seem to remember that you bubbled over with strong condemnation of him more than once."

"That may well be," said Dunois calmly and coldly. "But at the same time I never made a secret of the fact that the unity of the Kingdom is more important to me than anything else. When the King hurt that unity I objected strongly to his behavior. But now that he seems to be working for unity—I don't care why—I stand behind him."

Charles sighed with impatient annoyance.

"You seem to favor him considerably since he granted you an earldom," he remarked sharply. Dunois looked at him quickly and began to pace back and forth, his hands behind his back. After a brief silence he said curtly, "I deeply regret that you do not know me well enough to know that I have little use for titles and badges of honor, Monseigneur my brother. As God is my witness, I would rather be called Bastard of Orléans than anything else. I serve Orléans as I have always done, and Orléans is a fief of the French Crown. I hope I may never see Orléans follow the example of Burgundy and reject the King's authority because he thinks he is too great to be a vassal."

Charles rose.

"Do you suspect that I tend that way, brother?"

"I don't know what to think," replied Dunois with a shrug. "All I see is that you are offering your services in good faith to an affair which will certainly not promote the unity of the Kingdom. Peace with England—I can see the benefit of that and I shall gladly help you, my lord brother, to convince the King of it. But otherwise the cause you are supporting seems to me to smack of high treason. The rich can thank the ambition and intolerance of the feudal lords for their ruin. Must we repeat the same mistakes now that we are at the point of struggling up out of our misery? I understand your motivation perfectly." He turned and stood before Charles. "It's only natural that you should want to reassert yourself. But you will gain greater glory if you serve the true interests of France, my lord brother."

"You forget one thing." Charles' voice trembled with anger. "And that is that I owe my release chiefly to Burgundy. If he and the Duchess had not persisted and paid a considerable part of my ransom, I would still be sitting in the Tower, worthy brother. With all your love for the Kingdom, you could not reach the King and convince him to interest himself in me or our brother of Angoulême. It's only natural that I should be ready to render Burgundy service in return for what he has done for me."

"By God and Saint-Denis, are you blind then?" Dunois slammed the edge of the table with his fist. "While you've been here haven't you grasped yet what Burgundy is aiming at? Divide and conquer—it's an old saw, brother, but that's how he preserves his power. For fifty years the Burgundians have followed a fixed policy, that's obvious. Look around you, see how Burgundy grants favors to the low countries in order to be sure of strong support to the north and east of the Kingdom. Don't you understand his power? He is richer than all the princes of Christendom put together; no foreign power will be able to thwart him once he is firmly in the saddle. He has bought you, brother, just as he can buy anyone he wants. He will let you work in his own interest. I cannot forget that we had to fight in vain for years before we could restore our father's honor and get satisfaction for his murder in the rue Barbette—did they offer us compensation then?"

There was silence for a while. Charles kept his eyes lowered; Dunois stood unmoving.

"I am bound by my vows to Burgundy," Charles said at last in a stifled voice. "I cannot break my word."

"Go as quickly as possible to pay your respects to the King." Dunois put both palms flat on the table and leaned toward his brother. "The King is now in Paris. Speak to him before you go any further. You can render great service to the Kingdom if you can find a way to reconcile the vassal princes and the King."

Dunois looked searchingly at Charles, who stared thoughtfully at the papers before him. In this stout, flabby, greying man with his doubts and uncertainties, his fear of arousing displeasure, his eagerness to be of service, he saw little of the young warrior who had left Blois in 1415 to fight with the King against the English. Even in the past he had noticed that Charles was more amiable and more quickly inclined to indecision than other people, but he had never suspected his half-brother of calculated ambition, cowardice and stupidity.

"You would do well to listen to those who want to help you with advice and action, my lord brother," said Dunois more mildly.

Charles sighed and looked up.

"I have obligations to Burgundy. I don't see how I can withdraw my approval of the treaty of Arras, which by the way has never been rejected by the King, although he has never abided by its terms. I don't consider it treason to do what the King himself has done. The only thing I refuse to do is to confess that I am guilty of being an accomplice to the murder of the late Burgundy. I am ready, of course, to pay my respects to the King as soon as I can get away from here. But in God's name, brother, don't make my task more difficult by being obstinate. Let us both put off the requested declaration, it is only a formality."

"I won't do that willingly," Dunois retorted. "I refused to do it in '35 because I could not consult with you; now I refuse because I do not agree with you."

"Then I command you," said Charles vehemently. "I am still the head of our House."

"I'm sorry that you find it necessary to assert your authority this way." Dunois stood erect with his arms at his sides. "I obey you as my lord. But don't forget, Monseigneur, that during your absence, I served the welfare and honor of your House, body and soul."

"Forgive me, but I cannot retract the command," said Charles, lowering himself slowly into his chair. "I know that you will not desert me, brother."

"No, you're right there." Dunois gave a curt, bitter laugh.

"I remember," said Charles softly, without looking up, "how once long ago you advised me to conclude a pact with the enemy because you thought that if I did that I would be in a better position to serve the Kingdom in the long run. I followed your advice then, brother. You were only a young boy; I never reproached you later for leading me astray."

After these words both men fell silent for a while. Pensively, Charles moved his spectacles up and down on the sheet of paper before him. Dunois stared with knitted brows at the tapestries, gleaming with gold and silver threads, which Burgundy had ordered hung on the walls of the halls and apartments of the abbey in honor of his guests. Finally, Dunois formally requested permission to depart; he saluted and quit the room with measured steps.

About the middle of January, Charles came with his young wife to Paris, attended by a great retinue of nobles, pages, servants and soldiers. Burgundy had generously given up a part of his court suite to add luster to Charles' return to Blois. In addition, in all the cities which the Duke of Orléans passed through on his journey, noble families came to offer him their sons as pages or shieldbearers and their daughters as maids of honor in the hope that this would assure their children a good future. Beautiful gifts bestowed by the municipalities were carried along in wagons: gold and silver tableware, fabrics and tapestries, casks of wine—gifts which Charles had accepted with gratitude, because his own valuables had long since been sold or pawned. No less welcome were the sums of money offered by Bruges, Amiens, Tournai, Ghent and many other cities as contributions toward his ransom. No doubt it was all done to please Burgundy. Charles thought somewhat caustically that he must swallow all feelings of bitter shame over this charity accompanied by beautiful ceremonies; in truth, he could not afford to be proud.

So with Marie beside him, he rode into Paris in the midst of almost royal pomp. Richmont, accompanied by some high magistrates and courtiers, came to greet him at the city gates, but his arrival seemed to attract little attention. In the neglected streets with their ramshackle, peeling houses, groups of people stood here and there, watching the advancing procession with dull curiosity. That they were looking at the banners and ensigns of Orléans and Burgundy carried side by side aroused little surprise in a generation which did not remember the civil war which had raged thirty years before.

Silently, Charles looked about him, overcome by emotion. The city was gloomy, battered; the houses which had been chopped up for firewood during the last grim winter of occupation had not been rebuilt. Porches and shutters were missing from a number of buildings. The streets needed attention; they were full of holes and cracks and covered with refuse.

But when Charles lifted his eyes he saw the familiar outlines of church towers and castles against the sky.

Conversation dropped off; they rode side by side in silence through the somber filthy city on the way to the Hôtel des Tournelles which belonged to Charles and which had been made ready for him and his wife. They passed the palace of Saint-Pol, now vacant, neglected, defaced, like so many other royal residences in the city. No banners fluttered from the towers, the gates were closed with rusty chains. Charles looked up at the dark rows of windows, hidden for the most part behind shutters; here Queen Isabeau had died some years before, forgotten and uncared-for, a secluded invalid. She had been seen for the last time at one of the windows watching the coronation procession of her grandson Henry VI; after that she withdrew forever into the shadows of Saint-Pol.

"I intend to pay my respects to the King while I am here," said Charles to Richmont. "But where is he to be found at this moment?"

The Constable wrinkled his brow.

"Every day someplace different. He has no time to hold court. He travels from city to city, taking up details of business, searching out hotbeds of sloth and resistance, revising policies of state. I think you can find him in Sens, Orléans; at any rate he arrived there the day before yesterday."

"Then I shall send messengers to Sens to ask the King for an audience." Still frowning, Richmont cast a sidelong glance at Charles' pale profile.

"Don't expect the kind of reception Burgundy gave you," he remarked. "Here we have time only for hard work."

Charles began to smile. "Surely my royal cousin will wish to meet my wife and me, now that I have returned to France after such a long absence. He might want to talk to me about any number of important matters. I want to pay my respects to him not only as a kinsman but also as an envoy. Surely the King will find time for me."

"I see that you don't know him." Richmont gave a short, irritated laugh. "The King is an extremely suspicious man and his advisors are exceedingly sharp-witted. Do you know what they call him? 'Le Bien Servi'—he who is well-served. Believe me, those who serve him so well guard his welfare and the welfare of the Kingdom."

Charles' smile faded. He looked at Marie who rode on his right, pale with fatigue, shivering in her fur-lined cloak. She had heard nothing of the conversation.

"What do you mean by that, Richmont?" he asked, in a choked voice.

The Constable shrugged. "I wanted to draw your attention to something which you might not know yet," he said calmly. "Perhaps you will listen to the advice of one who is well-informed."

Charles could not help but think of certain events in London in the years 1417 and 1418. Silently he turned his head away.

In the days following his arrival in Paris he received envoys from the University, magistrates, a number of highly placed officials and priests who bade him welcome and offered him gifts; with great effort, in the impoverished city, they had collected a sum to be put toward Monseigneur's ransom. A solemn mass was read in his honor in Notre Dame; the church was adorned, precious relics were displayed, the great bells pealed, and a crowd of curiosity-seekers who had gathered in search of amusement in the square in front of the church, cheered when Charles and his wife came outside.

Meanwhile, the couriers whom Charles had sent to Sens cooled their heels in the King's anterooms. Scarcely a week after his arrival in Paris, the answer came back from the King.

"The Duke of Orléans is welcome, provided he comes accompanied only by a few loyal servants. No provision will be made for the arrival of armed men and a large retinue."

"What does the King mean by this?" Charles, somewhat displeased, asked Dunois, who had been with him for the past few days.

Dunois stroked his cheek. He could not help but smile at the surprise and disappointment evinced by his brother, who had been so sure of an enthusiastic reception.

"It means that you must leave all these Burgundians at home," he said quietly. "The King will receive his cousin of Orléans, but not Burgundy's protégé."

"Protégé?" Irritated, Charles flung the paper with its seal onto the table. "Everyone should understand that I do what I do of my own free will. I speak for peace out of conviction. It's partly out of gratitude to the man who ransomed me, partly from solidarity with my kinsmen of Alençon, Armagnac and Brittany that I support the aspirations of the Crown's feudal vassals. For that matter I too have a few legitimate complaints. No one should take me for a puppet."

"Go to the King and try to win his confidence," Dunois advised. "It will not be easy, but it is worth the effort. I have done what I could to temper his distrust. I have tried to make your position clear to him, brother. Now it's time for you to speak directly to the King yourself."

Charles stood before the hearthfire with his back to Dunois; he did not answer. He was extremely annoyed. What difference could it make to the King whether he came to Sens with a dozen or with a few hundred followers? It was not so much that he himself was fond of ostentatious display, but he refused to allow himself to be denigrated. He felt that he had already been humiliated enough. The King's demand was unreasonable; it seemed to have no other purpose than to demean the suppliant. Charles did not see how he could put up with it, especially since it also insulted those whom he represented. He would lose every shred of dignity, of authority, if he complied with the stipulations so condescendingly set by the King. Burgundy would not unjustly be offended if he, through Charles' person, was treated in this way.

"Tell the couriers that I am cancelling my visit to the King," said Charles coldly, without turning around. "Tomorrow I leave for Blois."

The summer sun burns on the houses of Blois, which lie scattered over the hill on the right bank of the river. Because of the prolonged drought the river has shrunk in its bed; the water, sparkling in the bright sunshine, is bounded on both sides by wide sand banks where children play all day long and washerwomen kneel at the water's edge. On the projecting plateau, a short distance up the slope of the hill, rises the castle, dark grey and weathered; but the shutters at the windows are painted bright blue and red, the ducal standards flutter from towers and battlements—from sunrise to sunset a procession of servants, pages, squires and officers of the Duke's household travels across the bridges and through the gates. After twenty-five years, a re-animated Blois once again shelters Charles d'Orléans within its walls.

Activity in the many narrow, steep streets and the crudely paved squares is increased by the presence of the ducal family. The rumble of voices and footsteps, the stamping of horses' hooves, the rattle of carts fill the city which for long years had echoed only to the murmur of brooks or the monotonous creak of a water wheel.

Stewards and kitchen and chamber servants can be seen walking among the stalls in the market as they used to do; on the meadows outside the city, pages and squires practice with bow and javelin. From castle yard and inner court the whinny of horses, the clatter of arms, reaches the streets of Blois once more. Often the young Duchess rides out through the fields with her ladies and her retinue in painted wagons, or on horseback, hunting birds in the deserted swampland on the other side of the river. Sometimes the noble company wishes to go boating on the Loire; on barges hung with streamers and tapestries, they are piloted downstream to Chaumont and Amboise, from which they return on horseback.

The people of the villages and farmsteads along the river hurry out to enjoy the charming spectacle; the noble ladies and courtiers in their bright attire sit laughing under the silk canopies on the ships gliding slowly past. The old happy days seem to have come back again—the golden days of chivalry when the cities thrived, the princes were generous and splendid and the people were well-protected. Those who live along the Loire in the region of Orléans and the lovely Touraine praise the Duke who has come back to them as a true prince of peace; they ascribe the new renaissance of prosperity, the restoration of order to these long strife-torn domains, to Charles' return.

In addition, to many he is a hero, a martyr; those who were still children when he left Blois remember only that he fought at Agincourt and languished in English dungeons. They have known the misery of war too well not to give the Duke high praise when they learn that he is working earnestly for peace, that he is trying to bring about a rapprochement between the King and the discontented princes. It cannot be denied that he throws himself wholly into his endeavors. He travels incessantly, returns for only a few days, then sets off again with his armed retinue and councillors to Brittany, Armagnac, to Bourbon and Foix, and to the north, to Hesdin in Burgundy where he meets the mighty Duke. When he is in Blois, he is rarely seen outside the castle. Each glimpse is treasured of that figure clad always in black, of that friendly face.

There is no complaint even when he proclaims an increase in the tax on wine, salt and fruit. Everyone understands that it is most important for him to collect great sums of money in as short a time as possible; won't he have to return to captivity if he has not paid his ransom in full in the course of a year? Don't the English still hold his brother, Monseigneur d'Angoulême, under lock and key?

For this reason the people of Orléans and the outlying cities and villages endure without a murmur what might under other circumstances have moved them to rebellion. After the anguish and anarchy of the war years, the severe military rule of Dunois, the uncertainty and astonishment caused by the King's new measures and reforms, the rule of Charles d'Orléans leads them back to the trusted ways of the past. Obedience and taxes are given in exchange for peace; the presence of the Duke creates the prospect of increased commerce, greater business opportunities, a new prosperity.

The noble lord himself is generous and kind-hearted; everywhere he is considered to be a national hero as well as an excellent poet. The ballads and rondelets which he sent occasionally from England to friends and kinsmen—letters in rhyme—are known outside the small circles of initiates; all men of letters have heard of them. Since the news of his homecoming has spread, scribes, bookbinders and illuminators have flocked to Monseigneur; they know that the Duke is a great connoisseur of books and manuscripts, that immediately on his return to Blois, he ordered his library brought from the cellar vaults of Font La Rochelle, that a few weeks later the books which he had collected during his captivity were transported by ships and wagons. The great folios were carried into Blois; Monseigneur's librarian has told bystanders where these volumes came from; they are the books which once belonged to the Duke's grandfather, Charles the Wise; the Regent Bedford had stolen them from the Louvre, but after Bedford's death Monseigneur had succeeded in gaining possession of the precious manuscripts in London.

These and similar stories considerably enhance the Duke's reputation; in addition, when he is seen in public, he has a good word, a friendly greeting for everyone. All the poor and homeless find a meal and lodging in Blois; no one knocks at the gates there in vain. He is the good Duke, "le bon duc d'Orléans."

How does Charles live since his homecoming? From the moment in the country road outside Orléans when two hundred small children stepped forward, with little flags in their hands, to bid him welcome, he has determined to justify the faith of the singing children and the elated populace lining the roads: he will bring peace, as a mediator he will end the misunderstanding between the King and his noble vassals.

For the first time since he set foot on the shore he sees clearly what he wants to do; he is now in a position to organize his impressions, to examine the facts which had confounded him during his stay in Saint-Omer, during his tiring journey, during the brief delay in Paris. When, after reaching the Loire, he rode through his beloved country past Gien, the fresh wind blew doubt and dissatisfaction from his heart. This is his country, this is the land to which he is devoted with all his being: the sloping fields, the broad river, the cities and castles entrusted to him since his early youth. This gently rising and falling land is, even in the winter, the garden of France, filled with color and life; brown and green hills, the houses and towers grey or russet and the sparkling river which changes at every bend—alternately silver blue or steel grey, ornamented with the sunken gold of the sand banks under the water, with small islands, with numerous ships.

Under this sky Charles cannot nurse a resentment against the King. While he rides on, feeding his hungry eyes, breathing in the fresh air, the odor of earth and water united in his lungs, he begins to realize what work he really wants to do. He does not want to choose a party, he wishes to be neither the leader of the feudal lords nor the King's servant—he wishes to be impartial, independent, to cooperate to bring conflicting interests into agreement with one another. What Burgundy desires of him he does not consider incompatible with his own wishes. He has promised his powerful kinsmen to visit the vassals of the Crown, to hear their grievances and proposals, and then to ask the King's consent to an assembly of the feudal lords at which they can air their objections and desires.

True, he suspects that Burgundy's plan is not so harmless as it seems; he is fully determined to take no part in any potential conspiracy. He will act only as an intermediary. As a consequence of the meeting convened by the princes, he will undoubtedly be given the opportunity to visit the King; perhaps it will be possible then for him to overcome the King's suspicions and recalcitrance, to show that he has come to play a role in the Kingdom which no one before him ever could have played, because there has never been anyone like him, who stands apart from all factions. When the King sees the importance of his task and recognizes the services of the mediator, the time will have come to discuss peace with England, to pursue step by step the path to an end of all hostilities between the two kingdoms.

In spite of his good will and zeal for the work, Charles cannot avoid the knowledge that a number of difficulties and disappointments lie in wait for him. He knows all too well that in practice he will not behave toward the princes with complete reserve. He is bound to them by blood ties and in addition he is dependent on many of them for his and his brother's ransoms. They have already made promises to him about that; he is afraid they will expect repayment not in money, but in services in another area altogether. Even during the welcoming celebrations in Orléans, Beaugency and Blois, he sends his couriers and envoys to the courts of Brittany, Armagnac and Bourbon to announce his impending visit. Preparations are being made in Blois for his departure; the young Duchess, sick and weary of travel, will not accompany him. During the few days of rest before his journey, Charles prowls once again through the castle and its grounds. While Marie, surrounded by her young ladies, stays in her apartments in the women's wing, Charles walks alone through the corridors and chambers where he had been accustomed to wander as a young boy, absorbed in thought then as he is now.

Much has changed in Blois; for years the castle was a fortress filled with soldiers, an important fortification in the Loire valley, a meeting place for commanders, a place where troops could be outfitted and exercised and supplies could be collected—all without hindrance. The years have left their mark on the castle. The rooms and apartments once intended to accommodate the ducal household have served other purposes. Before Charles' arrival, some tapestries were hastily hung, some pieces of furniture put in place. It is clear that these are the few things the creditors have not taken. Only the tower room where Charles lived as a young man remains unchanged; the bed, reading desk and chair, the chest in the window niche. On one of the dusty shelves lies his old psalmbook with its worn leather binding.

In that small room Charles remains standing for a long time, overwhelmed by memories. Here he wrote his letter to the King; here he once discussed the English auxiliary armies with Dunois—

here he lay at night staring, staring at the glow of coals in the brazier, thinking about the struggle against Burgundy, Armagnac's arrogance, about the need for money and the restoration of honor. All this is a lifetime ago, when he was guileless, ignorant and trusted everybody. Charles sighs and shrugs; slowly he descends the circular staircase, goes through the wooden verandas along the southern wall of Blois, now completely overgrown with vines, and walks through the series of chambers in which he had lived with Bonne. Involuntarily he walks over the dusty floor as cautiously as if he were on consecrated ground. The chambers are empty; no tapestries hang there any longer; the embroidery frame has vanished from the window recess. Gone are the benches, the tables, the prayer stool; only in the bedroom stands the bed with the green curtains where he dreamed his childish dreams, struggled with his childish anxieties, where he slept with Bonne. He touches one of the posts with his hand and stares at the bare planks, the threadbare bound curtains. His eye falls on a number of small scratches in the wood at the head of the bed. He moves closer, takes his spectacles from his sleeve. He bends forward and peers at the letters "Dieu le scet" scratched in the wood with a pin.

A profound emotion seizes the man who, wearing spectacles before his nearsighted eyes, stays on alone in the forgotten, dismantled room, the only thing which remains to him of the few truly happy days of his life: an old bed, a memory, a greeting from her who once slept in his arms. Here she lay, waiting, hoping, praying, feeling for the ring on her finger: "Dieu le scet." And once, on an endless summer night or on a stormy winter evening, to cheer herself she inscribed the motto "Dieu le scet" in the wood above her head.

With trembling fingers Charles removes his spectacles; blinded with tears which he restrains with difficulty, he walks back through the empty rooms to the inhabited part of the castle.

So in the year 1441 he travels to Nantes in Brittany, where the Duke has prepared a great reception for him. There he meets a number of old acquaintances who, to his annoyance, show him almost royal respect. The flattery goes against his grain: do they tacitly assume that he covets the throne? On all sides they offer him money and gifts; he must accept them gratefully in the name too of his brother of Angoulême. Among the noble guests at Brittany's court he finds his son-in-law, the Duke of Alençon, whose wife, Charles' daughter and only child, Jeanne, had died a few years earlier.

He does not much like Alençon with his polished manners and haughty demeanor. Bitterly Charles notes how relative the notion of kinship is; he feels no affection for this stranger; he realizes quite well that Alençon's display of courtliness exists only because of his own supposed political importance. He cannot get the thought out of his head that, beneath the veneer of gallant civility, things are going on in the court of Nantes which cannot bear the light of day. Too many meetings for his taste have taken place which are abruptly aborted when a non-initiate approaches. During the hunt and at mealtime there are exchanges of words and significant glances which he does not know how to interpret. They are hiding something from him; they do not dare to take him into their confidence. He sees that the Duke of Brittany and his nobles are able to move uninhibited through the streets of Normandy, which is still occupied by the English; English lords, including the royal herald, are seen repeatedly in the midst of the hunting, hard-drinking Bretons. Charles' son-in-law, Alençon, seems to be in the center of this group. Charles watches him, tries to tempt him to confide in him, seeks an explanation through cautious conversation, but Alençon gives vague answers, avoiding Charles' eyes.

This puzzling activity of the Breton nobles disturbs Charles all the more since it is known that in the government of England the war party, under the leadership of the fierce Humphrey of Gloucester, are once again predominant. Those who want peace with France, who have given Charles d'Orléans his freedom, who looked with hope to the results of their efforts, have been relegated to the background. The English troops in France are stirring once again. Charles listens in silence: the news of the King's victories in Creil and Pontoise provide him with food for thought. He understands why until now the King has resisted peace with England; luck has turned in France's favor. The King no longer needs to include what he has recaptured in battle, in order to negotiate a peace treaty: England is weaker than ever, torn by party dispute; Henry VI, the grandson of a madman, has begun to behave more strangely every day.

To a degree, the temporary ascendancy of the war party in England is advantageous to Charles, because these lords, who had worked incessantly against his release, cannot blame him if after a year he has not satisfied the stipulations of that release. If there is no change in the atmosphere in Westminster, he will enjoy a reprieve for the moment. On the other hand, he is overcome by helpless rage when he thinks of his hapless brother, who has been a prisoner now for thirty years and whose release depends on the struggle of those who want peace.

For months Charles is on the move constantly, a guest now here, now there, in towering castles, fortified strongholds; everywhere he hears the grievances of the lords against the King. Everyone joins him in the hope that the war with England will end soon—even though their reasons differ from his. If the chances of war remain favorable to the armies of the King, he will unquestionably drive the English out. If he succeeds, he will be more powerful than any French king in nearly a hundred years—and when the King's authority is unassailable, the feudal lords have little influence. Therefore they wish with all their hearts that peace will be effected before the King's power has been confirmed.

"Yes, exactly," says Charles thoughtfully again and again when they attempt in private conversations to make him a party to these opinions. "Exactly, certainly. . ." His past has trained him well. He can conceal his thoughts, listen calmly, answer courteously and never show anger, contempt or displeasure. To him this King is a strange, incomprehensible figure: at the outset he was a timid weakling, now from day to day he is becoming more feared and at the same time more respected. Charles does not yet know what attitude to take toward him. But toward the feudal princes he feels only distrust and a certain contempt. He realizes more clearly than ever how completely these men, all of whom want to be petty kings, subordinate the welfare of the realm to their own interests.

Heavy-hearted, he travels in October to Hesdin castle on the Flemish border where Burgundy awaits him.

His independence has sharpened Charles' insights. He finds the man with the wide mouth, the unfathomable eyes, who has invited him to Hesdin for an essential discussion, quite different from the distinguished, courtly host of Saint-Omer. True, both Dukes are surrounded by the luxurious opulence which Burgundy cannot do without: a castle filled with hundreds of followers and decorated with flags and banners. Wine and game are brought in heaped on wagons; precious tapestries, crystal and golden tableware are brought for the Duke from Flanders. At each meal minstrels, harpists, jongleurs, jesters and bards display their skill.

And here Burgundy and his son come striding, the ten-year-old Comte de Charolais whom he has brought with him, in stiff ceremony, amid bowing and kneeling courtiers who follow the varying daily rituals with painful punctiliousness. But there is, for Charles at any rate, a perceptibly essential difference.

At Saint-Omer he, whatever Burgundy's intentions might have been, was the guest of honor; but he comes to Hesdin like a vassal beseeching his sovereign. The man who is sitting beside him under a canopy of gold, sharply and coldly putting question after question, is a great statesman, ruler over a number of different territories. He who holds Holland, Friesland, Zeeland, Hainault, Gelre, Luxembourg, Brabant, Flanders, Picardy and Burgundy, as well as France-Comte, Bethel, Liège and Limburg united into a single kingdom, must indeed have the ability, to an exceptionally high degree, of weighing pros and cons so that they make sense, of serving a thousand conflicting interests and, in spite of everything, of maintaining his own power.

This man with his quietly controlled gestures differs strongly from him who spoiled Charles' youth; he differs from Jean the Fearless, with his passion, his toughness, his stubborn grim rage; Philippe, whom men call "the Good", possesses an effortless, innate royal ease, has an inner strength which overcomes almost any barriers existing on his chosen path to great accomplishments. The young Comte de Charolais, a princely figure in black and gold with the insignia of the Order of the Golden Fleece upon his breast, sits looking attentively at what is going on. Charles feels almost sorry for the lad who must one day take over and rule this awe-inspiring inheritance.

Charles tells Burgundy about his experiences. His host makes few comments; he sits erect and listens, nodding almost imperceptibly from time to time. Finally he issues his orders—at least Charles considers them orders—that now the King of France must be informed of the proposed conference of the feudal lords, and he must be asked to send *his* representatives as well.

"You will preside yourself, worthy cousin," says Burgundy, moving his large, shapely hand back and forth over the chain of the Golden Fleece. "You will lead the discussions and communicate the result in writing to the King. You will carefully explain all points, and you must not neglect to note your own grievances with the others. Finally, you will stress the fact that the princes of France demand that the King fulfil all the conditions of the treaty of Arras."

"What do you expect from this conference?" Charles was watchful in his turn. "Do you hope to intimidate the King?"

Burgundy shrugs.

"That remains to be seen, fair cousin. It is not clear whether the King's new determination and self-confidence is anything more than a mask. The conference will assuredly help to enlighten us about that."

At Charles' request, Dunois spoke to the King. Charles had expected some resistance, but the King, neither surprised nor reluctant, gave his consent to a meeting and sent his own chancellor to represent him. In February of the following year, the congress of feudal princes met in the city of Nevers; it was a purely formal affair with no other purpose than to demonstrate the unanimity of discontent.

Charles, who in his capacity as chairman had to listen to and lead all speeches, all arguments, all debates, was fully convinced, as early as the first day, of the dubious character of the assembly which had been announced as a conference "to advance the King's interests." The interests which were discussed were by no means those of the King. The Lords of Alençon, Vendôme, Bourbon and a number of others petitioned for restitution or gifts of land, money, manors, high offices. They all complained about the new regulations, about the fact that the King did not consult with them on important affairs, about positions of power of burghers like Coeur, de Brezé and Bureau.

Charles was confronted with the far-from-easy task of clothing these grievances and petitions in courteous, respectful language so that they could be laid before the King. Since he was expected to express his own desires as well, he noted in the document that he still awaited the restoration of the landed estates that had been confiscated from him in 1408; that he lacked the means to conduct himself as befitted his station, as well as to pay the ransom for himself and his brother of Angoulême.

Messengers brought the document to the King, who was inspecting his troops at Limoges. After a few days they brought back extremely unsatisfacotry news to the waiting princes. The King had listened to the reading of the document with impatient annoyance; finally, he observed curtly that he had no time now to reply to the lords one by one—they must be satisfied with his assurance that he would think over their demands and complaints. At the same time Charles received a letter from Dunois, who advised him emphatically to pay his respects to the King at once, without delay.

The King's Grand Master approached Charles who sat waiting in the window recess of an apartment looking out over the roofs and inner courts of Limoges castle.

"The King can receive you, Monseigneur," said the nobleman, bowing. Charles arose and allowed himself to be led through a series of small rooms hung with dark tapestries. At last they came to a door guarded by Scottish sentries; a few pages and members of the King's retinue stood talking together in subdued voices in the very small antechamber, once an alcove, that led to the reception hall. The conversation ceased as soon as Charles entered the room; obliging hands opened the door studded with iron figures behind which the King must be found. Charles saluted and went in.

The King stood in the middle of the room with his hands behind his back; on the wall behind him a curtain of embroidered cloth slid down in folds with a soft rustle, and light footsteps could be heard withdrawing into an adjoining chamber, unmistakably a woman's footsteps. Charles, kneeling in ceremonial greetings, glanced up at his royal cousin and namesake. He saw a man of average height with a large head, coarse features and light, distrustful eyes. The King wore a pleated brocade jacket which did not cover his thin legs with their bony knees.

"Stand up, stand up, cousin." His voice was soft, almost timid. "So we meet at last, in spite of everything."

He took a step forward and scrutinized Charles sharply as though he were looking for a resemblance in the face of his kinsman. At last he seemed satisfied; he half-turned and pointed to a bench placed on a dais. Charles followed him to the seat, suppressing a smile. He knew why the King had given him such a penetrating look: this shy, taciturn man had not yet reconciled the doubt awakened by his mother Isabeau's repudiation of him. He had been—Charles sensed this keenly—uneasy before his meeting with his cousin; he had feared that a certain resemblance between them would provide new material for his own disquiet and new scandal for others. For a moment they sat silently side by side in the dusky room; outside in the courtyard could be heard the neighing of horses, the sounds of men's voices; a hunting party was returning from an early ride.

"It was not possible for me to receive you before this," said the King, in his soft, unruffled tone. "I have been continually occupied during the past few months. Of course you know that the English are still trying to recapture land and cities outside Normandy. They are slow-witted. And in addition there were too many disaffected lords for my taste busy making life miserable for well-meaning citizens with the help of mercenaries and wandering rabble. Since I ordered the execution of the Bastard of Bourbon, they are singing another tune. I trust they see now that it is not to their advantage to turn against me."

Charles nodded in assent, but did not reply. The King continued. "Have you come here, cousin, to plead in person the cause of the vassals of the Crown and their partisans?"

"I would like nothing better than to be able to restore a good understanding between you and your vassals, Sire," Charles said cautiously. "But I am here primarily to greet you and to offer my services to you."

"Hm." The King turned his head brusquely away. Charles looked at his profile: the large jutting nose, the slightly protuberant eyes, the globular forehead. "You did not render me good service by placing yourself at the head of a group of lords who want to thwart me. In the past your name has always been closely connected with our royal House; your brothers have served me faithfully."

"I know that, Sire." Charles bowed his head again. "Believe me, I too am striving for peace and unity. After my return to France I have needed time to acquire an exact insight into the state of affairs in the country. Under no circumstances would I wish to place myself at the head of any group which seeks to curtail your power. I want only to serve as mediator. That is easier for me than for anyone else; I've been away for so long that I can scarcely be considered partisan any longer."

The King frowned and slowly shook his head. "Nevertheless I firmly believe that you had better give up your role as mediator," he said. It was very difficult to tell whether or not he was annoyed.

"If I need your services, I will definitely let you know, cousin. I have learned from your half-brother that you are willing to act as a go-between in the event we negotiate with England. At the proper time I'll gladly remember your offer."

"Forgive me, Sire. But I am not completely free to act as I wish." Charles stared at the King, surprised: how could anyone have taken this man for an irresolute weakling? He who spoke there was completely conscious of his own power; he chose his words with the calm self-assurance of one who knows the ultimate decision rests with him. "You should understand," Charles went on, "that it is extremely important to me that peace with England come soon. They would then undoubtedly be less rigorous about setting the conditions of the payment of my ransom and my brother's. They might even consider releasing my brother. As long as hostilities continue, it will be exceedingly difficult for me to raise the requested amounts within the stipulated time."

"Undoubtedly, cousin," the King answered patiently. "You may rest assured that I shall make peace as soon as a favorable opportunity arises. So far as your financial affairs are concerned, I am ready to meet you halfway. Because of your services to the Kingdom, you were a prisoner of war in a strange land for twenty-five years. We have not forgotten that. It is my intention to compensate you in a certain measure for whatever losses you may have suffered under those circumstances. I have decided to award you an annuity so that you may conduct yourself in the manner befitting your rank. In addition, a document lies ready in my chancellery in which it is stipulated that I shall give you a sum of 160,000 gold écus as a contribution toward your ransom. Be so good as to look upon this as a gesture of friendship."

"Sire!" Charles leapt up, astonished to the bottom of his heart. "I don't know what I can say. . ."

He detected for the first time a semblance of a smile in the King's sad pale blue eyes, and something else which he could not explain. Struck by a sensation of unpleasantness, he lowered his eyes and sat down again.

"Say nothing, cousin," the King said softly and calmly, "but do me a favor and return to your estates. You are settled in Blois, aren't you? A beautiful region. I can think of no place preferable to the banks of the Loire. I envy you." He sighed; his eye slid to the curtain which had been stirring when Charles entered. "It's a great pleasure to linger amidst fields and forests in the company of . . . of one who is dear to us. Thank God, cousin, that you have been vouchsafed this pleasure. It will, I hope, cost you little trouble to sever the bonds which hold you to certain lords? You acted only as a mediator. Besides, the congress is ended. I have been busy answering each petition separately, a long and boring occupation, I can tell you that. As for the Duke of Burgundy, what prevents him from reciting his grievances to me personally? Does he need a group of men who have no connection with the treaty of Arras to promote his interests? I'm ready to receive Burgundy or his spokesmen. Perhaps you can arrange this in due time, cousin."

The King stood up and walked slowly, somewhat stiffly, to the wide open window, past which pigeons, flapping their wings, flew continually back and forth, as though they were being fed at a neighboring window. The King, still smiling, stared outside, lost in thought. But suddenly his attention appeared to be caught by the noise of returning hunters in the inner court. He leaned forward and frowned; a line of pain ran around his large coarse mouth. Charles, who had followed him to the window recess, looked in his turn at the bustle below, at the nobles who stood talking together loudly in the center of the paved court, while servants and grooms led the horses away and collected the still-excited dogs. In this group a young man stood out because of his odd demeanor and slovenly dress. He had a sallow, sharp-featured face, lanky drooping hair and large hands. He stood with his shoulders slightly bent, his riding whip curved between his hands like a bow and glanced sardonically from one speaker to the other. Finally he said something in a low voice; the knights around him burst into loud, forced laughter which rang in Charles' ears.

"My son Louis," said the King, not without bitterness. "The thorn in my flesh, as they say. Your future King, cousin. Those who now turn against me and choose *him* as the pivot for these rebellions do not realize what they are doing. They think to use him, but believe me, he uses them all. The spider sucks his prey and leaves the shrivelled creature hanging in his web—one may take warning from that image."

The King sighed again and stepped back from the window. He glanced at Charles' surprised face and went on.

"The machinations of Monseigneur my son are not unknown to me, cousin. I know that he has corresponded secretly with Burgundy, that he repeatedly talks with feudal lords. I know that he encourages their oppositon to me. He does this only to upset me, although God knows that he hates no one in the world as much as he hates me. He has his own plans, he pursues his own path. Believe me, this treason within my own camp would be difficult to bear if trusted friends did not stand beside me. It is extremely important for me, cousin, to have good friends. It is worthwhile to be faithful to me."

Charles bowed again. In the quiet, dim reception room, face to face with the King, whose tremulous smile sorted oddly with his calm self-assurance, he was overcome by a feeling of oppressive uneasiness. The King's face seemed more enigmatic than ever. Charles did not know whether he should feel pity or aversion, suspicion or respect.

This man with his penetrating but timid sidelong glance had once been a sickly, nervous youth who bit his nails at receptions and chose to hide from all eyes; a weakling ruled by ambitious adventurers. Charles was conscious of a strong curiosity about the people who now stood behind the King. Unquestionably, the secret of his composure, his self-confidence, must lie in the nature of his support. Charles knew all too well that clever councillors and able magistrates could, by inducing a king to sign decrees and resolutions, give the impression that he was an authoritative and independent administrator. But which of these men behind the throne could point the way to self-discipline and self-control, the development of his own gifts, to an ailing, fearful prince? Jacques Coeur, perhaps, the banker, the King's councillor and moneylender, a well-travelled man, nearly as rich and powerful as a prince himself? De Brezé, Dammartin, Bureau? All these patricians whom he had heard mentioned—until now—only in disparagement? But he doubted that they could succeed where even Dunois and Richmont had once failed. There were many who believed that the King's mother-in-law, the skillful Yolande d'Anjou, had succeeded in bringing about the gradual transformation.

While Charles stared pensively at the figures on the tapestries before him, he thought he heard once more light rustling on the other side of the curtain. He recognized the sound: women now wore long trailing sleeves which rustled at every step and each movement. Between the folds of the curtain appeared the hesitant fingertips of a small hand. The King, who saw it at the same time, said quickly, "Worthy cousin, I regret to learn that you can be my guest for a short while only."

The fingers slid back behind the curtain. Charles knew that, deceived by the silence in the room, whoever stood there had assumed the King was once more alone. He smiled and looked away.

Later at dinner he looked attentively at the ladies of the court; wives of lords from the retinues of the King and the Dauphin. The Queen, with whom the King, it was well-known, rarely remained under one roof, was elsewhere. The ladies who sat quietly with downcast eyes amid even less cheerful courtiers—the taste in the King's court was for dull sobriety—seemed to Charles to possess about as much spirit as beautiful dressed-up dolls. It was not until the last day of his visit to Limoges that he found the answer to the question which preoccupied him. He was strolling, accompanied by a few lords from the royal retinue, in the gardens. The Dauphin Louis, who seemed to have gone out of his way to avoid him over the last few days, joined him now and lingered at his side between the hedgerows, the beds of clipped grass and flowering shrubs. He said little, but Charles felt his sharp, somewhat mocking gaze fixed constantly upon him. The King's words flashed through his mind: a spider indeed, who while apparently busy spinning his web, does not take his eyes from his prey.

"Greet your son-in-law Monseigneur d'Alençon on my behalf, if you should see him soon," said the Prince at last. "Tell him, if you will, that I look forward impatiently to news from him."

Charles looked into his dark, sparkling eyes.

"I was not aware that you knew my son-in-law so well, Monseigneur."

"We are actually very good friends." The Dauphin laughed shortly. "We can hardly do without each other."

A disagreeable sensation crept over Charles. Were they trying to lure him again into the dangerous world of intrigue? Was he supposed to recognize some sort of signal in the Dauphin's words? Was he perhaps being put to a test? He was seized by annoyance and distrust of Alençon: a man ambitious and even unprincipled enough to become involved, if necessary, in the most repulsive conspiracies. Charles was at the point of making his distance apparent to the Dauphin when the latter clutched him rudely by the sleeve with curved fingers. Charles looked up, surprised and displeased; with a nod of his head the Prince indicated a side path. Under the linden boughs some women approached, carrying armfuls of roses. She who walked ahead was dressed like a queen; a veil, delicate as a cobweb, covered only a part of the luster of headdress and necklace. When she saw Charles and the Dauphin, she stopped and curtsied deeply; then she walked slowly past with lowered eyes. She had a young round white face and a very small mouth. Charles glanced at her hands. He knew for a certainty that this was the woman who had waited behind the curtain.

"Don't you know her?" Louis the Dauphin whispered in his ear. "Her name is Agnes, Agnes Sorel, my royal father's mistress, and not only mistress but council and parlement as well. There goes the real ruler of France, Monseigneur; don't forget it."

Charles complies with the King's wishes. He returns to Blois for a longer stay than he has yet enjoyed. Now for the first time he has the opportunity to choose his apartments and make them really comfortable. He selects a series of chambers in the west wing of the main building with a view of the river. There his many books are arranged in specially constructed cases; there is the large table at which he likes to sit reading or writing; there the curtained chair can be pushed near the hearthfire or one of the windows, as Monseigneur wishes.

From the city of Orléans come new tapestries depicting the course of the Loire from its source to the point near Saint-Nazaire where it plunges into the sea. So within his own walls Charles can follow the beloved river, past castles and cities, between sandbanks and rows of poplars, between hills or high mountains, between vineyards and broad plains. And when these images seem somewhat lifeless to him, he has only to ascend two steps to one of the window niches. At the foot of the precipice on which Blois stands, he sees the water sparkling, he sees the leaves of the poplar trees gleam alternately bright green and silver grey in the sunlight, he sees the windmills turning on the bridge, ships gliding over the waterway.

Also in the multitude which surrounds him, individuals begin to appear. He appoints officials and functionaries, sets their salaries, assigns them duties. Many of them are Burgundians and Picards who joined him when he left Burgundy's court for Paris, but from day to day the number of servants who hail from Orléans and Blois increases. The Governor of the domain of Orléans is Messire Jean des Saveuses who succeeded the faithful, vigilant Pierre de Mornay; while Charles was a prisoner des Saveuses repeatedly crossed the Straits of Calais to deliver money to the banker Vittori. In return for these services Charles has heaped favors upon him. Des Saveuses is his right hand and his friend.

Then there are the court chamberlains, the gentlemen from Charles' Audit Chamber who enter income and expenditures on the books, and the tax collectors, the almoner, the clerks, the priests, the choirboys, the chamberservants with their staffs of tailors, cobblers, and furriers, the librarian, the armorer, the draper, the bookbinder, the goldsmith, the kitchen chefs and wine stewards, the cooks and scullery lads, the table servants and cup bearers, the gardeners, the stablemaster and his men, the horsemen and squires, the pages, the musicians, jesters, mountebanks and, finally, the man who enjoys the boundless confidence of the Duke and his household—Jean Cailleau, the court physician.

The Duchess has her own retinue, with maids and pages, harpists and fools, tailors and chamberwomen.

Living in the castle of Blois is like living in a small city; all day the stairs, corridors and galleries between the adjacent buildings teem with busy people who do their more or less important work with good cheer. All of them are partial to the Duke, who behaves like a lenient father, with a good word, a friendly greeting, a small gift at the proper time for everyone. He knows the names of all the children who play in the square and the inner court; he is always up to date on baptism and wedding celebrations, of those matters which bring sorrow and happiness into everyone's life. When anyone is sick he comes to see him; he sends Messire Cailleau with medicines and salves; he gives money so that necessities can be taken care of.

In his books and trifling occupations, in his interest in the people around him, Charles finds the diversion which he needs. In Blois, that hive of diligent bees, he forgets his worries, his bad luck. His brief political activity has left a bitter aftertaste, a feeling of disappointment, of failure, of futile effort. He has told Burgundy in careful phrases that he wishes to abstain from further participation in the assemblies of the princes; however he is always ready to ask the King to grant an audience to Burgundy or any of the lords who should eventually wish to speak personally with the monarch.

At the same time he makes it clear that he will always be an advocate of peace with England, and that he will take advantage of any opportunity to work toward that end. He writes in this spirit, too, to the Earl of Suffolk, who belongs to the English peace party. But when *will* the long-awaited opportunity arise? When will the King find the auspicious moment to put forward proposals, when will the war party in England come to its senses? Thinking about his brother of Angoulême, Charles is filled by despondency bordering on despair. How much longer now?

But there is more. Charles is worried about his son-in-law Alençon, of whom it is said that he is ready to serve anyone who will provide him with money for gambling and debauchery. He is considered to be a drunkard and a rake, untrustworthy and dishonorable. It is whispered that he has already, in exchange for money and favors, bartered away into English hands a series of forts in Normandy and Brittany. Again and again Charles attempts to approach his son-in-law through letters and messages, to tempt him to visit Blois. Charles would like to break the alliance, but he is held back by the thought of his grandchildren. He must now seriously entertain the possibility that his daughter's children may be his only heirs. The chance to have his own offspring seems dead; Marie, Duchess of Orléans, has a weak constitution; she has already been ill many times since her arrival in Blois.

In a confidential discussion, the physician Cailleau, shaking his head, has informed Charles of his conclusions: Madame is as fragile as glass: she is moreover anemic and suffers attacks of vague melancholy and listlessness.

The young ladies could tell him something about it: for days on end the Duchess stays in bed, weeping continually and refusing all food; then suddenly she wishes to bedeck herself as though for a fête. She orders her horse saddled or her boat prepared. Despite the admonitions and pleas of those concerned for her welfare, she goes out, in rain or sunshine. She laughs incessantly, appears untiring, gallops her horse through the meadows or stays all day on the water. She is as unpredictable as the weather in March; but her constitution suffers from this waywardness.

Charles nods and sighs, but does not reply. He knows that Cailleau, his old friend, is as aware of the source of Marie's moods as he is. He remembers Isabelle's tears, her fits of convulsive laughter; he had been too young then to be a good husband and now he feels he is too old to please his wife. He is well-disposed toward Marie; in his eyes she is a child with little in her head except concern for clothes, jewels, pleasure trips and similar things; she has birds and dogs, fools and musicians in abundance, a good horse and a whole retinue of young people around her. For his part, she may amuse herself to her heart's content; what could she want with the company of a man whose years of worry and affliction have lasted longer than her life? He doesn't want to trouble her; what would be the point? He is courteous and friendly to her and does his best to fulfil her wishes, but no one could expect him to behave like an ardent youth when he is one no longer. Never is it brought home to him more clearly how sluggish, fat and unattractive he is than when he walks beside Marie at receptions or on the way to church—a rather stout, grey-haired man trudging wearily beside a slim young woman who is taller than he.

When Cailleau thoughtfully suggests possible remedies, Charles shakes his head: pills and herbs cannot make Marie contented and happy. He watches her from a window above the inner court as she rides out among laughing, blushing maids, adroit young horsemen and frolicsome pages. Their clothing, in Charles' eyes, is ridiculous: fierce colors, crenellated and scalloped sleeves, loops of small bells, shoes with long, turned-up toes that constantly threaten to trip them. But they are young: warm-blooded, seething with a lust for life. He is filled with deep pity for Marie: is she doomed to wither at his side?

Sighing, he turns back to the book which lies open on the table. It is a day when Marie and her cortege have ridden out to celebrate May Day. They have planted a maypole in the flower-covered meadow outside Blois. He cannot distract himself with reading and study. For the first time in many years, for the first time since he foreswore poetry after Bonne's death, he picks up again the old copybook in which, during his captivity, he jotted down verse after verse. The bittersweet melancholy which he feels seems to him too narrow and transient for a ballad; he manages to capture it in a few rondelets. When the young people return laughing and singing from the meadow, carrying bouquets of flowers, Charles too has plucked his souvenir of the first day of May. Standing before the window he repeats under his breath the lines now written on the pages of his Thought Book:

Les fourriers d'Eaté sont venus	The servants of Summer have come
pour appareillier son logis,	to prepare his residence
et ont fait tendre ses tapis,	and have hung his tapestries
de fleurs et verdure tissus,	woven from flowers and green leaves.
En estendant tapis valus,	Spreading thick carpets
de vart herbs par le páis,	of green grass over the land,
les fourriers d'Esté sont venus.	The servants of Summer have come.
Cueurs d'annuy pisca morfondus,	Hearts long sunken in misery,
Disu mercy, sont sains et jolis;	Thank God, are now healed and gay.
Allez vous en, prenez pais,	Go away, find another realm,
Hiver, vous ne demeurez plus;	Winter, you live here no longer,
les fourriers d'Eaté sont venus!	The servants of Summer have come!

In the spring of the year 1444, Charles at last received the long-awaited summons from the King. The English armies of occupation, driven back everywhere to the coastline, were more than weary of the struggle. At long last the government in London appeared mellow and ready to renounce all its demands. Although the King of France continued to besiege the cities still held by the English, he announced that he would receive a delegation, for the preparation of which Charles d'Orléans would act as intermediary.

Charles was charged to enter into communication with representatives of the English government; immediately he sent couriers to Suffolk and Sir Robert Roos. He did not have to wait long for an answer. Suffolk wrote back in detail: the legation which would speedily cross the Straits of Calais would serve a two-fold purpose: to conclude peace, or at any rate an armistice and, in order to confirm the good understanding between the two Kingdoms, to negotiate a marriage between Henry VI and the daughter of a French prince.

Princesses of royal blood who were already betrothed were not to be considered; moreover, memories of the tragic nuptials of 1396 and 1420 were still fresh in both countries. "But," Suffolk wrote formally—Charles knew how strongly his erstwhile warden opposed the idea of a French bride on the English throne—"But we hear that there are daughters in the Houses of Brittany, Armagnac and Alençon."

Charles paid a visit to his sovereign to acquaint him with the

English proposals. The King rejected out of hand any alliance between an English king and a member of those French feudal Houses.

"Do they think I am going to admit the Trojan horse with my own hands?" he asked with his faint, bitter smile. "I charge you, Monseigneur my worthy cousin, to put yourself immediately in communication with my brother-in-law of Anjou; I can trust him without reservations. He has a daughter. It is our wish that you offer her as a bride to our cousin, the King of England."

So Charles began at once to prepare for the journey to Tarascon in the extreme south of the realm where Anjou lived; still mindful of his claim to Sicily, he always called himself "King". He was some ten years younger than Charles; from his father he had inherited a glittering series of sonorous and imposing titles and claims to crowns: he should rule—so he had been taught from childhood on—over Jerusalem, Aragon, Valencia, Majorca, Sardinia and Corsica, Barcelona and Piedmont. In actuality he possessed only the domain of Anjou, and the regions of Provence and Lorraine which his wife had brought to him as her dowry. King René—he was never called anything else—had, since succeeding his father, been obliged to wage one war after another to protect his rights, battles in which he had been defeated time after time, so that of so much worldly power and glory, of a kingdom which stretched from Spain to Jerusalem, nothing was left except the gleaming crown emblazoned on his coat of arms.

Along with the Duchy of Lorraine, his wife had brought him armed conflict with Burgundy. The results for René were defeat and six years of captivity in Flanders. During that enforced stay in Burgundy's court, it became apparent that René was a gentle visionary, an aesthetic dreamer. Burgundy freed him without compunction and saw his assumptions justified: in sunny Provence King René immersed himself in his many hobbies and bothered no more with politics.

"We have definitely settled all our business," mused King René, rising and drawing the folds of his wide, flowered brocade robe around him. "No more politics, worthy friend, no more of that. Let's enjoy the sunshine together as friends; here the good God grants us so abundantly all the joys which life has to offer. I have hardly had the chance to tell you how delighted I am at your coming here. We are brothers, dear friend, brothers, more firmly attached to each other than if we had been linked by bonds of blood."

Charles stood up too, somewhat dizzy from the heat and the blinding glare of the sunlight on the landscape around him. They had held their conversation under a spacious awning of tapestries in the open gallery which King René had had constructed, in the Oriental fashion, against the walls of his castle in Tarascon; one sat there as though one were sitting on a cloud high in the sky, with an unimpeded view over the richly variegated landscape.

The cool amber wine proffered by the pages seemed headier than its aroma might lead one to expect; Charles felt remarkably carefree, as though he had partaken of the nectar of oblivion. He took the hand which his host held out to him and allowed himself to be led inside the cool shadowy halls of the castle; lute players and minstrels accompanied the princes. They passed through many apartments adorned with Moorish mosaics; finally they went down some stairs.

King René clapped his hands and nodded to his followers: nobles, pages and servants stopped behind them. Charles and his host stepped together through a small arched gate cut into one of the outer walls.

"Yes, follow me, worthy friend, follow me!" King René looked behind him, smiling and nodding; his white teeth gleamed in his broad olive face; he made a grandiose gesture of invitation. Charles bowed in assent; he was somewhat taken aback but amused at the almost childlike pleasure of his royal host, who had confessed that he attached infinitely more importance to his visitor's poetic art than to all the honorable messages from the French and English governments together.

King René opened a little door, so narrow and low that they both had to stoop. When Charles looked up, he could not repress an exclamation of amazement. He was standing in a walled courtyard filled with blossoming trees and bright flowers; paved paths traversed the garden where three fountains played. Exotic, brightly colored birds sat chained to swinging perches set among the branches of the bushes; the air was filled with their penetrating sweet fluting and twittering and with the heavy fragrance of the flowers. The walls surrounding the garden were so high that only the tops of the trees on the other side could be seen. Above the garden and the treetops arched the dazzling deep blue sky.

On one side of the little door through which Charles and René had entered, stood a pavilion without walls; above a floor of large shining tiles a canvas had been stretched between poles; it drooped to one side to temper the light. Beneath that awning stood a bench, a slanted reading desk like the one Charles used and a table heaped with boxes, cases and folio volumes. To this bower King René, still nodding mysteriously, led his guest.

Charles entered the pavilion, feeling that he had left the everyday world for one of the symbolic fairy gardens described in the Romance of the Rose. He stared enchanted at the exotic birds and flowers, at the grass and leaves suffused with a greenish glow, while King René busied himself at the table and the reading desk.

"Look here now."

Charles gave ear to the gently urgent tone in which the request was made and turned around. King René had set out a number of small wooden panels on which were painted miniatures in brilliant jeweled colors, in the style of the Flemish masters whose work Charles had seen at the court of Burgundy. He was strongly interested; he removed his spectacles and leaned over to inspect the paintings.

"These are singularly beautiful," he said after a while. "Who painted them, Monseigneur?"

King René had watched Charles with quiet intensity as, one by one, he took the little panels in his hand; now he began to laugh. In his large, round face his jovial black eyes glittered like stars. "Do you really find them beautiful, my friend?" he asked happily. "That pleases me. I too find them excellent. I painted them."

"You have great skill," said Charles, surprised. "These are real works of art."

King René bent over the table so that his face almost touched the paintings; carefully he caressed the wood with his fingertips.

"Yes, they are beautiful, they are good," he repeated a few times in a pleased voice. "The colors are well-mixed. Look at how lovely that blue is—that cost me a fortune in lapis lazuli. But it's worth the cost, this beauty is worth it. I taught myself to paint when I sat in Flanders as a prisoner," he went on, looking at Charles. "That was a pastime for me, just as poetry was for you in England."

"Apparently you still derive much pleasure from it." Charles smiled and pointed to the dozens of paints, the reading desk, the brushes and jars for mixing the paints. "Unfortunately, the world claims too much of my attention; I cannot dedicate myself to the thing I love."

"The world, the world?" For the first time a shadow crossed King René's childishly good-natured face. "What do you call the world? Conferences, affairs of state, war, diplomatic maneuvering, money worries, obligations to all the world and his wife? Do you know what the world is?" He gripped Charles' arm and directed him to look once more at the panels: with his broad brown forefinger he pointed at the paintings: holy pictures, scenes from mythology, emblematic figures. "That is the world; there is the world for *me*," he said, his voice filled with affection. "During the hours I spent on that, I felt like a completely fulfilled man for the first time in my entire life. I am never so contented, so deeply happy, so filled with gratitude to God who created me, as when I sit here with my brushes and my colors and create little creatures, small worlds, on the wood. This is the world, Monseigneur my friend, and all things outside it are only dreams and illusions, lighter than smoke. Don't tell me that you don't know this already."

"I have often thought almost the same thing," said Charles thoughtfully, still smiling. "But I was never able to express the idea so clearly as you, Monseigneur. I have never dared to suppose that poetry could constitute the meaning and the purpose of my life. I thought that I had ... and have ... many other responsibilities to perform. My time does not belong to me alone."

"Friend, friend!" King René raised his hands and shook his head. His eyes began to twinkle once more. "You still have much to learn. You don't know yourself, esteemed friend. Be honest, confess that you really only live when you are thinking of poetry, or poetically thinking. I have had the privilege of reading a few of the verses which you sent some time ago to your wife in Rodez. Ah, let us not fall into comparisons, let's not name names, or mention Virgil or Horace whom we have learned to love and respect as great poets. The blackbird and the skylark know how to sing as well as the nightingale, and the fact that God has created them shows there must be room in the world for their song. Monseigneur, worthy friend, your songs are not the conventional rhymes which we all learn to compose at one time or another. Your heart is in them, they are warm and true as ... as ..." he waved his large hands back and forth, searching for the right word. Charles, still smiling, shrugged.

"It's certainly true that if one is touched to the heart, he will write good verse," he said lightly. He felt that he could never be able to speak so enthusiastically, so openly, as King René did.

"And what prevents you from loving with all your heart, from being overcome with delight or even with grief, if that's the way you feel?"

Charles followed his host out of the pavilion into the blinding sunlight; they were met by the intoxicating, bittersweet fragrance of roses and oleanders.

"When Madame Bonne d'Armagnac died, I asked in verse to be dismissed from the service of Love," Charles said, in his usual tone of jocular melancholy. "Since then I have hardly ever taken up the pen. I live under the protection of Nonchaloir—philosophical resignation, calm cool acquiescence . . . in that state one cannot be incessantly inspired to write verse. Although . . ."

He stopped and stretched his hand toward a cluster of flowers.

"In your enchanted court, my lord, I could almost imagine myself young and in love again. Yes, if I thought about that possibility long enough, I am afraid that rhymes and images would shoot up in profusion in my heart, like the flowers in his garden. I would need only to pluck them."

"And what stops you?" René's face was radiant with happiness. He seemed on the point of saying more, but suddenly he put his finger to his lips and nodded his head toward a flowering thicket. Out of the foliage came two white peacocks walking regally as queens; they moved their plume-crowned heads haughtily from left to right, letting their long, folded tail feathers trail behind them over the grass. When they perceived that they were being watched, they stood still and slowly opened their great snow-white fans.

"Monseigneur my friend," whispered King René, "don't our knights hold fast to the beautiful old custom of swearing especially solemn oaths on noble birds—herons, swans, peacocks? It seems to me that everything is conspiring to lure you away from your promise. Swear that you will not disavow the deepest desires of your heart, that you will no longer resist the muse who is our truest friend and mistress. Swear that you will no longer give yourself up to the sin of unhappiness."

For a moment there was silence in the garden which sparkled with light and colors. The peacocks moved noiselessly over the grass, the glossy leaves and fragrant flowers of the tall shrubs hung motionless against the deep blue of the heavens. Finally, Charles raised his right hand in a gesture of avowal. It seemed to him that he had never made a more significant promise.

Balades, chançons et complaintes	Ballads, chançons and laments
Sont pour moy mises en oubly,	Are put away from me and
Car ennuy et pensees maintes	forgotten,
M'ont tenu long temps endormy.	For ennui and crowded thoughts
Non pour tant, pour passer soussy,	Have long held me asleep.
Essaier vueil se je sauroye	But yet, to pass the lonely time
Rimer, ainsi que je souloye.	I should like to try and see
Au meins j'en feray mon povoir,	If I can rhyme as I once did,
Combien que je congnois et sçay	Although I know, I realize
Que mon langage trouveray	That I shall find my phrases
Tout enroillié de Nonchaloir.	All rusted over with Nonchaloir.

. . . . . .

Amoureux ont parolles paintes	Lovers paint with words
Et langage frois et joly;	And fresh charming language;
Plaisance dont ilz sont accointes	They know Pleasure very well,
Parle pour eux; en ce party	It speaks for them; I was once
J'ay esté, or n'est plus ainsi;	One of them but am no more;
Alors de beau parler trouvoye	Then sweet talk was cheap for me,
A bon marchié tant que vouloye;	I had all I wanted;
Si ay despendu mon savoir,	And so I spent my wit,
Et s'un peu espargnié en ay,	And if I have saved a little
Il est, quant vendra a l'essay,	It proves when put to the test
Tout enroillié de Nonchaloir.	All rusted over with Nonchaloir.

Mon jubilé faire devoye,	I should celebrate my jubilee
Mais on diroit que me rendroye	But they would say I surrendered
Sans coup ferir, car Bon Espoir	Without striking a blow, for Good
M'a dit que renouvelleray;	Hope
Pour ce, mon cueur fourbir feray	Has told me that I shall be renewed;
Tout enroillié de Nonchaloir.	So my heart shall be refurbished
	That is all rusted over with
	Nonchaloir.

During the early part of the summer the King received the English legation at Montils. For the first time in years the court set aside its characteristic sobriety: fêtes, banquets and tournaments added luster to the visit of the English lords. King René and his wife arrived; they brought their daughter Marguérite with them, a pretty girl of fifteen. Suffolk, charmed in spite of himself by the

King's bride, raised scarcely any objections when the French disagreed with Henry VI and his government about the terms of the peace treaty. The King of France was willing to give up Guyenne and Normandy as fiefs, but insisted on retaining sovereignty over these lands. After long discussions, over which Charles presided, a temporary solution was finally reached by which neither side had to give up an inch: an armistice was signed, to last for two years. Charles took advantage of this opportunity to discuss with Suffolk his own obligations to England: payment terms were set up. At the same time Charles and Suffolk signed a document which laid out the conditions, in minute detail, for the release of Jean d'Angoulême.

Although the embassy returned to London immediately after the discussions, Charles' work was not over by any means. The King, now that the hostilities with England were part of the past, intended to devote his time to the total annihilation of the marauding bands of mercenaries who still roamed the countryside; accordingly he instructed Charles to take charge of all negotiations and preparations for the marriage by proxy of young Marguérite of Anjou. Charles discharged this duty as conscientiously as possible, although he had no interest in that sort of activity. He felt very tired; the incessant travel to Paris and those places where the King made successive stops, was beginning to weigh heavily upon him. He was not involved only in diplomacy. He made use of his journeys through his own cities and landed estates to get the administration of his possessions in order.

Above all, he left no stone unturned to gather together the amount needed as an advance deposit on his brother's ransom. Whatever he managed to collect, either as a loan or a gift, he sent in installments to Suffolk's bankers, who would attend to further arrangements. Finally, in the spring of 1445, he received the news which he had eagerly awaited for so long: the guaranteed sum of 150,000 écus was now complete, thanks partly to regular contributions from Dunois. Jean d'Angoulême was about to cross the Straits of Calais.

Charles would have liked nothing better than to go at once to Calais to welcome his brother, but because of the nuptials of Marguérite of Anjou, he had to go instead to Nancy. King René had chosen the capital of his province of Lorraine as the scene of the festivities. He spared neither trouble nor expense to make his daughter's wedding the pinnacle of the art of courtly living.

From all parts of the country, princes and nobles streamed to Nancy to witness all the spectacles and to see the bride, in a dress strewn with silver daisies, being led by Suffolk to the altar where she swore loyalty to her lord and husband, Henry VI, King of England, in joy and sorrow, in sickness and in health, until death should them part.

All day long the great bells of the cathedral of Nancy pealed, and the people, beside themselves with joy at the conclusion of a hundred years of war and upheaval, could not stop cheering the young Queen of England, wishing her a long life, praising and honoring her as though it were she herself who had created the peace. After the festivities the court returned to the castle of Châlons, where the King had chosen to take up residence. Charles d'Orléans and his wife, following the example of most of the nobles gathered in Nancy, accompanied the royal cortege—not so much to attend the tournaments and contests to be held at Châlons, but rather at long last to greet Jean d'Angoulême who had sent word that he intended first of all to pay his respects at court.

Charles d'Orléans was one of the few noblemen who preferred the cool, quiet rooms of the castle to remaining outdoors in the tennis courts, the meadows and the hunting fields. He chose to spend his time in the library; the King had a fine collection of books, chiefly chronicles and histories. While Charles sat comfortably reading—so he whiled away the days until his brother's arrival—his young wife Marie sought and found, in the company of the courtiers, all the amusement and variety that her heart desired.

Among the knights who had come to Châlons in the hope of winning glory in passages at arms, was a young man named Jacques de Lalaing, who had had the benefit of being brought up at the court of Cleves. He had been a playmate of Marie's older brothers. Often, when she was a child, she had looked on while the boys were exercising, running or trying to break in their horses. When Jacques de Lalaing came forward to greet her at the court of Châlons, she was moved, almost frightened, to recognize this knightly figure as a vision from her childhood; the man who approached her in the splendor of his youth and fame—he was already considered to be an invincible champion at single combats and tournaments—seemed to her to be the Swan Knight of the legend, the hero whom she had once hoped would come to her over the Rhine. During the following days, Marie tended more and more to curse the fate that had allowed her only now to meet de Lalaing.

They saw each other continually because they were both part of a group who attended upon Margaret of Scotland, the young wife of the Dauphin. Around the crown princess, vivacious, restless and capricious, the celebrations never stopped; there were so many hunting parties, banquets, dances, strolls in the meadows, poetry contests and games of skill that Charles scarcely saw his wife. He was wholeheartedly delighted that she was enjoying herself in this carefree way, but not many days went by before he realized that it was not only the diversions and the sunny open air that brought the flush to her cheeks and the sparkle to her eyes. Preparations for the tournament were in full swing: an arena had been laid out, a stand built for the spectators and the masters of ceremony had their hands full determining the order of the single combats and mock battles. Charles' attention was drawn to de Lalaing, who was expected to be the victor.

Charles saw that the young man was skilled at sport and play; he was strong and handsome and knew how to comport himself with courtesy. It was also apparent that he was fairly taken with himself and was interested only in arms and competitions. He reminded Charles of a young cock strutting proudly and pugnaciously around a strange barnyard. The desire to joke about him faded, however, when Charles noticed Marie among the women who were taking pains to induce de Lalaing to wear their colors or their veils and ornaments as good luck charms during the tournaments. Soon it was no secret that two young noblewomen of the court, Madame d'Orléans and King René's daughter-in-law, were openly bestowing marks of favor on de Lalaing; he was at the side of one or the other at table, at dances, out riding and at the hunt.

Displeased, Charles followed the merry group with his eyes when they were all together in the banquet hall or the gardens. But he did not consider that this was the proper time to point out to Marie the folly of her behavior. Besides, he did not want to make himself ridiculous; there were already enough people who hesitated to congratulate him on the possession of so young a wife.

The day of the great tournament approached; expectations in Châlons rose even higher when it was announced that the King intended to take part in the tourney.

By chance Charles witnessed an encounter between his wife and Jacques de Lalaing that increased his worry and uneasiness. A beautiful house in the city of Châlons had been put at the disposal of the ducal couple; the members of their retinue were housed there too. Usually Charles returned late in the evening with his cortege; Marie not infrequently arrived from the castle after him. On the eve of the tournament the Duchess and her retinue had halted before the gate while Charles, attended only by a page, had just entered the obscurity of the arched doorway. Servants had dashed out holding aloft torches; by this light Charles saw his wife dismount, assisted by de Lalaing, who had accompanied her. Marie did not release the young man's hand.

"Jacques, dear friend," she said in a tone which Charles had never heard her use before, "when I was a child I saw you with my brothers. I have known you for so long that I believe I am not making an illegal request if I ask you to wear my colors in the tournament."

De Lalaing looked at her, smiling. "Madame, he who cares with all his heart for the brothers must also serve the sister."

"Jacques, you've been so busy the last few days preparing for the tournament that we've seen each other only to say goodbye in the evenings."

"Better late than never, Madame," de Lalaing replied in a subdued voice while he stepped back bowing. Marie's women had also dismounted and now approached to lead the Duchess into the house. Marie was visibly disappointed and uncertain; she seemed to be torn for a moment by an inner conflict. Finally she drew a ring from her finger and thrust it toward de Lalaing with a brusque, almost desperate gesture that brooked no refusal. Without waiting for a response she dashed through the arched doorway, brushing past Charles who had withdrawn into the shadows. She was so engrossed in her own thoughts that she did not see him.

Stands had been set up around the arena and hung with banners and tapestries; since Charles was condemned to spend the greater part of the following day there, he had ample opportunity to observe from close by that Marie was scarcely able to control herself. She showed no interest in the opening skirmishes between knights on foot in heavy armor. But her listlessness vanished when de Lalaing rode into the arena on a charger hung with gold and silver decorations. Charles saw that many eyes were fixed upon her; but his annoyance changed to pity when he became aware of the cause of her confusion.

On his helmet and his arm de Lalaing wore not only Marie's colors, but also those of the Duchess of Calabria, King René's daughter-in-law; he had taken care to protect himself from suspicion with a prudence that Charles found less than commendable. For both women the only recourse was to treat the affair as a joke. Madame de Calabria laughed and applauded in apparent unconcern, but Marie d'Orléans sat pale and motionless beside her husband behind the railing hung with tapestries, and did not speak a word. Charles, who was afraid that she was going to burst into tears, took her hand and pressed it hard. She gave him a terrified look, but took the hint to heart.

The next day when Charles returned from the solemn church service which marked the closing of the tournament, the King's heralds came to inform him that Jean d'Angoulême was expected to arrive in Châlons toward evening. Charles spent the succeeding hours in mounting restlessness; the meeting with his brother signified for him not only the fulfillment of a long-cherished wish, but also the end of all his political and diplomatic worries.

He was now fifty years old; his physical stamina, never put to the test during his years of captivity, was obviously not equal to a life of travel, often under difficult circumstances. He tired easily; dizzy spells and a pain near his heart dictated a quiet life. Besides, his eyesight was not good; he had already had a half-dozen pairs of spectacles made with succeedingly stronger lenses and he had a recurring fear that his eyes might fail him when he had most need of them. He wanted to go back to Blois, to spend a few quiet years on the banks of that sparkling river, at long last to fill his days with thoughts and occupations that were not vain or fleeting. Looking back on his life, he could find only a haphazard tangled cocoon of deeds and thoughts of which, after all, nothing remained except torn webs like those which hang in the hedges after an autumnal evening shower. He was sometimes troubled by the fear that when his time came, he would leave this life dissatisfied, embittered, disappointed, believing that he had missed every opportunity to gain peace of mind and real happiness.

Jean d'Angoulême arrived at the castle before the evening meal.

Charles was in the King's retinue; pale and upset, he looked on as his brother was led into the hall. He scarcely recognized the man who approached, bowing and paying his respects. An ample robe of state hung in loose folds around his thin body; he was somewhat stoop-shouldered and coughed from time to time. He had a large head, a lined, wrinkled face and mournful dark brown eyes. His hand, which he raised when the King greeted him, was so thin that the knuckles protruded. He spoke formally to the King in a soft, toneless voice, but his eyes were seeking Charles'. When at last the brothers embraced, they were overcome by bitterness rather than joy. Silently, each put his arm about the other's shoulders; each ran his eyes sadly over the face of the other.

My God, what ugly old fellows we have become, thought Charles. What a life we have led, he and I, since we embraced at Blois, so filled with noble, heroic sentiments, when he offered himself as a hostage. He must often have bitterly regretted his willingness to do that.

But in the days following the meeting, Charles had ample opportunity to perceive that in his brother's heart there were no feelings of regret or reproach. During his captivity, Jean d'Angoulême had become a pious, gentle, philosophic man; he had meditated a great deal, studied a great deal and read extensively. The world and all its turbulence seemed strange to him. He looked on at court life with somewhat childish wonder; to Charles' surprise he announced that he would like to take part in one of the round dances which were held after the evening meal. "I have never danced," he said apologetically. "I should like to try it once."

With a grave expression on his face, he performed the steps he was shown. But he did not let himself be lured into a second attempt. From that time on he was satisfied to remain an onlooker at the amusements of the young people.

At court the carefree stimulation of spring weather brought new excitement and new discontent. Everything seemed as dashing and festive as before, but under the surface streams and counter-streams were beginning to flow. The King had not let the pleasant summer, the period of peace and happiness after so many reverses, go idly by. While his guests amused themselves he, accompanied by Agnes Sorel, had attended the meetings of his Council; the new decrees, so long in preparation, were adopted, the plan for reforming and improving the army had now taken definite shape.

Charles prepared to set forth; his reasons for travel were not the same as those of his equals in rank. He was heartily sick of his stay at court. And more important than that, he thought he had better take Marie away before she inflicted damage on herself and her good name. Marie protested against leaving with tears and entreaties, but Charles remained adamant. They would go to Paris, accompanied by Jean d'Angoulême, to have a full discussion of the affairs of Orléans and the paternal inheritance with Charles' sister. The prospect of the journey and the stay in Paris could not rouse Marie from her state of dejection. She sat silently beside her husband in the coach, staring listlessly at the landscape bathed in summer sunshine. Charles would have liked to have been able to console her; he tried incessantly to think of ways to express his sympathy for her unhappiness, but he could not find the propitious moment for so intimate a conversation. He was afraid that any attempt on his part would only cause further estrangement between him and his young wife.

In Paris they took up residence in the somewhat dilapidated Hôtel des Tournelles, but they spent most of their time with Charles' sister Marguérite, Countess d'Étampes, who received them hospitably and with great joy. The problems of the inheritance and administration of the domain were settled amicably. Angoulême wanted to stay in Paris for a while, but Charles, grateful that his labors had ended, decided to leave at once for Blois. However, before he left Paris he wanted to visit the chapel of Orléans in the Celestine monastery; he had never been there before. For a long time he knelt in prayer at the gloomy stone slab beneath which rested his father's body and his mother's heart. A few steps away he saw the tiles with the family coat of arms set above the graves of his three brothers, whom he had never known.

He knelt unmoving, lost in thought. Perfect silence reigned in the chapel; a singular odor of incense and faded flowers hung in the air; sparkling motes of dust swirled in the rays of light which entered through the stained glass windows. At last he rose, sighing with the effort. In his prayers he had received no answer to the question which troubled him: whether those who slept here had found peace, whether they knew tranquillity, whether at long last their desires were stilled.

Charles joined his retinue where they waited outside the choir gates, in the church. Accompanied by des Saveuses and Cailleau, his court physician, he walked slowly past the altars and tombs on his way out. At this hour of the day the church was deserted; only one woman knelt praying before the image of the Mother of God, her face concealed by the folds of her headdress. While Charles lingered in the vestibule of the church near the statues of his grandparents— Charles the Wise holding a building on his open palm, Queen Jeanne with her tapering fingers folded in prayer—there was a loud commotion outside the church where the grooms were waiting with the horses.

Charles followed the gentlemen of his retinue who had rushed out together. A youth had tried to cut the purse of one of the squires; he had been caught immediately. Charles looked at the boy who was being held firmly between a pair of soldiers; a thin lad with a dark face and hostile eyes. He was nearly suspended between the two men; his sinewy bare feet were tensed, his eyes roamed uneasily. It was clear that he was looking for the first opportunity to escape. Charles, who knew what fate awaited a thief who was caught in the act, shook his head in annoyance—he did not know how to proceed with this boy. He had no desire to deliver the apprentice cutpurse over to the Provost.

"This means branding," he said curtly. "At least if it is the first time you have tried to steal."

"Anyway it is the first time I was caught," the boy said in the rough, bold tone of one who had grown up in the streets.

Charles stared at him, not without surprise. "If that is proven, then you go to the gallows. Do you know that?"

A spark of mockery glimmered in the youth's dark eyes. "What do you think? We live on the road to Montfaucon!"

"At any rate, you have a ready tongue," Charles said drily. "What is your name?"

The thin dark face tightened. "François," he muttered in a surly voice.

"What are you doing here near the Celestines? I should think you and your companions would be wise to stay in the Halles quarter or on the other side of the Seine."

François stared sullenly at the ground. But when des Saveuses remarked with irritation that Monseigneur surely did not need to give this boor the chance to defend himself, the youth said quickly, "I am waiting for my mother; she is in the church."

Charles asked one of the pages to fetch the woman whom he had seen in the church.

"If it turns out that you are lying, I will hand you over myself," he said sternly, while he drew on his gloves. The youth smirked, but he abandoned his fierce watchfulness; his body relaxed. When the woman was brought before Charles, she burst into tears.

Yes, that was her son, the nail in her coffin, the thorn in her flesh, she acknowledged, weeping, a youth like a devil, whom she could not keep at home, a youth full of tricks and caprices, as slippery as an eel and as cunning as a fox.

Charles gave the woman some money and then turned to François who had listened to his mother's words with downcast eyes but with his mouth twisted into an expression of contempt. "Do you know who I am?" Charles asked. The youth shrugged indifferently while he cast a quick glance at the banner held by the riders, and the trappings on Charles' horse.

"The King's family," he said gruffly. He looked again and added somewhat hesitantly, despite his show of insolence, "Orléans, I think."

Charles beckoned to the gentlemen of his retinue and prepared to mount. As he was about to set his foot in the stirrup he said, with a glance over his shoulder, "Let him go."

The men who held the youth released him reluctantly, but François did not hesitate for a second. Even before Charles was seated in the saddle, the young thief had vanished like lightning among the houses opposite the church.

In the hottest days of August the Duke and Duchess of Orléans arrived in Blois. Marie retired immediately to her apartments, suffering from a fresh attack of melancholy. Charles was worried; he could do nothing but walk back and forth absorbed in thought in his study, or sit in the coolness of a window recess, gazing pensively outside. One evening after supper he broke his routine and went to the series of apartments which Marie occupied, and had himself announced to his wife. Marie lay in bed, but she was not yet asleep. The chamber was full of young ladies busy putting clothing away in chests, carrying jugs and basins, preparing a night drink. Two small dogs ran under everyone's feet, nipping and yapping angrily at the chambermaid who was pulling the bedcurtains closed. Belon, Marie's dwarf, sat sadly in a corner, eating figs.

Charles' arrival created a great sensation: the maids vanished, stumbling and curtseying in haste and confusion, into a side room; it was extremely unusual for Monseigneur to visit the Duchess in her bedroom. Belon tottered, limping, after the ladies; only the dogs remained. They ran to meet Charles, barking fiercely. Marie sat up in bed and looked at her husband in alarmed bewilderment. In her muslin nightcap she looked like a child who is afraid of punishment.

"Lie down, Marie," said Charles reassuringly, with a soothing gesture. "Lie down. Forgive me for visiting you at such an unusual hour, but you have not left your room for days now. And I would like to speak calmly with you for once, ma mie. Allow me to sit at the foot of the bed. Could you perhaps get those creatures to quiet down? I fear we will not be able to hear our own words if they go on like this."

Marie clapped her hands; the dogs sprang onto the bed and settled themselves near her on the coverlet. Charles sat down carefully and gave his wife a friendly smile to put her at ease. But Marie remained nervous and fearful; the flush of terror did not leave her face. Charles sighed and ran his hands over his eyes for a moment.

"Do I frighten you so much, child?" he asked, shaking his head with a certain irony. "Surely you must know that I think only of your welfare. I have never desired what you did not wish to give me freely. You know me, Marie."

Marie hung her head, abashed, but did not answer. Charles went on, looking away from her.

"I know that I am a tedious old man, hardly attractive company for someone like you, ma mie. God is my witness that in my heart I have been bitterly sorry for you since the day that you had to accept me as your husband. I have reproached myself incessantly for not declining the marriage with you while it was still possible. We are a very unequal pair, child. I am fully conscious of the fact that I cannot make you happy."

He remained silent for a moment, staring with averted face out the window at the evening sky, tinged with yellow and as clear as crystal. "But look, that is the way things are now—we are bound to each other for life. For your sake, ma mie, I hope it will not be too long before you are free. Until that time we must try and live together. I know only too well what it means to have young, restless blood and be unable to allay your desires. Believe me, Marie, I know what you are going through. Because I lacked self-discipline, and because I was in despair and filled with impotent rage, I sinned during my exile; I was tempted when I was wretched, I desired what was not mine, and I took it. I forgot the dignity worthy of my rank and the honor of my House. Experience, bitter experience, has taught me that honor gives the deepest satisfaction after all. It seems meager solace and harsh advice, but unsuspected strength comes from the realization that one lives according to noble laws. The diamond is broken and cut so that it can sparkle as brightly as possible. Do I tire you, do you wish to go to sleep now?" he asked suddenly and gently, for Marie was leaning back against the pillows with her eyes closed. She shook her head in denial.

"Don't think that I came here to scold you, Marie," said Charles, attempting a jocular tone. "That would ill become me, I am not good enough to do it. But I have thought long and earnestly about how I could make your life easier, how I could provide amusement for you, how I could help you find a meaning and a purpose for your days. What we both greatly need here is a child to care for; therefore I have asked my worthy cousin of Bourbon to permit us to bring up his youngest son as though he were our own child. I hear that he is a pleasant, handsome lad, five or six years old. Tell me what you think of this, ma mie?"

Tears appeared under Marie's closed eyelids; she raised her hand quickly and wiped them away.

"Do you think that you would have enough to do if you looked after the little boy?" Charles asked, watching her with tired concern. Marie's lips began to tremble; she nodded.

"Then there are still all sorts of other things which could bring peace and forgetfulness," Charles went on cautiously; he leaned against the bedpost and fixed his eyes on a small star which sparkled in the still-light sky. "Here in Blois we have a hidden treasure of books, ma mie, for which great scholars envy us. You told me once that you can read Latin too—so a world lies open to you in which you can travel at will. There are so many landscapes and vistas to admire that one entire lifetime is not enough to see everything and understand everything. I don't know if I have spoken to you about my mother—but you know her story? For many long years she lived in loneliness and anxiety; it is only now that I understand how deep the sorrow was which she had to bear. But in adversity her nobility of character appeared. She did not complain, but she set an example for everyone. My mother sought and found solace in reading what wise men and great poets had written to direct us to a path in the impenetrable forest which life is. It is an image which was familiar to me when I was a child. My mother said once: Life is a long awaiting of God's peace. And I know that my father considered himself to be one who had irretrievably lost his way in the forest of long awaiting. We too seek a path in the wilderness, ma mie. Perhaps we shall wander inaccessible to each other, each in a different place. But shouldn't we try to find each other? Trust and sharing of views, these could bring us together."

Again he was quiet and turned his face toward her. Marie raised her eyes to meet his.

"Perhaps one day we shall reach the end together, the way out of the forest, where the meaning of our wandering will become clear to us. I know that the journey which I propose to you is fraught with hardship and danger. Perhaps I am demanding too much courage from you. Think about it, but believe that everything that concerns you touches my heart deeply."

Charles rose and nodded to his wife. "Rest well, ma mie." Marie did not answer; she lay motionless, gazing at the embroidery on the tester. Quietly, Charles left the room.

As soon as he returned from exile, Charles had sent messengers to his cousin, Filippo Visconti, Duke of Milan, inviting him to discussions concerning the domain of Asti which had been under Filippo's protection since 1428. According to Dunois, the agreement had been made on the condition that the rights of the protector would expire as soon as the legal heir and owner of Asti was in a position to exercise the rule himself. After a long delay, Filippo Visconti had informed Charles' messengers that he would return the domain in his own good time; but in spite of warnings, petitions and verbal demands, he had not kept his promises and the taxes went, year in and year out, to Milan.

Charles considered the possibility of selling Asti and its environs to his cousin, but Dunois emphatically pointed out to him the value to France of retaining such a strategic point on the other side of the Alps. The King of France still carried the title of Lord of Genoa, so if he should ever again wish to assert his authority there, the possession of Asti was of inestimable importance.

After Charles had returned to Blois, Dunois visited him almost daily. He too had left Chalôns; the summer fêtes had come to a tragic end with the sudden death of Margaret of Scotland, the young wife of the Dauphin.

"I don't know if I should mourn for her," said Dunois with a shrug. "She had a sad life. The Dauphin made no secret of his dislike for her; we were constant witnesses to the way he tormented her. The poor girl will have peace in her grave anyway. Now a violent quarrel has broken out between the King and Burgundy—or I should say that Burgundy is angry; the King always keeps himself aloof and lets things drift. He sees that in Burgundy's power lie the seeds of his own destruction. That Kingdom will surely crumble now that all that holds it together is one man's ambition.

"I believe that six or seven languages are spoken within the borders of Burgundy's territories; furthermore, all the Dutch and Flemish cities have their own law and privileges which they will protect with tooth and nail. Already deputations of burghers are coming to ask the King for help; the ones from Ghent have visited Chalôns many times. Believe me, the King is on the right road, the only road, to cure Burgundy's arrogance. By waiting to see how Burgundy's powers are dissolved through domestic uprisings and turmoil, the King will accomplish far more than he could through taking any stronger measures."

Finally, the matter of Asti came up for discussion. Dunois believed that it was time now for Charles to press energetically for the return of that territory; if necessary, the King should send representatives to Milan to make it clear that their patience was exhausted. Charles named his brother governor of Asti and empowered him to take whatever measures he deemed necessary for its restoration. Dunois had wanted nothing more than this; he decided to cross the Alps as rapidly as possible. However, before he could leave Blois for his own domain where he would make his preparations, there appeared—this happened in the last days of August—couriers from Asti with alarming news.

Filippo Visconti had died childless in Milan; on his deathbed he had named as his sole heir and successor his kinsman, the King of Naples, despite the fact that the latter had considerably less right to the succession than Charles, the son of Valentine Visconti.

It was immediately clear to Charles that he, by himself, was not equal to this flood of complications. He would have to give up his claims on Milan. If he wished to save Asti—the inhabitants of the domain, fearful of new unrest and violence, implored him not to abandon them to their fate—he would have to employ force to defend his rights, to protect his territory. He himself had no money to raise an army, and in any case because of the King's purges, there were no mercenaries to be found. In all probability the few remaining bands existed only on the other side of the Alps in the service of Sforza and other condottieri.

Nevertheless Charles had reason to believe that he would surely be aided by those who had more power at their disposal than he; Dunois had already gone to discuss the matter with the King, and a courier had arrived posthaste from Flanders to inform him that the Duke of Burgundy was acquainted with the situation and was not disinclined to grant assistance to his worthy cousin of Orléans. Charles understood perfectly well that for this offer he had to thank Burgundy's desire to thwart the King rather than any friendly solicitude.

So Charles quit Blois once more with a heavy heart. He hurried to Dijon where the Burgundian companies waited. For the first time in more than thirty years he rode again at the head of an army. He did not look forward to sitting on horseback wearing armor for the better part of a day. But the people of Asti were incessantly sending messengers, urging him to prepare the defense of his realm as rapidly as possible; they said that they considered him to be the lawful heir of Milan. While he rode on at the head of his troops, along the roads which led from Lyon to Tarascon—they would cross the mountains at the extreme southern point—Charles weighed over and over what the Lordship of Milan was really worth to him.

His grandfather's duchy was a valuable but extremely perilous possession; it would perhaps give him temporary power and wealth, but it would also force him to spend the rest of his life in disquiet and great anxiety. On the other hand, he knew that his brothers, his sister, his daughter Jeanne's children and his kinsmen in the House of Orléans expected that the assertion of his claim would increase their substance, honor the memory of his parents and preserve his mother's inheritance for her legitimate descendants. Their obligations had to weigh more heavily than his own desires.

After an extremely tiring journey in scorching heat, Charles finally reached Asti. He found the city—with its white and yellow-tinted houses set high amid hilly vineyards with a background of blue mountains—to be as beautiful as a vision. Bubbling streams flowed over crags and stony precipices to the fertile plateau which ringed the city; to honor Charles, banners in the colors of Orléans fluttered from the rooftops against the azure sky. But the delegations of burghers who came, wrapped in festive white garments, to meet the Duke outside the city gates exhibited a pleasure that was obviously forced. Inside Asti were couriers who had arrived a few hours earlier, bringing news of the defeat of the French troops at Bosco. Charles' captains, on learning this, decided that it would now be senseless and foolhardy to march against Sforza; they refused to spill the blood of their men in the massacre which would undoubtedly result from such recklessness.

Charles consulted with the city administration of Asti; not long afterward he sent three groups of lawyers and orators, each group with strongly armed escorts, to Milan, to the court of the French King and to Burgundy's court in Flanders. Those who went to Milan had been charged to draw the populace toward loyalty to Orléans; the messengers to France and Flanders would request reinforcements.

The Duke waited in Asti in the house of a notary. In a cool chamber, shaded by an awning, he passed the time playing chess with the physician Cailleau or with his chaplain, when he was not dictating letters or edicts to the secretary whom he had just taken into his service. This was a young man named Antonio who had a beautiful handwriting and spoke and wrote fluent Latin. He had attracted Charles' attention during the welcoming ceremonies when he paid tribute to the Duke by loudly reciting stately Alexandrine rhymes which he had written himself, and in which he compared the Duke with Aeneas because of his respect for the memory of past generations, with Cato because of his grave dignity, with Job because of his patience, with Ulysses because of his constancy in adversity, and which he concluded by wishing the Duke the military glory of an Alexander, the long life of a Nestor, the abundant offspring of a Piramus and the wealth of a Xerxes. Charles had listened to all this flowery praise and blessing with the necessary self-mockery, but he was amused by the young man's enthusiasm and imaginative energy. When, in addition, Antonio proved to be a zealous and capable clerk, Charles took him into his service and promised him that later in Blois he would appoint him to the post of secretary.

From France and Flanders came no encouraging responses; the unfolding of events in Lombardy, Sforza's victories, did not dispose the King or Burgundy to interfere in the Milanese affair in the near future. Charles realized that the vague promises they had made were tantamount to refusal. He disbanded his troops, since he could no longer pay them, and sent them back to their homelands. He too left Asti; not, however, without promising the people and the officials that he would make every effort to persuade the King of France or some other powerful prince to furnish him the means to assemble an army which could defend Asti against the menacing "protection" of Sforza.

Charles kept his promise; he did what he could. Instead of returning to Blois, he travelled with a retinue of trusted friends to see anyone who might be able to give some help in this affair. Although the roads in northern and central France were barely passable because of rain and snow, Charles crossed the country without allowing himself any rest. While he visited his friends and kinsmen and applied for help to the King and Burgundy, his secretary Antonio wrote letter after letter to his fellow countrymen in Asti, urging them in the name of his lord to be patient and have courage. Charles' efforts were futile: Burgundy made promises but did not keep them, and the King, wholly absorbed by a fresh dispute with the Dauphin, had no interest or inclination to attend to his cousin's problems. When, after a final interview with the King, Charles returned to his temporary quarters in the city of Tours, he had an attack of dizziness. Cailleau, who was nearby as usual, considered that he had the right this time to be seriously annoyed; Monseigneur made too many demands upon himself and refused to heed the warnings of his physicians. Nature was not to be trifled with; Monseigneur would now learn this for himself.

Charles, lying in bed with his left hand on his painful, irregularly beating heart, agreed silently with everything his physician said. He did not protest when Cailleau gave instructions to prepare for a return journey which would be covered in small stages. So Charles finally made his entry into Blois, to remain there at least for the time being. He who had ridden forth at the head of an army had to be brought back home in a litter, an object of curiosity and pity to the people along the road.

For the secretary Antonio, surnamed Astesano, the years of service to the Duke of Orléans slip by with the careless lightning-speed of the leaping, singing waters which flow through the city of Blois.

Antonio is almost as fond of Blois as he is of his native city in the Italian Alps; in one respect, he thinks, Blois wins the laurel: in the little old houses in its narrow streets dwell more beautiful maidens than the easily inflammable clerk has seen anywhere else. The longer he lives there, the more impressive the castle seems to him; he cannot praise the broad shining Loire enough, and not only to please his lord, who can sit hour after hour lost in thought, gazing at that silver-blue or green-black shining water which hurries, hurries to the sea.

As far as life in Blois goes, Antonio is of the opinion that he could not have been able to strike it luckier. In Blois the atmosphere is one of a perpetual holiday. People are lighthearted, always ready to laugh and joke and (a fortunate discovery for one who, like Antonio Astesano, wishes to gather literary laurels!) everyone is interested in poetry. More wonderful still, everyone *writes* poetry, although often with the aid of a rhyming dictionary. For poetry contests are the order of the day in the castle of Blois; they are, it is said with amusement, the Duke's only weakness. Nothing pleases him more than to gather guests, officials and servants around him after the evening meal when work is done, and propose a theme to them which they must then work into the form of a ballad or a rondel. After that, silence prevails for hours: there are knit brows everywhere, lips moving without sound, eyes staring vacantly into space.

When at last wine and refreshments are brought in, the competition begins: those who have successfully composed a verse step before the Duke and the judges—who change every week—and recite their work loudly. The Duke is all ears, he sits at ease on his bench, his black mantle thrown comfortably around him, tapping his forefinger softly against his lips, or toying with his spectacles. Beneath his snow-white hair, his dark eyes seem exceptionally large and lively in his faded, wrinkled face as he glances from one to the other. They look, to everyone who sees him thus, like the eyes of a young man.

Usually these poetry contests in Blois are extremely informal: the physician competes with the chancellor, the chief auditor with a chamberlain; the Duchess rhymes hard against a page or clerk, and the Duke has more than once extended the laurel wreath to his valet or to the chaplain of the castle chapel. But occasionally the great hall becomes more solemn, when Monseigneur receives high-born guests, or when a famous scholar or poet visits Blois; then the decorations and the preparation of refreshments receive more than ordinary care. Life in Blois is frugal, although the costs of maintenance are not insignificant, but when guests arrive no effort is spared. The finest fish, the best fruit, the noblest wine are brought and passed around and the Duchess orders her few really valuable pieces of tableware to be polished and displayed on the sideboards.

Antonio is enthralled by what the professional poets come up with; they are obliged by their calling to contrive ingenious rhymes, to employ exceptionally beautiful images, to sustain symbolism in the most precise way once they have chosen it. But all may be said to have acquitted themselves worthily of their tasks, to compose with almost offhand ease verse which is at the same time significant, clever and melodious, or so it *seems* at any rate to the listener who is nearly blinded by such a dazzling display of ballads, virelays, songs and rondelets. But the Duke has a sharp ear, a keen eye; he can instantly detect a false note, a bit of tinsel. If he nods his head thoughtfully, the poet can sit down satisfied. But when he allows a versemaker to come into his study and pushes a certain book with loosely folded pages toward him, requesting that he inscribe his ballad or song therein, then the poet may be certain that he has won the greatest praise Monseigneur can bestow—a place in the Thought Book. Many have seen it in Monseigneur's hands or on his writing table, but only a very few have had the privilege of reading it.

Monseigneur's verses are heard only when he takes his turn during a poetry competition; gazing pensively at a point on the wall or outside the window, he recites, in a soft monotone, what he has just composed. When he finishes, he comes to himself; he smiles rather self-consciously and gives a friendly wave to the next speaker.

Antonio Astesano has begun to write a great chronicle, in which he will record the history of the House of Orléans and demonstrate from documents on hand the legality of the Duke's claims to Asti and Milan. Monseigneur is interested in his work and has furnished him with much material. But as he writes, Antonio is troubled by feelings of sorrow. He will have to conclude the chronicle with the life of the Duke himself, for the House has no heirs. No son of Orléans will ever turn the leaves of Antonio's book; it will be no invaluable guide, but only a survey of forgotten things. Antonio is fully conscious that the prospect fills the Duke too with regret and bitterness; from the way in which, in the court or outside on the road, Monseigneur greets the numerous children who have been named for him—whom, at their parents' requests, he has presented for baptism—it seems obvious enough that he, more than any man, would have rejoiced in the possession of a family of his own.

Insofar as the Duchess is concerned, she behaves with more restraint toward the children who continually cross her path, but the impressionable Antonio finds her coldness more disturbing than Monseigneur's somewhat melancholy openness and good nature. The Duchess of Orléans has become, over the course of ten years, a pale, taciturn woman who—and this is noteworthy—takes great pains to support her husband in the management of the household at Blois, in the entertainment of guests and in the practice of good works. Madame still likes to hunt, preferably with falcons, but the time of boating on the river, of ecstatic horseback rides or round dances in the meadow, is over for good.

Very old people in Blois, who can still remember the late Lady Valentine, often say that the Duchess shows, day by day, a greater resemblance to Monseigneur's mother. Each time they see Marie d'Orléans sitting in the great hall or, from a distance, in the cool shadowed garden arbor, dressed in black as always, with an embroidery frame or a book before her and equally industrious court ladies around her, it seems to them that time has stood still for fifty years. Even the black wall coverings with the motto stitched in silver—Rien ne m'est plus, plus ne m'est rien—hang once more in the Duchess's apartments, and Madame wears the ornament which Duchess Valentine never removed after her husband's death: a fountain of tears cunningly constructed from silver and tiny glittering gems.

Fancywork seems to have become a passion for Marie d'Orléans; she busies herself chiefly with crocheting beads and buttons from Cyprian gold thread. Everyone has received these as gifts from her; Monseigneur wears them on his jacket and cloak, and they are threaded into his paternoster. It seems to Antonio that the Duchess is never cheerful or happy; she tries to be friendly to everyone, following her husband's example, but her heart does not seem to be in it. Even the little dogs and birds which she keeps near her always, she caresses absently. Now that Bourbon's son Pierre de Beaujeu, whom Orléans has raised as a foster child, has grown into young manhood, he no longer needs Marie's attention. If anything can make her realize profoundly that time gives no quarter, it is the presence of this tall adolescent squire who once—it seems only yesterday—entered Blois as a little child.

One day in the summer of the year 1456, Antonio set out at noon in company with a few other clerks from Monseigneur's office for the great hall where the repast was about to be served. They walked quickly through the garden, only pausing for a moment near the walled pond which the Duke, not long before, had had fitted with a fountain. Standing in a rock in the center of the pond was a bronze gargoyle. The splashing of the streams of water springing from between its lips, out of its nostrils and ears, was usually audible in the innermost chambers of the castle. But the fountain had been silent since that morning; there was something wrong with the ducts. The Duke, who had missed the familiar sound, had come to the well that morning, joking that he would die of thirst next to his fountain. Antonio and his friends mounted the broad stairs to the hall.

There the preparations for the meal were in full swing; under the supervision of the steward, Alardin de Monzay, three or four servants were busy putting tops on the trestles, unfolding the linen cloths. A youth ran about with a basket, from which he strewed fresh leaves on the floor. From one of the deep window recesses came smothered laughter; two of the Duke's pages stood there joking with Pierre the fool. The harpist, one foot resting on the steps of a bench, attentively tuned his instrument. Antonio went into another window niche, knelt on the stone seat and leaned forward to look outside.

The southwestern portion of Blois looked like a gigantic green-and-bronze-tinted tapestry. In the last few years vines had taken possession of nearly every open spot on the old wall. The village of Blois lay at the foot of the precipice in the burning midday sun. The river was low; the reflection of the sunlight on the exposed sands was so dazzling that Antonio involuntarily closed his eyes.

As he leaned on the window seat, dozing in the warmth, he caught the conversation going on among the jocular group in the next window niche. With exaggerated intonation, the fool was reciting a rondeau consisting of nothing but nonsense words, accompanied by the jingling of bells.

"Stop it, Pierre," said one of the pages. "In the name of anything you like, spare us from poetry for a while. If we aren't in church, we are rhyming. About love, about the four seasons, about the kindness of Madame the Duchess . . ."

"What do you want then?" replied another youth. "The Duke doesn't like the hunt and he is too fat for games of skill and horseback riding. Can you imagine him jousting?"

"He had fights enough when he was young, at least if you can believe the stories. He should certainly know something about what goes on. Don't forget he has been through Agincourt!"

The fool began to titter shrilly.

"We have another hero of Agincourt, gentlemen; only look at Messire de Monzay who stands there surveying the tables like a commander with his battlefields!"

"Hey, de Monzay, I didn't know that!" cried one of the pages. "Were you at Agincourt, man?"

"Hush, hush, hush!" the fool whispered so sharply that he could be heard in the farthest corners of the hall. "Do not bother Messire. He won't be happy to be reminded that the English stripped him stark naked and let him run away like that."

The pages laughed, half in derision and half in scandalized astonishment. De Monzay said, in a choked voice, "It would have been better for me if they had killed me, or sent me to England with the Duke."

"Man, you would have died from boredom on the other side of the Straits of Calais," cried the fool. "In that climate! I've been told that the fog is so thick in London that you can't see three steps in front of you."

"The Duke must still consider himself lucky that they let him go."

"He may well, but his purse still feels the pain." The fool uttered a terrifying series of moans and gasps. Suddenly he stopped and said in a normal voice, "Listen, the harpist is playing! There must be a lady nearby. Unless I'm wrong, even two ladies. There come a couple of the Duchess's young women, the two prettiest if I'm not mistaken . . ."

The easily enflamed Antonio Astesano, who was accustomed to wooing all the court ladies in turn—until now, however, in vain—hastily emerged from the window niche. The two young ladies, Isabel and Annette, floated gracefully into the hall. From their fashionable pointed hats hung veils of white muslin. They tried to maintain a dignified demeanor, but in their bright eyes sparkled the inexplicable, irrepressible delight that seizes maidens as soon as they enter the company of men whom they know they can tease. They glanced derisively with feigned hauteur at Antonio, who bowed, at the pages who gave them a friendly greeting.

"Messire de Monzay, the Duchess has left her chambers," said Isabel. "Monseigneur and Madame will be here shortly."

With a gesture the steward indicated that everything was ready. He clapped his hands; the servants, who had set down the plates and goblets and arranged the slices of bread in a great pile on the serving tables, lined up against the walls.

"Is it true that we will have a poet as guest again tonight?" Annette asked de Monzay curiously. This was the opportunity Antonio had been waiting for; even before the steward could answer, he sprang to the fore to give the requested information.

"Messire François Villon has arrived, a poet from Paris."

"From Paris, yes above all, *from* Paris," cried the fool shrilly. "He is banished from Paris, ladies, I hear he is a fine gentleman. Robbery, murder, whoring . . . and on and on. He stood once with the rope around his neck. We shall surely hear a different kind of verse this evening from what we heard last week when Monseigneur read a poem about the foolish hats-with-tails that you wear. Monseigneur will soon rhyme as creditably as a fool. Then I can do away with myself."

"Ah, don't mock," said Annette angrily. "Monseigneur is kind and courteous. We know perfectly well that his heart is occupied with other things besides our hats. He is only being cordial to us. This winter he gave me two golden écus, because I had lost all my money at cards."

"It is evident that *young* ladies especially know how to appreciate Monseigneur's qualities." The fool slapped his hands together once with exaggerated courtliness. "How many sixty-year-old men have the happiness to be consoled for the misery of life by so merry a young lady as the Duchess?"

The maidens exchanged annoyed glances. Annette said brusquely, "Monseigneur is not 'happy' and the Duchess is not 'merry'. Now keep quiet; they are coming."

Charles d'Orléans entered the hall through the great door; he led his wife by the hand. He wore, as usual, a loose, dull black cloak with no girdle. His hair was now completely grey and very thin;

his teeth were going bad. He walked with difficulty; the spring had been damp and he suffered from stubborn rheumatism. But anyone who caught his dark glance, who noticed the sensitive, ironic lines of his lips, the lively gestures of his still youthful hands, forgot quickly that Monseigneur had crossed the threshold of old age.

The Duchess looked half a head taller than her husband, who always walked with something of a stoop. Her long oval face, with its full cheeks and high forehead, was pale; around her mouth were lines that hinted at mournful resignation. The ducal couple were followed by members of the household; the chamberlain, the treasurer, the court physician, the librarian, the lords of the chancellery and the Duchess's ladies. Between the clerks and the scribes walked the guest, Villon, in a doublet that had been hastily cleansed of dust and dirt. From time to time he passed his palm over his freshly-shaven jaws. His eyes, dark and restless, took swift and sharp stock of the faces of the household and the interior of the hall. Charles and his wife sat down on the bench under the canopy.

"Take your place, Messire," Charles said to Villon, who remained standing somewhat uncertainly among the people who were going to sit at the lower end of the table. "De Monzay, bring our guest somewhat closer to us so that we may chat with him . . ." As Villon was seated, the Duke said to him, "I'm afraid you may find our meals here at Blois rather frugal. But our wine is good."

"I'm aware of that," Villon said. "I have had the opportunity to taste it more than once."

While the dishes were being handed around, Antonio Astesano who, during the customary prayer at table, had glanced stealthily at the guest from time to time, said to his neighbor under his breath, "The fellow looks like an outlaw."

"He is one, more or less," replied de Courcelles, one of the masters of the chancellery. "He roams around the neighborhood; he's usually drunk and he's always mixed up in something scandalous. It seems he wintered at Chevreuse."

"Chevreuse? But that's a nunnery, isn't it?"

De Courcelles winked. "The abbess is young and I hear that she likes poetry."

Antonio looked at the guest anew. Villon sat carelessly eating as though he were in a public house along the road. He held his knife constantly in his fist, even when his mouth was full. Meanwhile his dark eyes, sunk deep in shadowed sockets, flitted from one face to another. A barely healed rough red scar protruded from one of his thin cheeks. In his long, sinewy neck his adam's apple shot up and down as he swallowed. He looked, amid the well-cared-for courtiers of the Duke of Orléans, who sat quietly chatting and eating, like a ragged crow in a dovecote. From time to time he glanced sharply at his host, his mouth pulled wryly down at one corner. Charles, thoughtfully appraising his guest, met this glance more than once.

"What are you thinking about, Messire Villon?" he asked suddenly, with a smile.

Villon put down his knife. "I was thinking, Monseigneur, how much more pleasant this encounter is than our first meeting was."

"I was not aware that we had met before," Charles said, raising his brows. Villon laughed shortly.

"You may well have forgotten. I had the pleasure of speaking with you before the doors of the Celestine cloister in Paris when you visited there in '44. That is more than twelve years ago."

Host and guest stared at each other for a moment. Then Charles began to laugh softly. He raised his goblet and drank to Villon.

"Welcome to Blois, Messire François. I hardly dare to ask if your life has improved since we saw each other last."

"No, it is really better if you don't ask," replied Villon, in the same tone, while he raised his own goblet. "I hoped by the way to speak about other things with you."

"I am eager to learn why you have visited me." Charles gestured to the others to go on with their own conversations. Villon shrugged.

"I could say that I came here to serve you, or something flattering like that. The truth is, I was curious. They say you are fond of poets, you are more liberal and open-handed than many other great lords and that you yourself can write good verse. It would be rather convenient for me just now to have a safe shelter for a few days and nights. And it seems to me to be a beautiful opportunity to hear your poetry."

"It pleases me to note that you still come out with your opinions as frankly as . . . before . . ." Charles' lips twisted in an ironic laugh. "At that time you must have noticed that honesty of that sort holds an irresistible fascination for me."

"I am known as the worst liar under God's heavens," said Villon carelessly, "and I have earned that reputation ten times over."

The Duchess, who until now had sat silently eating—she took small bites and broke the bread with extreme care—raised her head and said mildly, with a quick, somewhat timid, suspicious glance at the guest, "Monseigneur, tell us something about the theme of the contest."

"I have two themes for today," Charles said. "I cannot decide between them, so you choose, ma mie—or else Villon must throw for heads or tails. This is the first theme: 'I die from thirst, sitting near the fountain.' "

Marie began to smile sadly, but Pierre the fool who, during the meal had sat on the arm of Charles' bench, called out in his shrill voice, "Ho ho, Monseigneur, that is poetic license, by your leave. The fountain in the garden is broken, I won't deny it, but how do you venture to say that you are dying of thirst with a glass full of delicious Beaune standing beside your plate? I am dying of thirst and, believe me, I'm not interested in rhymes at the moment."

Charles shoved his goblet toward the fool; the small crooked man sprang closer with a jingling of bells and quickly drank a few draughts. Villon repeated the theme: "I am dying of thirst, sitting near the fountain."

"The notion of thirst can hold no mysteries for Messire Villon," said Pierre, grinning; he climbed onto the arm of the chair again and nestled there with his shrunken legs crossed.

"The second theme," continued Charles, "is: 'In the Forest of Long Awaiting.' "

The Duchess made an involuntary gesture of surprise; she seemed about to say something, but remained silent, staring down at her plate.

"I choose the first theme," said Villon. "Usually I need more wine to be able to rhyme extemporaneously, but I shall try it."

Marie rose abruptly and said in voice so loud and cold that all the guests looked up: "I shall withdraw until the tables are removed. I have chosen both themes."

"You do not make it easy for yourself, ma mie." Charles came up out of his chair, amazed. Now they all rose, in the customary sign of respect when the Duke or his wife left the table. Charles, perceiving that Marie was displeased or offended for some reason, added courteously, "It goes without saying that you are perfectly free not to take part if you don't wish to. It's hardly a suitable amusement for a woman like yourself to be compelled to compose poetry on thirst and long awaiting. I take it, ma mie, that these subjects don't mean anything in particular to you."

Marie, about to descend the stairs from the platform—her ladies stood in a row waiting for her—turned and said, so softly that only her husband could hear her, "Monseigneur, I am childless."

The retinue remained standing in silence, watching her departure. Charles seemed suddenly tired and listless. He beckoned to des Saveuses and asked him to announce that the poetry competition would be put off until the following day. At the same time the chamberlain was told to announce both themes to those who had not been present at the meal, so that they could prepare in tranquillity. To Villon, who had witnessed this sudden change of mood with raised brows, Charles said, "Come with me to my study, Messire François. You will have twenty-four hours more to throw yourself into poetic creativity."

Villon followed the Duke to the library where an odor of parchment, ink and leather hovered in the air. Charles sat down carefully at the long table strewn with papers and, not without effort, stretched out his aching leg on a low footstool.

"Am I correctly informed, did they want to hang you in Paris?" he asked, signalling his guest to sit down wherever he chose. Villon had been looking up at the books in the tall bookcase. He shrugged.

"I had almost forgotten it, Monseigneur. What was really important I was able to put into verse for myself and the other rabble who were going to dance on the gallows."

"So you once mentally took leave of life," Charles said slowly, wiping his spectacles on his sleeve. "I should like to hear from you how it feels to have done with the world."

"It depends on how closely one is attached to life and the world," replied Villon; a spark of mockery flashed like a falling star through his eyes. "With the rope around my neck I could not feel that I had left much behind that was worthwhile."

"Then you are free, Villon. How does it feel to be really *free* of everything?"

"I did not think about that then. I sat on a pile of stinking straw in a dungeon of the Châtelet and scratched the lice from my rags.

I bartered my last meal for a piece of paper to write down my epitaph, that rhyme I mentioned to you just now: 'Brothers, who will live after me . . .' "

"There was no room in your heart for anything but a poem? And all that happened to you was nothing but the source for the writing of poetry?"

Villon grimaced and raised his long, thin brown hands in protest.

"God knows, Monseigneur, I do not deserve the good will of the muse. I have been untrue to her too often for the sake of more tangible charms. But she is the only one who is not fed up with me. In her honor I proclaimed a year and a day ago—'Blonde, brown or black, it is all the same, and woman's beauty vanishes like last winter's trackless snow.' "

Charles stared pensively at his visitor. He does not understand what I mean, he thought in disappointment. He can tell me no more than the others about what I want to know because this being-free, this not-being-bound is innate with him, as flying is with birds. He is bound by no chains of obligation; he is not pinched by any feeling of responsibility for so many lives, by the duty of being an axis around which a world turns, even if it is only a world of trifles. And the man does not appreciate his own freedom. How can I expect that he could explain to me what it's like to find no obstacles between oneself and the expression of one's feelings?

He sighed, gave a slight cough and put on his spectacles. Villon, who had sat quietly watching him, said suddenly, "A person can carry his own persecutor, his own prison, about with him, Monseigneur. He can—as you know—die of thirst even when he has the clearest water within his reach. To be free . . . not to be free . . . it is all relative. No one has to drag along more ballast than he wants to and he who allows himself to be bound is a fool. The biggest fools are those who wear shackles of cobwebs and believe themselves to be helpless."

Charles did not reply at once. With his head propped upon his hand he looked at his visitor—that thin, sharply delineated face with the shadowed eyes and the wide, bitter mouth, the face of a man who had lived fiercely and violently. Charles recalled the nervous vigilance, the disillusioned look of the youth who had been caught cutting a purse in front of the Celestine cloister; the face of the man who sat across from him in the quiet library at Blois bore no trace of youth, although Villon was not yet thirty years old. In that mask, only the eyes appeared sometimes to be vulnerable as they blazed for a brief moment with affection or enthusiasm. Charles, who was usually quick to strike a note of friendship with his visitors, found himself almost uneasy in Villon's company. More than the width of the table divided them: there was a whole world between them.

The setting sun gleamed red against the tapestries on the wall; from the leafy thickets at the base of the precipice a cuckoo called incessantly with a high, clear sound, and the poplars along the river rustled in the evening breeze.

"Someone has challenged me to a game of cards," said Villon suddenly. His voice sounded rough and indifferent once more as it had when the meal commenced. "Somebody in black and green with a bald head and a chin like a turkey cock."

Charles, startled from his thoughts, could not suppress a smile. "Messire Jean des Saveuses, probably."

"I shall have to hide from him; I cannot afford to lose." Villon shrugged. Charles groped in his sleeve and produced a purse of black plaited silk.

"I find it a very disagreeable thought that a guest of mine should walk through my house with empty hands. Take my purse, but don't make the stakes too high, Messire."

For a moment Villon looked at the purse with a grimace which was half challenging and half embarrassed. His hesitation was quickly overcome, however. He put out his hand and drew the small weighty pouch toward him over the table. At the same time he stood up.

"You are extraordinarily generous, Monseigneur," he said. He made a gesture as if he were going to bend the knee before his host, but Charles forestalled this mark of homage with a curt wave of his hand.

"Leave that, Villon," he said dryly. "Go now; perhaps des Saveuses is looking for you. Write a poem and win the match tomorrow. Good evening, Messire."

Villon, who noticed the change in the Duke's manner and in his voice, raised his brows, bowed swiftly and left the room. Charles sat quietly in the red-gold glow of the evening sun which now poured through the arched window.

"Here I sit imprisoned," he said, half-aloud, "in my old skin. A man in the declining years of his life—grey, fat and so exhausted and indifferent to the very core of my being that I create the impression of generosity." He shook his head and sighed; the sun disturbed him; he closed his eyes and turned his face away a little.

He had lived for ten long years in carefree, sunny domestic Blois, a world which he had created himself. Study, easy intercourse with friends and acquaintances, the secret bliss he derived from poetry—had satisfied him so fully that no room remained in his heart for other desires. The pleasures which had been denied him as a youth and as a man in the prime of life he now possessed in abundance. He was surrounded by devoted, affectionate members of his household. Yes, he could allow himself his small whims, his distinct peculiarities. He basked in the respectful, indulgent warmth of his surroundings. The outside world no longer mattered to him; he did not even want to know what was happening in the cities and territories through which he had once travelled, filled with a desire to serve King and Kingdom, or even to serve that distant vision: peace. That peace was indeed only a vision, a chimaera, he had been compelled to believe when, to his great shock and profound disappointment, the English, despite all treaties, all diplomatic protests, had proceeded anew to attack Normandy and Brittany. Since then the battle had raged incessantly in the coastal regions—sometimes to the advantage of France, sometimes not.

Charles had ceased to be engrossed in the results of the struggle, in the shifting fortunes of war; he turned a deaf ear when his courtiers discussed the tidings which messengers continued to bring to Blois. Yes, he did know something—he knew from his noble guests that de Brezé and Coeur had fallen in turn into disfavor and had been repudiated; that Agnes Sorel had died a terrible death; he knew that the people of Gascony, encouraged by the English, had risen in rebellion just when the King seemed to be shattered by grief and reverses. He knew that the Dauphin, after a fierce quarrel with his father which had lasted for many years, had been banished from court for life; he knew too that Burgundy, plagued by illness, was barely able to remain master in his own domains. The greatest cities of Flanders and Hainault, embittered by the way in which the Duke attempted to impose his authority, made known their opposition sometimes passively, often by force of arms.

All this Charles knew well. But it did not affect him.

He felt himself comfortably hidden, securely stowed away in the silence of Nonchaloir. The only disturbance he had to endure was the restlessness which poetic inspiration brought with it. All the conditions seemed fulfilled for a carefree, peaceful life. That in spite of all this he was not really happy astonished Charles anew each day.

A rustling noise at the door startled him; he raised himself, not without difficulty, and bent sideways so that he could look over the back of his chair. Marie had entered; carefully she pushed aside the tapestry which hung before the door and then moved it back again. She sat down opposite him on the footstool on which his aching leg had been propped.

"I hear you have cancelled today's contest, Monseigneur," she said softly. She always addressed Charles with formality. "Am I to blame?"

"It seemed to me that the subjects had aroused your displeasure," replied Charles. "It would make no sense to compete with one another in poetry when not everyone is in a contented and happy frame of mind. You know that I put a good relationship among my household above everything."

Marie nodded calmly, but her eyes did not lose their expression of mournful resignation. "I find both themes completely attractive. I considered earnestly the question of why you chose precisely these subjects which, each in different words, express the same feeling of helplessness, discontent. I thought that *you* were contented, Monseigneur."

"It is a question whether one ever finds the peace which gratifies the spirit." Charles removed his spectacles and, for a moment, pressed the thumb and forefinger of his left hand against his eyes.

"We can seek our consolation in God," Marie said quietly.

"Do *you* do that, ma mie?"

"I did not know that you were troubled, Monseigneur. I did not know that no fountain exists which can quench your thirst."

Charles raised his head and looked at his wife with surprise. He had never heard her speak that way before; it seemed to him that she was expressing what he had so often thought in secret bitterness. He leaned forward and took Marie's hand.

"I know a cool deep well which is pure and translucent and reflects God's blue heaven. If that clear water cannot slake my thirst, ma mie, it is because no cure exists for the drought which scorches me internally. And if in the forest of long awaiting I do not find the path which at long last opens onto a broad vista, then it is perhaps because I *must* go on wandering."

"I want nothing more than to share your thirst and to accompany you on your wanderings," said Marie, with downcast eyes. "It took me a long time to understand that this is a great privilege. But when I was ready to join you in that forest of which you had once spoken to me, I could not find you any more. Often it seemed to me that you had consciously fled from me, that you preferred loneliness to my company. And I thought that this was so because you had found in solitude what you had always sought: the spring which can slake your thirst, the path which leads out into the open fields. Because I did not wish to disturb your peace, I remained behind you, there where I would not trouble you.

"But I know now that you are not happy, Monseigneur, and I know also why. Forgive me for saying this to you, but whoever is self-centered and accepts love without giving it, feels depressed by day and lies awake at night, tormented by bitter thoughts. You are benevolent and friendly to everyone, but that is not praiseworthy because it costs you no effort. You do not really love the world or people, Monseigneur. You meditate only on yourself and live hidden in your own thoughts. And whoever beats at your door to gain entrance to your heart is not admitted. Forgive me, but it's the truth."

For a long time Charles sat in silence, with bowed head. Marie did not move. The light of the setting sun glowed on the walls of the library; in the crimson blaze even the images on the tapestries seemed to fade. A glass standing on the table sparkled with a ruby tint as though it contained the burning drink of the legends: those who moistened their lips with it forgot the world and were dazzled; they remained enchanted by love to the end of their days. But the sun sank below the rim of the window frame, the red light streamed back from the walls, the magical goblet became once more only a tumbler with dregs of wine at the bottom. Charles brought his wife's cool hand to his forehead and sighed.

"Forgive me, ma mie," he whispered. "Forgive me for having done you so great a wrong."

The members of the household who, after the card game, still sat chatting in the twilit hall, rose hastily from their seats when Monseigneur and his wife appeared walking hand in hand from the antechamber which bordered the library. But the ducal couple did not respond to their greetings; affectionately close to each other, they went by, walking slowly and silently. For a considerable time after they had passed through the vaulted door, the sound of Monseigneur's thoughtful footsteps could be heard on the stairs, along with the soft rustle of Madame's train.

On a certain day in the early spring of 1457, Jean Cailleau, Charles' physician and trusted friend, came to his master with a fairly solemn face. Cailleau had not lived at Blois for the last few years; he had become canon of Saint-Martin's abbey at Tours. If, however, he were needed at the castle, he came immediately as of old to let blood and make up medicines.

Around Easter the Duchess had begun to complain of feeling ill. Charles sent a courier to Tours to fetch Cailleau who set out at once to make the journey, partly by ship, partly by mule. He arrived at Blois much sooner than expected, in his dusty travelling cloak and with his heavy flat case filled with instruments and herbs. While he was with the Duchess, Charles waited anxiously and uneasily in the library. He had known for a long time that Marie did not have a strong constitution, but since the couple had become so loving and intimate, the idea of ever having to do without her seemed intolerable to him.

They had passed an autumn and winter in tender affection; daily they recovered what they had allowed to slip away from them during the sixteen long, empty years of marriage. With steadily increasing gratitude and astonishment, Charles had realized that his wife knew how to give him true friendship and deep understanding. In all the solitary hours she had passed over books and her embroidery frame she had been molding her mind and spirit to suit *his* needs. He perceived—a bewildering experience for a sixty-year-old man—that he was able to make her really happy. Marie loved him despite the fact that he was old and stout. This late bliss did not resemble in any way the radiant joy, the intoxication of youthful passion which he had known with Bonne. But how comforting, how safe, how peaceful it was to be together with such a gentle, understanding woman as Marie. Her illness alarmed Charles exceedingly; when he saw Cailleau's serious, calm face he could barely suppress his anxiety.

"How is my wife?" he asked, forcing himself to speak without emotion.

"Monseigneur," replied Cailleau with a searching look at Charles, "Monseigneur, my findings are these: Madame your wife is in blessed circumstances. Within half a year if God wills it she will be confined."

Charles sank into a chair and wiped the sweat from his brow. He was too surprised to speak. When he became aware that Cailleau was still watching him with grave solicitude, as though he doubted the good reception of his news, he began to laugh loudly, almost boyishly.

"By God, Cailleau, I have never received more joyful news in my entire life!"

Later he stayed for a considerable time in the gallery on the southwestern side of Blois, looking out over the land bathed in clear spring sunshine. The poplars along the river wore light green foliage; the hills were covered with young vines. The world seemed as wholly new and fresh as on the first day after creation.

Charles thought that he had never seen anything lovelier than his little daughter Marie. He had to laugh condescendingly when he heard people insist that all babies were terrifyingly ugly. He sat for hours lost in contemplation beside the cradle of the sleeping child. If he was not near her, he was thinking about her: did she have everything she needed, was she being looked after as carefully as possible? He competed with Marie in expressing his affection for the little girl. How profoundly interesting everything was which concerned her, in comparison with the things which caused turmoil in the world. The breaking through of a little tooth, the first step, the first word, provided Charles the opportunity to make his child the center of domestic festivities, to distribute souvenirs in her name. When the child appeared in her nurse's arms for the first time in the courtyard at Blois, Charles had three golden écus divided among the stableboys and kitchen servants who had not seen Marie d'Orléans before, with the request that they drink to her health.

In the summer, Dunois appeared in Blois with a great following. The brothers had not seen each other for a long time; Charles never left Blois and Dunois had had his hands full, year in and year out, leading the King's armies in Normandy and Brittany. That the English were defeated, time after time, that they had gradually been compelled to yield up all their conquests again, was thanks above all to Dunois' strong and skillful actions. The King, who had blind faith in him, showered him with favors: titles, gifts of land and sums of money. He had Dunois' birth declared legitimate, granted him and his descendants the right to bear the names of Orléans and Valois, and removed the bar sinister from his escutcheon. Dunois, who had meanwhile married, had accepted that prerogative for his children; he himself continued to cling firmly under all circumstances to the name which his father had given him and, as before, he signed all letters and documents with the words which he had heard added to that name since his youth: Bastard of Orléans.

Charles greeted his half-brother joyfully. Dunois had hardly changed over the course of nearly ten years; there were no wrinkles yet in his weatherbeaten, sunburnt face; no grey in his sandy hair; his green eyes were still as bright as they had been in his childhood. He was dressed in leather and mail; his escort was strongly armed. When Charles jokingly asked about the reason for this martial parade, Dunois frowned and said seriously, "I am travelling through, brother. I have just conveyed a prisoner from Paris to the King's residence, Nonette in Bourbon. I have to speak to you about it."

The news which Dunois gave him alarmed Charles, but did not surprise him. It concerned his son-in-law Alençon, whose behavior Charles had observed for so long with suspicion and anxiety.

The King, worn out by defeats and disappointments, had lapsed anew into seclusion, timidity and doubt, and had ordered the ecclesiastic authorities and the Parlement to initiate an inquiry in Rouen and Paris into the manner in which the late Jeanne, Maid of Orléans, had been condemned and executed. In the silence of his apartments the King, afflicted with illness and worry, was prey to morbid fears: he remembered that Agnes Sorel had once reproached him for his indifference to the fate of the Maid whom, in a sense, he had to thank for his crown. At that time he had brusquely rejected her advice that Jeanne's good name should be restored. But now he felt that his omission was wrong, that it was a sin which weighed heavily upon his conscience. He dared not die before he had discharged his obligation.

Among the many who came to Paris as witnesses in this matter was Alençon, who had spoken repeatedly with Jeanne. While he was making his statement, pleased at the opportunity to place the King's actions in an unfavorable light, certain letters were discovered on an English spy in Brittany. In these letters which had been written and signed by Alençon, the Duke expressed his desire to conclude an alliance with Henry VI, put himself and the inhabitants of his domain in the service of England, and supplied the names of coastal towns where an invading army could land.

The King did not hesitate; he immediately sent Dunois to Paris to take Alençon prisoner on a charge of high treason. In the castle of Nonette, Alençon confessed his guilt; he had acted, he said, because he felt he had been neglected and given short shrift by the King.

Charles listened in silence. He could not get over this news: the disgrace of Alençon, whose children were Charles' grandchildren, cast a slur on the honor of Orléans.

"This will end nastily for Alençon," Dunois remarked gruffly; he had distrusted Charles' son-in-law practically from the beginning. "It is pretty certain that all his possessions will be declared forfeit and the domain will revert again to the Crown. But I would be surprised if he got off with his life; the King seems firmly resolved to condemn Alençon to the scaffold."

"Will there be no trial?" Charles asked slowly.

Dunois nodded. "That is why I am here, brother. The trial begins in Vendôme on the fifteenth of December. The King summons you there to give your opinion of this business. Do not refuse," he added hastily, when he saw Charles make a movement of protest. "Our friends of Brittany and Burgundy have defaulted and it goes without saying that we will not see the Dauphin. If you are interested in salvaging whatever can be saved for your grandchildren, you must seize this chance to act as spokesman."

Charles went on sitting for a few minutes, his head turned away. "It goes against my grain to become involved once again in a questionable matter," he said at last. "Surely you realize that in order to accomplish anything, I shall have to plead extenuating circumstances for Alençon. But still, you are right. I shall prepare myself for the hearing."

The trial was held in the great hall of the castle of Vendôme. Stands hung with tapestries stood opposite and on both sides of the royal throne; on these platforms sat the great lords of the Kingdom, four rows deep: first, the vassals of the Crown and the princes of the Church; then the representatives of the nobility and the clergy, and finally those who would speak for the burghers. Armed sentries guarded the approaches to the stands and the open spaces between them. A great crowd of spectators filled the hall, overflowing outside onto the steps and into the corridors. At the King's right hand sat his youngest son and his blood relative, Charles d'Orléans.

The journey and the sojourn at the court had tired Charles greatly; he was not used to all this excitement. In addition, he was uncertain about the effect his words would have on a company most of whom wanted to see Alençon sentenced to death. Only the Archbishop of Reims and an envoy from Burgundy would ask for clemency, the first as a mere formality, the second chiefly to thwart the King.

From time to time Charles glanced at his cousin: he found the King sadly altered; his features were slack, his eyes restless; little or nothing remained of his authoritative tone, his self-assured bearing. Charles knew the reasons for the King's bitterness: the bad feeling between him and the Dauphin grieved him; he was troubled about the future of the Kingdom under such a rule and filled with regret that he could not give his beloved second son the rights that belonged to the eldest. In twelve years the Dauphin had not once visited his father; he ruled as he wished in his place of exile, surrounded by a household filled with people of unknown origin whom he had elevated to the nobility. That he was involved in other affairs as well became evident when, immediately after Alençon's arrest, he rode at full speed across France into Flanders and there sought safe accommodation at Burgundy's court. The King bent under this blow. To Charles he remarked with a sour, nervous laugh when the subject came up, "Burgundy does not know what he is doing; he thinks he will gain an advantage by harboring the future King of France. But he has let a fox into his hencoop!"

The King, motionless in the stiff folds of his robes of state, his face obscured by the broad brim of his hat, listened impassively to the distinguished speakers who came forward to air their opinions. After the words "death penalty" had echoed a number of times through the space around the stands, it was Charles' turn to speak. He stood up and descended the three steep steps with difficulty. He sensed that most of those present were watching him with disapproval and mistrust; nobody doubted that he would attempt to exonerate his son-in-law, or at least try to mitigate his punishment. Charles held the paper ready on which he had made his notes, but on second thought he hid it away in his sleeve with the spectacles which he did not need now. He bowed and turned to the King.

"Monseigneur! There are three things which must be considered when one is called upon to give one's opinion upon important affairs: the advisor himself, the person to whom advice is to be given and the matter under consideration. With regard to the first, it is written '*multi multa sciunt et se ipsos nesciunt*—many people know many things but they do not know themselves.' When I look at myself now and consider that I must advise you about your interests and those of the Kingdom, I find it a very risky undertaking on my part, who am neither wise nor learned enough to speak here after so many capable and renowned lawyers have had their say. I carry only a candle where a number of torches are burning. I beseech you therefore to take my good intentions into account if my insight should fail me.

"Concerning my second point—the person to whom I offer my advice: I see in you my lord and master and, in addition, my blood relative, to whom obviously I am accountable. Finally I honor you as my sovereign. And when I think about that concept of 'sovereign', then I realize fully the deep significance of it. For you are only a man like myself, of flesh and blood, subject to dangers, threats, adversity, diseases and other afflictions. That nevertheless you have succeeded in holding the reins of government in these very difficult times is for me a sign that your sovereignty has come to you as a gift from God, the King of kings, the Lord of lords. Therefore you are called Your Most Christian Majesty, and therefore all subjects of France must serve and support you as the representative of God's authority.

"Thirdly, the matter on which I must counsel you touches you and your family closely, since I, your kinsman, am bound by ties of blood and friendship to the accused, his father and his entire line." Charles then went on to recall that his father had concluded an alliance with the late Duke of Alençon, that he himself had been supported by the Duke and his vassals in the struggle against Burgundy, that an Alençon had died gloriously in the service of the realm on the field of Agincourt. While he spoke he was well aware that these were nothing but empty phrases; he knew only too well that old Alençon had never sought anything except his own advantage.

He tried another tack and dwelt on all those acts of Alençon's which could be looked upon as exercises of friendship and chivalry. He ransacked his memory to leave nothing unsaid that would place his son-in-law and the latter's father in the most favorable light possible. He besought the King to weigh good and evil carefully against each other and if he found that evil tipped the scales, to be merciful.

"For inasmuch as you are God's deputy, you must follow his example: 'You will do as I have done', He said, and 'As you have judged, so will you be judged.'

"I have the following advice to give you in this matter: in my opinion when we think of saving Alençon's life we must think of both his body and his soul. God has said, '*Nolo mortem peccatoris,* I do not want the sinner to die.' So you too cannot desire Alençon's death. Because his actions show that his common sense has failed him, and if he should now be put to death without the opportunity to amend his life and purify his soul, then all those who had demanded his execution would have neglected to give him that last chance which is every sinner's due. It is a greater affliction and torment to sit in prison for years than to die suddenly, for then one is delivered from earthly suffering. I know whereof I speak, because when I was a prisoner in England, I often wished that I had been slain at Agincourt.

"Therefore I counsel you for the sake of the security of the Kingdom to keep the Duke in safe custody, in whatever manner you deem best, my lord. It seems to me also eminently fair that you should have the right to dispose of his lands and possessions, but I .think that you should provide within reason for his wife and children. It is written, 'One may not wreak vengeance upon the innocent.' I implore you as a father to look after those who must now consider themselves orphans. Then it seems to me that you ought not to forget his servants and followers who bore no guilt in what occurred. Care for them, now that they have lost their livelihood. I declare before God, before you, my lord, and before all those assembled here, that I have spoken according to my honor and conscience, to serve the interests of the realm. At all times I would gladly, if that became necessary, put aside all my responsibilities and devote all my energies, to the best of my knowledge and ability, however scanty, to serve those interests. I have finished."

The King adjourned the hearing. It was obvious that he was extremely displeased.

In the following days it was no secret from Charles that his advice had not been received with favor. He could not help noticing to his dismay and regret that he was now viewed with the same dislike and suspicion that was felt toward Burgundy and the Dauphin. He noticed that he was being shunned; he knew that behind his back people were being told to keep away from him. And he learned that he had aroused the King's anger. Alençon's chances for clemency had not been increased by his appeal.

Suddenly Richmont, Duke of Brittany, appeared at Vendôme. What had put Charles in a bad light did not damage the King's former favorite and collaborator. Before long it was proclaimed at the meeting that the King "as a result of the petition made to Us by Our most beloved and cherished cousin the Duke of Brittany, uncle of the aforementioned Alençon" had resolved to change the sentence of death to confinement in a fortress. Charles d'Orléans returned to Blois.

Life in Blois flowed on from day to day in peace and benevolence. Charles read or wrote in the quiet library, sought and found fulfilment in his wife's company—they spoke together about things which interested them or sat side by side in companionable silence, she crocheting with gold thread, he with a book which actually he scarcely read—and diverted himself with his little daughter in the nursery, in the courtyard or the flower garden outside the walls. Little Marie was the apple of his eye; she was nearly three years old, swift of foot and swifter still of comprehension. He could not get enough of her small, clear voice, her dignified little lady manners. He gave her little psalm-books illuminated with miniatures, small paternosters decorated with red and gold beads, a little purse with tiny gold pieces to wear on her girdle.

When he and his wife left Blois to visit neighboring towns and castles, they took their child with them; Mademoiselle's flushed little face glowed like a rose against the black garments of the older couple. She was allowed to witness the solemn ceremonies in Orléans when, at the King's command, the Maid's honor was restored; the people of the region along the Loire, who had never ceased to love Jeanne and to honor her memory, moved in procession with burning candles, green branches and colorful banners to the bridge over which she had ridden in triumph into Orléans thirty years before.

Some time later a feast was given by the city in honor of little Marie d'Orléans: from her father's arms she watched the people dancing in the open air, and wine and spiced cake being set out for everyone on long tables in the market square. The Duke ordered the release of all prisoners from the city's dungeons. Among the pale people wrapped in filthy rags, shouting with excitement as they shoved their way out through the prison gates, was François Villon, who had been imprisoned some years before for a misdemeanor. With his usual directness he went immediately to pay his respects to Charles, who with a nod and an ironic smile pressed his hand and invited him to join the celebrations. Villon's sharp eyes saw at once where the Duke's affection and interest lay: in order to ensure continued favor for himself, Villon composed a song praising little Marie for her dignified, regal demeanor and comparing the three-year-old to the wise Cassandra, the beautiful Echo, the chaste Lucretia, the noble Dido. Charles was seized by a fit of laughter at this, but he was touched nonetheless, and gave Villon a generous reward and the privilege of coming and going as he pleased in the ducal residence.

About the middle of July in the year 1461 couriers brought to Blois the news that the King was dead. He had spent the last years of his life in the secluded castle of Mehun-sur-Yèvre, hidden away in its neglected rooms, suspicious and fearful of everyone who approached him. Finally, afraid that he was about to be poisoned, he refused to take food. He died of starvation and exhaustion.

Since the Dauphin had not yet returned from Flanders, the task of directing funeral arrangements fell to Charles. He traveled with a large retinue to Mehun to carry out this obligation. The King's body was placed upon a bier, conveyed to Paris with appropriate pomp, and there, after the mass for the dead, buried in the abbey of Saint-Denis.

On the thirty-first of August the new King, Louis, by the Grace of God the eleventh of that name, rode into Paris accompanied by Burgundy, his son and the Duke of Cleves. Charles was not part of the glittering procession which followed the King through the city:

he wished to make known by his absence that he no longer wanted a place in court, that he desired to withdraw from public life. From a window of his Hôtel des Tournelles he looked down upon the endless file of richly attired lords and their followers. He saw familiar faces: Dunois, Angoulême, Bourbon, Étampes and many others; under a canopy rode King Louis wearing white garments, but with a strange little black bonnet on his head, as though he wanted to mock the coronation ceremony. His face was as pointed, his eyes as malicious, as ever. He looked about sharply at the people along the way who were cheering him half-heartedly.

Charles saw Burgundy riding behind the King in a mantle sparkling with jewels; he bore himself as though it were *he* who was being led to his coronation. Charles watched him attentively; he asked himself if the whispers he had heard were true: that Louis, now that he had become King, did not appear prepared to grant to his protector Burgundy the place of honor on the Council and in the government which the latter had expected. It seemed that a violent disagreement had arisen between Louis and Burgundy's son Charolais. Moreover, the new King of France had declared curtly that he frankly found it excessive that Burgundy should escort him to Paris with a veritable army of courtiers and armed men; surely the King of France could count on a good reception without that.

Charles considered himself fortunate that he could now bid farewell to court life; he had no obligation whatever to King Louis, who most probably would have no further need of him. He was, thank God, too old for politics and diplomacy. With philosophical submission he allowed the stream of festivities and ceremonies to pass over him. While others danced and drank and did themselves only too well at the beautifully-decorated buffets heaped with fabulously costly food, Charles sat in a quiet corner, listening to the music. He remained in Paris chiefly to give Marie the opportunity to take part in the courtly amusements. She had, he thought, lived so long in seclusion; she deserved to go dancing adorned like a princess. But after a few weeks Marie announced that she had had enough of all these tournaments, pageants and banquets; she wanted to go home to her child.

Charles' thoughts too were incessantly with his small daughter, the more so since the King had let it be known in a manner which brooked no contradiction, that it was his intention to request the hand of Mademoiselle d'Orléans for his younger brother. Charles understood all too well where this must lead: if the King had made up his mind, Orléans would fall under his control once again.

In the spring Charles and his wife reached Blois, where they were overjoyed to find everyone well and everything in good condition. A few days after their return Marie, smiling, approached her husband who was standing in the library looking at a new manuscript.

"What is it, ma mie?" Charles asked absently; he did not look up from the richly illustrated page.

"Monseigneur," said Cailleau, carefully straightening the sleeves of his robe, which he had pushed up above his elbow. "Monseigneur, do you recall that we once—ten, twelve years ago—made a wager?"

Charles and the physician stood in one of the anterooms to Marie's bedchamber. Charles had announced that he would wait there while his wife was in labor. From time to time Cailleau came to tell him how the labor was going; there was, he repeated emphatically time and again, no reason at all for alarm.

"Wager?" Charles, who was constantly straining to catch sounds from the closed lying-in room—was it really going well with Marie?—could remember nothing about it. Cailleau kept his head bowed low while he fastened the laces of his sleeves.

"Yes indeed, Monseigneur. When I once told you that you could still have an heir, you wagered five hundred livres that that would never happen. My lord," he looked up, no longer able to suppress his delight, "my lord, I cannot tell you how pleased and thankful I am to be able to come now and tell you that you have lost your wager. Your wife has just given birth to a son."

The church bells pealed in Blois, Beaugency and Orléans, in all the cities and villages along the Loire. Flags and banners fluttered blue and gold against the summer sky, heralds traveled everywhere across the land to proclaim to the sound of clarions what the people along the roads already knew: that in the castle of Blois a son, an heir, had been born to Orléans. Those who visited Blois in those days saw that Monseigneur behaved as though he were rejuvenated; he still did not know how to express his delight. He distributed rich presents to everyone who came to congratulate him and entreated each one to pray for the child's well-being; he considered the birth of his son to be a miracle. While the bells of the district rang out, the infant was rocked to sleep to the tune of an old nursery rhyme— just as Charles himself had once been rocked:

> Orléans, Beaugency,
> Notre Dame de Cléry,
> Vendôme, Vendôme!
> Hark, we peal—what sorrow—
> All day, all night—willing or not,
> All hours, all hours!

Charles ordered everything to be made ready for the christening ceremony. The boy would be called Louis after his grandfather; his godfather must be his nearest blood relation—in this case, to Charles' annoyance, it was the King.

He hoped and expected that the King would refuse the invitation, but now it appeared that he had misunderstood his sovereign's character. Louis XI came, although in a far from benevolent mood. He, who as Dauphin had made use of the services of the discontented vassal princes and the ambitious nobility, had, after his accession to the throne, acted against this group more mercilessly than his father had ever done. Ignoring their objections and complaints, he had curtailed their privileges and restricted their independent control of their own territories. During the time when he was still feigning friendship for the great lords, he had learned many things which now proved very useful to him.

He had them in his power, he found their rage and disappointment amusing, but he remained on his guard. He knew quite well that they were conspiring against him; his excellent network of spies had given him all the names and facts which he needed. He bided his time, paying no attention to the hatred of the feudal princes. He had never heard the name of Orléans connected with talk of conspiracies; he suspected, however, that Charles would reveal signs of ambition now that he had a son.

On the way to Blois, the King had summoned one of his trusted retainers and asked him acidly, "How much truth is there in the little tale which I hear is spreading in Orléans and Touraine? Did Orléans predict that his son would wear the crown of France?"

The man could report only that an old woman had indeed said something like that to the Duke of Orléans.

"Hm," said the King curtly. "My worthy uncle of Orléans may be a dull old fellow, but apparently he has not been too dull and too old to make his wife pregnant. Keep an eye on him, the grey . . ." The King swallowed the epithet and signalled his servant to withdraw.

On his arrival in Blois, the King did not want to waste his time on compliments and ceremony. The baptismal procession was formed at once in the courtyard near the donjon; from there the noble company, preceded by torchbearers, set out for the church of Saint-Sauveur in the great castle yard where the Archbishop of Chartres welcomed the royal company.

The King, his lips pursed in an expression of slight aversion, held the child over the baptismal font; the infant, alarmed by the touch of less than loving hands, did what would, under other circumstances, have caused no comment. The King quickly delivered the baptized baby to his nurse, wiped his sleeves and said with a sour laugh, "Look what this child—his only achievement is to come into the world—Look what he dares to do!"

Charles apologized hastily for his son, and suggested that they move to the lying-in chamber, where the Duchess awaited the guests. The King walked ahead with his somewhat shuffling gait; apparently he felt no compulsion to laugh or make friendly jokes. He greeted Marie curtly, complained to her about her son's misbehavior and refused to remain in Blois for the christening feast. As he turned to quit the chamber, he stumbled over one of the tapestries which hung from the bed to the floor.

"This is the second time!" he said angrily; he jerked his mantle tightly around him and left the birth chamber without further ceremony.

Charles was soon to discover that King Louis was not a man who forgot quickly. The events in Blois seemed to have furnished the King with the pretence he had long sought to include Charles in the warnings and criticisms he directed to the feudal princes. He had been right in one respect: Charles had been stimulated by the birth of his son to renew his efforts to secure possession of Asti for his offspring. He applied with considerable reluctance to the King, who responded with obvious enjoyment that the thought of defending the interests of Orléans on the other side of the Alps was the farthest thing from his mind; he considered that he had the honor to be the friend of Sforza and not his enemy and he had no intention of fighting with him.

"Why not sell Asti to Sforza?" he asked at last, with raised brows. "You can always use the money, can't you, worthy uncle?"

Charles declined this suggestion and left to return home. Not long afterward the King dictated a letter to Francesco Sforza in which he said, among other things: "The Duke of Orléans does not want to give up Asti. However, it seems to me that his health is failing. I am quite sure that Asti will be there for the taking as soon as he is dead—and then we will also own his son."

Indeed, Charles was feeling far from well; for some time he had been suffering such violent attacks of gout that he could not walk without a cane. But it troubled him more that his right arm was stiff and painful: he found it impossible, after several fruitless attempts, to wield a pen. He was obliged to attach a seal to official documents to signal his approval, because he could no longer sign his name. From time to time his eyes refused to serve him; even with his strongest spectacles, bent forward over his book, he could make out nothing more than vague grey marks. He sought refuge with Marie, or in the nursery with his little daughter and his son— in that safe company he overcame his own fear of the blindness, the infirmity, which perhaps awaited him. As long as he was able, he wanted to act in his children's interest; he reproached himself bitterly for having wasted so many years in pleasant tranquillity. For his son's sake he had to enter into important relationships, to conclude alliances; to accomplish this he was prepared to go so far as to join the ranks of the rebel princes. He felt that he had no time to lose; death, or worse, the absolute helplessness of the living dead, could strike him suddenly and when he least expected it.

He sent messengers to Brittany; his nephew François Étampes had succeeded Richmont, who had died childless some years before. The young man promised his uncle to defend Asti by force of arms if necessary, to capture Milan and to stand by his young cousin of Orléans at all times. In addition, Charles ordered a marriage contract to be drawn up in great haste between his daughter Marie and his foster son Pierre, Bourbon's youngest son. However, before he could make an equally satisfactory arrangement for his son and heir, envoys of the always well-informed King had arrived in Blois with a proposal that gave Charles a new headache: the King offered his daughter

Jeanne as a bride for the heir of Orléans, in a manner which was more a command than a request. Charles, annoyed and upset, put off giving a definite answer from day to day in the hope that in the meantime the possibility of another arrangement would arise. And threats of serious disagreements between the King and the vassals of the Crown did in fact shove the matter of the marriage into the background for a while.

The princes, who had vainly attempted through petitions and personal visits, to effect the restoration of the honors which they believed were rightfully theirs, had finally realized what the King's objectives were: he wanted their participation in the administration of the Kingdom to be reduced to a minimum; he did not want them at his court, nor did he want their advice in the Council—for that, he would choose his own people. The cities and territories which he had peremptorily confiscated from them upon his accession to the throne, would not be returned. He said repeatedly that he would not allow his regime to be poisoned by a group of men who were driven and impelled only by self-interest and ambition and who had always shown hostility to any confident, capable sovereign. Charles, through his negotiations for alliances with Bourbon and Brittany, was embroiled once more in the affairs of the feudal princes; he had to declare his solidarity with the struggle of that group in which, because of his birth and rank, he held so important a place.

He attended the protest meetings convened by Brittany; that Burgundy's envoys appeared there at every turn did not please Charles. Their complaints and accusations far exceeded all the others in intensity: the King had occupied the cities along the Somme and, through men whom he had met in Flanders years ago, maintained relations with the rebellious commercial cities. Finally, the participants in the meetings decided to unite openly in a coalition "for the interests of the common welfare." They would gather together to show that the King's behavior was damaging to the landed interests and the honor of the Kingdom. But before they could proceed, the King summoned them—in a document which demonstrated how well-informed he was—to a meeting in Tours. The vassals of the Crown set out in a less than hopeful mood; they knew they could expect nothing good from a man who, for political reasons, had feigned friendship and familiarity with them for twenty years.

Charles came to Tours accompanied by Dunois; he was present at conferences presided over by the King himself. Coldly and sharply

Louis put his case to them once more, arguing that the measures he had taken were necessary because of the confusion into which affairs of state had fallen during the last years of his father's reign. In connection with the princes' demands, he made a long speech full of generalities about obligations, about obedience and loyalty. Finally he said, looking at the rows of faces with a somewhat sour smile, that he would be sorry if the maintenance of his authority forced him to victimize anybody.

The lords heard these words in silence. They recognized his iron will and his implacable antipathy. They had no doubt that the sole purpose of this meeting was to impress upon them anew, before they pursued their reckless path, the threat of the King's power. However, they remained resolute. Brittany, Bourbon, Anjou and, especially, Burgundy wanted nothing more than to take up arms openly against the man who had forthrightly said that he intended once and for all to crush the political power of the nobility.

Charles d'Orléans sat huddled in his fur-lined mantle—these December days were bitter cold—among the peers of France. He felt extremely tired, and shivered now and then as though with fever. Cailleau had advised in the strongest terms against this journey to Tours; in such damp raw weather Monseigneur was usually half-crippled with gout. Moreover, his heart had been troubling him again for some time. But Charles refused to consider staying at home; he did not want to give the impression that he would shirk his obligations to his kinsmen and allies out of fear of the King.

In the meeting hall in Tours, he regretted his obstinacy; his heart throbbed so irregularly that he could scarcely breathe; his feet were ice cold; it cost him a great effort to sit upright and pay attention to the words of the speakers. Once he nearly dozed off; Dunois nudged him gently. He came to himself in time to hear the King express his lack of confidence in the good faith of François of Brittany who was on such a friendly footing with the envoys of England and Burgundy. Charles' still-young nephew pressed his lips together in rage, but made no attempt to refute these accusations. When the meeting ended, he withdrew without saying a word. Charles, knowing that his sister's son was deeply wounded, determined to see the King and attempt to cleanse his name of all suspicion. It was of great importance to Charles to bind the young man to him: François of Brittany could be a valuable friend for his son in the future. The King granted Charles a private audience.

When Charles was announced, a few gentlemen were just leaving the King's apartments; to his deep amazement, Charles saw that one of them was Dammartin, who had been a trusted advisor of Charles VII.

"That surprises you, worthy uncle?" asked the King suddenly. He stood, Charles noticed, leaning his arms on the high back of a chair. "Go sit down—you look as though your legs will barely hold you. Great old age may be worthy of respect but its attendant symptoms are troublesome: tottery legs, trembling fingers, loss of hair and teeth—isn't that right, uncle?"

Charles sat down, startled by these caustic, derisive words. Passion and pride stirred equally within him, but he controlled himself; for the sake of his son's security he could afford to put up with a little abuse. "I remembered that Dammartin once aroused your boundless displeasure, Sire, because he served your father so faithfully," he said calmly.

The King began to laugh softly; he rested his chin on his fists. His body remained invisible behind the chair. That moving head, with its black eyes gleaming with malice and contempt, made a grotesque, almost terrifying impression. "Dammartin is one of those men who always remains loyal to the king—whoever the king might be—the born devoted servant—a possession not to be squandered. What didn't please me when I was Dauphin, I find excellent now that I am King, my worthy uncle."

"Yes, I have noticed that, Sire," replied Charles with a sigh. "Therefore I too have come to you to request your forebearance for my nephew, my Lord of Brittany."

"Not necessary! Waste no words on that, my lord uncle of Orléans. Spare me your meddling and your pretty speeches. I am not pleasant and courtly enough to hear your platitudes to the end."

Charles remained in his chair; he asked himself whether he had heard the King correctly. That Louis disliked him he knew very well, but surely his age and rank gave him the right to courteous treatment, at the least.

"You need not stare at me in such surprise," the King went on, in a tone of cold amusement. "I will readily admit to you that I have always found you an extremely stupid old fellow. If you had only half the brains which you think you have, you would undoubtedly be the wisest man in France."

"God knows that I have never held an exceptionally high opinion of myself. I willingly admit that I am old and stupid—but I have enough sense to know that such words are not worthy of one who wears the crown of France. And I am your blood relative, Sire."

The King sniggered again; he raised his hand and pointed a long, tapering finger at his guest. "You are my uncle, my father's half-brother," he said, visibly enjoying Charles' incredulous consternation at hearing these words. "I at least have never doubted that Isabeau, that slut, spoke the truth when she called my father—may God rest his soul—Orléans' bastard. Don't think that it disturbs me. On the contrary, better this than to stem from a lunatic."

Charles rose slowly. He had an answer on his lips. The King's malicious, grimacing face, his forefinger raised in an almost grotesque gesture, roused irresistible memories of the man who had once been held captive like a wild beast—the man who had had to be hidden from the court and the people because of his bizarre grimaces.

"I do not wish to tire you any longer with my presence, Sire," Charles said formally. For a moment the room sank into a grey mist; a strange buzzing filled his ears. I am ill, he thought, surprised, I must return to Blois. He heard his own voice as though it came from a distance; the words came slow, dull, with silence between them. "I deeply regret that you doubt the nature of my intentions—that you consider my actions to be meddlesome. All my life I have sincerely endeavored—sincerely endeavored—to serve my king—to fulfil my obligations to friends and kinsmen. I have—been—a—man—of peace . . ."

"Ah—." The King made a protracted sound to show his impatience and distaste. "Once more—spare me all the fine talk. What have you done, uncle? What have you accomplished in that long life of yours? How have you used the opportunity which was granted to you—more I know than to others—to maintain order in the realm, to preserve peace and support the royal authority? What have you, with all your good will and so-called wisdom, understood of the evolution we have undergone—of the real significance of the struggle which has been going on since my great-grandfather's day—between the Crown and the powerful forces who want to smash it to pieces?—For me you are already a dead man, uncle, a residue of something which has died without knowing it. In my eyes you are a ridiculous, foolish old man—you trot along good-naturedly with your peers who stretch out their claws in a last desperate attempt to grasp power.

"But it is over, lord uncle, it is over. Your time, the time when great lords were kings, is over. Henceforth there will be one King in France, one single King, by God's grace and by your leave, and that King will rule from the Pyrenees to the farthest border of the lowlands. He who dares to nibble at the cake will be sent from the table. Believe me, uncle, if any crumbs are to be picked up it will not be by the flashy, ambitious ne'er-do-wells with their gilt escutcheons and fine-sounding names, but by those who have made the cities great and prosperous, by the men behind the anvil and in the shipyards, by the weavers and smiths, by the merchants, soldiers—by each one with diligence and keen intelligence, even if he comes crawling up from the slime of the sewer. *These* I shall amply reward for their service—not a high-born weakling like you, uncle, who lets every chance slip through his fingers, who willingly lets himself be led by anyone who puts himself to the trouble of taking him in tow. Distinction, dignity, an affable manner—all at your service—but for all that, you did nothing worth mentioning for either king or country.

"Go back to Blois, putter about with rhymes and rock the cradle. God knows you could have been king, you could have spared the Kingdom a half-century of misery if you had had a drop of true ruler's blood in your veins. You could have stood where *I* stand now, instead of whining with humiliation and groping for the way to the door on trembling legs . . ."

Charles, who was feeling at the wall for support—he could not see; it was growing dark before his eyes—stood still.

"I never imagined that I possessed great gifts. When I was young, I often asked myself bitterly why so heavy a burden had been laid precisely on *my* shoulders, why I had to carry out a task which was too much for my strength. But now I know that each man over the course of his life receives an assignment which enables him to learn the lesson which he must learn here on earth . . ."

"And what have you learned, uncle?" asked the King, laughing softly.

Charles shook his head. Now all at once he felt thin and light, then again a leaden weight seemed to press him down to earth.

"I have been a slothful scholar—often wilful and easily distracted—but each day I learn to understand better—that in life people are not charitable enough to one another—and that he who is humble at heart—and sincere—can find and keep God's gifts, beauty and happiness—"

"Is that all?"

"Green grass in the sunlight—a child's laughter—and the beauty—the beauty of language—"

"Yes, yes." The King sighed with impatience; he no longer found the conversation amusing.

"That is only a small portion of the truth," Charles said with an effort, "but enough to make me realize that I know nothing. Since I realized that, I have had a deep desire to become truly wise. I am aware that what up to now I have considered reality is not reality at all. The world in which one wishes to be great and powerful and feared, your world, Sire, is an illusion." He coughed and gasped for breath. "I have not lived my life in vain. If I once . . . may have a glimpse of the real world . . ."

The King replied sarcastically, but Charles did not understand what he said. He lost all sense of time and place. It seemed to him as though he moaned, warding off a blow; as though he sought support from a friend whom he could not recognize in the darkness.

A long time later he opened his eyes; the darkness had lifted; he lay in deep silence. Against a background of green shadows, he saw the trusted face of his friend, the physician Cailleau. Charles tried to smile; he moved his lips but could utter no sound. Cailleau was looking at him so gravely, so attentively. It suddenly seemed inexpressibly soothing: that large, wrinkled face, drawn by anxiety and tension, hovering above his own. It made him think of something: once he had experienced a similar sensation—long ago.

He knew now what it was—his nurse had looked upon him like this when he was a little child lying in bed. He had tried then to lift his hand and touch the veils of her white headdress. He really could not help laughing at the memory: for a whole lifetime he had forgotten how it felt to be a small, helpless child.

In the greenery above his head, patches of light and shadow seemed to stir, as when the leaves in the treetops quiver above the forest path. The smell of damp earth and ferns, cool and fresh, greeted him; now here and there he could hear the rippling of a little nearby brook, hidden from view by leaves and underbrush. Charles sighed deeply in surprise and pleasure. After the heat and the dazzling brightness of feverish visions, the coolness of the wood moved him with inexpressible emotion. He began to move forward, hesitantly at first, as though he doubted his ability to do it. Slowly he walked beneath the trees, through long, silky, rustling grass. Birds and small creatures fled at his approach with a light whisper of wings and a rustling in the undergrowth. The sun shone through the foliage above his head; he saw the network of dark nerves outlined against the green-gold shading of the leaf. He had wandered alone, but at a turning in the path he saw a figure awaiting him. He recognized him at once: it was Nonchaloir, beckoning with a smile. But oddly enough, for the first time he had no desire to seek his company; he turned instead into the shrubbery.

While he struggled through the tall bushes, defending himself against the boughs which struck back with a rush after he had bent them to one side, he heard familiar voices all around him behind the dense forest growth: his small son cried, his little daughter, laughing, called his name, Marie spoke to him calmly and persuasively—and now it seemed to him that they were all talking together in a kind of chorus; his servants and friends in Blois, his kinsmen and allies: he could distinguish Dunois' loud, strong voice, Jean d'Angoulême's thoughtful murmur. He wanted to escape from them, he wanted to be left in peace now so that he could make his way, alone and unhindered, through the quiet cool forest.

He quickened his step; he pushed through the tender rustling greenness of the young saplings as a swimmer cleaves the waves—the acrid fresh odor of new leaves blew toward him and the splashing of the brook seemed closer now. He did not know what he would find at the end of the journey; he was seized by so overwhelming a feeling of anticipation that to return or even to look back seemed to him to be out of the question. It did not matter to him that the ground began to slope upward to a range of hills, that pebbles and roots hampered his progress, that thorny shrubs, stinging nettles and prickly foliage wounded his face and hands. He stumbled and fell but got up again and, head down, plowed into the intertwined growth around him. At times it seemed as though there could be no way out; the birds sang sweetly and enticingly in the cool leafy dome above his head, but he went on, warm and gasping, possessed by the longing to penetrate further, still further, to push on though imprisoned inextricably by twigs and branches. Who was holding him back, who was trying to keep him from finishing his journey?

The greenery receded once more into a twilit background. Cailleau's face came before him, large and hazy—it seemed to be asking him something.

"Where are we, Cailleau?" Charles murmured uneasily; he did not understand why he was no longer wandering through the shrubbery. Was this his goal?

"In the castle of Amboise, my lord." Cailleau's voice sounded very far away.

Amboise, Amboise, he thought in wonder; at the same time he noticed that the sound he heard was the murmuring of the brook. He waded through the crystal-clear icy water to the other bank; there the tree trunks rose high and smooth from the mossy earth. Far overhead he saw the sun-tinted leaves trembling in the wind. He ran forward quickly with an elastic step; and now from all sides, from the depth of the wood, Youth and Desire, Love, Joy, came toward him, a multitude of light-footed figures who cast no shadow on the forest floor. They were filled with the brilliance of the sun, which shone through the leaves; they were like figures in the windows of a church.

He walked past them with a smile and a greeting. Another procession approached with the jingle of harnesses and the clatter of hooves: the companions of his youth, his friends and comrades with whom he had hunted and gone into battle. But he did not stop to join them; he left them quickly behind. Bonne approached, barefoot, with a blue kerchief on her head; her large golden eyes lit up in a smile of deep happiness, and she stretched out her hand to him. He turned toward her, but the longing drove him on, past all those whom he continued to meet on his way—princes and kings, knights and priests, an almost endless procession of men and women whom he had once known. Silently and attentively, they watched him go by, as he hurried to plunge into the green depths of the forest from which they had just appeared.

Something sparkled before his eyes, someone slid something sweet and melting onto his tongue. High singing sounded very near. Only the odor which pervaded his nostrils made him realize what was happening. They were giving him the last rites. He was dying. He could not move; neither by word nor glance could he make them understand that he was still conscious. He felt himself shackled inside his body. For a few seconds he struggled hopelessly to make himself understood; my son, he thought, in mortal fear.

But now he heard the leaves rustling again, the coolness of the wind drew him irresistibly; he fled on through the soft grass that suddenly seemed very tall. Now he understood why this was so: he was a little child; bracken and plants reached nearly to his waist. The trees seemed as high as steeples. He stumbled on his path and fell. But within reach of his little hands he found the folds of a woman's gown, the fragrance of honey and roses. He got up and saw above him his mother's pale, lovely face. He did not stay, although he stretched out his arms, but slipped from the path into the shadows of the forest. He was alone among the terrifyingly tall undergrowth, the menacingly broad leaves covered on the inside with fine hairs, the virulently colored flowers with greedy biting lips and spiny tendrils. He cried for help, gasping for breath.

Now he was singed by pain. When he finally opened his eyes he saw, at the end of the narrow green path, dazzlingly bright light. There it is, he thought breathlessly, there it is. With a shout of joy and deliverance he plunged forward to meet the light.

Jean Cailleau, kneeling beside the bed, felt Monseigneur's pulse with his fingers, put his ears against his breast; slowly rose. He looked attentively and lovingly at the face, set in an expression of final fulfilment. After that he bent and gently closed the dead man's eyes.